PRAISE FOR

IN THE COURTS OF THE SUN

"An enthralling and original read, a stunningly inventive novel that will keep you turning the pages until the wee hours. With the sure hand of a master storyteller, D'Amato weaves together Mayan history, modern science, game theory, and the coming Mayan apocalypse to deliver a gripping read. Beware December 21, 2012!" —Douglas Preston, coauthor of *Gideon's Corpse*

"D'Amato's absolutely amazing thriller about the end of the world . . . takes over the late Michael Crichton's territory with a loud bang. . . . If you like historical thrillers and are as much of a sucker for time travel as I am, this one's for you." —*Chicago Tribune*

"A remarkable, unique, stand-out book. Prodigious in its scope, its originality, its ambition, its intelligence, and the mastery of its research. In a word: awesome. Or brilliant. Make that two words: awesome and brilliant."

—Raymond Khoury, author of *The Devil's Elixir*

"With a whirlwind plot and meticulous research . . . it really can't miss."

—*The San Diego Union-Tribune*

"Ambitious . . . a richly detailed, intellectually stimulating adventure through time." —*Booklist*

"Fans of the late Michael Crichton will welcome this engrossing SF thriller. As December 21, 2012, the date the Maya predicted would mark the end of the world, approaches, the Warren Group, a shadowy conglomerate, seeks to use technological advances to forestall disaster. . . . The period details are as convincing as those in Simon Levack's superb Aztec mysteries."

—*Publishers Weekly* (starred review)

continued . . .

"An exciting doomsday science fiction thriller." —The Mystery Gazette

"Fans will especially appreciate the vivid descriptions of the Mayans society, especially the insight into the Human Sacrifice game and the purpose of the Great Pyramid. *In the Courts of the Sun* is a refreshing, unique thriller."

—*Midwest Book Review*

"Sense of wonder, gonzo narration, and the best description of an alien civilization/secondary-world fantasy in a while; it just happens to be the historical Maya civilization circa 650 AD!" —Fantasy Book Critic

FURTHER PRAISE FOR BRIAN D'AMATO

"When a writer's voice is as compelling as Brian D'Amato's, you have to follow him no matter where he's going. . . . It's also satisfying—I mean really satisfying—to read a novel so bristling and humming with intelligence."

—Peter Straub

"The best first novel I've read in a decade." —Dean Koontz

"Fascinating and memorable. Definitely recommended." —*Library Journal*

"Ambitious and crackling with raw intellectual energy." —*Kirkus Reviews*

ALSO BY BRIAN D'AMATO

Beauty

In the Courts of the Sun

THE SACRIFICE GAME

BOOK II IN THE SACRIFICE GAME TRILOGY

Brian D'Amato

With Illustrations by the Author

NEW AMERICAN LIBRARY
Published by the Penguin Group
Penguin Group (USA) Inc., 375 Hudson Street,
New York, New York 10014, USA

USA | Canada | UK | Ireland | Australia | New Zealand | India | South Africa | China
Penguin Books Ltd., Registered Offices: 80 Strand, London WC2R 0RL, England
For more information about the Penguin Group visit penguin.com.

Published by New American Library, a division of Penguin Group (USA) Inc.
Previously published in a Dutton edition.

First New American Library Trade Paperback Printing, June 2013

 REGISTERED TRADEMARK—MARCA REGISTRADA

New American Library Trade Paperback ISBN: 978-0-451-41564-6

THE LIBRARY OF CONGRESS HAS CATALOGED THE HARDCOVER EDITION OF THIS TITLE AS FOLLOWS:
D'Amato, Brian.
The sacrifice game/Brian D'Amato.
p. cm.
ISBN 978-0-525-95241-1
1.Time travel—Fiction. 2. Mayas—Prophecies—Fiction.
I. Title.
PS3554.A4675S24 2012
813'.54—dc23 2011051637
Printed in the United States of America
10 9 8 7 6 5 4 3 2 1
Set in Keplar Std Light
Designed by Amy Hill

Manet alta menta repostum

Harold Steketee Sr.

1887–1984

There are strange things done 'neath the midnight sun . . .

A percentage of the author's proceeds from this series helps support various environmental, educational, and archaeological projects in the Maya area.

A NOTE ON PRONUNCIATION

Most Mayan words in this book are spelled according to the current orthography adopted by the Academia de Lenguas Mayas in Guatemala. However, I've retained older spellings for a few words—for instance, the text uses *uay* instead of the now-preferred *way* in order to distinguish the word from the English "way." Specialists may also notice that some words are spelled to be pronounced in Ch'olti, which usually means a *ch* takes the place of a *k*. I've italicized Mayan and most Spanish words on the first use, and dropped the italics after that.

Vowels in Maya languages are written like those in Spanish. "Ay" in Maya, uay, etc., is pronounced like the "I" in "I am." J is pronounced like the Spanish j, that is, a guttural h with the tongue farther back than in English. X is like English sh. Tz is like the English ts in "pots." Otherwise, consonants are pronounced as in English. An apostrophe indicates a glottal stop, which is like the tt in the Scottish or Brooklynese pronunciation of "bottle." All Mayan words are stressed on the last syllable, but Mayan languages are less stressed than English. Mayan languages are somewhat tonal, and their prosody tends to emphasize brief couplets. This gives the spoken language a certain lilt, which in some places I've tried to convey with dactylic dimeter, although readers may differ on whether this is successful.

A NOTE ON THE ILLUSTRATIONS

Readers of the first book in this series have asked about illustration techniques. Most of the pictures here were drawn on a pair of Wacom Cintiq monitors using Adobe and Andromeda software. Some of them incorporate scans of drawings in ink and scraping on scratchboard. Many of the glyphs were first sketched out in pencil by Prudence Rice.

MESOAMERICA

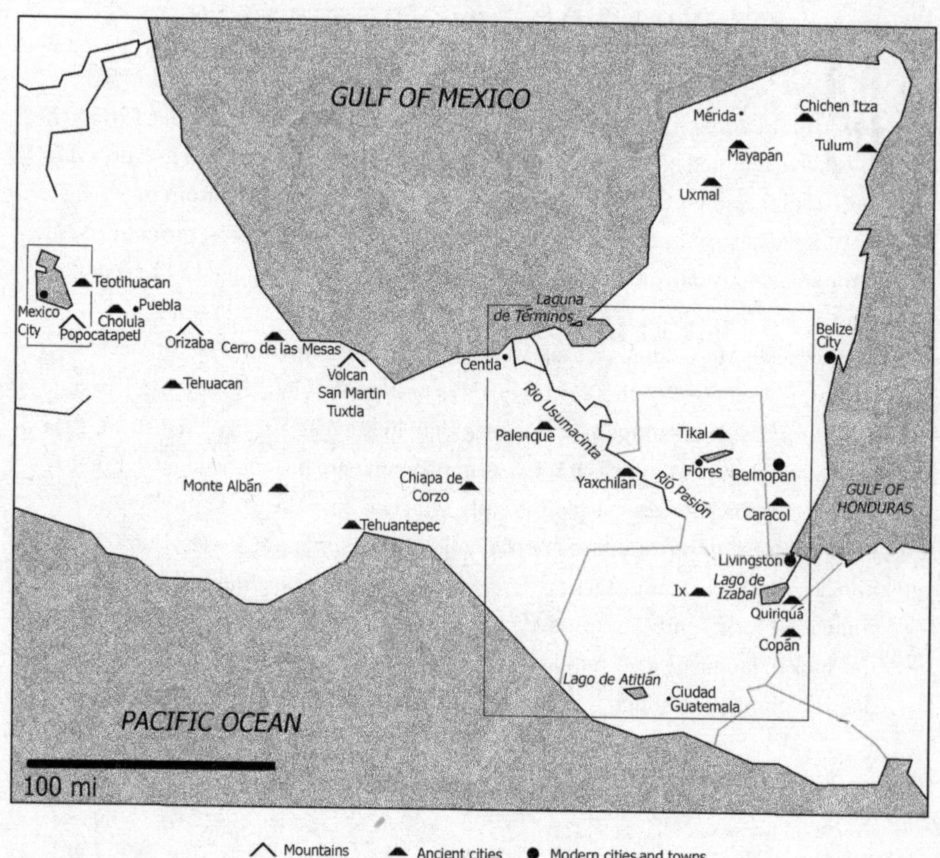

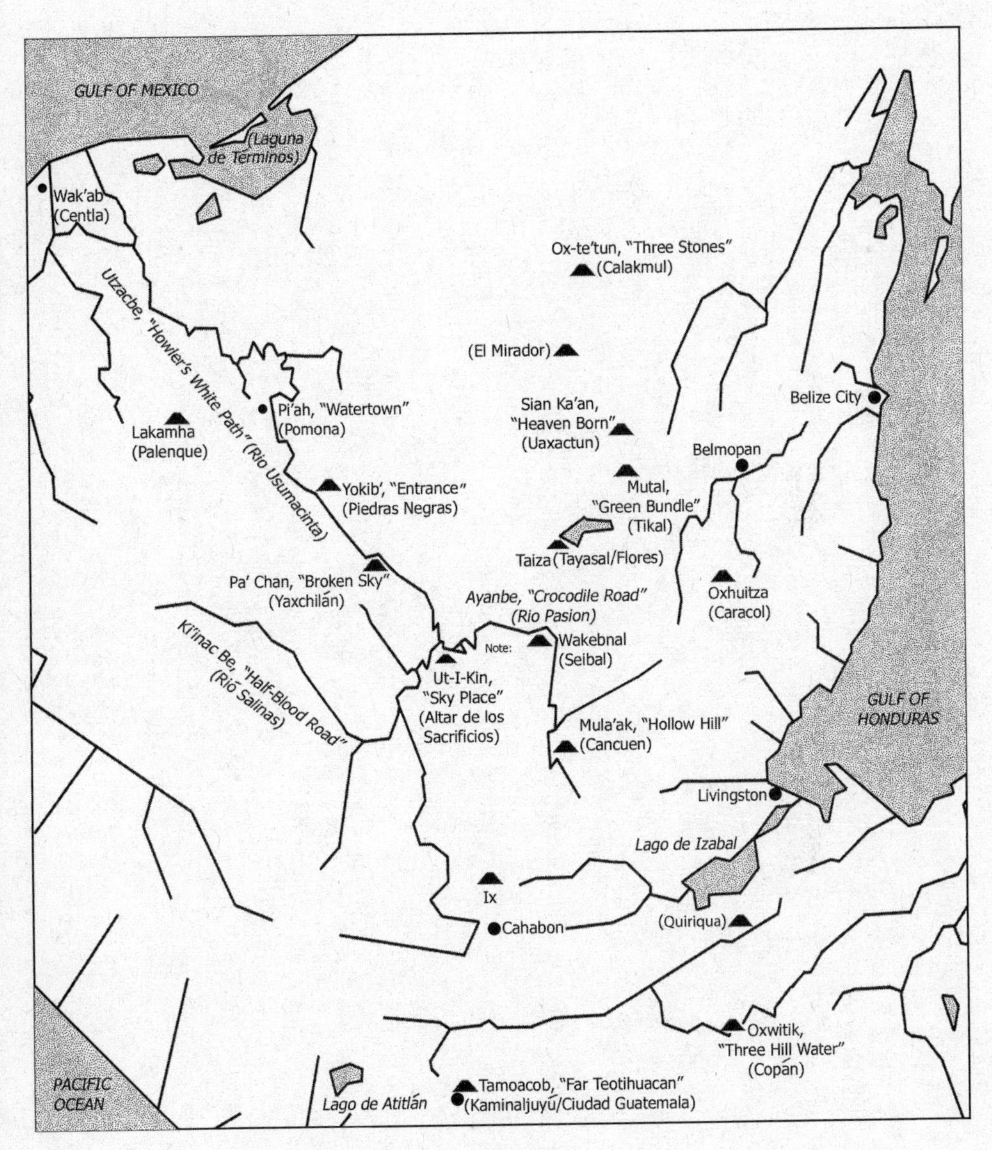

Detail

Ancient cities · Modern cities and towns · (Modern names in parentheses)

Note: this map shows only sites mentioned in the text

ZERO

Simple Experiments with Everyday Household Objects

Concept Sketch for Neo-Teo—Double Mul OC-A
Marena Park, Warren Interactive Entertainment

(0)

Why I Did It

By Joachim ("Jed") Carlos Xul Mixoc DeLanda

For General Release—
To post at noon, EST, on
December 19, 2012—
Contact: None
Indiantown, Florida, USA

4 Lamat, 12 Sac, 12.19.19.15.9

4 Sundog, 12 Whiteness, on the ninth K'in of the fifteenth Uinal of the nineteenth and last Tun of the nineteenth and last K'atun of the twelfth and last B'aktun

Thursday, October 30, 2012

5:42:08 P.M.

To All, Whom It Concerns:

. . . five . . .

four . . .

three . . .

almost there . . .

one . . .

zero . . .

tap.

Whoa.

That's it. I've done it.

Let me catch my breath here for a second.

Okay.

I didn't expect it, but just now, at the moment I tapped that icon, I—I guess I should say even I—felt a twinge, and more than a twinge, of that gray free-falling terror, that it was really happening, and that it wasn't reversible. Was there any guilt in the twinge? Hmm. Remorse, yes. Nausea that it had come to this? Sure. But guilt? I guess not. It won't hurt, for one thing. In fact, you won't even notice.

What I just did was—all I did—was I bought a hundred standard five-thousand-bushel corn contracts for February delivery, effective at the opening of the Chicago Board of Trade tomorrow. At 5:41:59 P.M. a bushel was at $7.10, so this only—"only"—took $3,550,000.00 out of my main Schwab account. I realize it doesn't sound like this transaction could be a very big event. Certainly not something that will end the whole place. I mean, end the world. And I don't mean just the world as we know it either. I mean the world, like everything.

But it will. According to calculations using Warren's latest (2.3 Beta) version of the Sacrifice Game software—a spectacularly accurate proprietary prediction tool, of which a little more later—the trade's going to drive up the price at the worst possible time. This will set off a very unfortunate sequence of events. Eighteen minutes from now, the second domino—that is, that's what I'm calling the second key event out of what I'm visualizing as a row of dominoes that will culminate in the end of us humans—the second domino will tip over as the Board of Trade software notices after-hours trading spiraling up at geometric rate that, just before it pulls the plug, will reach U.S. $1,244.02 per second. The third domino will fall exactly four hours and 21.02 minutes from now, as the Hang Seng sees a similar thing happening and suspends its own trading in all corn, wheat, barley, soy, and of course rice. And then, tomorrow morning, when the CBT opens at the ungodsly hour of 6:00 A.M., the fourth domino will fall as every hick trader and his adelphogamic brother jumps on the hay wagon and tries to buy as much—as many?—as much piles of staples as they can get their flippers on. At 8:48 P.M., Central time, the CBT will suspend all trading—Domino Number Five—and, on November 2, three trading days from now, the first of the food riots will start, in Dêqên Tibetan Autonomous Prefecture, in Yunan, China. That'll be the sixth domino. By the next morning, over sixteen thousand people will have died in the riots, mainly in Shenzhen, Dongguan, and Guangzhou—and those will inspire another, much larger riot in Gujarat—but we're getting ahead of ourselves. And anyway, by Number Seven you'll have seen a lot of all this on the news. So let's skip ahead to the morning of—well, you've already heard about the date. It's the big one, the one that's caused so much storm and stress. The last domino—it's a bigger number than nine, but smaller than, say, thirty-one—will fall on December 21, 2012, or in our reckoning,

that is, 12.19.19.17.19, of the fourth Overlord and the third Gold Sun. And on that date, just like a whole lot of kooks, New Agers, and pantophobics have babbled about for what seems like another thirteen *b'aktuns* already, that'll be it, the last of the last, the EOE, as we call it at the Warren Family of Caring Companies. The End of Everything.

For years now, when people heard that I was a Maya, they'd ask me what woo-wooey supernatural event was going to happen on that day, and I'd usually say something like "Nothing you need to know about." Or, often, just "Nothing." Well, now something's going to happen. Or, in an active sense, "Nothing." Only, there won't be anything supernatural about it. I'll have done it all myself. With my little cursor. Whatever humans are alive on earth, including the lady next door, the pope, you, the president, myself, and even the crew of seven aboard the International Space Station—who'll last a little longer than the others, but not much—will be the last humans ever. And, possibly, the last consciousnesses ever. I hope.

Why?

Well, because, it won't matter why, will it? In fact this whole exercise—I mean, writing this—seems pointless. I mean, to write a deposition for posterity when, if all goes well, as it will, there won't be any posterity. There won't even be any extraterrestrial archaeologists coming around to ask questions about the collapse of humanity. Most people will barely have time to read this before they wink out into zeroness. Still, I do feel that at least some of you, short-lived or not, deserve an explanation.

So, how did it come to this? Or, to put it more relevantly, How Do I Know This Is the Right Thing to Do?

Well, briefly, because I do. That is, I understand all the considerations involved, the math, you might even call it. Unlike almost anyone else, I can visualize the numbers involved, and unlike absolutely anyone else, I can comprehend what those numbers will lead to. And if you could follow it all, you'd agree with me. And you'd do exactly the same thing.

More clearly, I can understand how much human life is out there, and how much is coming. And I understand—and most of all accept—that over 99.8 percent of it, now, in the future, and always, is and will be sheer unrelieved agony. Pain. And no matter how many distractions and evasions people come up with, no matter how much gets spent on the denial industry, any honest person with an IQ over room temperature—that is, anyone worth asking—will admit that, to put it in the most ordinary and bathetic language possible, life sucks. I'm doing us all a mercy. And that's the beginning, end, and entire sum and substance.

I know, I know. Don't do us any favors. But this wasn't something I wanted. And it isn't something I'm making up. In fact, this ability—the ability to comprehend—didn't even come to me naturally, the way things do to crazy people. In a way, it took over thirteen hundred years. And also, I didn't make this decision so much for you and me, anyway. I'm doing it more for the kids. The coming generations. Yes, you and I are already well and royally fucked, but we can, at least, refrain from bringing any further consciousnesses into existence. It's the right thing to do. And actually, there are a lot of people—not just Schopenhauerian philosophers and their wannabe counterparts—who even know it's the right thing. But they haven't done anything about it. I think I have the will to do it—and the means, but especially the will—because I saw it with my own eyes. Or at least, I saw it with my intraregarding eye, through the lens of the Game.

Anthropologists would classify the Sacrifice Game as a sortilege divination game, something that uses counts of pebbles or seeds to investigate the future or, more rarely, the past. Playing it well feels like playing Parcheesi against God and winning. Although the Sacrifice Game is to Parcheesi as cooking a Peking duck is to getting a bag of Skittles out of a vending machine.

I'd been playing the Game since I was little. As some of you might guess from my middle names (below), I'm an ethnic Maya, a twenty-first-century descendant of those guys who built all those palaces in Mexico and Guatemala with the big wacko pyramids with the scary stairs and then, presumably, abandoned them. We tend to be confused with Aztecs, Toltecs, or Venusians. When I was five, when we lived in a village called T'ozal, in Alta Verapaz, Guatemala, my mother, who was a *na h'me*—a "sun-adderess," that is, kind of lesser shamaness—taught me a version of it that her mother had taught her, and which had survived, handed down in increasingly simplified forms, for hundreds of years. Two years later, in 1982, a Guate government death squad called the Mano Blanco disappeared my parents along with about a quarter of the village. Supposedly my mother died when they made her drink gasoline. I was in a hospital at the time for my hemophilia and eventually got adopted by a Mormon family in Utah. I kept up with the Game in my dreadful teen years and then in college I helped work out some of the theory of it with a professor of mine named Taro Mora. Unlike most economics/game-theory mumbo-jumbo, it really did do something, and eventually I learned to use it to make quite a bit of money in corn futures. Taro didn't come up with a mathematical solution for it, though, so the Game never worked well on computers. I went back to Guate a few times and tried to help bring the perps from the old regime to semijustice, but it was frustrating. I also became a frustrated opisthobranchologist and a few other frustrated things, but I never thought I'd do anything spectacular. And then, three hundred and thirteen days ago, on the fourth Owl and the fourth Yellowness of 12.19.18.17.16, or we could say December 23, I was approached by a woman named Marena Park.

Or actually, at the time I thought I was approaching her, but that's another kettle of verrucomicrobia we don't need to get into right now. She was—and is—an executive at the entertainment division of the Warren Group (or "family," as they like to say) of companies. It turned out she was a kind-of-famous game designer who was now, a bit oddly, I thought, coordinating a research project with my old mentor, Taro. And she wanted me to consult with them about a software version of the Sacrifice Game. And I would have said no, but they'd gotten hold of some new data: a description of the Game the way it was played at the height of the Maya Classic Period, thirteen hundred and forty-six years before.

The account of the Game was in a Maya codex, a screenfold book, that had just been photographed, and it had more in it than just a fuller version of the Game. There were "goals"—which you might, with a bit of tabloidal exaggeration, call predictions—going all the way up to the thirteenth b'aktun—that is, the so-called End of Time date in 2012. Of course, like a lot of entertainment companies, they were all very interested in the whole 2012 thing. Like they say, Mayan calendars sell like there's no tomorrow. And, almost needless to say, I'd never been into it. It had always been a bunch of New Age losers and disappointed Y2K conspiracy kooks sitting around in extra-large Jedi costumes and making up disaster scenarios out of Captain Future. But when I saw the new codex, the Codex Nuremburg—well, basically, among other things, it predicted the attack on Disney World six days later, on the twenty-ninth. Which, despite some recent contenders, is still, with 104,774 confirmed deaths and half a million casualties, the most deadly terrorist act so far. Not counting this one, of course.

So, to make a long—oops, too late—well, to at least cut the story off at the knees: after the DWH, the Disney World Horror, I got deeper in with Marena's people, and even met the head of the whole conglomerate, Lindsay Warren. The discouraging thing was that Taro's team and I didn't do too well at figuring out how to play the version of the Game we'd gotten from the Codex. But I found out they had another approach to it in the works, something pretty bizarre, or, well, at least pretty futuristic, although I guess not much more so than the Mars mission, glow-in-the-dark poodles, or your latest flexible-screen phone. They were planning to get data directly from the old days, and somebody from our era was going to go and pick it up. It wasn't exactly time travel. In fact, there are reasons why real time travel, where you'd send someone's body back to the past, was almost certainly always going to be impossible, no matter how advanced technology became. But there is a way to send energy. Basically, you can make something like a high-quality print of all the connections in Person A's brain that encode his memories, and then print that pattern onto Person B's brain. And—if you've adequately "wiped down" Person B's own memories, so that he doesn't get confused—Person B will believe he is Person A. Of course, you could use this process just to move consciousnesses around in the present day—and that's something I figured Warren Labs was gearing up for—but in this case, Person B would be in the past. Specifically, he'd be a Maya *ahau*—a king—who'd know or at least have access to the full version of the Game, or more technically, to the "nine-stone" version. And he'd have the resources to preserve that knowledge so that, thirteen centuries later, we could dig it up. And then we might be able to use that to save ourselves from whatever's lurking at the business end of 2012.

At first—or at least this is how it seemed to me at the time—the team hadn't been thinking of me as a candidate for projection into the past. Their first choice had been a younger student of Taro's named Tony Sic, who was from Mérida, in the Yucatán, and who spoke Yukatekan Mayan, and who'd worked at the CPR, the *Comunidad de Población en Resistencia,* in Ixcán, and who was even pretty good at the Game, although of course not so good as I was. But I convinced them I was the better bet. Either that or, as I've lately come to suspect, they were thinking of sending me all along. Still, what matters is that my consciousness got successfully downloaded, sent through what they called a desktop wormhole, and projected back to AD 664.

Still, things, as things do, started to go wrong before my duplicate self—whom I guess we could call Jed_2—even got there. He was supposed to arrive in the brain of an *ahau* named 9 Fanged Hummingbird, the king of the city of Ixnichi Sotz, or Ix for short, in the Sierra de Chama region, in the center of what's now Guatemala. He could just take over, watch some experts play the Game, and document everything. No sweat. Instead—according to Jed_2's letters—he'd turned up in the head of a star athlete named Chacal, who played the local big-time sport, hipball. It was something like how you'd imagine soccer if soccer balls weighed thirty pounds and were studded with razor blades. Chacal was about to roll himself down the local pyramid's steps as an especially humiliating sacrifice, as a kind of proxy to keep 9 Fanged Hummingbird in power.

But maybe I'm getting into more detail than we need here. The basics are that Jed_2—uncharacteristically—was resourceful enough to worm his way out of his sacrifice predicament, find out something about the Game, and, amazingly, make it all the way to Teotihuacan, the capital of the Mexican highlands at that time, to score some drugs.

(1)

The issue was that the high levels of the Game make demands on the human brain that the brain can't meet without chemical help. And in AD 664, which was the only time Jed_2 was going to get to hang out in Olde Mayaland, the main sources of the drugs had been monopolized by the two ruling clans of Teotihuacan. In fact, evidently this was one of the reasons for Teotihuacan's eight-hundred-year longevity as a capital city, but this has already taken up a pretty big fraction of the time you have left so maybe you don't need to learn any more history right now. Jed_2 made his way to Teotihucán and met with a personage who was illustrated in the Codex, a sort of nun named Ahau-na Koh, or just Lady Koh. And through her, he got hold of some of the Game drugs, but in the process he seems to have set off the fire that finally destroyed the city. Although his letter's a little reticent on this point. In fact his letters are frustrating in general and sometimes I suspect him, or myself, of editorializing. At any rate Jed_2 and Lady Koh's retinue made it at least as far as one of our prearranged search zones in Oaxaca, 270 miles from Teotihuacan. He buried the first cache of notes and Game drugs and, as planned, marked the burial spot with lumps of magnetite. There was a plan for him to inter a second set, along with his own body and possibly recoverable polymerized brain, in one of the royal tombs of Ix, although it looks as though he didn't get that far and now we'll never know. But back here—I mean back here like back now, in time—in

2012, Marena's team dug up the stuff without any trouble. Taro came up with a software version of the full nine-stone form of the Game and Warren's Lotos division came up with a synthetic version of the two types of drugs. And when I learned to play the Game on them, I—along with Tony Sic and several others of Taro's students in the Warren program—found that Jed_2 was right.

I guess we could call the *tsam lic* compounds "smart drugs" if that didn't make you think of G-Series Gatorade. They enabled one's brain to behave less like a brain and more like—I don't want to say like a computer, at least not like the sort of computer humans have invented, because it has a much more analogish, intuitive feel than that—but like some kind of cross between a superclock, a supercamera, and a super–slide rule. And we used it to avert the 2012 problem, or I guess now you have to say we thought we did. After a whole lot of hours using the Game to sift information—both from the Net in general and from NSA and other black databases—I tracked down a homegrown Canadian bioterrorist named Madison Czerwick who was just about to release a heavily tweaked version of a formerly military strain of *Brucella abortus*.

Now, I realize all this sounds like I'm getting a little flighty, but the proof's in the blood pudding, and in this case the Warren folks shared the information with the FBI and it checked out. And, using a multinational rapid response unit—just like in a Tom Clancy book, but without the colorful characters or expository dialogue—they grabbed Madison and isolated his tanks of bugs. And, when the lab at the CDC analyzed the stuff, it turned out that, yes, it really would have finished off almost all the human beings on earth, as well as the higher primates and a good fraction of lower primates, dogs, bears, pigs, and, for DNA-related reasons, toads, all right around the 2012 date. They even gave us all secret medals, which I guess are like invisible diamonds.

Still, the Game can't truly predict the future, since that can't be done. That is, you could always just do something that would change whatever you saw. And even if you couldn't do that, the Game's not some magic teleidoscope that sees all ∞ random events. That's impossible. It's more like a lens that focuses your perception on the strings of events that follow your potential actions, an optimizer that helps create a successful outcome, whatever random events occur. It enables a leap in reasoning power. And as the world becomes more programmable every day—well, let's say that as of now it's programmable enough.

As of December 10—Madison Day—I still hadn't taken the full leap. But two hundred and sixty-nine days ago, on March 28, I dove in. I played farther into the Game than, I'm sure, anyone—even One Ocelot, whoever he was—ever has. And at the extreme core of the meaning of today, I came to what felt like a sort of mountain with a cave at its peak, and inside that cave—which was bigger than the mountain itself and in fact bigger than all outdoors—I could see, or hear, or sense, the people of the future, all crying in well-informed fear of being born, begging not to be brought into the world. Or at least this is what I saw on a figurative or, you might say, symbolic level. To put it more abstractly, I experienced a massive growth in capability of empathy, which is a mental act that requires insight and imagination. I realized—*really* realized, for the first time—that no matter how many good or happy experiences a person has, the bad experiences still outweigh them. And this doesn't just go for the majority. It's true for everyone. And, more than that, when you're talking about people who aren't born yet, the possible good times they might have aren't benefiting anyone—since they don't exist yet—but they're definitely getting a benefit if they miss whatever bad experiences they're going to have. And I tried, but there wasn't any way to chip into the crystalline logic of this: For a consciousness, coming into existence was always, everywhere, and for all future times, a net loss.

Yes, it sounds like I just had an oversoaked tab of C20H25N3O and came out as leary as Timothy Loony. But, even according to buttoned-up-and-down corporate types—even according to the FBI, which has got to be the least imaginative bunch of bureaucrats on the rock—the Game actually works. And nothing I saw was outside the Game's—but wait a second. I don't need to defend myself against the charge. I'm not writing this to defend or excuse myself or to ask for forgiveness. I'm just writing it the way that, if you're the captain, you have a duty to inform the crew members of a battleship about the state of their vessel. And even if not a single one of the

~ 6,900,000,000 of you gets the logic, it still doesn't matter. If you could follow along and take this leap in understanding, you'd agree. You'd thank me. And if I weren't around, you'd do it yourself.

Of course, you wouldn't want to hurt anybody. Painlessness would be Number One. And Number Two would be the fact that even though you had a lot of money, you still couldn't afford, say, your own collection of atomic bombs. You'd have to work out a way to do it that would get a big payoff from a small amount of catalyst, something as easy and natural as, well, as—

Well, let's put it this way. On 12.19.8.9.19, 4 Thunderhead, 17 Flood, I naturally just gawped at the havoc along with everybody else. And as the initial shock faded, I started to wonder what about it besides the obvious—that it was all those people, that it was an attack on what you'd thought was previously safe ground—was even more disturbing than the sum of those things would imply. Was it that it took me as long as it did to realize it wasn't just a holographic trailer for some new Jerry Bruckheimer movie? Was it that you could actually feel some kind of presence there, that Luciferian grin in the gray clouds? Or was it, conversely, that there wasn't any presence, that behind the smoke there was just blankness, blankness, and even more blankness? For a while I thought it was just because it was beautiful, that it was the most spectacular event witnessed in living memory, even more than D-day or the atomic blasts, about the way the jets just disappeared and about those Beardsleyesque ostrich plumes of dust as the sand castles imploded, so that when it was over you found yourself not feeling the deaths but just that cheap after-the-fireworks feeling you get when you wolf down a big gooey dessert and then look ashamed at the empty plate, and that I was disappointed with myself for thinking that way. But at some point I decided that what really chilled everyone was simply how easy it had been, close to effortless, even, as though those Pillars of Dagon had been built expressly to the size of this Samson wannabe and all he had to do was stand between them and give a little push . . . or I guess one could almost just say how simply inexpensive it was, how all you have to do is hang out at the Halal White Castle or wherever young, underachieving, swollen-testicled hadjis congregate, cut a dozen or so of the most impressionable ones out of the herd, spring for a few thousand dollars' worth of flight lessons and a round of X-Actos, and suddenly it's the Decline of the West. For a little while, until their self-delusion apparatus kicked in again, quite a few people—despite all the time and effort people spend on making themselves feel like everything's okay, despite how denial, in various forms, has always been the world's biggest industry—folks came close to comprehending how much they lived in a house of cards, how much it was like they'd been keeping a glass bottle of lukewarm liquid trinitrotoluene on the edge of their coffee table and letting their kids and dogs run around, how—well, you get the picture. But on the other hand, if you were an aspiring destroyer—a "doomster," as we call them down at the Warren Family—it gave you a sense of limitless possibility. It inspired you to go it one better.

Which, incidentally, is one of the reasons I have to do this. 9/11 inspired a lot people, not just me and Madison. According to the Sacrifice Game Engine that we were now running on LEON, the Lab's main AI engine, there are at least sixty aspiring doomsters out there who have a good shot at killing ten million or more people. I can practically see them, beavering away in their basements on homebrew viruses, packing the remains of tossed smoke detectors into dirty bombs, refining hundreds of pounds of ricin, and on and on. Madison was unusually talented but not unique. So if I don't do this well, somebody else will do it, badly, in very short order. Any one of these losers could, and will, unleash his garbage at any moment. And from what I've had time to track with the Game, the scenarios aren't encouraging. The odds are good that the next few decades, and more, are going to be characterized by wars, famines, depressions, government repression, torturous deaths, wasting diseases, parents eating children and vice versa, and on and on. Things are definitely going to get bad, and bad is worse than people realize.

Like I say, the Game lets you read ahead and work out exactly what to program. By *read* I mean, in the sense of a great Go player reading a hundred moves ahead. But with the Sacrifice Game I was reading hundreds of thousands of moves ahead, in hundreds of thousands of much more complicated "games" all over the world, tracing a single chain through the latticework of contingency that would lead to—well, let's just say it leads to what I think is definitely the best available way to do it. Definitive, painless, and, once begun, inexorable. Now, *that's* progress. Eleven years, one month, and twenty days later, it took only one tap on a touch screen to trigger an event that, if there were anyone around to witness it, would make the World Trade Center event seem quaint. Now, *that's* progress.

Actually, there will be one near-witness: me. 4.564 hours—from the post time, the release time above, plus, say, four minutes for your reading up to this point—as I count down the quarter-seconds on the atomic clock, there'll be a moment when, as I'm wondering whether I could have made a mistake in calculation and the whole thing will be a nonevent, for, I think a little less time than one of those quarter-seconds, more like, say, 700,000 microseconds—about two *p'ip'ilob*—two blinks, as we say in Mayan—I'll see and feel things change around me, I'll notice that something huge and strange is happening, and for about another quarter second, just before I cease to be, I'll know that I hadn't made a mistake, that I'd gotten it all exactly right.

So, that's my whole story. And there's nothing left to do but wait for the bigger nothing.

Probably you still don't agree. But you would if—hmm, I almost said "if you were honest with yourself." Well, what with everything else I don't also want to put you down, but it's true. Just look around a little, check out the world a bit, and it seems as obvious as $a = a$. The average person just wants to—

Huh. Serendipity. Just while I was typing this bit, about the average person, I noticed a headline on my news screen:

Bridge Demolition Provokes
Soul-Searching in Akron

AKRON, Ohio—Its official name, the one on maps and signs, is the All-America Bridge. But so many people have jumped off since it was built 32 years ago that it sometimes goes by a less-welcome nickname: the Suicide Bridge.

Now the City of Akron has decided to do something about it, and plans to use more than fifteen million dollars of federal aid to destroy the bridge.

> Since the bridge was built in 1997, 468 people have died leaping from the bridge to their deaths in the Little Cuyahoga River Valley below. Police are called to the bridge to save would-be jumpers roughly twice a week. Neighbors below say bodies have damaged roofs. Four years ago, the city spent over a million dollars to build a safety fence, but this was circumvented by over sixty further jumpers. Mental health officials say the All-America Bridge has become a "magnet bridge": one with a reputation for suicides, therefore drawing more troubled people to try to jump off it.
>
> In approving the measure, the city has prompted a sometimes emotional conversation about suicide and mental illness, government spending, and Akron's image and future as it continues to remake itself and adjust to a new economy without the thousands of tire manufacturing jobs that once led people to call this the Rubber Capital of the World.

You could Google the rest, but you get the idea. And, really, who could be more representative of the general run than someone, anyone, from Akron, Ohio? Although I admit that four hundred and sixty-eight people is a hard-to-believe statistic. I mean, you'd think they'd have that many every couple of days. You'd think that by now the entire population of Akron, along with a large percentage of citizens from the neighboring communities of Cottage Grove, Barberton, and Cuyahoga Falls, would have taken the opportunity to jump. I mean, just typing the word *Akron* a few times has depressed me so much that I'm close to hanging myself right now with my mouse cord and not waiting around for the twenty-first. So why pull the thing down? If anything, you'd think the town fathers would just build a designated suicide platform up there, and put up bleachers and concession stands and sell tickets so that at least they could reduce the deficit. Or, if they absolutely insist on keeping their taxpayers alive, why not just work on making Akron less depressing? Although I guess that would probably cost more than a million dollars. A trillion? Infinity? Who knows?

So anyway, basically, they want it even if they can't ask for it. And I accepted the responsibility to give it to them. I didn't want to be the villain (*But y'are, Jed. Y'are!),* but without villains nothing happens.

And that's the whole reason. I'm not doing this because I'm frustrated or enraged at my co-workers or any of those postal things, although I suppose I'm as angry as the next gink. It's not because people are no damn good, although I've always had a deep faith in their awfulness, even before watching that toddler-in-the-microwave clip on Rotten Video. It's not because I think the real world is just some collective hallucination or alien holographic projection or veil of Maya or whatever. If only. Nope. The reason, the only reason, is that I spoke to the babies. That is, I met the unborn. All of them. I listened. And they don't want to be here. And I'm the person who's in a position to do something about it.

So, I have reason and opportunity. Do I also have the right?

I don't know. But I do tend to think that's a meaningless question. The only point is, like I say, I'm in a position to do it, and so I have the *duty* to do it. I didn't want to be the villain. Nobody does. But some are called—

PING. Ah. My imaginary internal alarm's telling me it's time to check in on that second domino.

Hmm. I'm almost afraid to look.

Okay. Not almost. I'm terrified.

Maybe if I don't look it won't have happened. Maybe it's all just a fantasy . . . maybe it can't happen, things like that don't happen, things stay the same, there'll still be things, there'll still be coffee and Japan and mornings, another season of *Battlestar Galactica,* there'll be parrot fish, crimson sea slugs, Fluffernutter sandwiches, snow—

Jed. You're getting maudlin. Stop. Get a grip.

I called up the price feed and scrolled down . . . slowing . . .

there it is—

. . .

Chix, chix, chix . Xkimik, xkimik. Ay, dios. Oh God, oh God. It's not true, it's not true . . .

But it is. It happened. I did it. It's happening, it's happening. *Todo por mi culpa.* All my fault. Oh my God, ohmyGodohmyGodohmyGod, OMG, O, O, O. *Ya estuvo.* It's done. There was that numbing swell again, like I'd inhaled a chestful of chilled helium. And there was just garden-variety terror, of course, and even a smudge of—well, I don't know if I'd call it, exactly . . . would I call it doubt? Cancel, cancel. It's done, Jed, it's done, even if I, even I, can't believe it's really happening, it is, it is, it is, it is—

Breathe.

Whew. Well, it can't be helped.

Okay. It's getting late, so I'll take a last question from the house. If the Game works so damn well, why don't you use it to show you how to avert all these horrible eventualities and make the future great for everybody?

Answer. I have. This is it.

Well, that's about it. And, like I—

Hang on.

Okay. I noticed I'd thrown up a little in my mouth and managed to choke the bolus of sour mush back down into the right tube. Okay.

And, like I say, you want it. Search your feelings and you'll find you crave release. Just like this mutilated dog I knew one time, you want it even if you can't ask for it. You'd thank me, if you could, for building us all a bridge out of Akron. And at least now you know. That is, you know all there is that's worth knowing, that the world won't end in fire, or in ice, or with a bang, or with a whimper, or even with a shrug. Just a click.

Very, very sincerely,

Joachim Carlos Xul Mixoc DeLanda

Joachim Carlos Xul Mixoc DeLanda

(2)

Marenad texted me while I was in the middle of writing my Dear Doomed World letter. She said she was back from Belize, and she was in her house, and I should come by. Wow, now what? I thought. And what do I tell her, besides nothing? I knew I wouldn't be able to resist, though. She still had a hook in me. Well, let's say a harpoon. And she knew it. Beeyotch. Anyway, I hadn't even been to her house yet, so I guess it was on my bucket list. Okay. I got the tanks into self-maintenance mode. I had some Fluffernutter and, just for clarity, a shot of *tsam lic*. It was basically the same proportional combination of the same two molecules as the drugs that Jed_2 had buried in Oaxaca, except that they were now synthetic, of course, and each with a few pairs of hydrogen atoms added for ease of absorption. It rocked.

I cleaned up and even got out a sort of nice gray summerweight Dormeuil jacket. Wait, is that a moth hole? FUU—oh . . . it's not. Just a speck of something. Polonium-210, probably. Whatever. I slipped on the jacket. Ahh. Now I'm an adult. Actually, since the unpleasantness at Disney World, I'd kept the garment all stocked up with my wallet, backup wallet, glasses, Purell wipes, SightSavers wipes, Q-tips, Twist-Em ties, Theraputty, Krazy Glue, grandessa, mandatory medication, optional medication, Adderall, OxyContin, Klonapin, clotting spray, wound dressing pads, blue Pilot Rolling Ball, Post-its, ToothTowels, Go-Between Plaque Stix, red astronomy flashlight, two competing telephones, the Gerber Suspension Butterfly Multi-Tool (which I much recommend), my real passport, my Warren-provided fake passport, nine blank checks from three different banks, about fifteen thousand U.S. dollars in premagnetic twenties, and a little nylon coin folder with twenty-five Krugerrands, which at the moment represented another seventy-five thousand, one hundred and two dollars. And a few other things, because, you know, one never knows. I checked the three working tanks again—I'd had Lenny replace everything after the Disney Die-off—and the apps on my phone that link to the tanks and the tank cameras, and then used the other new app to set the alarms and house cameras. I got my feet into a fully charged pair of Sleekers—just to show my support for the Firm, I rationalized— and selected an indoors-almost-appropriate hat. Wallet, keys, backup wallet, backup keys. Check, che—

Damn. I was feeling a subsonic throb version of the first two bars of "Transfusion." The alarm on my 1 phone. Time for another shot. Right.

I rolled up my female—I mean, left—pant leg and found a new virgin target on my inner thigh. Dr. Lisuarte, from Warren, had set me up with a PowderJect system that looked, irresistibly, like a better-tooled version of the 1946 Daisy Buck Rogers U-238 Atomic Disintegrator Pistol, and I gave myself a Ject of recombinant coagulation factor IX. *Fweeeeeeeeyup!* Ow. Fuck this, I thought. Well, it's not for much longer. Anyway, these days my clotting was nearly always up to at least seventy percent of normal, so if I wiped out on the Sleekers I'd still live to see the big quarter-second. In fact I barely worried about it consciously anymore, except still, if you've ever had any kind of hemophilia the whole world always feels a little different. Like for instance you're always a little on the lookout for sharp objects. It's like that feeling you get when you're sitting shirtless on that butcher's paper in a doctor's examination room and you look at the waste container that says SHARPS. If you're a bleeder, that feeling's permanent.

I went out, let the door suck itself closed, and listened to the motion alarms beep on. The overcast and 102 degrees and 79 percent relative humidity and no wind made you feel like you were stuffed in a box with a half ton of styro-peanuts and left on somebody's porch and not getting picked up. There was a top note of burning something in the air, over the bases of mold and fried crabgrass. Devil's Night, I thought. Starting a little early. Amazingly, I remembered to let the jacket slide off before I eased into the 120-degree interior of the Barracuda Thermador. It was a metalflake-mango-orange hardtop 1970 Plymouth that I'd gotten ten months ago, with the original body, engine, and drive train, and I called it that because the inside had been scooped out and replaced with all-up-to-code everything.

"Please tell me your destination," the car purred. Its voice was like the Stepmother's from the Disney *Cinderella.*

"How can I turn you off?" I asked. It didn't answer. Hell and corruption. It wasn't even the right voice. If this car could really talk, it would sound like Amy Winehouse. Should hire her to do it. Just a few phrases and synth the rest. Where was I going? the car asked again. This time I told it, out of sheer weakness. It suggested I head west on Magnolia Street. I obeyed. Indiantown looked like a neighborhood from *The Sims,* if there were a "seediness" option and you slid it up halfway. And today it seemed to be deserted. Everybody's hiding, I thought. Afraid of getting lynched by yahoos. Lately there'd been a rumor the Horror had been caused by some kind of Native American magic, and Indians had been attacked all over Florida. Sometimes I wondered whether that was what the "shoulder the blame" line in the Codex Nuremberg had been trying to mean. Except it didn't seem really plausible. I mean, that's too specific even for me to believe. Except, well, you never know. That One Ocelot was a pretty shrewd cat.

"Please make a . . . *right* turn onto Martin Luther King Boulevard," Car Voice said. I did, even though I knew another way and even liked it better. Damn. Getting servile like the rest of the sheep-men. Should've kept the old dashboard. On the radio, which of course hadn't really been a radio since 2003, a woman who kept telling you her name was Anne-Marie García-McCarthy was saying how a mob had stormed the Fort Polk army base in Louisiana and may have been fired upon. The Nation of Islam had issued a statement saying that the U.S. had declared war on the black population, who had to fight back by any means necessary. Time for a new catchphrase, I thought. She said that Dick Cheney, the mind apparently behind the DWH—the Disney World Horror—was still missing, but probably somewhere in Pakistan. She said spot gold had hit a new high of $3,004 this morning and corn, as we know, hit a new high after-hours. She told us her name was Anne-Marie García-McCarthy. Onto 710. It was pretty empty. *Future Site of Rockingham Vistas,* the first big video billboard said. That's what we need, more GCs. That is, what we real estate buffs call gated communities. *Windsor Forest—Based on the Masterpieces of Thomas Kincaid, Painter of Light®. Coke™ . . . Life Tastes Good®. Take Back Florida/ George Prescott Bush/ Republican for Governor.* An old Mustang with a scrolling LED bumper sticker: IN ANOTHER UNIVERSE, MY SON IS AN HONOR STUDENT. *Pilgrim Homesteads,* which I guess was code for a WASP-flight enclave. An anti-abortion ad scrolled by with an upset-looking fetus on it. No worries, little guy. You didn't miss anything. Anne-Marie was saying how analysts had thought that with statewide 30 percent unemployment more people would want to be police officers, but the opposite had turned out. Past the Baja Fresh and Fran's Anemones. They both looked closed. Damn. Fran used to compete with Lenny but I still got brine shrimp from her sometimes. *Federation Forest™. Enterprise Estates™.* Those were both for aging Trekkies. Actually, I only knew about them because they'd been developed by the "Warren Intentional Communities Family." They were big, but WICF's biggest hits were still the Golden Year Gothams, which were like whole cities made of nursing homes, and the Special Youth Plantations, which I guess were like a cross between giant day-care centers and reform schools. *Colonia Años Dorados™. Long John Silver's. Future Site of Pandora®.* I guess that one was going to be based on *Avatar™. Rancho Pasa de Uva™.* Or had I just made that one up? I looked back but couldn't read it anymore. God, this is stultifying. Well, this might be the last time you have to deal with the ol' Pike, I reminded myself. Even the last time you have to drive anywhere. Out over my left arm the big dirty orange sun touched the line of scrub behind dead orange trees. Six-forty P.M., I thought. Right on the dot. Just a hair west of west-by-southwest. Creeping toward the winter solstice on the Fourth Overlord. Which'll be the last one. Ever. Ever, everer, even more ever, Everest. OMG, OM—

Cancel, my other side said. That is, I call it "my other side," for convenience, but of course it can be either side, it's just whichever voice speaks second in my internal dialogue. Cancel, my other side said. Think Pos.

Okay. I passed the strip mall that had Reefer's Madness in it. They looked closed too. In fact the whole complex looked closed. Geez, it's like I'm already the Omega Man, even without doing anything. I kept repeating the happy end-of-everything thoughts, but still the boredom was so overpowering that at the four-lobe cloverleaf onto the turnpike I came within a few synapses of taking the crate up to 170 mph and ramming it into the uprights. Instead I just pulled up at the checkpoint. It could have been an ordinary toll plaza from "plaza" from thirty years ago, except for the brighter light, more cameras, and a trio of Rolly PoPos edging between the queues of cars. One of them waddled up to me.

(3)

"Hi there, welcome to Florida's scenic Ronald Reagan Turnpike," he or it said in the voice of, I think, Will Ferrell. Its wide black grin narrowed and widened roughly along with the consonants and the vertical black ovals that represented its eyes rotated thirty degrees in apical opposition, signifying childlike delight. "Could I jus' get a peek at your handprint real quick please?" He held out his right "hand," a thick four-fingered white glove with a round glass scanner in the center of the palm like a Jain dharmachakra.

"These aren't the droids you're looking for," I was about to say, but then I figured they must hear that a thousand times a day. Instead I just held out my hand, palm down. Green laser light flashed over it. Nanny Jackboots, I thought, except that I guess I should be glad now that I have stock in the company. Parts of the outfit he wore, and the whole Rolly Po-Po Program design, were Warren Group products. Marena'd shown me a brochure. It was from the Zerothruster division, which was all about mastering crowd psychology, and its current tagline was "The Fun, Fuzzy, and Family-Friendly Frontier of Nonconfrontational Law Enforcement." Basically the outfits were the regular water-cooled Explosive Ordinance Disposal Advanced Bomb Suits made by the Westminster Group, but since 9/11, when they'd started supplying them as character suits for Disney and Six Flags and other parks, Zerothruster had been facelifting the Nomex/Kevlar with poodle-furry flocking in "varied and cheerful designer colors," and adding big round outer heads that fit over the high collar and SCBA helmet and that featured "a wide array of designs customizable for cultural nonaggression and local correctness." This one was a black-and-orange neotenized cat with a teal-blue T-shirt that meant, I guess, that it was the mascot of the Jacksonville Jaguars, and an oversized round badge that said FLORIDA HIGHWAY PATROL.

"Good-o, guy, well, jus' gimmie a sec here," the thing's next prerecording said. The thing's left "hand" held a long angled stick with a camera on the end, and he started sweeping it under the 'Cuda. Was he watching the video with one of his eyes, or was someone or something else watching it?

"Hey, you're good to go, have a good one," the thing said. The words $14.50 RRT TOLL appeared on my bright new dashboard screen. Thanks, I thought. And enjoy being MicroHitler. For another fifty-two days. I merged law-abidingly onto the Turnpike. A blast of tianguiscore Dopplered by on the right at eight-five, coming from a Cutlass low-rider with curb sensors like catfish barbells and a young but obese Tejano hunched over the tiny steering wheel. Bet it could one-eighty on a peso at sixty-five. Well, I'm just an old square bourgie fart. Except why should I hurry? I least of all people ever to walk the earth. The Rapture's coming and it's *todo por mi culpa.* He zinged around an orange Yellow Van Lines truck and back into the right lane. Probably heading into the No-Go Zone, I thought. Some monster *delirio.* It's not a party unless you burn the place down at the end. Well, I agree. Have fun, hermano. Maybe I'll drop by on the way back from MP's. One of the odder things about the No-Go Zone was that even though some places were still clocking in at over 40 curies per square kilometer, since it covered over four thousand square miles, and there were about four hundred different roads leading into it, and since squatters don't much care about long-term health anyway, the police speculated that the population of the NGZ area had actually gone up since the Horror. I'd been there a couple of times to buy fake identity papers and it was actually kind of great, a whole sort of lawless Pirates' Nassau Town with a smorgasbord of meth, horse, crank, dogfighting, and preteen BJs, but actually not all that dangerous because M13 and a couple of the smaller gangs wanted to keep the carriage trade and policed the place themselves. Next, since it was a personalized feed, I got the malacological news: Sun-Min Hsu and Tobi Ramadan had described a species of nudibranch from the Line Islands area that they said might be eusocial, that is, divided into castes like ants and bees, although I couldn't imagine how that could be possible, and I actually do know a little bit about opisthobranches. Some people think nudibranchs are the world's most beautiful living things, with all the extruded gills and polyps in Fantasia-Phiokol colors, and other people think they're the ugliest, and most people haven't heard of them at all. Although to some other critter—to a lobster, say—they probably look pretty drab. Anyway, they have some unusual characteristics, including the almost unique ability to devour their prey and, instead of digesting all of it, incorporate some of its useful cells—cnidarians' stinger cells, for instance, or photosynthesizing algae—into their own bodies. I'd miss them. Except of course I wouldn't, because I wouldn't exist. And, experientially anyway, not existing is exactly equivalent to never having existed. So really we didn't have a problem. Anyway, after the Jedcentric news, for some reason the car decided I'd heard all the news and now wanted to listen to a feed called Last Age of Heroes, which seemed to be having a Stones/Byrds/Doors festival. Debuting at Marker 31, DHSMV had initiated another decade of postdeconstruction on the granny lane—INJURE/KILL A WORKER—$7,500 + 15 YEARS, a sign said, so temptingly that I couldn't imagine anyone resisting the offer. At the Kissimmee exit I voice-texted Marena that I'd be there in ten minutes. Why give her any more time to stage the place? See what she's really wearing, doing, reading, smoking, fucking, fisting, *et ceteris paribus ad foetidus hepaticum.* Right?

Marena's house was just outside the south city limit of Orlando on Orchid Island, one of quite a few residential patches that weren't only not abandoned, but were making a good-neighborly effort to muddle through as though things were normal. The faux-wrought-iron gate was open, but the dude came out of the guardhouse, made sure I was really me, and he was really polite about it. Classy. I tip-tired through the two S-curves of a long pink-concrete driveway flanked with close-packed pepper trees. There was a three-car garage, but Marena's Cherokee was parked on the side of the big circle, with two other dark SUVs behind it, and I parked in the front of the line.

At some point, I forget when, Marena'd told me that Walt had built her house during Epcot's early grand Utopian phase, and I'd thought she'd been exaggerating, but it turned out to be true, and the place was a nearly exact replica of some Frank Lloyd Wright house or other. From this side it looked a lot like the palaces at Uxmal, which is a Yucatec Maya city that was a big capital in the AD 900s, and which, incidentally, had been ruled by some of my ancestors, the Xiws.

I scrumbled out. Crack. Ow. Stiff. Getting old. Damn, it was stuffy. I re-pocketed my wallet and phone into my shirt and left my jacket on the passenger seat. Okay. Out of habit, I locked the doors. I looked up at NNE +30 degrees to see if I could spot Comet Ixchel but there was too much smaze. Okay, here goes. I toed on the microvibration, pushed away from the car, and skated—sorry, Sleeked™—across the cement. Sleeking felt like you were doing something between ice skating and old-time four-wheel roller skating, but since your feet were flat on the ground there was a sense like you were on a buttered Teflon tray. Basically, the deal was that the treads vibrated at a very high frequency, so they'd slip around even on an ordinary road surface, and then, when the vibe wasn't on, the action of walking on them generated electricity that they'd store for later, so there weren't any big battery packs. I guess if they'd come out when I was seven I would have gone monkey over them, but right now they weren't plugging my wound. Instinctively—already—I cut off the vibration with my big toes and came to a hard stop at the single doorstep. The car must have rung an alarm because before I got to the door a medium-tall Latino guy opened it.

"... Uh, Jed," he said. "Hi."

"Hi," I said. It was Tony Sic.

(4)

"Hi," I mumbled again. "Tony. Hi." At first I hadn't recognized him because he'd gotten a vicious crew cut. He was in shorts and a blue-and-white-striped Mérida Fútbol Club shirt with a big number 28. Huh, I thought. Huh. Wonder what's going on. He kind of stared at me. I felt a twinge of that old-rival feeling.

He asked how I was. I said better and asked him how he was. He said something. He seemed nervouser than usual. Were he and Marena having a thing? I wondered. She'd said she was getting married to somebody—but no way, she can't, can't, can't have meant she was getting married to Tony Sic. That was too ghastly to contemplate, and I'd been contemplating some ghastly stuff lately. Although why so ghastly, really? I didn't have anything against the guy. We were sort of competitive colleagues with the Game and I'd been terribly jealous of him when I'd thought he'd get to get downloaded into 9 Fanged Hummingbird, the Maya ahau, instead of me, and then when I'd gotten selected to go naturally I'd felt all guilty. He wasn't my William Wilson, but his story was quite a bit like mine. He was a Maya speaker, he'd gotten into academics and worked with Taro, and he'd even spent some time working for one of the CPRs, the one in Ixcán that isn't the same as Ix. Be nice to him, I thought. Remember, you're going to kill him. Along with everybody else, of course, but still.

Eh, *pues*. I stepped into the dry frigidity. I'd never gotten used to the benthic depth of air conditioning in El Norte. And never would. Sic motioned me to edge past him in the narrow entryway and I started to, but then he rattled a sort of nonobjective coatrack, and I said I'd keep my jacket on and there was a sort of awkward moment. We after-youed into a little sort of vestibule. There was a Geiger tube lying on the sort of radiator housing thing, charging from a big hazardous extension tentacle, and I had to get my feet over that, and then there was an orange SleekerBoard—it had kind of runners on the bottom like on a sled, and with what looked like a pretty heavy battery on its undercarriage, which I was sure Warren would deal with in the iterations to come, or would have, rather—which I guess belonged to Max, leaning precariously against the concrete-block doorjamb, and I avoided that, and then there were all the shoes, and I got around those and took three steps and then remembered it was an Asian-style house and went back. Instead of having laces, the Sleekers were spring-loaded to sort of intelligently release your foot when you toe a thingy on the side. I parked them next to sextet of Sic's big Diadora *fútbol* shoes. Sic seemed to feel like he was being rude watching me but didn't want to turn away from me, either, so he sort of backed away into the other side of the house, which didn't seem really like him. I got a spider-sense that there were other people around. Ashley$_3$, probably—Marena's housekeeper—and maybe her creepy driver with the ridiculously would-be scary name, Grgur.

"I'm in the orifice," Marena's voice called. Maybe she'd forgotten that I'd never been here before. Except that wasn't like her. I looked back at Sic. He kind of indicated that it was to the right. I went to the right, across pseudoglyphish cast flagstones, through a stony living room with a sort of squashed cathedral ceiling—maybe they call it a hut ceiling?—and through a high trapezoidal door into a dimly lit room with a big table smattered with monitors and hard drives. There were big French doors on the far side with a dark garden and a narrow pool glowing phthalocyanine blue. Something stretched up and—

Whoa.

(5)

The something had kissed me on the lower lip. It was Marena. She was in a sort of anthracite-gray, probably pashmina sort of top and a matching sort of bottom, with a sort of hairband thingie and a necklace with a hundred and eight garnet beads on it. Her face—it was a square, flat face, maybe too ethnic for a lot of howlies, but the sort of thing you really like if you like that sort of thing—her face was tanner, as expected, and it seemed more so because of big silver clustery Bucellati earrings that seemed clunky for her. She stepped back and sank to her normal height. She looked a little uncomfortable.

"Hi, that was nice," I said. She said hi.

I looked at her. She looked at me. I looked away first.

"You're looking really good," she said.

"Thanks." Damn, now if I tell her she looks good it'll sound insincere. Instead I started to tell her how she looked tan.

"No, I mean you really look healthy and happy and everything," she said. Really? I wondered. I'd thought I was moping, what with the Sic business and everything. "What's up?"

"Up? Nothing."

"Really?"

"Nothing," I said.

"You've been working out, right?"

"Well, I changed the fluidized bed filters in the sponge tanks."

"No, really, you're doing good, right?"

"Better never. I mean, never better."

There was a pause. You know how they say that when you're at a loss for words to talk about something that's in the room? So I looked around the room. There was a huge monitor on a big wooden easel, like it was an oil painting, and there was a sketch on the monitor of a sort of Mayanesque city, and I indicated it.

"Did you do that freehand?" I asked. She said yes. I said that was really something. It was too. The girl really could sketch. "That's what it'll look like from the plaza," she said.

"What will?"

"You know, Neo-Teo™." That is, she didn't pronounce the little ™ symbol, but I heard the name like it was there. "I mean, the analog version."

"By *analog* you mean real, right?" I asked.

"Oh, yeah, real life, full scale, inhabitable, the whole thing. I'm the first single person in charge of designing a city this large since, like, Peter the Great."

"Cool," I inarticulated. Marena talked fast sometimes, almost like she was from 1940s radio, and it could take one a second to digest what she'd said. I liked it about her, though. These days if you take a business-presentations class or whatever they always tell you to speak as slow as sloth shit, not just so the 'tards can keep up but because they've done studies where people think the same exact speech is more important if it takes two minutes instead of one minute. On the other hand, if you've ever been in, say, any software-development meetings of more than three people, you might have seen how there'll be two or three people who figure the problem out right away, and they work it out together speaking really fast with all this heavy jargon, and then when they've solved the problem they'll take a break and one of them will explain the solution to all the lesser minds. Marena was one of those two or three people. It's like, whoa, Brain on Board.

"Check this out," she said. She sort of pulled me around the desk area to a pair of low side tables. One of them was displaying a little crowd of vinyl dolls, or I guess you're supposed to call them action figures, and when I got closer I could see they were vinyl Barbie-gauge Maya mythological characters, all in that trendy sort of Jesse Hernandez Urban-Ocēlōmeh style. Each had its name in raised gold on its little fauxstone base. But even without the labels, "Jun Raqan," that is, Hurricane, would have been easy to recognize because of his single leg, and it wasn't too hard to pick out "One Ocelot," "1 Turquoise Ocelot," "Mam" (who, since he still turned up sometimes these days under the name Maximón, sported a nineteenth-century hat and bolo tie over his Classic Maya gear), "Waterlily Jaguar," "Ix Chel," and "Star Rattler," which was a long feathery snake with goo-goo-googly eyes and a lot of centipedalian legs. There was also a quartet of hunchbacked dwarfs in different colors, which they'd called "Northeast Chak," "Northwest Chak," and "Southwest Chak," and then a gang of creepshowy types, obviously the nine Lords of Xibalba, the Maya underworld. They'd named the tallest one, the leader, "4 Jaguar Night," and then his posse of eight henchmen all had names beginning with *S*—Scab, Skitters, Spine (a mastiff-sized fanged rabbit), Scald, Snatchbat, Scurf (a big disembodied head), Sarcoma, and Serpigo—who, to me anyway, looked more Cthuluish than Maya, but what do I know?

"Not those, this," Marena said. She edged behind the other table. It was covered with what looked like stacks of aerogel building blocks. She found a remote and clicked it on. The blocks filled with light and shadow.

Whoa, I said, or tried to. Anyway, I've left off the inverted commas because I suspect I didn't get it all the way out of my throat.

It was an architectural model of a futuristic Mayanesque city: pyramids, plazas, palaces, spires, towers, bartizans, barbicans, brattices, lattices, oubliettes, obalesques, clerestories, labyrinthories, minatourets, and zigzaggurats, all bathed in a late-afternoon glow and with the inhuman clarity of, say, a daguerreotype, or, to get flowery, something woven out of spun sugar by an army of tiny elves trained at the École des Hôteliers Gastronomiques. The table was only about four feet square and the model didn't even cover the whole thing, but every carved stone and enamel tile and copper-electroplated window stood out realer than real, so that there seemed to be more detail in it than you'd be able to see in a real city, from a good vantage point, on a clear day, with binoculars, and with the eyes you had as a ten-year-old. It really looked like something from the future. Although of course we've been living in the future for a while now, but still. And it wasn't holographic—obviously, because of the color—and it wasn't any kind of video, or—oh, right. I remembered. It had to be that new 3-D system they'd been talking about. *They* meaning Marena and her design team from Warren Entertainment. The Barbie Something.

"Have you seen it before?" Marena asked.

I think I still didn't say anything.

"I mean, the DHI?"

"Sorry," I said, "I don't know what that is."

"Doll House Interface."

"Oh, right."

"It's these blocks of aerogel with all these layers of plasma video screens like, sandwiched into them," she said. "So without the input it's almost transparent. The consumer version's still a few years away."

"Right."

"And then there's also layers of reverse-polarizers, so that makes the shadows. And then there's a lot of transparency, so you get color depth. And each little layer's twenty-four hundred DPI."

I mumbled how thrillingly advanced that all was.

There was a sense of movement somewhere inside the thing and when I squinted closer it turned out that the staircases on the pyramids were escalators. It sounds tacky, but the thing had such a what I guess you'd call a sense of unity that even that, and the neonish ersatz Maya gargoyles and animatronic caryatids and whatever, all seemed to be the right things in the right places.

"See, that's the Hyperbowl," she said. She picked up an oval block that was displaying a glass-and-titanium pyramidal shell and uncovered a playing field and tiers of seats.

"So, wait, you're going to build all this on top of the Stake?" I asked. That is, on top of what was officially called the Belize Olympics Complex. A stake is a Mormon mission, which was what it was originally, so that was what everyone called it around the Warren Family of Caring Companies.

"Well, eventually, that's the idea," she said. She handed me the oval block. When I squinted close at it I could just make out nets of gold wires and a black chip the size of the letter *M* in six-point pica. "After the games the Morons want their own boutique country. Basically it's a tax dodge."

"Well, it's always good to plan for the future." *End of Everything,* I thought. Hell. Don't think about it.

"Yeah. I guess, you know, now that they've prevented the end of the world, the Firm's getting right back to trying to own it."

"Right." *EOE,* I thought again. Damn. It really felt like I was thinking it in that Stephen King echo-effect punctuation, you know, like:

> Okay, so there I was, like, walking along, doo-dee-doo-dee-doo,
> and I
> *(End of Everything)*
> walked into the East Innesmouth Post Office and
> *(EOE)*
> the lady at the window, about whom much, much more in a moment, handed me a tattered, oddly heavy manila envelope wrapped in ratty twine, and I
> *(todo por mi culpabilidad)*
> opened it and . . .

You know.

"You sound doubtful," Marena said.

"No, I'm, I'm not, it, uh, it sounds . . ."

"Yeah, you are. What are you doubtful aboutful?"

"I'm not, I'm . . ."

"Hi, boss," Marena said.

"Hi," a ten-year-old boy's voice said behind me. It was her kid, Max. "Hi, Uncle Jed."

I said hi. He'd come up and was hugging me. I kind of hugged back but it felt really awkward for obvious reasons, like, because, you know. Okay, I'll say it. Because I was going to kill him. Had killed him. Fuck. I was starting not to feel so good. Coming up here had not been a good idea. He pulled away and looked at the Neo-Teo model. The afternoon-light effect had deepened to sunset cerises, and the stone and tiles on the "east" side—which was actually turned to the north—had gone to twilight blues and grays. Window lights and faux-neon signage, with Mayanesque glyphs in new Decoesque fonts, started flickering on. They made the place look a little more like the Syd Mead sets for *Blade Runner,* but without the grunge.

"Pretty godless, huh?" he asked.

"Your mom's very talented," I said.

"Tony says we can order whatever we want for dinner," he said. He'd gotten the Star Rattler figurine and was unsnapping its segments and reconnecting them in a different order.

"Whatever that's not Indian," Marena said.

"What do you do on Sleekers?" he asked me. He must have seen mine in the entryway. I said nothing much yet. "Lookit this," he said. He stepped back into the hallway, ran in through the door, and in what I guess was a parkour move vaulted one-handed over the desk, somehow avoiding the thicket of monitors. Evidently he activated his Sleekers in midair because he came down in a glide and, just as he was about to crash through the French doors, channeled his momentum into a scratch spin, pulling in his arms and spotting on my face each time. We said wow.

"Wait, that wasn't good," he said. "I'm gonna do it again." He did it again. We told him how great it was and how seeing it again would dilute our enjoyment of its surprising and utterly radical greatness. Marena asked what I wanted for sort of dinner. I started to say how, well, I hadn't been planning on making them feed me, but she wouldn't hear of it. She negotiated Max down to a "vegetarian array" of Korean food and he left to give the orders. Fuckez moi, I thought. I'd felt like a jerk before, but it had gotten a whole lot worse, that is, if it's even possible to be the worst person who ever lived and then get even more disgustingly evil. I'm the bad guy, I thought. Oh, well. He's still at the stage where things seem interesting. Better for him to just disappear before he finds out what the world's really like. Who's—

"Hey, don't rapture those Krispy Kremes," Marena called after him.

"Max is really great," I said.

"Oh, *définitivement,*" she said. "It's like a whole, it gives you a whole different set of priorities, about what's important, I mean, momming . . . hey, guess what he's going to be tomorrow."

"Sorry?"

"For trick-or-treating."

"Oh. I can't guess."

"Dick Cheney. He wrote a paper on him for Social Studies."

"Gosh."

"Hey, speaking of the date, I got something for you."

Oh, right, I thought. It's my birthday. Actually, for Maya folks your name day—mine was three days from now—is a bigger deal, but maybe she didn't know that. She handed me what was clearly an elephant-folio book, cleverly folded up in blue Genji-cloud *kozogami*. I coaxed it open without wrap rage. It was a book from 1831, von Stepanwald's *Curious Antiquities of British Honduras.* I must have told her how I'd lost my copy and ABE wasn't finding another.

"Wow," or something, I said. I thanked her profusely. I flipped through it. The copper engravings—and a few etchings—were as sharp as if they'd been pulled yesterday. "This is great," I said. There—

Wait.

Huh.

Hell.

The Citadel of the Ocelot Dynasty at Ixnichi Sotz in Ancient Days
As It Was Described by Señor Diego San Niño de Atocha Xotz

Curious Antiquities of British Honduras
By Subscription · Lambeth · 1831

(6)

You'd think I'd be beyond it at this stage, but I felt a welling up of some sort of good feeling mixed with some sort of bad feeling. I couldn't quite hit on their names, though. I guess the good one was like coziness or fuzzy-'n'-warmness and the bad one was . . . guilt? No. No way. Well, maybe. Dude. You're slipping. Undo, undo. You did the right thing. And you knew there'd be moments like this. You need to just get through the next fifty-one days. And there's only one way you're going to do that: denial. Right? Right.

"Okay, anyway," she said, when the little scene was over, "well, that gives us twenty minutes to finish that game."

"Okay," I said, managing to leave out the introductory "uh."

She steered me around to where there were two quadricolored Korean cushions on either side of an old and very thick straight-grained kaya-wood Go board, the one that had been in her now-closed office downtown, and which I figured was worth north of fifty K. You could just see the sunken pyramid on its underside reflected in the dark tile floor. She took the bowls off the board, set them down, opened them, and started scooping out stones.

"You don't like Indian food?" I asked.

"Hate. That stuff is *dirty*." The way she said the word it sounded like it was in that *Tales-from-the-Crypt*y drip font, like "**DIRTY**."

"I didn't know that about you."

"Well, I'm sure it's the last thing." She dug an old Insa analog chess clock out of somewhere, wound up both sides, and settled it next to the board.

"Oh, no, I'm sure there's lots I don't . . . you're a woman of mystery . . ."

"*You're* the mystery," she said. "You've got something going on." Marena started laying out the game where we'd left it three months ago, at the seventieth move. We'd started it at the Stake, during the Madison business, and a lot had happened since then, but—as I maybe should mention for the benefit of non-Go players in the audience—there wasn't anything outstandingly mentally acrobatic about picking it up again now. Actually, all Go players above a certain level can remember all their games and can pick up any of them at any stage. Also, as long as we're making explanations, maybe I should say how it might seem a little odd that we'd do this now, but only to people who don't play. No Go player wants an unresolved game hanging around in the air like a hungry ghost.

"Sorry?" I asked.

"You're not planning some damn thing for my birthday, are you? Because I'm not putting this one on my résumé." She snuck her right middle finger into the side of her mouth and, discreetly, bit on it.

"Oh, uh, sorry, no." *Mierditas,* I thought. I hate mind readers.

"So what's up? I bet you made another huge and foolishly attention-getting investment coup."

"No, no . . . it's just you haven't seen me for a while, that's all—"

"Uh-huh." She conveyed a mass of dubiousness. Hell, I thought. *(EOE)* I'm transfuckingparent. Better take off now. No, wait. That's even more suspicious-making. I looked up at the nearest one of the nine or so clocks on her desk. It was some I guess Masonic antique that said it was to . The next one in the row was an impossible-to-read skeleton clock—maybe it told the time in Xibalba—but the third one was highly legible: *"6:41,"* it said. *"Smartlite Sweeper™/Quartz USA."* Damn. The night is far-effing young. Damn. Okay, just stick it out. It's no biggie. Don't get para. All chicks have empath powers. Right? But she can't *actually* read your mind. Not without a whole lot of gadgetry, anyway.

"Nothing's up," I said. *(EOE! EOE!)*

"Are you sure—wait, hang on." She paused for eight seconds. I finished laying out the game. "Okay, just use the Amex number," she said. "Sorry," she said to me. Oh, that's why, I thought. I mean, why she had those big earrings. They were telephones. I mean, one of them was. The other probably had an extra condom in it or something.

"Okay," I said. I nodded. Marena nodded. I punched my clock. As it does, time seemed to slow down slightly. I'd decided on my move weeks ago, so I put it right down. She'd anticipated it and responded immediately. The world slowed down another five clicks. Despite everything else that was going on, despite whatever little secrets she had and despite the big deal-breaking secret I had, we were in Gametime.

And so it came to pass that there now followed about twelve and one-fifth minutes of silence, punctuated by six raps of stones hitting the thick wood. I always thought one of the most off-balancing things in life is when there's a pause at the wrong time, and this felt especially wrong, a strange interlude with nothing happening in the middle of—well, maybe it just feels wrong to me. Damn it, how can Korean food take so long? Like it takes time to open ten jars of assorted kimchee. I focused on the board. In the first stages of a Go game it feels like you're emplacing forts on a wide, desolate frontier. But at this point, almost halfway in, the stone pictures were coming into focus, crosses, flowers, a poodle, a long black staircase growing out of her second corner and bifurcating near the center into distended jaws, like the Star Rattlers balusters at Chichen. I pushed through a gap in the stairs and, maybe too fliply, hit the clock.

She didn't make a move. One minute. She bit down again on her presumably nonconforming fingernail, noticed she was doing it, and pulled her hand away and tucked it under her thigh. Two minutes.

"Damn," she said, at two minutes and eighteen seconds. Her biggest group was in real trouble. "This is not good."

"Sorry," I said.

"Not good. Maybe you should give me three stones next time."

"I shouldn't even be giving you two stones."

"I'm rusty, I've been running an empire and saving the planet and decluttering the kid's room and stuff. You should give me four stones."

"No way. With four stones you can beat anybody. Theoretically."

"Yeah? How many to beat God?"

"The world champion would be at a disadvantage by the fiftieth move with one stone against God."

"Uh-huh."

"Seriously."

"Hey, do you know what game I can beat God at every time?" she asked. "Without a handicap?"

"No, what's that?"

"Chicken."

"What do you mean?"

"Like with driving cars at each other, you know, how that kid got killed at the Colonial Gardens desert mall like, last—"

"No, I know, I mean, why, what do you mean about beating God?"

"Because—look, if one of the players is omniscient, like God, he loses. All you have to do is decide not to swerve."

"Wait, so God can tell you're not going to swerve, so he has to."

"Right," she said.

"Except if he's God he can't get hurt."

"What? Oh—uh, maybe. But he still loses."

"Are you sure about this?"

"Oh, yeah. They taught Max about it at Logic Camp."

"Huh. Well, I guess that's right."

"We used to play a chicken variant, like, we'd stand on like a wall and throw lightbulbs to each other, and we'd step back each time. Did you ever play that?"

"Well, I had a health—uh, no. We used to play *escondidas* . . ."

"What's that?"

"Like hide-and-seek."

"Oh, yeah." She looked at the board and then back up at me. "Did you ever play Time Machine?"

(7)

"What's that?" I asked. "No, I don't think so—"

"That's like—well, I'd sit in this spot in my room just like this." She closed her eyes and crossed her arms. "And I'd mark the exact—oh, wait, first I'd put on the B side of *Taking Tiger Mountain by Strategy*—and I'd memorize the exact date and time, and I'd sit like, still enough to stop time. And then I'd decide that exactly twenty years, like, to the second, I'd sit in exactly this same position with the same music and have exactly these same thoughts, and all the intervening time would be like it hadn't happened."

"Oh." I'd thought she'd meant some plasticky board game by Ideal or whatever. "Yeah, I guess I did play something like that."

"Really." She had a stone in her hand, but she wasn't putting it down.

"Well, yeah. Basically. I hadn't thought about it in a long time, though. And I thought I'd made it up."

"Maybe we both made it up," she said. She set the stone down on the side star point. It was a fine move, but it was still a book move. That is, not insightful. She hit her clock.

"I guess," I said.

"It's our psychic link." She smiled. It wasn't an ironic smile, or a wry, knowing, sardonic, nonconformist's smile, not even a humorous smile. It was just a sincere friendshipish expression. A rare bird these days, I thought. It was a smile like, we're hanging out and bonding and isn't that great. I felt a smudge of mistiness in the back of my eyeballs. Squelch that. Hard up. Don't forget how she made you a sucker. She conned you like she was Fa'pua'a Fa'amu and you were Margaret Mead—

"Or, I don't know," I said. "Maybe all kids play that."

"No, I don't think so. Just a few sad, introspective nerded-out kids."

"Yeah, maybe."

I cocked my head, closed my right eye, and looked at the board with my left eye to get a fresh look at the position.

"It's good to keep your different life stages in touch with each other," she said. "All those years just swish by."

"Yeah."

"Do you have any left?"

"Any what?"

"Any second parts coming up in Time Machine, you know, like, where you plan to sit in that position again and whatever."

"Oh. Yeah, I guess I do," I said. "I have one left."

"When is it?"

"Uh . . . January twentieth. At noon. Four years from now."

"That's great, okay, so maybe we should do something together then."

"Well, I don't—uh, okay." This topic was harshing my wave. I scooped up a stone and thwacked it down, a *hane* on her last point. Nothing board-shattering. I hit my clock. Maybe I don't need to find out what's the real deal with Tony. Maybe I should just take off now. No, don't. Leave now and she'll really know something's up. In fact she'll probably tell them to ratchet up the surveillance on you. Although that's kind of weird, she's a romantic interest and also your Stasi minder. Although the whole thing is weird. Well, NFML. Not For Much Longer. Just crush her flat in this one game, have two bites of bibimbap, and book. No sweat.

"Okay, it's a date. Even if we're both married to other people by then. Right?"

"Yeah . . ." I said. ". . . Why, are you getting married?" Damn it, Jedface, don't ask girls questions like that. Have a drop of sangfroid. Forget Sick Tony Sic, you lost, get over it. Anyway, what do you care? Nothing matters. We were all going to be dead in—no, don't think dead. Nonexisting—

"No, I'm not," Marena said.

I said okay, or something. I tried to look at the board, but the game was at that point where the stones start to look and even feel like pustules erupting on your skin, and you just want it to be over.

"Are you upset about Tony staying here?" she asked, a little muffledly because she was working on that fingernail again.

"No, I mean, he, you know . . ."

"I totally haven't touched him."

Huh.

"It's okay," I said, "you get, you get to touch whatev—"

"It's not a romantic thing, he's just staying here because he's, for a place to stay."

"What about that getting-married business?"

"That was a different guy."

"Oh."

"And I'm not sure about that lately."

"Oh. Okay."

"I mean—look, this is all getting into feelings and, like, feelings."

"Yeah. I have difficulty with those things."

"Hmm," she went. She sort of melted herself down into her oddly yielding Memory Foam cushions and stretched out prone.

"Maybe it's okay, whatever happens," she said, "maybe there's another whole world out there, like with that Mr. Bubble thing?"

"Sorry? I don't get the reference."

"The Crazy Foam, you know, those two guys from the Layton Institute with the bubbly verses, uh . . ."

"Oh, the bubbleverse," I said.

"Right." She was referring to this incident back in 1998 when a pair of Warren-funded physicists reported that said they'd created a bubble in the quantum foam and created another universe that, at that moment, was the exact twin of our own, but which, because of random perturbation, would exhibit divergent outcomes later on. It was purest bullshit.

"That's what I said."

"Uh, yeah."

"Do you think that's possible?"

"You mean, that they created another universe in their lab?"

"Yeah."

"Well, I, you know what Taro says, multiple uni—they're, you know, cheap on theory, expensive on universes. So, no, I don't, really. That's just something people say when their equations don't come out right, they say whatever's left over just slides into some other handy universe."

"Yeah, but they said they saw it."

"How would they see it? It's not in the same universe."

"Anyway, we'd be in it," I said.

"Okay, I don't know. That's what they said. And they said there was definitely not an infinite number of universes. There aren't even a lot."

"So how many are there? Like a handful?"

"Right. A few more 'n a couple."

"Five or six?"

"That sounds about right."

"Huh."

"Still, that's just my intuition," she said. "And every once in a while one of them forks and makes two."

"Fork in the road."

"Yeah. And then, you know, when something bad happens in one of them, it might not happen in all the others."

"Hmm. A very pleasant thought."

"Come on."

"Sorry," I said. "I don't know, maybe it's possible."

"Never mind. Heck."

"Maybe it's going to be alien probes," she said. "Running around the universe blowing up life-sustaining planets out of sheer pity."

"Humanitaliens."

"Yeah. Damn, damn, damn, damn," she said, five times in total. "Damn. We really nearly all died. Sorry, my mind's—I'm very free-associating."

"Do you mean with the Madison thing or just the Hippogriff thing?"

"Oh . . . I was thinking about Madison, but yeah, I also feel bad about those pilots sometimes."

"I wouldn't," I said. "Those guys dream about seeing action like that. They'd rather do one minute of real fighting than live to be a thousand."

"Yeah, I guess you—you're such a *guy,*" she said. "You get stuff like that."

"One crowded hour of glorious life."

"Yeah, whatevs."

I guess I mentioned the Hippogriff Incident in the press release, but just to clarify, we, or Warren Labs, were allegedly responsible for the incineration, on March 21, of two Fuerza Aérea Guatemalteca pilots, by, allegedly, an AIM-9 Sidewinder missile. It was an almost-major international incident that had exacerbated tensions between Guatemala and Belize, and even between Guatemala and the U.S. As of today, thanks to nearly sixteen million dollars of lawyering, Marena and the team and I seemed to have gotten away pretty clean, and even Executive Solutions still hadn't been charged with anything. But the whole thing had made it harder for the Warren Group to rock the boat anywhere in Latin America.

"Look," I said, "dying isn't—I mean, they probably didn't even notice."

"Why, you know what it's like?"

"Dying?"

"Yeah."

"Well, I'm pretty sure it's like, nothing."

"But apart from that."

"No, I mean, all I was saying was—look, the deal is, despite one's ingrained denial of it, the fact is that every time you fall asleep, you die. In fact you basically die every time you even just lose your train of thought. And when you die for the last time, for you it won't be any different, you'll just forget what you were thinking about and not start up again. I mean, you won't notice. The illusion of continuance is just pure nonsense."

"So maybe the world did end and we just didn't notice."

"Well, that's not exactly—"

"Or else the Bush administration covered it up."

"Well, then we wouldn't be making that speculation, though." She didn't answer, but she did look at me as though she was interested. "Actually, there are a lot of ways the world could end and nobody'd notice."

"You mean like if it happened too fast?"

"Yeah."

"How would that work?" she asked.

"Oh, you know, strangelets, earth-core perturbations, remote atom, atomic events from like naked singularities or whatever, um . . ."

"Well, that'd suck."

"I don't know, I don't think most people wouldn't even mind."

"You mean if they didn't understand what was happening?"

"No, I mean, even in advance, people wouldn't—I mean, look, half of them are at least wannabe suicidal anyway. They just don't want to deal with a lot of nooses and razor blades and guns and wreckage and starvation and fire and plague and stuff." I half noticed that we'd gotten into dangerous conversational territory, but, as so often, I didn't shut up. "They just don't want to see that shot of the top of the Empire State Building poking out of the water."

"Well, maybe. Still, that's only half of them."

"And the other half are just too dumb to be suicidal."

"Okay, but *everybody* dying is a bigger deal because then nothing means anything."

"You mean like it does now?"

"Well . . ."

"I mean, I wouldn't go that far, right?"

"Yeah, I guess."

"I mean, *mean*. You know, mean . . ."

"So anyway you think that's just, that's the boy of it," she said. "Like, those pilots died happy."

"I'm sure of it."

"God, you're so butch."

Huh? I thought. "Wow. Thanks," I said. "I wish I'd known that in high school."

"And it's like you don't even know it. Which makes it that much eroticker."

I mumbled something so incoherent I couldn't understand it myself.

"I can't get over how healthy you look," she said. "You're like, ruddy."

"Rutty?"

"Have you been working out?"

"Oh . . . I don't know . . ." I guess she's right, actually, I thought. Ever since I'd knocked over that first domino this afternoon—despite the occasional twang of guilt, and even despite some trepanation, I mean, trepidation, or, let's admit, fear—I'd felt this sort of . . . I guess, *warmth.* Hmm. Well, Jed, that's the evolutionary psychology of it. Chicks always dig guys who've killed a few people. Or, evidently, guys who are about to kill a whole lot of people. It gives a dude a glow, like the third month of pregnancy.

Marena flopped mustelinely onto her side. "Okay, questies. What if I started making out with you right now?"

"Uh, well, I'd certainly reciprocate, for sure, I'd—"

"Don't do me any favors—"

"No, I'm flattered, I mean—"

"Maybe I should get out my toy chest. You should see the thingy I just got."

"Is it like, an orgasmatron?"

"Kind of. It'll keep you going for, well, for a while."

"Going, like, what?"

"Well, not quite climaxing."

"Darn."

"Still, that's on the way."

"Really?"

"Oh, yeah. In the future, everyone will be able to sustain an orgasm for fifteen minutes."

"Wow."

"Yeah. The very near future. So get ready." She raised herself up in kind of upward-facing-dog position, stretched her head out on her long neck, and kissed me. I reciprocated. What if Max Sleeks in? I wondered. Better bar the door, Katie. Well, maybe he's used to such things. Hot mama.

"Call A-sub-three," she said. Pause. "Hi. Get me a half hour, okay? Yeah, Happy Rapture. Bye. Sorry." She got my head in her hands. Whoa. What seemed like a hundred and eight fingernails swarmed over my doubly naked scalp, and I saw as well as felt schools of that silver glitter that fireworks makers call drizzle effects. I try to take my hat off indoors, but it's a struggle, especially now after my head got shaved for the downloadings, and it was about the most gloves-offly intimate thing she could do, like she was slicing off my pants with bandage scissors. Wow, we're making out, I thought, like I was back in fifth grade. Now one of her other hands was fumbling with my groin area.

"How about you fuck me like it's still the end of the world?"

"Uh, mmm," I said. Okay, I thought, one last time, it's probably a good idea—but then at the same moment I thought how maybe I couldn't deal with it, and/or, more importantly, it was feeling like Jed junior wouldn't be able to deal with it. As they can, he could tell I was afraid of something. *Chill out,* I thought. *No fear. Fear is the woody-killer. Fear is the little death that brings total erectile obliteration. I will face my fear. I will permit it to pass over me and through me. And when it has gone past I will turn the inner eye to see the path where it has gone past on its path. And I will see that where the fear has gone there will be only a trail of tiny fearprints in the sands of the Erg. And only I will remain, picking grains of erg-sand out of my inner eye, like one whose water is frothy with liban and who has forgotten the ilm of his axolotls, one who—*

Can it, Muad'Jed. Get a grip. I got a grip on her head, but it didn't help. Marena came up for air.

"You're distracted," she said.

"No, I'm . . . I'm, I'm, I'm a simple soul today, I'm—"

"No, your sacral chakra's off-line. You're up to something."

"No," I said, "I'm just, you know, preoccu—"

"No, I think you're feeling distrustful."

"Well . . ."

"Okay, fine," she said. She pushed both of the buttons down halfway, stopping both clocks, and resettled herself in a lotosish position. "Look, tell you what, I'll give you three Truth or Deaths."

(8)

"Sorry?"

"You ask me anything, any one thing at a time, and I'll tell you the absolute truth, and then I get to ask you and et sequels."

"Sequentes," I said.

"Right. Boy, you're really on a Latin kick."

"Well, I'm a Latin American."

"Uh-huh."

"What's the death part?" I asked.

"You have to tell the truth, like, whole and nothing but. Or else drink hemlock."

"Is that a real game?"

"So I'll come totally clean if you will. Okay? Pinkie swear."

"Okay." We swore. Her pinkie nearly ripped mine off its metacarpal capitulum.

"You start. Ask me whatevs."

"Okay. You set me up, right?"

"In what way?" she asked. She didn't hesitate. She was a cool customer.

"All the time when I was explaining to you about the colored directions and whatever else about the Sacrifice Game and whatever, you actually knew all about it."

"No, I did not—I didn't know all that stuff, in fact I still don't understand it, in—"

"But like, when I—the first time I came to your office, you guys already wanted to reel me in, right? Taro'd said I'd want to see the Codex and you used that to bait me. Right?"

"Well, there's some truth to that, but you weren't the only—I mean, we looked up at least four others of Taro's students from when he was in New Haven and interviewed all of them."

"But when I begged you to send me you'd already decided to."

"No, not entirely."

"But you thought I'd be better at it, I mean, instead of Tony Sic, to zap back to Mayaland, but you figured I'd get spooked unless I thought I was convincing you to let me do it. Right?"

"We hadn't decided between you and Tony yet."

"But *you* thought I should do it and not Sic. You were being really deceptive."

"Well, okay, I'll say—but, I mean, come on. Would you say you're a very trusting person?"

"Uh, no."

"If you'd thought we had any—you wouldn't have gotten near us. Right?"

"Well, maybe I . . . I guess not." Any what? I wondered. Nefarious designs, I guess. Let it go.

"So I'll say yes, but now you're glad anyway, right?" Finally, she succeeded in severing the fingernail's last attachment with her left canine tooth.

"Okay, right," I said. "That's all I wanted to know." Somehow, now, it didn't seem like she'd done anything so bad.

She moved the loose nail into position with her tongue and started chewing on it with the same level of unself-conscious purposefulness my Jasus crayfish exhibit when they eat their molted exoskeletons. "Okay," she said. "My turn."

"Okay." Okay, I thought. Don't stiffen up. But don't flail either. Make normal-sized arm gestures. No hunching over. And if you have to lie, it's just like with a polygraph, you have to make yourself believe you're telling the truth. How'd I get into this? I don't have to do—except I still wanted to find out about what had happened in Guatemala. If anything. After all, she'd been down there for months. The last I'd heard she'd still been at the Stake, trying to get permission from the Guates to dig officially at Ix Ruinas. But maybe something more had happened. Or was going to happen. Maybe they'd found the tomb and there was more info in it. And if it looked like Jed_2's memories would get through, well, that would be huge. There—

"Okay. I think there's something big going on, and it's making you feel happy and powerful, but also you're a bit worried about whether it's going to come off. Am I right?"

Damn. Okay, I thought. Don't make any partial shrugs. No quick changes of expression. I checked my hands—that is, without looking at them, I thought about them. They were open with the fingers extended. Good. Okay. I focused on the bridge of her nose and, lowering my usual pitch a bit, said, "Yes."

"Okay, great. That's progress. So what is it?"

"That's a second question," I said.

"Okay, fine. You go."

"Okay. You guys are watching me. Right?"

"What do you mean us guys?"

"The Warren Spook Corporation."

"They're keeping an eye on all of us."

"That's not a good—I mean, I can tell I'm under surveillance."

"So what's the question?"

"Well . . ."

"Look, what do you think they're going to do? The Game—you're a Sacrifice Game specialist, right? It's like you're driving around with a trunkful of hydrogen bombs. We all are. They're watching me too, I mean, of course, and, you know, I think Corporate's being pretty reserved about it, frankly."

She had a point. "Well, you have a point."

"Okay, my turn," she said. "What did you do to make yourself so excited?"

"I wouldn't say I'm excited."

"But you are happy about something. Or relieved."

"No, I'm not—I mean, I'm relieved about the EOE."

"What's that stand for again?"

"The End of Everything."

"Oh, right. Okay, you're relieved that's not happening?"'

"Um, yeah. That's right."

"But that's not new. You said something new was going on."

"I did?" I had? I wondered. When? Or was she doing some hypno-thing on me? Bitch. Just be cool. Okay.

"Okay," I said. "I went very long on some futures a little while ago and I'm doing super well on them. I'm completely on Easy Street."

She looked at me. I tried to look back. Her eyes seemed bottomless. Finally it felt like I was staring into a gale-force wind. Fine, let her win the stare-down. I looked over at the Neo-Teo model. Most of the window lights and signs and had gone out, and its walls were a convincing range of deep-night blacks and blues.

"Well, that's great," she said finally. "Okay, ask me about Tony."

Huh. Well, maybe I'd passed, I thought. "Okay, well, are you and—"

Hell.

(9)

The main phone, the one in my key pocket, had pulsed—silently, but it felt as loud as if were standing in a foghorn. Time to check on the, you know. The thing.

I said something like "Hang on, I've got a call I've got to blow off," or something. I pulled the thing out. The CBT site had automatically come up on the screen. I hesitated. I looked closer.

Oh, Dios.

They'd suspended after-hours trading. The third domino had fallen. Oh God, oh God. I—I guess I should say even I—felt a twinge, and more than a twinge, of that gray free-falling terror, another notch of acceptance that it was really happening, that it was not reversible. My nefarious plan was working to perfection. *Todo mi culpabilidad.*

In a way, even—well, not in a way, forget the qualifiers—even I still couldn't believe it. I know I said that because of the Game and everything I'd become uniquely able to comprehend astronomical figures, humanly unfathomable amounts of money, of grains of corn, of suffering . . . but even so, the thing that was going to happen—let alone the fact that I'd made it happen—the thing that would happen in about four and a half million seconds was I think more than any human or maybe any consciousness of any possible type could ever comprehend. By definition, for that matter. You'd need a brain the size of the Hyperbowl, one that had been living for millions of years, enough parallelism to weigh the mass of lived experience, human, animal, and probably, now, even artificial, against that infinity-times-infinity of oblivion, you'd have to live, love, and lose a trillion times over even to glimpse how—

"Are you okay?" Marena asked.

"I'm fine."

"You were going to ask me about Tony."

"Okay, what about Tony?"

"What about him?"

"Are you and he having a thing?"

"No." She looked at me. I looked at she. Her eyes looked like she was—except, fuck, I thought, I really can't tell, can I? Accursed Oriental inscrutability.

"Are you having a thing with anybody else?"

"That's another question."

"Oh, come on."

"What are you, my mother?"

"Look—"

"Okay, fine. No. Nobody."

Naturally, I tried to watch for tells, but I couldn't see anything one way or the other. Damn, I thought. I'm at a big disadvantage here. I'd always had a little issue with facial expressions. When I was six I found a sheet in my Nephi K–12 folder—which was in a filing cabinet with a four-digit combination lock, as though that was going to hold me up for more than two minutes—that said I had "PTSD presenting as pervasive developmental disorder." That is, savant skills without IQ loss, but with defects of emotional affect. It's not autism, but it presents like it, as they say. So, for instance, you know how most kids get flash cards with words and numbers on them? I got cards with smiling or frowning or whatever faces on them, so that I could learn emotions. I couldn't even tell whether she was happy or sad just by looking at her. Telling whether she was lying or not would be like reading page 100 of a book while it's still on the shelf in the bookstore, in stretch wrap, and in Arabic.

"You said you were getting married to some jerk," I said.

"Nope. As of now, Octy is out." Octy? I wondered. Who the hell is that, Emperor Octavian? Dr. Octopus? No, don't ask and use up a question.

"Okay, my turn," she said.

"Right."

"What did you do that's making you feel so different?" she asked.

"Well, there's, there's that long shot on—"

"Okay, but why the hesitation just now?"

"Asking about the hesitation is another question already."

"Oh, for fuck's sake."

"Well—"

"Just—look, you have to answer the whole thing, you know, whole truth, not bits and pieces. Right?"

"Okay, fine." Pause. "I just went very, very long on the corn futures and I'm—look, the reason I'm not talking about it is I feel a bit guilty, uh . . ."

"Now you feel guilty?"

"Yes."

"And yet you're relieved."

"Well, yeah."

"Hmm. Apparent paradox."

"No, it's, like—look, I said, I'm making a ton of cash but the longs, that is, some of the stuff I'm doing is going to cause some hardship, I mean, in fact, there are going to be more famine deaths than there are already, and of course I'm just getting on the bandwagon, but I still feel really guilty about it." All true, I thought. "Okay?"

"Well . . . that's not the kind of thing I'm going to chew you out about, I mean, I work for Lindsay Warren, for God's sake, I'm going to hell in a Hummer."

"Well, thanks," I said. "That's it."

"Okay."

"Okay," I said. "What's happening with Ix Ruinas?"

"Sorry," she said, "that's a fourth question."

"Oh, for God's sake, come on, we're adults, and, you know, we're leveling with each other."

"Sorry."

"Okay, let's each agree to add a question."

"I'll tell you what, I'll give you the answer if you come back to work for us."

"On what?"

"On Neo-Teo. It'll be *the* art-and-life-and-everything work of the next century. It'll be fucking *Rome*."

"Well, that's great," I said—I didn't want to say, "Yeah, but the Warren Corporation makes *Caligula* look like *Heidi*," or some other forcedly snippy thing—"but you're the artist, designer, whatever, I'm just a code monkey—"

"No, seriously, we really want you on the team."

"Doing what?"

"Like, getting the imagineering and architecture into tune with the Game, more in tune with the new calendar . . ."

"What new calendar?" Have you been studying?" I meant studying the Game.

"Yeah."

"Great."

"But we are already missing your expertise. And it'll be fun to work with you. I like you."

"Oh. Thanks. Well, I like you."

Her body sort of constricted and extended. "Hmm," she said. "Maybe we're getting into feelings here."

"Yeah, I have a little trouble with, you know, feelings whoo whoo whoo feelings."

"Everybody has trouble with feelings."

"I guess."

"But, like I say, I do feel very fond of you."

"Thanks," I said. "That's great, I, feel fond of you." Hell. I really did, and it was cramping my act. I guess the takeaway is when you're planning to betray, destroy, and murder somebody and her child, bonding is not a good idea. Damn. It and I and everything all felt dark, evil, and not as inevitable as I'd—

"So let's hang out together and do this project."

"Thanks, but still, no, I don't have time, I mean, it'd take a lot of time."

"It'll take an hour a day, what's the problem?"

"I mean, I just don't feel like doing it." Except I was realizing that I did kind of feel like doing it. Or at least I was realizing that being here felt good. No, worse than that. I was realizing that I wanted to see what Max looked like in his little Dick Cheney costume, I wanted to see how the next Bond movie would turn out, I wanted to see whether she was right about that orgasm thing, I wanted to settle down in some gated compound and wake up with Marena every morning and go out together to feed the turkeys and water the soybeans and pull the corpses off the electric fence. Hell. Maybe these people really weren't so bad, I thought. Maybe even a nontrivial fraction of people everywhere weren't so bad, maybe people in the future would adapt themselves to be even less bad. Maybe I hadn't been weighing the decency fraction heavily enough, maybe I was wrong, maybe I'd made a mistake, I mean, with the EOE, maybe I had to stop it, maybe—

"Jed. You said you don't have time to do it. Not that you don't want to do it. Which is it?"

"It's, uh, the latter."

"Bullfuckingshitfuckbullcrapfuckingshit."

FUCK!!! I thought. I was sure I hadn't touched my nose or rubbed my ears or any of that stuff. Had I looked toward the door? Maybe she could spot microexpressions. Maybe that's how she got to be such a big deal in the competitive, high-stakes world of the international entertainment industry. I mean, besides talent. She could walk into a meeting and—

"Okay, *why* don't you have time to do it?" she asked. "What's going to happen?"

"Sorry, you're out of questions—"

"Fuck the three questions."

"*You* came up with the three questions."

"Then fuck me and the three questions, I'm asking you, as one concerned adult to another." She bounced up, walked to a built-in bookcase on the south wall, and dug a pack of Camel shorts out of their hiding place behind a copy of *Autodesk Maya 9 Fundamentals.*

"Okay, fine. Nothing's going to happen." Wow, I thought, she's feeling some real angst. Of course, one realizes that nobody ever really quits, but in her case, and with Max in the house—

"Again I call bullshit," she said. She lit a cigarette with an old blue-enamel Decoish desk lighter, came back around, sat down, pushed the Go board aside, and set down a big, heavy glass cigar ashtray in its place.

Pause. She pulled in a long, luxurious drag, vaporizing a full inch. Despite everything else, you could feel the satisfaction of long-denied addiction.

Damn it. I'd thought the Q-and-A was over, and I'd been thinking about something else—well, honestly I'd been wondering again what kind of name Octy was besides Roman/Shakespearean/Peakean—and then she'd come in and zapped me.

"Something's going to—" she started to say.

Pause. "What?" I asked.

"Oh, God—"

(10)

"—you mean you *don't have time to waste,*" she said. "You're sick, aren't you?"

"No."

"Yes, you are, you're like, terminally Pythian or something."

"What's that?"

"We've got to fix this. Lindsay'll pay the bill whether you've quit or not." The words came out bunched together.

"Marena, come on, stop. I'm not sick."

"Really? Well, something's wrong."

"I'm just not feeling top-tip, uh, tup—"

"You've like, seen that you're *going* to get sick, in the Game."

"Um . . . well . . ."

"*Fuck,* I *knew* it. Hell." She bounced up and around the Go board and touched my brow with the back of her hand. "Yeah, you feel a little squeamy. And your pupils are dilated, they're, like, like ripe olives, how much of the stuff are you on, right now?"

"Not too much, just the regular dose. It's nothing, it's like an espresso. Well, like nine espressos. Uh, -si."

"I want to get Dr. Lisuarte on it right now."

"No, I—"

"Why not? They made this mess, let's get them to clean it up."

"Look, sweetie, I don't want them messing with me any more right now, okay?"

"So who's going to deal with it?"

"Don't worry about it. I'm handling it."

"Handle what? What is it? A brain tumor?"

"No—"

"Fibrous lungs? Blood press—oh, my God, you're a hemophiliac. You're going to have a little stroke and it's going to wipe you out. Right? Shit."

"Look, however you're figuring out—well, I'm not sick. Ask me if I'm sick."

"Are you sick?"

"No."

She watched me for a few seconds.

"Okay," she said. Evidently, however she was reading me, she'd decided that last bit was the truth. "So, if you don't have time, but you're not worried about, about, uh, your own death, then. . . . oh, hell."

I know I said that her face didn't show things, but maybe I was just getting in a little ethnic slur there, because now something in her face did change, slowly but very noticeably, even to me. It showed fear, and it showed it unmistakably.

"It's me, isn't it?"

"No," I said, "It's—"

"*I'm* sick. It's that EVC thing again. How long do I have?"

"It's *definitely* not you. Honest injun."

She looked at me. She looked at me some more. One thing we auties and pseudoauties don't do too much, and which normals do way too much for our taste, is that normals fucking *look at you.*

"Okay, fine. So what is it, did you see something in the Game?"

"Nothing unusual. If I had you'd know about it."

Pause. As before, she looked at me and I looked back.

"So, so, what are you saying? You do know how you're going to die, we've established that. Right?" She took another drag.

"Well, uh—kind of, but it's a discouraging topic, let's talk about something—"

"How? How are you going to die?"

"I'm not going to tell you. I'm done."

"Okay, when? *When* are you going to die?"

"Not before any—not for a while, I don't—okay, look. I didn't want to get into this because I'm still really vague about it and I have to play some more sessions. But there's going to be a huge civil war in two years and we're all going to have to leave and go to, like, Iceland."

Again, she looked at me. Yet again, I looked back.

"That's not it," she said. "Come on, what's going to happen?"

"If you don't like that one, then I don't know."

"No, I know you've been looking in on the future, and you saw something big, but that wasn't it."

"Okay, fine—"

"Oh, hell, you found another doomster. Right?"

Better not answer that one, I thought. Don't answer anything, Jeddiot. Just stay mum, dumb, and schtum and you'll get out—

"That's why you're not going to die before anybody else, we're all going to die at the same time, you said there'd be other doomsters someday. And you've found out about one and you don't think you can stop him."

I shook my head.

"Or else it's some natural disaster. Right?"

"No," I said. "No asteroids, no tidal waves, no, no zombies, no lava . . ."

"Okay, so it's a nuke. Nuclear war."

"No, that's not it," I said.

"What is *it*? You gave off a guilty signal just now."

"It's—it's that investment."

"How many people is it going to affect?"

"I don't know."

"Is it going to kill more than a hundred people?"

"I—okay, I think so."

"More than ten thousand?"

"I'm not going to answer that."

"Fifty thousand deaths."

"I'm not answering any more. I'm done. I'm a jerk and that's it."

"How big of a jerk?"

I got my eyes detached from hers and swung them around the room. The clock said it was [glyph] to [glyph].

Out in the courtyard, the pool lights had gone out and without the contrast you could make out a hedge of I guess pepper trees beyond it. Over in Neo-Teo, *Eos Aimatiródactylos*—bloody-fingernailed dawn—was grazing the "east" facets of the roof combs. But somehow, inevitably, my focus gravitated back to her face. Our eyes locked.

She guesses, I thought.

She put the last inch of cigarette in the ashtray but didn't stub it out.

No. No, she doesn't. Just chill out. Just sit tight. Chill tight and sit it out. Shill sight tit shite chit . . .

One second. Two seconds. Was something changed in her expression? I couldn't look away. Yes, it was. Changing.

As of today I was thirty-eight short years old, and I'd already seen more than enough horrible stuff in my exile here on Planet Retardia, and not just on YouTube, either, all the things you'd pay a lot to be able to unsee, your second-grade class's gerbils in the act of maternal cannibalism, a tentacle-faced star-nosed mole, that photo of the six-year-old girl walking two steps behind her grandmother toward the gas chamber at Treblinka, a knot of eight dead naked toddlers in a six-month-old mass grave that No Way and I helped dig up in La Sierra when No Way and I were working for the relief corps of the CPRs, the Communities of Populations in Resistance, the unadulterated evil in the gargoyle face of Pope Benedict XVI, the giant toothy lamprey face of the Chunnel drilling machine, a woman in Mexico City with a huge facial tumor that made her head look like giant peeled pomegranate—but this, now, was easily the most horrible thing I'd ever seen, and I knew it was the most horrible thing I ever would see, not a fleshy gross-out or a monument of cruelty or an ugh-eyed monster, but, rather, just the slow, dark dawn of understanding in her eyes. She knew, I could tell that she knew, and that she could tell that I could tell that she knew. And I could tell that she could tell that I could tell that she knew. It was as though there were some kind of pneuma flowing between our eyes, like it feels with lovers orgasming together in bright light, but of course this was the hideous negative of anything loving, she was looking into me and seeing a wasteland of shit, a whole more-than-earth-size planet with diarrhea oceans broken by mountain-islands of stacked dry turds, and in my looking back I was agreeing with that assessment. A sound rose inside her, a rumble under her chest, and metastasized into something like a voice, but a voice that rasped out of some huge, recently dead thing buried in frozen ground:

"WHAT DID YOU DO?"

I noticed that my knees were cracking, and that meant I was standing up, slowly. I backed away from her, toward the big desk.

"I didn't," I started to say, "I mean, it's nothing, it's the right—"

"WHAT DID YOU DO?"

She bounced up and ducked around in front of me, as small, lissome people can. I jumped left and got the desk between us. Her eyes had an indescribable look—indescribable but not something I'd never seen, because I'd seen it in dying patients in the field hospitals at the CPRs, an expression of horror, horror and hatred and terror, or rather, I think, terror not for her but more, or maybe only, for her child, which is even more primal.

"I want . . . to . . . see . . . Max . . . grow . . . up," she barked.

"Marena, look—"

"How—can—you -k-kill—MAX?"

The forgotten Go clock ticked once. It ticked again. Tick. Tick—

"Max is Desert Dog," I said.

"What? What the fuck is that?"

"Nothing, it's just—"

"Is that . . . what you call all . . . call all . . . those . . . people you—"

"No, it's just, I know it's the right thing, it won't hurt, there's no way to—"

"Don't even tell me, you *fuck,* you, you, you . . . you think you're going to make that decision—you can't make that decision, you're not some like, wise being, you're just, you're a loser, you're a boring windbaggy geek loser, you're, you think you mean anything to anybody? You don't know anybody worth knowing, nobody's heard of you, you've never done anything remotely important, you're—"

On the last syllable of *important,* she darted to her right. I circled away, clockwise. She stopped, feinted clockwise again in kind of a Texas tango maneuver, and dashed counterclockwise, almost getting me, but I made it to the opposite side, so the French doors were at my back. Somewhere in my churning gray matter I realized something was off, that she wasn't acting quite the way she would normally, or let's say "normally," act faced with this information, that even though tears were almost squirting out of her eyes, she maybe wasn't yelling so loud as you'd have thought, but I didn't get the implication. Damn, I thought, I should just attack her and like strangle her or bonk her brains in or something right now. Except I didn't feel like it. In fact, I bet I'd never felt less like doing anything like that in my life—in fact, I felt like I wanted to hold on to her and shield her while the world vanished so that she and I could float off together like the shades of Paolo and Francesca, out into Earth-free space. God damn it, my other side said, you're a pussy after all. You'd think that someone who was going to kill everybody later wouldn't have trouble killing one person, but there's a difference between someone who kills for fun and someone who kills out of compassion, like, say, a veterinarian, and—

"You *shit,*" Marena said, "I was, I was, I was practically falling in *love* with you and you were *shit*. You were worse than shit. You're what shit would shit if it could shit."

"Yeah, I was just thinking along those lines." It was an idiotic thing to say, of course, but I was a long way from thinking clearly, and in fact I had just been thinking how I was one of them, Tamerlane, Hitler, Stalin, Mao, DeLanda, and then I was thinking how she was right, that I wasn't even an accomplished whatever like they all were, I wasn't a conqueror or a dynasty founder or even a good public speaker, I was the worst of all of them without even being in their league, just a loser who happened to find a way to make everyone else lose along with me, except even that was giving me too much credit because it was making me out to be at least a human being and I wasn't, I was the opposite of a human being, I was a smear of wriggling little verminettes that had to be immediately wiped off the ass of the universe—

"How do I stop it?"

"Just trust me, I saw the whole situation in—"

The click of a doorknob is one of those sounds you come to recognize unmistakably, and when I heard it behind me I instantly realized why Marena hadn't been shouting at me and in fact had been speaking almost softly, and that she must have said something that had activated her earring phone and—oh, right, in fact I knew what it was, it was when she'd used the words *call all,* that rang all the phones in the house—and—

"Hey, what's going on?" Tony Sic's voice said.

I snuck a peek over my left shoulder. He was in the doorway, about eight feet away. "Hi, Tony, nothing," I started to say, but before I got to the *-thing* part Grgur had loomed in behind him. I may have said at some point that he looked like Leonid Brezhnev's uglier brother, but now he looked like Leonid Brezhnev himself after going through the same gamma-ray-o-genic mutation that turned Ben Grimm into the Thing. He was in his goon outfit with the collar tips spreading over the lapels of the ill-fitting gray one-button sport coat. He was big. He edged Tony aside. There was an impression of motion on my right side and a shot of pain up my right thigh, and as I folded I realized that her foot had switchbladed into my knee—it was one of those low kicks Ana Vergara'd taught her—and I thought I was going to have to operate from the floor for a little while, but I surprised myself by getting my hands on the edge of the desk and holding myself up with I guess my arm strengthened by the epinephrine that sprays into your bloodstream so unbelievably fast when your amphibian brain decides there's a threat out there. As Marena came toward me I picked up a big old LCD monitor off the desk with my right hand and tossed it at her. She tried to bat it away but hurt her hand, I think, since she grunted, and as it fell, trailing cables, the edge hit her knee and her second kick stopped almost before it started. Run, I thought. Holy shit holy shite shat shot run run run run. My hand was on the handle of the French door and I yanked it up. It was one of those locks that open when you open it, if you know what I mean, and I slid out into the dark courtyard. Grgur was right there but I took the time to push the door shut behind me, since I figured it would buy me a good two seconds, and I turned and dashed out, with my stocking feet ouching on this sort of upscale little shiny black rocks. Bright light flashed on all over, like movie lights. I'm on camera, I thought. Oh, well.

"Jed's gone psycho," Marena's voice yelled behind me, and in the middle of the word *gone,* it switched from a normal yell to an iron scrawk blasting out of every speaker of every phone on the system, of which there were probably at least ten in the house and four outside. There was a slight lag between them that made the roar seem to be echoing off the walls of a vast crazy-angled canyon.

"GRAB HIM RIGHT NOW, NOW, NOW, NOW!!!"

I veered right. There was a sort of trapezoidal archway between the yard and the driveway, and beyond it there was an orange sliver of my car, and seeing the car must have made me reflexively thumb the key-card because there was the delicious *bwheep* of the door opening itself. The speakers started up. *"Ride the snake,"* Jim Morrison moaned, like he was breathing on my neck. Marena's voice was louder, though, even through the layers of car: *"NOW, NOW, NOW, NOW . . ."*

"... *NOW, NOW, NOW, NOW, NOW, NOW, NOW, NOW, NOW, NOW, NOW ...*"

Grgur's heavy feet scrunched on the gravel behind me and then thwapped on concrete, which means he was under the arch. I'm doomed, I thought, he's only like five steps back, I'll never get the door open fast enough, but there was a sort of a scrunch-and-thwack behind me and a growl, *"Sranje!,"* which I guessed was a cuss word in Urethrafuckistani, and I got the car door open the rest of the way and slid in and pulled the door closed. Reflexively, I touched LOCK ALL on the key card and the teeth inside the door snapped shut. I hit START and then snuck a look out at Grgur. He was just getting on his feet. What I guess happened—and it took me a few seconds to figure it out—was that since Marena's replica house was one of many expressions of the twentieth-century Prometheus' fascination with four-fifths scale, and what with the Lloyd Wright ceilings being low to begin with, and since the Grg was at least six foot six, the bastard must have scraped his head running through the archway. Good. The mighty V12 fired up on the second rev. Hah—

Whoa.

The supposedly ballistic driver's window had cracked from side to side. The sound was soft, meaning, I guess, that Grgur had come upon me and smacked it with his elbow. I peeled out backward past him, steering through the mirror, which was something I used to practice. I shifted, swerved around Marena's Cherokee, Ashley$_3$'s little purple carlet, and another two SUVs that were in the big circle. For a second I thought Grgur was going to climb up on my back bumper and try to hang on to the car while I drove, but I guess he was too trained for that sort of doomed effort because instead my last glimpse of him was as he opened the door of Marena's Cherokee. I shifted into first and floored it. Whoa. Too much power. Almost did a Tiger Woods. The big baby banked through the two gravelly S-curves, giving me that sickening feeling like I was in a canoe getting sucked into rapids. If that bastard thinks he's chasing me in that soccermommobile he's less of a pro than I thought, I thought. Although, of course, I might hit an obstacle or wipe out or whatever. Gate was still open. Thank Satan. As I passed the little booth I saw the guard inside was on his phone, probably talking with Marena. Too late, dork. I got through the residential streets in thirty seconds, running the stop signs, and in forty seconds I was on the access road to Route 400. Things were slowing down and getting clearer the way they do when the adrenaline really floods in. On the other hand, one's movements get jerky and stiff and you have to watch out for objects and things and stuff because you might bump—

Jim cut off and the car's phone rang. "Answer," I said. The line opened up. "Hi," I went on. "Sorry about all that."

"Jed," Marena's voice said. "If we don't catch you, please reconsider. Don't kill my kid. Please, please, please, please, please, please, please, please, please, please, please, please, please, please . . ." There was something that might have been either a sniffle or static and I wondered whether she was crying. I wished I could tell her what was what, that my motivation was utterly simple, that I'd simply seen something so horrible, or rather I'd worked out a truth that was so horrible, that I don't think even the greatest writer who ever lived could convey it, although maybe H. P. Lovecraft, with the whole thing about the Other Gods gnawing at the crust of the universe, would come closest, except even that seems almost hopeful compared to the bleakness I'd seen when—but this wasn't the right time for that discussion, even if Marena would have listened. I got on the ramp—and I know this is a bad time to brag, but I really took the speed bumps like Adrián Fernández—and onto the Teflon-smooth highway, north toward the orange glow of burning houses in Orlando proper.

"Do you like Max?" Marena's voice went.

"Sure," I said.

"Do you love Max?"

"This—I, listen, this train of conversation is, I'm not . . ."

"You do, I know you love Max, so why do you, why, why, why, why . . ."

"I know what I'm doing," I said. For some reason, at that moment I realized I'd left the nudibranch book behind. Damn it, I thought, my resolve was getting nicked up. Marena and Max and whoever were, like, real people, people with families, people who cared about each other, and I was just a fake person nobody including myself cared about, just one of those nowhere man losers who manage to take a few other people down with them, or in my case everybody. Damn, I needed to think about things. Maybe I was wrong, maybe I'd made a mistake, maybe—

Marena's tone shifted down. "I knew that samlet shit would eat out your brain," she said.

"It's *tsam lic,*" I said. "That means like 'blood lightning.' A samlet's like a fishling or some—"

"You're a junkie and like, true to form, you've gone—"

"It has nothing to do with the drugs."

"Sure. You're just like any other OD'ing psycho."

"Uh-huh." The needle crossed over to the sweet side of a hundred. There was a Chevy up ahead of me going just as fast. Evidently the police had given up on the area. Billboards passed me like pages flipping in a magazine: *Orlando: It's All about Options. Spartacus Jones, Opening December 19. Legoland Orlando.* I felt a thrilling lack of self-preservatory neuromodulators. When you're sure that death's around the next curve, suddenly you can deal with anything. What was too bad, though, was that I figured they had a LoJack and any number of other trackers on me, so I'd need to change cars pretty soon and kiss the 'Cuda good-bye. And for that matter, I could practically feel an itch on my scalp where the Warren Communications ROGS, the RapidEye Operational Geostationary Satellite, was tracking me from a hundred and forty miles overhead. And was Grgur actually chasing me? I couldn't see any fast cars behind me on the GPS. Weird. Maybe he'd decided the cars they had would be too slow and hadn't even taken one out. Just get downtown, I thought. They have everything. I clicked up a state police page that I'd marked, that showed where the manned checkpoints were and where they weren't. It looked like if I just kept on 27 and got off at Revolutionary Road, I'd get downtown without dealing with any PoPos. No prob—

"Jed, I'm serious," Marena said, "you're not thinking clearly."

"Look, yes," I said, "I know crazy people think they're not crazy, but actually I know I'm crazy about a lot of things, it's just that this *particular* thing—I mean—oh, fuck. I mean, it really, really checks out. That's like, suppose I said, 'two times forty is eighty' and you said that can't be true because I'm crazy, that's just—I mean, it's that level of certainty." The road went over an orchard that used to be a swamp and had tried to turn into an industrial "park" before the recession, and now was reverting to swamp. I passed six cars and a semi. There wasn't much traffic. Even though the Park District had been closed for months, a video billboard advertising the *Rainforest Café and the Tree of Life* was still running a loop of giant rocketing centipedes. Zoom, zoom, zoom.

"Jed, everything—"

"Mister DeLanda?" Grgur's accented voice interrupted. "We are go to ask you once and we are not go to ask you again. Stop the vehicle and wait of us. We know where you go. Understood?"

"Sorry," I said. Either he's bluffing or I'm toast, I thought. Maybe I should just aim this crate into the next overpass upright. I'd be out in a blaze of gory—uh, glory—and everything would still go on according to plan. But like Donald Pleasence in *Telefon,* I wanted to watch every little thing myself. Dimwit.

"If you do not stop, we are go to shut down your systems. Do you understand?"

"Put Marena back on and we'll chat," I said. I was passing a thirty-two-wheel car carrier with Aerostar vans packed into it like ticks in a wound. EXIT 29, a sign read. GAS FOOD LODGING.

"Mister DeLanda?" Grgur asked. "Listen. Get right now away from other vehicles. Understood?"

"I don't understand," I said. "Say again?" He can't be really serious, I thought. The variable constellation of molded-acrylic-slab fluorescent signage rose into view against the dark orange sky, Taco Bell, Quiznos, Gulf, Texacoco, Burger King, Jamba Juice, Chicken Itza, McDonald's, Arby's, a regular Amalthea's Horn of affordable dainties.

"We shutting down your systems," Grgur said again.

"Not understood," I said. Bullshit, I thought, hopefully. Still, I got into the right lane and slowed a little. If they were watching me I didn't want them to think I was taking the threat seriously, but then if he was telling the truth I didn't want to—

Pain shot through my nose and into my jaw and there was just grayness in my eyes and everything started happening in a confusing way, and I couldn't see a thing, just this wall of fog.

(12)

—but it wasn't fog, it was semisolid, and I couldn't get my arms around it to reach the wheel. Instinctively I stepped on the brake—I brake with my left foot—and the brake was engaging, but I could feel that the car wasn't quite stopping and at about this time I figured out that the gray stuff was the driver's-side airbag. There was a rumbling in the belly underneath me and a string of metallic pops as we slid over the line of flexible reflector posts. I could feel my testicles retracting. Cowards. One whiff of trouble and they go skittering back to the inguinal canal. The airbag was already deflating but the car was tipping alarmingly to the right, even though I thought it was totally flat around here, like one inch above sea level, but it was still just tipping and tipping and then there was all this scraping like it was driving over shrubbery and then it was just STOP, an instant absolute stop, and my right hand crunched against the lip of the dash screen and my forehead CHUNKED through the limpening vinyl into the lip of the dashboard with a blue flash of detaching retinas.

"Your ballroom days are over," Jim sang. "Your airbag has engaged and you have sustained impact," the 'Cuda gloated in its Maleficent purr, for some reason neglecting to cut off the music. "Exit this vehicle and seek emergency help immediately." An alarm preeped. *PREEEP, PREEEP, PREEEP, PREEEP*, it preeped.

"Mr. DeLanda, are you injured?" Grgur's rasp asked. I didn't answer. The most worrisome thing, I thought, with that sort of pedantic clarity that sometimes kicks in during a high-stress event, was that they hit me with the bag instead of just overriding the gearshift and putting the car into neutral, which would have brought the car to a gradual stop. Maybe they hadn't been able to spend enough time with the car to develop that capability. Or maybe whatever software they were using to run the car had just screwed up. But that didn't seem like them. By *them* I mean Executive Solutions. They were one of the ten biggest military-services vendors out there and certainly one of the two or three classiest, and they were usually very strong on detail. Except if it was just Grgur, maybe he's not so smart as the rest of them—well, you don't have to figure it all out right—

"Mr. DeLanda?"

"Fuck you, I'm in great shape," I almost said. Resist that impulse, I thought. If, I mean when, you get away, it's better if they think you're still dead in the car. Except if they'd wanted to kill me they could have, right? So maybe the deal is that they're nearby already and they wanted to mess me up enough so that I wouldn't be able to get away. So they crashed the thing delicately enough not to kill me but to keep me here. Well, if that was true they'd grab me pretty soon and I wouldn't be able to do much about it. And if the Executive Solutions goons got hold of me—hell. Even if I, say, killed a few people right now to get the cops to put me in the state prison, Boyle—I mean, Laurence Boyle, whom among ourselves we called Lance Boil, and who was one of Lindsay Warren's younger let's-say cardinal nephews—would find a way to get people in and give me a going-over. And it wouldn't take long. Lately there's been a media disinformation campaign about torture, trying to convince the public that it doesn't work and how you're liable to get false information, but the fact is that torture works just fine. Even if you've read only one or two manuals on the subject, these days, with just a recorder, some conductant, and a modified stun gun, you can basically get anything out of anyone in a couple of hours. Although I do still have that dirt on Lindsay Warren, I thought. Or actually it wasn't dirt on him, it was dirt that he and the other eighty Church elders had been hiding for more than a hundred and fifty years, scans of old letters by somebody named Sampson Avard, who was a founding elder of the Church of Latter-day Saints. No Way had dug it up months ago, before the downloading—I guessed from one of his antimissionary comrades in Ixcán, one of the CPR communities, which by the way is not the same place as the ruins of Ix—but he'd sent it to me on paper, to a FedEx store in Tampa that I used once in a purple moon, so I'd only just gotten and scanned in the folder a week ago. Just offhand it looked like dynamite stuff, really incriminating revelations, but it might take a while to use that sort of thing to threaten him. And I hadn't set up an automatic post. So it wasn't something I could do while I was being interrogated. If anything, they'd just get me to give it up. Hell, hell.

Hell.

So—well, hell. Might as well just sit back and wait. Just settle down to the big sleep. It's nothing. I'll get colder, I'll get woozier, and my thoughts will drift, and then, without even a click of the tongue to mark the spot, I'll lose my train of thought and I won't get it back, and that'll have been the end of everything of me, oh, God, the end, the end—

No, my other side said. No, no, no. Focus. "Open the doors," I said, slowly and clearly, but either the car didn't have good voice recognition or this was all starting to form a bit of a pattern. That's what happens when you let your gadgets get too smart. Other people can tell your stuff to do stuff. I pulled at the door handle but it was holding itself shut and the little peg just wouldn't go up. My face was hot. I pushed all the window-down thingies but of course those didn't work, and then finally I found the moon-roof button but that didn't work, either, even though everything else in the car was still merrily running along. I brushed a hair out of my face and felt a tiny, discreet spurt above my left eye, like there was a little kid there with an old plastic squirt gun filled with hot water. I looked at my hand. Blood. I felt a brush of THE FEAR, a stroke out of the reservoir of terror that all hemophiliacs carry with them always, which wasn't rational since I was doing away with myself and everything else anyway in fifty-two days, but of course rationality has nothing to do with it, or with a lot of things. I put my hand up again. The kid squirted me again. Another squirt. One of the supraorbital arteries. Oh, hell. Slip the juice to me, Bruce. Still, I'm factor IX'd up. In fact my clotting was at two and a half last time. Right? So it's not life-threatening. I found the overhead light and hit it and that at least turned on. The dashboard and the seats and door upholstery—which were all new tan real top-grain natural Napa buckskin and ungodly-ly expensive—were blotched and streaked and spattered with red that looked as shiny and opaque as enamel. I felt down my face and blood was running out of my nose in streams like wet snot. I rubbed some of the blood between my fingers. It's hard to tell, but it didn't feel sticky enough. Maybe the last batch of factor-IX I'd gotten was defective. Except that never happens these days. Does it? There was a larger, wetter stroke of THE FEAR. Head wounds are a big problem. There's never been much you can do about them, especially if they're internal, like in the nose. You can't tie a tourniquet around your neck.

Wound kit, I thought. In the, the thingie, the thingie between the seats.

Oof. Nnnnk. Ah. Got the thingie's padded lid open. *PREEEP, PREEEP, PREEEP . . .*

Hell. Junk in here. Too much crap. I scooped out handfuls of crumpled Post-its, low-denomination bills, used and fresh Purell wipes, coins, used and fresh Kleenex, pens, pen caps, rubber bands, wadded up fast-food receipts. Out, out, out.

No wound kit. No loose pads either. At least there was the Thrombostat spray and Surgicel pads in my jacket. Left inner utility pocket. Right. Hah. I got my hand on the little plastic spray bottle. I got it out. *Medique Brand Blood Clotter,* it said. *.2% Benzethonium Chloride.* Okay. Pads. They were the new kind, made out of shrimp cartilage, and they could pretty much patch you up by themselves, even if you were nonclotting. Gotta be in here.

Left patch pocket. No, not there. Right. No. Okay, wait.

Be systematic. Left lapel pocket. No.

Right lapel pocket. No.

Specially ordered inner utility pocket. No.

Other specially ordered inner utility pocket. No.

Key pocket. No.

Handkerchief pocket. No.

Left patch pocket. No.

Right patch pocket. No.

Silk-pocket-thingie-inside-right-patch-pocket.

No.

PREEEP, PREEEP, PREEEP, PREEEP.

Hell.

On the seat. No. In the crack of the seat. No.

Under the seat. I found my little flashlight and bent double and rooted around. It was all just sandy carpet and rubber mats and wadded Kleenex and metal seat thingies like cave formations in the red light. No. Not there. They took them. Not there. They really want to kill me. The Warren people really want to kill me. I was the Man Who Didn't Know Too Much, But Could Certainly Find Out Too Much, and they—except, then, why, if they went through the jacket while my car was sitting in Marena's driveway, why would they take out the pads and leave the spray? Or else—well, patch up first. Then worry.

I gathered some clean Kleenex, sprayed Medique onto two sheets, and packed one into each nostril. Woooffffff. This'd better clot. If you don't clot, packing doesn't do enough, the paper'll just keep capillarying up with your unviscous blood until you're the Scarlet Mummy. Okay. I wiped my forehead, sprayed up another Kleenex, and pushed it into the wound in my forehead with the heel of my hand. Yeoww. Huge juicy bruise there too. Okay. Hold on. Hold on. This isn't right.

Okay. Grgur'll be here any second. Got to get out of here. Take stock. Any other lacerations, contusions, or third-degree bruising? I wriggled and flexed and patted myself down with my right hand. Nothing apparent. Headlamp light slid upstream through the interior, and its source car zoomed past, and then another. Not stopping to help. Although of course they weren't supposed to anymore because of all the carjack kidnappings they did that way, in fact there'd been a whole campaign in Florida to get people to just call it in and if possible not even slow down, but of course now with police and fire stretched beyond the limit, calling did nothing. In the Loose Union of Socialist Banana Republics of America, one was basically on one's own. Cars passed. No cops. No good Samaritans. No ES goons. No Grgur. Keep up the pressure. I still had the bottle with my free hand and sprayed a little backward into my palm. I rubbed it between my fingers. Medique has a specific calone-ish smell to it. Hmm. I sniffed again. There was some of that smell there, but was there much of it? And there was alcohol in there, I could tell from the temperature, but wasn't there usually more? And as that evaporated the real thing had a milky texture and this maybe, well, I guess it did, or maybe it didn't . . . I mean, I'd been relying on the stuff for years . . .

No. This isn't it. Oh, hell. Oh, hell. They'd replaced the stuff with, I guess, just rubbing alcohol. *Rubbing alcohol.* Mean. Meanies, I thought, regressing. There was an upwelling of bullied-on-the-playground emotion like a flavored burp from a thirty-year-old meal. Mean 'n' cruel. Except I shouldn't talk (*EOE*), I guess. I took my hand away. The Kleenex was heavy with blood and slid off. Not sticky. Definitely not clotting the way it should. Oh, Christ. I was *normal,* for crying out loud. Hell. THE FEAR was crawling all over my body and through my mouth and down into my lower intestine. I was *normal.* I licked my lips but you can't really tell from the taste. I was *normal—*

Dr. Lisuarte, I thought.

She must have given me bad factor IX. I'd seen her only weeks ago, and she'd topped me up. Maybe she'd slipped me some—or what if it wasn't her, what if it was just ES? Then they'd had to have been slipping me some oral anticoagulant? Enoxaparin, maybe? Except that would take a few doses, and it had a pretty strong chalky taste that you'd think I would have—and anyway, why? Had that been the first part of a plan to kill me and make it look like my death was caused by my own old medical problem? Or had they just wanted to get me into a hospital where it was easy to keep an eye on me? Or was the anticlotting stuff some exotic preparation that only they had the antidote for so that I'd be dependent on them—no, that's ridiculous. Maybe—

Wait. Whatever they did, you don't have time to think about it. At this rate I'll bleed out in less than ten minutes. We had a professional-level situation here. I needed paramedics, at least, and really I needed an ER. Except then I'd be in Warren's evil clutches and that would be it. Anyway, there's hardly enough time for paramedics to deal with it even if they were right here. They don't usually carry thrombogen with them anyway, they'd just pack the wounds and put shock inflators around my legs, and that might not be enough. And anyway, I can't go to a hospital. Hospital = identification = police involvement. And police = Warren = torture.

Okay, go to Plan X. I hadn't seen any matches and I hadn't remembered packing any. So much for the survival jacket. Even Rambo's knife handle has matches. You dimwit. This is it. No. Okay. Think.

The lighter.

I fumbled and found the regular twelve-volt outlet and I pressed the thingie down, but it didn't stay down for a second and then pop out the way they're supposed to, so I tried just pressing it against the gash in my forehead but it turned out there wasn't any coil in it so it wouldn't heat up. Damn. Defeated by the Health Stasi.

Probably. Okay.

Okay. Got to get out. Gotta get out get out get out getout getoutgetout-getout.

"Five to one, baby, one in five," the Lizard King was still moaning, with what seemed like *Christine*-ish aptness. Blood was still streaming out of my nose like it was out of a fog nozzle. I swallowed. Glulg. Spurt. Gurgr. Spurt. Getoutgetoutgetout. No, don't panic. Chill, I thought. Just go to Plan Y. I wriggled into my jacket. Oof. Okay.

Huh.

PREEEP, PREEEP, PREEEP, PREEEP, PREEEP, PREEEP, PREEEP, PREEEP.

I couldn't get a good angle on the window on my side, so I powered the seat all the way back—at least that worked—and braced myself against the seat back and blasted both legs up against the glass of the soi-disant moon roof. It just popped out of the rubber seal, without breaking—a nice minor blessing—and I stood on the seat, untangled myself from the we're-strapping-you-down-whether-you-like-it-or-not shoulder belts, and wriggled up out of the moon roof. Whoa. Dizzy. *Really* dizzy, I'd stood up too suddenly without enough blood. Hang on. Okay. I got my legs out and sat on the roof for a second. The night had gotten cold. No. It wasn't the air. I was losing juice. Finally I let myself slide down over the rear windshield and the waxy shell of the hood. I got my hands on the grapefruit tree that had stopped the car, let my feet down, and melted over the grille onto the centipede grass.

PREEEP, PREEEP, PREEEP, PREEEP. Cars roorshed by. A siren. I looked around. Nothing. Just wishful imagination magnifying the tinnitus in my cochlea. Okay. Stick to the factuals.

I heaved myself up. Okay. I waddled over the bent-down wire-and-lathe fence and wobbled onto the gravel shoulder. Okay. Bye, bye, Barracuda. Step, step. My feet felt asphalt.

Where? What?

What now? Get out in front of a car and wave and make it stop? No, not likely to work. People are too paranoid. As well they should be. They'll just keep the doors locked and run me over and then tell me they've called Officer Friendly and that he'll be here any hour. Got to hoof it. Huh. I'd passed a Walgreens four minutes ago but that was way too far. Okay, Plan Yuzz. Have to do fast food.

I started lurching toward the exit ramp. Down to the McDonald's. It was farther away than I'd thought. An eighth of a mile, maybe? About three hundred steps. And if you figure you'll bleed out in fifteen minutes, that's—no, don't figure. Just do it. Step. Step. Ow. Ankles ache. Feeling woozy. In a few minutes I'll be thinking so unclearly that I'll forget why I was doing this, and I'll sit down for a second to rest and that'll be about it. Oh, God, oh, God. My fingertips were numbing. Numbening? Oh, fuck, I was fucked, I was fucked. As I got under the first of the tall sodium lamps of the sort of rest-stop area I noticed my right foot was leaving a bloody footprint. A literal one, for once. Brrrdrrrrdrrrr. Cold. I've had it. Dun 4. I've had it. It's over, it's all—

No. Press onward, Lemmiwinks. You might make it. Stranger things have happened. Frogs have lived a hundred years cast in cement. And not just Michigan J. Frog. Ninety-year-old ladies have survived shit that'd kill a wild yak. I kept lurching toward the big M solar-path glyph, dragging my osmium feet through the clotting air. Step. Step. Come on.

Step.

Step. I found the little Ziploc of green OxyContin 80mg tablets in my watch pocket, popped eight of them into my mouth, and chewed them up. Ick.

Step. Step.

Better take a few Adderalls, too, I thought. I did. Four. I chewed them up and gooked the paste under my tongue. Okay.

Step.

Cold. Step. I can't make it, I thought. No effing way. Anyway, why bother?

It's only another seven weeks. That's nothing. You might as well just pack it in now. Except you don't want to give them the satisfaction. You just want to be the last one out the door so you can turn off the lights yourself. And how dumb is that? Step. I washed down the Oxy 'n' speed dust with a swig of blood. Step. Step. O Christ Jesus on the Cross, just let me get through this, O Jesus Resurrected, O Lord of the Flail, Lord of the Spear, O Baby Jesus, O studly thirtysomething Jesus, just give me a break, O Black Jesus, O female Jesus, O phosphorescent polystyrene Jesus of the Dashboard, O any Jesus . . .

Step.

Step.

Step.

It took forever to get to the McDonald's, and then I remembered that what I really wanted was Burger King. I looked up. There. It was a little farther away—too far away—on the other side of the big rest-area lot. Still, it was worth the extra effort. McDonald's fries their hamburgers, but Burger King flame-broils.

(13)

The glass door opened itself, welcoming me into the cheerful golds and reds of the "restaurant"'s sit-down area. It was as bright and frigid as high noon at the South Pole. I counted ten patrons sitting in four groups, although since one of the groups had five people and nobody was sitting alone, there must have been something wrong with my math. I decided not to let it bother me. They were of varying ages but all of them were paste-white, overweight, and dressed up for Halloween as—among other things—Warcraft orcs, Dormammu from the Doctor Strange movie, Little Fat Mermaids, Seven Death from the Neo-Teo game, and hydrocephalic vampires. At least it was the best possible night of the year to be a fugitive. Most of them looked up, stared, and then went back to chewing their cuds. The Force is with me, I thought. On my way to the counter I tried to disguise my limp and nearly stepped on a discarded plastic fork. Watch yer step, I thought. Fork in the road. The sort of boy behind the counter looked just like Kaspar Hauser, Animal Boy of Nuremberg. He had slow sloe eyes, a pretty big spatter of acne, and a tag in his ear with a barely visible microphone wire curling out of it toward his mouth. There was a black chunky woman in the back, by the drive-by window, who didn't even look up.

"We'come to Burger King, we're cookin' up s'm grea' Vegatamales™ today, may I ta' y'r order, plees?" Kaspar asked, not giving my gory "costume" much of a look. His voice was like Butt-Head's without the wit.

I managed to flop my torso onto the counter and drag my legs up after it.

"Uh, I'm sorry, you cain't go back thur, guy," Kaspar stammered out.

"I've been severely injured," I said. "You'd better call the police and paramedics." I let myself down on the other side, leaving five thick red drops on the counter, and half walked and half fell into the food-prep zone.

Hefty Black Woman didn't look around. "Any Vegatamales™ with that for today?" I heard her ask into her microphone.

"Uh, sir? 'Scuse me!" Kaspar said.

"I have to perform an emergency medical procedure," I said. Remember, he's probably illiterate, I thought, noticing that he had a pictoglyphic keyboard like the ones they make for lab chimps. Use short phrases and simple action words. "I'm a doctor. I've been in an accident."

He stared.

"Please call nine-one-one," I said, just to give him something to do.

I looked around. Two prep tables, steamer, chopper station, refrigerator, freezers, sinks, combi oven, mixer station. Nice layout. Reflexively, I took two blood-sticky steps toward the first-aid kit, which was hanging in its undoubtedly OSHA-mandated spot on the wall over the first worktable, but then I remembered I was past that stage. Go to Plan Wum. Fast methods for fast times. I got some napkins out of a dispenser and blew my nose into it as hard as I could. From the way the blood sprayed out I guessed the wound was on the right side. Good. There was a straw dispenser by the mixer station and I dispensed two. Luckily for me they'd switched from plastic straws back to presumably greener paper ones.

"Sir, I cain't let yuh back here," Kaspar said. He was pressing a button that he must have been told to press if anything happened outside his competence zone. I staggered forward to the big deep fryer, pulled off my hat, and set it down on the control panel. The unit had four wide bins, one with a big drift of French fries tanning under a red lamp, two others holding big empty frying cages with detachable handles, and one covered with a square lid with a big knob in the center. I lifted it off. It was full of about six inches of polyunsaturated vegetable oil that I figured would be around three hundred and fifty degrees. A Panthalassa-size ocean of pain.

The deal about cautery is that even though it's too tricky to recommend generally, it's always been effective. If you just stick a hot poker in an arrow wound like in a John Wayne western, all you'll do is burn away the healthy skin from around the hole and make things worse. It's more something you use for interior wounds, on organs like the liver that can't be stitched. Or you use liquids, like in the American Civil War, they used hot tar. Obviously there are better options now, and the instruments that do still come in military field medical packs are a lot more advanced. Still, even these days, in Pakistan, for instance, a lot of Marines, and maybe most of them, carry about ten sets of strike-anywhere matches in their Bug Out Bags, duct-taped together in bunches of ten and twenty. And if the worst case comes to pass in the absence of a medic, they light up a bundle, stuff it into the wound—even a bullet entrance or exit—and, if they're still conscious after that much pain, pull it out when the heat's gone. This has saved a lot of lives by controlling bleeding when the medics were a long way off, or when, like I did, one had a reason not to go to the hospital.

Okay. Entering the World of Pain. It's always just an angstrom away, on the other side of the Carrollian looking-glass.

"Uh, I'm sorry," Kaspar said, "we're not allowed to let cus'mers behin' the cou'er, um, even for emer'e'cies."

"Just give me a second," I said. I screwed the straw as far as I could up into my right nostril. "Don't upset yourself."

"Sir? Sorry, I cain't let yuh do that."

"Did you get nine-one-one?" I asked. I took a deep breath, bent down, and snorted a blast of hot oil up into my sinuses. It was like a Grucci chrysanthemum shell went off in my head, those same silver brocades and the water-drum boom from the report component, while I, or rather not so much I but my more basic selves, my amphibian and insect brains and the flatworm brain way down in the gut, were all sure that that I was dead. People think stubbing a toe or breaking an arm or getting zapped by a stun gun is painful, but it's not in the same league, game, arena, or continent. You stay sane through those things. With this, for some time it wasn't me there at all, just a mad snarling vicious thing, and then when it was me again, there wasn't room for any thought other than the surprise that I was alive. At some point I noticed I was still screaming, and after I'd made myself stop

I noticed I was writhing around on the floor. Some of the oil had dripped back into my throat and I thought my throat would swell up so that I couldn't breathe. I should order a milkshake, I thought. Later.

"Uh, sorry, sir, but I can't let you back here. There's a public telephone by the restroom." Kaspar had his hand on my shoulder. I took it and used it to pull myself up. I looked at him. My vision must have tunneled in because I had to move my head to see his name tag, which said his real name was Herb.

"Herb, I appreciate your concern," I rasped. My voice sounded like Karl Malden playing Satan. "And I know you have to follow proper management procedure to run this restaurant efficiently."

Okay, next item. Head wound. I eased toward the back of the kitchen. The grill. "But if you get in my way, as soon as my team of security professionals get here, and that'll be in about two minutes, they'll torture you and your co-worker to death with a Makita cordless circular sander. After that they'll take your IDs and look up your families and kill them, too, if they live anywhere in the area." I got a quarter-inch of paper napkins out of a dispenser and folded it into a mitt in my right hand. "So, Herb, seriously, please, make this easy for me. My way right away. Right?"

I stood in front of the flame broiler. There were two big iron grates, with patties charring on the right one. The left one didn't look hot, so I just whisked the burgers away and lifted up on the iron grate. Too heavy. Takes two hands to handle. I folded a second paper mitt, crouched, and pushed up. The grate rose up. I stood up and poked through the layer of volcanic rocks that covered the heating elements. The bigger the better. I picked up the largest lava stone I could find in my left hand. The napkins smoked but didn't catch fire. I pressed the smoother side of the rock into the wound in my forehead. This was a different order of pain, colder, more like diving into liquid nitrogen. It wasn't easier to deal with, though. My body knew it had to get away, so much so that I thought it would split into two pieces like it was tied to two cars going in different directions. I could hear my head sizzling like Canadian bacon. I screamed again, I think even louder.

"Sir? Are you hurt?"

No, I thought. I'm fine, can't you tell? I turned. I could only see a little bit of him, just his face and hat, like I was looking through the wrong end of a pair of binoculars. I pushed past him and staggered to the exit door on the side with the drive-thru window. There was gray stuff around him and a smell that shouldn't be there. Oh, hair, I thought. Yes. The front section of my hair, short as it was, was on fire. Evidently I'd spattered oil on it and the rock had ignited it. No problem. I patted it and it went out, I think. The pain rose again and I screamed again. Whoa. Okay. It's out of my system. Damn, that was a whopper freakout. I took a quick look back over the counter at the eating area, expecting to see Grgur walk in the front door. He wasn't there. Neither were any other new visitors. ES must be having problems, I thought. Well, don't fuck a gift horse in the mouth, et cetera. Okay. As I'd learned from No Way back in the day, drive-throughs are the fugitive's best friend. Let's go car shopping.

Side door. EXIT. Right.

Step, step—

Whoa. Who are you?

A dude—who I guessed was the Manager on Duty, finally alerted by the panic button—had strode in from somewhere in the back and was blocking my exit. He was big, blond, about thirty, and, as seemed to be de rigueur, somewhat overweight. I noticed I still had the lava rock in my left hand. He said something about how I had to stay where I was and wait for the police.

"Thank you, sir," I said, keeping my eyes on his eyes. I pressed the rock into his paunch. It sizzled. He emitted a high, shrill scream, almost louder than the ones I'd just produced myself, and his body recoiled, although, I guess reflexively, his right arm threw a sort of halfhearted haymaker punch. I just crouched under it—it wasn't coming fast enough for me to claim that I ducked—and I edged around him. There was a three-AA flashlight hanging in its own OSHA-mandated spot next to the first-aid kit, and I took it as I left the food prep area. Damn, if I'd known pain like this existed I would have crawled back into the womb and lived there for the next eighty years. Although it had made me forget about the cold.

"Sir, excuse me?" Herb asked somewhere behind me. I looked around. My vision seemed to have opened out a bit, and I could see that he was still back at the grill station.

"You've been great, Herb," I said. I went out. The patrons looked up to watch me leave, but only one or two of them stopped chewing.

(14)

The car at the head of the drive-thru line—a first-generation Equinox in Navajo Nectarine—had its window down, I guessed waiting for the rest of its order, and I edged forward to where I could see the driver.

A woman. Young. Plain. White. Fat. Bewildered by life.

Perfect.

Okay. Plan Um.

I held up the flashlight in that underhand cop style and flicked it on.

I don't think I've mentioned this, but actually I have a pretty deep voice. "Police emergency!" I said, in as authoritarian a basso as I could manage while also reining in my chattering teeth. I flashed my American Malacological Society membership card. "License and registration, please."

She obeyed. The license said she was Miss Kristin Dekey, 24, of Winter Haven, not that I cared, but I felt I had to look at it long enough to seem official. I tried to hand it back but she was fumbling in the between-seats thingie for the registration. The woman in the passenger seat blinked at me. She looked enough like her to be her twin sister, except all crackers look alike to me, so who knows. "I'm sorry, I can't," Kristin was saying, "I'm sorry, I have um, I have a proof of insurance, here, I'm not sure, the registration, I'm not sure where the registration is, is this going to be enough to, I'm sorry—"

I took the piece of paper. Pretending to look at it used up twenty seconds, but when you're impersonating, it's a good idea to get the subject used to the idea that you're who you're pretending to be before you tell them to do something unfamiliar. And the best way to do that is to put them through whatever rituals are most familiar. If you do it right, even if you're, say, a five-foot Chinese teenager in a Gothlita dress—or if, like me, you're covered in blood and your hair is smoldering and there's smoking bloody charcoal scab all over your face—by the time they sign the report they'll swear you were six foot six, wearing a full police captain's uniform, and looked like Clint Eastwood.

I gave the paper back and took out the larger of my still-jammed phone. "One Adam thirteen," I said into it. "I *am* in pursuit of suspect *in* a civilian ve*hic*le, over. Ma'am, you and your passenger *must* exit your ve*hic*le." As normals usually do, she obeyed. Her vehicle mate took longer but also got out. Instead of both backing up, though, they sort of sought each other out and met in front of the car, standing there like they were going to confer about something. I got in and leaned over the open door.

"Ma'am, for you own safety, please step away from your vehicle." She did. I said the same thing to her twin. Her twin did the same thing. Then, she thought of something.

"Are you hurt?" she asked.

"Hey, are you really a policeman?" Kristin got it together to ask, too late. I got in the rest of the way, slammed the door, reached over and slammed the passenger door, found the thingy that locks all the doors, locked all the doors, got the thing in gear, and took off.

Ahh. Freedom. I—

Oh, hell, I thought. I'd left my hat back in the kitchen. I thought of going back for it, realized that was ridiculous, and then got worried that just the fact that I'd considered it meant I wasn't thinking clearly. Focus, Jedface.

Up the ramp. On the off ramp, on the other side of the highway, my abandoned Barracuda was lit up with halogen light. Above it, a helicopter swept a second light around the car in a widening spiral. Hah, I thought. They're way behind. Way.

Onto 400. Forward. Upward. *Ad astra per atrocitas.* I adjusted the seat and wheel to suitable positions for nonporkers. The highway straightened out and pointed the Equinox toward the burnt-orange glow over the No-Go

Zone. My hands were still shivering and my teeth were still chattering, and I was tired and light-headed, but I wasn't quite in shock yet, and if I held on to the four quarts or so I had left, and if I kept making adrenaline, I'd keep going for another few hours. Just need to be supercareful until I find a dealer . . . well, the last time I heard they were selling blood packets there, so they ought to be able to get factor IX too . . . and maybe some thrombogen, a few burn packs . . . top up the O negative . . . hmm, while I'm at it, pick up some Oxy or at least some Hydro, and a saltshaker of the old benzoylmethylecgonine. Maybe a Glock 36 and couple of Heizer DoubleTaps, and a few hundred rounds of HydraShok. And a papered ride, of course. I just had to stay ahead of the ES people. And the way I'd set it up I knew I'd manage it. Finally my paranoia was coming in handy. I'd set up four different legends, of varying degrees of detail and remoteness, and if I cycled through all of them over the next few weeks they'd never catch up. ES was top-shelf, but nobody's resources are unlimited. Of course, they'd be using the Game to find me, but I'd be using it to stay ahead of them. And I'd be doing it better.

I passed a row of abandoned detoxification trailers and a tossed-aside ROAD CLOSED barrier. There were more cars here, all heading to the twenty-four-hour cop-free party zone. The fugitive's first rule is that the more people there are around, the harder it is to find the one you're looking for.

Past eighty. Hmm. There's a slow-pokin' cat. I passed him on the right. I voiced the car's "radio" onto commodities news. The Dalian and Zhengzhou had both just suspended trading. The fourth domino had tipped over right on schedule. Well, it's out of my hands. Need to just sit back and wait.

EOE, I thought. Well, they deserve it. Factor IX indeed. They'd been planning to kill me for a long time.

And she knew it.

Marena was no damn good.

People were no damn good. Even dogs were no damn good. Even lichens were no damn good. I'd done the right thing. I was doing the right thing. I let myself feel a full blast of elation, not just the kind that comes after you make a narrow escape, but the deeper kind you get when you know your future's assured. By the time I passed the abandoned checkpoint, I knew I'd make it.

Mission good as accomplished. Fifty-two days left. Or, counting down by seconds:

Four million, four hundred and ninety-two hundred thousand and eight hundred . . .

Four million, four hundred and ninety-two hundred thousand, seven hundred and ninety-nine . . .

Four million, four hundred and ninety-two hundred thousand, seven hundred and ninety-eight . . .

Four million, four hundred and ninety-two hundred thousand, seven hundred and ninety-seven . . .

ONE

The Scorpio Carfax

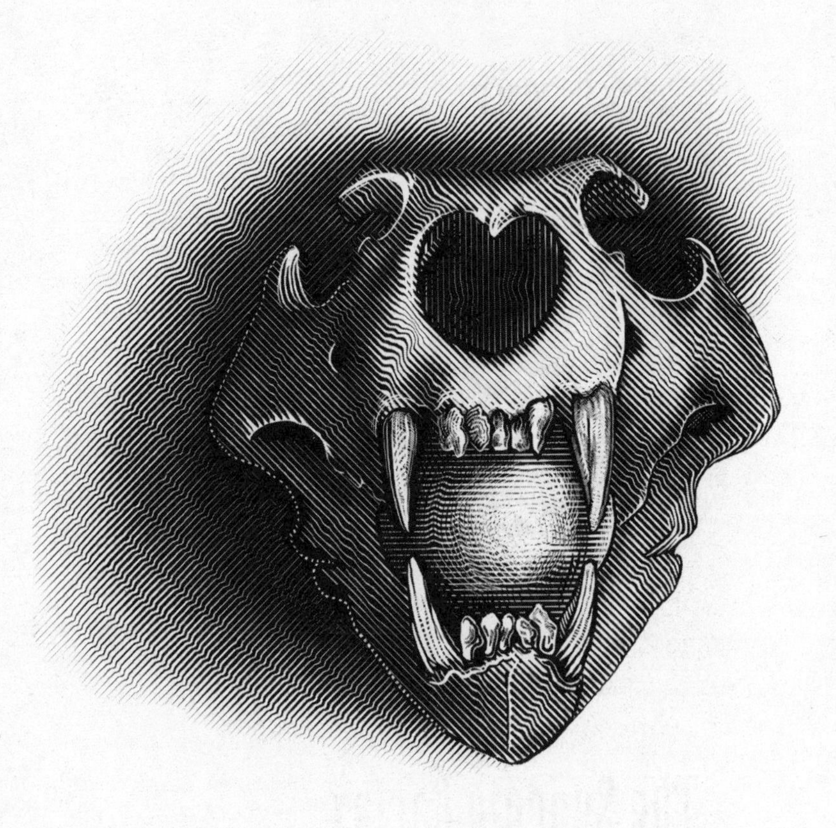

Jaguara Skull with Jade Sphere
Recovered at the Ruins of Ixnichi Sotz

Curious Antiquities of British Honduras
By Subscription · Lambeth · 1831

(15)

The world had ended eight days ago, just as Lady Koh had predicted, on 4 Earthtoadess, 5 Vampire Bat, 9.1 1.11.12.17—or, in Gregorian terms, on May 1, AD 664. Or, at least, almost everyone here—and I really mean almost everyone, that is, the entire population of Mesoamerica and large swaths of North and South America—believed that it had. Today, the eighth in the new lineage of suns had just died at 289 degrees west by southwest, and still the light on the Altiplancie Mexicana, that is, the altiplano, the Central Mexican Highlands—was a disconcerting diffuse maroon, like they say daylight looks on Venus, hadn't changed since dawn, and it was the same as it was yesterday and the day before. The faint path curved around a stand of scrub pines and up a gentle grade toward a line of wrinkled mesas. We hadn't seen a living person for at least a thousand rope-lengths now—a little over four miles. And we hadn't seen a dead one for least three hundred. At least not a whole dead one. Just a few odds and ends.

We still smelled them, though. It was really true that you never got used to that cadaverine foulness, the indescribable foetor that the 1945 generation brought back from the camps riveted in the snuggest fold of their brains and which they wanted to forget more than any other memory. Rotting flesh, burning flesh, and burning rotting flesh. It's not just the worst smell in the world. It's truly the worst thing at all in the world. And this is in a world that's full of unsavory things.

Thousands, and thousands, and thousands, I thought. And more thousands. Poor bastards. Well, bless 'em. Even before this latest apocalypse, I'd estimated that suicide was at least the second main cause of death around here—second to starvation, that is, not counting deaths in childbirth—and now it was obviously a strong number one. And it probably would be for the fore—

Oops, I thought. If there's one cliché I of all people really ought to give up, it's "the foreseeable future." Let's just say the self-immolations would go on for a good long time. Thousands, and hundreds of thousands. In the seventh century—that is, now—Central Mexico had the largest and densest concentration of people in the New World and one of the densest in the world. There were thousands of villages and scores and scores of—hmm, I said *scores,* so I guess I've already been here long enough to start thinking in base 20—and dozens and dozens of full-scale hundred-thousand-plus-population cities. Corn was simply a hugely efficient, labor-unintensive crop, and a corn economy left people enough time to build purely ceremonial buildings, craft meticulous luxury goods, maintain troops of full-time athletes and entertainers, squander food in potlatch orgies, and kill, capture, torture, and sacrifice each other not out of any necessity but just for the sheer kicks. According to Michael Weiner, the Warren Group's resident Mayanist, population here would have doubled in the last forty years, and in the next forty, despite the dip of the last few days, it would double again. Still, right around here, settlement was patchy. The populous river valleys were separated by wide swaths of near-desert, and up here we were in a high area without aquifers, on crappy soil that would never be cultivated. So it was on the Chocula team's map of good areas to bury the gear. Although the gang would be amazed that I'd come this far from Ix. They—

Jeg jeg jeg jeg jegjedjwhzzeeew?

It was the long guggle of a nightjar.

Jeg jeg jeg jeg jegjegjegjedjwhzzzeeeew?

To almost anyone, even to a Mesoamerican who wasn't a member of our sixty-two-man column, it would have sounded natural. But it came from one of our front-runners, or I guess we can call them recon men. They were fanned out about forty rope-lengths, or ten minutes' walking, ahead of us.

Jeg jeg jeg jeg jegjegjedjwhzzeew?

Jeg jeg jeg jeg jegjegjegjedjwhzzzeeeew?

The call itself meant that there was a crossroads four hundred paces ahead of us, and repeating it four times meant all-clear in all four directions. Good.

A red deer darted across the path ahead, redward, that is, eastward, running away from the fires. One of the guards behind me must have looked like he was going to throw a javelin at it, because I heard Hun Xoc give a let-it-go whistle. We weren't here to hunt. Anyway there were still so many animal refugees running in front of the fires you could net almost anything you wanted, field rats, jumping mice, hares, rabbits, armadillos, ocellated turkeys, quail, and even Mexican silver grizzlies. You'd have thought the villagers around here would have trapped and eaten them already, but I guess they believed they wouldn't need food. After all, the world was still ending.

There was—were?—was a handful of skeptics, of course, master manipulators like Lady Koh or my adoptive stepfather, 2 Jeweled Skull. Or even Hun Xoc, who was pretty sharp. Or myself, who doesn't count. But the bulk of the public had either been reborn—like Koh's trail of eighteen thousand or so followers—or raptured, like the millions who had killed themselves or died in the fires or who were now starving to death or dying in interpolity raids.

Step. Step. Steppedystepstepstep. The pines gave way to ocatillo and prickly pear. Every so often we passed giant century plants, some of them two stories tall, like frozen land-mine explosions, with sawtoothed leaves that were so thick and wide you could walk out on them and bounce up and down like you were on a diving board. There—

Huh. I saw something.

Stop, I touched on Hun Xoc's back. He touched the blood in front of him and the order to halt traveled through the three bloods ahead of him. Around here—I mean in Mesoamerica—the ranking hotshot usually came last. But on this job, the senior blood, Hun Xoc, was breaking protocol by marching near the head of the file, and he kept me behind him. Oh, by the way, "blood" is a literal translation, but it does work in English. Or Elizabethan English, anyway, like "young blood." *"As many and as well-borne bloods as those,"* as I guess King Philip says. In Ixian it could mean any warrior-age male from one of the "great houses," that is, from the ruling class.

The halt rippled back down our column, through fifty-seven other men all the way to the rearmost, the last of the four sweepers raking over our trail. I signed to Hun Xoc that I was going on alone. He edged aside, reluctantly, and tilted his head, asking me to be more careful. The bloods in the vanguard closed around me, but I pushed through them. Did they not see anything? I widened my eyes into the unnatural dusk.

A figure sat at the crossroads, a hundred paces ahead of us. A man. A man with a cigar. It wasn't as though he materialized, and in fact he looked like he'd been lounging there a long time, but I'd just looked there a few beats before—when you're marching, you develop a rhythm of looking at your feet, and then look around, and then look ahead of you, and then repeat—and I hadn't seen him. And none of our forerunners had noticed him or they would have given us an owl screech.

I turned and signed to the *sitz',* the fourteen-year-old boy, behind me. His provisional, preadulthood name was Armadillo Shit, and he was my *k'ur chu',* my "fellator," or I guess if we want to be delicate we can call him my squire. Or if we want to be indelicate we could call him my bitch. Every blood had at least one. It was kind of a Spartan *erastés*-and-*erómenos* system. The *k'ur chu'ob* who survived all the hazing—about forty percent, I figured—would, eventually, get admitted into whatever society it was, in this case the Harpy Ball Brethren Society. Like *jonokuchi* Sumo wrestlers, they did everything for us, including, shall we say, wiping.

He came up alongside me and spat drinking water into my eyes. I rubbed my face dry on his manto and looked again. The figure was still there. He wore a long orange-and-black-striped manto and a wide straw traveling-trader's hat, almost a sombrero, that gave him an incongruous nineteenth-century-European-peasant look.

I walked forward, alone. The gentleman readjusted his hindquarters on the dessicated and defanged barrel cactus, took a deep drag on his cigar—it was a green Palenque-style stogie as thick as a Churchill—and studied me.

Hmm. He looked familiar.

I switched my gait to the deferential Ixian halt-step and then stopped four paces from him.

He let out a snake of blue smoke. I squatted, and touched the ashy ground. He didn't speak, so I did.

"Salud, Caballero Maximón," I said, and then, remembering when we were, I saluted him again with his older name: *"X'taca, halach ahau Mam."*

He answered in Spanish, though. *"Hola, cabrón. Estás que Cholano gringo de San C."*

I clicked yes. His Spanish was rustic but awfully good for someone who, technically, probably hadn't spoken it regularly for twelve hundred years.

"Están buenas Pirámides."

"¿Perdón?" I asked. Oh, right, the cigars I'd given him back in San Cristóbal Verapaz. Back in the twenty-first century. *"Ah, cierto. Claro, yo soy . . ."*

"Maybe you can score me some more of those sometime."

"Oh, *seguramente*. I'll go by the Great House humidor in BC."

"Buen reparto," he drawled, after largely resolidifying. The way he talked about it, it sounded like it had happened yesterday, not thirteen hundred and forty-eight years in the future. Although that's how it is with guys like that, time just—or I guess you could call him a deity, although the English word doesn't get the flavor, and anyway in the old days, to be polite, we just called them "smokers"—the deal is, with beings like that, time just rolls off them like scandal off Reagan. He took a long drag and blew out a plume of smoke that uncoiled as slowly as a satiate python.

Damn, I thought, now this is what you call a strong hallucination. As soon as the idea came to me, though, Maximón seemed to fade a bit, so I put it out of my mind. He might still come up with something of value. The thing was, there's more in your mind than you realize. And when you're in someone else's mind, like I was, the whispers just keep on coming. And some of them strengthen into voices, and some of those solidify into, well, into something like I'd just seen. And some of *those*—not most, because then you'd be just another crazy person, but some—can be worth paying attention to. Especially in a place like this. Like everybody's here in the old days, Chacal's brain didn't think hunches and insights came from within. They came from the smokers, like Maximón. And sometimes the smokers saw something in your head that you'd forgotten, or that you'd never noticed, but which was still something real.

"So," Maximón asked, "how did you make your way to this glittering b'aktun?"

"I sent myself here," I started to say, "into the skin of this hipball player, as you see—"

"What self is that?" he interrupted.

"Well, I mean, yes," I said. "It's not exactly my self, it's that my memories, they got . . ." Damn. I tried the word *pach'i*, "printed," like in a seal on wet clay: "They got printed and sent back here."

"What are we in back of?" he asked.

"Well, that's true," I said, "we're not really in back of anything, I mean, to here, earlier, than . . ."

I trailed off. "Lllll," he went. It was the Mayan equivalent of "Hmm."

"I still have Chacal's brain," I stammered out. "But it has the higher-level type of my twelfth-b'aktun memories, from Jed." It was all the things that had happened to me, I explained, all the English and Spanish skills, the emotional habits, everything that made me think I was Jed DeLanda, and it had all been downloaded out of my head, encoded into a form somewhat like a holographic film image, and directed at a target brain, wiping out that brain's own higher-level memories in the process. As far as current understanding of the universe went, it was the only possible process that was even close to time travel—a term that, by the way, we avoided, the way intelligence pros won't use the word *spy*.

He took another monster inhale. Did he get it? I wondered. Or did it all sound like nonsense? Or did he know it all already? I can't do this forever. Somehow—and Chacal's reflexes were a phenomenon I'd come to heed, without understanding them—I felt the troop was getting restless. Wait, I signed behind me. The sense of motion on the hairs of my back faded and disappeared. One good thing around here was you could talk to the air and people wouldn't think you were crazy, but just in tune with one of the folk of other levels, the Unheard, Unsmelled, and Unseen.

"So," he asked, "are you Jed or Chacal?"

(16)

The words came out as smoke. Or, rather, what happened was, the smoke from his cigar contorted into a rising pillar of Ixian cursive glyphs, and at some point I noticed that I wasn't hearing him speak, but just reading the vertical column.

"I don't know," I said. It was a question I'd been asking myself a bit lately, in a different way. At first, of course, I'd felt like I must still be pretty much like the Jed, for clarity let's keep the convention and say Jed_1—who'd stayed back—"back"—in 2012. But things happened to me, and I saw things, mainly disturbing things, and I did things—not all, or not even mainly good things. And I guess I'd changed because now, when I thought about the other Jed, the one we're calling Jed_1, I thought of him as, well, not as a total dolt, maybe, but certainly as a lucky but clueless naïf who wouldn't know shit from Shinola, and it was only going to get more so, even if I got—hmm, I was going to use the word *back* again, but it's bugging me. And, come to think of it, what *does* Shinola look like? Maybe I don't know so much as I—

"And so," he asked, "what ill chance has brought you into this vexed wilderness?"

"I came to plant a message in the Earthtoadess," I said.

"You mean for your *n'aax caan*"—the expression meant something like "favorite dominatrix" or "pussy-whipper prostitute"—"in the thirteenth b'aktun."

Uh, right, I grunted. Should I offer him something? I wondered. What did we have with us? We'd brought jade celts worth about six hundred adolescent male slaves, just in case we had to trade our way out of something, but I didn't think he'd want them.

"That Marena of yours, *tía buena,*" he said, smacking his lips once.

I just nodded. How did he know about that? I wondered. Well, I guess he knows a lot. Not everything, like Jehova would, but still a lot. You've got to watch this guy around the ladies. I remembered something my mother had told me when I was six or so, how in her hometown in Honduras, back when her grandfather was young, one day all the men went off to fight the Spanish and left Maximón at home to protect the women, and then when the men came back, the women were all pregnant. So the men flayed Maximón alive, and hung his skin on a monkey-puzzle tree. But the women were so devastated that they made the men set up his effigy in the church. And then he didn't stay dead for long anyway.

"So you need to find a quiet spot," Maximón said.

"Yes. Exactly."

"Quiet for how long?

"Like, four b'aktuns," I said. About fourteen hundred years.

He raised his head and, leisurely-ly, looked over his left shoulder, toward the west. You could just see a low orange smudge, not the sun but the reflection of Coixtlahuaca, the nearest of the hundreds of cities burning in sympathy with the destroyed capital, Teotihuacán. Lady Koh's caravan was between us and the city, back almost half a *k'intaak*—that is, a *jornada,* a day's journey. We couldn't go much farther if we were going to come back and meet up with them before dawn. And we couldn't be walking around like this in daylight, even if the daylight was going to be as dim as twilight. Some village bumpkins would still be alive somewhere, and they'd spot us, and the word would get back to one of the Puma Clan's hit squads, and that would be it. They'd have our guts for G strings. On the other hand, if the gear was going to keep for thirteen centuries before Marena dug it up, it would have to be pretty damn out in the boonies. Dang, darn, damn.

"Lllll," Maximón went. He took another drag and blew a smoke snake that read, with the formal, archaic voice of written Mayan, "I would try up yonder." He pointed northeast with his lip toward a pair of twin mesas. "No one ventures there." He used a continuing indefinite tense that meant not now, not before now, and not ever. "Even our grandfather Rucan 400 Shrieks"—that is, the east-going Whirlwind—"refuses to dance there." I almost didn't get the last part because as soon as I was reading each word, it would start dissolving.

"Okay, *buen consejo*. Thank you, señor."

"No problemo," he said. He said it orally this time, and in Spanish. And the abruptness suggested that the interview was over, but I hesitated.

"Yes?" he asked, a little impatiently.

"Oh, I was, I was just wondering if you over me might have noticed anything farther down the road."

"You mean the road to Ix?"

"Well . . ." I said.

I was getting the feeling that he knew the answer already, and was asking me just to see how honest I was, or how I'd justify what I was doing.

". . . yes," I finished. It was supposed to be a secret—that is, when we got into the lowlands we were going to lead the people to Ix and not toward Palenque like Lady Koh had given out.

"You'd better watch out for the Pumas and the rest of the pack," he said.

I know that, I thought. But I just clicked—an Ixian gesture that meant "yes"—and then, redundantly, nodded.

By *pack* he'd meant, like, "pack of cats." That is, the remnants—numerous remnants, I should say—of the feline clans of Teotihucán and its hundreds of satellite cities. They'd regrouped after the unpleasantness and were out gunning for Lady Koh and anyone connected with her.

"We'll manage it," I said. Be confident. Chicks and gods dig confidence. And it was true, right now I was ahead of the game. Especially with this Lady Koh thing. I knew a star when I saw one. She already had her eighty thousand–plus people under her little blue thumb. And she was just getting started. And for whatever reason of her own, to the extent that she understood my plans to preserve the Sacrifice Game and get myself back to the last b'aktun, she approved of them. "And I'm going to get the hell back too."

This time he didn't ask "Back to where?" and I was sure he understood that I meant back to the twenty-first century. If one can use the word *understand* in this context.

"You're not worried about Severed Right Hand?" Maximón asked.

Zing. Maybe I'd sounded a little too flip there. Watch it.

Hmm. Severed Right Hand's name had come up around Koh's council mat, but he was kind of a shadowy figure. Supposedly he'd been a junior member of the synod of the red moiety of Teotihuacanian, that is, the war clans, and he owned only two bundles of pink reeds—that is, he was only eighteen years old. Yesterday, according to Lady Koh's G2, he—well, of course we didn't call them G2, we called them *b'acanob,* "whisperers"—hmm, let's say, according to our intelligence units, he'd already killed the remaining patriarchs of his own Swallowtail Clan, and had captured the next two Puma duarchs and most of the surviving synodsmen.

"Maybe I should be much more worried," I said.

"Severed Right Hand is quite energetic," Maximón said. "And he's just adopted another twenty-eight thousand bloods."

I clicked three times, respectfully, meaning, "Please go on."

Maximón said that Severed Right Hand was now commanding at least four thousand *veintenas,* that is, platoons of twenty. About fourteen thousand of those were full bloods from the Puma clans. They were experts with the javelin launcher, the Teotihuacanian signature weapon, and they'd be the hardest to fend off if there was a direct battle. He'd set up his mobile headquarters at Tehuacán—which, despite the similar name, was not the same as, or even a satellite town of, Teotihuacán. It was two jornadas due whitewards, north, of us. He'd brought along what was left of the city's council of four hundred, which he now dominated. And he'd sworn to capture all the Rattler's Children and give their heads and skins to the Green Hag, a sort of fresh-water elemental who'd been the elder patroness of Teotihuacán.

Severed Right Hand was claiming that Koh—or, as she was now styling herself, the Great-Elderess of All Star Rattler's Children—hadn't just foretold the city's destruction, but had caused it. The claim had the advantage of being basically the truth, although this hadn't seemed to have hurt Koh's standing with her own followers. Even our cleverer clan leaders, the ones who'd gotten the gossip about her machinations, seemed more loyal to her than ever. So even though the official motive for the now-unavoidable civil war was, as always, revenge, it was revenge in the Maya sense of capturing Koh's *uays*.

More specifically, Teotihuacán had been like the Lourdes, Jerusalem, Rome, and Mecca of Mesoamerica, and anyone who could have destroyed it was vastly powerful. If Severed Right Hand captured Koh and, through torture, annexed her uays—her most active souls—her powers of prophecy and domination would accrue to him. Her former followers would be constrained to obey him, since his uays would hold hers within his skin. He would become both the avenger of the destruction of Teotihucán and its prime beneficiary.

But even with all that, the main reason they were after us, like the real reason for almost anything, was economic. The displaced Puma clans had lost most of their wealth and they needed negotiable items to trade for new homesteads. And every family in our völkerwanderung had brought as much of their high-value gear as they could drag, jewelry, celts, top-grade blades and obsidian cores, textiles, feathers, furs, raw jade, gold dust, and even some chips and pebbles of unworked turquoise—which we called *xiuh,* a proto-Nahuatl word, since there was no word for it in Mayan, and which was the latest almost-unaffordable sensation from the farthest edge of the world's bleached northeast. The greathouse lineages had also brought thousands of rubber-sealed baskets swelling with about a hundred varieties of spices and drugs, and thousands of examples of the sort of jade objects that we twenty-first-centuryites would call "art." And, especially, they'd brought slaves. Although they weren't really like old-world slaves. Maybe it'd be closer to the Cholan sense to call them "thralls." For one thing, there wasn't any clear line between slaves and nonslaves, since even rich clans were like slaves in respect to their local ruling lineage, and then that lineage was like slaves to the ahau, and then, the ahau was a slave to his most deified ancestor. And the slaves could be from any ethnic group. Still, they could be ordered around, and sold, and eaten. Just as, theoretically at least, anybody could be, all the way up to the ahau. And he could get eaten by the smokers.

Anyway, the point is that we—the long train of Koh's followers—were, despite our bedraggled look, a seductive target. And we wouldn't be able to put up much of a fight. Most of the support for Koh's Star Rattler Society had come from Teotihuacán's white moiety, the peace clans, who were related to the red war moiety through mandatory exogamy, but usually didn't train their own sons as warriors. Our caravan had about eight thousand bloods with war experience who'd come from other Rattler-pledged clans, but they weren't well organized like the Teotihuacanian infantry, or, yet, very well coordinated with each other. To say the least. And we had a few thousand Maya bloods from the expatriate Ixob Ocelot lineage and some allied Maya trading clans from Tik'al and Kaminaljuyu, but they already weren't getting along with the Teotihuacanians. Finally, at the bottom of the social pyramid, we were dragging along about eighteen thousand families of thralls. About twelve thousand of these were warrior-aged males, nonbloods who we could send in to fight, but who were armed only with pikes and weren't effective in battle except as a buffer. And their kinsfolk—well, they fetched and carried, and their young folks took care of the greathouse males' sexual needs, and they were meat on the hoof, as it were—but really, most of the time they felt like a liability.

The upshot was that in a direct fight we'd be in trouble. We'd agreed—we meaning Lady Koh, her provisional council of clan patriarchs, and I—had all agreed that our best strategy would be to just keep moving as fast as possible and draw Severed Right Hand away from his logistical support base in the Valley of Mexico.

"Severed Right Hand seems to be holding his own against your Lady Koh," Maximón said.

"You mean in the Sacrifice Game?" I asked. She'd told me that she played against him every night—long distance, of course, and by the equivalent of telepathy. And then in the mornings she'd issue orders accordingly.

"Yes," Maximón indicated, somehow.

"You're right." He seemed to be fading—I mean, visually—and my voice started hurrying. "In fact it seems like sometimes he knows where we're heading before we decide to go there."

"Of course, it's really his advisers playing."

"Oh?" I asked. "Who are they?"

He said they were five nine-stone players who'd worked for years for the capital's twin synods, and who were so permanently *in camera* that nobody, not even the synodsmen themselves, knew their names. Supposedly they didn't have tongues, and they spoke only in a house sign language, and they had white skin, like vestal virgins, and two of them were over a hundred and twenty years old.

"Well, that's good to know," I said. It sounded like it was just hocus-pocus.

"And they also say he's a great *hun sujri,*" he said. Now he's really got to be jiving me, I thought. The word literally meant "skin slougher," or, to save syllables, let's say "molter," that is, a skin changer or a metamorphoser, someone whose animal uay was so unusually strong that it could transform his physical body. It especially applied to people with big-cat uays, Jaguars and Pumas. They were known for metamorphosing into cats, of course, but they also supposedly sometimes appeared as boys, as capturing-age bloods, or as old men, depending on the occasion. And the most powerful of them were always adding to their stock of new uays, human and animal.

"Which of his uays would you over me guess that he'd favor?" I asked, trying for a nonconfrontive reply. That is, what would he likely metamorphose into?

"I'd keep an eye out for snatch-bats," Maximón said. He meant the big *camazotz* vampire bats, *Desmodus draculae,* which had a longer wingspan than any of their related species that would survive into later centuries. They were fearsome-looking suckers.

"You wouldn't happen to know whether Severed Right Hand is planning to attack us right now, would you?" I asked.

"He has his own problems," Maximón said, or his glyphs said. "He'll wait to cut you off at the Río Capalapa." His outlines seemed less distinct than ever.

Wow, I thought. How did he know that? Or, what I mean is, how did I know that? I mean, you only get out of these things what you already have in there somewhere.

Hmm. We were still four solid jornadas from the Capalapa. Send a runner back to Lady Koh? Except I don't have any evidence. We could reroute the march west, and then go south along the Mixteco instead. But that's a pretty big deal. Anyway, he could be wrong. That is, I could be wrong. Severed Right Hand could attack us tomorrow. Better wait and get back to her and then send out some recons and try to confirm.

"Thanks," I said.

"You'll be all right if you hurry." He said something else, but I couldn't read the last four glyphs. Damn. Ashes. I rubbed my eyes but the glyphs, and Maximón, looked blurrier than before.

"Thanks."

"*Dominos Nabisco*," he said, orally. Did I hear that right? I wondered. "And also with you," I said. I started to back away from him Maya-underling style, but after only ten steps all I could see was the tip of his cigar floating in the infrareddening haze.

(17)

"We're turning whiteward," I signed to Hun Xoc, shielding my hands with the drape of my manto so the men wouldn't see that I was actually the one in charge. He didn't ask why, he just gave the order, signing over his turbaned head so that everyone could see. We marched to the crossroads and turned onto the left path.

The redirect took up about fifteen hundred beats—around twelve minutes—because we had to signal the front-runners, and then they signaled that they were coming back to show us what they insisted was a path in the right direction, although when we got to it I couldn't see it. We marched—well, let's say "slogged"—toward the nearest mesa of the low northern sierra. If I remembered right we were about eight thousand feet above sea level now, so up there it would be nearly nine thousand.

This had better be the right decision, I thought. What if I'm really losing it? Maybe the fact that the Maximón thing had been so realistic was something I ought to worry about. Maybe I'd gotten a whiff of psychoactives back when we were raiding the Puma's pharmacopoeia, and they'd taken until now to kick in. Or maybe it was the neoplasm. I mean, the brain tumors that would have been seeded by the downloading. They had to be getting big enough now to start causing problems. I'd picked up roughly two sieverts of gamma radiation that had zwapped an image of my memories into Chacal's brain fifty-one days ago. The Consciousness Transfer Protocol and the downloading routine and everything were all amazing technology, but the downsides were that there was damage to the host brain, the host spinal cord, and a few other vital areas. I figured the body I was in was good for another seven months or so, tops. Sometime around the thirteenth k'in of this uinal—in the Gregorian calendar, say, before January of 665—I'd be too unhealthy to function at all normally. Well before that time, I'd need to be signed, sealed, and entombed. And we'd just have to see whether I'd get delivered.

Well, don't stress on it. Except should I really be taking Maximón's advice? I mean, it was really my own advice, but if I was getting screwy . . .

Well, even so, if I'd learned one thing from these Olde Mayaland folks, it was that—well, actually, I'd learned a few things, but one of them was—it was that your brain isn't one thing. The way they put it, you had sort of a stable of different souls. Some were human, some were animals, and some, like your *ik'ar,* your "wind," or let's say your breath, were practically mineral. And if you were clever, you let them talk to each other, and you made sure they all listened.

The crew and I struggled up the slope of crumbled sandstone. Finally we gave up on dignity and climbed on all fours, with our feet turned outward for extra grip. Still, I slid more than once, ripping cuts in my forearms. I kept looking around and seeing, with a reliable little chill, how small our troop looked against the cyclopean landscape. Like I said, I'd only brought twenty-two porters, four Harpy Clan bloods counting my adopting brother Hun Xoc, Six Ixian Rattler bloods, 7 Iguana—the Harpy sacrificer—and our head outrunner, 4 Screaming, with his own crew of nine, and a few other miscellaneous functionaries. It wasn't enough to fight off even a single veintena of actual soldiers. If they found us.

The slope leveled out into a wide oval tableland that floated over the ash shroud around us, so that it felt like we were in a crater on some C-class asteroid. We posted lookouts at the rim and I marked three hundred and fifty paces to the nearer center of the oval and signed to Hun Xoc. He relayed the command to the porters and they set down their packs, put together their wooden shovels, and started digging. Hun Xoc and his two porters and I got out a forty-arm's-length right-triangle surveyor's cord and marked out the four smaller holes where we'd drop in the lodestones. In the twenty-first century, they'd be brazenly visible from any of Warren Communication's microwave-sounder satellites. Before that was done, the crew hit rock, four arm-lengths down, but they changed their wood shovels for picks and kept at it. Hun Xoc, the other bloods, 7 Iguana, and I all sat on the piles of rubberized bags and watched. Greathouse bloods didn't do dirt.

We waited. Maximón had been right about the wind. Lord Papagayo had been walking strong on the plain, but up here when you dropped dust out of your hand it fell straight down. Weird.

We'd brought six nearly identical terra-cotta round ovens, each about twenty finger-widths across. Each one was wrapped in rubberized deerskin so that it looked like a half-deflated yellow beach ball. Inside each of the vessels were two more nested terra-cotta bowls with a layer of wax between them. So each round oven had only about forty cubic inches of interior space. Still, one of these interior spaces held four duplicate screenfold books with my notes on the Game, copied, two tiny jadeite bottles of the refined tsam lic compounds, toads and other critters mummified six different ways, and two folded miniature feather-cloth Game boards, all packed in expensive Cholulan rock salt. I hoped it would give Marena and company enough information to stave off Armageddon. Still, I couldn't just slack off. Even if they got the package—well, I was pretty sure they'd get it, but let's say even after they got it—there'd be a chance that without the sort of specialized knowledge and skills I was picking up from Koh, they wouldn't be able to use the Game effectively enough to stop all potential doomsters. If we wanted to be closer to certain, I'd have to get my working brain back, with all its precious cargo. Or most of it.

The other five round ovens held various counterfeit versions of the stuff, convincing enough, I hoped, to satisfy any treasure hunters who might get the gossip.

After four hundred times four hundred beats I strolled over and looked in. They'd gotten down another two arm-lengths. Good enough. We started them on the second hole, one rope-length—about twenty-one feet—west of this one. Again, we sat and watched. Armadillo Shit picked fleas out of my hair. The flint pick heads struck showerlets of sparks on the bedrock. Hun Xoc told them to speed it up.

He's right, I thought. They're working hard, but they don't seem eager to finish.

They know.

Well, it can't be helped.

After another hundred-score beats they'd finished fifteen holes. Enough to fill the Albert Hall, I thought. All right already. I signed to 7 Iguana to get ready, and he opened his pack and took out a short muffled mace, like a ball-peen hammer with its head wrapped in rubber tape.

(18)

We buried the rest of them, raked over the scars, and spread gravel and cinders over them as realistically as we could in the half-light. I didn't even tell Hun Xoc which of the vessels was the important one, although he might have been able to guess from the pattern of the other nine holes. Each of these—the smaller holes—received a heavy rubberized deerhide sack the size of a bowling-ball bag. Five of the bags were full of very ordinary rocks in a big wad of wax. The other four, the ones forming a perfect two-rope-length cross with the primary vessel at the center, were full of chunks of meteoric magnetite, which I'd bought thirty-one days ago at the fetish market in Teotihuacán, at a cost equal to about fifty good adolescent male slaves. The magnetite was also, of course, in a big wad of wax. I figured it was probably overkill, but why cut corners on your signature project? As the men filled in the holes I rotated them around a bit, hoping they'd get confused. Not that it would matter unless we got stopped unexpectedly—

Bdrdrdrdroododoodoot. We all froze.

A pygmy-owl hoot. Also just detectably artificial. It was the outrunners. Seventy beats later a silhouette materialized on the north ridge and held his hands over his head, palms down, signing "No danger, but wait." A hundred and thirty beats later—a Maya beat was a little shorter than a second, so say about two minutes—4 Screaming, our chief outrunner, was standing next to us. His rubber-soled-sandaled feet hadn't made even a slight crunch on the cinders and packed gravel. His name was 4 Screaming, but despite his name, he was silent and permanently furtive, and like all the outrunners—actually they were called *k'antatalob,* "sniffers," because around here you usually smelled your enemies before you could see them—he was long-legged and wiry, with pocked skin smeared with deer feces.

"No Pumas," he signed, "but there are tracks half a day north, and in Coixtlahuaca we counted about twice four hundred skinless bodies." The Pumas—who'd been the leading war lineage of Teotihuacán, and whose remnants were following Severed Right Hand—routinely flayed their kills, animal and human. He started to go through the list of the towns and paths and milpas where they'd seen the biggest concentrations of corpses, but after a minute I just looked at Hun Xoc—who was senior to me and nominally the ranking captain but who was easygoing enough to be basically acting as my second-in-command—and flicked my eyes northeast. Hun Xoc signed for 4 Screaming to take his squad that way as far as possible for two-ninths of a night—about four hours—and then report back again.

4 Screaming took thirty beats to sign to his squad, and they all took off again without even asking for drinking water. God, I thought, these guys are tough as jackboots. Gluttons for punishment.

Well, good for our side. We could keep digging.

By eighty-score beats before dawn, or what would have been dawn under normal conditions, the top of the mesa looked exactly like it had when we'd gotten here. To me, anyway. To an experienced tracker, it—well, you can't cover everything, I thought. Better to get the hell out of here even if it's not perfect. Anyway, there was still wood ash falling. That would even it out a bit. I gave the signal for the crew to reassemble at the southeastern rim of the basin. Without being asked, thirty-eight of the men squatted in two rows of nineteen, facing northwest, toward their birthplaces. 2 Hand—another adopted son of 2 Jeweled Skull's, who was also officially senior to me but who was increasingly acting as my third lieutenant—went down the rows, taking their offering letters. We'd burn them to Star Rattler at the next celestial date. The first one signed that he was ready and our *nacom*—our untouchable executioner—squatted behind him and hammered, or almost just tapped, once, on the back of his head, driving the occiput into the brain stem. The sound was as soft as if he was hitting balsa wood, not bone.

The porters loaded the bodies onto the empty sleds and started to pull them down the mesa. They'd be defleshed and, presumably, brought all the way with us to—well, to wherever we were going, which was a bit of a vexed issue—and then stored in the Star Rattler's ossuary. It wouldn't do to have any of their cranky uays hanging around here, leading some warlock or fortune-hunting wraith or whatever back up here to the basins. On either side of the trail, every so often, you could just make out one of the outrunners lurking along, making sure that none of the much-reduced crew ran off. But it didn't look like they would. The thing was, these days, you really could get good help. Or, to be less flip, these guys counted themselves among the lucky ones. Around here, the rodent-uayed—that is, ordinary people—didn't do much better in the afterlife than they did here on the zeroth level. Most of their multiplicitous souls would just wander around and eventually starve. After all, nobody among the living would bother to feed them, or at least not for long. These guys had guaranteed, if not lavish, support in the next levels. They wouldn't have to be slaves to one of the Nine, or even to the Thirteen. They could relax a bit, finally, and work their way toward what everyone aspired to: oblivion. And it would take them only twenty years or so. Only the feline-uayed stuck around for any length of time—not because immortality would be fun, since it wouldn't, especially when people on the zero level started to forget to send you blood and tobacco—offerings—but because they had a responsibility to keep an eye on the other members of the clan, living, dead, and unborn.

And besides, I thought, Koh had insisted. Right? It couldn't be helped. Except, no. Don't try to shift the responsibility, Jed-head. You had the witnesses iced and that's all there is to it. And, not even very indirectly, you've accounted for a lot of other poor bastards over the last few few *tunob*. And, frankly, it's started not even to bother you very much. You're just another realpolitiker. You evil fuck.

We humped back southwest down the long grade. The porters kept begging for the honor of carrying me, or at least pulling me on a sled, but Chacal's body had been feeling like it was getting soft—he'd been a top athlete, after all, before all the excitement started—and I insisted on marching. I wore out another pair of rubberized sandals on the scurf. That's five so far, I thought. 4 Screaming rematerialized and he and 2 Hand and I had a quick, silent confab. He said Lady Koh and her entourage had moved six-score rope-lengths up the line already, so we adjusted our course to intersect hers, branching off our previous track onto a new route that zigzagged down out of the high ground into charred scrub and then into damper air and what you could charitably call rolling meadows. Each of the recently abandoned milpas—that is, corn-and-squash fields—had a scarecrow of sorts in the center, usually a dog skull with a ragged cape on a tall stick, with strings of bird femurs and clamshells clicking and clopping in the occasional breeze. It was as though somebody'd mandated that everyone go out of their way to make things as creepy and depressing as possible. It looked like some of the corn had been harvested, too young, but most of the pinkie-sized ears were burnt and withered on the stalks, with a few popped kernels standing out like big whiteheads. Even this far south the drought had lasted fifty-six days so far—since the eruption of San Martín—and everything had burned as fast as Chinese dead money. It seemed like even the rocks burned. We'd seen villagers spreading the fires around their houses, torching their own granaries and huts with their wives and children screaming inside them.

It wasn't logical, but the average Mesoamerican still seemed to think that the world needed some help ending itself, and there'd been a thousand orgies of self-immolation all the way from the Sonoran Desert to what would be Costa Rica. We'd seen whole families staked out alive on the ground for the insects and vampire bats, kids peeling strips of loose arm skin off exhausted but conscious oldsters and eating it like it was Fruit Roll-Ups, mothers killing their toddlers by forcing pink-hot pebbles down their throats, a thousand things you wish you could unsee. And by now, except for the animals on the run, there was basically nothing left. Fuck Severed Right Hand, I thought. He won't be able to feed his troops around here. Ten more days and he'll lose interest. Why was he so determined? It can't be because of the tsam lic. According to Koh's informers he had his own sun-adders and they were rebuilding the pharmacopeia in Choula.

There's got to be something else going on that I don't know about. Maybe

I should confront Koh about it? Except, in general around here you didn't get very far with direct questions. Just watch her, I thought. Watch and deduce. Then when she gets the people to wherever they're going—hmm. Well, I needed to get back to Ix for my last act. That is, the entombment. But the refugees—well, even if the Maya lowland zones hadn't been agriculturally exhausted yet, the way they would be in two hundred years, there still wouldn't be enough unclaimed farmland in Ix's orbit. If they could even learn how to do that kind of bog-reclamation planting, which I doubted they would. People don't learn. Lately, Lady Koh had been saying that the Rattler had shown her the site of a new city, in the coastal flats on the farthest marches of the Harpy Clan's red territory—that is, somewhere on the Quintana Roo coast. The current deal was that 2 Jeweled Skull would provide an escort for safe conduct to the site and give her lineage the area in perpetuity. But it sounded vague to me. And most of these people wouldn't get nearly that far anyway. We had food for another forty days or so, but once we were into the dry season, it was . . . hell. It was depressing.

Don't think about it. Anyway, you did the main thing, right? Maybe the Lodestone Cross bit was going to be enough. Maybe I'd already just become the biggest hero since Hercules. Since Jesus, for that matter. Maybe I was done here. Maybe I can just relax. Except not. Still ought to go through with the backup plan. Get back to Ix. Get the ol' memories back to Marena. Do the full meal deal.

The light faded to a more delicate shade of scab. 4 Screaming's second-in-command came up and signed that they'd sniffed a large crowd of strangers to the northeast. They couldn't tell yet if they were the Teotihuacanian soldiers, but we picked up speed. They asked to carry me again and I said no. Oddly, despite everything, I felt pretty good.

At the end of this Grandfather Heat's youth—about ten A.M.—the breeze shifted up and we smelled our caravan. It was basically that same aroma as when a really hard-core homeless person shuffles onto the subway and everybody risks a ticket to cross between the moving cars rather than stay even fifteen beats in the presence of the indescribable hell stench. But what was odd about it now was that to me, coming in from the cold as it were, it smelled reassuring, or even pleasant, like home. I guess it really is all context. Hun Xoc touched my arm and pointed ahead at ten o'clock. At first I couldn't see anything and then I made out a human figure against the brown sky, levitating two rope-lengths over the scrub. As we got closer I could see it was a lookout, or as I've said, a sniff-out, one of our shortest, scrawniest, and sharpest-eyed bloods, wobbling in a sort of a crow's-nest on the top of a tower woven of weeping bamboo. It looked so flimsy you wouldn't think it could support a squirrel. He signed down to us that things were clear. Another came into view behind him, and then another and another, so that as we got close to our line of march there was a whole troop of them, like a thin reflection of the dust-wreathed caravan below. You could squint and just imagine that it was a camel train on the Silk Road, headed toward Samarkand. Nights in the Garden of Allah. Song of the Sheikh. Midnight at the Oasis. Ah, zee Englishwoman is a thoroughbred which no man has yet dared to ride. Bring her to my tents, Hasan. Have zee serving girls anoint her with essences of oud and Ubar and drape her in the finest Murshidabadian silks and suchlike. I will school her in the ways of the Rif. *Blue heaven, and you, and I, and sand, kissing the moonlit sky . . . the desert breeze, whisp'ring a lullaby . . .*

I was used to it by now, but I suppose to the twenty-first-century eye one of the odder things about this place—I mean Mesoamerica, or for that matter the entire New World—was that everything was single file. Even if you had a hundred thousand people on the move, there were never even two of them abreast. The thin human snake just slid on forever, curving over both horizons. 2 Hand—Hun Xoc's younger brother and, unofficially, something like my second mate—came out with a veintena of men to meet us and said that the number of Koh's followers had gone up by a fifth—again—just while we were away, so despite our adjustments we'd still come in about four thousand marchers behind the great woman and her entourage. 2 Hand called her "the Elderess," which made me wonder whether he was starting to believe some of her hype. Bad sign. We cut through the line and jogged ahead on its southern side, with what they called the Iguana River, a sad yellow trickle at the low point of the long Nochixtlán Valley, on our right hand. It was light enough to see faces now, although today's sun wouldn't show itself. I passed—or to be socially correct I should say "my bearer, my scarefly, my weapons valet, my faithful fellator Armadillo Shit," and I passed—a delicate-looking fourteen-year-oldish girl who was pulling her family's big ratty old travois single-handedly, or I guess I should say single-headedly, since it was drawn by a tumpline that cut deep into her forehead. There was a mole a half inch below the right of her hornet-stung lips, just like the one on, hmm, some actress, who was it—oh, yeah, Claudine Auger, the girl who played Domino in *Thunderball*. Her mother and sisters were walking in front of her, and her father, a brother, and four other male relatives sat in the sled, taking it easy. Patriarchal fucks, I thought, although I should mention that the four male relatives were deceased, just masked mummy bundles sitting as stiffly upright as Quaker ministers, so they were probably pretty light. But then there were also three big hearthstones on the sled, and one of those big wooden Teotihuacanian host statues, the kind that have all the little statues inside them, and a bunch of other bundles that I guessed were just more garbage, and I was on the verge of going up and shaking the paterfamilias and screaming, "You *fuck*, first, you get out and pull the sled, and second, you toss those dead guys and the other crap right *now* and fill up every waterskin you've got, and beg, borrow, or steal as much rock salt as you can *possibly* drag, and then *maybe* you all have a chance of lasting another twenty days, you FUCKHEAD," but of course you'd have to tell everybody the same thing and the important thing was to keep a low profile and get yourself and the tsam lic critters back to Ix, and anyway you couldn't argue with these people. Or any people. Then there were three loners, each dragging a fresh or—let's say "still unprepared"—corpse. There just weren't enough defleshers to go around, even though they were working day and night, stuffed with extra rations and sitting in unaccustomed luxury on special sleds as they picked over the bodies with their inch-long fingernails. And they were hurrying. It was lousy mojo—obviously—if the dogs got any of you, but even so a big scurfy pack of them seemed to be making its whole living following the catafalques. When the bones finally dried out, an engraver would carve their owners new names—that is, their postholocaust, Koh-given names—into the ulnas and tibias. Although you'd think there wouldn't be time for such niceties. But even with fire, starvation, bandits, disease, and troops of more novel apocalyptic horsemen, everybody found the leisure to give themselves new names, brands, tattoos, tooth decor, and whatever else. Craziness.

The next big group we passed was a clanlet of well-to-do Swallowtail-affiliated traders, about fifteen blood family members and two veintenas of thralls hauling them on eight extralong sleds. On the last sled, three eight-year-old girls, who looked like triplets, fanned the patriarch with huge chocho palm leaves that had recently been blanched and then dyed blue-green. Which, I guess, is getting into more detail than necessary, but I wanted to mention it while I'm thinking of since it became an issue later: all of Koh's followers who could afford it wore or carried something in her signature turquoise-blue shade—there were vats of the indigofera dye on special sleds—so that from a distance the procession looked like it had been sprinkled with periwinkle blossoms. Something old, something new, I thought. Something borrowed, something askew. And something too nauseating even to name. Still, they all thought they were part of a larger being. And despite everything, there was an element of fun to it, or if not quite fun at least adventure. For most of them this was the first time they'd been away from their home ground. For that matter, some of the women probably hadn't ever been two rope-lengths outside their hamlets. This was the primary event in their lives, and in their family's lives, all the way back to their first ancestor at the first birth of this sun on 4 Lord, 8 Seed Maize, 0.0.0.0.0., that is, August 11, 3113 BC, and ahead to their last descendant, who, of course, would die on the last 4 Ahau of the last b'aktun, in AD 2012.

There were about three hundred big palanquins in the high-rent district of the line. They varied in size and opulence but they all had arrays of cushions and big round wicker roofs covered with embroidered cloth, so that they looked incogruously like psychedelicized Conestoga wagons. Lady Koh held court on the largest of the palanquins. It was only about eight arms wide—still wider than any of the others—but about forty long. Right now there were sixteen people sitting on it and forty carrying it. There was a breeze, but another gang of thralls carried a portable windbreak, and the feathers on the mat barely stirred. A squad of guards ran alongside on each hand. There was a strong smell of monarda—a kind of horsemint that upscale valets crushed and strewed around their masters—which didn't much cover up the hellish odors, and under that a hint of what people said was the breath of Koh's most secret uay, and what a modern person would call her signature scent. When I'd first smelled it I'd described it to myself as the opposite of the smell of cinnamon, and now, after what seemed like years, I still didn't have a better description. But I did know, now, that its main component was enfleuraged from what I was pretty sure was a species of *Brassia,* the genus of orchids that mimics spiders, and that as far as anyone seemed to know, it was unique to her and her close followers.

Koh's guards all knew Hun Xoc, but it still took a while to pass through their circles. I was already doing rage-abatement breathing by the time my bearer finally set me down on the edge of the platform. It rocked just a bit as it moved along, pleasantly boatlike. Koh sat in the turquoise center of a feather-cloth Sacrifice Game board two arm-lengths square. Her eyes were closed and she was mumbling to one of her uays in some animal language. There were eight members of the *popol na*—the mat house, that is, the council, up here, and they greeted me and went back to talking among themselves. They were all in expensive gear, but it was still a pretty motley crew. Crüe. Whatever. The youngest of them, 14 Wounded, was eight *tuns,* that is, a little less than eight solar years, older than I was. He'd been the trade representative in Teotihuacán for my adoptive clan, the Harpies, who were the richest family in Ix besides the ruling clan, the Ocelots. Or they might now be even richer, because of the Ocelots' gigantic debts, except it was harder to put a value on things here than it was back in the twenty-first. Anyway—oh, except there was one who was younger, Koh's Steward of Invisible Things. His title meant he was something like a legal counsellor. His name was Coati, that is, kind of a raccoon. I'd barely met him back in Teotihuacán, but now he was with her every minute.

The group had started as a temporary meeting of the major greathouse ahaus, but now it had hardened into a government. Well, whatevs. The other seven people on the platform were attendants, fanning us and whisking away the screwflies. None of them looked at Koh. Ordinary folks who saw her face might get scorched by her captive lightning.

Hun Xoc manuevered next to me and squatted. I kneed to the edge of the Game cloth. It was strewn with jade and quartzite pebbles, and after a minute I could see that she was using it as a battle map. A long line of turquoise pebbles, stretching diagonally from the center of the white quadrant to the upper corner of the black one, represented our caravan. The clusters of pink quartz that approached it on its north side were Severed Right Hand's army, and it looked to me like they were color-coded like in an old Kriegspiel layout, darkening as they became increasingly hypothetical. But beyond that I couldn't read what she was up to. There was at least an equal number of other stones, mainly black and yellow, distributed in other zones of the board, and aside from the fact that they had more to do with time than space I couldn't tell what they represented. For all I knew, some of them were just there to confuse the other members of the council.

Well, if so, it was working. They were all stone-cold killers and word-is-law patriarchs, and now they were sitting patiently, waiting, speaking in hushed mutters, and casting apprehensive looks at her as we jogged along. Either they all believed she was getting her orders from a higher authority, or they figured enough of the others believed that none of them wanted to question her.

When I—

—Ow. Damn. One of the scareflies had gotten a hair into my eye. I glared at him. He quaked in terror, almost literally. And I almost felt guilty, but I got over it. I watched Koh. She moved two of the black stones. She was as unhurried as though no one else was there.

Hmm. *When I know more of tactics than a novice in a nunnery,* I was going to say. Well, our own nunnery novice had certainly convinced these cats that she knew something. Just two tuns ago—I would have said "short tuns" if they hadn't seemed longer than python turds—Koh had been just one of the more promising young members of the Orb Weaver Sorority. It was an elite group of epicene veneratoresses to Star Rattler, high-stone sun-adderesses who usually wore men's clothing so that they could operate in male spaces. Although now she was wearing bits of both male and female clothing. And as far as I knew, this was her own idea. She was becoming all things to all people.

Geez Belize, I thought, I've created a monsteress. I gave this girl her start. I mean, I was the one who'd contacted her in the first place, because there was a picture of her in the Codex Nuremberg. But the Codex wouldn't be written until long after this, sometime in the 1100s. And it wasn't clear from the Codex whether she'd still be alive or not *after* she became a big deal. She could end up like Jesus and be dead for a hundred years before the franchise really got going. And if she turned into a martyr, most likely she'd take me down with her. Well, don't worry about it. I was still pretty useful to her. Wasn't I? I mean, I knew stuff nobody around here knew, not even her. I could even still mix up some gunpowder if she wanted me to, although of course I didn't want to call that much attention to myself. Somebody'd say I was a dangerous scab-caster—like a warlock—and every other ambitious blood would be looking to off me.

The mumbling stopped. Lady Koh raised her eyes, and they met mine, and, without actually moving a single muscle of her face, somehow she conveyed a smile.

(19)

After that, Lady Koh made eye contact with each member of the council in turn and then, instead of speaking, took her hands out of the folds of her manto and signed in Ixian hunting language. Every once in a while, when there was a name that didn't translate, she spoke a syllable or two to fill in. "He'll march ahead of us, at least to the oxbow," she signed. "Then he'll retrace his route and wait for a west wind dawn." She moved the largest and brightest of the pink quartz pebbles southeast of our position and then back alongside us, illustrating the maneuver. The idea was that Severed Right Hand would want to come at us with the sun rising behind his men and the wind in front so we wouldn't smell him. It sounded reasonable. "So we need to have *iik* and coals ready." That is, when they attacked, we'd be ready to run baskets full of burning chili peppers upwind, to try and blind them.

"Smoke is for first-time-menstruating nongreathouse second-born girl daughters," 14 Wounded said. Needless to say, but I'll say it anyway, the expression sounded better in Mayan. Anyway, it meant that smoke screens were a cowardly tactic.

There was a pause. Cowardly is good, I thought, but I didn't want to start defending myself on the point, so I just kept walking. Set a good example, I thought. Quiet, uncomplaining, impervious to pain, stoic—*ow*. Sticklet in my left sandal. Damn. Ow, ow, ow. Why me? *Ow, ow, ow, ow, ow*. I shook it out. Okay. The trail went over a dry gulch and the platform swayed like a jet in a pocket of low pressure. You could hear thousands of callused and/or sandaled feet padding on gravel.

Finally Coati held up a hand with the thumb and first two fingers touching, which meant basically, "Insignificant as I am, may I yet please speak?" The members of the popol clicked their tongues for "yes."

They looked at Koh. She signed "yes."

"All great-alliances collapse from stomach parasites, not predators," Coati said. It was a well-known line from some old masque, but 14 Wounded didn't say anything more.

Koh and her privy council spent some time working on the new set of signals they'd give for advances and retreats. She stipulated that after the battle—which, I guess, they all figured couldn't be avoided—her followers would regather in a village called Place of the Ticks, on a defensible bluff two jornadas to the southwest. From there the migration would bear due south for two days, and then turn east along the Atoyac River to a site on the coast just south of what would later be called Veracruz. She'd resettle them there, she said, and reseat the Star Rattler's *mul*—that is, very generally, "pyramid." And after that, Koh and I would go on to Ix by the inland water route, with a small escort of two hundred and forty Orb Weaver bloods and a hundred and ten nonblood supporting families, meaning about another two thousand people.

The council lasted for two-thirteenths of the day, that is, about three hours. No one could leave until everyone agreed it was over. And in fact, unless one of us drastically changed rank, whenever any combination of us sat together again, it would be in the same relative positions and oriented toward the same directions. There were also twelve people who were allowed in the room but had to sit outside the circle: four servers, two of Koh's monkey-masked clerks, a silent guy in a striped outfit who was named 0 Porcupine Clown, and who seemed to be kind of Koh's court jester, 1 Gila's accountant and two guards, and our own two calligraphers. And, because tonight would belong to Serpigo, who was the most dangerous of the lords of the dusks, there were four censers pacing counterclockwise around the perimeter of the circle, trailing clouds of geranium incense out of their hand burners.

Finally one of the this-meeting-has-to-end votes carried. The bigwigs crouched backward away from the circle and went back to their own families. Hun Xoc stayed. Coati rolled up the Game board, the attendents folded the wicker covering over the four of us, and Koh and I got to speak almost in private.

She said that while I was away on my burial excursion she'd sent four runners forward to 2 Jeweled Skull, my adopted father and the ahau of the Harpy Clan. They were going to—wait, maybe I should mention a few other things about old 2JS. When I'd received Jed$_1$'s mind up on the Ocelots' mul, 2JS had unexpectedly been in the same tiny room with me, and he'd gotten a bit of scatter, enough of my memories to speak English and Spanish and understand quite a bit of what I was up to. But he hadn't gotten enough of me to, say, understand that the images he had of airplanes weren't a species of friendly condor, or that the computers he remembered me using weren't silent marimbas with captive souls inside. And he was still very much himself. There wasn't enough of me in there to confuse him about who he was, the way I'd been confused at first about whether I was me or Chacal, the ballplayer whose brain I was, shall we say, staying in as a guest. Luckily for me, Chacal's sense of self had faded away pretty quickly. But 2 Jeweled Skull had never become me. And knowing so much about me hadn't exactly seemed to help him empathize with me or my plight. He'd been angry. And I guess he'd had a legitimate beef. But he'd tortured me pretty badly to get me to pull myself out of his mind, and then, when I'd finally convinced him I couldn't do that, he'd gradually figured out a way to turn the situation to his advantage. He'd sent me to Teotihuacán to break the Teotihuacanian monopoly on tsam lic, the Sacrifice Game enabling drugs, and now here I was.

Anyway, Koh's runners were going to repeat to 2 Jeweled Skull—in a Harpy House code language that they themselves didn't understand—the message that I and the other Harpy bloods who'd survived from the team he'd sent, along with Lady Koh and a small Rattler-blood escort, would be sempiternally honored to attend the great-hipball game in Ix on Ixlahun Chuwen, Bolonlahun Yaxk'in, that is 13 Howler, 19 Redness, or July 14, forty-nine days from now. But they weren't going to mention the great migration. He will have heard about it anyway by now, she said. Calling attention to it would just raise the issue of what we intended to do with them. What if Koh didn't manage to found her shining-city-on-a-hill and we turned up in Ix leading a hungry multitude?

I moved back to one of the long, narrow Ball Brethren sleeping toboggans—for some reason they had a team of four watchdogs pulling it today, instead of the usual pairs of thralls—and crashed between two of my teammates. It was male-on-male cozy in a way that would have weirded me out as fagophobic old Jed. We trudged on through the night. What I thought were low stars behind the smoke turned out to be bonfires up in the hills that loomed invisibly on both sides of the trail. Just before the next dawn an alarm went down the line. There were always hairless dogs barking, arfing, and yipping, but some of us could distinguish the voices of the actual watchdogs, and when their pitch went up, it meant we were under attack. The Teotihuacanians were ahead of us, just like Lady Koh had said, but somehow they'd managed to ambush two veintenas of our forerunnners and they were closer than we'd allowed for. Ahead of me Koh gave the first of her coded commands. Armadillo Shit stripped off my wristlets and anklets and other rank signifiers and wrapped me up like I was a low-clan elder. My manto looked normal, but it was made of quilted cotton filled with sand, which pretty effectively stopped most thrown darts. Naturally, Koh had prohibited me from fighting. But for some reason—maybe it was emotion carrying over from Chacal—I realized that, irrationally, I really, really wanted to get my hands bloody.

Well, resist that impulse. It didn't matter. Right? Why should it? I shouldn't care about these people. *Those I fight I do not hate,* I thought. *Those I guard I do not love.* Except maybe I did. Already I could hear the moan of long bull-roarers and the grunts and occasional screams from up ahead. Then there was another hoarse sound, children screaming through megaphones. It's a pretty hard sound to describe, like cats in traps, maybe, but more sort of bagpipish, so much so that I wondered whether bagpipes had first been invented to imitate it. Severed Right Hand was torturing some of his youngest captives. Then there were the ringing sparks of flint points in the last dark, like little stone bells, and the barely audible click of darts leaving the spear-throwers, and the hisses and sizzles as the first of the flaming spears came in. The line started to smell like a giant pit latrine, as all battles do, plus vomit, and with the addition of chili smoke. Jaguar-Scorpion battle-cries welled up and the Rattler bloods started screeching coded instructions to each other—we did have war cries, by the way, but I never heard any that were like that whoo-whoo-whoo thing the Plains tribes do in old movies—and at the same time one of the Harpy bloods who was shielding me put his hand up to his face and picked a thin blowgun-dart out of one eye, like a long flowered thorn stretching out forever. Even in the firelight reflected off the smog-roof I could see the point was wrapped in the black-and-yellow-striped skin of a harlequin creeper. I suppressed a flinch. You couldn't let anything faze you in front of these people. But if you could just suck it up, you were almost home.

We crouched with our shields up and backed into the crowd of Rattler bloods behind us. The blood who'd been hit broke from the group, turned around with his bloody wink, and saluted us—our salute was generally more of a casual "Hey, bro," than a military deal—and ran wobblingly off to charge the Jaguars while he was still alive. While that was happening and before it was over a runner came through from Hun Xoc and led us farther back into a narrow pass. Koh's entourage was already in the center. They set guards at each end so that if it looked like we might get cut off on one side we'd get ready to break on the other. I listened, trying to separate the code-calls from the screeches and the whirs of whistle-spears, but couldn't get anything. It was still too dim to see detail. Someone was pushing through to us. It was Hun Xoc. He said the outrunners didn't think Koh had been singled out yet, so neither had I. We should just dig in. In the meantime 1 Gila had taken a division south and was going to come back in from the east with noise like there were a whole lot more of us.

Well, the plan sounds—oh, wait. Who the hell is 1 Gila? Okay. The largest Teotihuacanian war clan that was solidly bonded to Koh and her Star Rattler Cult—and so were declared enemies of Severed Right Hand—were the Lineage of the *Acaltetepón*, that is, *Heloderma horridum*, the Mexican beaded lizard. 1 Gila wasn't the patriarch of the clan—that was his much older uncle—but he was their war leader, and he was probably Lady Koh's most powerful supporter.

Okay.

Well, the plan sounds great, I thought. Yup. You've got my blessing. I asked about our second-largest battle-ready group, 3 Talon's contingent and the rest of his Mexican Eagle Clan. Or let's be correcter and say "Caracara Clan." Hun Xoc said they were fighting other feline clans themselves, but that as far as he could tell they'd already split off. Just before we needed them. The spies said they were going to consolidate in a fortified Caracara town about four jornadas west of the Valley. We didn't know what they'd do after that. Probably they'd try to start another Teotihuacán-like city nearby with themselves in charge, although we knew from history that it wouldn't be such a big deal. Anyway, they didn't want to tell us much or make commitments, but since they were in shit with the cat clans they wanted peace, if not necessarily union, with the Rattlers. Nobody wants to fight on two fronts, except for crazies like late-period Hitler.

For a while things didn't look good. 1 Gila's people, who knew the area, could tell which different vendetta squads had taken advantage of the collapse of government in the region and come through ahead of us just from the number of headless bodies tied up in trees. The number of white buzzards overhead seemed to double every fifty-score beats and it started to really bug me, I couldn't stop thinking about how hot and sour they must feel even way up in the air, all these fat suckers with their little heads like barbed penises, just slacking around in these high, agonizingly slow interlocking spirals, the most patient birds in the world. But by the end of the day—the day that was already being called the first Grandfather Heat of the fifth family of suns, "the Grandfathers of Heat to be born after the end of the earthly paradise"—it became clear that in this case bad for others was good for us. At noon we met the main body of Koh's Rattler Newborn, or converts, which was listed at fourteen thousand but was obviously triple that if you counted women and children and thralls. About a third of Koh's followers from the zocalo, that is, the plaza, had been killed by the Jaguars or by the fires, but the ones who had gotten away credited her with saving them. Most of them had picked up their extended families in the suburbs—who knew her prophecy already—and packed up whatever they had left to follow Koh to the Promised Land. Of course, they didn't know she hadn't yet decided where that would be.

And Koh's *k'ab'eyob*—"rumorers," rumor spreaders, or I guess we can call them advance men—had also done their job. More and bigger towns joined us every day, and more and more clan leaders pledged themselves and their dependents to Koh. Her runners ran up and down organizing them, adding the blue-green band to their colors, having them swear impromptu oaths, setting marching and foraging orders, whatever. She'd brought cases of cosmetics along—as always, first things first—and her dressers worked on everyone, from Koh on down, making us look more like a real royal entourage and not a messed-up gang of escapees.

By the old age of the first Grandfather Heat, the sun, as we headed into what would later be Puebla, our line stretched out so far that someone could go off-road and take a nap at the head of the first file, get woken up two- or three-hundred-score beats later as the last stragglers passed, and then, if they could afford bearers, have themselves run up to the front of the line again. Koh's clowns ran up and down the sides of the line, under the direction of her favorite Porcupine Jester, and entertained the marchers with lampoons on the Pumas.

Finally, just as the same Grandfather Heat died, another round of messages went up and down the line between Koh, Hun Xoc, 1 Gila, 14 Wounded, and me. Without meeting in person we reached a consensus that we—"we" meaning us greathouse leaders and our core bloods—couldn't afford to camp. We didn't have enough guards to resist a full assault from the Pumas, so we'd have to stay on the move or they'd have time to set up an ambush somewhere. We had only fifteen suns left to get back to Ix before the big great-hipball game, barely enough for an ambassador with staged porters, let alone an army. So the Rattler Fathermothers and 14 Wounded's posse and the Harpy bloods and me and the other hotshots kept going through the night, carried in stages by bearers who'd collapse exhausted at the end of their stint and sleep in the side-scrub until the trail sweepers in the rear guard prodded them. The heralds ran ahead to tell potential converts to wait for us so they could help carry the leaders. Mao had the Long March, but if this one got that kind of press it was going to be known as the Fast March. Or the Scatterbrained Dash, or something.

But, incongruously, it had a festive side. Since there was no question of secrecy, Koh had dancers with royal blue-flame myrtle-berry torches swirling in snake-coils ahead and behind her three palanquins, so that from a distance we must have looked like a long trail of glowworms with a single turquoise-tinted chemical mutant in the center. I thought it was silly of her to mark her position. But Koh was surrounding herself more and more with the trappings of divinity in other ways too. She asked for her pledged followers to get special perks and rationing, as opposed to other people we had in our train, and after some hemming and hawing even 14 Wounded said okay. Up and down the line and up and down the social scale she was the main subject of conversation, people repeating themes she'd started herself. She'd used old stories about One Ocelot's daughter to make herself seem like the fulfillment of a prophecy, the same way that, much later, the nations that Cortez co-opted would spread rumors that he was "fulfilling" a prophecy that hadn't existed before.

From what I could tell, she played the rest of the Star-Rattler Society pretty well too. Each of the high-ranked members of her order, including the nine-skull epicene adders, of which Koh was one of nine, advised and took care of a troop of dependents, generally lesser clans and villages that had converted, but also some individuals and smaller families. And Koh never made an overt statement against any of them. She cultivated her seniors in the Sorority—only three of whom were with us anyway—and played down her separatism. She had to get a coalition together but also position herself as a new dispensation, a kind of popular outreach. Forty days ago, before the Last Fourth Sun, the majority of the Rattlers' children hadn't specifically been Koh's own followers, or even much aware of her. But now, after the Pumas had attacked all of the Rattlers indiscriminately, Koh made it look like she was in charge of the resistance, and thousands more had come over to our side. Or her side.

Embarrassingly, I still hadn't learned that much about the Star-Rattler's children, who were a secretive lot, and even though I was considered adopted into it I hadn't seen any of its rituals. When they'd appeared on their mul during the vigil it was as spectators of the Jaguar-Scorpions' procedure, not as participants. But the religion, if you can call it that, really was an improvement on the old ancestor cults. It had a certain glorification of poverty and austerity, and not in the same way as the flesh-piercing tortures of the old ruling class. Although there was still plenty of that. It was more meditative and Theravada-ish, the kind of thing that would become the New Age bullshit I generally love to hate, but as I saw more of it I realized it was just another kind of human technology that drew on people's fatalism in a different way, maybe even in a needed way. In the old clan hierarchies, someone from a dependent family would kill himself if his greatfather-mother said to, because otherwise he and his children would be doomed to nearly everlasting agony. But people under the sign of the Rattler seemed more stoic, happier with the austerities of life and death, I guess because at least they got a smidgeon of respect and a better deal in the afterlives—not pie in the sky yet, but a promise of, at least, some goddamn rest.

Very few of the new lower-lineage converts ever saw Koh personally, but some of their leaders did, and from what I could tell they were impressed. They'd talk about how the Rattler's Children foresaw things that other people couldn't, how the great serpent's venom could wash the cataracts out of their eyes. In order to keep the blood of their lineages alive through coming generations, each of the new apostles had a special charge to follow Lady Koh into the realms of the next suns. Her intimates had become a fanatically loyal core, and no matter how many more she wanted to attract, she followed Lenin's dictum in advance, that a handful of committed souls is better than an army of unmotivated mercenaries.

And Koh naturally took to statecraft. She sent emissaries to all the main Orb Weaver and Caracara families, to some nonaffiliated clans, and even a few to disaffected cat families. Apparently her literacy had been a big deal in Teotihuacán, and one of her businesses had been having her scribes keep records and accounts for the less literate Teotihuacanob ruling families. She'd even been part of a project that was writing down Teotihuacanob history—which had been kept in picture and textile writing with oral supplementation and whatever—in the Teotihuacanob language written with a system of Chol characters, and she'd hung on to some of the manuscripts. Other rulers had already sent messengers asking for copies, and she had a whole three monkey clans—that is, calligraphers, who, impressively, were able to write with a tiny brush while they were swinging in sedan baskets—

and she kept them all busy every day. In fact, since the histories had been rewritten to make Koh look good, I suppose you could even say that she was grinding out paper propaganda.

And maybe it would have an effect, I thought. Maybe things were less desperate than they felt. Maybe enough of the lowland clans would support us that we—except, wait a second, who were *we*? If "we" meant the leaders of the Rattler's Children, maybe "we"'d do all right. But if "we" meant the Ball Brethren and the other traveling contingents of the Harpy clan—well, then "we" were going from being Koh's saviors to being her guests. And around here it was a short step from "guest" to "hostage." But that would change when we got to Ix, right? Maybe. Anyway, when we did get back, it wouldn't hurt for me to have some pull with the Muhammadess of Mesoamerica. If we got back. If the Ixian Ocelots didn't pick us off first. If Koh hadn't gotten too uppity by then. If the Lord be willing and the cricks don't rise. If, if, ifffff.

At the birth of the next sun there were still some fights going on ahead and behind the safeish central area reserved for us VIPs and the captive Scorpion-adders, who were trussed up in padded sleds. At least every twenty-score beats or so some gang from some third-rate cat family would rush one of the straggling groups in our train, like a cougar picking the sickest-looking bison out of the herd, and a few of our bloods would have to run forward or back to help drive them off. But we headed south on the main Caracara road, through the later Texcoco along the east edge of the great lake, passing thousands of other refugees, south and up into the highlands, toward what would later be Ciudad Oaxaca and was now called the Citadel of the Valley of Clouds and Steam.

(20)

What? Whoa. Off balance. And awake. I was awake.

My bearers were having trouble keeping me level. Rock me gently, for Chrissake, I thought.

I uncovered my eyes and squinted up at the rusty sky. There weren't any stars or obvious change but somehow you could tell it was near dawn. I sat up. Someone was coming up alongside us. A runner.

"You over me, my elder brother 10 Red Skink Lizard?" my flanking guard asked, using my numbered code name. "Five Score and Two is coming, my elder brother."

I rolled onto my side, steadying myself on the edge of the wicker pallet, and the guard nearly looked me in the eye and looked down. He wasn't supposed to stare at VIPs. It was another beige dawn already and the wind was picking up. We were in a wide valley between five-rope-lengths-high mesas, bristling with tall hardwoods all recently killed by the changing water table. When a breeze came through, yellow leaves dropped off their branches as fast as those cards flying up when you've solved a hand of Freecell Solitaire.

Hun Xoc's palanquin came back alongside the file and settled next to me, his bearers expertly turning in place and reversing direction so that he was running alongside. He looked princely reclining under his quilt. Fiddle-dee-dee, I thought. Wonder what the poor people are doing today.

"The whistlers have come back with word from our sun-eyed venerand, the quick of speech, our greatfather 2 Jeweled Skull," he said in the Harpy House code-language. The "whistlers" were a Kaminaljyob mountain tribe with a tonal language that could be whistled or even played on flutes, and we used them as code talkers. They'd said that 18 Jog, 2JS's nephew, was going to meet us in one of the last towns before the Third-Sunfolks' Boneyard, as they called the Tehuantepecan salt flats. I asked how many suns away the flats were and he said three or four. 10 Red Skink Lizard will be painted and ready, I said. I didn't even ask whether it was possible that the message was a fake from the Pumas or their relatives in Ix, the Ocelots. Communications was one thing the Harpy House did have their act together on. Before we'd left, Hun Xoc had memorized thousands of columns of word substitutions, and he and 2JS used each pair only once, so that a given word never meant the same thing again, kind of like a one-time pad. Every important message from us to 2JS and from 2JS to us was carried by at least four teams of covert runners, each on a different route, and one or two had probably been intercepted and interrogated. But no one could make anything out of a string of nonsense words, not even an NSA mainframe and certainly not the Ocelots, no matter how psychic they were.

Since that was the end of the formal conference Hun Xoc asked how I was and I said fine. Maybe you and I can kick a ball around sometime today, I said. He said that sounded fun. He had to go back and pass the news to 14 Wounded, who was leading the rear guard. He reversed his porters again and disappeared.

Well, this is still tapirshit, I thought. If any of these guys had their act even remotely together they'd get together and swear out a treaty and go back to peacefully exploiting their thralls. In fact, Koh and I had even discussed trying to reach some understanding with the feline clans—the Ixan Ocelots and Severed Right Hand's Pumas and the Caracolian Jaguars and all the rest of them. Realitywise, there wasn't any reason why they couldn't.

Except that they just wouldn't. All over Mesoamerica, the avian and feline lineages had always been at daggers. And they always would be. And the other clans—the Rattler's pledges and the other families with totems that weren't birds or cats—would always be making an alliance with one side and then with the other. These people were like any other mafias, they thrived on vendettas. It was part of their soup. They counted on fresh booty to keep them solvent. It was like Israel and the Muslim states, even their gods hated each other, despite their being the same.

And now, after the fall of Teotihuacán, both sides had absolutely nailed their colors to the masts. And as far as the independent parties went—I mean the Rattler's pledges—well, even though both the feline and avian sides saw the Star Rattler cult as a threat to their hegemony, the Rattlers had been in bed with the Harpies for more than a b'aktun, and now there was just too much bad blood for us to even approach the felines. Koh had to support the Harpies right up through the moment the Harpies—gods willing—took control of Ix. And even then the Harpies wouldn't kick the Ocelots out. Instead they'd blood themselves to the clan and become Ocelots themselves. The whole thing was cray-cray.

Still, if I wanted to get back to 2012, I'd have to go along with it. It was going to be up to me to build a whole tomb for myself, and set up the sarcophagus and mix up the jelly and lay out another set of lodestones and a hundred other things, and there wouldn't be any way to do that on Harpy territory while the Harpies were under constant attack. Even if the Chocula team found my tomb in one of the Harpy catacombs instead of in the main Ocelot one where we'd planned to put it. Which I couldn't count on. No, no, no. We simply had to take over the whole place. Even if it didn't feel possible.

For that matter, right now I didn't see how I could get everything together before my brain gave out. Hell, hell, hell and corruption. In fact, it didn't even feel like we'd make it to Ix. All these people around gave you an illusory sense of security, but Severed Right Hand's forces were just too big and too well trained and on three sides they were all the fuck around us. If we dug in someplace nearer than Ix—anywhere other than a real city—even with stockade fences and an endless water supply and a stock of stored corn, we wouldn't last a month. And then Ix would be just another hostile city, and my chances of getting in there and pulling off an entombment on the sly would be, I don't know, roughly the same odds as Mel Gibson's winning the Nobel Peace Prize. If anything, I should try to make sure we stick to the Ix plan. Basically, get back to Ix, use my Unlimited Personal Power to help 2 Jeweled Skull take the place over or at least reach a favorable truce with the Ocelots, get my tomb built, mix up the necessary compounds, seal myself in, and hope for the best. Getta condo made-a stone-a. No problem. Get in, get down, and get out.

And the first thing to do was hook up Lady Koh with 2 Jeweled Skull. She'd be the next big thing, so it'd be doing him a favor. Scratch his back, et cetera. Even if he was in trouble with the Ocelots, the Harpy Clan was still probably the richest family in Ix, and he was still the head of it. Right? In fact, maybe we should just let everyone know we were going to Ix. As of now, only the leaders knew about it at all. Our given-out destination was Kaminaljuyu, which is, or used to be, where they put Guat City later on. Otherwise all we'd said was that we were going to go through what was later called Oaxaca, and which was now a heavily populated collection of little city-states that had been part of the Empire. On the other hand, if we told anyone, the cats could head us off. Or 9 Fanged Hummingbird could get ready for us, or something, maybe better not . . .

I lay back and even started to doze off, but then heard something shiveringly familiar:

"1 Porcupine Ass caught two of the three man-beetles."

I got a shiver for no reason and then it took me a beat to realize it was only a couple of amateur beat-keepers somewhere ahead, chanting verses for drinking-water rations, timing how long each blood could keep his mouth under the waterskin. And they were using the same currently popular song that the Ball Brethren, and their guest bloods from the other Ixian clans, had used to mark the time-outs on that night—definitely the worst night of my life, and there were plenty of other contenders—the night fifty-two days ago when they'd dressed me up as a deer and hunted me down:

(Drink) He ground them up in one big pot, he threw (stop)
(Drink) Twenty blue seed-corn skulls into the pot (stop) . . .

Well, things were different now. The world might be ending, but at least I was in with the in crowd.

(21)

My dresser—not Armadillo Shit, but an attendant who was even lower on the totem stele—came up with my urine bag. Ahh, *redivivus*. He gave me a shot of cold cacao out of a dogskin, checked and oiled my feet and tied on a fresh pair of running sandals, and ran off-road to bury my excretion so that nobody'd get hold of it and work action-at-a-distance curses on me. Go for it, guy, I thought. Do whatever you gotta do. I had them put me down and I broke into our near-jog. The thin stony air felt detoxifying. I went off-path for a minute and could see Koh's three identical palanquins a score or so rope-lengths up the line. I guess the idea was that if we got raided they wouldn't know which one she was in. The defile opened out into a high plain between extinct volcanoes, still showing the grid of an ancient city, speckled with dead scrub oaks and dead agaves and ocatillos and my namesake firebushes and all crawling with mating-drifts of black ladybugs. Oddly, there were still flakes of wood ash following us from the house fires behind us and they swept across the overgrown courts and twirled into Grasshopper pranksters, dust-devils, dervishing goofily ahead of us toward the old temple precinct. A few bloods were out in the ruins, canceling old cat-related zoomorphs. We didn't want to leave a specific trail, even though there was no way the track sweepers in the rear could really eradicate the traces of so many people. Some "pastless clans"—people who, in the twelfth b'aktun, we'd call the homeless—had squatted in the old palaces, but when we came through they waddled away from us like dazed postnuke mutants and peeked out from behind charred adobe walls.

By the sun's death we'd come into the Knife Mines. It was a glistening black rockscape of flash-frozen lava spatters, basically a holograph of a few seconds in a geologically violent day that, tradition said, was the starting date, 8/18/-3041, Gregorian. The white sky turned red, meaning that our ancestor, the Great Eastern *bacab*—timebearer—was coming out to watch us, and as the red deepened he blew a different wind our way, one with a fertile eggy scent. I could feel magma throb through the ground, radiating almost-reassuring maternal energy from the giant watchful presence ahead. Out beyond the bluffs green sheet lightning crackled up along the rim of the sky. Wind rose and Hun Xoc decided that since it might cover our tracks we should move the whole chain from the main road to a smaller trail. To get there we had to strike across this Ishtar-Terra-ish plateau in the dark and it was a little extreme, you couldn't hear anything and most of the time you couldn't see Thing Zero, so there was no way to get bearings and Hun Xoc's Rattler guides were navigating by literature. Lightning would coil around overhead into repulsive knots, and for a beat you'd see everything in all-over powdery light like industrial fluorescents. By morning we were in a long north-south valley with a few dead trees all tilting in the same direction, away from the Deer, that is, Virgo. The only good part was that the villagers sold us some snow from the peaks. We insisted on having our own chef make it into guava-pickle slushies.

The ash cloud was all around us now, as though we'd gone through a big door into a world all modeled out of gray Plasticine. Once I thought some of the ash flakes were alive and then realized they were clouds of mating whiteflies. Every village we passed had the corpses of at least a few sacrifices staked up in the scrungy little zocalos, usually good-looking little kids, but in a lot of different stages of decay. There was one style of doing it where the stakes went up through their anuses and came out their mouths. Some of them looked like they'd had their hands or feet burned off when they were alive to put them in sympathy with the Toad's fiery mood. Obviously the offerings hadn't helped, though, and a lot of the villages were abandoned. Sometimes there were drifts of old offerings of yams and manioc and dogs that were way too magotty and dessicated to eat, but our small chain of captives grabbed them and gnawed on them anyway.

By the death of the fifteenth new sun we were in the asphalt swamp around the Toad's Cigars, cracked flats pocked with sputtering vents. When a gas bubble would tear up through the sticky crust the bloods would invariably say "She's hatching another whopper," or something, like they were saying "gesundheit." The great cinder cone grew imperceptibly on our left, jarringly regular with the same forty-nine-degree angle as the Rattlers' mul in Teotihuacán, silhouetted against its own dust and streaked with thin glowing pink seeps that folded and congealed into scoriac glaciers. The guides made us veer west to detour around something called Xibalba-Chen, Deathland Well, which from what they said must have been a crater lake that spurted out tons of carbon dioxide. Supposedly it had killed a whole lot of people and animals. We picked our way through a plain of fumaroles and steaming mineral wells down to a path along the Atoyac River, southeast through the Sierra Madre del Sur past Etla and Mitla, places I'd thought I knew pretty well from the twenty-first that were now unrecognizable, even though we passed less than a jornada from the city they later called Monte Albán. I guess some of it was beautiful but I remember mainly monotony, the smell of the runners' skins crisping in the sun, the fatal localness of the jillion little no-name hamlets, all beginning to feel the domino effect of the continent-wide wave of depression that had started in Teotihuacán.

We'd abandoned thousands of the slower travelers when we'd doubled our pace, but the heralds were still going ahead, proselytizing villages and irrigation societies, making private visits to village cargo-bearers and promising them positions of power in return for the support of their war bloods, shrugging off threats from the greathouses, trying to overwhelm the old hierarchy by numbers, the same old story. By 16 Jaguar we barely had to do anything, we'd come up on a town and the people would hear the rattle-flutes and rush outside, strewing monkshood and fringed gentians in front of Koh's train, and crouch by the side of the road, looking into the ground, chanting Koh-songs the heralds taught them as we walked through the middle of this weird audience that couldn't see us. Then as they'd fall into lockstep behind us you could hear their travois poles scraping on the gravel in this unending hiss, and I could feel our bloods' probably misguided optimism growing, especially when they came back from an audience with Koh. At least the girl had charisma. No matter how many people our outrunners said were chasing us, no matter what rationing and logistics and disease crises we had, no matter how panicked Hun Xoc and I were about getting the hell to Ix before the big hipball game before somebody could head us off, practically everybody seemed to treat the whole thing as a big holiday. Anyone close to Koh was a celebrity. The younger bloods gambled over who'd get to be in my third circle of "pets," that is, guards/valets. That was outside, or on top of, the ten Rattler bloods who were assigned to protect me and my inner "sleeping circle" of three Harpy bloods. And I wasn't even one of the major stars.

Before 24 Jaguar—the new incarnation of Grandfather Heat—rose behind the brown clouds, the whistlers said the Harpy emissaries were less than a sun away, and that there were only twenty-two of them. It was all about runners around here, like in a Greek tragedy, the way messengers keep coming in and saying "My King, I bear dreadful tidings from Paedophilopolis," or whatever. Which maybe means those plays were more realistic than I'd thought. The king and the chorus and whoever were all hunkered in their bunker out of harm's way, and all the dangerous stuff really *did* happen offstage. Anyway, before the sun's midlife crisis we got hit by a rainless sandstorm called the Razor Wind. Ash sand burrowed into our leggings and rubberized sandals and our most tightly wound bandages and salved-together eyelids, and the skin painters covered us with salves and balms and ointments and shit, to the point where my testicles were frozen in this lake of goo, but it was either that or chafe city. No one could look ahead, you could only peek down once in a while at the trail in front of you, and most of us were holding on to some rope or rag dangling from the ass of the person in front, like circus elephants. After a quarter-sun Hun Xoc had to call it quits and sent word down the line for a noncombat halt. We were at a nothing old town called Coloa to triage the wounded bloods. A lot of them would have to kill themselves. The village wasn't situated right to be much of a refuge, but 2 Hand spread our guest mats and set our backrests in the little mud council house. There were only two other decent buildings. We designated one for the emissaries and one for the captive Pumas. The bloods converted the square into a barracks and the converts overran the rest of the town, trying to find shelter, haggling with the locals, scrounging through garbage heaps for critters to munch on, crows, rats, anything that would normally be shooed away. Some of the converted families set up pathetic little offerings and started chanting. At first I thought they were praying for Koh, but as I listened more closely I could tell that as usual they were just praying *to* her.

14 Wounded ordered the porters to get the palanquins and sedan chairs together because he insisted that every and each blood had to ride into town just ahead of Lady Koh. Giving ourselves airs, I thought. It was like how people hire a limousine to take them to an event three blocks away because they need something to step out of. But then I didn't say anything because it occurred to me that the idea might actually have come from Her Worshipfulship. Maybe Koh was a little insecure herself.

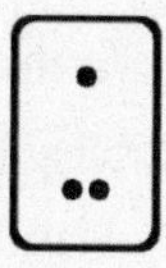

(22)

At our Grandfather Heat's next birth we met three of the Harpy emissaries. They'd been among the bloods who'd adopted me in the cave, way back in the day, before we left for Teotihuacán. We exchanged cakes and did a whole "welcome, my brothers" trip. They kept making jokes about how 2Hand had lost weight during the trek, how his eyes had sunk so deep into his baby-fat face that they looked like two black pebbles in a bowl of dough. Actually, it really was like coming home, I felt a little cozy in spite of myself. Still, gloom hung over the situation like, I don't know. I guess like gloom. Like, basically, a whole lot of hanging gloom. If the Harpies didn't win the great-hipball game we'd lose everything, including the fillings in our teeth. Or at least the jade fillings. Maybe they'd let us keep any wooden ones.

And we wouldn't win. The hipgall game would be worked. And the fix would be tight. If we won, it would be like getting a real upset in a World Wrestling Entertainment event. It couldn't happen. If the Harpies persisted in trying to win anyway, the ball game would be called against them, the Harpies would object, and a fight would start, which the Ocelots were confident they would win. Then they could justifiably take all the Harpies' possessions and probably a good chunk of them as captives. After that, the other raptor clans in the area would retrench and make deals with the Ocelots.

It was dark inside the *audencia* tent and the sand over the hide-covered smoke holes sounded like a cymbal brush on a floor tom. I kept thinking about the all the converts outside, huddled in their little camps, their exposed skin shredding away. We sat in an abbreviated version of our circle, with the three leaders of the Harpy delegation in their hereditary spot at the eastern point, and then Hun Xoc, 2 Hand, 1 Gila, 1 Gila's eldest son, two of the old greatmothers from the Rattler House, Koh, Coati, and me. We could each have one attendant behind us and I'd picked Armadillo Shit. As I said, normally a woman wouldn't be let anywhere near here, but just like Alligator Root was kind of a third sex and could go in the women's courts, Koh and her greatmothers could come into ours. A couple of the town cargo-bearers scurried around setting out basins of fish oil and big wide-rimmed pots of rock-heated water. We were the biggest thing that had ever happened in town and they'd already all sworn sempiternal devotion.

2 Dead Coral—one of the ordinands under 20 Blue Snail, who was 2JS's sort-of in-house heirophant—was the head of the delegation, and even though he was being friendly he gave me a touch of the creeps. He greeted us speaking as 2 Jeweled Skull, which took a while, since it was a ritual form, like telling you how to insert the metal fitting into the buckle and how items have tendency to shift during flight or something. When he got to the actual news from Ix it didn't sound good. Like I may have said, 2 Jeweled Skull had been called out by 9 Fanged Hummingbird, the ahau of the ruling Ocelot House of Ix, to a hipball game, kind of like a trial by combat. In this case the stakes were the Ixian Harpy Clan's stores and trading rights against the heads of the Ocelot Clan's Emerald Brethren, that is, their hipball champions. Basically it was a way to scale down a civil war. But from what the emissaries said, this one wasn't likely to scale it down too effectively. Most likely the ball game wouldn't even get to the second half.

Of course, the subtext of all this was that 2JS was really asking us to relieve him, and hoping to win the battle with our help. 20 Blue Snail—a duckbill-mask-wearing underling who was 2JS's best Sacrifice Game player, but who wasn't even in Koh's league, or even mine, lately—took some time comparing long lists of bloods and auxiliaries on both sides, but the gist was that 2JS and his pledged allies would have about forty percent the strength of 9 Fanged Hummingbird and the Ocelots. If our convoy got back to Ix in time, Koh's forces would easily tip the balance. Then the other Raptor clans would step in and help 2JS, and the Ocelots would be recent history. 2JS would become at least the de facto *k'alomte* of Ix, maybe keeping 9 Fanged Hummingbird on as a puppet ruler. Maybe he'd even take over completely, although since the k'alomte always had to be a cat, to do that 2JS would have to get himself adopted into a feline clan.

At any rate, the Ixian branch of the Star Rattler cult would become Ix's most powerful non-clan-based organization. Koh would set up shop near the Star-Rattler's mul—which was in a good location in Ix, "downtown," I guess you could say, but which currently wasn't large and wasn't very well funded—and 2JS would have to keep her and her followers happy. And one of her conditions would be that the ruling coalition would have to build my tomb, to my specifications. And if that got done in time, I could get the gel mixed up, get buried per the ROC specifications, and the next thing I knew I'd be back in the merrie olde twenty-first century with a headful of Sacrifice Game expertise and a revitalized Will to Power.

20 Blue Snail said even though the Ocelots had gotten the gossip from Teotihuacán about our role in wrecking the place, they still couldn't disinvite us. We'd be welcome as clansmen of the Harpies. Delegates from both cat and raptor clans were coming from all the important cities of the highlands and lowlands. Even Severed Right Hand was officially invited, although since he was still only at Ka'an, near the coast, he'd be too far away. And for every official guest there'd be at least ten peripheral people arriving in Ix over the next few days, vendors, traders, smart oddsmakers and destitute addict gamblers, prostitutes, clowns, wandering families, whatever.

Finally, 20 Blue Snail said the buzz was that Koh's Star-Rattler's cult was growing "in four directions," that is, all over the world, and that 2JS was interested in helping serve Star Rattler. Koh was impassive, of course. I couldn't tell whether he was just flattering her. Then, as though it was an afterthought, he mentioned that the date of the ball game had been moved up two suns. He said it was for some astronomical reasons, but also that the Ocelots were behind it. Anyway, it gave us only eleven days to get to Ix.

There's no way, I thought. The fastest marching rate for the whole army—even discounting the elders, the women, children, the sick, the dead, and the inessential baggage—couldn't possibly be over a jornada, that is, about thirty miles per day, and we had over three hundred miles to go in eleven days. We could do it if we forced four or maybe even just three extra marches, but the line would get strung out and even the bloods would be exhausted when they entered Ix. I looked at Hun Xoc and Koh and could tell they were doing the same calculations. As far as I knew no group this size had ever moved that fast. We'd have to set a record.

Hun Xoc asked permission of the rest of the circle to speak in house code.

Everyone signaled that it was all right.

"The Lady Koh's four hundred clans won't make it," Hun Xoc said.

"They'll have to seek asylum somewhere else."

Not true, 20 Blue Snail answered in the same language, Koh's children can't stay outcasts for much longer.

What he meant was that the main thing Koh needed was to stabilize her base. She might be able to afford to keep the cat clans as enemies for a while, but to do that she'd need to reach some sort of stable rapprochement with as many of the other international (to use the word loosely) ruling families as possible. As of now, she could count only the Fog lineage and the rest of 3 Talon's aerial clans, and maybe the Ixian Harpies, as friends. Settling respectably in Ix as an invited clan leader—at least temporarily—would be her best chance.

I looked at him. You couldn't read anything under the duckbill mask. I couldn't stop thinking about how much he looked like one of the plates in this nineteenth-century book on the Maya by Stepanwald. I pretended to ease myself back and used the motion to sneak a look at Koh. I had the feeling she understood what 20 Blue Snail was saying, and that he was right.

They passed the speaking cup to Lady Koh.

She asked when we'd have our meeting with 2JS. I guess she didn't want to deal with anyone but him and you couldn't blame her.

He can't come outside Ix to meet you, Hun Xoc said. From the way he said it I got the feeling 2JS was under polite house arrest. 20 Blue Snail said we wouldn't all be able to talk when we got near the city, either, we'd be in a ceremonial procession and under constant observation. It was going to be like an inauguration or royal ball. For now, all we could do was accept the invitation and get there.

Then we need to get a few beats alone with him just before the hipball game, Koh said.

20 Blue Snail said he'd try. And if a fight breaks out, what then? he asked.

The Rattler's children will support their host, Koh said.

The Ocelots won't let all of your followers into the court district, Hun Xoc said. At most they'll let in two or four hundred of the highest bloods. The rest will have to stay as close as possible outside and wait for our signal.

Koh signed that was good enough. We voted "agreed."

(23)

You could have individual conversations in the "smoke," the after part of the mat circle, when you were all just hanging around, not necessarily at your own position, and it was even considered polite to doze off. Sleeping's a big part of bonding. It's hard to describe the cozy factor of the huge foster family and my growing place in it. The clan definined who and what you were so strongly and so completely that, as naturally as F = ma, you'd be willing to die for it in a beat. It, and not you, was you. Anyway, at the southwest end of the round room, Hun Xoc, 1 Gila, and 2 Hand were getting their knee calluses massaged and drinking out of the balche pot through long bullrush straws. On the white side, I mean, the northeast side, near the little door, the two Rattler greatmothers were still sitting bolt up on their backrests and chatting together, smoking and weaving elaborate shrouds on little hip-strap looms. Coati was stirring the fire. The emissaries had already done their big leave-taking, so they wouldn't have to go through it again, and Zero Porcupine Clown had taken them off to their own over-storm house with a bunch of the Rattler Clan's sex workers and gamblers, a few of whom were also trained listeners and mnemonists, just in case they said anything. Koh had told the gamblers to let them win. Most of them would escort us to Ix, but a couple of runners were going to rush back to 2JS as soon as the storm let up. I was reclining on top of my two dressers and pets, and the younger brother was rubbing oil into my feet and ankles, which were still scabby from volcanic ash. I guess maybe that sounds a little odd. But it wasn't in a sexual way. In fact, none of us were supposed to do any sex on the trip, even though the local chicks and dicks all wanted to service us godlings, because the adders said our semen trail would make it easier for Severed Right Hand's hit squads to track us. I was just leaning on them because they were used to it and it was cold and I was entitled to the service. There was more touching in general around here, although if you touched someone you weren't supposed to that was it for you. Supposedly Shang emperors used to sleep on *mounds* of people. Anyway I was just calming down enough to close my eyes when Koh kneed over to me. Her big quilted turquoise-blue manto was tied a little like a giant stiff bathrobe. My dressers propped me up into a more formal attitude. Koh settled into her position on the mat and unrolled another world-map version of the Sacrifice Game board, a less elaborate traveling model. On this one the central circle represented our own army or migration or whatever, and she piled stones in it representing how many different types of people we had, 62-score full bloods, 9-score sick or wounded bloods, 410-score scouts, dressers, and calligraphers, about 700-score converted men and roughly 1,202 score converted women and children, 812-score porters, 2,108-score thralls and captives, and over 3,500-score stragglers who really didn't have any reason to be with us. Of course, the Star Rattler societies in other cities were revitalized by Koh's success, and they were pledging tens of thousands of new converts, but until her chickens got here she wasn't counting them.

She subtracted stones for how many of each grade of person we were likely to lose to raids and how many to attrition and starvation. A lot of people don't have a head for logistics, how many bowls of gruel each soldier ate per week or whatever. They want to hear how a lone hero won a whole war single-handed. Koh was the opposite. She wanted to reduce the uncertainty as much as possible before she even started to do her really serious calculations.

Koh set out carved disks representing the major cities, with a saucery green one standing in for Ix, and then started laying out glyphic stones into them. I recognized the stones that represented 2 Jeweled Skull, 9 Fanged

Hummingbird, Severed Hand, 3 Talon—who was the patriarch of the shall-we-say "international" alliance of aerial clans—and our troops and followers, and a lot of the other clans, and us. But in general I could still understand only about ten percent of her visualization. Pretty soon she was using little brown seeds that represented hypotheticals, often in doubles and triples. She positioned the hit squads that were chasing us in four different possible spots. She guessed at food sources and weather along the route into Ix. And when she'd come to the end of her own knowledge she started asking me things. What did I think the other Caracara Greathouses were up to? How much has 2 Jeweled Skull asked them for help? What was his real relationship with the small Rattler Society of Ix? Why hadn't the Ixian Rattler Feeder responded to her messages?

Why do you think the Ocelots are so confident? she whispered.

I said I guessed that actually a lot of them were terrified by the end of Teotihuacán, but that some of them were thinking they might be able to fill the gap and carry on the business of the empire with a bigger cut for themselves. They'd have to get rid of the Harpies first, though, and so they'd spent quite a bit in bribes to the supposedly neutral hipball officials, probably much more than 2JS could afford.

But 20 Blue Snail-Shit makes 2JS sound confident, too, she said.

I said maybe it was 6's job to put a good spin on things.

Koh said she thought 2JS was pretty smart. He'd have to have something worked out, some unpleasant surprise for the Ocelots that wouldn't depend on what we did.

I looked at her. I mean, into her eyes, which you just didn't do. Normally her eyes—even the one surrounded by her light skin—were as cowled and tragic as if they'd been been painted by Pontormo. But now they were transparent. And they weren't tragic. They were wary. I could tell she was thinking that 2 Jeweled Skull—in exchange for the safety of his own house—might sell her out to the Ocelots.

"2 Jeweled Skull set this up," I said. "Your guilt is his."

"He might deny that," Koh said. "Now that more

Feline-clan bloods hate my house than hate his."

If he turned you in they'd get him later anyway, I said. She didn't answer, but from her face it seemed that she realized that was true. The Ocelots would renege. They knew he was bound up in this from the beginning and they'd never forgive him.

"And once he's won will he need me around?" she asked.

"He'll need the tsam lic, and a nine-skull adder," I said.

"I'm not so sure," she said, "he'll get those from
9 Fanged Hummingbird, as soon as he captures him,
If he even thinks he needs the Game at all."

Koh added two uncertainty stones to 2JS's stack. I could feel my loyalties dividing. She must have seen it in me, because suddenly she started backtracking:

"I trust my father 2 Jeweled Skull," she said,
"I wouldn't plot against him, and I'm not
Positioned to; I only want to shield
Our followers, and leave them an escape
In case another city crumbles on them."

I said I guessed that sounded like the right thing to do. Sometimes Koh's forties-Picassoid face would seem all limpid and transparent and I'd feel all cuddly with her—not that I'd ever touched her myself or anything, but just kind of homey and peaceful—and then her face would go opaque again like that glass in Marena's office and it was like I was alone in an observation room.

Koh unrolled what I thought was a smaller Game-mat, but it turned out to be a detailed and relatively naturalistic map of Ix. "The ball court's isolated here," she said, running her little finger down its trench. She was right. The whole temple district had originally been built on a hill surrounded on three sides by a shallow irregular lake, kind of like a miniature San Francisco. Since then the lake level had been raised and palace plots had been extended out into the water, so the temple district was surrounded by wide canals, like the Rialto in Venice. The temple district included the five largest of Ix's hundred and ten muls, six hipball courts, the Ocelots' emerald-green greathouse, the council house, and the original sacred well of the Ocelots, which was now fed by aqueducts from the surrounding mountains but was still surrounded by a garden that included a few of the original celestial poison trees. There weren't any solid bridges on the east, north, and west, just floating pedestrian barges that could easily be moved. Even if we were armed and ready when we took our places in the stands, we'd still be in the center of the Ocelots' ward, separated from the mainland by the mountains behind the Ocelots' emerald-and-scarlet mul. Two hundred of us could be trapped and picked off without much trouble. I figured the odds of something unpleasant happening to us on the court, either during or right after the ball game, were at least ten to one.

So what can we do about it? I asked. Not go? Set up shop somewhere else?

No, there are other things we can do, she said. We may not be able to pull another Teotihuacán, but we can do something like it. You might have to be the one to carry some of it out, though.

¿Yo? I thought. Little *moi*? Why me again, because I'm the odd man out anyway?

Always me, me, me.

Because you're such a genius with the ball, she said, answering my thought.

Chacal was the genius, I said, and he's gone. She just sat there and looked at me, like she knew I could still play as well as before. I kind of felt she was right too. Despite everything I was feeling great these days. Finally I said fine, sure, run it by me. I can deal.

She said as an antepenultimate plan she thought we might disguise me as one of the lesser-known ballplayers on the Harpy team and try to get me into the *halach pitzom,* the great-hipball game, for a couple of rounds.

"Then you could score a ring or two and win," she said.

"The Ocelots would have to really cheat,

And might not even get away with it."

Whoa, I thought. Hang on a beat.

I said it sounded like fun for me—my cocktail of Chacal neurotransmitters was already perking up just at the thought of my getting onto a court.

She said imagine the reaction. The fans would go wild, although she didn't put it that way. Maybe they'd all give you some big hero thing and you'd be able to take over.

I said that sounded a little too good to be true.

Well, anyway, she said, whatever happens it would at least distract them. They'd be off their stride.

I asked for how long and she said she didn't know.

So then what? I asked.

Then we go to the antepenultimate plan, she said. Great, I thought. The ultimate plan, as always, was just to kill ourselves as quickly as possible. All right, I thought, what's the *pen*ultimate plan? I asked her, as whateverly as I could.

She held out her dark hand out and, slowly, turned it palm-downward. "I'll show you," it meant.

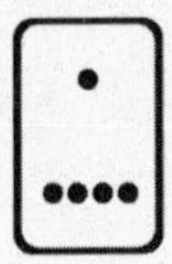

(24)

Just in sight of the Cloud People's main citadel, which would be the site of Oaxaca City, there was a place I knew well, with a tree, eventually a rather famous tree, that—which? Who?—that would still be alive at the end of the last b'aktun. I led Koh's caravan a half-jornada off the route to camp there, and she and I fasted and prepared for a session of the nine-stone Sacrifice Game. We'd agreed that I'd be the only querent, and only her dwarf and Armadillo Shit would be attending.

The big cypress wasn't big yet. In fact, it looked less than a hundred years old, and it divided into three trunks near the base. So it wasn't one that you'd ordinarily think of as a major branch of the Tree of Four Hundred Times Four Hundred Branches, the tree at the axis mundi that penetrated down through the hells and soared up through the holes in the centers of the thirteen skies, the tree the Teotihuacanians called the Tree of Razors and that the Motulob—the citizens of Tikal—called the Tree with the Mirror Leaves, and that, in the twenty-first century, generally gets called something like the "Maya World Tree" or even "the Mayan Yggdrasil." But I convinced Koh that I knew what I was talking about. We started at the naming time of Lord Heat, that is, noon. Twenty arms west of the Tree there was an ancient well surrounded by a five low stone cisterns, each about two arms across. The westernmost cistern had been filled to the brim with fresh water, and Koh sat on its west side, facing east. I sat on its eastern side and, instead of presuming to make eye contact, focused on her hands. Twenty bloods, under Hun Xoc's command, sat around us in a loose circle with about a fifty-arm radius. The sun went under a rainless cloud shelf. Her dwarf handed her a jade offering basin, with coals still smoldering in it under the ashes of offering paper, and held it up in front of her forehead to stand in for the sky.

I looked down, into the still water. Koh looked down. We nodded to our reflected souls. They nodded back, almost immediately. Koh brought the basin sharply down onto the rim of the cistern, cracking it into pieces and scattering sparks out of the cinders. Without flinching from the embers that burned her palms, she pushed everything into the water. The shards sank and the coals and ashes floated, sizzling.

> " . . ." she said. That is, in the ancient language,
>
> *"Teech Aj Chak-'Ik'al la' ulehmb'altaj 'uyax ahal-kaab Ajaw K'iinal . . ."*
>
> *"You, Hurricane, who sparked Lord Heat's first dawning . . ."*

I took over:

> " ," I said, *"Teech kiwohk'olech la abobat-t'aantaj uxul kiimlal,"*
>
> *"You over us who foreknows his final dying,"*
>
> *"Teech Aj k'inich-paatom ya'ax lak . . ."*
>
> *"You, sun-eyed coiler of the blue-green basin . . ."*

Hmm. I paused for a second. What's the next part again? Oh, right. I started to go on, but Koh broke in and finished the sentence herself:

> *"Teech uyAj ya'ax-'ot'el-pool ya'ax-tuun ch'e'e . . ."*
>
> *"You, jade-skinned carver of the turquoise cistern . . ."*

I snuck a glance up at the tree. Mayan languages tend to classify things more by similarity of shape or function than by differences, so that, for instance, insects, bats, and birds are all the same class—and the Maya skeleton of my borrowed brain did the same, so that the tree, which was and is, as I've said, a cypress, became in my sight, also, a latex tree, a calabash tree, and especially a ceiba tree, *the* ceiba tree, *ya'ax che, Ceiba pentandra,* the kapok tree, the cotton-silk tree, the Generous Tree. It was thorny and umbrelliform, pustuled with phantom orchids sucking its red muculent sap and clouded with Cynopterus sphinx bats harvesting its scoriac nectar, and its branches spread at a curve as steep as the cissoid of Diocles. And then, without seeming to change, it was also a stone tree like a titanic stalagtite, and then it was a stratovolcano, higher than Orizaba, but, of course, upside down, with its buttress roots worming up through the thirteen shells of the sky.

> *"Teech te'ij acho'oh jul-che'o'ob,"* Koh went on, *"uchepiko'ob' noj k'ahk'o'ob,"*
> *"You, there, whose hissing javelins strike wildfires,"*
>
> *"Meent utz anuhko'on wa'ye' ti' amosoon."*
> *"Deign to respond to us, here, from your whirlwind."*

She sunk her dark ring finger in the water and stirred up a cloud of asphaltic steam.

"I can smell him," she said.

She meant 2 Jeweled Skull.

She paused. "He's more you than you know."

I almost broke protocol and asked her what she meant, but she'd moved on, up the trunk of our now-internalized tree, zagging and zigging through the forking branches, setting stones down so fast that sometimes she just let me guide her hand without even looking at the board. Naturally, we had a hell of an edge, since I could use my—well, let's not be modest, I could use my encyclopedic-ass knowledge of Mesoamerican, world, and economic history to guide her. But even so, as I think I've touched on a few times without having the stamina to really go into, we had to deal with the cosmic frustration of not being able to see within our own event cones. That is, what would happen to me, or to Koh, or to people we could influence directly, and so on, those events were still in flux. But as we got farther into the future, paradoxically, things became clearer. So, for instance, we knew the ceremonial district of Ix would be abandoned within the next *k'atun*—the next twenty years—but we couldn't pin the date down more closely than that. But the abandonment of Motul—Tikal—was more certain, around 949, and then we both knew and saw how Chichen would be overthrown by treachery in 1199, how the next *may* capital, Mayapán, would be destroyed by the Xiu in 1441, and then the whole world would—nearly—disappear in the plague, in 1515, nine years before Tonatiuh, that is, Sun Hair, Pedro de Alvarado, would finish it off—nearly—in 1524. The b'aktuns of slavery and pain after that were, of course, well documented, and we crawled together farther and farther out onto the thin green twig of the last possibilities, past the Disney World Horror, past Marena finding—thank God—the Lodestone Cross, and toward a very likely End of Everything, a doomster named M something, in the north, somewhere—Canada!—and then, they—yes, they, we, we stop him!, and then—

Wait.

"The one from the north is not the last," she said. Her voice was starting to quaver from the strain.

"Not the last doomster?" I asked.

"No." She ran out of seeds. She scattered again, and, again, climbed up past M. Again, she couldn't see any details of the last one, the one we had to worry about. Oh, God, I thought, oh, Jesus, oh, oh, hell hell. "I can't see him," she said. "He's too close to you."

"Is it someone I know?" I asked. "Someone I may be going to know?"

"*Erer k'ani*," she said. *Maybe*. A pearl of sweat rolled down her light cheek, over the border into the dark side of her chin, and dropped onto the white margin of the board, where it touched the rim of the cistern.

She scattered again. She shivered. She winced, brought up her dark hand, and screwed its heel into one eye and then the other, as though she'd been staring at the sun.

"*Erer k'ani*," she said again.

Pause. Ten beats. Twenty beats.

"The Celestial Rattler has shed seven skins," she said. "But it"—

incidentally I'm using "it" as the pronoun because Mayan is ungendered—"won't shed another until another until the birth of 4 Ahau. And with that skin, you'll know that its two heads have parted destinies."

Foolishly, I looked up. It was only a few four-hundred-beats after noon, and, to boot, the sky was still overcast with smoke from the wildfire, but even so I thought I could see the Rattler's body, the Ecliptic, sidewinding across the sky's ninth shell.

Everybody's probably heard the folk unwisdom about how you can tell how many years old a rattlesnake is by counting its rattles. And most folks now probably know that of course this isn't true, because although they do gain, roughly, one rattle each time they slough their skin, the little suckers don't necessarily shed only once a year. Anyway, the *tzab*, that is, the Rattler's rattles, were the seven stars of the Pleiades cluster. Koh meant it would gain a new rattle, a new star, just before the end date.

It sounded unlikely. From what I could recall, there were a few possible protostars in the nebulae surrounding the formation, but nothing that made astronomers think there'd be an eighth Pleiade any time soon. Or, rather, that one would have been born around, say, AD 1500, when the light that would strike the Earth in 2012 left the cluster. As to the two heads parting destines, I had no idea what she meant by that. Sometimes Star Rattler was depicted with two heads, not like that poor two-headed fer-de-lance they'd had at the Hogle Zoo, but with at one on each end. That's the way it was on the double-headed serpent scepter, the one 9 Fanged Hummingbird carried on state occasions. Maybe she just meant there'd be a big saddle point on that day, something to make a decision about. But we knew that already. There had to be more to it than that. I started to ask her to clarify, but she waved me off. "That's all," she said. She stretched out her bare light arm and swept the stones off the board. Game over.

"Thanks to you over me," I said. "And—"

"One more thing," she said. "It's someone you know of, but whose face you've never seen."

(25)

That was all.

Well, fine. Now, what the bleeding hell did she mean?

We tried again and again, of course, and then, when the tsam lic had worn off, we went over and over the game. Night fell, or maybe just happened. Koh's shall-we-say praetorian guard prowled around us with increasing impatience and eventually with real alarm, begging us to rejoin the army. Finally she got me to admit that I accepted it, that is, that I accepted the fact that everything I'd done up until now had been useless, that the notes and the jars of tsam lic and the Lodestone Cross burial and all that I'd been so pathetically proud of wouldn't stop the real doomster, and that if we wanted to work out who the doomster was, or how to stop him, or anything more specific than what we'd just seen, we'd have to play the Sacrifice Game on a vastly larger scale. A human game, specifically. And if *that* didn't work I'd have to get my brain back to the twenty-first century in relatively good condition. Either way, we'd have to get back to Ix.

Sometimes—at times like this, I'd say, especially—one might as well just go with the cliché: I was crushed. Yes, it'd be nice to come up with a more clever word than *crushed*, but really, why bother? *Crushed* pretty well does the job.

What surprised even me, though, was how much I wasn't crushed just because I was a lazy slob and I'd thought I could relax. It was that I—even

I—was rather annoyed, in fact more than annoyed, in fact, let's say again, crushed—that the world was still doomed. And I even realized that I cared about it in the general sense, not just personally, that even if I died back here from my neuroblastomas or in a ball game or by the flint dagger or the wooden sword or whatever, even if I didn't get back to the thirteenth b'aktun to see Marena and the gang and catch the next season of *Game of Thrones,* I still wanted the good old crazy ratty loathsome ridiculous old world to keep rolling on.

Okay. Look. We can do this, I thought. We're young, we still have a lot of our health left, we're capable, we know more stuff than anybody else in the whole world. Just go with the best bet. Get to Ix and help 2JS get put in charge of the place. And in return he'll help us get together a human game. No sweat. Right?

Wrong. Oh, God are we fucked. We are so very fucked. Royally fucked we fucking very are—

Cancel that. Buck up. Man up. Gird your loins into the sticking place. Forward, crawl.

At the Isthmus of Tehuantepec we turned yelloward off the commercial track and onto a single-file path through what they called the Protectorship of the Brown Ants. It was the floor of a Devonian sea, coarse calcium sand made of diatoms and crinoid stems and the scales of ancient armored fish. The dunes gave evidence of nocturnal use, musky ropes of fox scat and the parallel-gash tracks of sidewinders, but daylight was dead. Sometimes we'd pass a lump of armadillos, poking around like big sow bugs and licking ants off crumbled lobes of brain coral. Supposedly some of the convert-bloods behind us complained that we were leading them into Kikilbaj, what the Aztecs would later call Miclantechutli, the desert graveyard at the zeroth world's ragged edge. They kept flipping out about the celestial Puma and Jaguars who were supposedly spying on us, and they were constantly doing all sorts of pathetic little rituals, combinations of bribes, apologies, foster adoptions, and threats. In the unfashionable rear of the now seemingly endless procession, families were offering their younger children to the lords of their hearth fires, making them swallow ashes or ramming hot stones into their eyes.

Another Puma band hit us again that night and we lost four bloods, fifty porters, and three or four hundred thralls. It was only the worst in a long and repetitious string of attacks. Things weren't going well. At dawn Hun Xoc, speaking for Lady Koh, called a war session. There weren't many good ideas. Finally 1 Gila suggested we split the forces in two. 1 Gila would take the main body—Koh's "Four Hundred families" of converts—and would continue southeast along this route. They'd take our palanquins and standards and some of our dressers, so that they could put together look-alikes of me and Hun Xoc. The rest of us, the Harpy bloods, 14 Wounded's group, and Koh's officers, greatmothers, and "capturing bloods," would get rid of our markings and detour southwest, heading the long way down the coast in a much smaller elite unit. Hun Xoc and his squad would stay with us to escort us to Ix, and the other ten emissaries and runners would go with the Four Hundred families. Severed Right Hand's men would almost certainly follow the bigger group.

It sounded like the right thing tactically but it was a cold move. The untrained converts would be way out in the breeze drawing fire. Koh might be sacrificing half her converts. On the other hand, there were a hundred and sixty score of them now. Even if only eighty thousand made it to Ix they'd be enough to tip the scale of the battle in 2JS's favor.

Anyway, Koh eventually agreed and 1 Gila's plan carried the day. At one point Hun Xoc took me aside and said he was a little nervous that 1 Gila would just take off and not make it to Ix at all, but after kicking it around for a while we decided that really they had nowhere else to go. They were marked outcasts far from their now-nonexistent homes, and at this point they'd either get to Ix in a hurry or get eaten. And some of them would get through. We worked out routes that would get both of us into Ix at the same time: The big army would take the direct route to Ix, marching in daylight, and we'd have to hustle around the long way at night.

I functioned. I sat on the strategy committee. I advised Koh. I played a running hipball game whenever the army passed a usable court, and then, as I slept, my bearers ran me to the next court. And I got some of my skills back, nothing like what I'd been as Chacal, but still not bad. But it happened in this smog of despair, that feeling like you've suddenly realized that the world is constructed entirely out of damp corrugated cardboard, and of no further interest because, no matter how elaborately and even artistically you cut, fold, paint, and arrange it, damp cardboard is still just damp cardboard. Only, this time it wasn't just in my mind, it was really the case, the world was going to wink out just as it would be getting interesting. Even though I was way back here, that is, "back" here, in 664, it felt as though the end was going to come tomorrow, later today, in an hour, in a minute, before the end of this sentence, now—and really, in terms of historical time, let alone geological time, it was only an instant away. Oh hell, oh hell, oh hell, oh hell.

Weirdly, though, Koh seemed to understand. She kept surprising me that way. I mean, with what she could understand. And even though the end of the thirteenth b'aktun would be so long after her own time, when everyone she knew would be lucky even to be bones and not just dust, she still wanted the world to continue. Although I think she mainly thought of it in terms of wanting her descendants to continue, but even so . . . anyway, just after the birth of the next sun we were slogging along on the south bank of the Río Coatzacoalcos, and I was curled up in my palanquin cursing the day I was born and all other days and all others who had been born, and she had my bearers bring me alongside her and, as we jogged along, she started a conversation—almost a modern-style conversation between equal and skeptical people and not an Olde Mayaland–style formal court exchange.

"Writing it all down wouldn't be good enough anyway," Koh said. As far as she was concerned, the Game was such a subtle and physical art that only directly transmitted skill was worth anything. "You have to show your eagle a way to your b'aktun"—by my *eagle* she meant my primary uay, like my self, or as we'd say, my brain—"and you need to be there yourself to ask Star Rattler to sacrifice another thirteen of the segments of his body, to give your world another thirteen b'aktuns."

"I can't say I see a likely route," I said.

"We'll plan the route together, at the human game," she said. "*K'ek'wa'r.*" That is, "Double strength," or, roughly, "Courage."

I signed a thank-you-next-to-me.

I have something to show you, she signed back.

Ix in AD 664

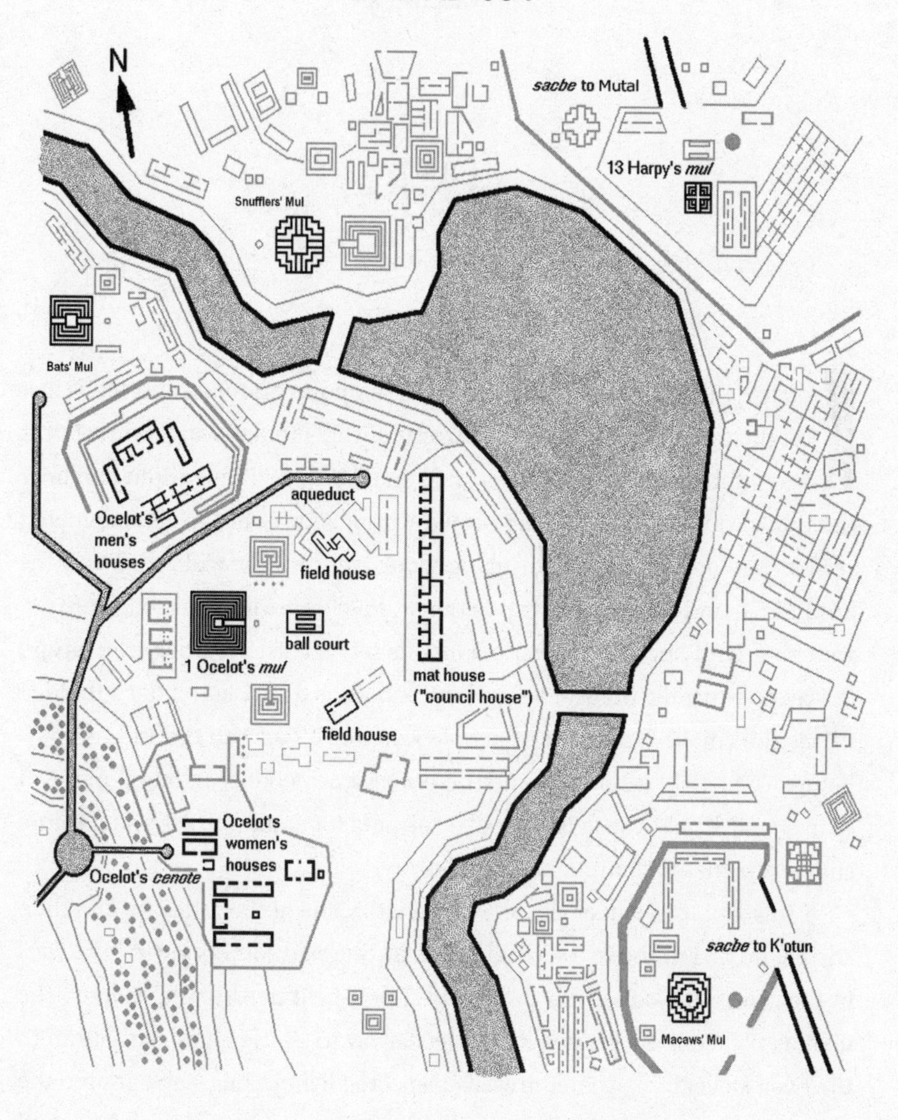

N
sacbe to Mutal
13 Harpy's mul
Snufflers' Mul
Bats' Mul
aqueduct
Ocelot's
men's
houses
field house
ball court
1 Ocelot's mul
mat house
("council house")
field house
Ocelot's
women's
houses
Ocelot's cenote
sacbe to K'otun
Macaws' Mul

(26)

Koh had her wickerworkers weave us a temporary ramada and set us just off the towpath alongside the Atoyac River. The day was steamy but it was cool under the cypresses and you could smell the tannin and hear the brown noise of the rushing brown water. Four of her deafened guards set out jars and baskets of drinking water, set up four wide rush screens around us, and took up their positions crouching with their backs to us, watching. Hun Xoc and a few other bloods sat at a distance, between us and the river. Armadillo Shit sat behind me and Koh's dwarf sat on her shoulder. It was the smallest number of people Koh and I had had around us since before we'd left Teotihuacán, and there wasn't any chance of our being seen or overheard, but even so, Koh looked around for a minute, listening, before she took something out of her bundle.

It was a polished deer rib. She dipped it in one of the little jars and then stirred the rib around in a second water jar. She said something to her dwarf in their personal code. The dwarf slid down, held her breath, covered the first jar, picked it up, carried it ten steps away to a little channel that ran to the river. Delicately—to her it was a respected living thing—she poured the water into the channel and then, not delicately, she dropped the pot and lid down in after it, shattering them.

I looked down into the drinking-water-pot. Cripes, I thought. What I'm getting is that this is some potent-ass shit. Koh took a dried marigold out of her little kit, picked a single tiny petal off it with a pair of horn almost-chopsticks, dipped the petal into the jar, stuck the tweezers into the mat like a double mast with a single wet flag at the top, and covered the jar. She moved a little myrtle torch closer to the petal, dried it, took it off the tweezers with her fingers, and tore it in half like it was a tab of LSD. She popped one of the halves in her mouth and gave me the other. I could practically hear Grateful Dead music playing in the background. I put the petal on my tongue.

"Boiling this doesn't much hurt its power," she said,

"They'd have to steam-distill their drinking water."

The exact word meant "steamed onto cloth," but it meant distill. Which no one would do anyway. With only clay or wood or leather or whatever vessels it was hard to boil water in big quantities, and people were in the habit of relying on mountain-spring water diverted or fetched directly to their homes. In Ix the drinking-water system was separate from the irrigation systems, which in turn were separate from the water in the artificial lake and the canal system, which was much more tannic and saline. Supposedly all the "sacred original" water, that is, the pure water, came from the Never-Empty Font of Waterlily Ocelot, the central reservoir of Ix. The huge cistern was fed directly from two cold underground streams that burst out the side of the hill. It was the heart of the city and the umbilical cord of the world, the Tree of 400^4 Branches, woven when the Earthtoad was a soft-shelled egg. Water was more holy the more upstreamness it had, and when it came out of the earth and for some time thereafter it was under the direct control of the Ahau, the Lord of the Fertilizing Waters, and it fed the cities' twelve drinking-water fountains and then, farther down the line of impurity, the whole system of floodgates that let the *ahauob* program the city's irrigation cycles. The Ocelots had always owned the water, and it fed hundreds of little fountains through the city, both on the Ocelots' peninsula and on the surrounding mainland. It had been one of the foundations of the Ocelots' power since the beginning of the city as a tiny irrigation society over a thousand years ago.

"On the court you'll face their garden,"

she said, pointing at the spot,

"Their goal's three hundred paces from the well
On their great-mul's female side. Run for the mainland,
Pretend to drown yourself, and release the bag,
And hold out till the Ocelots' eyes fog over."

Sure, I thought. *I bought an unction of a mountebank.* I said it all sounded a little wacky, although of course I didn't put it that way, I said it as well as possible in the high-equals language we were still using with each other. Even if all that went exactly according to plan, the minute people started freaking out from the usual water, the Ocelots would switch to some other source.

We lit cigars.

And how long do you think it will take them to feel it? she asked. Do you feel anything?

I said no, not really. Maybe my tongue felt a little numb and frisky, but I wasn't giddy or anything. Given what a long day it had been I felt totally in control.

"Well, listen, if you take the court," she said,
"You can always have this with you just in case."

I said something along the lines of "Sure, whatever." You're delusional, babe, I thought. I guess again she could tell what I really thought because she said something like "Well, we may not need it anyway," lit another pair of cigars, and handed me one. After a few puffs we exchanged cigars. It was a gesture of extreme hospitality.

I leaned back on Armadillo Shit and puffed. We exchanged cigars again, completing the little ritual.

"Just now this picture flew through me," Koh said. "What would you say to it?"

I pointed to my ear, meaning that I was listening.

"If you could really move your ruling uay from one skin to another," she said, "then you could stay on this level forever. You wouldn't have to paddle downstream through the canyons." She meant I wouldn't have to die.

That's right, I said. I could just possess someone younger. She was right. I'd thought about that particular implication of the consciousness transference only a couple of times. But there wasn't any reason it wouldn't work. You wouldn't have to invent all the gigantic neural nets and zettabyte storage networks and everything else you'd need to make a mechanical substitute of the brain. You could just have yourself copied and zap into whoever. Or if you felt bad about killing someone that way you'd just clone a few babies of yourself, keep them drugged and unconscious until they get to a good brain-size age, and then use them as vessels. It might be a good growth industry to get into, I thought, another few billion for the Warren Organization.

Still, I can't do this from here, I thought. Let's not build castles in the air. Deal with the here-and-now here and now. And then if you get Back to the Future you can take care of Marena and Lindsay and the Warren Group and the whole unholy crew. Right?

Warren. Lindsay "Big Data" Warren. Christ allwhitey. Back to Square Zero. Hell.

Everything I'd gone through in 2012 seemed pretty remote. Once in a while I'd even catch myself thinking it hadn't been real, that I was just a regular Maya ballplayer with delusional paranoia and a lot of imagination, and I'd have to remind myself that no old Maya dude could have made up the history of the entire Western world, no matter how clever he was.

And how clever am I? I wondered. Maybe Koh's right to worry about 2 Jeweled Skull. Maybe I should worry more. Maybe I didn't worry enough about coming here in the fucking first place. Maybe I hadn't been that thoughtful about that whole business with the Warren Corporation.

I don't know, Idunno, idddnnnow. I was getting pretty sure that Marena wouldn't have gone to all the trouble of dealing with me if she hadn't been thinking of sending me even then, from before the beginning.

Maybe Tony Sic never really wanted to go in the first place. The more I thought about it the clearer it seemed. They'd needed somebody inconsequential, so naturally they'd chosen little *yo*. Fruck. Yuck. Well, the joke's on me—

HOT! OUUUCH, *TA', TA', TA'!* Shitskies! There were all these scalding drops of water on my face and I brushed them away. Confusion over us. Somehow I was lying on the ground and Armadillo Shit was rolling on top of me, squealing a little like he was in pain. Orange flies. Two bloods were pulling on me and we all fell back I squinted into the dark forest, toward the river. Hun Xoc and another person were rolling over broken pottery and pools of liquid. There were a couple of big thumps, Hun Xoc butting his head into the other person's face. I looked around for Lady Koh and couldn't find her and then it turned out she was behind me. She had a funny expression and at first I thought she was in pain but then saw that she was laughing silently. She'd gotten a few drops of hot stuff, too, but her dwarf was already daubing them with ointment, like one of those movie makeup people who rush in and redoes your entire look in the two minutes between takes. I looked back at Hun Xoc. The others were holding him up. The man he'd butted with his head was still on the ground, mashed and moaning. You couldn't make out much of his face anymore, but his threadbare manto had been newly edged with Lady Koh Blue, which implied that he was one of the village elders who'd been adopted into our household and was, supposedly, serving us.

Well, I thought, I guess he really had tried to kill us. But I was laughing so hard that it took everyone a while to explain to me that it had been an assassination attempt, that the dude had tried to throw a pot of boiling oil into our faces. They also explained that we were under attack again, but even though I could hear the alarm calls and the whistles of bull-roarers, it still all seemed incredibly funny to me, no prob, no sweat, no brain, no pain, and I still couldn't stop giggling.

They bundled me into a sled and we took off. I squinted up at the beige sky. It turned pink and then green and then, oddly for a sky, it disappeared. Boy, I guess that crud really does creep up on you after all, I thought. So let's see, if it had taken about a hundred-score beats to hit me last night, it might take three times as long in cold water, so maybe you could count on over a half a day of delay. Maybe Koh really had a point with that stuff.

Nobody'd gotten anything out of the village greatfather who'd tried to kill Koh or me or both of us. The other elders said he had been out foraging the day before and had probably gotten co-opted by the Pumas then. The Harpy bloods started to kick the other elders around but I was pretty sure none of them had anything to do with it and got them to let them go. My good deed for the month. Well, the year. Lifetime. It was hard to even tell them what I wanted since I was still cackling like a moron, but Hun Xoc asked Koh whether I'd had too much wild tobacco—which was strong enough to be hallucinogenic in medium doses—and Koh said probably. She didn't want to tell the Harpy Clan or even the Rattlers about the earthstar compound until the last possible moment, in case somebody got captured and turned.

Again, embarrassingly, I giggled. Maybe things weren't really so bad.

(27)

In the youth of the fifth sun following we were in a desert again, and a sixty-blood Puma raiding party somehow got ahead of us under cover of a sandstorm. For a while our bloods dug in and protected our flanks, but by dawn it was clear from the long-distance way the Pumas were fighting that they were just trying to hold us up until the main body of troops under Severed Right Hand could get to us. So we started off, without even going after them. It's like in Go, sometimes the more you ignore the opponent and don't even deign to respond to what he's doing, the better off you are. We kept our convoy in the closest thing to a real defensive march formation we could manage but took some losses on the flanks. Hun Xoc led a party of running spearmen ahead and then back, to try to come up on the Pumas from the rear, but they kept ducking into dry-gulches and getting away. You still couldn't see much out here, it was like those crummy overpriced photos of Mars.

All during the march that day we—I mean we fearless leaders—ran back and forth and counted and formed up the squadrons. As soon as night covered us three hundred and twenty of us hotshots split off from the big line. 1 Gila's whole group and thirty-one score Rattler bloods were with them, so they weren't defenseless. But we hardly sent any Harpies with them, only a score of 14 Wounded's men and four Ixian Harpy bloods. Good luck, guys, I thought. Have fun taking the heat. Poor bastards.

We rubbed deer feces on our calves—like all Mesoamerican warriors, we dragged along big baskets of the stuff—and silent-marched all night, without audible signals and on new rubber-soled sandals, and camped at dawn under the last stand of trees at the edge of a plain that led down to what I think was later the Río Mezcalapa. It seemed we hadn't been followed. At dusk we crept out into the flats and down a long, long incline into marshes of scrub cypress and hyacinths. It seemed like ninety percent of the ground was impassable bog. I couldn't believe how much you'd have to go the long, long way around, how you'd see a destination hill ahead and have to zig and zag in the opposite direction to get there. I remember mainly wasted time and angst, the pi-r-squared longer everything took. I got the feeling we were avoiding some places because of their bad mojo even though the routes we took were actually more dangerous. I marched or rather jogged myself almost all the time now, building up my lung capacity for the possible ball gig, even though I could still have done the rickshaw thing if I wanted everyone to think I was a total wuss. Dopamine from the exertion kept fogging my head and sometimes I couldn't even remember who was planning what, I kept breathing "Did I miss something, did I miss something?" as a running-mantra. Did we all miss something? It all kept shifting. What didn't Hun Xoc tell us? What was Koh really up to? She and I talked every day but somehow we never got around to what she was thinking, it was always what I thought everyone else was thinking. Anyway, she was spending most of her time now interrogating the captive Pumas. Just after the birth of the Grandfather Heat who was also the grandfather of the sun of the great-hipball game—that is, two days before the game—we pushed through into the high forest road along what would later be called the Grijalva River and stopped to meet with two of Koh's runners from her "Four Hundred," her army of converts.

The runners said that 1 Gila's Four Hundred had lost nearly a fifth of their men and more of the women, but they'd also picked up a few villages, even without Koh, and they were on schedule. Hun Xoc sent a different pair of runners back with a message for them to head through the Macaws' Pass into the Harpy House's hunting preserves, on the east side of Ix. From there 2 Jeweled Skull's men would get them as close to the city as possible, less than a hundred-score beats' march away from the red eastern gate. We also decided to send the three Scorpion-adders and the sensitive cargo-sleds with them instead of taking a chance that the Ocelot inspectors would ask to go through them, even though the really major stuff was in false bottoms under boxes of Koh's rattlesnakes.

And when we get the word to them, they move in, Koh added. The runners went off and we moved out again, marching in daylight. We were late. In the next sun's middle age, near what they later called Santa Cruz, we got onto the great western *sacbe,* a laser-straight causeway with a whitewashed macadam under blue mirage puddles and spews of heat distortion. I hoped we looked fearsome and dragonish, sliding down the immense walkway like a spiny caterpillar on the edge of a porcelain cleaver. If it weren't for the curvature of the earth we could have seen Ix at its vanishing point far to the east, surrounded by yellow corn plots and orchards. Seeing my ancestral country in its prime—even all withering in the drought, it still looked a lot more prosperous than it would in the bad old twenty-first—made me feel kind of homesick, I kept wondering what Marena would say about all this. She'd have all sorts of isn't-this-fun *aperçus.*

At dusk runners from 1 Gila came in and said the Four Hundred Newborn Clans were at Two Kinds of Jade, near Palenque, which meant they were behind schedule. Hun Xoc sent them back with a message to double their pace again even if they had to split off a temporary camp for the stragglers and leave them behind. It wouldn't do for us to get into Ix if they weren't around to back us up. On our end he forced an extra march overnight and we managed to sight the glow of festival smoke from Ix before dawn on the day of the big ball game. Monkey accountants scampered up and down the line doing the final count—we were down to only about eleven thousand bloods and forty thousand porters—and telling everyone to look peaceable. Even though the road was a free zone we were over Black Macaw territory and had to be cool and act like we weren't an army, just acquaintances of 2JS's. A quarter after the zenith, outside Ix's fourth and outermost circle of palisades, the signal for "weapons ready but not visible" came down through the file, like a wave of motion through our collective centipede. 9 Fanged Hummingbird's runners had come up. I pushed forward to the back of the van and watched the little conference. One of Koh's palanquins was there, but for all I knew it wasn't the one with her in it. The Ocelot ambassadors were all decked out in their signature emerald-green under their tetrahedral parasols and speaking in this really haughty lilt, dandies from the capital slumming it out in the hinterlands. They recited a formal invitation to the great-hipball game, which would start after dawn at the Second Twin Setting, which meant about three-hundred-score beats from now. They made it sound like a huge favor and a big deal, like getting tickets for the Super Bowl. Then, before Hun Xoc could respond, they said they only had room for two hundred of the Rattler's guests—it was understood that they meant only blooded clan members—and couldn't properly receive the rest in the city.

So what, it wasn't supposed to be up to them, I thought, if one of the competing clans had room for a lot of guests, that was their business. Fine, fine, I thought, we'll crash the afterparty.

Hun Xoc stood facing them in the direct sunlight. He took his time about answering, not even flinching at the deerflies biting him. I wondered if their biting meant rain was coming. If it did, Koh's idea with the earthstar compound was screwed from go.

It was a bit of a tense moment. If we didn't accept, it would be an insult and an excuse to start a fight right now. We were in the weakest possible position, uncamped and tired. Since we were on settled hostile ground, our scouts hadn't been able to check out our flanks. If the Ocelots hit us now they'd be dug in with an easy retreat and we'd be way out in the breeze.

Hun Xoc had signaled that he was ready to answer.

"We all accept with thanks," he said, "but how

Can we desert our children on the road?" he asked.

The Ocelots drew back and conferred. Evidently they didn't want to wait here while the runners got the answer to 9 Fanged Hummingbird and brought back his response. Eventually they worked out that we'd all go into Ix, but that a hundred and twenty of our bloods would have to stay as "guests," that is, really, hostages, in the Ocelots' grounds on the mainland, far from the temple district. Hun Xoc agreed and made the division, taking the best fighters with us in our two hundred and leaving the others in the lurch.

We said greatfathers-protect-yous and did a few little extreme-unction-ish rituals. We'll never see them again, I thought.

While that was going on covert runners from 1 Gila came in at the back of our line and we had to wait for the damn Ocelots to leave before we could talk to them. 1 Gila's news wasn't good. He'd been slowed down by a bad raid and had had trouble making the split. When the runners had left they were still only at Ch'uuk sal—"Sweetwater"—which was still over a full normal day away. We sent back a message asking how much of the force could he get to Ix for the ball game, assuming the first ball dropped on schedule, exactly at the death of Grandfather Heat. I kept asking stupid questions. How long would the hipball truce protect us? Would the Ocelots come after 2JS after the festival, or during it, or even during the ball game? Finally even Hun Xoc told me to quiet down. By full sunlight we'd hired four hundred local porters to carry us into Ix and got the hell going. We wanted all our bloods to be fresh and feisty and ready to kick some head.

(28)

It was hard to see much of the actual city through all the kites, banners, and offering smoke, but I remember thinking, "Wow, Ix is *huge*!" I realized I hadn't gotten much of a look at the city before, since my first visit had been a little rushed. Not that it was endless like Teotihuacán, but it certainly wasn't a couple of pyramids in the middle of a jungle. It was more like the central cluster of the nine main mulob were there to focus the hundreds of acres of comfortable houses and the thousands of acres of shantytown sprawl. The Harpy Clan's own mul—which was named One Harpy, the seat and personification of the founder of the line—was the closest from this angle and just spiked up overhead like superheated smoke from an old-fashioned space rocket. I'd never gotten a good look at it before. It was steeper than the others, almost a sixty-degree angle, and red on each side with the directional colors banded through on the north, west, and south. The sacbe branched southwest and we descended four levels into the plain of the valley. The terraced slopes on either side were studded with rows of hundreds of nearly identical compounds, and at least in this district the different sides of most of the houses were painted in the colors of the directions they faced, and the whole thing had a sort of cubist bop to the staggered blocks, like they were all lit with yellow light from the south and black light from the west and so on, no matter what time of day it was. But it wasn't like Teotihuacán's brutal crystals, it was all organic, smoothed over at the corners, and the closer you got to the center of town the more everything sprouted a luxuriance of grotesque vegetal ornamentation that I really can't describe the effect of, it was just so *much,* forests of multicolored grandfather-poles, tree-people, cornstalk-people, their heads bursting Daphne-like into ceiba-branches that trailed off into long, thin streamer-kites fulgerating against the pewter clouds. I guess you might get something of the volume of the overload by walking around inside a Buddhist temple in Sri Lanka, but the style was different, all shadowy and obsessive, and *outlined,* every little thing darkly haloed like it was sealed in an infinitely flexible membrane. I got a shiver without knowing why and then realized we were passing a mural of myself, as Chacal, winning the *tun*'s *halach pitzom* against 6 Hurricane at Snapping-Turtle Lake, with a big "in memoriam to the greatest" inscription with all my dates and scores, and I felt this huge flood of vicarious pride or something and had to force myself to cool it. As we crossed the first bridge we could see the canals and the big oxbow around the temple precinct were choked with ceremonial canoes, all draped in cotton banners and red-and-pink geranium chains and flying giant sun-disk kites. A contingent of Harpy bloods had met us and were walking alongside Hun Xoc, code-whispering about arranging for the converts. They'd be able to get inside the valley but they wouldn't come closer than the second circle of palisades without starting a fight. Bloods and dependents from all different clans, even some Ocelots in their distinctive emerald trogon-feather half-capes, crowded the low walls of the causeway and pushed against the flanking bloods trying to get a peek at Lady Koh. They shouted the same questions over and over, mainly asking for predictions on the big hipball game. Somebody begged her to curse the people who'd raped and "sealed" his four daughters, but he got shouted down. A rumor had gotten around that Koh was powerful enough to call the Rolling Head without harming herself. In general, a curse involving the Head was so powerful it would kill the curser as well as the cursee. But if you were really major, you could do it and survive. Anyway, she ignored the issue. We turned off the sacbe down the steps toward the courts. The city was dressed in its beyond-festive great-hipball game atmosphere. Every surface had been redyed with fugitive overlays, cerulians, violets, and magentas, and oiled and buffed and reoiled, and it all sparkled in the peach light. I kept wanting to look over my shoulder and had to remind myself that was stupid, if they attacked us now we couldn't do anything about it.

We crossed the Second Bridge and passed under the Black Gate and into an alley between the rows of low stone dressing-room buildings that bordered the court precinct. It was male territory, but I guess since Koh was a liminal being it was okay for her to be here. Anyway, she had her two male epicene-attendants holding translucent blue-green feather-fans on either side of her head so that symbolically she'd never stepped outside her holy space. I could hear the players gearing up inside the screened-and-guarded rooms, and beyond that the crowd in the stands, that nervous pre-bloodsporty rustling growl. We passed a couple of vendors selling drinks of hot water at drought prices. Good, I thought, people's home cisterns are probably pretty much empty. If there was a battle the soldiers and fires would eat up the rest of the stored drinking water in a few thousand beats.

The Harpy bloods ushered us—I mean Koh and her dwarf and two of her handmaids, and then 2 Hand, 14 Wounded, and me, and our attendants—to the back of what you might call the Visitors' Field House and through a little anus-door into one of the few tiny hipball-game changing rooms that wasn't in use. I wished Hun Xoc were with us, but he'd had to go through a special purification. When my eyes got used to the interior dark I saw there was a one-fifth-scale statue of me in a niche—that is, myself as Chacal, the ballplayer. It wasn't a good one, just a mold-made workshop multiple, but it was still disconcerting. There were figurines of 3 Balls and 1 Big Peccary and these other legendary players alongside. Two more Harpy heralds were flanking the draped mouth-door on the far side of the room, which led out to the Ocelots' ball court. There were nine of them, but the great-hipball court was by far the biggest. It smelled like sweat and analgesic ball-oil. There needs to be a stronger word than *nostalgia* for the effect of smells like that. It just shot this jump-through-the-roof rush through my Chacal side, all buzzed up with pride and confidence and determination, but on my Jed side it coughed up all this bad stuff from high school in Nephi, the locker room and the sports doctor's office with the rolls of adhesive and the Pam Anderson poster on the wall and all these loutish athletes coming in to get taped up before they went out on the field, and me sitting there blue-icing a bruise I'd gotten from a free weight in my Remedial Physical Education program, and just having to sit and plot my revenge while I took all this shit about being an aboriginal faggot freak. And now I was a big shot in this environment. The biggest. I mean, really, you have no idea how huge I was. It was like it was 1999 and I was Michael Jordan and everyone thought I'd died in a space-shuttle accident, but really I was walking around looking at displays of myself in the video stores at O'Hare Airport. In two minutes there'd be so many people there that the floor would collapse. Just wait, I thought. It's comeback time.

2 Jeweled Skull's heralds crouched in and flanked the door.

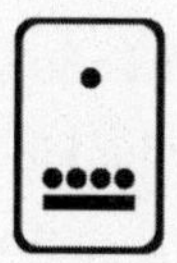

(29)

"And here my sons are," 2 Jeweled Skull said, "and Lady Koh of the Rattlers, and her backrests and flutes."

He meant her supporters. He went on a bit, doling out bits of praise. Hmm. 2 Jeweled Skull was saying all the right things, but there was something different and older about him. Maybe he just didn't look so scary as he had when I was the new kid in town and he was towering over me with torture implements.

He teetered over to me, embraced me in that stiff dancey way, and gave me a ceremonial battle-saw. It was a three-arm-lengths shaft with a handle beaded in the pattern of my names and captures, with its last two feet widening into a flat wood blade inlaid with circular pink spondylus shells and edged with double rows of perfectly matched triangular blades of iridescent-yellow obsidian, like the nose of a golden sawfish.

Whoa, I thought. Usually I was just frustrated by the whole hyperflattering flowery speech thing but for once it didn't seem like just empty form, it really meant something. It was corny but I was getting all misty and glowy inside.

"You tilt your basin of blood my way," I said, correctly. "Perhaps
You've just mistaken me for someone else,
I who am unreliable, I of vice, of shit,
May I not think myself a worthy receiver."

Yeah, I really did good, didn't I, I thought. I felt, just, like, warm. Even the long aftertaste of the time he'd tortured me just made him seem more fatherly, in a sick way, I guess, but I couldn't get distance from the feeling. Anyway, I could understand how he'd felt. After all, he's old, I thought. He was carrying over sixty solar years, which was old for a Maya, or a preindustrial person from anywhere. Maybe it was up to me to take care of him now. He acknowledged everyone else in correct order but cut the exchange of speeches short. Judging from the tone of the beaters out on the court, the first ball would drop in eight more measures of four thousand beats each, that is, about two hours, which would seem like a while, but 2 Jeweled Skull had so much meeting-and-greeting to do that there was barely enough time to get him into position. Between the beats you could hear the crowd making urgent crackly sounds, like kids opening presents.

Please take asylum here, 2 Jeweled Skull said to Lady Koh. He touched a bowl of chocolate. His herald handed it to her.

"Star-Rattler's Brood would accept your too-bright offer,"

Koh said, before touching the bowl,

"But our children have a gift as well for you."

She meant the tsam lic and the three captured adders.

"But they aren't here yet, and we come with unbent backs."

At the risk of being obvious, "with unbent backs" was like saying "empty-handed."

2JS couldn't just say "Oh, yeah? Then when the hell are they showing up?" As host it was his position to say "Oh, that's all right, anything's fine, come anytime." The mode we were speaking in made it all about whatever you weren't saying as opposed to what you were. It was like *Strange Interlude,* you pictured everyone speaking out loud through a mask and then whispering what they really meant on the inner side.

"Our messengers say your children only entered
Our fields this morning," he said, "but we all hope
They'll join us for our moonrise victory feast."

It was Koh's turn to make a quick decision. She took the bowl of chocolate, held it in the "accepted" gesture, drank, and sent it back.

"And please take this as our pledge to serve our host

With all our numbers, genius, blood, and sight," she said.

She handed Coati four long blue military-macaw tailfeathers, which he handed to the herald. 2JS accepted them. Everyone didn't quite sigh with relief, but there was an okay-let's-get down-to-brass-shit feeling. We sent out the peripheral people so that counterclockwise it was just 2 Jeweled Skull, Hun Xoc, 2 Hand, me, 14 Wounded, Lady Koh, Coati, and Hun Xoc.

We all squatted in the tiny dark hot room, not wanting to sit on the stone floor or to take the time to set our mats. Coati set a Gila figurine in front of him to acknowledge that he was also speaking for them.

It was 2 Jeweled Skull's position to start.

There was a pause.

Our backup troops, the Rattler's Newborn, were just fucking not here.

You couldn't blame 1 Gila or anyone for the delay, but it was still a crisis that could sink the whole thing. The mood was shifting from an if-we-keep-our-heads-we're-going-to-rock feeling to a maybe-we're-in-trouble-no-matter-what-we-do feeling. 2JS and I looked at each other. We both wanted to get away and just catch up, but this was one time work really did have to come first.

"So then," he said, "after the end,

We may have close frontiers on all four sides."

It was a super understatement, like saying "It's going to be a bumpy night." I looked at Koh. She looked at me and we both looked at Hun Xoc. It was like, damn, maybe we're screwed. We're leftovers-to-be. We came all this way and we were still fucked. I felt guilty about it, I'd walked them into the worst possible situation when we all shoulda stood in bed.

The troops' getting behind schedule hadn't been any kind of a shock. It had more been one of those things where something's just a little uneasy-making, and then it gets worse and worse, and as it gets worse you also realize how significant it is, until by the bitter end you're wondering how you could have let the seed of the situation sprout in the first place.

Laughter, or what might be better described as frantic giggles, seeped in from the crowd outside. Probably the contortionists and animal jugglers had come on, which meant it was later than I'd thought. Then the mockers would come on and then the first ball would drop at the instant the east end of the court fell completely into the shadow of the Ocelots' emerald mul. The timing was partly because otherwise one side would be trying to score goals into the low sun, but mainly because the ball was an astral body, so you wanted to launch it only when it wasn't competing with the sun.

Hun Xoc asked how many bloods we really had to count on when they did get here. He didn't use any of the code languages. I guess we're sure nobody's listening, I thought. Still, this whole side of the court was supposed to be Harpy territory for the duration of the festival.

Coati answered that we had at least thirty score coming, but to keep in mind that at least fifteen score of them were loosely trained, not yet full bloods. There were also about ninety score nonmale supporters. It was a huge army by Maya standards and respectable even by Teotihuacanob ones. More than enough to tip the balance if it was deployed correctly.

Coati asked Hun Xoc whether there was any sense that the Ocelots knew the Rattler's Brood was headed this way.

Hun Xoc said apparently not. He said the Harpies only had one informer left inside the Ocelots' inner household, and she might not even be an accurate source, but that at least as of this morning they all thought Koh's converts were still heading southwest to Kaminaljuyu. Evidently 1 Gila had even sent a couple of advance parties to Kaminaljuyu and back just to increase that impression. As far as Koh's presence here at the festival went, the Ocelots seemed to think she was swinging by here to pick up a few deserters and family members from the Harpy House to add to her army of converts on her way to her presumed new city in the south.

And so, if the Rattler's Brood is just beginning to trickle into the preserve now, how fast could the first of them get to the gates? 20 Blue Snail asked.

Coati said 1 Gila and the managers of the Harpy preserves would know better than she would. But from the latest runners he guessed at least a quarter-day, which meant by Vega rising, about two A.M. And if we wanted them to show up armed and briefed and formed up into any kind of battle array and not completely exhausted, it would take longer. Even if we sent word to only send the bloods, and to send them at a run, we were still looking at an arrival time of Jupiter rising, or a little before midnight.

Hun Xoc started to make some kind of crack about Coati's name, but 2JS cut him off.

Unfortunately, 2 Jeweled Skull said, the ball game won't last half that long.

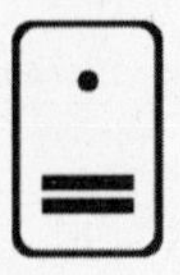

(30)

I'd say everyone looked around at each other, except around here one didn't eyeball people, so it was more as though we all sensed around at each other.

2JS said that tonight the Ocelots would make sure they'd win before the crowd got tired, before they'd even peaked, and while there was still plenty of time for them to contest the outcome if they needed to. And the best time for them to start the fight would be right at the end of the hipball game, when their crowd was the most pumped. And they'd pull something even faster if they got an inkling of armed Rattler troops coming close to Ix. The instant the Rattlers show themselves, the maximum time we'd have remaining to win the game would be the time it would take for a spy-runner to get from 2JS's preserves to 9 Fanged Hummingbird, and for 2JS to issue instructions. Which could be as little as four hundred beats.

And without the Rattler's Brood, how long could we hold out in a direct fight? Koh asked through Coati.

Over a day if we were back at Harpy House on the mainland, Hun Xoc said. But 2 Jeweled Skull and the rest of us are going to be cut off in the temple district. Even supposing we dug in at the council house or one of the field houses, we'd last less than a quarter-day.

14 Wounded asked for the floor. So, then, our father, he said, what plans do we have?

Uh-oh, you're out of line, I thought. You don't have the seniority to question 2 Jeweled Skull. On the other hand, it wasn't time to stand on ceremony. On the third hand, they didn't think of it as ceremony, they thought of it as the way the universe was.

2JS answered, though. If they cheat, he said, or if they overstep their wager, we'll fight them with whatever we've got. He said he'd position a blowgun squad among our supporters in the stands.

Blowgun squad? I wondered. Did that mean he'd acted on some military-strategy idea he'd picked out of my head? Wasn't he afraid of a Cosmic Censor who doesn't exist? Were we better prepared than he was saying? How much wasn't he telling me? This is no fun whatsoever, it's just completely frustrating.

But beyond that? 14 Wounded asked. His voice was getting a little shrill.

Beyond that there's nothing more we can do, 2 Jeweled Skull said. 9 Fanged Hummingbird would get all sorts of kudos for finally capturing us. In fact, he was counting on the fact that Severed Right Hand was only eleven days away—although 9 Fanged Hummingbird would certainly need to be unusurpably in charge of Ix when Severed Right Hand arrived.

And what support can we count on from the other aquiline clans? 14 Wounded whined again. That is, clans related to the Harpies of Ix, the Caracaras of Teotihuacán, and the sixty or so other Eagle lineages throughout Mesoamerica. It was a serious question but more than a little indelicate and it wasn't at all right for him to pile one question on another like this.

2 Jeweled Skull said that his main effort during the last eighty-five days—besides training the team and holding out against the Ocelots' little raids and tax assaults—had been solidifying his support with other clans, both aquiline and feline. But when he'd appealed directly to the Eagle clans of Motul and Caracol, they'd turned him down. It had been an unpleasant surprise.

We should never have let 1 Gila split our forces, 14 Wounded said.

Whoa, I thought again. Dude, you're getting yourself in trouble. 14 was kind of a goofus but I almost felt a little sorry for him. I tilted my head to the left and they passed the right to speak around to me, like an invisible microphone. Wasn't it also true that the Ocelots would let the ball game run a little while first? I asked.

Hun Xoc said that was correct. The Ocelots usually liked to hold off pulling the first fix until at least the ninth ball or so. Otherwise the public—which really meant the guest royalty and village cargo bearers, not so much what we'd call the actual masses—might feel cheated themselves.

I asked what kind of a cheat he thought the Ocelots were likely to use.

Well, first, he said, since they'd had the two best Harpy players disqualified—and he added that the Ocelots probably set them up to get caught with prostitutes and how if we got through this he was going to have them skinned and salted—the Ocelots simply had a better team. So they might win fairish and squarish anyway. But if things weren't going their way by about the hundredth point, they'd probably do one of three things. There might be bad dead-ball calls against us, the equivalent of out calls. They might have set a couple of our own Harpy players to throw a point or two. Even though the players on both sides were supposed to be sequestered before the hipball game, people do get turned when their families are threatened. And if for some reason all that didn't work, they might bring in a loaded ball.

2JS said no, they only had one informer left in the house, and he couldn't help with the game.

What about Koh's earthstar stuff? I wondered. But of course it was too slow-acting for this gig. As it was, we might all be dead by morning.

Damn.

We are in trouble. Weareintrouble weareintroubleweareintrouble.

We just need another ten-score beats or so, I thought. That's not a lot.

I asked who was on the Harpy team.

Hun Xoc said 24 Pine was the coach—he was one of Chacal's old mentors, the one they called the Teentsy Bear—and 9 Dog and 6 Cord were the starting strikers, or strikers. 3 Deer, 1 Black Butterfly, and 7 Sweatbath were the starting blockers. They were all decent players, kids I'd played or trained with in the past, but not stars. It was a solid defensive backline but they'd disqualified our serious strikers. 6 Cord, who had the nickname "Drunken Wildcat," was fast and fierce and might be good for three or four goals, but he couldn't score and keep on scoring. The nine substitute players were basically just the usual second line from the old days, with a few rookies. Nobody major. All of the team's really good players had gotten lured away back during 2JS's tax trouble, even before my aborted sacrifice on the mul.

I asked who the starting five were on the Ocelots' team.

They said 2 Howler, 4 Howler, and Under 5 were the defensive line. The Howlers, whose enemy names were "Flabby Bitch Monkey" and "Even Flabbier Bitch Monkey," were really just a couple of thuggish Ocelot greathouse bloods who liked to beat people up and think of themselves as ball stars. Under 5, who had the nickname "Mudbag," was more of a famous guard than an effective one, totally over the hill compared to me, that is, to Chacal. They said the blind-side striker—or left striker—would be Emerald Immanent and the open-side striker was 20 Silence.

Hmm, I thought. Both of them were truly dangerous players, professional ballplayers temporarily adopted into the Ocelots. Still, I thought I could deal with Emerald Immanent. Despite his name he wasn't really that quick. In fact his current nickname was "Suffocation" because he tended to just mash you against the banks until your lungs collapsed. I'd played two games of one-on-one hipball with him and won both.

20 Silence was a different story. We'd played against each other only once, in the big game at Blue Stone Mountain, and had pretty much run circles around each other the whole time, while most of the other players, on both sides, got hamburgered all over the court. He was a true no-sell, a real glutton for pain. We'd won, finally, but it hadn't been his fault. That had been one of my last big games, and since then 20 Silence had become the leading scorer in what you could loosely call the league. His most popular nickname was "400 Weasels." He was the one who'd killed those backs in the hipball contest that Hun Xoc and everyone had been talking about on our way up to Teotihuacán, the one who'd pulled 23 Crow's eyeballs off their optic nerves after 23 Crow scored that incredible goal. It had been kayfabe, of course, but even so, he wasn't just a heel. He was also a point machine. Even so I thought that with a good striker our team could put them away without much trouble.

Which other Ball Brethren are ready to play? I asked.

That was 9 Fanged Hummingbird's brilliancy, 2JS said. He made sure our best players left us just before he challenged us. And after that we were such underdogs nobody would join us, they were afraid of getting killed or sacrificed.

What about the handicapping? I asked.

He said we hadn't been able to negotiate much and keep our face.

But they won't stop the hipballs with us ahead, I said.

He said no. If they did we'd pick up too much popular support from outside clans that had taken long-odds bets on us.

And if we could delay the contest, I asked, wouldn't it be better for the Rattler army to stay down for now and come in after dark anyway?

We can't delay it, Hun Xoc said. If you weren't there when the first ball fell, you lost.

Fine, I thought, anything you say, we're fucked whatever we do. I asked what they thought would happen if we won incontrovertibly, even though I really knew the answer.

Hun Xoc said the Ocelots would start yelling that we cheated and start a fight anyway. So we were looking at a fight whatever we did. The best thing for us to do would be to keep ahead without actually winning. Until our troops were ready. But the Ocelots might pull little things during the game, bad calls or illegal traps. We'd need to be good enough to stay ahead on scoring even if they got away with some of that stuff. We'd need to score beyond what they could take away.

Maybe we need a ringer, I said. The phrase wasn't really like "ringer," of course, it was more like "one who has hidden his strength," but it was the same idea. I said a good striker could keep the score nearly even until we got our act together.

All the good players are being watched, Hun Xoc said. It was probably true. There were only a few ballplayers in the world who were capable of going head-to-head against 20 Silence. And even though pitzom was a team sport, the outcome usually depended more on matching one-against-one than, say, basketball.

So maybe I should just go in and play, I said. I'd keep us ahead and drag the game out as long as possible.

Silence. I resisted looking at anyone's face.

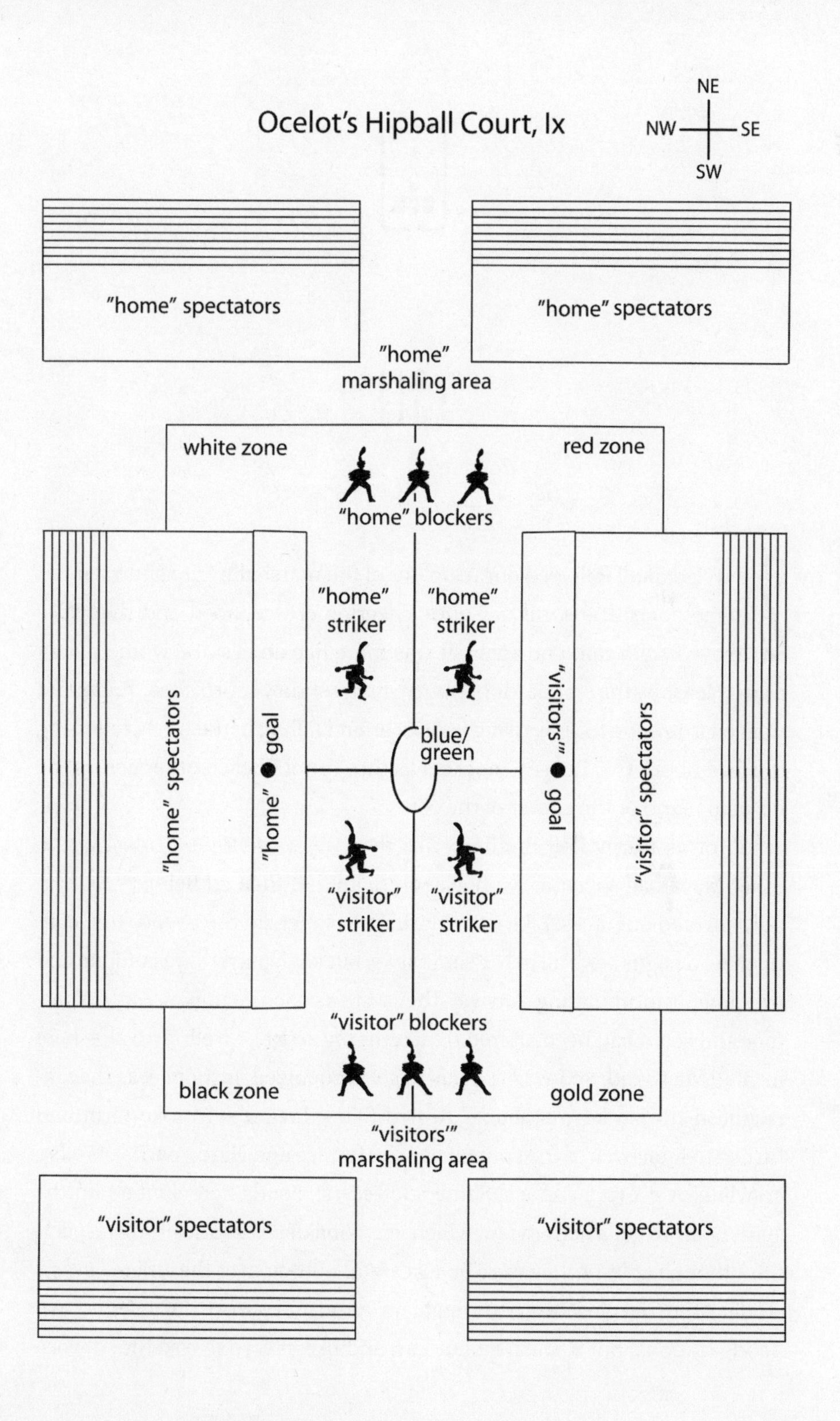
Ocelot's Hipball Court, Ix
NE
NW
SE
SW
"home" spectators
"home" spectators
"home"
marshaling area
white zone
red zone
"home" blockers
"home"
striker
"home"
striker
"home" spectators
"home" goal
blue/
green
"visitors'" goal
"visitor" spectators
"visitor"
striker
"visitor"
striker
"visitor" blockers
black zone
gold zone
"visitors'"
marshaling area
"visitor" spectators
"visitor" spectators

(31)

2 Jeweled Skull followed our team out of the marshaling area into our red home zone. The shrill not-quite-cheering crescendoed and then rose above itself again and again. It was more like an ecstatic whine than a roar, at least by the standards of twenty-first-century sports fans. The sound sloshed from side to side, rising in one ear and falling in the other, following the lead of our two houses' mockers as they taunted each other across the no-man's-land at the center of the court.

All of us Harpy Ball Brethren, like the Ocelots' team and most of the other Maya ball societies, wore elaborate animal-themed helmets that totally covered our faces. Like with Mexican wrestlers in the twenty-first century, the designs were all in the same style, but each player's was unique and presumably intimidating. Anyway, they were as good as masks. And my tattoos and scars had been altered right after my arrival—well, "arrival"—here in Olde Mayaland. So I wasn't likely to get recognized. Just once, as they introduced me under my alias—"10 Red Skink Lizard"—I broke form and turned to look back at the council house. Harpies and Harpy partisans were crawling over every surface. Some adolescent bloods had climbed up the spirit poles to get a better view, which was considered idiotically disrespectful, although at least they were being careful not to cover the effigies' eyes. I studied the Harpies. They'd brought in an armory-worth of taken-down hand weapons. But it wasn't a hot day, and like everyone else they'd worn layers of feather cloaks—which would get thrown down to their favorite big scorers—and you couldn't tell. Despite all the tension, the Ocelots had let us into their precinct without searching us. It just wasn't done. That is, no one ever brought anything but nonfunctioning ceremonial arms into the ball courts. It wasn't like the Old West around here, with people wearing guns around town, if even the Old West was ever really like that, which I kind of doubt. And it wasn't like flying in the U.S. in the twenty-first century, dealing with brownshirts from the TSA. Anyway if the Ocelots got the drop on us and found the weapons, it would be more than enough justification for liquidating the entire house. I snapped my head back around, facing west, toward the ball court and the beyond it the high, steep-sloped emerald wedge of the Ocelots' mul.

From overhead the ball court would have looked like a huge capital *I*, with east at the top, and with two symmetrical banks on either side of the vertical bar. The top of each bank was a flat platform, or reviewing stand, where the highest-ranked spectators stood. Each bank had a sloping apron that descended to the level channel of the playing field at a forty-two-degree angle, so the structures were like truncated and elongated pyramids with their flat tops about five vertical Ixian arms—twelve feet—above the playing surface. The two bars of the *I* were marked by low boundary walls but open to the ground level, so that the VIPs could get to us. Beyond these end zones crowds of less important spectators could watch from the grounds surrounding the court and from two main vantage points: On the east, the wide swell of steps leading up to the long façade of the council house, and on the west, from the scarlet-and-emerald dawnward stairs of the Ocelots' mul, although the eighth level and the temple above it—where I'd first found myself in Chacal's mind—were empty. Also there had been tiers of extra wooden stands built for this one occasion, fed by a whole network of steps and catwalks behind the official platforms. Greathouse bloods' hipball games had always been restricted events and the courts weren't designed for the public. There were no seats, since there wasn't any point having them. People would just jump up from excitement anyway, the way no one ever really sits down at rock concerts. Even 9 Fanged Hummingbird stood up for hundred-scores of beats in the 105°F+ heat to watch a game. The playing trench between the platforms was brightly painted, divided into the four directional quadrants, with a long line east to west down the center of the trench and a short north to south line bisecting it at the center of the court, so that each color area was about the shape of a capital *L,* with a quarter-circular bite out of the top left corner where it intersected with the jade-green circle of the central face-off zone. The circle was about a half-rope-length in diameter, say, eleven feet, with an eight-fingers-wide round greenstone block inlaid in its center. There were also two other stone markers set into the playing surface, one at each point where the top of the lower bar of the *L* intersected with the east-west middle line. The actual goals were three pairs of pegs jutting out from the vertical risers at the top of the sloping banks. They faced each other across the trench, one pair at the center and a pair on each end, in line with the markers. Only the central pair of targets was really important. Each was roughly a ten-inch cube. But really you don't need to know any of that to understand what was going on in the game. You get a notion of it if you think of it as body soccer with a bowling ball.

The Ocelots' goal was carved as a defleshed sky-cat and stuck with emerald-green macaw down, just for this event. The Harpies' goal was carved as an earthtoad and, more cheaply, painted Harpy red. I felt all fat and stiff and Megazoid in the padding, like a penis swollen with Viagra. The area beyond the court boundary—which I guess you could call the sidelines—was crowded with VIP punters and a few high-caste bookies, looking us over as though we were racehorses in the paddock. Our team started to strut around the end zone in roughly counterclockwise paths, sawing the air with our hand guards. Our wood-and-leather yokes—big horseshoe-shaped protective belts—bounced off each other like old-time bumper cars. The players who'd stayed here kept looking at me. They, but only they, all knew who I was, and supposedly they'd been briefed about what to do. But they were still freaked out that I was alive and with them. I was still playing as "Red Skink Lizard," presumably an obscure relief player. My disguise, or new identity, was still holding up. It might not last once I started playing, though. Not if I used any of the old signature moves. I stopped pacing and tucked my head down under my helmet, like I was praying. 2JS came up next to me. He didn't turn his ornament-swollen head, but he spoke to me in our house language and so low that no one could hear us over the shouting.

"And am I going to lose another son?" he asked. He was referring to five foster sons and two biological ones, including the one he'd sacrificed in my place, who had already died on him. And he was talking about the hipball game, not the battle we were anticipating afterward. Full matches at these stakes were pretty dangerous. I—or rather Chacal—had played twenty-eight full great-hipball games, four of them with nearly identical rules and timing. But that was an exceptional record, and people had been killed around me in almost every match I'd played. The general feeling was that an athlete's career was so short anyway that you might as well die on the court. And one effect was that ballplayers started playing more recklessly as they get older. Emerald Immanent and a couple of the other Ocelot players were just at that age when you expect them to give it absolutely all they had, which could mean taking you with them.

I said the closest thing to "I'll be careful."

2 Jeweled Skull said that if I survived the ball game he wanted me to get off the court and into the middle of a special squad of Harpy bloods led by 7 Wind, who was another of his sons. They had instructions to get me the hell out of there, off the Ocelots' temple promontory and out to the Harpies' mountain *milpas* in the east. Then, even if 2 Jeweled Skull was killed or captured, I'd still have at least a chance of getting back someday and setting up my special tomb.

I said I thanked my father but that I didn't want to desert him.

He said playing under a new name—that is, not for my own prestige—was enough.

I said I was worried that we'd be cut off from the mainland. Actually, I was trying to get him to open up about what he was going to do. If anything. He said he had sixty score nonbloods from dependent families—what you could call the bulk of the Harpy infantry—waiting outside the eastern gate. They hadn't been told anything beforehand, though, and they were just now being briefed on what it was their Father of the East, that is, 2 Jeweled Skull, needed from them. Also they weren't allowed to touch spears, blowguns, or saws, and could only fight with clubs. Still, they had barges ready and were going to lash them together and lay planks over them, and try to get across the canal from the Harpy Quarter to the council house, bypassing the permanent bridge, which of course the Ocelots were guarding. After that, the Harpy clubmen were going to try to take control of the council house and give us at least one relatively secure base on the peninsula.

2JS also said a messenger had come from Koh's followers saying they were only six-hundred-score beats away. But their scouts had run into Ocelot patrols, and since we didn't want to tip them off, the Rattlers were going to hold back until they got the word the hipball game had started.

So maybe we'd be all right.

"Well, okay, dude, great, let's go," I said in English. "Well, sheesh, this is a long way from the United States Chess Federation Interzonal at the Springfield, Massachusetts, Hyatt Regency Resort Hotel and Convention Center, isn't it?

2 Jeweled almost smiled. It was enough to give me a little shiver. Maybe it was like Koh had said back under the Tree of Mirror Leaves, that he'd gotten a bigger dose of me than I'd thought. I'd been pretty sure that he just had bits and pieces, random beads that he couldn't string together into a coherent Jedditude. But being in on stupid little private jokes took a pretty advanced level of understanding someone. Maybe I had a way of growing on you.

"We'll just Win Through Despondency," I said, "Harnessing the Power of Self-Loathing." It wasn't a gem, but he smiled and then chuckled, and then I did, and for a beat we couldn't stop laughing, it was like, we're like twins, we grew up together, we're homies, we're just chillin' out—

A Harpy messenger came up and signed that the Ocelots were ready. 2JS waved him away. Our talk was over. He blessed the team with his cigar and left to take his place on the platform. I looked after him for a beat as he walked west. I hadn't realized how lonely I'd been feeling without him to talk to about stuff. He was the only one around who actually understood.

I looked up and peeked around. The muls were all dressed for the occasion, draped in gigantic feather-embroidered tapestry mantles that had last been unfolded at the sheaving of the fifth katun before this one, eighty solar years ago. They were crowned with huge headdresses of radiating tree trunks tufted with ribbons to imitate giant feathers, and trailing necklaces of huge feather-flowers in the air. Uay-animal floats slid deliberately through the walkways, levitating up and down steps and spinning in the squares. The lacework superstructure above the city was filled with kites and papered torch-cages like big multiple lanterns. Effigies of the ahaus *and* bacabs *and* various sun-adders stood in the upper steps of the mulob, holding the lords' places while their flesh bodies were down watching the ball game. I tucked my head down again.

Damn, I thought. There'd been so many things I wanted to ask 2JS. How was he dealing with the debris of myself inside him? Was he more me or less me than he'd been eighty-five days before? Or was I already so different now from the Jed that entered him that it didn't matter? On top of everything I was feeling, maybe not teary, but a little misty.

Out in the center court the hazing contest had segued into the actual challenge to the match. I could hear the Ocelot negotiator offering to double the purse and the Harpy negotiator accepting. Better not whiff out on this one, I thought. Actually, I hadn't been stellar in our last practice on the road. But maybe with an impossible challenge, Chacal's ballplaying genius would come through. Right?

I smelled something. It was Koh's cinnamon-in-reverse perfume. I broke protocol and looked up.

(32)

Koh and her eight-person escort had gotten into the east zocalo and were pushing toward the end zone. A gang of high-ranked Ixian Rattler converts followed alongside, throwing passionflowers and blue-curl blossoms on the path in front of her and waving petition bundles tied with big bright knots. I signaled to Hun Xoc, who caught the eyes of the rest of the team, and as I drifted over to the boundary line as casually as I could they pressed in behind me. She came up as if she were just scoping out the players. I didn't look at her. Her escorts held up their traveling screens around her, as though they were shielding her from the sun, but actually to keep the Ocelots from seeing her talk to me. It wasn't unheard-of for a major sponsor to talk with the players before a ball game, although it must have been the first time in a while that the sponsor had been female. I kneeled down on the court surface and she did the same, so that we were all alone in the sweaty jungle of legs.

What if they don't get here as fast as we think? Koh asked without a preamble, in her own sign language.

I said I didn't know.

"This is my burden," she signed, meaning her fault. She seemed pretty upset under her poker face. I didn't know what to say, either, I felt bad about having gotten her into this and angry that she wasn't getting us out of it like she'd said. It was like "Sorry, it's my fault," "No, it's *my* fault."

She asked something else.

I said I couldn't understand. She leaned her head toward me, over the boundary line. They're making me sit on the Ocelot side, she said out loud, in one of the code-languages she'd taught me, one we hadn't used before. It wasn't a whole separate language, it was more like Carney or Ubby-Bubby, where you inserted nonsense syllables, but it wasn't something anybody else would be able to figure out right away.

What do you mean? I asked, not believing I'd heard her right.

As she explained it, this guy named "8 Smoking Peeper," who was the head of Star-Rattler's cult in Ix—the one Koh's messengers hadn't been able to reach—was standing in a swirl of emerald on the Ocelot side, of the north lateral platform of the court, and he'd asked for Koh and her attendants to come and stand at his right hand. The Ocelots had co-opted him. And even though Star-Rattler didn't have much of a cult here he was her primary relative, and it was something she couldn't say no to without starting a fight. She had to be gracious about being chaperoned. It was a big deal for a woman to be allowed to watch the match at all.

It was a teeth-gnashingly clever move. Even besides almost certainly setting her up to be captured. One special feature of pitzom as it was played here in the lowlands was spectator participation: each person on each of the two main platforms—the Harpies standing above their goal-peg on the south and the Ocelots above theirs on the north—was allowed a short stick like a miniature hurley called a hatchet or *baat,* another onomatopoeic word close to the English equivalent. Oddly to the twenty-first-century way of thinking, interference was allowed. Whenever a ball bounced up close to the favored spectators, they would lean precariously down over the banks, stretching out their *baatob,* trying to deflect the ball away from their goal or, if it lobbed high enough, to swipe it toward a member of their own team. Since the longest-armed supporters could barely get their short *baatob* down within an arm length of the goal, the bats connected only when the ball lobbed too high, and the spectator-participants ever really influenced the ball game on only a couple of shots. So it worked the supporters into a frenzy without much affecting the score.

But the serious deal was everyone who stood on one of the platforms was officially in the ball game, on that side's team, just like the ahau in the center, playing through his proxies below. So the Ocelots were forcing Koh to "play" on the Ocelot side, even if no one in her group even touched a ball.

Dammit. Maybe the Ocelots weren't so dumb as we thought. I wondered how much they guessed about 2JS's part in the end of Teotihuacán. I can't believe nobody had thought of this, I thought. No, believe it. Incompetence is forever. She was as good as captured.

Say you have a commitment to stay here, I said.

That's not a good idea, she said, they'd take it as a huge insult and start the fight now.

She was right.

This isn't good, I said, they'll capture you in a hummingbird heartbeat.

I know, she said. She said maybe they wouldn't get to torturing her right away. If the battle goes all right you can surround the Ocelot House and trade me out.

Right, I said, but we both knew it was too much to count on. There would be too many screw-ups, it was just the way things are. Do you still have the earthstar blood? I asked. The earthstar compound.

She said yes.

I tried to remember what I knew of the layout of the Ocelot district. We weren't far from the most-holy *ch'en,* that is, in Spanish, *cenote,* a giant half-sunken cistern. In this case it was the main source of drinking water for the south bank of Ix, and it had been a cornerstone of the Ocelots' power since before the third sun, an ever-gushing font of calc-free H_20, like Elisha's Spring at Jericho.

Well, maybe I could actually do it. We'd have a ready-made diversion, that was for sure. And down on the court we wouldn't be surrounded by Ocelot guards like the bloods in the stands.

Hmm. I really might be able to get there. Just out the west end of the court, into the popol na's zocalo, that is, the main plaza, into one of the Ocelot compound's "women's doors"—which ought to slow down any pursuers a bit—and then onto the roof and up one of the aqueducts straight to Grandmother's House. No threat, no sweat.

I'll run for the Great Cistern, I said. If it looks at all possible. Maybe that'll give you some extra time even if they get ahead in the battle.

She thought about it for what seemed like about sixty-eight beats.

I'll try to feed Lord Earthstar, she said. She meant she ought to do an offering to get him to release the full power of his dried blood. I gestured like, okay, whatever. I was being pretty tough, I have to admit, but then I ruined the effect by telling her not to let any of her people know we were going for the Great Cistern. It was kind of an insult to tell her that, because it was like saying her bloods might crack under torture, but she didn't seem to notice.

She whispered to Coati.

Don't let them give you any water in the basket, I said. By *basket* I meant the place in the Ocelot house where they kept high-level captives under suicide watch. Like the one 2 Jeweled Skull had kept me in.

I don't drink water anyway, Koh said. It was kind of a drought-season joke, like "Lips that touch water shall never touch mine."

Coati came back and handed Koh a red-and-white-wrapped *uah'ach,* a sort of ceremonial nine-layered tortilla bread women were supposed to give to players before the ball game. Koh messed around with it for a second behind her screens, came forward, and presented it to me over the wall of the pen. I gestured "Accepted," tore open the dyed corn-husk wrapping, and took a bite. It wasn't very good.

Koh spoke to Coati again in the same language. Get to 2 Jeweled Skull, she said, or if you can't get to him, get to Hun Xoc. She told him to let them know what's going on with the earthstar compound. Maybe they could get back to Harpy House and hold out for a day or so. Make sure they keep it quiet as long as possible, though, she said.

She turned back to me. *"Xka' nan'ech lo'mob kutz,"* she said. "Smoke faster than the flies can bite." It was sort of a casual jokey leave-taking salutation, like "Be good." She left. The commotion behind her guards picked up, the Ixian Rattler's Children shouting questions at her in this sort of respectful howl, asking for predictions on the score like she was a combination of the Dalai Lama and Nick the Greek, which, in fact, she basically was. I thought she was going to ignore it, but all of a sudden she turned inside her semitransparent screens and spoke through Coati:

> *"Now, 10 K'atun, 1 Deer, 11 Thought,"* he/she said,
> *"Before the thirteenth ball rolls up the green,*
> *Look out for ingrown blue hair knots in your walls."*

(33)

There was a trough between the waves of shouting and then a higher crest as the people started reacting to it and asking what she meant. I didn't get what the *carajo* she was talking about either. It was like, ease up on the Delphic Sybil trip, babe.

I watched her turn and lead her escort back down the walkway, around the east end zone of the court, and up a side ramp onto the south platform, through hundreds of hostile-looking Ocelot princes in jaguar skins and emerald-green feather spikes, all of them probably waiting for the signal to grab her and rip her into bite-sized morsels. They saluted her and she had to salute back like we were totally honored to be with them. Ocelot guards moved her forward toward the lip of the court, to where the Ixian Rattler-adder was standing at the coveted second rank. Lady Koh and the Rattler Adder greeted each other in public sign language. I pictured little thought-balloons bubbling out of each of their heads saying *I'm going to kill you.*

She was totally isolated up there. If a fight started, our bloods would have to roll down into the playing trench, claw their way up the slick bank to the opposite platform, and try to grab Koh before the Ocelots behind her pulled her backward. They'd never make it.

Nobody seemed to be watching me. I bent down like I was messing with my sandal, tore open the nine-layered tortilla with my teeth, and pulled out something I recognized, a whitish, double-bladdered bag. The earthstar compound.

I dusted some cornstarch off the bag and handed it behind me to Armadillo Shit. I pointed to my hip padding and he reached in through the quilted layers, positioned the bag in the hollow on the left side of my groin, and tied it down with slack ends of weasel gut from my yoke harness. I stood up and Armadillo Shit whisked some bits of offering-confetti and torn-up betting contracts and morning-glory blossoms and dyed feathers and crap out of my helmet.

A long *"Eeeee,"* a sort of performatively awed gasp, spread through the stands and away into the city. The Ocelots' hazing team had just brought out a captive harpy eagle, and some of the Harpies in the stands tried to get down to the court to rescue it and had to be held back. Meanwhile Harpies' mockers had brought out a baby ocelot, and from what I could hear they were starting to yank it around on its leash and poking at it with skewers. I'd say the audience went bananas except that's not a menacing enough fruit. Torturing specimens of each other's totems was basically a declaration of war. This thing wasn't ending with the last goal.

DOOOONG.

It was a note like a chord of D, C, and F sharp way down on the black keys at the left end of an old Boesendorfer, and it came from a slit-gong made from a cedar tree the size of the body of a 707. Hun Xoc walked past me, his waist yokes swinging in opposition to his steps, forward into the playing trench, and took his marker. Only three players from each side were allowed on the court at one time, but including the coaches there were six people on each team. Everyone on our team had a name with the word *red* in it, so our coach "Teentsy Bear" was really named 3 Red Pine, and Hun Xoc's full name was 1 Red Shark. Red Beak was going to be our other starting striker, or forward, and then 5 Red Wedge—we called him 5-5—would be our starting "zonekeeper," which was like a goalie. Red Cord and I were going to be on the bench at first and then substitute in when they needed us.

On the Ocelot side, Emerald Feral Dog—the coach—was going to start Emerald Immanent—a giant, who must have been at least five six—and Emerald Howler—the one we called "Fat Monkey-Bitch"—as strikers. Their starting zonekeeper was going to be Emerald Snapper—"Fatter Monkey-Bitch"—and Emerald Screecher and Emerald Jog were the bench. Emerald Immanent was making not-quite obscene gestures up at the Harpy stands.

I'm going to pop you, you fat fuck, I thought. Up in the stands the drivers were chasing away a vendor hung with gourds of hot honeyed and salted pine-tea and sweet cacao. A couple of independent bookies hopped acrobatically through the stands taking last-minute side bets on individual players. I checked my personal inventory, the same little pre-ball-game ritual I always did. I felt the weasel-gut cords holding my knee- and elbow-padding. I untied my main torso harness, loosened it slightly, and retied it. If it was too tight it could cut you. An *insei* came by with a charger full of rosin and ashes and I dipped my hands in it and spread it over my arms while he rosined my feet. From here I could see most of the Ocelots' emerald mul past their end zone, and beyond that a bit of the eastward curve to the mainland, and above that and to the right a glimpse of the wall-and-platform complex that surrounded the Ocelots' sacred Great Cistern.

Maybe it really could be done, I thought. Stranger things had happened. It'd be totally unexpected. Surprise. Surprise, like that Ana Vergara said. Surprise is your copilot—

I noticed everything had gone completely silent.

9 Fanged Hummingbird's music started, a single giant flute, getting nearer and nearer. The crowd in the Ocelot stands parted and a tetrahedral box floated into the center of the stands on the shoulders of dwarf bearers. The box was covered with iridescent emerald-green hummingbird feathers, like something that had dropped from a Platonic heaven onto the shoulders of 9FH's two attendants. He could see clearly through the screen, but to us on the sunlit side it looked as opaque as enameled metal. As they set the box on the mat-throne at the highest riser the shrill cheer-chord rose again, each side repeating its chorus over and over, off-rhythm with the other side, trying to drown them out: the Harpies chanting, "*Ch' uchu' b'aj, jab k'eseic k'uul, ch' uchu' b'aj, jab k'eseic k'uul,*" *We shine up high, we tear off your jaws, we shine up high, we tear off your jaws, we shine up high, we tear off your jaws,* and the Ocelots chanting, *Chupa'yal bak, chuyu'baj tox, We flash bright-dark, we chew on your hearts.* Down on the court we saluted him:

"You far over us,
Lord of the Razor,

You far over us,
Lord of the Javelin,
You far over us,
Closest to One Hurricane,
You far over us,
Dearest to Iztam Na,
You far over us,
Ruby-browed Captor of Eleven Wind of Motul,
You far over us,
Sun-eyed Captor of Sideways Coatimundi of Caracol,
You far over us,
Avenger of the capture of Sixteen Ocelot,
You far over us,
Retriever of the skull of Four Ocelot,
You far over us,
Captor of eighteen times four hundred bloods and sixty-one bloods,
You far over us,
Subjugator of twenty times twenty cities,
You far over us,
Lord of the Twice Four Hundred Cities,
You far over us,
Overlord of four hundred times four hundred towns,
You far over us,
Nine-Fold King of Sacrifices,
You far over us,
You out of range of our offerings,
You far over us,
You over the four hundred times four hundred times four hundred thralls under us,
You far over us,
You far over all those over us,
You far over us,
Earthquake-born, whose real name no one can guess,
You far over us,

Whose manifest name is 9 Fanged Hummingbird,

Deign you to look down over us,

Grant us your clear sight extending far, far over us, protecting us,

You, far over us,

Overlord,

9 Fanged Hummingbird."

Then, as slowly as sufi dervishes, we spun around and around to salute the four directions, the two competing ahauob, the five great houses of Ix, all these visiting indignitaries, Lady Koh, the lords of the dawns and the lords of the dusks, and other notable guests from as far away as what's now the southern shore of Lake Nicaragua. As Hun Xoc used to say, we practically saluted our own asses.

There was a blast from a tree-horn. The temple precinct sank into silence like debris settling after an explosion. The cantor launched into his megaphoned spiel,

"Now twenty, fifty-two, two-hundred sixty," running through the litany of great exploits his generation of the greathouses of Ix had endured on this court, and encouraging the young players of today to try to match the skill and stony resolve of the players of old even though they'd be bound to fail and everything, on and on. I was only smoggily aware of it. The referees entered in their long feather robes, one from each corner of the court, censing the trench with their big twisted cigars. Their decisions were final and could be capricious, but they were all over seventy years old, without children, and serious about the hipball game as a sacrament. And they were all from a single presumably nonaffiliated monastic clan, and it would be almost but not quite unheard of for them to slant the calls toward one side, since their order's survival had traditionally been dependent on its impartiality. Still, a corrupted individual could always have been planted a long time ago—

The cantor had finished his recitation. While you could still hear the outlying criers had finished repeating it the Master of Hipball—or *Magister Ludi* as we *Glasperlenspiel* fans might translate his title—announced the stakes.

"Four hundred score dependents each," he said.

The main bet was always supposed to be *chunchumuk*, even money, but it was bartered out in a complicated and, I think, kind of artificial way. While he talked, punters and bookies in the audience were already holding up fingers asking for nine-to-two odds against the Harpies, which even I thought was on the long side. I remembered I'd forgotten to get my own bet in and then decided it wasn't important. The Magister Ludi was about to finish when 2 Jeweled Skull's herald's drum sounded. The chanter let the herald take the floor.

The herald said that the Harpies asked to raise the stakes by wagering One Harpy. He meant our first mul and the temple—including the support or family membership or loyalty or service or whatever you'd call it—of One Harpy himself, the founder who'd brought such wealth to our clan over the last nine hundred and fifty-eight solar years. Basically everything we had, including our name.

The side betting stopped. There were a few murmurs in the silence. A crow cawed an alarm far off to the east. Bad sign.

The Ocelots took a few score beats to respond. When they did, their crier said they'd see the bet, but he didn't stake the Ocelots' mul and founder. Instead he put up what you could roughly call the equivalent, in loyalty, real estate, hunting and fishing rights, salt works, and slaves. It took forever to list everything, but it didn't sound fair to me. Still, we accepted it.

There were another eighty beats of expectant silence. I couldn't see 2 Jeweled Skull but he was probably conferring with his in-house bookies. Finally, he accepted.

The side odds went to seven to four and there was a whole new spate of what they called "hero bets," durations and spreads on individual players. I figured that about half of the city's entire year's economy was going to redistribute based on this one match.

Two pairs of untouchables entered the trench. Each lifted a round-bottomed cylindrical jar of powdered pigment on long tongs and balanced it on the top head-plate of each of the square target pegs.

There were some very complicated rules to hipball, kind of like international ice hockey rules, with a lot of checks and balances in the scoring, but basically a hit on the other side's target peg was worth a point, and a ball that came up over the top of the peg and either broke the pot or knocked pigment out of the pot scored four points. There weren't any ring goals on this court, or for that matter on any other that I ever saw in the old days, although they eventually became famous because of the much later court at Chichen Itza, which of course became a tourist attraction in the twentieth century. Which supposedly they gave James Naismith the idea for basketball. Sometimes players practiced by knocking the ball through a big wooden hoop that they rolled on the ground. But using rings in the ball game itself must have started later. Anyway, the first side to score nineteen points won. But—weirdly, but maybe not coincidentally, almost like in modern Ping-Pong or tennis—you had to win by three points. And just like in those games you could go back to "deuce" indefinitely. If you faulted the ball over your own rear goal line, a point went to the other side. You didn't switch sides. Each team had two substitute players, but that was it, and if more players got knocked out of the ball game it came down to last-man-standing.

DOOOONG.

A brace of bearers brought in the doeskin-wrapped ball Hun Xoc had brought back from 31 Courts, holding the too-potent bundle with wooden hands, and tied it to the service cord. An umpire inspected the knot, signaled, and the ball was hoisted up, hanging above the central marker stone.

"Now, One, Two, Four, Five, Seven, Nine, Thirteen," the Magister Ludi chanted, switching from the second-person plural imperative to the apostrophic tense you used only when speaking to gods,

"Now Twenty, Fifty-Two, Two Hundred Sixty,
O Night, O Wind, O Day, O Rain, O Zero,
Now, guests, inspect 2 Creeper's blood-boiled head."

2 Creeper had been the greatest Ixian ballplayer in living memory, but he'd sacrificed himself thirty-nine solar years ago after an ankle sprain. The Ball had been wound out of white latex around 2 Creeper's cranium as a hollow center—to increase the bounce—and then baked black and studded with painted thorns, like little nails. Finally the ball had been purified in two

kinds of blood and then washed in original water boiled over the offering fires of both houses' grandfathers-nests. It was bound on a little below its equator by thirteen turns of a multicolor-stranded rope, and as the last of the ribbons dropped off, the service cord began to unwind. I smelled that old fight-or-flight charge building up in the players around me, joints quivering ever so slightly, weight shifting, glands shooting that rich *watch out* cortisol mixture into spinal cords no matter what kind of kamikaze ethic their upper brains had been washed in.

"Li'skuba hun," the chanter called. "Ready for Ball One."

The sunlight clicked behind the mul, but guava light reflected into the court off the eastern roof-combs like they were vertical lakes. They wouldn't set torches for over thirty-score beats. The bookies called last bets and then hushed up. The right strikers tensed their muscles for their springs, front feet ready to disengage from their lines at the sound of the ball striking the central marker. There were four beats of global motionlessness as the spotter watched the dying sun.

There were thirty-nine beats of silence.

He held up his hand, and, delicately, brought it down in a cutting motion.

There was a stirring and an intake of breath in the crowd. The Magister cut the end of a taut cord attached to the railing of his chair. The end of the cord seemed to dart away from him like a blue racer, and it whistled down to the court and up through three different loops to the ball-sac and the ribbons around the ball uncoiled and fell to the side, exposing the dark sphere. In proportion to our body size it was about as big as a basketball. Knocking it around with your bare flesh was like playing hackysack with a cannonball, and if you got off balance the ball could maim or kill you.

The untouchables scurried out of the court. The referees stepped behind the end-zone line. The rope unraveled faster and faster and just as the ball began to free itself the Magister Ludi called out "PIIITTZOOOHHM PAAYY-EEEE*EEEEEEEEEEEEE!!!*," which I guess the closest thing to in English would be **"PLLL—***AAAAAAAAAAAAAAY BALL!!!!!*

(34)

The knot unraveled, but the ball seemed not to fall but to hover for more than a moment and then to sink reluctantly into the thick air, slowly accelerating down into the round central marker, building up to real speed in the last arm of its fall, and then there was a hollow *CHUHN!!!*, the sound marking the exact demarcation between yesterday and today for all Ixian historical time.

"Chun," the cantor called almost simultaneously with the sound. In ball language *chun* was the word for base or "trunk" or "root," since the markers were sections of branches of the tree path to Xibalba. So the cantor's play-by-play was kind of like Yoruba talking pressure-drums, it both imitated the sounds of the ball game and gave out names and moves and positions, and the whole rap radiated out from the court in a widening circle. Listening to the city was like hearing hundreds of big antique radios picking up a broadcast through some thick medium that slowed it down to much less than the speed of sound.

Before you could see the black sphere rise off the marker the right-hand strikers had already closed in, Hun Xoc from our side and Emerald Immanent from the west. The ball drooped down again into their double blur and you heard flesh slapping on flesh and then the crisp hollow sound of the ball on a hollow yoke. The head cantor shouted, *"Bok!,"* the ball word for "yoke," or "bone" or "horn." The word was so close to the actual sound that it seemed like one of the echoes off the sloping banks, as the batteries of criers relayed the call out into the suburbs and hamlets and out the roads far through the hinterlands. Village adders memorized it at the first hearing. Troupes of hipball-adders interpreted it based on where the hit came from, by whom, on what beat, and a hundred other considerations, and the human reverberations rippled through signal- and runner-relays out through IX and Ix's four hundred towns and beyond, out to the corners of the four quarters and up and down to the buds and roots of the Big Tree, the Tree of Four Hundred Times Four Hundred Branches. But of course here the ball-time was moving on ahead, and before the echo had gotten to the second relay circle, beyond the court district, the ball had angled up and hit the Harpies' goal peg, and there was a wide liquid clap on the huge clay-cylinder scoring drum. The cantor shouted, "*T'un!*," which imitated the sound of the ball on the hollow peg but was also the word for "point."

The referees signed that it was legal. A big whooshing spitty whistley hiss rose out of the Ocelots and their partisans, the equivalent of applause, all breaking against a tide of stamping feet on the Harpy side, the more satisfying Maya equivalent of boos.

> "*T'un Bolom, kam-chen Bolomob,*" the first chanter sang, that is,
> "*Goal, Ocelot, one–zero, Ocelots.*"

The circles criers repeated the call, "*T'un Bolom, kam-chen Bolomob.*"

At the goal the players retreated behind their end-zone lines. A pair of untouchables ran in and caught the ball together with their gloved hands. One of them stood on the central marker, holding the ball, while the other purified it with a dusting of blood ashes out of a pouch. If the invisibles were like stagehands, the untouchables were a bit more like ballboys. But since they touched the court surface and the blood and the dead and most of all the ball, they were irrevocably polluted.

"*Li'skuba ka.*" Ready for Ball Two. I was getting that racehorse-at-the-gate feeling that I'd burst if I didn't get out on the court. The first invisible faced west and threw the ball underhanded up into the air, expertly dropping it down on the Ocelots' emerald-green rear marker.

"Chun," the chanter called again. Emerald Immanent got the tip again and yoke-bounced the ball upward, controlling it—*"Bok"*—and passed it gently off his shoulder arm.

"P'uchik," the chanter called. The word both meant a hit on the body and imitated the sound of a ball hitting flesh and then snap-disengaging from oiled skin. Emerald Howler, the other Ocelot striker, caught the pass on the side of his yoke, *"bok,"* and knocked it ahead and right, angling it off the sloped masonry wall like in old-fashioned court tennis.

"Pak," the cantor called, imitating the crisp solid sound. It was also the word for "wall." Emerald Immanent had already run downcourt and positioned himself under the dropping ball for a shot at the target. The crowd noise fell to near silence and all you could hear was the warbling play-by-play chants and the players' grunts and the squeaks and cracks of their sandals. It wasn't that spectators weren't allowed to talk, but that the game absorbed your total attention, even if you couldn't see it happening. The crowd was so fascinated they actually shut up and let the intensity build until it was released in the paroxysm of applause at the end of a tense play, or a goal, or a death.

5-5 came up fast and blocked Emerald Immanent's shot, but Immanent shifted, faded back, shoulder-passed back off the wall to Emerald Howler—*"P'uchik pak"*—who yoked it up perfectly up into the underside of the Harpy goal: *"Bok . . . t'un!"*

> *"T'un Bolom,"* the score-adder called, *"wasak-chen Bolomob."*
> *"Goal, Ocelot, two–zero, Ocelots."*

Whistling blasted out of the crowd. It was two hundred beats later before the players settled into their positions and the head invisible served out the third ball. Emerald Immanent got it again and tried the same run-and-feint and back-pass to Emerald Howler, but this time Hun Xoc was there and he intercepted it, pulling the ball out of the air with his wrist-guard and sending it south to Red Beak. It was a signature move of the Harpy School. In most courts around here hipball was more like soccer, because you couldn't touch the ball with your feet or your hands. But Ixian rules were a bit different, and we each wore a lizard-skin-wrapped wooden extension on the underside of our wrists, extending up into the palms, and you could bat or deflect the ball with those. Even so, the ball was so heavy you couldn't get much force on it with your arms. And of course you weren't allowed to catch it, not that you'd want to. Really, it was too heavy to launch seriously with anything but the braced weight of most of your body, and if it had any major momentum behind it you'd have to add some of your own as well. In your big yoke, which came nearly to the nipple level, and the roll of cotton padding peeking up over it, you felt gravity siphoning up through you, and as you received and launched the ball it felt like you were negotiating between a good-sized satellite and the pulling power of the earth. Sometimes you'd have to use your shoulder or calf or even upper arm, but you wouldn't want to and no matter how hard you were you flinched against the weight. So the idea was to shoot with your hip-yoke whenever possible—which let you get your full weight behind the impact—and then to use your calf, shoulder, thigh, upper arm, and finally the palm guard, in that order of preference. Using your head would be a bad idea.

Red Beak kneed the ball south, low into the red expanse of the Harpy wall. Hun Xoc dove after it falling on his knees, blocking its rebound with the top angle of his ornate yoke. The ball settled down into the groove, reverberating between the wall and his yoke like a pinball caught between electric bumpers, the criers imitating the accelerating beat, "*pak, bok, pak, bok, pak-bok, pak-bok, pak-bok pak-bok pak-bok pakbok pakbok pakbok-pakbok pakbokpakbokpakbokpakbok,*" into a blur of sound. Hipball was a dignified game, a stolid ritual, an act of worship. But it was also a much faster game even than basketball, at least as fast as jai-alai or Ping-Pong.

Emerald Immanent recovered but Red Beak backed away from him into the Harpies' end zone. The main territorial rule was that neither team was allowed into the other's end zone, which in our case was the left half of the east half of the court, a red area shaped like a backward *L*. So in this match that meant the Ocelots couldn't step on red and the Harpy clan couldn't step on emerald. Each side's blocker couldn't leave the zone but the strikers could go anywhere but the enemy's home quadrant. You couldn't keep the ball in your zone for more than four bank- or body-bounces, though, and if the ball hit the level floor on your half of the court, it was out and you had to turn it over to the other team, but this hardly ever happened. The ball was too bouncy and the players were too good. Any one of these people could have body-juggled a cinder block and kept it in the air for scores of scores of scores of beats.

Red Beak waited for Hun Xoc to get between him and Emerald Immanent, and then took a slow run up toward the peg, working the ball with short flesh-dribbles onto the north wall. He shot and missed. Emerald Snapper got the ball and passed to Emerald Howler. Howler shot and missed and Hun Xoc got the ball. The deal was that it was nearly impossible to shoot for a goal from the enemy's side of the center line, although "backward goals" and even error goals off the opposing team did happen. And since there was only one really good spot on your side to shoot for the opposing goal, the ball tended to follow a fairly set course. You'd gain possession, get the ball into position on your right side, and then charge up along the right bank, shooting ahead and up to the right at the other team's peg. If you missed the peg, the opposing team would almost always gain possession. Then they'd do the same thing, they'd set up, make their own run and shoot for your goal, on your left side, and then you'd get the ball back and repeat the process. So even though there wasn't a net, the design of the court itself created a back-and-forth motion and a general counterclockwise draw, like the endless left turn on a racecourse. And the same centrifugal force tended to keep the two teams separate, although not enough to prevent a clash or two. Despite how dangerous it was, it wasn't really a contact sport, at least in theory.

Hun Xoc worked the ball up the north bank, "*bok, pak, bok, pak,*" and suddenly took a long shot, like a three-pointer, sending the big black planet nearly into the Ocelot spectators' baatob, and even though the ball seemed to miss the goal, it grazed the fragile jar of dyed marble powder. The jar wobbled and fell, trailing emerald-green plumes.

"*Waak'al, waak'al,*" the chanter shouted. The word meant "explode," that is, a great-goal. The Harpy partisans went wild with a special hiss-cheer you used on big points. It wasn't that stupid Mexican trilling thing, though, like they encourage you to do at tequila bars in the States. It was more like ten thousand panicked crows. The boot-stamping sloshed welcomely over to the Ocelots' side.

"Halach tun Kot, lahka tunob Kotob, wasak tunob Bolomob," the chanter called,

"Harpy Great-goal, 2 Ocelots, 4 Harpies."

Maybe we're okay, I thought. The invisibles scurried in to clean up and replace the jars. The Magister flashed his hand-mirror and the fourth serve fell. Red Beak got it and shot. Miss. Emerald Immanent trapped the ball, took two dribbles up the south wall, *"bok pak bok pak,"* and shot, *BOK.*

Miss. Too high. I would have made that. Goddamnit, lemme out there. The ball arced up over the stands and a Harpy spectator, as per custom, deflected it back down—

But something was wrong, the guy in the Harpy stands should have passed the ball to us, but instead he'd deflected it the wrong way, back toward the Ocelots. Emerald Immanent leisurely repositioned himself, got the rebound, and shot again. He hit the peg.

"BOK T'UN WAAK'A!" "Great-goal! 6 Ocelots, 4 Harpies."

On the Harpy side the sort-of-boos coalesced into *"keechtikob, keechtikob, keechtikob,"* "spies, spies, spies." Whoever'd batted the ball in the wrong direction was getting pretty badly torn up. Even if he swore that it was a mistake there was no way they'd believe he hadn't been turned by the Ocelots.

Still, it wouldn't work twice.

On the next serve Hun Xoc got the tip but Emerald Immanent and Emerald Howler charged on him so fast he passed the ball back to 5-5. The pass overshot and 5-5 missed it. The ball hit the red bank and bounced over our zone down into the trench, about to go out. 5-5 leaned out to make a save and got the ball back in the air, but he was off-balance and fell onto the white, out of the Harpy Zone, which gave the Ocelots a point without a goal. The umpire signaled and the cantor started to call out the new score—

"7 Ocelots, 4—"

But before he'd finished he was cut off by the sound of oiled skin chalkboard-screeching on the clay-packed surface and then a bone-snap as Emerald Immanent's yoke collided with 5-5's upper body. Then, before I could see anything, both teams had bunched into a scrum over the two of them and the drivers were already pulling them apart. Emerald Immanent had made it look like a mistake, but of course he'd charged at 5-5 and checked him the instant 5-5 was out of the red zone.

Everyone pulled apart. 5-5 was sort of sliding along the red bank, leaving a dark stringy bileish trail. The percussionists had mimicked the sound of fighting and now they were using maracas and notched sticks like bear calls to imitate the sound of blood spraying out of an artery and splattering on the ground.

The hell of it was that touching an opposing player wasn't a foul unless it was a definite attack. And naturally the umpires didn't call this one. The offending player was supposed to go through all kinds of apologies or be ready to fight. Emerald Immanent was already running through his mea culpa in a sarcastic tone. 5-5 was trying to say something, too, but when he realized you couldn't understand what he was saying through his mouthful of bloody mush, he started signing that he wanted to stay in the ball game. Hun Xoc was walking him off the court at this point but 5-5 was resisting and just to humor him Teentsy Bear told Hun Xoc to let his brother go and back away. 5-5 took one half-step and then fell forward on his face, rolling over on his yoke like a canoe on pavement, with his lower right leg bent bassackward. On the other side of the court the Ocelots laughed and imitated the fall.

"7 Ocelots, 4 Harpies," the cantor said again.

The untouchables swept up with their round handleless brooms and sprinkled oil and pigment onto the surfaces. Two of our invisibles carried 5-5 off, back through our end zone to the offering table. His leg swung in a circular motion, like his knee was a ball-and-socket joint. Shit, I thought. He didn't look good.

Teentsy Bear calmed everyone down and sent in Red Cord as our new zonekeeper. The fifth serve came down fast and our side wasn't quite together. The Ocelots got an easy goal.

"8 Ocelots, 4 Harpies."

They changed balls for the next serve and each team had a little time to retreat behind the end zone and huddle. One of our ball surgeons came up and told us 5-5 was dying and 2 Jeweled Skull had given word that he was going to be considered the first sacrifice of the ball game.

We all looked at each other. Nobody broke their hard-ass face.

Damn.

Another misconception about the Mesoamerican hipball game is that the losing team got sacrificed. Or at least that wasn't usual. What actually happened was that different offerings followed the match on each side. In general the losing side would see its defeat as a sign that their gods weren't happy with them and they needed more gifts to the gods, so they'd sacrifice some people to them. The winning side might sacrifice a few of the people to their gods, just to say thank-you. Sometimes it was opposing players, if they'd been playing for each other's lives, but otherwise the offerings were just thralls or whatever human stakes had been put on the table. But sometimes the losing team would be so mad they'd end up killing the winning team, especially if the losers were more powerful. Whatever happened, only the gods always came out on top.

I said something—I forget what—to Hun Xoc. You weren't supposed to be able to see anything in his face but I knew him so well I thought I could see a lot. And it wasn't just anger, it *wasn't* all boiled down to violence like I think I talked about a long time ago. There was anger there, but there was this big aquifer under it of just plain surprised sadness there, that childlike disappointment that the world was such a ghastly place.

The team was passing around a wide, shallow basin with a faecaloid pile of cigar stubs smoldering in the center. I rubbed my thumbs in the ashes.

> **"Great One Harpy,**
> **Now protect us,**
> **Guard our goal zone,**
> **Please, Great Harpy,"**

I whispered, and marked four ascending dextral streaks over each of my nipples—which were dyed blue, and just barely exposed over the mass of my ball yoke and hip padding—to signify that my presumably debilitating grief over 5-5 had already burned out and I was ready to be an instrument of his revenge.

"Chun!"

(35)

At the first bounce of the next serve, Emerald Immanent got the tip back to Emerald Howler. Howler dribbled once and passed it back to Emerald Immanent. He shot. A miss. 5-5's replacement set the ball up for Hun Xoc, who took a long shot. Miss. *"P'uchik bok, pak, bok, bok BOK."* The ball was getting back into its counterclockwise orbit. Emerald Immanent shot and missed high. There was a *"Baat"* back to the Harpies, a good one this time. Red Beak shot but missed. Emerald Snapper picked up the ball and passed to Emerald Immanent but Hun Xoc was there to intercept the pass and knocked it back over the line toward our end zone. He undershot but Red Cord dove forward on one knee and just before the ball hit the red floor he made a spectacular save, the Willie Mays catch of the day, sending the ball high up to Red Beak. He set up for a shot but Emerald Howler was there and checked him and quicker than you could see everyone had mashed into a ball again, and the drivers were separating them, but then somehow Emerald Snapper was still dribbling and Emerald Immanent was out of the scrum, got the ball, and hit the peg.

"Nine goals, Ocelots

And four goals, Harpies."

Was that legal? I wondered. I flipped through Chacal's memories but I couldn't find another situation when the drivers were on the court and someone scored anyway. This is fucked up, I repeated, fucked up, fucked up.

Hun Xoc and Red Beak got loose from the scrum and staggered back to their markers. Red Beak didn't look like he had too many serves left in him. I deserted my waiting-marker in the little bullpen-marker and stepped in front of Teentsy Bear, collaring him in the middle of his signaling to Hun Xoc.

I've got to get in there, I said.

He snapped at me. "Wait," he said. "We're going to put everything into the next two balls and then I'll move you forward if I have to." He went back into the scrum.

It's true, I thought, I was way out of line. And Teentsy Bear didn't have the awe of me a lot of people had. It was like the way Phil Jackson used to handle Dennis Rodman. I got another loneliness wave in spite of myself. The ball societies created this intense sort of sports-academy family/rival relationship. The moment you felt you were being excluded from the group you just wanted to hang yourself. Calm way down, I thought, that's not you, it's not a real feeling, it's a relic from Chacal.

Serve 7. The ball went around sixteen times. Neither team was letting the other strikers get off good shot. Finally the ball caught the underside of our goal peg, *"T'un!"*

And then, there was a piff of powdered pigment.

> *"Wakal t'un!"*
> *"Eight goals Ocelots,*
> *Six goals, Harpies."*

No effing *way,* I thought. That ball did *not* touch that bowl. Cheat, cheat. Strings attached. Wiggly peg. Pea shooter. Something. Hun Xoc and a bunch of the other Harpies were looking up at the umpires, too, and a few bloods in the stands were shouting at them, but the umpires didn't do anything. Fuckers.

Nobody called for a check. Bogus. Shame.

Waves of grumbles were spreading through the Harpies' stands but so far no one was going to challenge the umpires.

At this rate we could be toast in two more serves.

Emerald Immanent got the eighth tip. Red Beak rushed at him on his unsteady legs. Emerald Immanent shot over Red Beak's head. *BOK.* Red Beak couldn't get his arm up in time. He just jumped and blocked the shot with his face. There was just this *blchufff* sound. Something happened that looked like what used to happen in this machine that used to grind up eaten-out coconuts outside the company store on that finca in Livingston. It was like a big dirty blender, and my dad would throw the sucker into the gadget's eel mouth and one instant it was this solid round thing and the next it was just this gooey pulverulence and strings of yellow pulp. Hun Xoc didn't break his game, though, he scooped up the loose ball, dribbled once, and took a close, easy shot, turning the Ocelots' goal vase into a cloud of emerald shardlets.

"Harpy great-goal, 13 Ocelots, 8 Harpies."

The Harpies weren't sure whether to cheer or clap—that is, clap their hands against their chests to express their disapproval. We were ahead but we'd lost two players and used up our bench. The Ocelots still had their substitutes intact. Goons. Personally, I guess I should have been more upset about Red Beak but I was so pumped up that I was going to get in the ball game.

They carried Red Beak off the court. Cash in his chips, I thought. He's as dead as the novel. Yes, we have no more forwards today. I stared pleadingly at Teentsy Bear's hands. He looked back at me. I felt eight different hormones blasting into my medulla and a huge erection popping against its tortoiseshell cup.

Come on. Come on. The untouchables hoisted up a fresh ball. Come on—

Teentsy Bear's hand coughed and then signed *Go.*

Yes!

Before I could walk forward Armadillo Shit put a wad of chili-flavored chewing gum into my mouth. It was more liquid than the twentieth-century-and-later kind, and it was laced with cocaine that had been traded over unimaginable vast distances from the far south, from a whole other world. Kind of a combination tooth protector and combat pill.

"Hit me," I said. Armadillo Shit slapped my right cheek. I slapped him back with the back of palm of my left hand and stepped out into the court.

You could smell how pumped the crowd was. My feet found the warm-friend welcome of my marker through the latex soles.

The ball knot unraveled. My body automatically shifted its weight from side to side, my toes hooking over the edge of the marker, my yoke twisting left and right around my upper waist like a heavy tire, settling into the groove of the supersensitive and super-sturdy Motown bump-swings that were every ballplayer's dominant lifetime rhythm. A few beats ago I'd still been aware of all these confusing conflicting feelings, gratitude to and love for 2 Jeweled Skull and also all these competing worries about Lady Koh and Marena and my own objectives, and now they were all just wiped out as I felt the centrality of the face-off marker, the elevation of the targets, the volume of warm air between the banks, and especially the vectors of my teammates and opponents.

The ball was about to disengage.

I snuck a hand down into my eyedazzler sarong-swags and tightened the inner knots on my yoke-padding.

I flexed my iffy ankle. I felt like I could jump over the mul. Gonna pop a pot of powdered pigment, I thought. Poppety poppety pot. The ball dropped, more slowly than ever this time, the world slowing as I sped up.

"Chun!"

I was there before I knew it and my hip connected, my mass transferring inertia into the sphere, and I had that rush back again. Of the few things I can tell you for sure, I can tell you that it was more satisfying than getting your Louisville Slugger square into a twelve-inch regulation softball.

Hun Xoc got the pass. I got around Emerald Howler as he passed back to me. "*Bok.*" No problem. I shot. *"BOK."* I missed. Whiff.

Emerald Snapper got the ball. Emerald Immanent set up and scored a great-goal.

"Seventeen goals, Ocelots,

And eight goals, Harpies."

Long time away, I thought. Don't get discouraged. Come on, focus.

I noticed the torches had been lit. In the violet twilight the court was weirdly multishadowed and dichromatic. I looked at the sky. Need another watch, I thought. Come on.

Hun Xoc was watching our coach. Teentsy Bear was watching the other side. I turned and caught what he was saying.

They're going to trap you between them, Teentsy signed to Hun Xoc.

I'll take care of it, Hun Xoc signed.

Not allowed, Teentsy Bear signed. Even if we get a goal or two while they're beating you up it doesn't matter. If you're out of action we're rat bait.

Red Hun Xoc signed an "Understood." The tenth ball came down.

"Chun!"

(36)

Like Teentsy had said, Emerald Immanent pretended to try to make the tip and then he and Emerald Howler came together at Hun Xoc. Just as they were about to trap him, and without looking, Hun Xoc faked a stumble. I got the ball and back-passed to Red Cord. He bounce-passed back to me. I came up to shoot. Howler was about to nail me but Hun Xoc was there and jumped high up in front of him, waving his arms and puffing out his cheeks into a frog face. I shot but just missed the peg. Emerald Snapper got it and passed. Emerald Immanent shot, missed, and then instead of recovering dove into Hun Xoc and gave him a good bump, but Hun Xoc rolled himself up like an armadillo and slipped away backward, back into our home zone. He was the best at that stuff. Red Cord had gotten the ball and sent me a lob pass. I shuffled four finger-widths closer to the north bank. My old systems were still responding, everything flowing pretty well.

Apex. Down. I got my hip into place and braced myself and *"bok,"* yesssss, ball! Ball! Ball!

Correct angle.

Dodge. Around. Successful. Under.

Ball. Ball. Now.

"BOK!!!"

I got the black sun just at the right nanoinstant and the feeling was like nothing else, so delicate, so powerful, so round, so firm, so fully *boked,* so violent even though you're just standing in one place. It's hard to explain how visceral the impact is, I guess if anything it feels most like doing a "dig" in volleyball, or hitting a chester or header in fútbol, I mean, soccer. Or like the way you can launch another person on a trampoline. When you hit the ball with your body the contact's just erotic, it's like you're a slit-gong ringing out this incredible chord made up of all your different nerves, pain, pleasure, position, everything, it's globally refreshing like every one of your two hundred and six bones pops out of its socket, shakes off all the accumulated pressure of time and gravity, and snaps back into place better than ever, and you just buzz and ring afterward like you went through this electroshock degaussing.

I could feel I was going to make the shot, so instead of a follow-through I dove forward, rolling over along the oiled bank before he could get to me. I couldn't see the jade dust falling on me, but t seemed as though I could feel it.

Score! GREAT-SCORE! GREAT*SCOOORRRE!!!*

"*Li'skuba wasak.* 17 Ocelots, 12 Harpies."

On the eleventh serve Hun Xoc shouldered in a great-goal, bringing the score to 17 Ocelots, 16 Harpies. As of now Hun Xoc was the top ballplayer in the known world. I got eye contact with him and his exposed cheeks flashed or implied a smile under his mask. Floods of pride welled up in my chest or heart or wherever such fountains well.

On the twelfth serve I hit a single, for 17 Ocelots to 17 Harpies. It wasn't spectacular, but it was a whole new game. The cheering went on and on and on. And—the—crowd—goes—wild, my mind looped over and over, in the weird even spondee of Howard Cosell. The Harpy clansmen and partisans and even what you might call "undecideds" were all really roaring this time, like stir-crazy cats in the middle of winter in the old Lion House at the Bronx Zoo, the way when they really got going that reverb would just soak into all the tons of masonry around you until the whole building was like a big old bronze alarum bell. I rolled back and south into our home zone and into a cloud of trash talk, a little afraid the cats were going to pile on top of me even after the call, and didn't look up until I saw the red paint under me. A big shadow passed on my right, Emerald Immanent glaring suspiciously at me, thinking of hand-smashing me even though the ball was dead. He didn't do it, though. Even if all the umpires had been fixed they'd have to call a *si'pil*—a big fault, like a sin—and take him out of the game.

"You're gonna get balled," Emerald Immanent muttered. "Balled" meant getting trussed and wrapped up, alive into a big-old ball and kicked around unto death. I was about to say something snappy back but thought better of it. He'd know my voice on the first syllable. It was kind of like if everyone thought Michael Jordan had died and then he came back to play as a rookie with a different number, darker skin, repositioned eyebrows, no moustache, a beard, a blond Afro, and no tongue. If he hung back people wouldn't pick up on it, but if he started stuffing basket after basket a few people would start saying how much he looked like Jordan, and the word would spread, and in a few minutes the whole stadium would be talking about how he *had* to be His Airness, and the word would spread, and . . . well, anyway, I wouldn't stay unrecognized for long no matter what I did. But there still wasn't any point tipping cards right away. I was still an unknown scrub who'd just had a lucky shot.

Marker. There. Mine. My spot. My marker.

The thirteenth serve came down. I was there exactly right for the tip but something was off, it was like the ball just caught and paused in midair for half a beat. I'd overshot and tried to step back but by the time the ball had actually fallen Emerald Immanent had gotten a good line on it. He passed it back to Emerald Howler, who took a leisurely shot and made an easy great-goal.

"18 Ocelots, 17 Harpies."

The ball had been rigged with a nearly invisible gut cord, and it had hesitated just long enough before it snapped the line to throw us off. There was rustling in the Harpy side of the crowd. I looked up at them and heard the word *"si'pil,"* major cheat.

Damn.

I'd been in a couple hipball games where somebody switched in a lopsidedly weighted ball, but with those you could call for an examination. If you looked at this ball you probably wouldn't see anything. And somebody'd rolled up the cord. It was a good one.

I stood there, looking around like an idiot. Or, as Forrest would say, like a idiot. No call. The elder Harpy bloods were calming the others down. As they should have, I supposed, but it still rankled.

Like I said, they had to win by three. Just a regular goal, I thought. Can't pull that one again. No tricks. Don't think about it. Just like any other point. Play hard. Give it the old Bulldog try. Handsome Dan. Rah.

Fourteenth serve.

"Chun."

Red Hun Xoc got the tip. Emerald Immanent was hanging back now. Letting the game come to him. Emerald Howler was tied up guarding me. I faded back into our zone, letting the pass hit the bank on my right, and then got back under it and scooped it up. I shot way low and missed on purpose. Emerald Snapper got the ball and sent it to Howler.

Okay, here's *my* trick, I thought. I was downcourt in three steps, onto the black and all over Howler before he could pass. He hip-dribbled low against the angle of the bank, trying to keep it away, but I darted under him and knocked the ball toward me with my knee and in less than a beat I'd balanced it on my right wrist-scoop and shot it way back upcourt into the red. Hun Xoc knew what I was up to—he and I had run this move a hundred times—and he was there.

I twisted away, faked north, and then blasted back up the middle of the court, tiptoeing on the line between the neutral black and the off-limits yellow, and dove into our home zone just ahead of Emerald Howler.

Hun Xoc picked up the ball and dribbled it twice up the white zone toward the Ocelots' goal. I barely signaled at all but he knew what I was getting at. Just before Emerald Immanent was on him he back-passed to me.

I shouldered the ball up at a long angle, darted around the two-person crunch, and picked it up again on its downward arc. It was something I'd practiced so often from such an early age that I wasn't even aware of it.

Emerald Immanent was the first to clock what I was going for but Red Hun Xoc got in on my left and kept him off me. Emerald Howler got around, though, and checked me on my left side, cracking the front of his yoke into the underside of mine.

"*Kaaxtik u bak'el it*," he said through his grunt. "Better clench your asshole." I tipped right, braced myself on the chalky slope with both hands, and kicked backward at his knees. Emerald Howler dodged away. I guessed that he'd figured the most urgent thing was separating me from the ball, not attacking me, since I was about to get torn apart by the rest of his team anyway, so he'd leave himself open. And he did. As he settled himself and got his yoke down into the path of the descending ball I jumped back and caught his right wrist-guard in the crook of my left arm and twisted backward, straining against it. He was this incredibly strong guy, just a squat chunk of muscle and breakage-enlarged bones like a twisted oak stump, but after a beat I got him over onto me, the ball coming down and bouncing off the cotton beneath his yoke, and as he rolled over to try to crush my legs with his yoke I got my left hand up and too fast for anyone to see it I ripped his nose plug out of his septum, and sort of deflected the spray of blood into his eyes with my hand while I rolled backward. He'd gotten hold of one of my waist straps but I pushed against him with my legs and I finally snapped away, rolling over again once, and I was back on my feet. Hun Xoc had managed to pick up the loose ball and, as he got his last bit of juice together, set up and shot just over my head. He hit the peg dead on, but the vase didn't move.

"19 Ocelots, 17 Harpies."

Qué el fuck? I thought, No *wakal tunI*? He fucking tipped the jar, what did they do, glue it on?

I looked up at the stupid little clay pot. It was just hanging out there, like, who, me? And he'd just sent a brotherfucking earthquake through its little fucking peg.

"The Harpies request inspection of the bowl," I started to yell out in formal Chol, but Hun Xoc was already on top of me and he practically stuck his hand down my mouth.

Shut up, he said. He moved me back into the red. Emerald Howler and Emerald Immanent were on their feet and running in place at us, held back by a fog of invisibles.

Let's go, Hun Xoc said. We teetered back to our markers along the north wall, leaving bloody handprints.

On the fifteenth serve, the Ocelots fouled us, for 19 to 18. Yay. The sixteenth ball made twenty-eight circuits—an unlucky number—but just as I thought we were getting a line on it Emerald Immanent's lob shot grazed the peg, lightly but fair and square.

"Ocelot great-goal, 20 Ocelots, 18 Harpies."

The Ocelot side whipped up into a cheer orgy. One point away. Bastards.

Finally everyone quieted down for the serve, and then there was a signal that 2 Jeweled Skull had asked to raise the stakes by what was basically the amount of his personal treasury. It was the signal for the Harpies to get ready for combat. I looked up into our Harpy stands. The three hundred or so war-age bloods were bouncing around and waving their baatob like innocent spectators, but if you were looking for it you could see, just from how still they were, that something was going on. They had a look like the nonexpression of a Japanese gymnast doing an iron cross on the hanging rings. They were dressing each other for combat under their mantos, popping the nuts off the points of their blowgun darts, untying the knots of their mantles and heavier ornaments so they could slip them off at a *p'ip'il*'s notice—at a blink—tying obsidian knives and saw handles around their upper arms. It was slow going, you had to be careful not to cut yourself or the person you were dressing. Obsidian's really nothing to screw around with. The edge of an obsidian blade is only one molecule wide, and it can part the molecules of your flesh like it was going through air, often nearly painlessly, so that it takes you longer to notice you've been cut. They still use—or I should say they were going to use—skin scalpels with obsidian edges in the twenty-first century. In any pitched battle with obsidian weapons, about half of the combatants were always hash in a flash, like they'd fallen through a stack of windows from the pre-safety-glass era.

Could the Ocelot spies see something was up? I wondered. Or was it so subtle that you had to know it was happening to catch it?

The signal came down that Fanged Hummingbird had seen the raise. There was another blast of commotion. I got Hun Xoc and Red Cord into a kind of a huddle and got my mouth onto Hun Xoc's ear.

If this turns into a fight we have to head into the Ocelots' compound, I said. West.

Why? he signed on my arm. He was planning to stay here and fight it out.

We have to get to the Ocelots' tree, I said. There's something I promised

2 Jeweled Skull I'd do. I didn't want Red Cord—or even Hun Xoc, I guess—to know about the earthstar compound. Better they thought I wanted to ring or somehow poison the Ocelots' celestial tree—which would be a reasonable goal, actually, ritually speaking. It would be like killing the clan.

Hun Xoc signed that he didn't want to run.

I started to try to tell him the old thing about how we weren't running, we were just advancing in a different direction, but I tripped over the words. It wasn't that easy to translate an English phrase into Chol, or at least it wasn't for me.

We're not running anywhere, I said, I have to *ajma-xoc*. It meant "follow what our father says." It was incontrovertible. Come on, I thought, switch hats. You're not a ballplayer right now, you're a commando.

He demurred again. I insisted. Finally he said "Agreed" by contracting his shoulder muscles.

It'll just be the three of us and six of Koh's guards, I said. Maybe not even that many. We can still make it, though.

Listen, something's going on, Hun Xoc signed by tapping my yoke.

What? I asked, but I heard it.

"Kot Chuupol! Ile Kot Chuupol!" It was Emerald Immanent's voice.

He'd recognized me.

(37)

"*Kot Chuupol! Ile Kot Chuupol!*"

His voice was like he was trying to throw up, except loud. You're supposed to be silent like your stupid name, I thought. *Ch'uupul* was a Chol word for like gay or queer—not in the okay sense of a epicene, but in the sense of being a willing bottom—so the most popular insult-name for me was just something midway in sound between that and "Chacal."

"*Yan Kot Chacal!*" he yelled. "It's Harpy Chacal!"

Just ignore them, dear, I thought.

"*Yan Chuupol Chacal! Yan Chuupol Chacal!*"

I was sort of half-aware that a couple of people up in the Ocelot stands had heard Emerald Immanent identifying me, and they were having mixed reactions. Some of them were more than a little spooked and kept on rhubarbing about it. But I was too pumped to pay much attention. The chanter and Magister and beaters and everybody just went on with what they were doing, cruising through the protocol on inertia.

Anyway, the serve went out. Hun Xoc got it and passed to me. In the femtosecond I spent looking at him I could see he was too winded to make another goal run himself. In a normal ball game, with more bench players, he'd have dropped out already.

I passed back to Red Cord. Just get me a good shot, I signed to Hun Xoc. Red Cord passed back to me.

Okay. No point holding back now.

I scooped the ball out of the air and passed it back to Hun Xoc and fell back and turned, setting up my signature run. I mean Chacal's signature run. It was like one of Lebron's dunk-in-the-post, I'd perfected it over so many repetitions it was almost one motion and felt completed as soon as I swung into it. I built up speed and ran up the red wall, like Donald O'Connor in *Singin' in the Rain.* I was giving myself away, but I was like, Fine, I don't give a fuck, I'm doing my transcendent little dance and nothing's gonna stop me cause I'm the Duke of Earl.

I turned like a skateboarder just above the lip of the wall and dashed down, building up momentum, and diagonally across the alley and up the Ocelots' emerald-tinted wall. By the second step up I'd revisualized my path up the bank, felt my speed, yep, everything in place, THE TIME IS NOW!!!

I came to that moment of perfect equipoise where I was standing motionless like a fly at this crazy forty-five-degree angle. I felt the wind from Ocelot spectators' fists as they swung at me, not quite connecting. The goal was only six arms ahead of me and three arms above. Hun Xoc yoked the ball up to me like he'd done a thousand times, and it came up just as I was falling, nearly right where I wanted it, so that I could gauge its stately spin by a pink spot of bloody chalk-dust, and I dug my wrist-guard into the black moon and just fed it right into the side of the vase. I could see the bloom of turquoise powder as I fell out of my equilibrium and as I rolled I could hear the chanters squealing above the cheers:

"20 Ocelots, 22 Harpies." You could tell from the chanters' voices that this wasn't how it was supposed to go. They'd been sure the Ocelots had a lock. Well, choke on this, I thought. One more.

Hun Xoc got the eighteenth serve, set up, got a solid hit on it, and grazed the peg. Somebody'd checked me, and I'd fallen over. But as I hoisted myself up I could see a tiny but incontrovertible wisp of blue-green dust.

We did it, I thought, but as the chanters' voice swelled into a chorus of "*Kax kot, kax Kot*," "Win, Harpies, win, Harpies," I could hear, closer and louder, Emerald Immanent's voice, and then Emerald Snapper's, and then two, and four, and then what sounded like a hundred other voices, all screaming:

"Yan Kot Chacal!" "It's Harpy Chacal!"

I staggered toward the central marker. There were Harpy bloods chanting back, *"Kax! Kax! Kax!"* "Victory! Victory! Victory!" and the Ocelot crowd shouting, *"Tuus! Tuus! Tuus!"* "Deception, deception, deception." Nearer, I heard Hun Xoc's voice.

"Chokow pol!" It meant "crazy" or "Crazy Man," another common and somewhat more admiring pun on my name. But he used it only as a warning. I turned. All I could see was this big black thing but I ducked in time for it not to tear my head off.

4 Blue Howler had scooped up the dead ball and yoked it at my head.

What's going on? I thought kind of dully. I was still endorphined out. Ball was supposed to be an elegant game—at its best combining the artistry of rhythmic gymnastics with the excitement and finesse of men's lacrosse—and now it's turning into Australian football. Howler ran at me, following the ball. I turned like I was going to run away and then dug my right foot into the bank and pushed off the angle between the floor and the sloping wall, stopping myself. Howler skidded into me from behind. I hunched forward and pushed my rear end back and felt the left prong of my horseshoe-shaped yoke connect with bone. I rolled forward and was on my feet again. Howler was sliding in a clockwise arc down the bank, leaving a wide black streak. The crowd loved it. I crouched into a "turtle," expecting a tackle from Emerald Immanent, but it didn't come. I looked up. Red Beak had gotten hold of him. Not for long, though, it looked like. Behind them I noticed Emerald Snapper and the two Emerald bench players running at us. Snapper was huge and big-boned and I thought for a beat that I'd had it, but he got off balance and as he fell toward me I got his head right on the sweet spot of my yoke. There was no crack, it was more like just a quiet *glutch*. Whatever, I thought, yeah, forget the damn Marquess of Queersbury rules, let's take the buttons off the foils. As Snapper fell back he got a hand into my yoke and pulled me down onto the slaughterhouse floor. I managed to roll away before he rolled onto me and flattened me. Emerald Immanent was coming back around on my right. The umpires' drivers and both sides' invisibles were already out on the court, trying to shield the players they were assigned to.

"Lothic ekel ytzam," Howler yelled from the other side of the court. Basi-

cally it meant "You're taco meat," except *ytzam* was this really cheap sort of pemmican that the pastless clans ate and sold. It was known for having all sorts of squirrels and bats and bugs and mud and shit in it.

"Chikin ukumil jotzpaljal," I said, scooping the ball out of the air with my hand shield. "Your shrunken dick is showing." That particular word for *shrunken* meant like with a shrunken head. I launched the ball off my yoke in an arc over his head. It looked like a good lob, but I slipped on blood and fell backward. Up in the stands what had been everyone arguing at once was devolving into everyone shouting at once. Out at either open end of the court, where some of the Ocelot and Harpy partisans overlapped, I could hear a few little slap-fights starting, the kind that turn into big ones. Some of the Harpies were cheering my name, that I was Chacal, I guess figuring I was back from the Underworld.

Where's the ball gotten to? I wondered. I rolled over on my stomach—with all the padding we were wearing, falling over was one thing that didn't usually result in an injury—and for a beat I could see Lady Koh's eyes watching me, unblinking and seemingly calm, penetrating through the swirls of motion and feather confetti. I thought about signing up to her but it was too far, I'd have to gesture too loud. Ahead and behind I could hear younger bloods were pouring through both end zones into the playing trench.

I noticed Hun Xoc's hand under my arm. He pulled me up. Both sides' bloods were overpowering the drivers, who only had these short ceremonial maces anyway, more just regalia than practical weapons.

Hun Xoc tensed as Howler came at us again. Howler hit him. Hun Xoc skidded back into me on the bloody floor. I toppled over and there was what seemed like two minutes where Howler was kneeling, looking down at us and babbling through a cluster of little bits of teeth and glogs of foamy mucus, something to the effect of how he was going to fuck us with a barrel cactus, one after the other. I just gritted my teeth and grunted back. Finally there was a crack as Hun Xoc got to an almost-standing position and brought one of his palm guards down on Howler's head. Howler stopped sputtering. I pulled myself upright, clawing onto one of our invisibles, and got my hand on Hun Xoc's shoulder. There was all sorts of jewelry and expensive clothing falling down from the stands and you couldn't see much, but the main problem was that we were already getting moshed between all these fans, which was usual enough for us except some of them were armed with obsidian-flake saws, and like I said, compared to that shit syringe needles and razor blades seem blunt by comparison. I climbed half-up someone and looked around for Koh. I couldn't see her but a squad of six of Koh's Rattler bloods, the ones she'd promised me, were sliding to us down the north bank. The rest of both sides of the crowd took that as a cue to start oozing down the banks into the trench. That's it, no more play, I thought. *Les jeux sont totalement faits, copains.* Fear, fear, foes, fuck—

Four of Koh's Rattler guards got through and pushed through the knots of churning flesh on the court and kind of enclosed Hun Xoc and me, like an amoeba swallowing a pair of paramecia. Finally they got us up on their shoulders. I looked up and finally picked out Lady Koh. Like us, she was totally cut off, completely separated from the main body of the Harpies. She was gesturing at me. Go for the well. I climbed up on one of the guard's shoulders and looked west over all the headdresses. The V of the court's canyons looked invitingly open, with the emerald Δ of the Ocelots' mul sticking up inside it. I can do this, I thought. Anyway it's not really like being brave, it's just like you're 99.44 percent definitely fucked anyway so why not spend your last minutes of freedom doing something a little wacky? Anyway, it's not that far. We need only about two minutes of misdirection.

I looked back up at Koh. She kept signing. Go for the well. Go for the well. Well, well, well. She added an "urgent please." *Ko'ox tuun!* Go. Go. Go. Gogogogo**GOGOGOGO!!!!!!!**

(38)

Koh's entourage closed in around her like bees in a ball around their queen. Above us and to the right some of the Death House guards were trying to get through the crowd and jump down at us, but they were all tangled up in the spectators' capes and scarves and jewelry, like the victims in that bombing at Harrods. The hipball music was still going on, imitating the sounds of fighting. Maybe the musicians just kept playing as a way of staying musicians and not becoming combatants.

They carried us west, over the Ocelots' end-zone line. Keep your head up, I thought. Win through intimidation. The Ocelot bloods and partisans parted in front of us, not like the Red Sea, though, more like they just wanted to get a look at us before they decided whether to tear us apart. We got past the players' pen, out into the small zocalo between the Ocelots' end zone and the beginning of the three tiers of steps that led up to the razor stairs of their mul, rising up only about four rope-lengths away. The long emerald-green-stuccoed stone wall of the Ocelots' clan house was on our left side, and beyond and behind that there were two actual semiresidential sections of wood and plaster climbing up the rising ground. The nearer one was for women and the higher, the holier one was for men. Beyond that I could see the top of a gaudy ceremonial wall worked with deep frets and triangular crenellations and behind that a long red-and-green smudge, the manicured and pollarded treetops of the Ocelots' poison garden, surrounded by a thorn wall. It wasn't really that far.

I told them to put us down. They did. I yanked off my helmet and arm protectors. At the Ocelots' equipment house some big mean-looking guy stepped out in front of us like, hey, what's going on? I threw my damn stuffed rodent in his face and he ducked in this comical way. It was this magical talisman flying at him with its sharp little claws. I fished a little shell knife out of my crotch pouch, cut the cords off my outer swag of quilted padding, and tossed it to one of the youngest Ocelot bloods in the crowd like it was a major souvenir, which I guess it was.

I am Chacal! I declaimed. Everybody stared. I've gone to Xibalba and brought back the Razor Ball! I was overexcited and shifted into English. "By the bomes of Crom, you're all horsemeat! Shop smart—shop S-Mart!" I was about to add that I was going to sic the United Fruit Company on them. Emerald Immanent was still down on the court behind us, shouting for his brothers to grab us, but he must have been still blocked by the Harpy invisibles. I stepped up onto the first swell in the sea of steps. My little squad followed my lead, surrounding me in an oval formation. Eight steps. Nine. The first tier intersected with a second tide of clear-edged waves and ripples, black flats and green risers scraped and buffed and finished like a Noguchi marble. And the Ocelots let us through. I guess we had a fear edge because—for most of them at least—it really was more like I'd transformed into Chacal than like I'd just been in hiding and then disguised. There was a kind of incomprehension of the whole idea of disguise; even when people wore the costumes of the gods, they were taking on that identity, not just dressing up, and it was a very serious deal. Plus, a lot of the people around the end zone were visitors to Ix, and weren't prepared for a fight. And of course we were still officially their guests in a place that took hospitality seriously. We were just eight little dudes in the middle of their turf and there was plenty of time for them to rush us. And maybe most of all, they weren't yet sure whether it was part of the show. They were all watching the fights erupting down on the court and spreading out into the stands, and wondering what the shot was, whether the panic was the beginning of another Carthaginian catastrophe, what was expected of them, whatever. For one reason or another, for about forty beats we were in this limbo between action and reaction, where if you just walk straight up, if you don't look even slightly nervous, you can get away with a lot.

We edged closer to the Ocelot house on our left. Just a little farther. Their emerald mul loomed on our right. We came up level with the women's residential quarter of the palace. I guess *gynaeceum* is the right word for it, but who cares. It wasn't all walled up like the residences in Teotihuacán. There were still no windows, but there were all these alcoves and inviting little doorways. Bevies of Ocelot women looked down over us from their sort of harem balcony up in the roof gardens. I got my knife down under my back padding and cut into the straps on my ball yoke.

We're going through there, I tapped on Hun Xoc's arm. His eyes picked out the same door I'd scoped out. It was only twenty steps off but I resisted the urge to run. I turned to the captain of the Rattler guards and he'd obviously picked up on what we were doing. He seemed pretty eager to follow my orders. Koh must have told him his life was totally at my disposal. It was one of the good things about a feudal caste system, you really could get good help once in a while. Or at least dedicated help.

There was an explosion of combat yells down on the court. Don't look around, I tapped. I finally twisted off my ball yoke and swung it in my right hand like a battle club, trailing beaded straps on the steps. I kept wishing we'd had time to rehearse this. I veered left into the alcove. The door was just red-oiled quilted deerskin set into the high wall. It was tied down on the inside, but it opened upward and I sliced through the top left thong-hinge. The Rattler leader took my cue, cut the other four, and wrenched the door down. By now there were Ocelot bloods pressing in behind us, asking what the hell we were doing, and our outside Rattler bloods had their maces up. The first six of us pushed into a tiny sweat room and out the far door into a tiny enclosed square courtyard. There were all sorts of freshly dyed cotton festival yarns laid out drying on the floor. There was only one other door into the court, on the far side, and five or six Ocelot women, with undressed hair and wearing only damp emerald-and-white huipils, scampered out through it, but one little round old grandmother just stood in the middle of the space shrieking at the Rattler captain, telling him over and over how we were wrecking all her stuff, and before I could say anything he swung his hand flail through her eyes, taking a chunk out of the bridge of her nose, and she just stood there still squealing until she eventually keeled over. I'm not proud of it, but I just went ahead with what I was doing, maybe feeling a little queasy. I'd gotten kind of inured to this stuff.

Hun Xoc got the Rattlers to pick up these big dye barrels and throw them out the door at the Ocelot bloods. As they dodged the kegs I could see past them for a beat, down into the canyon of the court complex about two vertical ropes below. It was a confused mass of hand fights between ballplayers and partisan spectators, but I could see Emerald Immanent and Emerald Howler's standards were coming up through the crowd toward us. It meant they'd gotten their trainers and supporters together and were leading them after us in an organized pursuit. The nearer Ocelots looked indecisive to me, though. They were more interested in rushing down to the court area to save 9 Fanged Hummingbird and their other royals. It was like you see at stadium riots or fights at rock concerts or political rallies, the sound and fury covers a lot of plain Brownian motion, the ninety percent of indecisive stuff that happens before, during, and after anyone comes to blows.

The captain left two Rattler bloods to hold the door. We need to get to the mainland, I lied, a little too loud, hoping that the people behind the door heard me or that the rear guard would get taken and talk. If word got back to the ahau it was pretty essential that they assumed we were trying to make a break for it, that we were trying to get onto the curved walkway around the south side of the peninsula and back east to the mainland. And like I said, Ix was a canal city and didn't really have streets, so to get anywhere you had to either go by boat or practically walk through somebody's bedroom. I hustled everyone else across the courtyard to the far door. Already a couple bloods had gotten on top of the wall we'd come through. I went in first, even though I wasn't normally allowed to take the lead. I was too important. I got into this little dark smelly hallway and around a couple crooks and nannies toward the right, uphill. It would have been confusing but my directional sense was another thing that had improved a few thousand percent since I got here. I pushed into a little cook yard, out its trash door on the other side, and through an open alley into one of the food-prep courts. Dozens of the women's household cooking servants milled around squawking, not knowing what to do. I noticed I was laughing again, partly from adrenaline and whatever but mainly because it was getting like one of those Bond movie chases where they always overturn fruit carts and the irate peddlers shake their fists after them. And what seemed funniest was that we were actually getting away with it so far. For these guys it's still fresh, I thought. This kind of commando strike was outside the protocol of Mesoamerican warfare.

For the first time I could really see how Cortez was going to be able to take over the whole continent against ten-thousand-to-one odds, how when your thinking is totally outside the system, the people in the system have no way of dealing with you. If you do something that just isn't done, most of the time, you win. The Rattler captain handed me a short mace and I tied it on to my left hand. I pointed to a low red fabric door in the center of the west wall, a moon-path door. Hun Xoc went up to it and started slashing through the fabric door—it was a quilt of rubberized cotton stretched over a wicker frame—but I could feel the knot of bloods behind me hesitating, like the door was radioactive. Ix had basically four overlapping webs of footpaths used by different classes of people. We were going to take one of what they called "fanged-rabbit-blood walks," which were segregated routes to special wells used only by menstruating women, all painted red on the insides and roofed with red tent-cloth. No male would even think of walking on the polluted ground.

We're going that way, I repeated. Hun Xoc and the captain seemed up for it but the other five Rattler bloods just gawked at me.

Everybody's a fucking superstitious insubordinate schmuck, I thought. Good help indeed. You could *never* get things together, nothing *ever* worked. And things never *will* work.

Hun Xoc got a handsaw and stood in front of the nearest blood and ordered him through the door. The kid was terrified but he still started to make some objection, something about how it wouldn't be good for us. While he was still talking, Hun Xoc reached down into the kid's scale-patterned apron, grabbed his penis and testicles, knocked his legs out from under him, and whipped the short saw under his hand. The kid barely made a sound. Hun Xoc stood up and tossed the kid's bloody genitals at one of the other bloods. They splatted on his chest and flopped jiggling on the floor.

"You'll take the women's path as men right now,

Or we can make you women first," Hun Xoc said.

The amputee sucked in his whimpers and tried to stand up, and the rest of the crew just stood around silently. It was a weird moment. The bloods seemed to be really considering the alternative.

I pushed in through the shredded leather into the creepy mauve light.

(39)

A couple of old greathousewomen were in the tunnel and freaked out and scuttled off. I stuck my head out. Finally the amputee limped for the door, and one after another the rest followed him. Maybe they figured it was okay now because the streaks of blood down his legs added realism. Hun Xoc prodded from the rear.

We went about twenty rope-lengths west and south and two rope-lengths uphill through the twisting walkway to another courtyard, a so-called "moon-blood latrine," where the unclean water from the female compound emptied into the "excremental water" of the canals. There was a cistern in the center fed through an open half-log pipe from the mountain above. We all boosted each other up onto the roof terrace. The culvert led up to a branch of the great southern aqueduct. Hun Xoc climbed one rope-length up the intricate relief into the culvert. I followed him and the guards came after me and we crouch-ran uphill in single file, stepping on the sides of the channel, trying not to slip on the trickles of water. It was twilight but with the damn big moon it was just too bright. So much for under the cover of darkness. There were spatters of coded alarm cries behind us. We'd definitely been spotted. The aqueduct zigzagged up the slope and at the first bend I got a view down to the Ball district.

Usually fighting around here was more like a series of little duels than a battle, but this was different. There was still a knot of Harpy bloods in the center of the northern platform, and each one had a long blowgun. It was the same story on the steps of the council house, except the Harpies there were arrayed in a four-deep line, with the ones in front aiming and the ones in back loading, Frederick the Great style. They must have snuck in the blowguns broken down into two or three pieces, I thought. And then at the last minute they'd twisted them together. Meanwhile the Ocelots had taken control of the court floor as well as their back and some of the east zocalo, but there seemed to be as many dead and dying Ocelots as live ones. I heard a Harpy whistle that sounded suspiciously like a signal to load, and then the wet sound of hundreds of darts sliding into spit-wet breeches. A bunch of Ocelots charged up at them but the Harpies fired a single volley across the court into the wave of bloods. It sounded like a huge cough and hiss. I couldn't see anything, and the Ocelots certainly couldn't, just this invisible tidal wave of poison rolling at them at four hundred feet per second. Five out of six Ocelots pitched back and sank into the mass of emerald-speckled bodies. A second wave of Ocelots somehow sped up and rolled at them before the platform squad had quite gotten themselves together for a second volley—

What's going on? Hun Xoc asked. I'd stopped running. I looked around and he pointed down to the zocalo. There were about twenty or twenty-five people definitely on our tail and Emerald Immanent was definitely the ringleader. They'd been slowed down by the crowd and were still at least four hundred beats away, but it was still disturbing, we'd gotten less misdirection out of the situation than I'd hoped. Some of them saw us looking at them and shouted to us to stop and come join the party.

Nothing, I signed to Hun Xoc. I got myself together and ran on uphill. Yeah, what the hell *is* going on? I wondered, but I knew the answer. 2 Jeweled Skull—my brain mate and adopted and spiritual father—had been drilling his Harpy bloods. He'd taught them to keep together in a tight body, seek cover, lay down fire, and most of all don't try to take live prisoners, all the most basic stuff from a pre-radio-communications military perspective. But it wasn't obvious in a wigged-out chivalry system. I mean, in Europe it had taken hundreds of years just to get the generals not to ride out in front of their troops with a flag labeled SHOOT ME.

I turned another zigzag. The Ocelots probably hadn't even expected them to aim to kill, I thought. If anything they always expected an opposing force to drop back out of missile range and challenge individuals to come out and fight.

Fabulous. Maybe 2 Jeweled wasn't in so much trouble as I'd thought. I certainly could of, should of, and really would of figured he'd come up with something. What would he think of, after all? Probably the exact same thing I would think of.

Would it be enough for him to win? I snuck another look back and down. The Harpies were throwing wounded bodies down into the irregular charging chunk of bloods. They're acting cleverly for once, I thought. Maybe they do have a chance.

What did that mean? Something I wasn't thinking about. No time now.

About six rope-lengths farther on—one vertical rope-length above the highest roof of the Ocelots' greathouses—the aqueduct passed over the Ocelots' mountain's southern walkway, and we dropped down onto the stuccoed surface. It was pretty narrow, just a processional path that led down from the peak through stepped passes to the inner yellow gate to the Snufflers' quarter and out to the mainland. There was no railing or anything on our left, just a one-rope-length drop down to the level of the lower terrace. The emerald wall of the Ocelots' poison garden was on our right hand. It was only half a rope-length high but it was topped with a big nasty crucifixion-thorn hedge, the kind with the two-finger-width needles. Behind us, about two hundred paces back, the causeway intersected with a more major route—which meant two people could almost walk abreast on it—leading from the inner rectories of the mul complex up to the top of the mountain behind it. There was a bigger gang on our tail now, charging up the main route only about a hundred paces away from the intersection, frustratingly clear in the zinc light. They'd figured we were heading for the mainland and had just gone around the women's house. I didn't see Emerald Immanent's standard but I was pretty sure it was them.

We can make it, Hun Xoc said. He gestured ahead and down to the canal. I could see a few emerald-sashed figures on the causeway—Ocelot partisans—but not anyone we couldn't get through. I'd forgotten that Hun Xoc still thought I was going for the mainland. There seemed to be new

Harpy blowgun squads out in boats in the canals. Beyond that there was fighting in the Snufflers' quarter, but from this distance the battle looked purposeless, like a red ants' raid on a black ants' nest, a thousand higgledy-piggledy games of ritualized tag.

We have to break into groups, I said. I noticed that we'd lost Armadillo Shit somewhere. Whatever, don't think about it. I picked out two of the Rattler bloods and ordered them to go hold the path against Emerald Immanent's hunting group. Their captain repeated the order and they didn't hesitate, they just charged down to certain death. I turned around south again because there was something going on. Two Ocelot guards had come up out of nowhere ahead of us on the path, and a couple of the Rattler bloods were fighting them off. I'd thought it would be deserted up here, wasn't everybody supposed to be watching the ball game? The Rattler captain smashed one of them on the head with his mace but the guy just staggered a bit and kept coming and he had to hit him another few times to get him down. The other Rattlers had gotten the other gardener down to the ground and were working on skinning his face—they weren't into that scalp thing around here, by the way, that was strictly for low-life nomads from the deserts north of Teotihuacán—but the captain told them to skip it and they straightened up. There were already another bunch of four or five Ocelots behind them, coming up toward us from the yellow gate. I wondered how they'd been alerted. I looked around. There were only five of us, one still bleeding and limping from his emasculation.

We can make it, Hun Xoc signed in the direction of the Yellow Gate, we can get through them.

We can't make it, I signed back.

?!?!? he signed.

I pulled his face in front of mine so that the Rattler bloods couldn't see and gestured to the wall with my eyes. He looked into my eyes—which was like a really aggressive, inquisitorial thing to do—and I gave him a look like "It Must be Done!" and he accepted it.

I pulled the Rattler captain over and whispered into his ear. You're going to take the last three of your bloods and my standard and get down to the Yellow Gate, I said.

He started to object. Koh'd probably told him he couldn't leave me no matter what. Then he thought better of it and ran off at the head of his little group in that awkward way you run on unfamiliar ground at night. They won't even make it to the gate, I thought. The amputee limped after them but Hun Xoc said, "Not you," and pulled him back. He didn't have much mileage left on him.

Just the two of us left, I thought. Better anyway. Hun Xoc boosted the amputee up onto the wall and made him lay his torso prone over the thorns. I could hear him biting through his lips to stifle his shriek. Behind us Emerald Immanent's posse was only just around the curve of the causeway, less than a hundred paces off. Hun Xoc lifted me up onto the amputee's hot, oily back. It shivered a little as it crunched down into the spines. I couldn't resist taking a quick look back down at the court. It looked like Harpies had sent shock squads around through back alleys to come up behind the Ocelots' formations and attack their flanks. What had happened to Koh?

Don't think about it, I thought. Just take care of your end. I hopped onto the poor bastard's seventh cervical vertebra, grabbed his pigtail with both hands, and vaulted over his head down onto the invisible foliage below. Hun Xoc climbed up him and slid down next to me. I got my head up out of the dewy sego-lily leaves and looked for the cistern.

Eyes. Hot orange-green eyes in a scary-clown face, a jaguar colored with blue powder. I looked into the eyes and breathed. It was a big jaguar, just watching us in that lazy-alert way.

I am not afraid, I thought, and started counting. At twelve the cat turned and disappeared between a pair of these twisty ancient trees all inlaid with arabesques of tourmaline and spondylus shells. It was a weird transition from the urban setting we'd been in. Behind me Hun Xoc was ordering the amputee to get off the wall. I guess he hadn't even seen the jaguar. He pulled up the kid's bloody face with both hands and pushed it upward. The amputee must have gotten the idea because he arched his back and pushed himself off the thorns with what must have been his last erg of free will. I listened to him clatter onto the causeway.

It's got to be that way, I thought.

I pointed. I pushed up and hunt-ran around the trees, uphill of the cat.

(40)

Hun Xoc followed. The trees were boxed in milpas set in check-dam terraces, laid out just like any poor person's garden, or anyone's garden, anywhere else in Mesoamerica, the same exact 91.2 by 92.2-foot rectangle with the same orientation to Kochab. *Jotzolob* ran between the milpas, uncultivated trenches that were combination dirt sources, rock dumps, irrigation channels, and flood ducts. My feet automatically found one of the main channels and we headed "upwater," toes gooshing into the muddy bottom. The trees on either side gave us a little cover until we came to a clearing with intersecting aqueducts and four giant bulbous stelae of the Ocelots' Watching Greatfathers sticking up in scarlet, emerald, and black against the deep cobalt sky. It was getting too dark to see things clearly. I did a quick headcheck and climbed up out of the trench onto a milpa thigh-high with marigolds. A couple of these big flightless birds, rheas or something that the ahau kept as pets, walked stupidly toward me, maybe expecting me to feed them. Scram, I thought. Behind a grove to the south a couple of old Ocelot gardeners hobbled away from us to spread the alarm.

It didn't look guarded, though. I guessed no one but the highest Ocelots would ever think of coming in here anyway. You can really do a lot with taboos. Just hang out in places where everyone else thinks they're going to get fried by the bad mojo. Of course, they still get you eventually, but it does take them longer.

I got to the cistern. Too little. It wasn't the right one. This wasn't the actual source, just a way station, one of a bunch of little holding tanks. Their main feeder culvert sloped higher up the ridge toward the east slope of One Ocelot's Mountain.

Damn. The place was a lot more detailed than Koh's stupid model.

Higher up, I signed to Hun Xoc. I ran. That spot on the ball of my right foot was itchy. A weird red bird flew over my head and cut into the leaves in front of us, and after a moment I realized it was a *lem-lem,* a barbed throwing stick, basically a boomerang that doesn't come back but which flies a lot farther than an ordinary stick. It took me another two beats to realize that meant Enemies Behind.

How far?

Left. Around the corner of a thick pepper grove. I dropped down into the prickly gulch. A point on the mace on my left hand cut into my thumb. Hun Xoc dropped down into the nettles next to me. We were both gasping too hard to say anything. I edged over to him through the wet stalks and held on to his arm. I put my head against his chest for a beat. He reached forward down into my *wex*—I guess you'd have to call it a loincloth or a breechclout or some other ridiculous term—and held on to my penis, trying to calm me down. Just a little casual military homoerotism. Breathe, I thought.

There can't be that many of them. Some of them must have followed the Harpy standard. How far away were they?

Well, at least two terraces below. We can make it. Stay out of sight lines. It'll still take them two hundred beats to find us up here. Well, one hundred. And also, those guys had just been watching the match, so they weren't even winded. Except for Emerald Immanent, but he was just supernatural. I couldn't resist bringing my foot up to scratch it. There was something there.

My foot couldn't feel my fingers. And when my hand felt my foot, it felt too big.

"I'm stung," I said, "the male foot."

Hun Xoc let go of my Jed junior and took the foot in his hands. I could feel him digging the dart out of the puffy wound with a shell knife, but the sensation was far away. I listened to him him suck-and-spit. A timeless craft. Too late, though. I'm fucked, I thought. Oh, cripes.

I'm over the limit, it's payback time. TILT, GAME OVER, INSERT ONE TOKEN FOR ANOTHER PLAY, 12, 11, 10, 9, 0.

Hun Xoc rubbed dirt into the wound to stop the bleeding. I noticed I wasn't dead yet. It was like when you're stoned and you look at your watch because you think you've been wherever you are for days and you're going to be late for whatever and it's only five minutes later.

We're going the wrong way, I signed on his chest. You down-this-way go. I up-that-way go.

I stuck one eye up over the curve of the slope, like it was on a stalk, and looked around 220 degrees. I got an impression of figures advancing on us without really seeing them.

I know what I'm doing, I signed. I'm ready.

We looked at each other. He made the sign for "accepted" and vaulted up out of the ditch, running through the south *jotzol,* parallel to the rise of the peak. I jumped out and headed at right angles to him uphill. The trees ahead were wilder and thicker. They'd been allowed to branch relatively naturally because the area of the Source was the house of Chac. It was like the way an ahau's house was always just sealed up and never touched after his death, unless his heirs enlarged it or an enemy canceled it. Something made me look left. Below me Hun Xoc seemed to trip and fall, knocked back and then jerked forward off his feet like a roped steer. He'd probably been hit with a string club, kind of a big sharp yo-yo. I looked around. I still couldn't see the attackers but I could hear them stomping through the bracken below him, not bothering to be quiet. It was one of those instant-decision moments. Go and charge the Ocelots and try to disentangle him? But if I stopped, there wasn't any point anyway. I turned and kept going. There was a breaking-glass sound of Hun Xoc's mace going through jewelry and skin and an exhalation of air. We were both going to get taken in less than a minute anyway, I thought. Complete the objective.

Left.

Hun Xoc. Damn. Don't think about it.

The trench leveled out. This has got to be it, I thought. I spun around twice. The crest was laid out like a big rustic pyramid, with a cyclopean platform in the center and relatively straight hewn steps leading down to the four directions. There was a rough star of clothes and jewelry and human and animal gristle and bones on the platform, like the offerings had been laid out carefully but then picked over by the jaguars. Where's the cistern? There wasn't even any aqueduct.

I ran around the platform, kind of frantically. No well.

Stairs. Back down. No, up. Stairs too big. Everything wrong size. Clearing. Same one? Hump in the center. Maybe that's it.

No, too small.

No, that's it. I picked out the main feeder aqueduct that led into it from the spring source in the side of the mountain. I hadn't seen it before because it was covered over with U-shaped limestone slabs, almost like a regular old pipe.

Okay, Tonto. Just across this little clearing here. One milpa. Fifty-four regular steps. Fifty-three if you stick out your chest at the tape.

Just go.

I've got about ten more beats of total freedom, I thought. In that amount of time I can do whatever I want.

Just don't look like you're going for the well.

Just go.

Okay.

I dashed out. They came out to meet me.

Thirty more steps. I was limping. I couldn't feel my leg at all. Numb past the knee. Probably not anything fatal, I thought, they really want to bring you in kicking. Assuming they've got their act together. "We're going to kill all the men, rape all the women, and steal all the cattle," I yelled. "And for Gog's sake, get it right this time. *Disperse, ye rabble, die, ye scurvy scum, argghh, die!!!*"

I'll never really get this down, I thought, I just can't take it enough to heart. Twenty more steps. I could tell there were about a billion people around, or at least it seemed like a billion, but only one was really close. Keep going, he's not on me. No, he's on me. I had to turn around. Of course, it was Emerald Immanent, surprise, surprise. He just had to do his whole hero thing and add "Twice-Born-9 Chacal-Capturing" to the front of his name. If Emerald Immanent didn't cover himself with glory they'd all just be on top of me all at once in about two p'ip'ilob, and they'd just take group credit for the offering.

Emerald Immanent, the Ocelots' star striker, slashed at my bad leg with a long-handled hunting saw, trying to hobble me. I rolled behind one of the steles. It had about a fifteen-finger-width diameter and was coated in smooth, thick, black, white, and green paint like it had been dipped. There was the swish of air over a sharp surface and a dramatic constellation of sparks as his flints glanced off the stone. Tiny shards spattered through the air and one of them got into my right eye. Great, just what I needed.

"Kuchul bin ycnal," Emerald Immanent growled. "You're a runner." It meant I'd abandoned the ball game because I was afraid we'd lose.

"Xejintic ub'aj," I said. It meant "Vomit on yourself" but it was like saying "Bullshit." I didn't have any voice left, so I kind of stage-whispered it.

"Lothic ah tabay," he said. "You were beat."

"*You* were beat," I said. "Beat, beat, beat."

I let go and bolted for the well. Someone had gotten ahead of me. I butted into him and twisted around him to the side of the cistern. My hands grabbed relief-work starfish-glyphs and I could feel the firm resonance of the hundreds of cubic tons of water on the other side. It was streaming fast despite the drought, still more than enough to serve the whole city. The rim was only at chest height. Just get over it, I thought. The guy grabbed my pigtail but it was still two-thirds fake and the extension pulled off in his hand. More people grabbed at me. I edged back and rolled up onto the wide lip, trying to look like I was panicking. The octagonal opening was only a rope-length across. I could feel negative ions blasting up out of it and I was all refreshed all of a sudden, somehow thinking clearly even though my body was a firecracker string of unbearable pain. They were dragging me down off the rim. You've got to act more, I thought. Otherwise you'll be giving it away. It's not enough to just dress up, you have to act. I wrenched up and back, shifting my weight to pull at least one person up with me. The blood got his elbow around my throat as I edged us off-balance and we tipped back into cold.

(41)

People used to tell me I remember everything, but of course there is too much of everything for anyone to remember. It's really just that the type of things I do remember are different, like I might be able to quote the script of a movie I've seen, but I wouldn't be able to say whom I saw it with. Movies and other things tend to exist in a sort of limbo memory space. And for a while after we tipped back into the Great Cistern, events for me shifted into that unmarked class of sliding space-time. Maybe in another way it's like if you're listening to something or watching a movie on a disk and you've hit the REPEAT button and then fall asleep in your chair while it loops over and over. You might remember the scenes perfectly clearly, but not how they fit together or which repeat you saw them on. It was like an in-and-out dozy state when you might be sort of remembering a dream while you're dreaming it, or getting ready to dream it again and sort of seeing it coming and getting ready to remember it. It never quite seems to be happening at the time. Instead it's like you're visualizing what's going to happen or trying to make sense out of what's happened already, and even though the events are all clear enough they're not correlated against any clocks, internal or external. I certainly remember that feeling of knowing we were irrevocably off-balance. I don't remember falling or hitting the water. I think my heart stopped for a beat and a half. I realized the blood I'd pulled in with me was still choking me, and I remember reaching over with my right hand and finding a shard of obsidian that was still stuck in my left one. I got it out, tightened my fingers around it, twisted my arm back, found the protuberances of the blood's left floating ribs, felt up the costal arch, and cut through under the base of the sternum. He reacted but his grip didn't relax and I could tell I didn't have much consciousness time left. I got the feeling we were still sinking instead of floating up, maybe because of all his quilted padding and heavy spondylus shell wrist cuffs and ankle cuffs and everything. I dug the knife in again, got the tips of four fingers inside his skin, finger-crawled up under his xiphoid process, and cut through the diaphragm up into his hot pericardial cavity. I was in the wrong position to get all the way up to his heart but I found the inferior lobe of his left lung instead and grabbed it. It felt like a wet sea sponge. I yanked on it and it mushed and collapsed, but it must have triggered some real alarm because the blood's whole body spasmed so that I could push clear of him. I gasped at the release and a croquet ball of water forced itself down into my throat. It was about halfway pleasant because I really did need a drink but more pressed into my lungs and I got a blast of preconscious reptile panic.

Last thing, I thought. I dug the bag of earthstar powder out of my crotch and fumbled with the knots. I couldn't get it open with my shredded hands. Some of the shard was still stuck in the metacarpals of my right hand, though, and I stabbed the side of the little bag, twisted a hole in it, and punched the bag inside out though the hole, releasing trails of numbing death through the water. I even managed to cut the bag off its thong and let it sink, although consciously speaking I'd forgotten that it had been weighted with pebbles. I floated.

And that was basically it for a while. I don't remember being wet, although being underwater doesn't feel wet anyway. I do remember gazing at the circle of faint sky-blue below me, the opening of the well—although it was really above me—and considering whether to blow the rest of my carbonized air supply out through my lungs and die in one of the most pleasant ways possible, in the center of a jade sphere in the hands of the well gods, listening to the resonance of the water, room, womb, tomb, flume, shroom, plume, room, whoomb, boom, twroooowmb, twoooooommmmmmm.

TWO

The Taste of Screams

Figurine of a Diety Impersonator in a Duck-Billed Mask
Found Downstream of the Ruins of Ixnichi Sotz

Curious Antiquities of British Honduras
By Subscription · Lambeth · 1831

(42)

There's no memory in there of my being grabbed. But there was a moment somewhere when my numb wet head seemed to swell to mul-size in air that felt like dry heat. Grab air. Nose full. INHALE, no, hard chunk. Spit it out. Spoot it eett, *GET IT OUT!!!,* and there was this sensation of swallowing myself, like the way if you put a dragonfly's tail in its mouth it'll eat until it dies. At some point I realized that someone stuffed my left hand into my own mouth, the embedded shards of flint cutting through my upper lip. I blew my nose and opened one nostril and managed to breathe through that.

I think after that there's a longer period that I don't remember at all. And in a way that's sad because the moment of your capture is one of the most important in your life. It's a sacrament. But I don't remember hearing my captors' speeches, or my saying any of the little poems of submission, or anything. I do remember wearing ceremonial bindings, like the ones I'd been wearing on the mul, and I remember being in total dark smelling dead people near me. They smelled like they'd been beheaded, maybe, or eviscerated, which lets them drain a bit so they don't get quite so smelly as people who die from disease. You don't usually smell in dreams, I thought. Does that mean I'm awake? My swollen tongue scraped against cakes of blood on my inner cheeks. My leg was cold and big but when I finally got my bonds twisted around so I could reach down and feel it, it didn't seem to be around.

There was something fleshy there, according to my hand, but it was utterly numb, like I was touching someone else's leg, and it seemed swollen like I had elephantiasis. Before, after, or during that whole dark period I remember being prodded and surrounded. I reached out and felt their fur leggings. They were made of baby-ocelot skin, the kind only 9 Fanged Hummingbird's personal guards got to wear. What's happening with the earthstar compound? I wondered again. Is it working? If it's working, some people should be acting strange by now. They should be acting too happy, anyway. Right? Or maybe they're onto it. Maybe they're being smart, they're only drinking water they've held on to for a while. Hell, hell, hell.

Ow. Someone kicked me. I think someone ordered me to get up and walk and I think I tried to tell them I couldn't. I also don't remember being dragged or carried, but at some point I was in a different, fresh-air space, probably a treaty tent. I was with four other high-ranking Harpy bloods. We were all gagged, but from what we could grunt out in tonal language it seemed like none of us knew anything about the outcome of the battle. I was pretty sure none of them were major homies of mine. My messed-up right hand felt all big and fun and floppy where it had contacted the earthstar powder.

I remember the neutral-zone weave of the big trading mat they set me on, all by myself, which meant they were doing a special deal for me. I automatically took the captive's hunched position but I did get my head up long enough to check out what was being offered on the other side. You always want to know what you're worth.

It was a tray with a set of four stuffed quetzals, symbols of safe conduct out of the area. There were glyphs burned into them but I couldn't read who they were from or who they were for. Voices started up all around. I recognized one of them but couldn't place it and then realized it belonged to 18 Jog, who was 2 Jeweled Skull's favorite nephew. His name meant a critter halfway between a jaguar and a dog. Other voices haggled for a while in ambassadors' dialect. Apparently this was a pretty big deal. I felt like a pricey prostitute. Finally heard enough to get that some of some of 9 Fanged Hummingbird's commanders were buying their passage into exile—or maybe even 9 Fanged Hummingbird's—with a number of captives, especially me.

Maybe we were getting somewhere. Maybe the earthstar stuff had worked. Maybe Lady Koh's army had gotten the upper hand somehow. Hot spit. Maybe.

They struck a deal. An Ocelot guard took the birds and handed my leash over to Hun Xoc.

It took a minute to register. Four cheers for our side, I thought. We dun it. We grabbed the gold, won the battle, war, big bajoor, whatever. *Victoria!* I was getting something close to a flood of relief, but I was still too freaked to really latch on to it. Hun Xoc led me through a low door but as I got up I collapsed again and I remember only a little bit of getting brought into a small off-square Ocelot courtyard. The walls were frescoed with cat immortals. Some of the younger, less powerful ones had simply been canceled by gouging out their onyx eyes, but the main ones had been placated with flowers and smears of blood. If 2JS was going to take over, he'd have to get himself adopted into the Ocelots' clan and start courting the Ocelots' gods' goodwill. To be in charge of Ix you really had to be an Ocelot. It was an Ocelot town. I guess it sounds silly, but everybody just knew that jaguars were the mightiest creatures and if you were on the very top, you were descended from jaguars. You couldn't just change the title.

They took me to a round raised platform in the center of the courtyard. I checked out the sky, maybe for the last time. It was just a parallelogram of overcast and white smoke but I could tell it was sometime in the morning. I could hear a few far-off Harpy war shouts but none close by. Things still looked a little droopy and I wondered whether I was thinking clearly, even aside from exhaustion and blood loss and poison darts and whatever, and I thought maybe I wasn't. I guessed I'd gotten a brush of that stuff during my little dip. They pushed me down on a convalescence mat and a couple of dressers started working on me, rubbing ashes and perfumes into my lacerations. They gave me soothing warm beverages and prechewed honey tortillas. At some point I heard shells and cabochons tinkling and saw 2 Jeweled Skull had come into the courtyard. I was so glad to see him I would have wet my breechclout if I hadn't been emptied during my latest period of unconsciousness. He came over to where I was sprawled out on the mat, which was a big deal for him and a big honor for me. He was all decked out, the ultimate example of how you could be loaded down with ornament and still not look ridiculous. The blue circles tattooed around his orbitals made him look cool and mysterious, like you were seeing his eyes through sunglasses, and he had his black pyrite mirror on his forehead, like that third eye thing doctors used to wear.

"My son is a four-hundred-blood capturer," 2 Jeweled Skull said to me. It meant I was going to be seated in the Harpy clan as an *ahau*. It was the highest promotion you could get besides becoming a bacab, like 2JS, or the ahau of ahauob, like 9 Fanged Hummingbird. I've arrived, I thought.

"Your game has been recorded as a win

For the Harpy House,"

he said. Also a very big deal. I mumbled an unofficial thank-you and started one of the short speeches of congratulations on his "capture of the center of the world," his taking Ix. He cut me off.

"Our win has yet to be solidified," he said. On the west side of the courtyard, the public side, a messenger came in with a dispatch 2JS had to deal with and he took his leave for a moment, using an among-equals form. Evidently he was really busy. I'll just hang out here for a while, I thought. Me and the rest of the big shots. Relief soaked into me again. Except, wait, I wondered, where's Lady Koh? There were four-hundred-tesseracted things I had to ask her. Starting with whether she'd remembered to tell all our friendlies not to drink the water.

I started to get up. The dressers couldn't hold me down because they didn't have the authority, so they let me get halfway to standing. Then they caught me as I keeled over. I heard 2JS talking with Hun Xoc and some of his commanders.

You have to wait, I thought. I looked up at the sky. I don't know whether I faded out or not but at some point later 2 Jeweled Skull had come back again and was asking me if I was all right.

I said I felt ready to play another ball game right now. He smiled.

And something in the smile—

Something wasn't quite right. I'd been about to ask him whether they'd told him not to drink the water, to make sure he knew about the earthstar compound. But there was something—hmm.

I've never thought of myself as a great judge of character. When other kids in grade school were learning spelling from flash cards, I had a special set of cards that were supposed to teach me emotions, like it had a face with X's for eyes and a tongue sticking out and I was supposed to check off the word *disgusted.* But maybe Chacal was a better judge. Or at least he picked up on the vocal microtones of a lie, or inimical pheromones, or something. Anyway, somewhere in Chacal's lower brains, the cortices that scent danger on a reptilian level, somewhere in there a neuron fired that said *Don't tell him.*

And I didn't. Instead, I congratulated him again on the victory. He said thanks, it was nothing—part of the polite protocol—and then said it looked secure but had cost the Harpy House a lot of bloods. I said that was too bad but that they died "in the right place," as we put it, and he said yes. I asked him if I could ask him a question. He said fine.

I asked—or inquired politely—whether Hun Xoc or 5-5 was still "in the middle level," that is, alive.

My son 5-5 is dead, 2 Jeweled Skull said. My son Hun Xoc is missing, and not claimed by the Ocelots.

I said the necessary things. After that I was expected to ask, "And who else of our family have we lost?" to which he'd recite the list. Then I'd ask, "And whom have we taken?" and he'd recite that presumably much bigger list. But we didn't do any of that. I guess he'd gotten enough of me to be a little less formal. Instead he said we'd hear the triumphant speeches later, around the conquest feast, but that he had to go see to the repair of the palisades. He said he was already digging a dry moat across the "Right Shoulder," the narrowest part of the northern pass into the valley.

I asked if I could ask about something else.

He said all right.

I asked whether he knew where Lady Koh was.

I don't know, he said, we had to win without Lady Koh's help. Which is why "win" may still be a bit of an exaggeration.

I held my right hand up to my mouth, with the palm open, and rotated it to the right, meaning, "That's hard to believe, tell me more."

2 Jeweled Skull said that he'd seen images from my memory in his mind, historic battles and formations of paper soldiers over vast map tables, and

that after I'd left he'd drilled a squad of a hundred of his best blowgun marksmen as an archery-style firing line. He'd broken the families up into smaller units and told them to keep fighting even if their lords and standards were captured, just like I'd tried to do back at Teotihuacán. He'd done everything right. Lady Koh's army never showed up, but despite inferior numbers he'd taken the temple-district peninsula and most of the city.

But we're still vulnerable, he said, we still need the Rattlers' help, and Koh's army isn't here.

I said that even if Koh had been captured by the Ocelots, 1 Gila was supposed to be bringing in the Rattler army anyway.

He said the equivalent of "Well, we're waiting."

I asked whether he had any idea what had happened to Lady Koh after the ball game. I was getting this dizzy, ripped-off, betrayed feeling.

2 Jeweled Skull said that if the Ocelots had captured her he would have heard about it. They would have offered to trade her. Either she'd sold us out and made a deal with 9 Fanged Hummingbird, or somehow she'd had her guards spirit her away at the very beginning of the battle, or maybe she'd gotten out some other way. If she had made a deal with the ahau of the Ocelots, that is, 9 Fanged Hummingbird, it would mean she was coming back later, with him and Severed Right Hand, to retake Ix.

So 9 Fanged Hummingbird is still alive and outside the city? I asked.

Yes, he said. I think Koh may have been plotting with 8 Smoking Peeper, the Ixian Rattler feeder. Maybe that whole business with the Ocelots getting 8 Smoking Peeper onto their side was just an excuse for her to get away from us. It was setup city.

But the Rattler army was in our own territory, I said. The border patrols out there would have to know where they are.

I haven't heard anything, he said.

We looked at each other.

Dang.

I started to make a formal apology. It wasn't like I'd vouched for Lady Koh or anything, but still, I guess I should have seen this coming.

2 Jeweled Skull said I'd done more than any of his other sons had ever done for him.

I gestured, "Thanks to my Father," and he gestured, "Accepted."

There was another pause. Behind me 2JS's commanders were impatient to go. He looked past me at them and gestured for them to wait another ten beats. He looked back at me. Under all the fooferaw, he was starting to look like a worn-out old politician.

I said I supposed no one from 1 Gila's squad had given him the Scorpion-adders or the tzam lic either. He can't know about the earthstar drug, I thought. Can he? No, no way. Koh and I'd kept that one too close to our vests. Didn't—

"No," 2JS said. "They haven't given me anything."

I didn't answer. He asked whether I had gotten any idea of where Koh might have gone. I said no.

Was there anyplace they talked about in the region? he asked. Anywhere they might have supporters and space and cover, where they could go to regroup?

I said I didn't know of any. If anyone had set something like that up, it would have been 1 Gila.

And Lady Koh never told you anything? he asked.

I said no. I thought we'd talked through everything, but evidently she fooled me. I'm a fool, I'm a porcupine, I'm not worthy.

"Nothing?" he asked again.

"No," I said, "I didn't—"

I paused like there was something in my throat.

2 Jeweled Skull looked at me.

I looked back.

He'd looked at me that *way,* with that same scraping-the-back-of-your-skull look he'd had when he first interrogated me such a hard, if not long, time ago, and I understood.

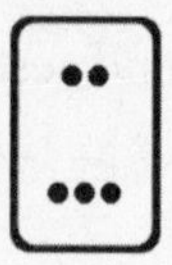

(43)

Without any perceptible change of expression, his eyes shifted to that look that—hmm. It's that look . . . let me think . . . okay. Instead of trying to describe it, let's do this. If you have a dog, there's a way to see this that involves scaring yourself. Make eye contact with your dog, command her/him to sit, and reward the behavior with a strip of turkey jerky or bacon or something your dog loves the smell of. Keeping him/her sitting, and keeping up eye contact, take another strip and hold it in front of your face, right between your eyes. Your dog's expression will shift ever so subtly, but, if you've done it right, the shift is terrifying. Something in his face had something of my own mind in its expression, something I could read.

2 Jeweled Skull thought I might be in league with Lady Koh, and he could tell that I could see it in him.

He looked away from me and waved the commanders out of the little courtyard. Suddenly it felt all private, just him, me, the two dressers holding me, his two heralds, and Hun Xoc.

"Well, listen, if you were Lady Koh, where would you be?" 2 Jeweled Skull asked in my own nearly unaccented English.

"Dead," I said. Hmm, I thought. Guess he'd picked up a little more of my old Jed-mind than he'd let me realize eighty-two days ago.

Idiot.

"Well, I guess it's nice of you to let the old veil slip and everything, though," I said in English. "Finally."

"Oh, well, yeah, sorry," he said, in practically a Jed voice, just a little higher and older. "You know, I didn't want you to get confused."

"I was already confused," I said.

"Anyway, it's nice to have someone you can talk to, right?" he asked. No kidding, I thought. Just hearing English spoken again was sending my emotions into a stupid, automatic tailspin.

"Right," I said.

"I just wanted to double our chances, you know?"

"I know." I was getting dizzy from the flood of homesickness and had to bite my lip to keep myself from crawling over and hugging him. Maybe we could just go crack a couple of hot cactus ales and grab some cheeseless nachos and kick back and chat about whatever—

"So maybe we can work together on this," he said.

"Uh, yeah, and whichever one of us lives is going to go back?" I asked.

"I don't know," he said, "maybe we'll both go back. There's room in the tomb. Twombsome with youse'm. Tomb with a viewm."

"And they'll load both of our memories into Jed-Sub-One?"

"Sure," he said, "I mean, maybe it's possible, I've been thinking about it a lot and I don't see why not."

"Nonsense," I said.

"Give it a little thought. They can probably do it. We just have to make sure they do. Whichever of us gets uploaded first has to make sure Marena girl does the other too."

"Yeah, sure. That won't work and you know it."

"Well, let's try it."

"No way," I said, "You'll off me a long time before that happens."

"Why do you think that?"

"Because it's what I'd do."

"No, it's not."

"Yes, it is," I said. "As you well know. We're going to off the Jed that's back there, aren't we?"

"What do you mean?"

"That Jed that's there without our memories, when everything we've been through gets uploaded into him, that Jed, Jed-Sub-One, he's going to basically die," I said. "And we don't even care. That's just the way it is."

"Hmm."

"It's survival of the shittiest. Why are you even asking me, do you think Chacal's brain is so stunted I couldn't work this stuff out?"

He grinned. "Well, I had wondered about that," he said. "Chacal's ideational skills and everything."

"Chacal's brain's as smart as Jed's was," I said. "Maybe not so fast on calculation, but on spatiotemporal it's way ahead."

"How nice for you," 2 Jeweled Me said. "Well, whatever. Anyway, maybe we can work out a deal."

"I guess—"

"I mean, if you can't negotiate with yourself, then, with whom?"

"Mm," I said. "Yeah, I was just about to say that." This whole thing was bumming me out, I felt naked talking with this hostile version of myself. It's disturbing enough just to watch yourself on video. "So, you're just good old Jed, right?" I asked. "You're totally in control of 2 Jeweled Skull."

"Believe it or not, yes," he said.

"I don't believe it," I said. "You're still 2JS. I mean, 2JS's running you."

Don't let his newly cozy persona fool you, I thought. You're not really talking to yourself, I'm talking to my personal body snatcher pod-person.

"Listen, there was as much of a chance of my getting killed here as your getting killed out there," he said. "The main thing was just always just getting the tsam lic back."

"Sure," I said. Somehow he wasn't touching my heart. "If you're so hip and everything, why didn't you do something really amazing? Maybe you should have built a machine gun."

"Well, I didn't want to rock the boat too much," he said. "I was still in a bad spot here, you know, no matter how cool you are somebody can always get you."

"Yeah."

"The blowgun squad's enough and enough is always correct. I don't want to trip the Cosmic Censor or anything."

"There is no Cosmic Censor."

"Well, I just thought somebody might hear about a machine gun or something so it wouldn't work. Or something."

"I guess."

"Anyway, everything's pretty secure here. I'm not worried. Unless we can't find Koh."

"Great," I said. I could tell he meant that he had the whole tomb setup ready to be installed. The folgerite, the gel stuff, everything. He was planning to head back for the bad old latter days right on schedule.

"I just wonder whether there's something you're not telling me. And I do need to learn that Sacrifice Game business." He was trying to sound casual about it, but of course he was as nervous as I was. If Koh was dead there wasn't much of a chance that he'd get very far with the Game. Especially not with setting up a human game. According to her—and although she could be cagey, I believed her on this one—there were only a few other living people who knew how to do it, and they'd been scattered with the fall of Teotihuacán. Maybe one or two of them were in Severed Right Hand's camp, but even that wasn't certain.

"Ask the Ocelots," I said.

"That may be a bit difficult," he said. "They're a recalcitrant bunch. Anyway, I had to let 9 Fanged Hummingbird go just to get you back. For which you're welcome, by the way."

"Thanks."

"It's okay," he said. The English words sounded odder than ever in this context. "Anyway, we should talk to Koh. And I don't want to risk running around looking for her."

"I don't know where she is," I said. "Why don't you just bring out your nefarious instruments and we'll get started on proving it?"

"Listen, we're twins," he said. "We're even better than twins, we're clones."

"Clonies. Cronies," I said.

"If we fight we're just fighting ourself."

"Come to me, my son," I said in the deepest voice I could manage, imitating James Earl Jones playing Thulsa Doom in a Geraldine fright wig in *Conan the Barbarian*. Needless to say, he knew exactly what I was referring to. He laughed. I know I always laughed out loud whenever I thought about that scene.

"Come on, think about it, if I'd let you know I was just like you, you might have come after me. Right? How could I know what you were going to do? The right thing was to make it as possible as possible for you to get the Sacrifice Game. And meanwhile make sure everything here was ready."

Well, it was the kind of thing I would have thought of, I thought. Except I wouldn't have done that to myself. Would I? No. I don't think so, anyway—

"I hear you got along well with Miss Koh," he said.

"Well, yeah, pretty well."

"So maybe she told you what she was going to do."

"Well, or maybe not," I said. "Maybe she didn't trust me."

"No, I think she probably told you something. Or gave you something to do, maybe. Maybe you were supposed to mislead me."

"Oh, I'd never do that."

"No, there's something," he said. It seemed we were having a stare-down contest. "I ought to know."

"Uh, okay," I said. This is getting weird, I thought. It was like when the Tin Man finds his old "meat head" in a cupboard in the eleventh Oz book and they don't get along with each other. More of a monologue than a dialogue. Except it was also like I was one of those split-brain patients whose right hand didn't know what the left one was up to.

"Tell you what," I said, "you give me my command back and I'll go find Lady Koh and bring her back here and we'll all talk."

"I don't think so," he said. "You'll probably come back with an AR-15 and take me out."

"Well, so, like they're going to say, if you can't trust yourself who can you trust?" I asked.

"Yeah, that's the problem," he said. "Listen, we're short on time."

"Sorry," I said. There wasn't much more to talk about. Except for the stuff he didn't know, he knew everything. If you know what I mean. The first dresser, who I guess was now officially a teaser, held me a bit tighter while the second went off to get something.

And Koh had run out on me too. Silly me, I guess I'd thought a deal was a deal and we'd all live happily ever after. I guess I hadn't really been ready to play in the big leagues. Where the main difference is the rules. Lack of.

Or maybe she was regrouping, planning a second raid.

No, she'd probably given up on the whole project and headed farther south. Leaving me stranded.

2 Jeweled Skull gestured over my shoulder to the teaser. I got the first little hit of that deep-down fear-bloom, when it feels like a little hole just opens in the bottom of your stomach and all this crud starts trickling out. The second teaser kneeled down in front of me.

Think, I thought.

Maybe Koh hadn't told them about the earthstars. I guess I'd just kind of assumed she was getting the word to them. Maybe she hadn't told anyone. Maybe she wanted to take out everybody.

And nobody'd told him they'd picked me out of the Great Cistern. If they had he'd have gotten wise to what had happened in about a yoctosecond. And he would have told me he was taking care of it, just so I wouldn't have any lingering hopes.

And it's only twelve hours since I dumped the stuff, I thought. At most. The Harpies wouldn't have started drinking the affected water until a couple of hours ago. That meant there might be a few people just starting to feel the effects pretty soon. Even longer if it was as slow as Koh said it was in cold water.

It's going to be a hot day, I thought. They'll taste the water for the usual poisons and they'll all be drinking up a storm. And they'll be having a victory party then anyway. Maybe nobody'll wise up until tomorrow, even.

Don't tell him. Maybe he'll even drink some of the shit himself. If you only don't tell him one thing, that's it.

The jerk, I thought. Bad timing. He should have cozied up to me a minute longer.

"So, what's Miss Snake up to?" he asked.

"She wouldn't really tell me," I said. "We didn't talk that much, I wasn't up to her social class."

"Liar," he said. "Prick on fire." The teaser pulled my penis out from under the little padded ball-loincloth and held it in his right hand.

"You can't mess with me," I said, "I'm 400-Capturing 9 Wax Ahau." The teaser gently inserted a little reed-skewer into the tip and pushed it three fingerwidth up into the urethra. It was pretty painful. 2JS crouched down closer to my face, reading me, looking for something. It wasn't just like there wasn't any warmth there anymore. He'd never had warmth, exactly. It was like he looked like the lethal injection room at the Terre Haute Correctional Facility, nicely decorated but not a place you want to be. But something in his face was also mine. My stupid, goofy expression, all transformed into something crisp and efficient. I got a wave of that "Give Up!" feeling, like you get in chess when you get down a piece early in the game. Stifle that, I thought. Come on. Be Muhammad Ali. Bounce fucking back.

Think.

He's pretty eager for me to give up Lady Koh. That means he thinks she's coming after him.

Okay. Think. Get to that glassy-calm cool state. Take the long shot. Plan L. What would a Starfleet commander do in this situation? Think, think, thinkedy-dink—

EOOOOAOAOAAAAEEAEEEAEEEAEEEIIIEIIEIIIIIYIYIYYYY!!!!!

The teaser was blowing chili-water up into me through the reed. I tried to flex my eyes and suck the tears back into their ducts, relax the face, relax the face.

Thimk. What actually happened?

Maybe our whole expedition to Teotihuacán would have worked for him anyway, even if we hadn't brought back the tzam lic, because the main idea was to distract the Ocelots' attention from 2JS's preparations. And when 2JS was sending us all those messengers on the road about how much trouble he was in, it was all just bullshit. He had to create a balanced effect. The impression that the situation was dire enough that we'd believe in his air of resignation when we got here, but not so dire that we wouldn't get here at all. 2JS planned to use Koh's force to fight his battle for him, then blame it all on her and turn her and the other Rattler leaders in to Severed Right Hand as a peace offering. And 2JS would stay on the throne here in Ix, without threat from the Ocelots. *No mierda,* Miss Marple.

And then if Koh didn't make it to Ix, 2JS was planning to defeat Severed

Right Hand with his Frederick the Great squad, and then turn her and the other Rattler leaders in anyway, from a distance.

The teasers jerked my head down and there was another blast of pain, a column of magnesium sparks up through my abdomen into the roots of my hair, and when I was sane again I realized they'd blasted the chili extract up my ass with one of those enema things. The arc of pain seemed to descend for a moment and then somewhere inside me the two blasts met and interacted somehow, and it was like I was a mother parthenogenic fly, being eaten by my own ten thousand babies. Find the gray zone, I thought. Not many people know about it, but far out in the sea of pain there's a not-unpleasant island.

2JS signed to the second teaser to bring in the others. Time to quit screwing around and start the real show.

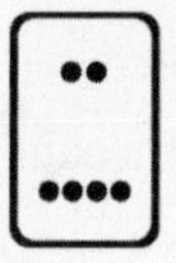

(44)

They strung me in the center of the platform and set Armadillo Shit on my right, a little ahead of me and facing in so I could look at him. They'd trussed him up in a fetal position, stuffed him into a big wicker jar, and poured wet lime-plaster down around him so that only his head was showing. I gave him a "Sorry" expression and he gave me that pathetic anything-for-you-boss devoted-underling look back. There was a ring of morning glories around his panting head. The setup was artful in its way. I guessed they were going to keep him alive as long as possible and just see what happened. I shivered at it a bit, but I could understand their fascination in the experiment. It's like the way little kids' curiosity is totally cute, but it has a cruel side. I'm not proud of being receptive to it, but that stuff has an allure that's hard to explain to Fifth-Sunfolks, that is, citizens of the twenty-first-century. You have to think of that stage that children go through. I guess it's usually around the ages of nine to fourteen, at least in the industrialized late-capitalist West or whatever. Anyway, at some point in there, most kids, especially the boys, are obsessed with really gross-out stuff, including theoretical if not actual torture devices. Supposedly they prefer whatever toys seem most repulsive to their parents. And we still had a lot of that sensibility. I mean we, like, the Maya ruling class. Twenty-first-century sophisticates would dismiss it as preadolescent humor, but we thought of as tragicomic religiotheatrical art.

Come on, think, I thought. Maybe last chance to think for a while. Come on. Get it straight. I was having trouble getting it together. I was still a bit more disturbed by the possibility that Koh had abandoned me than by the possibility of spending the next twenty years in continuous and indescribable torment.

Okay. 2JS never had any intention of honoring his commitment to Koh. He wouldn't need a rival in Ix later anyway. Once he was entrenched in Ix he'd need peace with the Ocelots, the Pumas, all the other cat clans, everybody. Right? Right. He'd want to become one of them. He'd have zero reason to keep his word. Except for his family bonds. Which he probably cared less about since he'd gotten an infusion of relativism out of my consciousness. My little contribution had created a monster—

They brought in Hun Xoc. He'd been knocked around a bit but not badly wounded. The Ocelots had probably let him take out two or three of their bloods in order to get him alive. They tied him to a prefabricated scaffold in the Good Thief position, a bit in front of me on my left. I looked at him like "Sorry, I screwed up," and he looked back like "No, *I* screwed up." Otherwise he just looked confused. Why was his father doing this to him? Because he hadn't played well enough in the ball game? One of the teasers started playing with Armadillo Shit, tweaking his face with a thistle stalk. Just a warm-up act. No more massages, I thought. No more fixing up extensions for old 9 Wax's hair. I was getting a little sad. Squelch that. Armadillo Shit's breathing was already quick and shallow and it got worse. I wondered what his skin felt like. Lime is corrosive. Another one tied a thong around Hun Xoc's left elbow, twisting it tighter and tighter with a stick.

Damn, I thought, I blew it. I nearly had it, just forty-seven days left, and I failed. Fail, flail, frailed.

Maybe it's okay if 2 Jeweled Skull goes back instead of me. I mean, instead of this me.

Except it's not, is it? If he does go back he's going to do something rotten. There's just something bad about that guy. Maybe I was a bad influence on him. No, maybe he was always bad. I don't know.

I was sure he wouldn't do the right thing, though.

2 Jeweled Skull's attendants put an ocelot-pelt cushion behind him and he

sat back on it, nibbling a honey tortilla and watching us like we were TV. Trying to act casual. It's not going to work, I thought. He's worried something's up.

"Ti ku ti bin xot u cal tumen," 2JS said to Hun Xoc. "You (inferior) have shat in our house." Suddenly he was all Chol court language again.

He's not me, I thought, 2JS isn't me.

I was pretty sure. I wasn't running 2JS, or rather, the other copy of Jed_1 wasn't running him. He was running himself. It wasn't because he was being such a bastard and I was such a great guy or anything. It was just because I really would have handled everything a little differently. Maybe worse, even, but differently. It's hard to explain. Somehow you could tell this guy was still thinking like a Maya ahau. Not like screwed-up little me.

"Please offer me, my father," Hun Xoc said.

His arm was puffing up like a nuked hot dog.

"Your brother's parasite came here to wreck us,"
2JS said. "It's just a gut-snake speaking through
The mouth of Son Chacal's decaying skin."

"This blind, unworthy non-son didn't know," Hun Xoc said.

He said he didn't know what he was being asked for or how he'd screwed up. No kidding, I thought. 2JS can't really be expecting Hun Xoc to know much. They'd brought him here more for my benefit. What did Hun Xoc really understand about me, anyway? Not a lot when you got down to it. I'd really leveled with him, almost as much as I had with Koh. But he wasn't the intellectual she was. I was sure he expressed it all to himself in terms of familiar concepts, wandering *uayob* and whatever. He thought I was still Chacal somehow, like Chacal's disembodied spirit had visited this weird place during a night journey. He'd asked a lot about the seventy-eighth hotun but I'd always had to simplify my account. Certainly I'd never been able to really explain how engines worked or anything. He'd been interested in it but it was like Strange Tales of Another Dimension to him, he'd never apply any of it to his own experience—

2JS signaled again. One of the teasers had a short wood-and-flint bone saw, and he positioned it on Hun Xoc's forearm, just below the elbow, and pulled the first stroke. Purple deoxygenated blood sprayed up like beads, turning red in the air. His teaser twisted his arm slightly, directing the spray away from himself and into Hun Xoc's face. I hadn't been watching but my own teaser had gotten another mouthful of chili water and blew it up into me, farther this time, while someone behind me squeezed the enema bag again. Staccato sting-rolls spread out of my groin and through every micrometer of my earth's-diameter-length network of arteries and veins and capillaries, and congealed into a mesh of razor wire. When I could think at all again I waited for the pain to slide onto its descending curve. It was the only part where you could get anything together mentally.

Okay. I retreated into chess mode. Next move. Other side. On track. Think. I visualized a pudgy little Hercule Poirot doll waddling around in my head, stroking his mustaches and pointing out inconsistencies.

What's Koh doing?

Maybe she'd gotten herself killed somehow. Or maybe when she saw she was going to get captured she'd just cut herself with a poison ray spine. Maybe she didn't want to be traded out to what was, after all, just another enemy. Maybe 1 Gila took control of her troops and didn't tell her.

No, that's ridiculous. They're fanatically loyal to her. She has Unlimited Personal Power. Her armies are still out there somewhere, waiting for something.

Okay, Logic.

Koh hadn't trusted 2 Jeweled Skull and she wouldn't trust the Ocelots either.

She'd anticipated that 2 Jeweled Skull would sell her out once he'd used me to lure her to Ix. She never had any illusions about what would happen to her once she helped seat 2 Jeweled Skull on the Ocelots' Emerald Mat. She knew he would have come after her next. Even if he wanted to promote the Star-Rattler cult after he came to power, he'd to do it through manipulatable venerators, not through a headstrong leader like Koh.

Okay. So she saw it coming. She knew he'd fuck her over, so she told the Rattler Children to stay away. No wonder we didn't get any word from the twelve Harpy emissaries all that time, I'd bet a buck she issued orders for 1 Gila to kill them immediately so they couldn't report back to 2JS.

For that matter, she'd probably set up 1 Gila's idea to split the forces in the first place. That whole thing was just an act. Okay.

Koh's still out there, with her army, or what's left of it. Okay. So when Koh's army didn't show up, though, that actually surprised 2JS. Right? Right. He'd been counting on them to take the heat in the fight. The idea was to co-opt them and then sacrifice them once they put him in a good position. Even so, though, his blowgun squad carried the day.

Okay. So what about Koh's long-range plan? What was she up to? Or more to the point, what was she up to with me?

Maybe I was only good to her for the well run. Koh couldn't have sent her own squad to the well because then 2JS would have wondered what they were doing there. The most convincing story would be that I was trying to escape. It would keep him from thinking about where I was when I was captured—

"Where were you going when they took you?" 2JS asked Hun Xoc.

"The mainland," Hun Xoc said.

"To do what?"

"To meet someone, that's all I know," Hun Xoc said.

Ah so, I thought. 2JS thinks we were going to meet Lady Koh. The teaser twisted off Hun Xoc's forearm and started working on the other one. To my right they were peeling strips of skin off Armadillo Shit's cheeks.

2JS walked over to me, reached out, and took my chin, like he was thinking of pulling my jaw off. His hand left little images of itself trailing after it in the air. Evidently I was still pretty messed up.

"So, Koh has something up her cunt, right?" he whispered in English.

"Sure, she's heading for Kaminaljuyu," I lied. "By a west-coast route. She's going to regroup her force there and decide on the next move."

"Bullshit," he said. "If there's one thing I know about it's what's going on in fucking Kaminaljuyu." He reached out and touched my jaw with a sharpened index nail.

(45)

"Well, it *is* a secret," I said.

"Listen," he said. "Jeddy face. Buddy."

"Yeah?"

"You know you can't last, right?"

"Uh, yeah," I said.

He was probably right. It's not totally true that everyone cracks eventually. Hun Xoc would never crack, for instance. But I wasn't that strong a character anymore. I wouldn't hold out all the way through to a horrible death. I wasn't Chacal, I was Jed, and Jed was just a mixed-up punk kid.

"So let's not mess up the whole project just because you're disappointed that you're not going to be the one going back. You do want the project to work, don't you? You *do* want to keep the world running. Jed?"

"Yes?"

"Are you following me?"

"Yeah," I said.

He let go of my chin. He's rushing, I thought. Even if my Jedness would weaken me it might still take hours to get me to talk. A couple of days if I was really motivated. And normally he would have expected to wait that long. The teasers might work on you for months, until they were sure you'd do anything to just be killed without another session. Everyone was so hard around here that if they were ever actually trying to get information out of someone, the levels of pain and time involved multiplied exponentially. And if you were the victim, the general wisdom was that the only thing to do was to be so maddeningly bland that they'd kill you ahead of schedule.

But if you were the interrogator, if you rushed the process you might kill the subject. Or drive him insane, or at least make it actually take longer. It was a bad idea to allow for less than a couple of days.

So 2JS didn't think he had a couple of days—

The attendant behind me held my head up and my eyes open. 2JS took a pinch of dry chili strings in two fingers. I got in a last, and I hoped scornful, glance at him. He held his hand up and delicately blew the threads into my eyes. At first it just felt like I'd peeled and chopped a mound of onions in a couple of beats, there was all that tearing and burning and itchy-nose liquefying way back up in my sinuses and the needing to blink—although in this case I wasn't able to—but as the powder worked its way up into my eyelids and down and around into my tear ducts it got to a whole different level, buzzing heat bubbling up into explosions of dry-ice bergs spiking through cracks in my skull.

"Jed?" 2JS asked.

Come on. Think of something really, really plausible. Something that'll take a while to check out.

"She's coming after you," I said. "I gave her all these plans and she's building onagers and crossbows and shit right now. She's going to level this place."

"Yeah, sure."

"Blowgun squad indeed. Fuck that, you should have come up with an antiartillery squad."

"You're not convincing me," he said.

"Fine," I said. Don't say anything more, I thought. That's the worst thing you can do. Stick with the one story. Eventually he'll start asking about it again. Catapults. I could hear sizzling and smell burning flesh and skin. They must have been holding Hun Xoc's stump against a hearthstone to cauterize it. The hot tears streaking down my neck felt acidic, like they were loaded with salts of despair. 2JS asked Hun Xoc something but I couldn't hear what it was through the popcorn cracklings in my ears. Hun Xoc answered that he didn't know. His voice sounded pretty normal. It must have taken a big effort. This kind of test of will was a big deal in a blood's life. If you screwed up and cracked it meant your uay was shit-weak, but if you were cool you were in like Flynn. It was something you almost looked forward to. Attaboy, I thought. Just try not to mention where I was going when they caught you. Please.

I guess right around there I passed out for the first time of the session—and like I said, way too early—because the attendants were holding my eyes open and one of the teasers was spitting drinking water into it to clear it enough for me to see what was going on. Servers were setting up two tripod stands on the lip of the platform in front of us, with big steaming dishes right out of a cookhouse. The attendant behind me released my right arm and I was instantly rubbing it into my eyes. Even a little relief really is blessed. It felt like I'd just won the lottery. Fuck, itching is really something. It needs a stronger word than *itching*. A server took the lid off the first dish. It was just a stack of *waah*, tortillas. He peeled off one and handed it to me. The other server took the lid off the second. It was Hun Xoc's forearms, quick-baked over a big eternally hot river-stone and then infused with chocolate ale and sliced in almost a spiral cut down to the bone. Very Morton's. The tattoos on the wrists had been touched up with food-paint and the hands were arranged to sign "I traitor." I closed my eyes but my head-holding guard pried my eyelids up with his fingers and turned my head back down to the dish. The roaster peeled off a well-done strip from the end and they guided my hand to roll it into my tortilla and moved it up to my mouth. I wasn't thrilled but at this point I was already like, anything to put off the next inevitable, so I just chomped into it. It wasn't too good. Everything tastes like ostrich. They made sure I swallowed and moved over to Hun Xoc.

"Please taste yourself," 2 Jeweled Skull said in Chol, laughing under his breath in a way I wouldn't have. "We mixed 9 Wax shit with the sauce for you."

Hun Xoc just clicked his tongue twice to refuse. They started force-feeding him. He was laughing a little himself. 2JS took a tortilla with a good slice of Hun Xoc in it and chomped into it with his old filed teeth. On my right they were blowing salt water on Armadillo Shit's raw cheeks, and he was cracking, but just babbling gibberish. They didn't even pretend that he might know anything. 2JS must have been getting impatient because he signed for the attendant behind me to hold my eyes way open, and he came over and held a sharpened-nailed finger up to my right eye. He didn't ask anything, he just chewed.

"Like I said, I told Koh everything," I whispered. That earthstar shit had better be working, I thought, and I almost thought he could hear me thinking, GO EARTHSTAR! GO EARTHSTAR! *Don't* say it. Don't even think it. Keep him focused. "I gave her the recipe for *gunpowder*. You're fucked through the dick with a battle saw. She's going to bomb this place back into the Stone Age. Oh, sorry, we're still *in* the Stone Age around here, aren't we—"

He poked his finger into my eye. There was a flash and the feeling of a balloon popping all through the right side of my head, and then I could feel him prying out the eyeball and ripping it off the optic nerve. It was painful, but not more so than some other things I'd put up with lately. It was really just that instinctive urge to protect an eye, the panic and the helplessness, that was tough to take.

He held my deflated eyeball up to my remaining left eye. Its pupil was dilating. A pink drop of vitreous humor stretched out and finally dropped off.

"This sucks," I said.

2JS said something you could translate as "Your ball days are over. Would you like me to take the other ball as well and put out your sun?" But it was kind of an untranslatable pun, since he used the same word, *k'iin,* to mean "ball," "eye," "day," and "sun."

"So you're giving up on the English?" I asked. He put his fingernail against the eyeball. "I don't need that eye either," I said. "Not if I'm going to be looking at you, anyway. You look like if Margaret Hamilton had been in *Once Were Warriors*." I was still acting blustery but actually I was worried I was about to crack, getting to that point when the doctors of pain really do become a lot more frightening than death, just flailing on this macker of panic. The pain and the idea of blindness were heavy enough but 2 Jeweled Skull's character was another whole level of pressure, I was fighting his insight into character and his near-mirror-perfect insight into me especially, fighting his old dominance over Chacal, fighting his Jedness, it was rough. Maybe I'll just tell him what's going on and we'll all laugh it off later. No, wait. Squelch that. Cold out. But instead of using up the other eye he wiped his finger off while one of the teasers stuffed my empty eye socket with chili strings. At first it was just shrieking sound and flashes of lightning, my reptile brain thinking I'd been frozen and dropped and shattered, and then it peaked and settled into a long, slow shriek of the razor wire through the vessels, shark-skinning all 862 receptor neurons from the wrong side, the inside. For some reason I came out of it singing, "I don't care, I don't care," like Judy Garland in *In the Good Old Summertime*. I could hear tears dripping out of my eye onto the mat, but was pretty sure everyone could tell they were only from laughing. Someone threw water over me to shut me up and get my attention.

"This is your last chance for me to just kill your friend," 2JS said too impatiently. "Otherwise he's going to be a twenty-year captive."

"Well, I just have to let him go," I said. Just don't tell him, I thought. Don't tell him about the earthstar compound, and don't tell him what Lady Koh's planning to do. Just those two things. Anything else is fine. Just hang on to those for a little longer and . . . and . . . well, and then there's at least a chance, a slim chance . . .

2JS gave the order to gag me. The teasers started packing up Armadillo Shit, who I guess had died. If I was going to talk like that, 2JS wanted to talk to me alone. He turned for a last stab at Hun Xoc. Three fingers were sticking out of his mouth in an actually pretty comical way.

Your skin tastes sour, 2JS said. Like you're nervous, like you're lying. Where did 9 Wax go after he abandoned you? He pulled the fingers out of Hun Xoc's mouth.

He ran south, down the path to the yellow gate, Hun Xoc said. There were traitors from the Snuffler clan waiting there to meet him. They were going to smuggle him to Kaminaljuyu.

Whoa, I thought.

Hun Xoc had figured out I'd been going for the well. Maybe he'd heard about the earthstar stuff or maybe he just figured out that something was up.

Either way, he was lying for me. It was unheard of.

Even I was shocked. Resisting your father wasn't just individual disobedience. It was irreparably damaging the family's eternal uay. It was heavy business.

"Behead me, please," I said in a flood of resignation. No need to be flip. Just get it over with. Just don't tell him. "I don't know anything, just offer me. Make me holy."

Hun Xoc looked at me. His eyes had sunk into that steely war face, that don't-tell-them-anything-no-matter-what expression. I signed "Agreed" with my remaining eye.

Which was about it for a while. Maybe they blasted me again. I can't have blacked out right then, but whenever I did go under I must have lost the time just before.

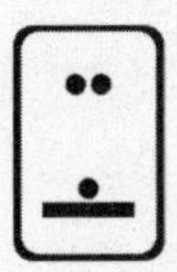

(46)

I realized I was awake again, but there was a minute or so before I could remember where I really was, and instead I thought I was back in the hospital in K'oben, where I'd been when my parents were killed. It was all soaked with gallons of urine and just this solid despair when you don't even know what despair is. I'll remember that smell forever, I mean, at least once per minute between now and forever. Anyway, at some point I figured out that I wasn't a fantasizing sick little kid anymore, I was in this really unusual situation, and I wasn't in a cinder-block building or underground or anything, I was just bandaged over my eyes, and I was in one of an array of captive baskets set in rows like livestock pens. It was stuffy but there was a ventilating shaft overhead. At some point I realized Hun Xoc was nearby. But we just identified ourselves with the usual apologies and it's-all-rights, and didn't say anything else. They were hoping we'd start talking. Idiots, I thought, of course I wasn't going to say anything. I wouldn't say anything if we were tied up outside in the middle of a desert for a year and I was *sure* no one was listening. We worked out an alternating "beater" job position so we could keep track of time. My roughly eight-hour shifts were from what we figured was dawn to noon and then from dusk to midnight. Sometimes I got tired of counting time by Maya beats and started to do it by running through the B side of the Beatles' *Abbey Road* album over and over. It's 19.2 minutes long and it's so easy to hum it's like "Happy Birthday," you can keep time with it and still think about whatever else you want. Maybe we'd be here for years, I thought. Maybe 2JS had worked his thing out and we were just being stored until we cracked. Or didn't. Twenty years is 547,500 *Abbey Road* B sides. When it wasn't my turn to be the clock I just drifted in and out. When you're a bound prisoner you get to a stage where you can't sleep, it's just too uncomfortable, so you sleep in patches, conking out and starting awake again. At about twenty-six hours into our confinement torchlight came in from one side under my bandages and someone pulled our heads up and poured water back into our mouths. Probably the giggle water, I thought. Who cares. Anyway, we'll get to check it out. The guard didn't change or even loosen the bonds. Although I already felt I was sensing where the spy was, about one rope-length behind us. No matter how quiet he was being you could learn to distinguish it from the breezes outside. At thirty hours, the flies started biting. At least they stuck to my left side for some reason. Maybe it was wetter. A better spot for their eggs. At thirty-one hours in I started to smell a black tinge of *Clostridium*, the herald of gangrene, from my poisoned right foot. Great, I thought, on top of everything else. I just lay there, straining my right wrist-rope in a circular motion against its wicker cleat that, in a couple of years, might even wear it through, feeling my scabs crinkling, skin rotting, my body just turning into bits of dirt. My okay leg could feel the heat from my bad leg's decay. I'm just a compost bin, I thought. Postconsumer. Consumed. There weren't a lot of events. Sounds rose and fell outside, all too confused to read. They could have been a battle, a party, a herd of moose, anything. Once in a while a pair of red rats ran under the baskets. I made friends with the columns of flies and *Pediculidae* lice surveying me for development. The thing is, pure despair isn't really that interesting to talk about. After a while, even pain gets boring. Forty-one hours into our confinement, right after my morning clock shift, the wind died down and the rot wafted up again.

"*The water,*" 2 Jeweled Skull's voice said.

I contracted like a poked sea cucumber. I'd thought we were all alone in here. Guess the old guy hasn't lost his New World ninja sneak-up skills. Oh, hi, I thought, sorry, I thought we had the flat all to ourselves.

"It sounds like you're in trouble," I whispered. I didn't have any vocal cords working.

"What is it in the water?" he asked. I felt one of those sharp fingernails gouge through my cheek, but I was getting passive about that stuff.

"I told you she was coming after you," I said. He poked his nail farther into the back of my tongue. I guessed he was trying to say I should answer the question.

"I don't know," I gagged around his finger. "Is there some kind of witchcraft afoot?"

"I'm going to execute your bitch, Hun Xoc, now," he said in Chol.

That sounds good, I said. Is that all right with you? I asked, switching to the "equals" tense Hun Xoc and I used. I heard him grunt yes. But instead 2 Jeweled Skull and someone else started untying me, probably getting me together for another visit to the dentist. I held my breath and pushed it up into my head, straining against myself, what I guess they call red-turning or "doing a raspberry" on the playground, but it was really an old torture-victim's trick. Because it was dark I got away with it and passed satisfyingly out.

(47)

My head got half-going again as they carried me through the open alleys of the Ocelot House and out into the upper zocalo. It was already past noon. Dry-wood-and-lime-smoke hung in the still air. Burning buildings. Somehow there was a sense that the bottom had dropped out of the city. My eye was weird where the teaser had sprayed water on it, it was all jumping around and unfocused, but one of the first things I noticed was a Harpy guard crawling around on the floor, spitting and repeating the same thing over and over, *"Kot wuk, Kot wuk, Kot wuk,"* that is, "Here's my favorite auntie, here's my favorite auntie." Well, that's a good sign, I thought. The earthstar compound was having its desired effect, at least on one person. They passed me down steep steps. There were shouts and the noise of multiple ball impacts that, from the flavor of the echoes, I could tell were coming from the Great-Hipball Court. It was nearby, but I couldn't tell in which direction. Finally I got my eye working and I could see we were on the raised platform in front of the Council Mat House. I didn't have a great sense of depth, and I had to keep swinging my head around to get a wider field of view, so it took me a minute to see that some kind of combat was still going on out in the yellow and red quarters. There were a few lackluster one-on-one fights nearer to us, more like street fights than warfare. We descended to the level of the temple district, down through an almost visible boundary layer into an inversion filled with the miasma of decaying bodies, a beyond-belief stench like opening up a month-dead walrus on a sunny beach and rubbing your face in its fermented gastric juices and self-digested tissues. It wasn't just human, it was also fish decomposing in the canals, with a faint anise scent over everything else. Outside my little escort there were all kinds of people eddying around, castes and clans who would never normally be mixed together, everyone flopping and bumping, saying things that didn't make any sense. Some of them prancing around in luxury clothing and headdresses that weren't theirs, something you'd absolutely never do. One group of Bat House bloods was sitting in a circle, throwing thorn-spiked balls back and forth at each other and crying like little kids with temper tantrums. Maybe Koh's buying me out, I thought. On the other hand maybe the Ocelots are buying me out.

The guards carried me past collapsed wood stands, around little fires and puddles of alcohol and vomit and through the Ocelots' emerald-green end-zone into the main trench of the ball court. Its floor had been neutralized with a layer of thousands of pink geranium blossoms, but otherwise it was a mess, with bits of clothing and weapons and blood all over the stands and platforms. They carried me out over a lake of petals to a big Harpy trading mat that had been laid out in the center of the face-off zone. I didn't see 2JS anywhere but from the way the attendants acted I got the sense he was behind me, watching. There were Harpy guards standing at the banks and on each end zone, but I noticed one of them was unconscious at his post and another two were nibbling on his bare feet, tearing off strips of skin and swallowing them. Looks good, I thought. Some kind of fight erupted behind me and I looked around, but it was just another Harpy blood sitting on the ground and shouting. He was all wild-eyed and foamy at the nose. He started kicking out at his brothers, who stood back and urinated all over him. The far end-zone was mainly pyramidal stacks of bodies, ready to be dealt with but not getting processed. A few were squirming but at least there were more dead ones than live ones. It was a perfect day for the horde of the flies. Some of the corpses hadn't even been stripped of their elaborate-ass festival regalia. It was like those photos of British officers frozen in the Crimea, where they're wearing all this fancy stuff but they're still really messed up. Through the eastern V of the court I could see a bit of the wide steps up to the council house. It all looked like the ratty tail end of a late party, people stagger-dancing and flapping their arms. Harpies with victors' blossoms and untended captives, bloods who had fought against each other a little while ago, were sitting motionless next to each other, staring into nearby infinity. A little Ocelot boy sat on a soldier's dead body, pricking himself over and over on the chest with a spearhead.

Psyche, I thought. Fabulous. I'd been worried that the shit would be too diluted. Not that I was out of the frying pot yet. Trade me out, I thought, they'd better be trading me out. Come on, Koh, babe. Trade me out. A ten-man treaty party was advancing from the other side of the court, but I couldn't make out who they were since they were all in neutral clothes. The Harpy negotiators set me in the center of the trading mat. Again. I wondered whether my stock had gone up or down and tried to check out what was on the other side, but it was just a stack of tied screenfold tribute books and another damn dish of clay tokens I couldn't read through my one messed-up eye. I held myself up for a beat, saw that under their mantos the other traders were Rattlers' Children, which meant they'd come from Lady Koh.

I rolled back on the down-soft fabric. A big fly, her abdomen filled with eggs, lighted on the outside corner of my sighted eye. I blinked but she wouldn't go away. It was too likely a spot. I was too relieved to care much, though. They turned me over to a team of dressers, because I remember being in a neutral-color tent with a couple of people working on my leg while a surgeon rubbed yellow cocaine syrup into my empty eye socket. I whined a little and he gave me a ball of corn silk soaked in cocaine and morning-glory paste to chew on. I couldn't move. Maybe it was for my own good. They really took charge of you around here. It wasn't just that I'd been tied up half the time. It was like ninety percent of the time I was treated like a week-old baby. Or like a cow going through a packing plant. I thought about asking him to cut a chunk out of the bridge of my nose, like the Duke di Montefeltro's, so that I could see a bit farther to the right. But I decided maybe I'd had enough folk-medical abuse for one day.

At another point, which I guess must have been later, I could tell I was lying prone on a fur pallet in a stone room. It was all blue and glowy and I wasn't alone. There was this incredible itching in the ball of my right foot. I tried to scratch it, and my arm actually seemed to work, but I couldn't find the foot anywhere. Eventually I felt for my penis—great, it was still around, I thought—and then followed my leg down from there with my hand. The leg ended in a crusty cauterized stump just below the knee, but as I viciously scratched the stump it felt like I was scratching my old foot again with penetrating electric fingers. Absolute bliss. I felt for the bone at the core but it had been plugged with wax.

Where's what's left of me? I giggled. At this rate all that's going to come back to Marena will be a brain in a vat. If that. Vat. Bat. Vein in a brat.

I exploded into a sneezing-fit—someone must have stuck some fish-tincture up my nose, kind of like smelling salts. I rubbed my eye. Warm oily hands turned me over and held my head up toward the light. The far walls were covered with the wings of blue morpho butterflies. Lady Koh was sitting at its center, looking at me out of the heart of the cerulean bloom. She had a wooden dish on the table in front of her, and inside the dish I recognized my leg, dry-cured and dusted with cinnabar.

(48)

The thirty Grandfathers of Heat between July 16, the day Koh traded me out of captivity, and today—13 Motion, that is, January 22, 664 AD, the first day of my combined wedding-and-seating festival—isn't quite a total dropout. I remember stuff. But I was in such a flaky mental state that either I don't remember what came before what, or I think I must be remembering the explanation of what had happened to me that someone gave me later instead of the actual occurrence. And trying to sort it out seems like a labor of Penelope.

In fact, having my coiffure done in the once-in-a-lifetime Hero Twins Senegalese-twistesque style—which took them over five hours, mainly because my natural hair was still only two inches long and they insisted on hitch-knotting each strand of the extensions on separately—is almost the first thing I can remember as a definitely time-marked event. I remember thinking how I'd come a long way—how Koh was in charge of Ix, and how pretty soon she'd put me nominally in charge by marrying me—and how much I still had to do. I had to organize a human Sacrifice Game with Lady Koh, and play it until we got to the 4 Ahau date of the last b'aktun. And even if we didn't come up with anything—well, since I'd buried the Lodestone Cross cache, I'd learned what felt like ten times as much about the Game. Maybe even if I didn't get my brain back, it would still be enough to make Taro's version of the game sufficiently powerful, powerful enough to neutralize the 2012 dooomster. So I had to write that all down in a form that, if I didn't make it back, Jed$_1$ would still understand. I had to take over 2 Jeweled Skull's ROC gel operation and make sure we had enough of all the different compounds. I had to get the tomb in order. I had to figure out how to bury myself in a way that would ensure that my tomb would be undisturbed. And those were only the main things. Each of them needed hundreds of other things to get done first, even to have a chance of working. And I was already getting double images and microblackouts and spike headaches and other brain-tumor symptoms. And before I could do anything else, I had to heal my leg and my eye and get at least half-functional. I lay still for days on end in a tiny pinkwashed room that adjoined a different, smaller sweat-bath, kind of a celebrity hospital and detox center, just feeling my wounds itchily stitch themselves together. I'd lie there doing yoga eye-exercises with my one eye, moving my focus as slowly as possible from upper left to lower right, repeating the process hundreds of times, getting comfortable with the most interesting pocks and cracks on the stucco ceiling. I wasn't exactly depressed in that way where the whole world seems like it's made out of Homasote, but I was definitely fuged out and totally exhausted, with a flavoring of that resignation you get to when you know you're really broken beyond repair. Sometimes when I'd fall asleep a tattoo scribe would sneak in, rub anesthetic into, say, my upper arm, and when I'd wake up there'd be a sore patch with another row of twenty head-glyphs and the name of each captive I'd supposedly taken. Of course I hadn't actually captured anyone, but Lady Koh had dedicated their blood to me because I'd made it all possible. Becoming a capturer was like being a "made" man in the Mafia, where you're sort of certified by performing a killing.

Koh had thoughtfully traded Hun Xoc out of captivity too. He hung out with me a lot. His arms had healed, although you could see the crescent cross-sections of bone in the center of the cauterized crust at the stumps, and exposed bone is painful, especially in cold weather. He'd had fake arms made of human skin stretched over wicker, with stylized hands like flowers, that fastened onto studs in his stumps. But when he was hanging out with me he'd have them taken off and let one of my male nurses massage him with oil. Of course I kept asking him and everyone about the battle. He said that before we'd even gotten to Ix, Koh had told 1 Gila and her main body of troops to stall for another two days after first being sighted by 2 Jeweled Skull. Koh had made sure that the Ocelots and Harpies would fight each other as long as possible, so that when her own troops came in, the Ixob would be exhausted as well as drugged.

I'd gotten the earthstar compound into the well a bit before midnight, and it wasn't until the evening of the next day that the first Harpy bloods who'd drunk from the water system started to feel unusually happy. Of course most people attributed the elation to their great victory, and what with the fog of the aftermath of the battle and all the balche drinking and premature feasting and raping and pillaging and whatever that went on after the Ocelots' military structure fell apart, the drugged water had spread through most of the city and especially most of the Harpy clan before more than a couple non-judgment-impaired people had realized what was going on. Best of all, it had taken out five of 2 Jeweled Skull's eight commanders along with their troops. It hadn't gotten 2 Jeweled Skull or 9 Fanged Hummingbird. They probably drank only rainwater. Certainly their food was tasted, stored, cooked, retasted, and then selected at random. Anyway, it had been plenty.

From what the dressers said I gathered that Koh had let 2 Jeweled Skull think she'd retreated northeast, and then kept moving her band of converts around the perimeter of the Harpy Clan's scouting range. Supposedly she'd even let a couple of her doubles get captured just to throw the Harpies off. And then, when the earthstar drug hit, she'd moved in her big old ragtag horde in the confusion. Supposedly the short siege had been more like a bunch of parades converging on a riot. She'd pushed through to the lake in less than half a day and then used her numbers to block the bridges and cut off the peninsula and the temple district. By late that evening the holdout Harpy bloods had collapsed most of the Ocelot compound around themselves. And by now—I mean by 13 Motion—there wasn't any real fighting still going on, just a few fires still burning in the north and west where Ocelot-allied clans had torched their granaries.

I still didn't really know what the hell was going on, though. Had Koh really won? Was she really in charge? Had 2 Jeweled Skull really lost? What had happened to 9 Fanged Hummingbird? How had Koh gotten away to begin with? Hadn't she been sitting in the middle of all these Ocelot bloods at the hipball game? All of whom had been primed to capture her?

I closed my eye. Don't even try to understand right now, I thought. *The answers to these questions and more . . .*

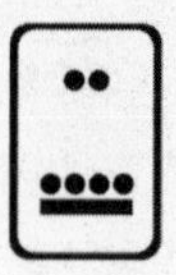

(49)

"Now the Southeastern peak breathes blood,"

the Wedding Symposiarch sang,

> *"So now unfurl the newborn warlord, peacelord,*
> *Sun-eyed avenger, Lord of Morning Twilight,*
> *One Turquoise Ocelot. And now face Coldwards*
> *And now to Whitewards, now to Knownwards, now*
> *Enthrall to him and face the Unrevealed."*

And in fact the orange steam all around me was so fierce that when they lifted me out I did feel newborn, in fact prematurely born, and as I began scraping the extruded sebum flesh-worms off my open-pored swollen skin with cockleshells it felt like they were carving me out of a protostellar cloud. This second room was like a tepidarium, cooler and lighter than the sweat bath, with a slatey predawn glow dripping through the oculus. The beat was clearer out here, although I didn't need to hear it at all anymore since I was sure my heart had been permanently tuned to it. At this point it was like the world ticking on forever. Or at least until 4 Ahau, 2012. My dressers rubbed a base coat of harpy-eagle oil into my spongy white flesh and began clothing me, or rather wrapping me, tying my long red cotton wex with a complicated female-style knot like a pillow in my lower back, a knot that was only used at weddings. You're always getting dressed or undressed around here, I thought. It's all before and after, you're always getting ready to make an offering or coming back from making an offering and getting ready to make another offering, and the actual thing was usually over in a beat. They inserted a new plug in my lip, a female one, and fresh spondylus shell spools in my ears, and an embroidered anesthetic herbal ball in my empty eye socket to soak up the tears.

I'd be appearing in women's clothes—and Lady Koh would be in male clothes—because we were going to be a sun-telling couple. That is, we were both father-mothers. I guess the cross-dressing sounds a little odd for a wedding, but actually you could still sometimes see Maya shamans wearing women's clothes at harvest festivals in the twenty-first century. Anyway, like a lot of things, it had to be done this way. One thing I could be sure of was that Koh had checked every detail.

Lady Koh needed to marry me. Or, rather, she needed to marry the Ahau and K'alomte of Ix. The Classic Maya world wasn't so gynophobic as, say, Islamic society, but women who wanted to run things still had to do it through their menfolk. Or, at best, in the Yaxchilanian and Ixian and other traditions, they had to be widows of the ahau. Which was what she'd be in a few months. I'd be as canned as Charlie the Tuna and she'd still be corking along. And if she conceived a male child with me, that would be even better for her. She could reign until he was blooded, at fifteen or sixteen, and then, undoubtedly, keep him tied to the huipil strings. Or if she didn't, she could either adopt an Ocelot baby or even fake a pregnancy and just pick up some kid from the slave market. So I was a convenient choice. And, as the miraculously revivified Chacal, the semidivine hipball legend who'd predicted the San Martín eruption, I was, especially with Koh's spin-doctoring, even a popular choice with a large slice of the public. Of course, a lot of folks still viewed me with extreme suspicion. But things had changed a lot in Ix, and throughout Mesoamerica, over the last tun, and people had come to accept events that, before the destruction of Teotihuacán, would have seemed upside down.

Even so, though, I was lucky. Koh could have set up somebody else, probably one of the younger Ocelot bloods. So I was pretty sure that Koh's real motivation was that she really wanted me to get back to the thirteenth b'aktun. I still wasn't a hundred percent sure why. But I wasn't ruling out sheer goodwill, or, let's say, sheer sense of duty. She saw her role as a protector of her lineage, and if she could protect their descendants long after her death, her uays would remain powerful long b'aktuns from now. They might even grow more powerful. After all, despite everything she'd learned from me about astronomy and physics and even twenty-first-century thought in general, she was still a believer.

And, also, she had 2 Jeweled Skull in her custody.

I hadn't seen it happen. Koh's men had surrounded him during the Earthstar riots and, amazingly, had taken him alive. Now she had him in a basket in what had been the Ocelots torture pavilion, with two guards watching him at all times so that he couldn't commit suicide in some clever way like, say, biting a chunk out of the inside of his cheek and swallowing his own blood until he bled to death—something that had, in fact, been done more than once by twenty-year captives.

On the other hand, a lot of the Ball Brethren and the other Harpies were still loyal to 2 Jeweled Skull, so we had to treat him well and keep up the polite fiction, which of course nobody believed, that I was taking over the Harpy House at his request. And, I suspected, Koh was cagily holding him in reserve. If I got out of line she could always reinstate him and get rid of me. Just one more reason I had to watch it.

My two dressers stood me up. My stump sank into the wicker cone of my shell-inlaid leg—which was made from the femur of someone larger than I'd been, and carved as a snake with its head straining forward where my foot would be—and they wove it onto my knee with gut straps. It still hurt a bit inside despite all the analgesic salves. They combed my hair with a brush like a whisk broom and oiled it, scented it, corded it, beaded it, bound it, tasseled it, and attached the extensions. They wrapped me in a long red skirt with obsidian-mirror stars and sewed me into a sort of feather-woven tunic. My new valet fastened wide neon-orange spiny-oyster shell cuffs around my upper arms and jade ones just above my wrists. Another back-sash went around my waist and they draped a white-jade beaded sort of poncholike thing over my shoulders. My hairdresser coiled all the complicated hair into a bun and set it into what was kind of like a spangled turban with a stuffed *muan* bird on the top, a combination critter made of several other birds with the head of a baby caiman and the beak of a condor. Then they dusted me off.

The cantor crouched out through the tiny door first. He was a famous neutral-clan professional adder from Kaminaljuyu, whose poetic name was On The Left, and who I guess you could also call the toastmaster or the master of ceremonies. He was serving as the head of my marriage-sponsor party. The dressers half picked me up and handed me out to him. The little room had gotten full of hot and sour breath and carbon di- and monoxide, like we were inside a big smokers' lung, and now the fresh air sucked on me.

We were in the same inner courtyard of the Harpy House where 2 Jeweled Skull had stored me in a scavenger's-daughter body basket a billion psychological years and 244 days ago. The square of sky looked like an old chalkboard with Eos's talons scraping on the eastern side. My two marriage-sponsors stood at the west side of the court: 24 Pine, that is, Coach Teentsy Bear, who was taking the part of my *halach ayadoj,* that is, the equivalent of my godfather—and an elder Harpy named 4 Wren, whom I'd adopted as my surrogate father. I'd sent for Teentsy when I heard he hadn't quite been killed during the battle, and he and I had gotten pretty close again—again, that is, in that he'd been close to Chacal. I was less crazy about 4 Wren. But Koh had been adamant that dynastically and politically speaking he was the only real choice. Our main problem now was legitimization. Anyway, the sponsors' roles were just ceremonial. Elders had to be brought in as go-betweens and surrogate parents in the marriage negotiations, which were supposedly kept secret from the bride and groom—although of course in this case Koh was running everything.

The six of us left the compound through the west door, headed through an alley between high fretted walls, and went down a swept and red feather-strewn stepped walkway toward the ghatlike steps leading down into the canalized lake. Guards in black night-raid paint kept pace with us on either side, with more ahead and behind, part of a rotating squad of sixty full-blood Rattler guards. Since they weren't part of the official entourage they had to protect us from a slight distance, but we'd kept them on high alert. The Snuffler and Macaw clans and their dependents were as resentful as ever, and what was left of the Ocelot dependents were obviously still in a murderous rage, no matter what cessation oaths they'd sworn. Well, what fricking ever, I thought, we're going to take care of all that tonight. And if they didn't like it they were in for yet another little purge. I was becoming a big believer in the Seven Habits of Highly Effective Stalinists. And Habit number 1 was "Kill First, Interview Later."

The Rattlers had repaired the floating bridge to the occupied Ocelot compounds and the court precinct. Ten of our dark guards crossed and stationed themselves along the bridge before we even stepped onto the rustling wood. We went single-file, first the so-called godfather, then the so-called father, then me, then my two dressers, then On The Left, the cantor, and finally a beater striking a muffled water drum, so softly you could barely hear it—since the procession to the bride's family's house was supposedly a secret, even though, again, everybody in town knew about it. From here you couldn't see the peninsula that connected Ix's temple district to the mountains behind, and the encrustation of muls dotted with watch fires in the cold mist looked ageless and aloof, like the island of Mont Saint-Michel. At the far end of the bridge we could just see the newly enlarged Rattler House, which had been built on Ocelot grounds just north of the council palace. The sky and its reflection had shifted to transparent Prussian blues with strings of Swainson's hawks, coming through right on schedule, uncoiling across them. An osprey stooped down into the water on our left and disappeared with barely a splash. I was afraid it wouldn't come up, but finally it resurfaced with a big catfish writhing in its talons and made its way heavily shoreward. If the fish had dragged it down everybody would probably have thought it was such a bad omen they would have called the whole thing off. Yesterday one of Koh's spies had said that some bloods from the Snuffler clan had heard about the wedding and were going to try to stop it. They'd been behind more than a few "little disturbances," or what you might call civil unrest or gang squabbles, over the last ten days, and they were getting more belligerent despite or because of Koh's death squads. So everyone was a little edgy.

In the center of the bridge we met the spy. He came within twenty steps of us, wheeled around, and ran back to the Rattler House to warn Koh's relatives. He was an expected part of the act. We stepped down off the bridge and up the steps to a small zocalo that led around the corner of the high council house and into an approach to the fresh serpent-headed wall of Koh's new compound. There were squeals. Fifteen or so young girls—either Koh's unmarried female relations or Rattler neophytes taking the part of them or some combination—blocked the entrance to the front court and started throwing pebbles at us, yelling that they weren't going to let us in, they knew what we were up to, and they weren't going to let me take Koh away from them even if we chopped them into little bits. I held my left hand over my last eye. The stones got larger and we backed away. Teentsy Bear must have actually gotten a painful hit because he yelped, a real rarity for him, and seemed about to start cursing the girls back. Of course, the little altercation was just another hoary ritual, but Teentsy had zero sense of humor and tended to take things too seriously. On The Left nudged him from behind, telling him to chill out. Sports types never knew how to behave.

> *"Blue-green daughters here, four breaths, please, four, jade daughters,"*

the cantor said, appearing from behind us.

The girls eased up on the damn rocks. The cantor walked up to them like Gandhi walking up to a line of British troops.

> *"A red blood begs for rest beside your hearth,"* he said.

The gals calmed down and let him through. He entered the compound. We waited. After four hundred beats—about six minutes and fifteen seconds—the cantor appeared again, made the sign for "patience" at us, and went back in. We stood for another eight hundred beats. The deal was that he was supposed to be begging Koh's parents to let us inside. I wobbled a bit on my snake-foot.

The cantor came out and gestured for my sponsors and the girls to follow him in. Still, I stood for another twelve hundred beats. The dressers touched up my face paint and dusted me with a sort of blue-clay talcum powder. The beater kept thumping. How did he stand it? I wondered. He was just a human clock. He must be crazy. Come to think of it, professional beaters did tend to act a little odd. The girls gawked at us while, at the same time, trying not to look interested. Finally the cantor came out a third time and gestured for me to come in. I told one of my dressers to run and get the gifts, although if they were on the ball the porters would have already followed us here. I blood-walked alone through the gate into the little courtyard. The first person I recognized was 3 Talon, the Caracara father-mother and aerial-clan patriarch, whom I'd last seen on the burning mul at Teotihuacán. Since he was Koh's godfather he stood to the left of the single door to the house. 1 Gila, who was taking the part of Koh's "father," stood on the right. Lady Vanilla Orchid, Koh's mother—her real, biological mother, by the way, brought with On The Left, at some risk and expense from Kaminaljuyu—stood way to the left, near the girls, between the charmingly named Lady Creosote Bush, Koh's sort of mother superior from the Caracara Clan's Orb Weaver Sorority, and Lady Sourdough, who had kind of the same relationship to Koh in the Rattler Society. Two Rattler monkey scribes crouched on a single mat next to the north wall, ready to take down everything anyone said. The giggle of girls crowded against the south wall with their backs to us, which was considered their most respectful position. I have to admit, purdah systems do have a certain eroticism. When women seem like a totally different and inaccessible species they're maybe more violently attractive.

There was a pair of Rattler-blood guards at each corner of the yard, and a lookout crouching on each corner of the wall above them. One of Koh's hunchbacks unrolled a reed trading mat, about one rope-length square, and I squatted on its eastern threshold side, with my back to the gate to show that I didn't have any enemies. I saluted everyone in order, first 1 Gila—calling him "father"—and then my own so-called father, 4 Wren, and then this wife of his who was playing my mother, and finally Koh's mother. I'm using the word *salute,* but really there were dozens of different sign-greetings, everything from banging your nose on the ground and licking the dirt to just stiffening up a little, and which one to use depended on who you were and whom you were talking to. Then there was a little interminable speech I had to say and a triply interminable speech back from each of them. Basically I just said, "Hi, my name's 9 Wax, I'm not worthy," and they said, "Hi, yeah, we know."

My porters trooped in behind me ahead of cue. One of them stood behind me, holding a tall capped jar with my preserved leg inside, just to show that no enemy had gotten it and I was still, officially, a whole person. The head bearer laid three big balls of fresh highland jade, all ready to be worked, in the center of the mat. She stepped back as the other porters started laying baskets around the stones in radial arms, and then followed after them, counterclockwise around the mat, lifting off the close-woven lids. She started with the dishes in front of me, clusters of popped amaranth seeds held together by bright red achiote syrup and molded into Chak figurines, coiled strings of an especially rare kind of tiny chili pepper that supposedly made you bear male children, red manioc wafers and roasted mamey sapote, sweet potato meat sculpted into rabbits and parrots like baroque marzipan, and finally a vat of powdered cochineal extracted from what I figured must have been around two and a half billion cactus-scale *Dactylopiae.*

(50)

The server moved right, counterclockwise, and opened dishes of transparent-white luxury cornflower cakes like communion wafers, stacks of creamy-looking squash-seed pralines, and a set of four twenty-pound blocks of pure highland-spring salt carved into statuettes of the dwarf yearbearers, and, in a big bundle with claws and a head, the skin of a pure white bear from God knows how far north. Meanwhile the toastmaster launched into his speech on my behalf. It was a set form personalized for the occasion. First he went through all the work I'd supposedly done for Koh's "parents." Ordinarily, if you were from, say, a middle caste, you might have to help them with stuff for years, if you wanted to get a desirable wife out of them. But I'd basically gotten all that waived based on the heroic services I'd performed, "rescuing" her from Teotihuacán and winning the ball game and everything. Next he went into a spiel about how great I was, and finally he pointed out some salient features of the gigantic bride-price I was paying. Which I guess wasn't a total sham—after all, a lot of Harpy land was going to Rattler immigrants—but of course Koh had really done all the negotiating and banking and gifts and everything herself. Anyway, I guess all weddings are at least a bit of a sham. While he was talking the server moved to the western quadrant, directly across the stones from me—practically at 1 Gila's feet—and started revealing trays of long black vanilla beans, strings of savory dried black water-bugs from what's now the Lago de Nicaragua, which supposedly made you immune to skin diseases, jars of sinister-looking black mushrooms, inky rolls of cured sharkskin, and finally twenty bricks of preservative linden leaves each wrapped around twenty smaller bundles of anise-scented avocado leaves, each of which contained two hundred and fifty-six sinkhole-grown cacao beans, roasted and ready for grinding. The last quadrant, on my left, started with baskets of papaya and pineapple strips from the islands crystallized in squash-flower honey. Next there were baskets of preserved marigolds, what they call Mexican tarragon, from Choula, and calabashes filled with orchid honey from the cloud forests, and last an item from Panama, still a recent novelty: a nine-string beaded breast-necklace of four hundred turquoise-eyed hummingbirds sculpted in hammered gold. Then the human gifts trooped in and squatted around the borders of the overflowing mat, two master carvers to work the jade, four dyers to handle the cochineal, and ten female chocolate mixers—who'd had been specially raised just to process and prepare chocolate drinks—each with her own clay grinding board and wood roller and her set of tall jars. The trickiest move they did was pouring the hot chocolate-infused liquid from one of the tall jars to the other, over and over, to raise the foam on it. The bigger the head of foam on your chocolate, the hotter shit you were. Anyway all sixteen servants were going to work for Koh's household for the rest of their lives.

There were only two more presents to go. The first was my own idea, one I'd had made so that she could be surprised by at least one thing, not that gifts around here were supposed to be surprises. I unrolled its case and laid it next to the hearth-fire stones myself. It looked like an ordinary ironwood hand flute, but it was actually chromatic, with six-hole transverse fingering and pitched to D, instead of to the double-pentatonic minor scale they used around here. I'd started the project a hundred and twenty-six days ago, the day Koh introduced me to my severed leg, and it had taken until now to get it tuned and to the flautist to play it. I'd adapted the fingering to the Teotihuacanob style, so she could deal with it, but it would still put out scales no one here had ever heard before.

The last item was definitely a not-least. With an air of finality, the head bearer laid three accordion-folding tribute books across the cold hearth-fire stones. Each book was bound in plucked eagle skin and filled with tribute lists and coded maps representing rights to a hundred and eighteen villages and thousands of acres of Harpy farmlands. They were the only really serious part of the bride-price.

Enough, already, I thought. I'd been thinking of throwing in twelve bloods a-blooding, eleven dwarves a-dwarving, fifty-four other items, and a vulture in a prickly-pear tree. In fact—even though I know it sounds like some conspicuous-consumption event à la the Duc de Berry or the Miller Sisters—this wasn't even the most elaborate royal wedding. Supposedly, seven hundred and twenty days ago, at the wedding of 1 Chocolate of Caracol, the eight-year-old groom had had four hundred thralls killed just for spectacle, without even offering them to any particular immortal. Of course, he might have been another victim of bad publicity.

The so-called in-laws looked everything over. If only Marcel Mauss could see this, I thought. Finally the room servants started gathering up the loot and 1 Gila said it was okay for me to enter the fucking house.

The room was big, maybe about the size and shape of the Oval Office—which isn't that big—and except for an opaque screen of state at the back it was totally empty. Not for long, I thought. The two sets of parents and godparents sat on mats at the right side of the door. Teentsy Bear and I sat and faced them from the other side. The girls and the other female relations crowded behind the screen. It was rare for women ever to see men eating, but Koh was making an exception for her mother and my surrogate mother and the various godmothers. 1 Gila sent a "runner" to go get the High Midwife, who was probably watching everything through a hole in the wall anyway. A bearer brought him a basket and he took out a long *halach wex,* that is, your basic loincloth but very fancy with tiny scales, that is, beads, showing my glyphs and dubious accomplishments. More than a couple seamstresses must have gone blind getting the thing ready in just twenty days. He presented it to me with a presentation speech and I accepted it with an accepting speech. Before I was done everyone snapped into a respectful attitude. The high midwife crouched in.

She was an old Rattler greatfather-mother and besides being a midwife she was also what you might call the Rattler Society's head. In a way, in the context of this one ceremony, she was the most important person here.

She saluted my father, Koh's father, my mother, and Koh's mother.

The toastmaster did the same. The bridal family struck "welcome" poses and saluted everybody else, in order of precedence, by name, with me last. Then the toastmaster saluted everyone again, with me last. I saluted back. Finally the midwife launched into her spiel to Koh's parents. She said I obviously wasn't good enough for their daughter, but since I'd worked so hard maybe they should go against their better judgment and let Koh come out of the gynaeceum. Finally, Koh's parents gave in. One of the girls ran to get her. I counted two hundred and ninety-three beats before Koh appeared in the door. The strata of encrusted ornament seemed to grow out of her flesh, even the smiling jaws of the giant nurturing snake around her head didn't so much seem to be a separate creature swallowing her as another part of a compound animal, antennae coiling in, under, around, and through her in stitches too complex to follow, fangs curling over her cheeks and around her neck down to her male-Rattler-adder pectoral insignia—and the two shrunken heads looking up from the sides of her wide belt set with eighteen Mixtec crystals, each of which was carved, in intaglio, with her portrait glyph:

She was all backlit by the morning sunlight and looked new-hatched just for display, like the mouthless imago of a male tiger moth on a milkweed, drying its wings. The four parents rose. I turned my head so I could see her with my right eye, even though it was gauche for me to move. My right eye—I mean, the one that wasn't there—had developed this kind of nondarkness, this absence, like the part behind your head where you can't see. It's not dark, it's just nothing, like death. At first it had just looked dark over there, like it was shut, but now I was this visually lopsided person.

Koh squatted at the threshold, morpho scales and quetzal and macaw plumes fluttering like she'd just flown down for a beat from her gemstone forest on the surface of the sun and she was still shaking off drops of thermoluminescent liquids that deliquesced in the air, leaving flakes of spiced copper-leaf floating to the floor. She held a long *k'inil wal* in her dark hand, sort of a long combination fan and fly whisk, basically a bunch of thin cloth streamers and strings of flower-petals on the end of a rod, with a perfume sachet at the base, like a Japanese *hare* stick. Her face would have seemed blank if there hadn't been a hint that something was unbearable to her. The effect was childlike or even frightened, and I almost thought that through everything I could make out some emotion, maybe even that same old bittersweet song twitching at the curved border between dark and light that ran just left of her left eye.

(51)

I still wish I could say Koh decided to marry me because she was crazy about me, but I don't think that was the way it was. I think she found me intriguing. Or at best fun in a liberating way. More than once during my convalescence—that is, when she had a free minute to drop in, and wasn't busy booting up her new empire—she said she owed me for my silence. She used the words "*makik uchi,*" "meritorious silence under torture."

I hadn't spilled the beans on the earthstar stuff, I hadn't sold her out to 2JS, and so she was going to honor her promise to force the five Ixian clans to make me ahau of Ix for the remainder of my section of the cycle. But like I say, that wasn't the main reason either. What she really needed to do was to legitimate her name. As a first step I'd already been installed in absentia as head of the Harpy House of Ix, that is, I had to take 2 Jeweled Skull's former position and titles. I got the feeling from her—as much as I could get out of her, in my little room, with her monkey secretaries there, and the sounds of construction outside—that legitimating me had been one of her trickier behind-the-scenes manipulations, and even though her army was in control of Ix it had taken more than a few little assassinations and exiles. But Koh was never one to say anything had been difficult. It was always fait accompli, no prob. I could hardly even get her to talk about how she'd gotten away from Ix and back to her army after the first battle, or ten thousand other things, although I did get a notion of what had gone on that I figured was close to accurate. Evidently Koh had let herself be "protected," or really captured, by the Ocelots. Then, when 2 Jeweled Skull had taken over, she'd bought her freedom by giving him the tzam lic drugs and apparatus and three captives that he thought were the Scorpion-adders from the Puma House of Tamonat. The trade probably helped make 2JS overconfident, and certainly it gave the Ocelots of Ix fewer bargaining chips. But at some point after Koh had rejoined 1 Gila, 2JS probably found out the Scorpion-adders were impostors. At any rate he sent people after Koh to kill her anyway. After that Koh had managed to stay ahead of the hit squad—who killed two of her doubles—until they got the gossip about the bad situation in Ix and gave up.

But during the second battle for Ix—"after 2JS's short reign had collapsed in a hallucinogen-sodden rout," as I liked to think of it—Koh had had to trade 2JS the three real Scorpion-adders to get me out. She also had to let him go, of course, and he'd probably taken them with him in his retreat force, which she said was only eight score or so bloods. I figured Koh had probably mastered the tzam lic anyway and didn't even need them anymore.

I felt not quite like a pawn, maybe, but definitely like a commodity. Still, Koh had kept to her end and gotten me out and that meant a lot, even if I was just part of her bid to establish herself. It all got me to thinking about my whole thing, what was going on and what had gone on before, I mean, before the downloading. I'd just look up at the lengthening cracks in the new plaster and flip through images of my life, trying to think of things that would distract me from my itching stump.

I asked Koh where she thought 2 Jeweled Skull had gone, and without answering that—annoyingly, a lot of people around here didn't exactly answer questions, they just sort of commented on them—she said that she thought she might be able to take him again, and that there were people working on tracking him down. I figured she meant the Caracara Clan of Teotihuacán, the ones she'd invited down here along with everybody else. Even back on the mul in Teotihuacán, when she was talking to 3 Talon and I hadn't heard what they were talking about, she was probably already making that deal, that if she were in charge she'd help the Caracara Clan of Teotihuacán expand into the Ixian area and would deed their leaders some choice formerly Ocelot land—on the condition that they turn over 2 Jeweled Skull. She'd probably convinced them that he was a danger to the house anyway.

Which was true, kind of. Or at least he was a loose cannon. In the end 2JS was too much of a fraidycat. He didn't take his new information far enough, he couldn't get his head around the various paradoxes my consciousness had brought him, and really it was no wonder he'd gotten confused and screwed up.

Koh was curious. I mean, she had curiosity. She couldn't get enough history. She made me go over and over the dates and events of the Conquest until she could recite them herself, which she did with a kind of morbid relish. She'd spent her whole life training to figure out just a little bit of the future, and as good as she was at it, for her it was at best like being blindfolded and given ten beats to feel her way through a cathedral. And then suddenly here was someone who'd actually seen it. She was fascinated by the idea of a time when women were closer to the social equals of men. She kept asking whether I thought of women as equal in every respect, and I said I flattered myself that I did, except it was obvious they weren't as good as men at collecting baseball memorabilia. She couldn't get enough of whatever I could remember about powerful women in Old World and latter-day New World history, and she'd just sit there filling my sickroom with cigar smoke while I told her about the three Cleopatras, Zenobia, Joan of Arc, Sor Juana Inés de la Cruz, Catherine the Great, Margaret Thatcher, Eva Perón, Madonna, Hillary Clinton, Rigoberta Menchú, Marena, Jenny McCarthy, whoever. She asked whether women fought in wars and I said combat still—and of course I'm using the word *still* inadvisedly—wasn't so popular with them as it was with guys. She asked a lot about war, to the point where I thought she might be thinking about training a crossbow squad. She still didn't get the captives thing, though. She was like, what's the point if you have to give back your trophies? Nor did she grok the concept of an equal-opportunity society. In her world you either baked tortillas or whacked your enemies—or, rather, watched your hirelings whacking them—and if you didn't, you were a social nothing, no matter whether you were an architect, a great fresco painter, a Rattler monk, a cantor like On The Left, a flesh picker, or her much-loved favorite dwarf.

Nerds are forever, though. As I might have expected, she made me go over math more than any other subject. She wasn't too impressed by Arabic numerals—which are actually Indian, by the way, that is, East Indian—but she was amazed by trig and higher equations and, especially, game theory. Sometimes, after a couple of hours of giving her Probability 101 problems and watching her work them out on a bean abacus, I'd start feeling like if I'd wanted to teach freshmen I'd have stayed home, but I don't think I ever quite lost patience. Anyway, she was a quick study. She was less interested in art and literature and didn't get the notion of art for art's sake, whatever that was. But that stuff is hard to describe. She asked about modern musical scales a couple of times and I tried to demonstrate them but Chacal's singing voice was one thing that wasn't much better than Jed$_1$'s. We made paper helicopters and airplanes and unit-origami crystals. She loved them so much she refused to burn them. "They'll rot in a few revolvings"—seasons—"anyway," she said, which was true.

At first I thought I was just opening up to her because I was lonely, but I have to admit I got to liking her. Obviously she reminded me of Marena in a lot of ways, except Marena was all screwed up and sassy-talking and flashily brilliant, and Koh was graver and about a million times more spiritual. Koh had a stately centeredness that would seem chilly. To twenty-first century Westerners, she'd have made Gong Li look warm. As exceptional as she was, she was totally Maya.

Which did ultimately become a source of friction between us. At one point when she'd dropped by late in the afternoon with some accounts she wanted me to look over she'd mentioned that two villagesful of Ocelot partisan captives were going to be offered at a "racing feast" that night, that is, just for entertainment. It meant that everyone was going to get popped, including the smallest kids. And if I knew anything about the behavior of victorious bloods, Rattler or not—who were mainly just pumped-up corn-beer-soaked teenagers, after all—the civilians were going to be in for a bumpy time. One thing they were doing lately—that is, one of the trendy torture fads—was making the captives swallow little bags of bean flour, one after another. Then they'd force water down their throats and the poor bastards would puff up with beans and gas and explode. Another one they'd probably do at the same event was this thing where they'd tie the subject on top of a stump and force him to kill himself with a little hook, ripping at his own veins. The idea was that if he wasn't dead by sundown they'd stake him up and leave him for the birds. Anything where the subject was given a choice was considered more interesting.

Anyway, I told Koh I wished she'd tell them to just cool it. She said I could make humanitarian laws when I was in charge.

I said it didn't matter what I did, that she should do what she oughta do. I started laying this whole trip on her about personal responsibility and innocence and everything.

She asked how many people I figured had died in agony in this k'atun. When I didn't answer right away she asked how many I figured had died badly in the seventeen hotunob between ours and yours?

I said between ten and twenty billion, but that it didn't make it all right. One does what one can, I said.

She just said it sounded like the so-called twenty-first century was a lot worse, and without any dignity besides.

I agreed but said it wasn't my fault.

Fault is treachery to your own family, she said. Not doing the ordinary thing with your enemies.

I said maybe she had too many enemies and not enough family, but the minute I said it, it sounded like Deepak Chopra or something. Anyway, I wasn't going to change her on this issue anytime soon. Koh wasn't a cruel person, she was just from her own patch of the space-time curve.

So maybe in some ways we really were too different. At least she didn't have self-esteem problems, I thought. No hesitation in asserting authority. She was a textbook illustration of how, no matter how patriarchal the society, a few of the very smartest women always manage to get themselves put in charge of things. Even if she had to get hitched to a weirdo like me.

But she and I couldn't spend much time getting more acquainted. There were still problems. On the day of the ball game 9 Fanged Hummingbird had been counting on the fact that whatever happened with 2 Jeweled Skull, the

Puma coalition under Severed Right Hand was only eighteen or nineteen days away. Now—that is, now at the time of the wedding—he'd camped north of the later Palenque, only four days away, undoubtedly trying to find out if Koh was solidly enough in charge to get a defense together. At least she'd entrenched her position enough to force Severed Right Hand to be careful. And if she stayed on top of things and shored up her defenses, he might be reluctant to attack the city at all. Supposedly his troops were feeling the water shortage and the distance from home. But it wasn't anything to get flip about. Anyway, one way or another, I let her get everything together and here we were.

Koh looked up. My "father" 14 Wounded crossed to her and took the end of her k'inil wal, her fan, in his right hand. She inclined her head and said the equivalent of "Yours" or "At your service," calling him "Father" for the first time. He handed the fan to her own "father," 1 Gila, and she saluted him in the same way, and then she greeted her mother, and finally my so-called mother took her fan and helped her up. An attendant folded up the door cloth and let in about twenty other relatives, or I guess you'd say guests, Alligator Root and Koh's other advisers, and Hun Xoc and 14 Black Gila, and basically the whole gang. Koh and her party took their mats on the right side of the door, facing the so-called parents. I was in the middle, facing the screen in the back, sort of linking the two sides. Sometimes at these things there was another big screen down the center of the room to keep even the closest-related women separate, but in Ixian society, at least when I was there, it was considered classier for the women just not to look at the men and be sure to eat a course after the men were done with it. The whole thing was who could look at whom, the married parents could look at each other, the toastmaster could more or less look at everybody, the thralls couldn't look at anybody, Koh and I could look at each other, a cat could look at a queen, whatever.

I suppose all the ceremony sounds pretty silly to us modrin folk. But when you were living it, it was different, it was obvious how crucial it was. It wasn't just bearing, it was an attitude. It kept everything together, it made life bearable, it was like you could make every gesture a work of art, like life was danced, and the main virtue was to be a great dancer. When it worked, you got what everyone wanted most from the world—applause. It was like everyone got the chance to be an actor in this grand, ornate drama of church, state, and media all in one.

We could hear sounds of a crowd outside, families from our dependent clans who'd heard about the procession over the bridge and had followed and been allowed onto the peninsula. It sounded like it was mainly kids asking for handouts. The guards had orders to keep them quiet but to hand out honey tamales to everyone, and then to everyone again and again. So the throng would probably triple by the end of the meal. Some of the cantor's apprentices were addressing the crowd, repeating his version of what was happening in the forbidden court.

Each set of parents sat and saluted the Toastmaster again, one by one and in order. 14 Black Gila ordered his servitors to bring in the marriage table. It was large and low, like a Japanese tea table, newly built for this occasion and scheduled to be destroyed immediately afterward. Waiters brought out miniature canoes full of fresh water and poured them into tripedal basins.

> *"Now take the basin, wash each other's mouth,*
> *Each other's hands,"* the cantor said, *"and taste,*
> *But not too greedily, not to excess."*

Oh, please, I thought. Enough with Big Nanny. But of course I did exactly as he said.

(52)

That was basically what I did here now, go along with things. Uncomplainingly. The head brewer set a huge tub of balche in the center, bristling with long drinking reeds, and all of us—I mean all the men—crowded around and sucked the pot down to the bottom, like the visual cliché of a nineteen-fifties teenage couple drinking out of the same milk-shake with two straws. A pourer refilled the pot with a weaker dilution and the women did the same. Next they handed me a pot of smoking tubes, thin reeds filled with ground tobacco and orchid aromatics, and a stack of tube-rest dishes, like ashtrays. I wobbled up, put the pot under my right arm, and passed them out to the men in order, starting with 1 Gila, handing the tube from my left hand to the recipient's right hand, like it was a spear. Next I handed out the ashtrays, from my right hand to their left ones this time, like they were shields. I sat down and we puffed as the food came in. It had all been transported here from the Harpy House, right behind the gifts, in big braziers.

The first dish was a roast giant peccary ornamented with arching bay branches, a gift from my father to Koh's father. They went through the whole presentation and acceptance thing. 1 Gila sent it back to his storehouse, presumably for later consumption. The next dish was a roast stag, with the same garnish, a gift from my father to the toastmaster. Nobody ate any of that either. On The Left gave it a puff of blessing smoke and sent it off to his house. Finally they brought in the real dinner, all in individual casseroles, one of each item for each guest serving the flesh foods clockwise. There was kind of a choked disturbance at the far end of the room, near the screen, and for a beat I thought the Snuffler Clan really had gotten someone in here to bust up the party, but as I stood up I could see the head bearer had whopped one of his underlings. The servers had to carry the dishes in the palms of their hands, never by the rims, no matter how hot they were, and the guy who was on the floor and crawling out of the room had evidently gotten his thumb in the gravy. I reminded myself to tell Hun Xoc—who was acting as my first lieutenant—not to let them kill him.

Everyone ate pretty discreetly, almost furtively, in a way. Like On The Left said, it wasn't good to make noise or seem to be eating too greedily. Certainly we all had better table manners than most people in, say, the U.S. in the early twenty-first century, although that's not saying a lot. We also had to keep quiet while Koh's mother and so-called father asked the toastmaster to explain our marital duties to us, and then we all had to listen to his speech. It went on forever in spite of Koh's instructions to cut it short. Come on, come on, I thought, it was nearly noon and there was much more serious stuff to take care of, even before the end of the sun. And then we still had to get everybody ready and announce the human-piece version of the Sacrifice Game. It was going to be a long day's journey into night.

Back on Meet Your Ex-Leg day, Koh'd said that the hundred and twenty days I would spend recovering from my poison-illness and various "sacred wounds" was just enough time for her to make me into a nine-stone adder. She'd asked me about the visions I'd had, that is, the dreams, and she'd interpreted them and said I was on the right track. And she'd taught me the necessary things about the basic Sacrifice Game, all the things my mother never taught me, things that had taken six hundred years to forget, how to count without looking at the pieces, how to read ahead without looking at the board, how to count yourself down into a divination state without using any drugs, how to listen to your blood and feel its lightning striking different parts of your body, how to lay your body out over the board and the world so that the lightning would really mean something, a location, a time, an event. She said I'd been good when she played the first Game with me and now I was getting great, that I was a natural even though I was learning so late, all that stuff. But she also said she didn't think I'd ever get more than a few k'atunob ahead. "You have to have it pressed into your skull when it's still forming, like your forehead-board," she said. She'd had Lady Creosote Bush sit with me and teach me when Koh was away. CB was her superior in the Orb Weaver Sorority and a higher nine-skull adder than Koh, although I suspected not so naturally talented. She was eighty-four solar years old, certainly the oldest person I'd run into around here, and she'd witnessed the great city-wide version of the Sacrifice Game they played at Teotihuacán in 604, sixty years ago.

We were going to try to duplicate it here in Ix. The human game would need at least two hundred trained adders. We'd requisitioned two hundred and forty from the towns in Ix's orbit, and another fifty-one had come, as gifts, from other city-states as far away as Motul. Most of them would be only at the one- or two-stone level but a few would be more advanced. Most of them wouldn't survive.

I was relieved, of course—well, *relieved* seems like a weak word—that Koh was alive and in charge. But I was still totally dependent on her for the success of my ultimate goal, and I didn't want to blow it. It seemed that she'd been working on the Game, learning how to dose the scorpion drugs and everything, but she certainly hadn't shown me anything about that level of it and hadn't even hinted at what sort of move would get us past the next cycle. I was still pretty nervous about the whole thing. It was getting late in the trip and I still hadn't learned anything about what was going to happen in 2012. And what made my position even more touchy was that before he was recaptured, 2 Jeweled Skull had supposedly killed the remaining Scorpion-Puma adders, the ones Koh had traded for me. So Koh—and possibly Lady Creosote Bush—were the only people in Ix who could still play the nine-stone version of the Sacrifice Game. Any other players of her level anywhere in the area would be with the old Ocelots, allied with Severed Right Hand, and totally out to get us. Koh said she was going to support my project and make sure I was entombed correctly. But she wasn't going to tell me anything about the highest level of the Game until after we were married. And I hadn't been in a position to object. So despite things seemingly going my way at the moment, I was still feeling some random perturbation. Calmate, Jedderina, I thought. Prenez une gélule de chill.

The toastmaster finished and we heard the rataplan of five kinds of popcorn in the courtyard outside, meaning we were getting to the wind-up phase, which wasn't exactly dessert but was more like snack foods. Koh and I didn't eat anything anyway, we spent the whole time serving each other's families, which in our exalted case didn't mean running around replacing cups but redundantly badgering the servants to do it. There were nine kinds of starchy-liquid drinks to keep track of, thick manioc beer, goo drinks made of tiny mucilaginous salvia seeds like thin Jell-O, soured *posolli* dough like sickroom gruel, corn mush like Cream of Wheat flavored with cacao butter and colored with cinnamony *Tagetes lucida* marigold pollen, all these things that I guess sound gross but actually you get into them after a little while. It's reassuring stuff. Soul food. For the last course the mixers I'd just given them formed up around the table and poured the achiote-dyed chocolate back and forth, over and over, raising high blood-red froth heads, sprinkling a few drops each time to each of the four directions. The women couldn't drink the chocolate either. Not fair, I thought—

A little death-scream came from behind the blue featherwork screen at the far end. I jumped up. There was a shout from a guard:

"Ch'aatol!"

Assassin.

(53)

The feather screen had canted over but the Rattler guards had already converged on the sound, closing off the view. The toastmaster stopped his spiel. Hun Xoc got to me and he made me sit down, his mock hand pressing dryly on my shoulder. I sat. I caught Koh's eyes. Ignore them, they said. She gestured to the toastmaster to go on and he started again. She looked back down at her dish in that demure bridal way. I listened. One of the girls was still making noise but it seemed like the guards were already calming down after the first shock. Someone had made his way in and nearly gotten to the main wedding party, which wasn't good. They probably weren't assassins, though. More likely just outcasts who'd been liquored up and sent in to slow us down.

I looked around the table. Some of the celebrants looked uncomfortable, but they did the right thing, which was the cool thing, which was to go on with what they were doing like nothing was out of the ordinary. I could hear more screaming outside. One of Koh's men was already whispering to her, telling her what had happened. I made what-the-hell-is-going-on? gestures behind my back until one of the guards got into whispering position behind my shoulder.

"Yellows," he said, meaning the Snuffler Clan. I clicked "Understood" and asked if anyone had been hurt in here. He said he didn't know, but that the intruder had been taken. I looked back at Koh, but she wouldn't look at me.

It's getting too late in the day to deal with this, I thought. Had she left enough time for everything? It's frustrating when there's just no way you can ask.

Finally, by the time the speech ended, everything had quieted down, inside and outside. Well, that was efficient, I thought. Shrugged that one off pretty fast. Part of the job. No sweat. I could still hear my heart beating, but I hoped nobody else could. I knew Koh and Hun Xoc could see my nostrils flaring, but they wouldn't hold it against me. They knew I'd brought twenty-first-century cowardice along with me, and by now they thought of it as one of my charming flaws. I caught Koh's eyes again. She didn't look worried. The servers cleared the dishes and table and took them out to the bonfire. We all drank and smoked again, and washed our hands again, and Koh and I stood up. On The Left signed for us to stand together and we walked tentatively toward each other like two red-footed boobies gearing up for a mating dance. He stood behind us and tied the long corner of Koh's embroidered half-cape to the tail of my huipil. He held up a plate of tiny milk-white honey tamales. Koh picked one up. I picked one up. She fed hers to me. I fed mine to her. That was it. The guests stood up and we all trooped out, still in order, out the little throat-door. The courtyard and walls were crawling with Rattler guards. Someone had definitely tried something, but this wasn't the time to ask about it. We all paraded sunward around the serving room under an arch and into another larger courtyard, covering what had been a whole section of the second council zocalo. Its new walls were festooned with orchid-strings and the floor was invisible under drifts of pink geranium petals. At the far end the freshly built windowless bridal house looked like a pink sugar cube with a door in it. The sky overhead was settling into that too-blue afternoon color. We led the procession as slowly as possible to the door, kicking up little pink dust-devils. Koh stooped through the entrance cloths first. I followed. My valet, dresser, hairdresser, and flautist followed me in. Koh's maid, dresser, hairdresser, and head vocalist followed her in. Finally On The Left stooped through the door, stood in front of it with his legs apart and his arms on his staff, and watched.

The house had two rooms. The first was just a cubical chamber with a tiny oculus and a brazier in each corner casting mottled red ember-light over walls encrusted with stars of red conch shells. There was a high raised sleeping shelf in the back with four big bat-skin cushions and four hammocks. In the center there was a low stone altar table and a small hearth with a little white-jade corn-grinding stone and cylindrical *metate*. The second room was a sweathouse, opening off to the right. It didn't have any furniture, just mats and jars and a hearth in the center. I was feeling a little twitchy and getting an exuberant erection. The musicians had come into the courtyard outside. They slowed the downbeat to one out of four and took the drone chord up a third. Koh led her three attendants into the sweathouse and strewed geranium and bay-tree leaves over the floor while the girls poured resined water over the hot stones. My attendants unplugged my jewelry, unwound all my stuff, and untied my leg, storing it all on a wicker mannequin. The four women crouched out of the steaming door, their clothes dripping, and I crouched in. My valet undressed and followed me. I sat and sweated for four hundred beats. My hairdresser undid the big football of female hair from the top of my head. It was hard to sit still. I looked down at my tattooed glans poking out of the foreskin like the head of a killer whale through an ice floe. Whoa, that's really something, I thought. I guess it sounds like I'm bragging. But it was Chacal's body. My valet scraped me down. Since this morning I'd already developed another coat of sweat-goo. But it was cleaner goo. Finally they moved me back out into the main room and stood me up, balancing me on my meat leg. Cool air whisked over me. Koh was standing next to the sleeping shelf, facing me and Flipper the Self-Willed Dick. My dresser rubbed male-manatee oil into me and dusted me with metallic-green beetle-shell flakes. I watched the maids peel off Koh's last layer of fabric. Her body was proportioned differently from the western canon, maybe something like one of Maillol's young nudes. Or of course you can see a bit of the feeling of it in Classic Maya statues, like there's a figurine of a weaving woman from Jaina Island—which was a sort of Isle of the Dead off the Yucatán, like the San Michele in Venice—in the Griffin collection at the Princeton Art Museum that has that same boneless strength. Koh was a bit taller and more willowy than the average Maya, and it made me feel a little runtish. I'd thought it was because she had Teotihuacanob ancestors but now I guessed it might be related to her polydactylity thing, chromosomal trisomy 13 or whatever it was. She had two smaller vestigial nipples, each about four finger-widths below her regular ones, and two more little moles each three finger-widths below those, each set of three strung on a subtle hint of a seam like the lateral lines on a fish. The dark patch on the right side of her face continued down her neck and over her right clavicle, slanting left over her left breast, leaving her stomach and hips light, and then looped back around over her right thigh and slanted left again, leaving her right leg light to just above her knee and throwing her entire left leg into darkness. On her right side the three dark nipples popped out of the light ground. It was like she was a spiral-extruded soft ice cream cone imperfectly dipped in chocolate coating. I guess it sounds maybe grotesque but it was incredibly beautiful, with her perfect wide face and perfectly rounded limbs. Her genitals appeared to be normal, although of course they were hairless like most Maya's, with chocolate-dark labia peering out of her light pubis. Her dressers started oiling her with a mixture presumably from a female manatee.

The servants weren't eyeballing us in the face, of course, but they were watching our every move to see whether we needed anything. Still, we were both so used to them and so dismissive of them as people that there was still a certain sense of privacy in the small room even though there were eleven people in it. Actually, On The Left was the only one here who made me feel a little uncomfortable. But he hadn't moved from his post in front of the doorway and wasn't going to. My flute player eased into a little rambling Lester Youngish solo theme I'd sort of written to go along with the sort of sad march they were playing outside, nothing that would make it sound like jazz or anything, but still a super novelty. I could see a little bit of surprise and maybe interest behind Koh's blankness. Probably more about the music than about me.

Koh let them dust her. She moved to the sleeping shelf. She had a sort of geisha grace, but the style was less twitchy, without that white-silk stiffness. There was more flow, more gravity, I guess less yang and more yin. I'd only rarely seen any twenty-first-century Indians moving that way, like my mother, a little bit, when she was sewing. Maybe it was a little like Javanese ballet movement, but without the sort of apologetic gestures. But really, it's silly to compare it to anything else, it was its own thing. Come here, my little Frigid Queen, I thought. Koh's singer started improvising a listlike erotic prayer to my Mayaland swing theme. On The Left shifted as though he was about to say something, but didn't. His deal was just to sit here and witness for both families that we didn't pull any last-minute substitutions or anything. With royal marriages everyone really wanted to make sure of what they were getting.

They lifted me onto the shelf. Koh's dresser fanned her. My dresser fanned me. Koh kneed over to me. I balanced myself while my valet held my knee stump. Her maid took my bursting penis and guided it clinico-choreographically into Koh. The instant I was enveloped by that ridged cylindrical tongue, what self-control I had over whatever aphrodisiac had been in that damn tamale just evaporated. My hips jerked back and forth involuntarily and I was basically just fucking away, which I guess is at least a good way to break the ice. Koh reciprocated. There was a lot of pressure and speed down there but I was still surprised that Koh had an orgasm almost immediately. She stifled it a bit but there wasn't any doubt. It was like a teenager's orgasm. First sex all over again. Koh had had plenty of sexy fun with her maids and women-in-waiting or whatever in the Star Rattler Society, but not with any men. So I guess maybe it was the novelty. Although it wasn't a whole Buster Hymen thing. Virginity wasn't such a big deal at this level, somebody as major as she was didn't have to prove anything.

There was definitely something drive-in-movieish about it for me, though. Like I guess if you're a guy, especially, and if you grew up dealing with primitive, superstitious peoples, like say the middle class in the U.S. in the 1970s, you might have been making out with someone and for whatever reason this person didn't want to slide for home. So you staggered back home or out to the car or whatever and started masturbating and your testicles were so swollen like two Jiffy Pop bags, pebbles of cum overflowing and backing all the way up into your ductus deferens, so that it actually took minutes of near-pain to get into org-mode, and then when you got over the hump you just exploded in a total agony that submerged any more delicate pleasure sensations you might have gotten but which knocked you into such a long slide of incredible release—as you lay aching and groaning in this rain of semen—that you still might give quite a bit to reexperience that intensity. So, yeah, anyway, this was like that. When I could hear again, On

The Left was giving the scene his little "well done" blessing. He left. The servants poured balche over the four pots of embers in the corners of the room and left, too, tying the door behind them. We had about nineteen minutes, which we had to spend together to keep our putative child from being polluted by Koh's looking at any other person. I wondered whether I really would get her pregnant. It was an odd idea for me. Except if I had a kid with Koh it wouldn't take after me anyway. It would be like Chacal. And of course, even if Koh and I didn't conceive, she'd either have a kid with someone else or just commission one secretly and pretend it was hers.

Koh sort of slid out from under me and I sank prone on the olingo-skin cushions and looked at her. We were more or less in bed together and more or less alone in the twilight steam.

She started giggling and tied my hair back out of my face. As a rule, I can't say the Maya were very cuddly, but there was definitely affection there. Although she didn't seem into oral stuff. We messed around a little more and I was trying to get her to come again when she said she appreciated how I had a lot of different ideas but she thought she still basically preferred sex with women. She lay back and played with my penis, pulling the foreskin over it and then pushing it back. She said it reminded her of the ovipositor of one of her wasps because of the way it was striped. I bent down and tried kissing her again but it just wasn't one of her tropes of demonstrating affection. Mouths around here were more for biting and chewing and getting yours near someone was like an attack. I said it was like when she'd put the drugs into my mouth seventy-four suns ago, but she still wasn't into it. Cuddling was different too. I'd see something as a sexual preliminary and she would see it as juvenilizing. Like the way some people like baby talk and some people can't stand it. I stroked her, though, from one nipple down to the next and back up the other side, over and over and as lightly as possible so that I was really just gliding over her almost nonexistent body hair, and she did like that. She sat up and started checking out my stump. I blew air over her to cool her.

I'd been thinking for a while about maybe getting Koh to come back with me. Back to my old overripe turn-of-the-century hood. I imagined myself bringing her around to meet the folks. *Hey, dudes, this is my main squeeze, the Dragon Princess.*

I asked her.

She laughed in a you-idiot way. She had dynasties to found and enemies to plunder and everything. Despite her natural curiosity she wasn't even remotely intrigued by the notion of coming to Florida like an e-mail-order bride and trading in her growing rack of shrunken heads for Prada suits and publicity agents and dinners at the Delano. She'd seen a bit of the future and had decided it wasn't much.

Which you couldn't argue with, I thought. I'd been getting all bittersweet and misty and now I was starting to chuckle a bit myself. Watch the mood swings, I thought. Anyway, she was right. Anyway, even if I did get her in my casket with me I didn't really know if it was even possible to upload her consciousness or whatever on the other end. You should have asked about that, you dwurk, I thought. And anyway, who was I going to get for a donor? Was I going to run around like some murdering body-snatcher preying on the innocent to keep my vampire bride alive, like she was Jessica Harper in some Dario Argento movie? Had I lost every last shred of decency?

I changed the subject.

"So may I ask," I asked, "do these fingers work as well as the others?"

"Yes," she said.

"Are they weaker?"

"A little weaker than their aunties," she said, meaning her pinkies. "And they do hurt sometimes. This one doesn't have a nail." She wobbled the artificial or rather commissioned nail. It was sewn on through a piercing in the flesh below. I stretched and looked at the ceiling and held her ear. We'd hit one of those great natural pauses like it could have been anytime, anywhere.

"Chocolate and deer is the gift of this sun," she said. It meant it had been a good day.

"Utz-utz," I said. "Very good."

"It's time, now, though," she said, using the word that meant "this very instant."

I asked what she meant.

"I have to light the cooking stones," she said. "Female orb weavers always eat their mates."

(54)

I was a little freaked out, to say the least. I just sat there for two beats, and then eight, wondering whether to run for it. Although of course there wasn't anywhere to go. Get outside to Hun Xoc? No, they'd be holding him too. My eye darted to the doorway. Koh's nacom, an old skin-blackened Rattler sacrificer, was crouching in it with a long-handled flint knife.

Lunge forward. Grab Koh's neck. Try to hold her as a hostage.

No. Won't work either. They'll pry me off her in two p'ip'ilob. She owns this place, I thought. I've had it. Serves me right for dealing with these fucking headhunters.

I looked back at Koh. Her look said it was all all right. Thanks a lot, I thought. The nacom kneed toward us. Four Rattler assistants came in behind him, lifted me up, and laid me over the little stone altar table in the center of the room, holding my arms and legs lightly, so that my back wouldn't break. The nacom sprinkled purifying balche over me, said his little invocation, and touched his flint knife to my Adam's apple, like he was lighting a fire with a long match. I felt an ultrasharp stone hook catching a fold of my skin and then drawing a long, nearly painless line down my chest. The nacom put the knife aside, put his unclean hand over my abdomen—dangerously close, but not quite defiling my skin—and lifted up a bright-red achiote tamale, sculpted into a stylized heart. He handed it to Koh. Shockingly—I guess it was part of her New Deal religion, showing that she was immune to the pollution of death—she broke off a piece of the crust and swallowed it. Evidently the Orb Weaver Sorority had toned down this part a bit since the even badder older days, back between the time when the Oceans Drank Atlantis and the rise of the sons of Aryas. Novelty baked goods, I thought. Yet another example of Koh's terrific sense of humor. You never knew where you were with this chick. I leaned back, listening to my sweat and urine dripping on the stone floor. Koh was giggling a little bit. Laugh it up, I thought. She was always pulling stuff like that, riddles, gags, infantile practical jokes. Gullible me. Yuk, yuk.

The rattler ordinands moved me down onto a bobcat-fur-covered pallet and started washing me in three kinds of water and four kinds of sand, purifying me after sex and death and whatever.

I've got to have a talk with Koh Babe about this shit, I thought, it's not funny and it's wearing me down. A couple more brilliant moments like that and I'll be the only white-haired aborigine between here and Iceland.

I guess she's just testing me again, to see how cool I can be. Well, the SATs are over, sweetheart. I've been cool enough. I raised my head up on one arm, even though it wasn't a pose anybody seemed to use around here. Another four-kid Rattler troop had crawled in with a human-size tray. It had a full-size corn-paste figurine of me, very cleverly done, all dressed in the exact same ceremonial clothes and ornaments with the same tats. I watched Koh undress the figurine and bite into the right hand and the cornflour-cake doll-face. Thank God there wasn't any fake blood inside or anything. She pushed her finger down in its chest cavity, replaced what was left of the heart loaf, poured balche over the open wound, and sent the whole thing back out to the Orb Weaver Sorority feast table. Go for it, I thought. Take, eat, barf, whatever.

I looked over at Koh but she was supervising the damn ritual washing of her private parts. I sat, watching, breathing hard. They finished wiping me and started dressing me, again, this time in male clothes. Koh let her team sew her into a plain white huipil—which only the highest muckamucks got to wear—and then kneed over to the hearth-fire stones. She uncovered a jar of water and a jar of blue corn, soaking in water and lime. Good morning to you, too, I thought. Well, so, that was fun, how about brunch?

I sat patiently, getting worked on, like an actor being made up for a monster role, listening to that *krik, krik, krik* of the grinding stones. That sound really is like nothing else, I thought. Koh's having to make symbolic tortillas seemed a little demeaning to me. Here, honey, I'll do that. I'm a sensitive hubby. Don't get dishpan hands. Oh, well. It was probably the last time she'd ever make them herself anyway. She wouldn't have to do it six hours a day every day of her life, like the rest of the gals in this hemisphere.

Eight hundred beats later we reemerged from the house dressed as the joint heads of our united clans. We could hear a crowd outside the gate, mainly kids and festivalgoers from the dependent clans—that is, the closest thing to a middle class—getting free food from the overflow of the wedding. They were giggling and everything but a little awed to be on the peninsula. The whole holy district was off-limits most of the time, but welcoming now.

We formed up in the courtyard, getting ourselves together, Koh and I in the center of the wedding party, with all of us surrounded by Rattler guards with big round shields of iridescent blue-green trogon feathers. The attendants moved the food aside and started packing it up for incineration. We listened. These guys had better be on cue, I thought, but before I'd finished the thought, I picked out that unique roar far away. A nonet of Ocelot musicians, playing the Ixian peace song on long boxwood horns, were coming up on the crowd from the southwest, from the direction of the great zocalo.

On The Left stepped out through the gate, leading two porters carrying the oracle box. It was an arm-span square and pearl-white, woven out of the stripped shafts of egret feathers. The person inside it was, supposedly, a hundred and sixty years old. But of course that was hype.

We heard the guards on the outside making a space for him in the center of the crowd. The horns came around the council house. Plaster walls buzzed in the roar. I imagined the crowds drawing back and doing their varieties of dirt-eating moves as the Ocelot procession came through.

Our band blasted out our entrance chord. The cantor gave his little speech of welcome and the screen of guards fell back, and the twenty of us, Koh and Hun Xoc and the Gilas and our flanking retainers, were all suddenly visible to all these people, real people, like, let's meet the public.

Na'at ba'al, the cantor said, relayed through his megaphones. The crowd yelled back its welcoming response, somewhere between a reedy cheer and a chant.

I felt all exposed. It had been a while. On The Left asked the crowd if they were ready and they answered that they were. The tone of the expression was something like "Yes, thank you, what are you going to do for us next?"

I tried to listen for signs of trouble in the chord but I couldn't get any. Koh had had thousands of Rattler families adopted by other clans, so they were interspersed through the crowd, and the others were going along. And at least half the remaining clans really were crazy about us, they thought I was literally the gods' gift. It was really only the Macaws and Snufflers we had to worry about. And any recidivist Ocelots. Well, at least, no matter how resentful any of them were, they weren't showing it. They were going along with the shills.

What was our danger quotient on this? Like they used to say, oaths sworn at spearpoint were always worth a little less. I wished we could have controlled better who was coming into the temple district. Normally only people belonging to one of the clan temples on the peninsula would think of coming here. And every family had its spot, so you sort of knew who you were getting. Any group of infiltrators would have been spotted by the people they were trying to stand with.

And Koh's guards and their guides—that is, local people who helped them recognize other local people—had been out around the clock, ever since the battle, turning the place into a police state. But still, you couldn't search everybody, or even recognize everybody. The main thing to do with something like this was just for us to keep isolated, stay out of any conceivable kind of projectile range, and then get the hell out before people got too drunk.

The chief herald blew his special trumpet for the first time. It was a long whine like a giant router with a two-inch bit, air raid, ground raid, water raid, ascending into a long squeak like an ulna whistle, and then there was nothing.

(55)

Just a few more little tests, I thought. Testlets. Testes. Just quizes, really. Before the Human Game, anyway. That would be the real test.

I waited. The crowd waited. And I was sure the sun waited, and that the semidomesticated flock of scarlet macaws that had been circling around their nest niches on the Macaw clan's mul were now hanging motionless in the air, but of course that was one of those chronopathological brain spikes I'd been getting lately. The silence before had been really a rustling, breathy silence, but this silence was nearly absolute, just a hint of breeze and the eternal beat pulsing in my syncopated ears. Then there was a static apogee moment when the silence maybe sounds like rustlings that might just be ancient sounds, from long-gone b'aktuns, still echoing through the canyons, and then a point when that suspicion of sound had definitely become rustlings and making-readies, something dressing itself over a subacoustic drone. The drone sank into the subsonic hum of long, long approaches, something getting bigger and bigger until you can't believe its size, Plutonian barges and giant coal-burning trains dopplering through perpetual fog.

At first it was obviously coming out of the citadel at the top of the mul, but it was picked up and echoed and reechoed above and below, the echoes anticipating each other too fast for sound, either too clearly from too far away or too diffuse from much too close, the space way out of joint, and then it all petered out into a crackle of gibbering from the oracle in the box.

There was still a test I had to pass before I could play the human-piece Sacrifice Game. Get ready, I thought. I'd trained for this to the point where I was sure I could do it backward, but even so—

Cancel that. Don't think fail thoughts. Just don't screw up.

> *"One Ocelot may show himself, he says,"* the interpreter said,
> *"When he learns what happened to the bloods who came*
> *And fed him over this k'atun, who claimed*
> *His rights and titles. Where have they all gone?"*

On The Left answered:

> *"Those bloods abandoned him,"* he said. *"They lied*
> *When they said 9 Fanged Hummingbird would be here now;*
> *They ran off under thorn trees, under bushes.*
> *Tell Ocelot, 'Look down on us and see*
> *What's happened,' and we'll show him, and we'll wait*
> *For his response, his judgment, we attend."*

There was a crash on a rack of clay bells as the clowns entered out of the council house and poured down the steps, pretending to slip and fall and roll in their padded parodies of the bacabs' vestments. The crowd broke into a sea of relieved laughter. At least they did laugh a lot around here, I thought, whatever else they did. Koh's Porcupine Clown, the one I'd seen in Teotihuacán, bounced out of the ahauob's entrance and tumbled down the stairs in a ball, crashing into a table of ale pots and coming up out of the splinters and foam with one of them on his head like a top hat. He rolled a long way in his ball, his feather suit collapsing, and then sprang up and staggered around, blindly bumping into people, blinking under his bandit-banded makeup. People were collapsing from laughing. By this time the invisibles had cleared a Sacrifice Game–gridded square in the center of the zocalo, and the actor personifying me spun out into the green center uncoiling a long geranium-flowered umbilical ribbon. He was covered in red wrappings with down tufts to show that he was still a baby, and his big mask was a 3-D version of my head glyph, or what you might call the logogram of my name, not anything that resembled me personally. Actors strutted out personifying 9 Fanged Hummingbird and 4 Orange Skull—that is, 9 Fanged Hummingbird's elder brother, who died in the fifteenth yellow k'atun, AD 726, before 9 Fanged Hummingbird took the mat. They all paraded once around the square. The 9 Fanged Hummingbird giant crept up on 4 Orange Skull from behind and chopped off his lime-gessoed wicker head. Can't he just do something classy, like drizzle poison in his ear? I wondered.

I could tell the polyrhythms were speeding up. 9 Fanged Hummingbird started chasing the Chacal actor around the square. Chacal popped himself off his umbilical cord and hid behind an ember pot. The actor playing 2 Jeweled Skull of the Harpy House crept in, reacted to 4 Orange Skull's headless body, grabbed Chacal, and pulled him away into the red zone of the Sacrifice Game grid. 9 Fanged Hummingbird mimed looking around, but couldn't find them.

"2 Jeweled Skull took 9 Wax into his ball-school
In Blue Stone Mountain, far, far East, in safety," On The Left said.

We were totally rewriting history, of course. Especially my—or Chacal's—undistinguished genealogy. Chacal wasn't blood-related to the Ocelots at all, he was just a dependent-clan provincial kid who'd shown early talent and gotten himself into the league.

Still, the same old story gets 'em every time. I hoped.

9 Wax—now called Chacal—became the greatest ballplayer ever, of course. The actor did a couple nice stunt versions of my spectacular saves. Then pretty soon the 9 Fanged Hummingbird character suspected who he was and tried to sacrifice him. But then there was the eruption, well-suggested by batteries of tree-drums and long ratchets. Our hero fled to Teotihuacán, destroyed it apparently single-handedly, brought the Star Rattler—in this scene, a long-jointed wooden snake—back to Ix, and challenged 9 Fanged Hummingbird to a big hipball match. The square filled with

acrobats wearing huge full-head masks like toy bobble-heads, one for each of the famous ballplayers. The tumbler who was playing the ball knocked the Ocelot champions' heads off one after another. And invisibles scurried in and cleaned up the stage for the war. It had all taken less than a half an hour so far but I was getting impatient. I knew how it came out. Warrior-mimes faced each other across the square, advanced one by one, and paired off into slow-motion duels. Up on the four cedar poles the twelve acrobat kids spread their Harpy-ancestor wings and let themselves drop. Their gut cords unwound from the pole, spinning them counterclockwise in widening gyres down toward the eastern crowd. The Ocelot ancestors crept out on the western side, not just giant cats but Ocelot-catfishes with bulbous bulging-stomached popcorn-stuffed suits so big each outfit took four jaguars' skins to make and jutting jawless faces waving long flagella and feelers and trailing hairy barbels. They didn't look ridiculous, though, they stalked forward with that wary catty deliberation behind each silent pad-placement and it was really kind of disturbing. They grouped on the raised border of the zocalo, two rope-lengths in front of where we were standing, and watched. Down on the battlefield the Harpies were winning. 9 Fanged Hummingbird turned and ran to his ancestors for help, but they rejected him and pushed him back into the ring.

> *"You're weak and treacherous,"* the cantor said,

imitating the voice and language of the Ocelot Ancestors.

> *"Bring us our heir, the son of our greatfathers,*
> *And seat him on the mat, or you'll be slaughtered."*

The 9 Fanged Hummingbird character spun around frightenedly and ran off. I guess On The Left's going to do all the voices himself, I thought. Is that supposed to make it more arty? Down on the battlefield the Ocelot bloods seemed to be getting the upper hand again. The 2 Jeweled Skull character ran back and forth, trying to show as clearly as possible that his side was in big trouble. Finally he ran up to the Chacal character, who was dispatching another Ocelot blood at the extreme southeastern corner of the court, just below the Star Rattler's blue-green mul.

"My son, 9 Wax, help us kill the Ocelots," the cantor said in an imitation of the voice of 2 Jeweled Skull.

> *"I can't kill my own family,"* "Chacal" said.
>
> *"Then stop the battle,"* "2 Jeweled Skull" said. *"Take*
> *The Ocelot's mat, and also take my mat,*
> *The Harpy's mat, and sew the two together,*
> *Unite both great-greatfathers in one blood."*

Wow, this really is bullshit, I thought. That wasn't at all the way things happened. Would the guests really believe it? Except don't even think that way, I thought. Believing it doesn't matter. It's about whether the ones who know what actually happened can deny the truth. And of course they can. That's what people are good at. It's *media,* for God's sake. Right? And everybody'll go home and tell two friends about what they saw, and they'll tell two friends, and by tomorrow afternoon it'll be like it all really happened.

The Chacal character pointed his saw at the sun. The clashing warriors in the battle separated and froze into listening attitudes. There was a long, long hiss from orchestras of maracas, like shipyardsful of woodworkers running sharkskin over lignum vitae. Everyone—including guards and watchmen who were supposed to face their posts—turned and looked toward the Star Rattler's mul. The low sun hit its façade flat-on and saturated it with light filtered to a pure spectrum-band of cadmium-orange deep through the still-omnipresent ash roof. I smelled that smell again, the one that followed Koh, more insistent now, and as smoke curled up like fangs out of the mouth of the high sanctuary something emerged and flowed down the stairs with the deceptive nonmotion of a lava flow and rolled coiling into the zocalo, sidewound forward, tasting the space, and then reversed itself and slithered up to the peak of the mul again, its head passing its tail at the top, and then as its tail thrashed it slid down again with horrible purposefulness and coiled in the zocalo's blue-green central zone, scattering the warriors, and oriented itself to the invisible milky way. It paused, licking the air with jointed tongues—they were made like those novelty wooden snakes that bend sideways but not up and down—and then wriggled warily toward us across the court, its movement so perfectly snakelike or rather centipedal that it was hard to shake the sense that it was alive. It had that angular movement that isn't really movement, where the thing just shifts mysteriously from one spot to another without seeming to be in between, without crawling or even sliding, more just sucking itself obliquely forward by torsion building and releasing and building, surfing on the liquid sine wave of the universe, and for a beat I realized it was lining its side-stars up with the earthstars of the mulob, remaking or mirroring the astronomical moment, Antares setting and Saturn in the Crab. It drew itself up at the apron of the Ocelots' mul—which had been emerald and scarlet but was now black, scarlet, and Lady Koh's signature blue-green—and reared back, flaring its ruff like a horned lizard and inflated its chest like a mating quail's. It seemed to be about to speak and then it puffed its cheeks to bursting, like a frog's, and extended its eyes on long stalks like a slug's, feline-slitted pupils rolling round and around, inspecting us. It opened its mouth, and first nothing and then a sound came out, a gurgling of petrified glyptodonts bubbling up out of tar pits, a wheeze and release like sneezing out broken glass. A dark-green flood of writhing globules vomited out of its mouth, separated into lumps with legs and hands, and rolled blindly over the stones squealing in mock pain, dwarves dressed as toads covered with glistening thick oil that mimicked digestive juice. The dragon coughed, shook its head, unfolded and spread its thirteen pairs of wings, opened its jaws again, and spoke:

"Star Rattler calls One Ocelot: Show yourself."

(56)

Everyone on the dais drew back from me so that I was exposed to the crowd. I teetered up four low steps to the next, smaller platform, the foot of the stairs of the pyramid, a half-rope-length above everyone else. I was alone except for a tall wrapped stele lying in the center of the landing, ready to be lifted and slid into the big hole under its base.

The crowd reacted, although it wasn't anything you could hear. This was already the first stage in climbing the mul. It meant I was committed to respond to the oracle's challenge. The whole thing was considered a test. Which I guess is obvious, except it wasn't just testing me personally. If Ocelot accepted me and infused me with his uay I'd supposedly be strong enough to establish Ix as the seat of another thirteen-k'atun cycle, the way Teotihuacán had been the seat of the previous one, and then Ix would get a whole lot of goodies. Of course, now that the Teotihuacanob coalition had fallen apart, other cities would immediately contest the claim. But everyone was still taking it kind of seriously. Too many snafus from the ruling family and people would start losing confidence. Motivation, I thought. Human resources. Give 'em a leader. *Ein Volk, ein Führer*. The Ocelot interpreter took out a half-calabash basin. It passed hand to hand like a collection plate, first through the great-bloods on the level below me and then through part of the crowd below them. Each person who got it unwrapped a single small green chili pepper, *Capsicum frutescens,* a variety so hot that it was used only for torture and poisoning fish—and dropped it into the gourd. The full basin came back to the interpreter. He mashed the chilis with a pestle—*the vessel with the pestle has the brew that is true*—I thought added a shot of balche, and stirred it up. An ordinand handed him a blue sacrificial cord with ocotillo thorns woven into it. He showed the rope to the crowd and coiled it into the basin, tamping it down with the pestle. He let it sit for a minute and then pulled it out to show how it was soaked with chili water and covered with little yellow seeds. There wasn't going to be any possible question about it. Nothing up my sleeve.

I turned to the mul and gave it the son-to-father salute. Except for its staircase its entire bulk was draped with the twenty-seven original *halach popob,* cotton-and-feather weavings rippling over its nine blue-green courses in waves of gold, black, and scarcely believable unfaded Gobelin reds.

Thirteen of them hadn't been unfolded since the seating of 4 Rabbit, in the first sun in the first tun of the eighth red hotun, 493 AD, at the last quadruple conjunction of Saturn, Venus, Mars, and Jupiter, two hundred and fifty-six years ago. The interpreter handed me the cord.

Okay. Right. No point waiting, I thought. Not everyone in the crowd could see everything, but the great-bloods on my left and right could see plenty.

Can't fake this one. Nope. Come on, get it over with.

I unwrapped a fresh stingray spine, handling it gingerly like a communion wafer, and tied it to one end of the cord, like I was threading a needle.

Go for it. Goferit. Gfrt.

I untied my little loin-package and took out my penis. It was a little embarrassing, not because I was showing it off or anything but because it was looking kind of puny, pulling its turtle-head into its long foreskin. Shrinking violet. Shying away from the coming inevitable.

Hard up, little dude.

Now, now, NOW NOW NOWNOWNOWNOWNOWNOW. I held up the shaft, slid the spine into the underside right above the bulb, and slipped the point forward in the space between the loose skin and the deep fascia and poked it out again just under the corona, pulling the thorn-thread after it.

The first mental state I was aware of was disbelief, amazement that I could be feeling like this and still be alive. The interpreter set the chili-coil basin down on my left, placed a larger terra-cotta trencher in front of me, and dropped thirteen triangles of blue sacrificial paper into it. He seemed to check the menstrual flow out of my glans and then stood back. I was too aware of the scores of great-bloods leaning in closer, watching for even a grimace or twitch of pain that might show I wasn't the one. I dangled the cord down over the mound of paper, scattering red dots, and kept pulling it through. I watched the blood flow out of my groin, out over the ribbons on my legs, down into the trencher, spilling over its rim and off down the stairs and into the world, the inside becoming the outside, the most-private written out for the universe. It made sense. I pulled it through, hand over hand, as slowly as possible. It was the longest rope in the universe. And the thickest. It made the VSNL transpacific cable seem like a piece of dental floss. Come on. Too late to whiff out now. Go. Go. Go. Go. The heat of the capsaicin had already spread through my body, buzzing my eardrums and activating tear ducts I tried to choke off, but I did manage to just stand there, not jumping a rope-length into the air and screaming like I really had to do but just pulling and pulling, hand over hand, until it sank into its own groove. It was only while these things were happening that you could ever explain to yourself why we did it. I mean, pain has its own world and its own allure, but it's not describable after the fact. When you get down to it we did it only for the only good reason to do anything, that is, just for the hell of it. It was just suffering for its own sake, or for its own clarity. When you become a connoisseur of agony it gets like anything else, like any acquired taste, you get into controlling it, you learn how to distribute it through your body and through time, how to teeter on the very edge of your expanding personal limit without falling off into insanity. It teaches you to separate yourself from your body and swim out into the ether. You learn how to distinguish four hundred different shades of pain. A ton of stuff. And as far as I know it's a lost art, like knapping a statue out of obsidian.

I pulled the last thorn-knot through and out with an explosion of droplets and coiled the end of the bloody cord into the offering-trencher, and now the aftermath was already setting in, quarts of endorphins sloshing through my capillaries. Pain releases you from yourself and returns you to yourself. The interpreter took the trencher, raised it and showed it to the sky caves of the four directions, and set it down on a brazier. Curls of blood-smoke slithered up and out, my essence sent into the farthest reaches of the great gas-cloud. It made sense.

I stood there wobbling a bit in the warped gravity. It might have been just a figment of my lack of imagination, but I thought I could hear sniffing, the big cat checking out my scent. I teetered backward and caught myself. Watch it. I was feeling dangerously good. One thing I can guarantee is that that moment of recovering from intense pain is the truest peace anyone can ever experience. Especially if it's self-inflicted pain. If you can dive into what you're most afraid of and drift there and not swim up until you're good and ready, everything gets different, the world looks all washed and every vertex of reality's ten billion polygons a second is shard-keen against your Malpighian skin, like you're a sphere of holographic film picking up every photon reflected by every facet of the world.

An acolyte knelt in front of me, squeezed tiny globs of anesthetic honey-lime into the two wounds on my penis, and wrapped it up again in its bloody bands. The sniffing sound segued into something like a purr. My mask came down over my head and my backrack attached itself to my torso, tying itself on with four hundred biting laces in eight hundred invisible hands.

He says to come a little closer, the interpreter said. How did he hear him from this distance? I wondered. Was there somebody else relaying sign language? Well, ask about that later. You can't be an expert on all their little secrets. Remember, they've been staging these things for a long time. They know what they're doing.

I positioned myself at the first step, sideways to the incline. The stairs had fantastically high risers, twenty-two inches according to the BYU map, and we were small people, so as I stood flat on what was effectively the first step, the one above it was above my knee, between it and the level of my groin. To raise myself up it I had to balance on my peg, lift my intact leg with its stilt-shoe as high as possible, like an *élevé* in ballet, position it on the upper step, shift my weight to it, and pull the peg up after me. I'd had them drill a shallow hole at the edge of each step, kind of like on Captain Ahab's deck path, so I could fasten my hidden sole-spike into it between steps. But as I took the first one and wobbled on the pull-up I had trouble getting it in, and when it did slip in I tipped over to that side and panicked until I teetered back upright and found my center of balance. Whoa, I thought. Watch it.

Cripes. Two hundred and fifty-four steps to go. If I pulled this off, it really would be because of divine intervention.

The beaters signaled the next step. Okay. Next. Go. I had to move up one step every five beats. We hadn't made any allowance for the fact that I'd been maimed. If we changed the requirements or faked it at all, I'd lose too much of my already leaky credibility.

I'd rehearsed this, of course, on a forty-step mock-up. But I hadn't been brilliant and I'd been too sick to risk the drinking and blood loss. And it was getting breezy, and dark. And mainly I just wasn't feeling too good. It wouldn't have been so bad without the damn towering beaky Eagle headdress, I thought. And without the claw-foot Elton John platforms, of course. But I was starting to feel like with them I didn't have much of a shot. I raised my foot but somehow I flicked my vision upward, toward the sanctuary, and my Cyclops eye somehow let an awareness of depth into my head.

Uh-oh. I'm in trouble.

The stairs just went up and uppity up, but it wasn't even the horribly steep fifty-one-degree angle that had really hit me, it was the unbrokenness of the span, the subtle strangeness of the absence of railings, absence of landings, absence of turns between flights, the lack of all those little-noticed amenities that all stairs in the rest of the world always have. The stairs projected utter antihumanism, architecture as weapon, not just a complete disregard for comfort and safety but a will to grind you down, to trick you into climbing and then to make you slip and saw you into pulp. There'd never been and wouldn't ever be anything like these stairs in the architecture of the entire rest of the world. You're nothing against them, I thought. Call it off.

Nope. Don't even think about it.

They'll tear you to bits. Even now. They don't love you *that* much. As far as I knew, all the kings and adders who had fallen had been posthumously disowned and wiped out of the records. It was one thing you just couldn't wuss out on, the risk of being on the stairs was an essential bit of realness in the trial by ordeal.

I pushed up to the second step. I felt synovial fluid squirt out of my knee. I cracked and wrenched and got my peg into the hole almost on cue. Really, I could handle these stairs in a jiff, I thought. I mean if I weren't also crippled, drunk, blood-poor, and in stilts—

Stop whining, I thought. Just shut up and deal. Third step. I blasted myself up faster than I was supposed to. My sweat-drenched foot slid forward on the plaster. Christ, watch it, watch the hell out. Slow down. Save it. You aren't the athlete Chacal used to be. You were able to play that one ball game okay but it's pretty much spoiled you for anything else. Not even counting injuries sustained since then. Chill. Beat. Fourth step. I could feel eyes pressing on my back, my clansmen and their clansmen, adders and bloods and dependents, all looking up at me, or rather to me. I could feel their need to trust, feel all the responsibility, all that stuff that sounds so dopey. Something was clicking into position beyond fear and resignation. I guess I'd have to call it a comprehension of the particularity of the moment, or of the brittleness of existence, but it was more abstract . . . anyway, only two hundred and fifty-two steps to go, I thought. No big whoop. Fifth step.

It sounds like I'm bragging but in spite of everything else that had gone on in Mayaland or anywhere else, and no matter what else I've ever dealt with, walking up those stairs in that condition was the single most extreme thing I've ever forced myself to do. It still feels like it took longer than my entire life before and since. I remember the unique ache of each and every step, so that every number between one and two hundred and fifty-five has an indelible association. The only thing I want to really crow about, ever, is finishing that climb, because I went on for a long time after I'd made up my mind to give up and die.

So anyway, I made it but it was like I'd never do anything again, and I don't think I really remembered who I was. There was a vibration of relief in the air behind me, but nothing I could hear over my blood-roar. The top level of the mul really had four sublevels, the scarlet level of the floor of the sanctuary, a black step leading up to that, a wide turquoise apron-step below that, and a second narrower black apron-step before you got on to the stairs proper. I got my peg into its hole in the lip of the threshold stone and looked up into the mul's throat. It was ringed with nacreous barbs like the grinding mouthparts of a lamprey eel. I wavered on my flesh leg, the void behind me sucking on my back, pulling me into the big easy. Watch it. That was exactly how I'd blow it, I thought. I always screwed stuff up that way. I'd finally get through everything and get back here with the drugs and the girl and get it all set up great and then I'd just wipe out at the very last beat. I found my center of balance and let the roaring fade until there was silence everywhere.

> *"Ahan Bolom,"* I said. *"Wake Ocelot,*
> *White North, black West, yellow South, red East, and turquoise*
> *Here and near offer you our corn, our children."*

There was an intake of breath that faded into another purr and then into a rumble of compression like the Ross Ice Shelf getting ready to calve, and then it drew itself out into a long rattle and a crack, like lava rolling off Mount Erebus into the volumes of layered ice. I knew it was the orchestras around me cutting the scaffolding out from under their tree drums and letting them collapse and smash onto the flagstones, but even so at the last snap it seemed to me that One Ocelot appeared against the hemorrhaging sun and called me into the citadel. Fire flared up in his mouth and eyes and light flashed out in irregular rays through the smoke, flickering with a greenish aurora-borealis tinge. The flares had been rolled from refined wax-myrtle berries and mixed with whale oil and the whole thing was brighter than any artificial light anyone had seen since the seating of 9 Fanged Hummingbird. The crowds below went weirdly silent. I stepped forward, up onto the second apron, forward, up the two steps, and into the hole in the sky. It seemed bigger than outdoors, even though there were all these cat people—most of them mask-enhanced mummies but a few with living bodies inside—around me and all this heat and light, the fire reflecting and rereflecting off walls mosaicked with polished pyrite, the flames not regressing infinitely like they would with a smooth glass mirror but jumbling together in a kind of metallic fog like a whirlwind of gold watch springs. The oracle came up behind me and led me into the adoratory, the holy of holies, the Kodesh Hakodashim as we Hebrew buffs would call it. It was all full of jars and vases and big pots on hot braziers. I knelt down on a hot mat. In front of me, 6 Murmuring, a captive tortoishell jaguar lay prone, unbound but heavily narcotized on a wide, slightly concave altar. The hierophant squatted on her left and set a short table between us, with five little tamales on it, each the color of its direction. The blue one in the center was bigger than the others. Each of the four outer tamales was studded with tiny sea-urchin spines, and each spine was wound with that same black-and-yellow skin from poison-dart frogs. The oracle backed out and headed down the steps.

I looked around. The shapes around me looked so unsavory that I closed my eyes again. I wobbled, a little still dazzled from the smoke and the fresh darkness. A voice cawed:

"Now still you aren't our flesh."

(57)

There was no one else in the room. Blood drained out of my head. Hallucination? No. Hidden somewhere. Speaking tube. Yes. The stone god in front of me probably sat on a vertical pipe that went down to the tombs and the caves. Really, those things were pretty common, I remembered, there are spirit tubes in pyramids all over Central America. It's just that the archaeologists all had said they were just spirit things. Like, nonfunctional. But not in this case, the hierophant really was down there. Maybe there were other adders down in the caves with him. Did 2JS know they were still alive down there? I'd have to ask him, if I could convince Lady Koh to let me near his cage for more than a minute. Did Koh know? Did the sitting oracle know where they were, and how to get in there? The oracle had called him with the beat. Did that mean you could ring them up anytime the same way, or did you have to set up an appointment—

> *"As when I felt you first you still trail death,"*
> the sandstone voice said in old court language.

I didn't know what to say, so I mumbled some line from On The Left to the effect of how the inevitable is also the necessary.

> *"You want to read your own k'atun,"* he said.

He meant the future. I said yes.

> *"Then tell me what I'm going to do with these,"* he said,
> *"And if you're right, I'll give you one of them,*
> *And if you're wrong, you don't get anything."*

I had to get him to give me the blue one, which was baked with the blood of Ocelot and would make me speak for him in the zero level. Otherwise they'd force one of the others into my mouth and I'd be dead. Or, like he said, he wouldn't give me anything. In which case I'd also flunk. And he'd give a sign, and when I came out one of the offerers would execute me with a blowgun, and in a few minutes they'd be rolling my corpse down the stairs.

Fine, I thought. All very *Matrix avant la lettre.* Whatevs. I love riddles. Give me a beat.

(58)

"You're going to keep the yellow tamale, the red,
And the black and the white one," I said. *"You won't give me those."*

There was a ten-beat pause.

Gotcha. *This statement is false,* you bastard.

"Then take and eat," he said.

I took the blue tamale and put it through the mask's mouth and into my real one. I chewed it up. It was fine. Earth felt the wound. I swallowed—ow.

Blue liquid sprayed over me. The baby ocelots or cubs or whatever they were—of course they were people, but not only hadn't I heard them come in, but I was losing track of what things looked like—were blowing ink into the cuts in my genitals. Sizzling sounds rose up in the little room. Outside I could hear giant birch-bark kazoos imitating the gurgling sounds of birth. One of my ears popped, and suddenly my head was filled with a luscious comforting smell, like movies and sleepovers. A stone bell tolled twice, the signal for me to slit open Six Murmuring's abdomen. I did. Someone handed me a smaller flint scalpel and I reached in and up, far, far in, and finally found her heart, and, with difficulty, cut it out.

They lifted me up and spun me around and around, rubbing ashes in over the ink, cutting off my costume and weaving me into a new one, strapping wide ribbons around my ankles and wrists, uncording and combing and recording my hair. And change the oil, too, I thought. Finally they draped Six Murmuring's skin over my shoulders. Somehow, while time had raced around me, she'd been sacrified, flayed, hastily tanned, and cut and sewn into a crude manto. A hand fed me a tamale with part of her ground heart inside, and as I swallowed it the uay of a hero, the grandson of One Ocelot, raised his head inside me, shook the ichor out of his hair in a cloud of garnet beads, and looked around. There was another pop and another and then more all around. It wasn't my ears, I thought, maybe it was the stone rending itself asunder molecule by molecule or something, and then I realized it was corn popping, pouring out of the heated pots. I faced the mouth-door. Some of the cubs had ball scoops and were shoveling the blue-white molecules out through the opening like snow, down the steps and into the breeze. From below it would have looked like the mul's cat-head was foaming at the mouth. Cool air coiled around me. I stepped outside, into the big blue-green room of the zero level, and even though I kept telling myself not to get carried away, that it was just an act, I really felt that I was being born out of a wound in the pericardium of the sky.

I watched the white blossoms falling down and away onto the living surface of the city, every visible facet sprouting people like buds on a branch. Infinite focus pressed in on me, the expectation of the human cornrows of bloods and pledges and dependents all sorted into their levels, all staring at me, or rather at the costume that was wearing me, emphasized perspectivally at the apex like Christ's head at the vanishing point of Leonardo's *Last Supper,* acquiring the power of the converging mass of the city, the biomass, the constellations of mountains, the earth and the ocean, and the twenty-two layers of the universe. I felt like a mother spider with thousands of children I wanted to let feed on my own body. Every surface was garlanded with people and I could see into the eyes of every one of them. I stepped to the edge of the threshold stone and stood. The people answered my rebirth with a vast sort of happy vocalized hiss, drawn out on and on, longer than the ovation for an opera diva's farewell. It was both a welcome and a collective oath of allegiance, or more specifically what we called a "breath gift," theoretically, at least, as binding as a blood gift. Each person was breathing one of his, or, in a few cases, her, souls into me.

"Our younger brothers, younger cousins," I said,
I need all of your help in planting me,
In seeding me, 1 Turquoise Ocelot."

It was the closest an ahau would come to a populist invocation, since I was asking for a sanctification—or more accurately a "speech gift"—from each individual. The mouth of my mask, I guess like the much earlier ancient-Greek kind, was carved to work as a small megaphone, so my voice carried and echoed before the human echoers picked it up. But I wasn't satisfied with the tone. It was still too reedy. To really lead a mystery cult you have to have The Voice. Orpheus, Manson, Jones, Koresh, Applegate . . . and just to give them their due credit, 9 Fanged Hummingbird and 2 Jeweled Skull, had beautiful voices. Anyway the crowds answered all together, like a Greek chorus. Which I guess was also a ritual thing before it turned into a stage device.

"*Kimak kimak*," they said. It was like saying "Gladly" or "Of course."

"*Xtalan*," I said four times to the four directions. "We thank you" or "we will remember you."

"*Oxlahun ueceb uchic yn uecic,*" the crowd chanted. The formula was as ingrained as a Hail Mary had been for me in the twentieth century:

"Now still our breath is yours, your sap is ours,
We are your roots, you are our trunk, you branch
Out to the unrevealed four thousandfold . . ."

Each voice was individually pitched to its caste and its clan and its place in the clan, so that you could almost pick each individual voice-loop out of the wall of pitched breath.

Of course, the whole thing was an exchange of obligations. We—I mean, we hotshots—threw these big parties to pay the Morlocks back for all the shit they had to go through, but then we also had to keep making each new party even bigger and wilder than the last one so that it would put them under more of an obligation to us. In Kaminaljuyu and some of the other cities the royals were more blatant about it, begging the public to help them out of debt and even sending out collection boxes. Koh and I had tried to be more circumspect. We'd be making offerings in the name of all the clans and their dependents, and then the clans would show how grateful they were by sending their adders to play in the city-wide Sacrifice Game, as a wedding- and seating-gift to us. And then we'd reciprocate by seeding the k'atun. Which meant reading the game, using it to divine what the weather would be and where to settle people and how to lay out the fields and everything else, and, incidentally, reaffirming or redistributing the various clans' rights and privileges—hunting rights, shares in the irrigation systems, hereditary dress and regalia, client villages, clans of thralls, and much more besides. On my own end, the offerings had to go down right or I'd lose a lot of popular confidence. To put it mildly. I had to show I could do the job.

The central zocalo had filled up since the masque but now a troupe of twenty terror-clowns whirled out into it and cleared the spectators away with a jerky choosing dance, creeping up on a spectator as though if they caught him they'd offer him as a sacrifice, and then as he got away turning and leaping at another. The bacabs' oblationers followed them out into the floor, four of them from each of the five clans, each team trailing a long blue rope. They were elect elders, unmasked but weighted down with ornament, and they stomped out in converging spirals, sucking energy out of the earth with a sort of springy flat-footedness. Rigid white fabric wings extended from their thighs, like dragonflies' wings, and as the spirals contracted into spins the centrifugal force pulled blood out of cuts in their hips until the white had all gone red. It was a pretty showy way to make a blood offering. They clustered in a circle in the center of the zocalo, crushing their limp red wings between them, and reeled the ropes in after them. Meanwhile the Porcupine Clown had worked his way into the line like the fool in a morris dance, dancing along with them and then suddenly braking and disrupting their rhythm. He grabbed the lead oblationer's position and led the line off its course, like Charlie Chaplin with that parade in *Modern Times*. The crowd loved it. Porcupine was the only real clown allowed in the zocalo during the gifts or the City Game. Koh had ordered him not to actually mess up anything, but just to relieve some of the tension for the spectators.

Finally the old men got their act together and brought the first gift to the base of the mul. It was from the Snuffler House, who had backed 9 Fanged Hummingbird before all the unpleasantness and so owed me the first gift. And more. Big-time. I'll deal with you guys later, I thought. They unwrapped the gold cloth and presented him to me. From what I could see from way up here he was an appropriately beautiful full-blood boy just heading into puberty. The ocelot-ancestor personifiers did this thing where they made these big "surprise" reactions, like they were noticing him for the first time, and then closed in around the teenager and started dancing around him like "We're going to eat you, we're going to eat you," or whatever, and then they sprang at him and covered him up, twitching their tails above them in slow increments, mimicking cats nibbling their live food. Next there was a blast from a clay kazoo and my nacom walked out and into the orange-and-black tangle. The ocelots turned and backed off, like they were relinquishing their food to the leader of the pride, and the nacom took the prisoner's rope and led him to the stairs. Four invisibles fell into line after them and the little procession started up toward me. The chant was segueing into a sort of fugue, as familiar to us as "Row, Row, Row Your Boat" is to American preschool classes, but it had a sort of haunting expectant interrogatory half-melody. Which I guess isn't very specific, but it's tough to describe music anyway. And now there were teasers prodding screamer captives too—different captives—somewhere I couldn't see, and the screams made it more like a burning than any kind of singing. But they gave it a completeness, like you needed the pain at the edge of the chord.

(59)

When the nacom reached the lower apron of the adoratory, I stepped back into the shelter of its mouth, just behind a wide brazier. The attendants laid the kid down on the plain stone table. The nacom bent over him, purified the boy and then his long-handled flint knife with his cigar, slit the kid's stomach horizontally with a single motion, palmed a smaller knife, reached in and up, worked for a moment inside the abdominal cavity, severing the heart from the aorta and vena cavae—and then pulled out the little red muscle. An attendant held up a dish. The nacom set the heart in the dish, slit it longitudinally, opened it up like a book, and studied it. He turned upstage to me, let an attendant wipe the blood off his arms, and then signaled that the signs were good. I signed the go-ahead, and the attendant ran up past me and tipped the heart into the brazier. I listened to it sizzle and breathed in the sausagey smoke. The different sections of the crowd-orchestras reacted, hitting high notes of relief on a long, slow melody that overlaid the bass line, while the kid's body rolled down the stairs to the holy chefs. One down, I thought.

The kid had behaved really well and didn't even seem drugged. It reflected well on the Snufflers. And on me, too, I supposed. Sometimes you'd be happier if you could get your captive to scream, because you just wanted to humiliate him, but a lot of the time you'd be happy if the victim took it like a mensch, since you wanted to show how hard you were by capturing somebody that tough in the first place. This was more in the second category. Also, there were some occasions when you wanted your adders to divine from their screams, but at a time like this if they freaked out it would just help spoil the invocation.

The Macaw Clan's oblationers unwrapped their gift. It was a little boy on his first public-name-date anniversary, which meant he was nearly four years old. They led him to the base and the invisibles mimed hoisting him up to me on his flowery-strung blue ribbon, actually lifting him up, placing him on each step, and lifting him onto the next. The Macaw boy wasn't too heavily drugged, either, and by the third step you could see that he really was terrified, he'd realized in some way what was actually going on, and he slid into something between a whimper and a screech.

I guess all this is going to make me completely unsympathetic. Right? I'd made my peace with what was going to happen earlier, when I was going through the wedding rehearsals with Koh's stand-ins—but I suppose I was still just a fuck to go along with it. Of course, I didn't see any other way. I was just following orders.

And remember, this was a big ceremony and we still only did nine or ten people, which isn't exactly a holocaust, right? I mean, it's not great, but at least we didn't do those big wholesale blowout sacrifices like the Aztecs supposedly did later. They'd go through ten times that many people on just a regular day, probably before breakfast. Although on the other hand, I'd recommend getting captured by the Aztecs, instead of the Maya. Since we—I mean the Maya—were a lot more creative torture-wise. At least the Aztecs just killed you.

And anyway, consider the context, right? We—I mean we like us Ixob dudes again—we were emulating God by being as mean as possible. God obviously enjoys killing little kids, right? At least we didn't pretend that God *doesn't* enjoy torturing innocent people, or pretend not to notice.

And anyway, I did feel queasy, I did feel sorry. But where do I get off mentioning it anyway? Sorry doesn't muck the custard.

Down in the zocalo my own Harpy clan was unswaddling their gift. It was a former foster brother of all of theirs, now disinherited: 18 Jog, 2 Jeweled Skull's favorite nephew. He'd been sewn into the 2 Jeweled Skull costume from the masque, but he wasn't the one who'd actually danced 2 Jeweled

Skull. We hadn't trusted him to go through the motions. I focused across the plaza at the central room of the Council House, where 2 Jeweled Skull was being forced to watch from his cage, but it was too dark in there to see him.

The invisibles stripped off 18 Jog's regalia and unwrapped his team of five dwarves. They were so fattened they looked table-ready, like kids in turkey costumes in a school Thanksgiving play. But they weren't official sacrifices, either, and weren't going into the communion pot. They were just there because 18 Jog was still a greathouse, captive or not, and still deserved attendants to keep him amused on the road out of this level. Dwarves always work. The invisibles led them up, 18 Jog walking stiffly—he was twenty-three solar years old and, from what I could tell, not so quick or forceful as his famous uncle—and the dwarves followed, struggling up the high steps, trailing veils of tinkling laughter from the crowds. To me they didn't look very aesthetic, more like Grock, Loopy, Scuzzy, Sullen, and Retarded, only without the beards, but really they were matched and trained and must have cost a lot. Anyway the audience had been waiting for a finale.

They came to the threshold. 18 Jog just stood there like Jesus until they stretched him over the table. I could hear a couple of his joints popping. Maybe Koh's people wanted to make him scream. But really it wasn't a good idea. Anyway since he was a full-blood captive there wasn't much chance of it. At most you'd get a little unconscious vocalization at the instant of death.

The nacom purified 18 Jog's face and chest. I walked forward, let the nacom blow smoke over my halberd, and set its central hooked blade on 18 Jog's neck.

Now, as you probably noticed, so far I hadn't done any of the actual killing myself. In general you didn't want to get that close to the death-breath. So you let the professional sacred outcastes take care of it. You really just wanted the recipient—Ocelot, in this instance—to give you the credit. It's like you want to throw the party, but you don't want to have to cook everything yourself and hand-feed it to your guests. But in this one case I was expected to do a few little things, although I'd still let the nacom give the coup de grâce. It was okay partly because 18 Jog wasn't a captive I'd taken with my own hands. It was like how when you were hunting it wasn't cool to eat anything you'd bagged yourself.

I held 18 Jog's forehead with my left hand, turned his head toward me, made an incision under the earlobe, found the condyle of the mandible, and severed it from the temporomandibular ligament. I turned to the other cheek, did the same thing, handed my long-handled knife to one of the ordinands, pushed 18 Jog's forehead back so he couldn't bite me, hooked my right thumb around his lower incisors, and pulled off his jaw. A little sunshower of blood spattered down around me and saliva sprayed up out of the ducts. I held the jaw up and whirled it around four times. The tongue was still flapping and trailing pink drool. I tossed it down the stairs. The ordinands stood up 18 Jog to show him to the crowd, teasingly tilting him back and forth on the lip of the precipice. He tried to launch himself over but they kept catching him. The crowd went wild and a few sections lost control of the chant. I wasn't feeling good about the whole thing, but I've got to admit—just to get rid of any vestige of sympathy you may have for me—that at the same time I couldn't help not quite laughing but at least being aware of how ridiculous 18 Jog looked at that moment, with his front teeth sticking down into nothing and his big head wagging around on its little neck. A jawless person is just really, really funny-looking. They handed me my knife, turned him back upstage to me, and I cut into his abdomen longitudinally above the navel. He had abs, not a six-pack or anything, but still abs, so it wasn't an easy cut, but I got through it in one motion. I got a little dizzy for a beat, maybe from stage fright or conflicting motives or something but maybe more just from the feeling of parting that thickness. Cutting into living flesh is like that feeling of spooning into something soft that keeps its shape, like pudding or cheesecake, and taking out a smooth half-oval. There's some basic fascination in creating that hollow area. Maybe surgeons feel that all the time. Still, I got it back together, handed off my knife, reached in and up with both arms, and tore through the diaphragm with my nails. *This little curtain of flesh,* I thought. I found the heart, and held it for a beat. I guess it's obvious that it must be an odd feeling to hold a still-beating heart in your hands, but it's hard for me to say exactly why. I guess you could get a sense of it by holding a bird and thinking about crushing it to death. It's got that same incredible power at the vanishing point of the lines of repulsion and fascination.

For some reason I looked at 18 Jog's face and his eyes contacted mine. He didn't seem angry or panicked or anything, he just had that swooning relaxed look you get when pain goes over the edge.

The heart wasn't what we were after in this particular procedure. It would go into a special giant batch of *atole* later on. I let go of it kind of reluctantly, twisted my hands down and behind it, and found the liver.

It's a heavy, fragile, floppy organ, but I found and cut the vena cava and the portal vein, got both big lobes out—along with the gallbladder—and plopped them into the dish. An acolyte wiped my hands with palm oil. I took the dish, turned, and walked up into the sanctuary. It was darker inside now but there were still flares burning and a single feline acolyte crouching in the back next to the heirophant's casket. I set the basin down on the old great-mat. The acolyte lifted the old man's torso. He looked at me and then bent down over the liver to inspect it. I came forward and watched. He turned it over. It seemed like a big, healthy, blood-rich sucker, but then he reached into the fissure between the left and quadrate lobes, and pointed to a smelly little abscessed necrosis, like a popped tube of anchovy paste. He looked at me.

"All right for now, but not for later," he rasped. Or, well, his voice was a little thinner and finer than a rasp. "He sanded"? "He emeryboarded?" "He nailfiled?" Anyway, I knew I wouldn't get any more out of him. He was set on being difficult. I thanked him, did my little obeisance, and walked out back to the threshold.

> *"Kimak-kimak,"* I said. *"All's good to swim,*
> *Forward, four times four hundred solar years."*

The crowd answered with a din like a giant cave full of sea lions. Just to show off, the ordinands released 18 Jog and let him stand on his own for a beat. He just stood there for five beats. His chest and legs were solid red but he was still alive. Finally he tried to take a step toward me but tilted forward, and just as he was about to fall into my arms the acolytes caught him and held him while the nacom expertly sawed the rest of his head off his body and handed it to a preparator-acolyte for wrapping. There was almost no blood from the neck. The ordinands released the body again and the nacom nudged it downstage, over the lip of the saw-stairs. It tumbled over and down almost noiselessly. The crowds went silent for a beat and then slid back into a softer, more awed-sounding cycle of the chant. I felt this wave of protectiveness of them, and I could feel how grateful they all were, love and relief rising off them like heat waves. Sacrifice can create this incredible bond, maybe the strongest bond you can have with more than one other person at a time. And especially with throngs of people you haven't met. There's this community epiphany, you get a rush of shared exaltation of surviving on together. You know so clearly you've all felt the same thing and lived through the same little terror, it's like you've just had sex with everyone there.

They rolled the next batch of sacrifices down the stairs alive, just to get the party mood going again, first Loopy, then Retarded, and then Jock, Sullen, and Scuzzy all at once. Since the atole was finished it was all right to pollute the stairs with inferior blood. They bounced over and down and around and around, glortching and squealing, their movements defining five separate arcs from living to dead. To the audience—I almost said "to my family"—it was pretty much the funniest thing in the world. Great sense of humor, guys, I thought. I shoulda brung some tapes of *The Benny Hill Show.*

An acolyte tapped the platform next to my foot. I turned. He was offering me a regulation-size ball, freshly wrapped out of white rubber ribbon. Its glyphs said 18 Jog's head was inside, just in case there was any doubt. I took the ball and held it over my head. I could feel the inrush of breath underneath me. I threw it down the steps. It bounced higher and higher as it fell lower, finally arcing high into the crowd, and then bobbing from one lucky person to another as they hipped it back and forth across the square.

Pitzom pay-ee, I thought. Let the Game Begin. I signed for Koh's escort to bring her out. The hissing rose up again from Star Rattler's mul. The snake poured down her steps again. The crowd below scattered aside. The mul's temple doorway, recently resculpted as Star Rattler's giant mouth, vomit-birthed a big blue egg-box and flicked its rattle against it. The egg exploded and Koh emerged headfirst, like a baby, in a cowl of metallic green beetle shells sewn in a celestial map onto a manto pieced from the skins of four hundred black iguanas.

(60)

She floated up the steps toward me, twice as tall as her actual height, carried by a pair of dwarf bearers hidden under her long star-scale-skirt. Four of her own attendants followed her, two steps behind. It was a little out of the ordinary for her to be here and there'd be some muttering among the oldsters. But really, since the gifts were over, women could step on the holy ground without polluting anything. Anyway, things are gonna be different around here, I thought. Sisters are doing it for themselves.

I reset my stilt-sandals on the sharp lip of the threshold and nearly fell forward again. In the smoke and the amethyst half-light things seemed closer than they were, even without depth perception. A new set of Harpy Fliers had climbed the poles and were spinning downward, and the Ocelots were dancing through the costumed celebrants, rocking and almost falling, strutting and voguing, uninhibited but also totally controlled. It wasn't like a nightclub or anything, actually it was just the old men who were supposed to really dance, and the others just sort of bopped. But the righteous dub ran through everything. It was so different from the dour, stale Teotihuacán vigil. It had a sense of beginning. A lot of the spectators and dancers were popping off into orgasmic trances, but even so, they still kept pulsing to the same gemütlich beat. There's really nothing nearly so powerful as tribal fellow-feeling. And as I watched the rough edges of artifice disappeared and I forgot the dragon had legs, or that there were ropes holding the fliers in the air. The revelers' masks fused to their flesh and pulsed and rippled and grimaced. I could feel my smile flowing through to the scales of my jade mask, everything meshing. The dancers' back racks unfolded into pulsing mating displays, the gods' power rising off them in clouds of musk, and it wasn't a ceremony anymore but the event itself, gods kicking up the world just for the hell of it a long time ago, now, and again. It was a childlike feeling but it also had this brooding, shrouded purposefulness to it, and a bittersweetness about how I was part of a we, and how we were all so pathetically grand, so hopeful, so alive, I got this love-twinge and felt tears soaking my face-padding. It sounds sappy but it's really comprehending the quiddity of whatever it is, the what-it-is-ness, how limited it is, how much we could love only each other, that really gets you. Twenty-first-century people haven't lived at all, I thought. You've got to go for it, you have to string yourself along the thread where sex and violence and pleasure and pain and egotism and oblivion all intersect on the intensity graph, to this point of exhilaration without concepts, just thereness, that pure no-doubt living-goal insects feel, and if you haven't gotten there at least once it's like you've been looking at the ocean through a window without ever swimming in it. Or at least that's the way it seemed at the time.

Koh rose up in front of me. Invisibles spread the ancient great-mat at the edge of the platform. I stepped onto it and sat down—so slowly that it took over a minute—facing north, so that when I looked over my left shoulder I could see the vertiginous rush of the Steps and the whole roiling zocalo. Actually, the entire area between the two great pyramids was considered a kind of ball court. But it was at least a hundred times the area of an actual playing trench, much too big for humans to play on. Instead the balls were the planets and moon and sun. Normally it just worked on its own, slowly, but in this one ritual Koh and I were going to bounce them forwards ourselves, and use the people to mark where they might land.

The dwarves set Koh down four arms away from me, facing me—that is, south—and slithered off, back into the sanctuary, keeping low so the crowd couldn't see them. Down in the forum the invisibles were clearing everyone off the central square, an area about three rope-lengths on a side. It had been pumiced and buffed and freshly repainted in the color zones of the five directions with the full Sacrifice Game grid superimposed on it like a squared-off spiderweb. Finally, I thought. The Human Game. Let's go.

Koh's attendants snipped off her blue-green-goggle-eyed snake-jaw helmet and instantly started constructing an Ocelot queen's coiffure and headdress in its place. She was pretty much giving up her old role as a sort of nun to Star Rattler. Still, marrying me was the safest plan for her. Later—not much later—before I entombed myself, I'd announce at the popol na that Koh was going to continue ruling, as the mouth of my uay, and then, eventually, as regent for her son, assuming we were going to have or secretly adopt one. And meanwhile, with me out of the picture, Koh would keep working to unify the Ocelot and Rattler factions until the situation was stable enough for her to relocate. And—at least until the twelfth b'aktun—that would be my contribution to posterity.

She and I saluted each other, but she didn't say anything. An attendant set a covered Game-table between us.

Down in the forum the invisibles swept and oiled the Game grid. Alligator Root, Koh's crier, sat two stairs below us, wearing a thin black mask, like a domino mask, fastened over his eyes with wax. At least she hadn't had him blinded.

The first fifty-nine evaders—or poison oracles—walked out and stood at their posts at the center of the tetragon. Each one held a pair of sticks and they wore tall zero-masks. One of the leading one's sticks was a big red-streamered staff, twice as tall as he was. Next the fifty-eight masked catchers took their places around them, seven at each of the eight star points and two in reserve outside the grid. Each of the catchers had a little drum on a stick. The hundred and seventeen players had all been chosen from four- or five-stone adders from trusted dependent clans, which meant they could all feel the blood-lightning and count like they had little abacus cashiers in their heads. But presumably it also meant that they wouldn't know enough to direct a City Game on this scale, or to remember it and take the knowledge with them. They'd picked the thirteen evaders from among themselves, by cleromancy, and tattooed them and studded them with the patterns of the sidereal scorpion, and fed them on liver and deer's blood to make them strong. And for the last ten days they'd all practiced every hour they were awake. Each one would be, in a way, playing his own separate game, and the totality of games would magnify the totality of the master game.

The Game beaters started on their clay water drums, in time with the beat of the universal festival, but more insistent.

Let's go, I thought. Letsgoletsgoletsgo. I still couldn't quite believe that the Human Game was really happening. It was like—well, I don't know if it was like anything. But if it worked, I'd learn what I needed to know, what we all needed to know. And then, knowing . . . knowing . . .

"You know, at best I'll only see the moves," Koh reminded me. "You'll have to interpret."

I said I knew that, and I thanked her again. She smiled, like, Hey, no problem, we're just hangin' out anyway, right?

As I think I mentioned, as far as anyone knew, this was going to be the first City Game since the one played in Teotihuacán k'atuns before. And given the way the art was dying out, this might turn out to be the last one anywhere. This Game was supposed to be a public demonstration of my ability to read the future, but it would really be Lady Koh who was doing the seeing, and she and I would be playing for our own reasons. And, if all went well, nobody else would find out the farthest-off or the most important things we'd see. We'd throw them a few solid predictions about the next few k'atuns, and keep the rest to ourselves.

Koh lit one of her green cigars—the kind with chili and chocolate threaded through the tobacco—took a hit, and passed it to me. I puffed. She started the invocation. As I think I started to say at some point and then lost track of, it was in the old heavily metaphorical adders' dialect, and—especially in a heavily accented language like English—it's hard to get a sense of the swing, which it don't mean a thing if it ain't got. So I'll make this a bit closer than a paraphrase, but less than a translation. Okay, Jedketeers? Right. Here we go:

Koh:

"You, Hurricane, who sparked Lord Heat's first dawning,
You over us who foreknows his final dying,
You, sun-eyed coiler of the blue-green basin,

You, jade-skinned carver of the turquoise cistern,
You, there, whose hissing javelins strike wildfires,
Deign to respond to us from out your whirlwind."

Koh looked up, not at my eyes, but at the emerald-green mask of One Ocelot on my pectoral sash. I hesitated, cleared my throat, and launched into my first response.

Jed:
"We who are only dust motes in the whirlwind,
We, born at sun's fall and gone before its dawning,
Who will be waiting for us by the hearth fire?
Whose hands will polish our bones beyond our dying?
Will our skulls just bounce on the floor of the fresh-sea cistern?
Will the potters rebake the shards of our shattered basins?"

Ahau-na Koh:
"You, Cyclone, grant us a perch below the basin
But over the clouds, above the wrecking whirlwinds:
An overlook above the fourfold cistern
Where we can scatter the seeds of coming dawnings
Where we can count their growings and their dyings
Where we can spot young floods and fresh-sparked fires."

Jed:
"Where we can warn our heirs of nearing fires,
Where we can feel the first cracks in the basin
And cradle our lineage and forestall its dying,
Where we can hear them crying in the whirlwind,
Where the entire talley of their dawnings
Reads full and clear, above the yawning cistern."

Ahau-na Koh:
"You at the center of the turquoise cistern
Show us the gold southwest fires,

Let us see redward, through the sierra of dawning,
Southeast to where the horizon meets the basin.
Guide us northeasterly through the bone-dust whirlwinds,
And even northwest, through the soot-black dunes of dying."

Jed:
"So that in ages far beyond our dying
Our daughters can still pour offerings in your cistern,
Our sons can still feed blood-smoke to your whirlwinds,
Our thralls will always tend your altar fires,
Pouring you chocolate from brimful basins
Through all the days undawned but now soon dawning."

Ahau-na Koh:
"Dawning we bake our bodies and smash them dying."

Jed:
"We shatter our basins and drown them in your cistern,
And snuff our last fires to steam, to slake you, Whirlwind."

Koh scattered the seeds and whispered their position to the cantor. He called them out and the human pieces took their places. She waited five beats.

She made her first move.

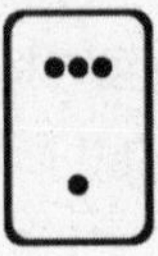

(61)

"*One death, one wind, four thought, sixteen, nineteen,*"

Koh said, immediately giving the last date from the Teotihuacán City Game. She'd basically just skipped ahead about four hundred solar years, to Gregorian 1225. I'd thought she'd guide the adders to it, ease them into it a bit, but maybe she wanted to see if they knew what they were doing. The nine clumps of adders broke up and shifted somehow and for a beat the plaza seemed like just a jumble, like the human crystals had just dissolved in solution, and then they coalesced into a new octalinear pattern, and melted again and lined up again. Even though I was expecting something like it I was totally taken aback. It was definitely like something. Not anything biological, something from physics or technology, I don't know what, maybe like hundreds of those Pac-Mannish magnetic polarities coursing through the domains of a synthetic-garnet bubble-memory chip. What was actually happening was each adder was walking forward, on the beat, out onto the lines separating the points of the grid, the interstices interspersed between the intersections, earth-marching from his old position to a new one determined by his individual count of the days and cycles, which in turn were all different because each person represented a different cycle that he counted on his sticks or his drum, and each person's cycle was a unique mathematical progression that ignored some beats and, say, triple-counted others, and then redirected his progression based on the people he intersected in his nonrandom walk. On a human scale the movements had similarities to reconstructions I'd seen of Renaissance minuets, and there was a flavor of Gujarat stick-dancing, or like I said, the morris dance. But even if it was dancelike it was so obviously not just for effect, they were all really doing something. Or building something. They stopped.

Two evaders had been taken out in the shuffle—that is, intersected with and caught by a catcher— but they didn't kill them since it wasn't necessary yet, they still weren't really counting ahead. The pair just slunk off don't-notice-me-ishly through the forest of erect catchers, as neatly arranged in their staggered ranks as North Korean parade soldiers.

> *"Now wait,"* Koh said, her herald repeating. *"Now*
> *He goes on seething, now she's resting, breathing."*

She meant they were supposed to hang out where they were for a beat. The catchers looked impatient, gesturing at the remaining evaders like they were trying to grab them from a distance. I would have thought it was insubordinate, but it really meant they were already trancing into their roles. Koh's attendant set her Game board on the table, and positioned a close-weave basket and little brazier on the mat just upstage of it. Koh undid the knots and uncovered the board. From where we were sitting the cleared Game-zone in the zocalo below us and the board in front of us both seemed about the same size, like if you had two eyes you could look at one out of each eye and focus them together to get a stereo view. The attendants descended onto the apron beneath us and spread out to the edges, so that no one would be so high as Koh and I. Unless you counted the old trog-in-the-box.

Alligator Root must have signaled the drummers at the first sight of the flame, because in unison they launched into double time.

"First runner, move to fourteen Night," Koh said.

I moved it. My role in this thing was actually pretty mechanical. I was just supposed to translate the positions of the human pieces onto Koh's board and wait for her move. "You can't keep track of all the strains," Koh had said at some point, I forget when. "You need someone to hold them down."

Alligator Root called the move out to the zocalo. The runner with the red streamer walked circuitously to his new position. The colors were going Disney on me, like the ninestrips of Technicolor they used in the Bahia sequence in *The Three Caballeros*. About thirty-one thousand, four hundred and twenty people on the peninsula, I thought, and then I realized I'd guessed the number by counting the people in a small section of zocalo and multiplying it out, and it had taken me less than a beat. I felt like I could count a swarm of a million-plus bats coming out of a cave. Not even. I could instantly count a swarm of midges floating up out of a dead whale by counting the legs and dividing by six. Just for the hell of it I made up a couple of integrations, did them in my head, and checked them. Right on. My Jedman powers were coming back. I could see the parabolas like they were giant intersecting towers of Lego bricks, warm colors for even numbers, cold for odd, metallic for prime.

The blue of Koh's face was seeping into the regular flesh tone, and vice versa. I sniffled so I wouldn't have to wipe my runny nose. Gods didn't do stuff like that. I ran through a few distribution tables, 0.5040, 0.5438, 0.5832, 0.6271. I let a tear or two fall out of my eye and socket. I was feeling a little restless and weak and everything. I can handle this, I thought. I reached into the jars, counted out a red corn-skull for each runner and a blue one for each catcher, and reset the position on the world-board around us. It's hard to describe, but it seemed to me like the mul we were on was just the central peak of an unimaginably vast plateaued landscape. Koh thought for twenty beats and twenty more.

"Two entering, twelve striking, northward eight," she said.

Her herald repeated it and the catchers and quarries shuffled again, separating and weaving together like threads on an invisible Jacquard loom, multiple warps coming up through the weft, heddles and treadles and shuttles and lams. There was a moment of near-stasis as the lead runner moved upward through suns of the same name again and again, days from the past turning up in the future, and then the catchers and quarries added up their combined and respective totals, each called out his result, and then each moved again, that much farther forward on the basis of the others, blasting through progressions it would take *Encyclopaedia Mathematicas*—full of tables to even hint at, and then they'd melt into a different rhythm, like gears on a Pascal adding machine, the Quarries spiraling away from the meshing circles, stately, microscopic, and terrified, until one of the Quarries was caught between two catchers, and they all stopped while the nacom walked out and strangled him with a red-and-blue ribbon.

Invisibles carried the body off the court.

The idea here, briefly, and to put it in a way Koh wouldn't have, was that the closer you are to death, the more of your own event cone you're able to see. Not many of the human pieces would survive the Game. But their counts would be preternaturally insightful. It was cruel but effective.

It was already dark. No twilight in the courts of the sun. Who said that? Damn. Forgetting things. The Usher Gods had lit torches inside tall vertical cylinders of oiled rushwork, almost like giant paper lanterns, and the rows of them glowed in lavender and deep sea-snail purples. Two skeletons flopped up the stairs of the mul, only a hundred and ten steps below us. They weren't really supposed to be on the mul, but this was kind of like an anything-goes Mardi Gras where all the roles are reversed, one of those masters-wait-on-the-servants kind of things, and I guessed it was okay as long as they couldn't get up here or see the board or whatever. I looked at Koh but she was way too out there to get distracted. I could probably have leaned over and kissed her and gotten zero reaction. Koh's Porcupine Clown flop-danced up after the skeletons, staggering and reeling on the edges of the steps like Harold Lloyd in *Safety Last*. He shouted at them to get back down off of there, and then, when they didn't, to jump. Even I had to laugh, he was really kind of a pantomime genius, like Grock or David Shiner. I'd never seen anyone move like that. For a beat he seemed to be walking along my arm and I realized I'd lost my scale and couldn't tell which was bigger, the insect board in front of me or the human one on our left, or the celestial one overhead. I tried to focus on the blue-green center of the board. At least it was easier than if I'd still had two eyes. Turquoise really is an excellent color, I thought. There just wasn't enough of it around. I have got to get more turquoise stuff. Koh intoned another little number jingle, programming the interactions faster now. Without any warning the main runner, the one with the staff, seemed to get caught between two human points on vast intersecting ellipses, and the other catchers rushed in like T-cells rushing to spin a net across a wound. The main runner handed off the streamered staff to another runner on an adjoining square, and the nacom executed him, and the array settled again. The other runners were off in the Northwest, still pretty isolated from the hunters, but at this rate they might not last the length of the game.

Koh regathered her seeds and counted them out again, shifting back and subtracting, and gave the herald another directive, and the human net dissolved and reformed, the invisible spider spinning her a dewy web and eating it and respinning it and eating it again. I was beginning to see a bit of a pattern in it, not more than the kind of vague sense you get when you look at a long row of successive calculations and try to guess the function they're coming from, but for a beat I thought I had a notion of how the Sacrifice Game had grown, back when things didn't change so much, when technology and population increase were barely factors at all, and the main thing was just to keep going, not to stay on in a bad place, not to get caught by bad weather, and the tribal knowers nurtured the craft over those big empty millennia between Late Paleolithic and Historic, working out settlements, summer and winter camps, lookout fortresses on the frontier, dividing territory, spreading alliances out into space and time, locating the freeholds for new families, seeding new cross-pollinated strains of humans out into the vastness, the universe focusing into the great-great board, and that focusing into the miniature one, and that one focusing into our brains. And all the time, like I keep saying, it wasn't any magic or fortune-telling, it wasn't supernatural, it was just a big human computer, and to run it right you had to be a kind of symphony conductor. And, as you know, if you're a classical music fan, with a tricky composition, some conductors just get it and some don't. Koh was one of the last of a tradition that just knew or felt some mathematical trick other people had forgotten, something about spotting potential catastrophe points way in advance. She was at 910 AD. 1353. 1840. Oh, my God, she's going to do it. 1900.

There was a burst of laughter below us. Porcupine had dragged the skeletons off the mul and was threading through the elders' mats on the long, high stone benches that took up south side of the Game zone. He had a long drinking reed, twice as tall as he was, and he'd snuck it into one of the elders' balche-pots and drunk the whole thing in one draft. The old man who was holding the pot had turned back to it and just now found it empty. He saw from the reaction of the crowd that something was up and he whirled around, but Porcupine ducked behind a fat old guy next to him, grabbed a big tamale out of his dish, and replaced it with a sort of rat-baby doll. The victim looked back at the tamale, did something almost like a real double-take, jumped up, spotted Porcupine, and threw the dish at him. Porcupine deflected it and backed off, dancing nonchalantly over the low tables. It was like a *Candid Camera* thing. The audience was in hysterics and a couple people threw expensive shawls at him to show how much they loved it. Porcupine picked up the shawls with a flourish, struck a pose that was like the equivalent of a bow, and took a bite out of the tamale, except it was the rat-doll. He spat it out and made a disgusted face. The crowd was roaring.

The beat divided into fourths, each one a complete miniature of the phrase of the polyrhythm. I heard Koh's counter click resolutely on the board. Eye on the ball, I thought. I looked down at the move. It felt like my boulder-sized head would roll down and crash through the board. She'd moved the sapphire again, back to where it had been in terms of days, but according to the hotun-count she was already at 10 Alligator, 20 Jaguar, 14.8:4.56. AD 2002. I started to wipe a too-tickly tear from under my non-eye, the hell with my regal fucking bearing, but it felt like my hand was in a plutonium boxing glove. What if I got too much of the tzam lic? It was good for playing a thousand moves ahead, and for Koh and I to communicate wordlessly with each other and everything, but I knew from experience that the hangover could be a bear. How'd I gotten this much out of a few puffs on a funny cigar? It must be some new recipe. Did Nurse Feelgood really know what she was doing? She might be able to sprinkle Agent Orange on her Shredded Ralstons, but the rest of us—

Squelch that thought. Don't worry. At least I now knew what the big deal was about this stuff. Bet if I live I'll sleep for at least a week. Below us Porcupine had gotten back on the mul again and was teetering along the fifth step, holding a shrunken Dzonotob trophy head—which he must have yanked off somebody's court dress—in front of his own white and black-masked face and working the mouth up and down.

"Help help, help help!" he ventriloquized. "How did my body ever grow so big?" He forced his right thumb in through the neck and wagged it through the mouth like a tongue. His left hand pretended to turn the reluctant head around, pulled it down to his crotch, and forced it into sucking motions. He howled. He'd gotten two other fingers of his right hand up behind the shell eyeballs and pushed them out from inside, making them bounce bug-eyed. Meanwhile his left hand had found a bowl of white atole and as he pretended to come he shrieked, blasted the gruel up over himself in a milky shower, pushed the head away, and shook himself off like a dog.

Charming, I thought. Japanese game-show humor. Next vee have zee socolate-mousse wrestlink—

> *"Six sproutings, fourteen witherings,"* Koh said.

She was at August 12, 2005.

> *"Next fifteen rainings, eighteen crackings; next,*
> *Six sparkings, twenty-seven darkenings."*

The beat divided again into sixteenths—about the length of a p'ip'il, an eyeblink—and the branches of possibility spread out at such a steep curve that they almost headed into reverse, like the umbrella profile of a ceiba tree with branches that curve out almost to the horizontal, but never quite droop. I could see there was some equation there. If only I had room to write it down in the margin of my brain, I thought. My fingers were aching from setting and resetting the seeds, but it didn't affect the performance of my autopiloted hands. Koh moved her sapphire right through the equivalent of 2007 and out toward the rim. I thrashed along after her. She was down to two quarries. The sun and moon and the two Venuses flashed their ellipses over the board, and it churned underneath them motokaleidoscopically like heaps of floating rhinestones going down a drain, although really I could have been either seeing it or just imagining it. The catchers closed in on the last runner. Koh came to the threshold at 2012.

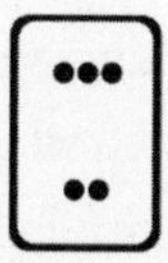

(62)

The runner was surrounded at the northwest corner of the board, cut off at the edge of the world. It was like Koh and her avatar were checkmated, there was nowhere for the sapphire to escape to. Oh, shit, I thought, that's really it, the end, the end, the end, the end. I looked up at Koh. She was still studying the board. I saw movement at the nose-edge of my right eye and bent down to focus on the board again. Koh was definitely seeing something, she'd made another move in her head, but I couldn't imagine where. I tried to see what she was seeing on the board but it was all murky and distorted like the lens in my eye was melting. Koh picked up her sapphire and moved it toward the center of the board, like the runner was somehow jumping over the mass of catchers.

Something touched her shoulder and she looked up. The Porcupine Clown had gotten all the way up to our level and was leaning over Lady Koh herself, flirting with her like he was trying to lead her down into the zocalo. Was he supposed to do that? I wondered. Wait a beat, I thought. Koh stood up and I thought she was laughing but then I thought maybe something was actually wrong, the Porcupine was hugging her, and she wasn't just being a good sport in the act, she was really struggling. Where were the guards? I wondered, but of course it had looked like just part of his act. I jumped over the table at them but I was too groggy and the Porcupine was too fast, he was already over the lip of the sanctuary and rolling down the steps with his arms and legs wrapped around Lady Koh. I lurched down after them but my Ahab leg slipped out from under me and I slid down into the arms of one of the guards. Attendants were bouncing down the steps below me and for a beat I thought Koh had rolled down all the way, but as I screamed for them to get me down, DOWN!!! Porcupine had fetched up on the tenth step below us, caught by a ball of belayed guards, and I saw some of Koh's robe in the knot. I couldn't hear anything over cataracts of blood through my ears, but the guard got me down to them and I sort of slid down into the cluster, held by a couple of the roped guards while a few more of Koh's attendants rolled down, leaving spatters of blood on the white stairs. Some of her other women and a couple of attendants were coughing and gagging like they had rocks stuck in their throats. I got my hands on Koh's crushed brittle headdress and threw it aside.

I thought for a beat that she'd smeared her face paint, because the white parts of her skin were a purple I couldn't imagine was real. Below her the three bloods who'd caught Porcupine were sprawling back on the edge of the platform, gasping for breath and choking. Another one had gotten his quill costume off and was trying to ask him the eternal question, who'd sent him, but the clown's tan skin was already turning to blueberry-black and there was a huge maroon erection popping out from under his raggedy underwear. His chest was pocked with little sticks.

I got Koh's head into my hands. She had a surprised, disgusted look. She said, "You—"

"It's all right," I said stupidly in English, "you're going to be great. Right?"

She didn't answer. Foamy snot was running out of her nose and mouth and her open eyes were getting that matte finish. There were little sticks stuck to her face and chest and I picked one out of the underside of her chin, automatically holding it by the side. It was smooth and tiger-striped, a spine taken from a living scorpionfish, with a neurotoxin that kills by suffocation. They'd been woven into Porcupine's suit, mixed in with the hard-oiled black feathers that mimicked quills, and when he'd hugged her some of them had gone into his own flesh too.

"Get water in her NOW!!!" I screamed in Chol. I got my hands around the back of her head and blew air into her mouth, but there was just this whiffling blob of mucus in there. I turned her over and tried to Heimlich her but she wasn't responding, she was just a lump. I started hitting her but there was nothing. You're dreaming, this shit's lethal at half this dose. I yelled for someone to help me get the fucking quills out but they didn't know what I meant because I was speaking English again and then they were afraid to touch her because they weren't allowed. Alligator Root appeared and he and I pulled them out. Each time they left this blob of thick-looking blood. An attendant had gotten a pot of water and we tried to get her to drink, but there was nothing, and I made them find an enema gourd and we forced some down her throat, but she wasn't really swallowing. I screamed to Alligator Root that there must be some antidote, that he had to run and get the surgeons, but of course there was no antidote. If they really knew one thing around here it was poisons. I got on top of her and started stupidly trying to massage her heart back to life, crashing down on her and breaking her ribs like I'd forgotten how to do from No Way's survival books, but I just rolled off the stair and nearly tumbled down after the others, it was like we were on the steep slope of an icy mountain with barely any friction keeping us in place and it seemed for a beat like the whole knot of guards and attendants was going to come off its moorings and go rolling down the saw stairs, but one of the bloods got to me and tied me to a sacrificial rope with a scarf—he didn't want the rope to touch my skin—and I got so upset at him for messing with me and not doing something for Koh that I elbowed him in the face and he skidded off down the blades of the stairs. I'm a jerk, I thought. I grabbed the enema gourd and sprayed water in her face. No response. I grabbed her puffy blue tongue and pulled on it. Nothing. Okay, still not too late. Miracle worker, right?

The well, I thought. We're going to the Great Cistern.

No. How cold is that, fifteen degrees Celsius? That's nothing.

The lake in the caves. How cold? Eight degrees, ten degrees?

Hypothermia temperature. But not brain-keeping temperature.

Jelly.

GET HER IN THE JELLY NOW, I mind-screamed, and then tried to put it into Chol, but it was already too late for that. Even if I could get her down there it would take hours to mix up the stuff.

Air too warm here. Come on. Get her down there. Two minutes, three minutes max. Otherwise her brain would have rotted to irrevocable stupidity. I yelled for them to get us down. The attendants held me while they practically sledded down on their ragged rumps. Face it, you're fucked, I thought. The flying finger fucks. I was even crying, which was pretty silly in the context. It was probably mainly just about what a fuckup I was, am, and would be. She was the greatest and you're the pits. About one beat faster and you would have gotten her out of there. We slid to the bottom, into a slick of blood and wheezing bodies. I got Alligator Root's ear down to my mouth.

Get us into the Ocelot caves now, I said. They picked me up and wound Koh into a sheet and the bloods started parting the crowds ahead of us, cracking their flails and blowing kazoos, and the crowd did scatter, but by the time we'd even gotten to the steps up to the mountain path behind the Ocelot mul I could tell it was already ten minutes since the attack, and then it took another ten minutes even to get to the first mountain shrine that led down to the caves, and it was way, way, way too late. Brain dies within two minutes. Dumb. Retarded.

You were supposed to be her primary guard, you know, I thought, you were her husband, after all, you little freak. Big shot, right? Sitting on a big smelly pile of rubble with a dead girl and no—

Snow? Could have had her dumped in snow. Could have had a giant tub of snow always ready. A couple of hundred runners working round the clock to keep it stocked, that's all it would have taken. Save her. Take 'er back.

Brain rotting. Dead, dead. Dead, my lords and gentlemen.

"Send forty running teams," I said. "They're going to Ice Mountain. For a hundred times four hundred bags of snow."

Alligator Root looked at me. I looked back at him. He didn't move. I looked down.

No point. No point. It was four days' run away.

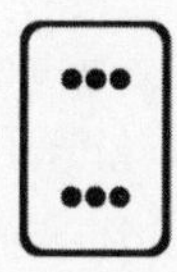

(63)

"*We had a burden,"* I said. *"Your final act*
On the zeroth level can be to honor it."

2 Jeweled Skull didn't answer. I peered forward into one of his dry, sewn-open, upside-down eyes. He wasn't even pretending to tune out, he wanted me to see how damn bloody yet unbowed he was. He'd made himself pass out into some kind of trance a couple times over the two and a half days since Lady Koh's death, but the teaser had put a stop to that by force-feeding him peccaries' adrenal glands.

"Tell me what it is," I said again. I thought I saw some kind of insolence well up in his eye and in spite of myself I thought about Lady Koh again and just lost it for a beat. I started hammering his ears and nose with both hands. Pink lymph-thickened blood spurted out of his tear ducts. I guess that stuff really ran to your head. Anyway, that ordinary level of pain was barely registering at this point and after a beat I fell back, sitting down hard on the war mat. I looked up at 2 Jeweled Skull. He was hanging upside down on a blue-and-yellow scaffold inlaid with pink cowries, draining into a one-arm square basin carved from black serpentine. There were only five other people with us in the tiny courtyard, Hun Xoc, Koh's herald Alligator Root, my teaser, and his two assistants. Normally there'd have been an audience, but this gig wasn't for fun. I'd worried about Hun Xoc's being there, but he didn't seem too upset about the way we were treating 2JS. Generally your adopted father was someone you were expected to beg to die for, but either Hun Xoc had gotten enough of my influence or he was rebellious enough to begin with to get over that. In the little square of sky above us noon sun and overcast alternated on what seemed like even two-hundred-beat cycles. At midnight tonight it would be three days since the assassination and I had that sour cigar-stub feeling in my stomach that you get only after your lack of sleep shifts into its warning phase. A fattened dog was barking somewhere nearby like an unanswered telephone, but otherwise it seemed quiet enough. It was an illusion, though. Outside things had way degenerated.

Ix was already in near chaos, for a hundred reasons. A couple of rival prophets had come up after Koh's death, probably working for the Snufflers. One of them was from the Rattler Temple of Ix and was trying to take over Koh's whole act. Fights were breaking out between the Rattler partisans and the Snufflers and Skull clans. There was a question about 1 Gila's loyalty. Most dismally of all, Severed Right Hand and the feline alliance were only a few days away. The beat he'd heard about Koh's assassination, he'd marched triple-time for Ix without waiting for resupplies or reinforcements. We'd expected him, of course, but his speed took us by surprise, and even though we had every able body digging moats and putting up palisades, there wasn't much chance of getting a defense together. At least, not unless I wanted to train and command another western-style blowgun troop. Which I didn't have time to do. It was already only five suns until 20 Cayman, which was my own personal outer limit. It was way past time for me to take the money and run, only I didn't have the money. Lately Hun Xoc—who I'd made my first minister—had been saying he'd rather torch the whole city now than let Severed Right Hand get hold of even some of it. The idea made me feel kind of *Brennt Paris?* but I was starting to consider it. I could tell my brain didn't have too many more days of functionality left in it. A month and a half, maybe, on the outside. And now without Koh looking out for me I couldn't afford to pass out somewhere in front of people and maybe get separated from my tomb complex. I wanted to stay right here, to keep supervising the assistants as they finished making the gel compounds, and make sure the sarcophagus and the tunnels and everything were rigged to go at a moment's notice. If I suddenly got worse, I'd need to get down there and get into the stuff, and trust Hun Xoc to finish closing off the crypt and dealing with the upshot of my autosacrifice. But that would be iffy. Hun Xoc was bright, but there was no way he was going to pick up on the chemistry and the engineering in time, and I was sure that the toastmaster was already intriguing with the Ocelot ministers . . . well, anyway, I wanted to see that everything was perfect myself.

I signed for the attendants to lower 2JS so I could reach him without getting up and I scooted over next to his head. His mouth was open and dry and his breath had some foreign rot element in it that was really hard to take. The teaser had drawn a sort of map like an acupuncture chart onto his body, with little glyphs with dots. I took a medium-length reed skewer, dipped it in a dish of a nonlethal dilution of scorpion venom, and turned it slowly into a dot just beneath—or now above—2 Jeweled Skull's earlobe, drilling into the attachment of the facial nerve. For a moment his neck and torso quivered like he was lying on an old vibrating bed from some honeymoon motel, but there was no vocalization and the next beat he had it almost totally under control. I moved the point farther down in tiny increments like it was controlled by a Trac-Ball, feeling for variations in his current of trembling. Supposedly there was no kind of toxin that was more painful. His sternocleidomastoid muscle contracted and writhed under my hand again, but his face held on to that willed blankness.

God dog, I am such a twonk, I thought. Koh had mentioned back in Teotihuacán that 0 Porcupine Clown had been a gift from 2 Jeweled Skull, and then I'd just forgotten about it.

She should have thought of it herself, though. Anyone can be a sleeper assassin, even somebody who hadn't been planted so openly. Well, damn it. She'd had a lot to think about and it slipped her mind.

For most of the last three days, when I hadn't been fiddling with 2JS, I'd been staring at a Sacrifice Game board set up to Koh's last move. Of course I hadn't been able to make anything out of it. And of course we'd consulted everyone, Mask of Jaguar Night and the other Jaguar-adders, the three Orb Weaver mothers Koh had brought with her, all the independent adders I could get hold of, everyone who was even just a six-stone player or above, and they were all stumped. Nine-stone players just knew something that eight-stones didn't know.

So all I really had to go on was that last moment with Koh, when she'd said "you" and looked at me with a sort of surprise. What had she meant? Was me getting back somehow essential to the events she saw in the future? And had she meant me, or the other Jed, Jed_1, who I'd left back in 2012?

As I said, 2 Jeweled Skull had supposedly killed the two remaining nine-skull Scorpion-adders Koh had brought back from Teotihuacán. Even so, we went through the trouble of interrogating the men who'd been with 2JS when Koh captured him, and finally we tracked down and identified what was left of the Scorpion-adders' bodies. They brought them to me in three big baskets, but it was way too late for CPR and we weren't going to get much out of them.

And as I also think I said a long time ago, there were only four other Maya cities with nine-skull adders attached to the cat mat, and none of them were friendly. There were six cities in the north, none of them friendly either. And no matter what kind of commando squad I could come up with or what kind of deal I offered, there wasn't much chance of getting to one of them, interrogating the nine-skull, and getting back, all within a few days.

I was coming to realize, of course too late as usual, that there had been a dynamic at work here no one had put into words. Teotihuacán had been in severe economic decline for over a hundred years, and its two great families knew as well as anyone that its collapse was inevitable. The only thing that had kept the Empire going for the last several decades were the sun-adders, the custodians of the Sacrifice Game, shoring up the bloated, decaying city with the accumulated awe value of their predictions. And for whatever reason—maybe because of pressures from each other, more than pressures from outside—instead of spreading the Game knowledge, the leaders of Teotihuacán had restricted it, allowing fewer and fewer players to reach the nine-skull level and keeping the ones who did near-prisoners in their own city, the way Lady Koh had been. Like most rulers who realize their power's fading, they'd preferred to hang on to the scraps of loot as their edifice collapsed around them, and to take whatever they could to the grave. The whole culture of the Sacrifice Game was in deeper decline than I'd realized. And as I knew from later history, it was just a matter of slow entropy before the whole Maya civic culture would decay in its wake.

Even so, if we'd had time, we might have been able to get hold of some other nine-skull players eventually, even if we had to lose ten thousand bloods in the kidnap raids. We might even have been able to play another City Game. If we'd had time.

But the Jaguar hierophant of Ix was the only one we had a real shot of getting to. Which was easier said, though. The hierophant was still down in the Old Cats' Cave—which I pictured as a smoky bar with an octogenarian jazz combo—somewhere near the other end of the speaking tube he'd used to phreak me out when I was up on the mul. It was part of a complex of dry chambers past 9 Fanged Hummingbird's tomb, deeper down on the way into the wet caves that supposedly led to the river to Xibalba.

Evidently, 9 Fanged Hummingbird had hidden the guy and his caretakers down there at the beginning of the siege, twenty-nine suns ago. And he'd provisioned them for a couple of months and sealed them off. And then he'd put another set of doorkeepers in the cavern above them, in the Ossuary—which was the only entrance to the Cats' Cave—and barricaded them off with instructions to kill the Jaguar hierophant and then themselves if anyone but he or his representative came to get them. Which meant there was a code you could give to the doorkeepers to get them to let you through. Most likely it was a symbolic object that you'd lower down through one of the air holes in the barricade.

After that, what must have happened—as Hun Xoc, Alligator Root, and I worked it out after questioning Mask of Jaguar Night—was that 2 Jeweled Skull got the hierophant's pass key from 9 Fanged Hummingbird. Probably 9 Fanged Hummingbird used it as a bargaining chip to get 2JS to let him go. Then, when Koh took over, 2 Jeweled Skull did exactly the same thing as part of his deal. After that, just like Koh had told me, she'd held out the possibility of releasing the hierophant to the Jaguar Society. She promised Mask of Jaguar Night that she'd let the hierophant out after the seating, and he made her promise that the hierophant would administer my final ordeal for admission to the society, as always, through his damn tube. And Koh had said okay in order to let the Jaguars—theoretically at least—still be the final arbiters of who was who.

Mask of Jaguar Night and the Jaguar-adders had even been talking to him through the damn tube during the time before the seating. But obviously the hierophant didn't know the pass tchotchke.

And Koh hadn't told anyone else. Not even Alligator Root. Or at least he said she hadn't wanted to put him in that position and I believed him. She was a close-mouthed gal, and anyway, he didn't have anything to gain from keeping that secret. And Koh had told him she wanted to help me. There didn't seem to be anyone else who knew. 2 Jeweled Skull had killed 9 Fanged Hummingbird's two ministers, and his own ministers had killed themselves before Koh captured them. For that matter, we just had to hope that Koh hadn't changed the code. And so here we were, in this stupid position, trying to get it out of 2 Jeweled Skull, and it was like trying to extract mercury out of cinnabar with a cigarette lighter. It's like, really, you'd think that without computers and encryption software or even electricity or even metal locks and keys or whatever, you wouldn't come up against problems like this. But actually these guys worked hard to make it all more complicated. It was like how in the seventeenth century, before they had safety deposit boxes, everybody's office desk had about a hundred little secret compartments in it.

I was ready to try anything, of course. I'd had Mask of Jaguar Night yelling and banging and calling for the hierophant through the tube, but he wouldn't answer. He hadn't even left a message on his machine. And we had a team of foundation thralls digging down to him, exposing a flight of stairs from the mul sanctuary to the chambers underneath that had been filled in eighty years ago. But since it had to be done silently so as not to alert him, it was going to take days. Anyway, even if we did get to them, the hierophant and his society would follow orders and kill themselves if we cut through to them without giving them the right pass sign.

I'd even suggested we try to strike a deal with Severed Right Hand, that maybe 9 Fanged Hummingbird could give us the key in exchange for a peaceful surrender. But as Hun Xoc and Alligator Root said, 9 Fanged Hummingbird might not even still be alive. Severed Right Hand may have gotten rid of him. And even if they did make a deal with us, why should we believe them? They'd probably give us the wrong passkey and the guy would be dead by the time we got in. Also, if we surrendered the city without trashing it, 9 Fanged Hummingbird might dig up his old tomb again, no matter how many boulders I'd piled above it, and my pickled body would be out in the cold. And time's pretty cold. Anyway, "peaceful surrender" wasn't really in these peoples' vocabulary to begin with.

So finally I'd said they were right. I could hardly stand the frustration, though. Knowing right where the guy was and not being able to get to him. I could tell I was working on an ulcer, on top of everything else. And torturing 2JS wasn't helping. I mean, not only hadn't it gotten anywhere so far but it also wasn't making me feel any better. I would have probably tortured him anyway, of course, after what he did to Koh. But now I had to be careful about it. I pulled the point of the skewer back, slid it onto the mastoid process, and, starting delicately, scraped it against the bone.

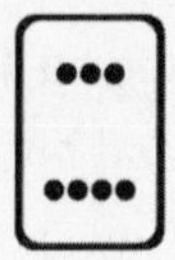

(64)

Despite himself, he moaned. I drew the point back and across more slowly, and he grunted more. Just like, shall we say, intimate relations, torture gives you that deep, instantaneous reaction from the other party. You have to look for rhythms and be responsive to whether this pain is on an escalating scale from the last one. It's also like the intimacy of playing a good game against a clever opponent. They're like three vertices on a triangle.

2JS's face didn't change, but the grunting peaked and then faded and I had to stop before he passed out from the pain. The teaser crept over, undid a padded cotton binding from around 2JS's shoulder, and started massaging his neck. It was important that none of his limbs got numb. Come on, crack, I thought. You're either going to tell me what the signal is or you're going to memorize every square micron of a continent of pain nobody else has ever even visited. I'm going to make a skinful of chili peppers feel like Marena's memory-foam pouf. I was learning. Like they showed in that test, almost anyone can enjoy being a torturer, as long as someone tells them it's the thing to do and how to do it. It's for the whole family. The teaser selected an enema bladder and squeezed a few drops into 2JS's mouth. It was a triple-refined balche flavored with vanilla and honey, almost a cordial. 2JS swallowed involuntarily, even upside down, and I could tell he was getting the pleasure of it despite himself. The idea was to keep offering rewards and respites at odd times, to get him down to an animalistic level of stimulus and response. Torture around here was like a martial art in Asia, it was something to do stylishly, or sometimes comically. In the twenty-first century there were basically two conflicting raps about torture. On the one hand big organizations like the U.S. Army tell their commanders not to interrogate using torture because the subjects will tend to just tell you what they think you want to hear. The second rap is that no one ever holds out for long against professional interrogators. Personally I think they both have some truth to them. It's true that the first thing a subject usually tells you is whatever he thinks you want to hear. But that lasts only as long as you can't check his information to see whether it's accurate. If you can check the information, the next thing is that the subject has to trust the interrogator, at least that if the story does turn out to be accurate, he'll either stop torturing him or at least, for instance, give him a knife to kill himself.

Aside from that stuff, though, I think the second rap's truer. As far as I know, whenever you hear about someone who's supposedly held out against torture, it turns out it's because the interrogators screwed up. Otherwise, in general you can forget it. Pain's just too large.

But getting something specific out of a Maya blood was a different story. It was a touchy thing, even though my teaser was a ninth-level master and definitely knew what he was doing. 2 Jeweled Skull was beyond tough. He was getting weaker, and at this point he was just pure will. But I got the feeling he could easily die from pain overload several times before he'd tell me Thing One.

So we'd tried most of the usual non-pain-related tortures first. We'd slashed and desecrated his mats and planned murals of him losing the hipball game in various cowardly poses. We'd paid people to run around spreading rumors about him and then brought in people who'd heard them to make fun of him. We'd gotten together as many of his ancestors' remains as we could find and let starving dogs teethe on them while he watched. But maybe he'd made his peace with that stuff already, because it didn't have any effect. Maybe it was because he had so much of me in him, he had extra distance on the situation.

And we'd offered him bribes, of course. Men, money and an escape route. We'd offered to kill off some of his old enemies, almost anything he wanted within the realm of credibility. But he was just totally obdurate. Maybe he could tell we were in nearly as much trouble as he was. Or he didn't trust any of us at all no matter how many witnesses we brought in. Or he was just set on cheating me of the pleasure of seeing him crack, cheating my world of its chances for the future.

So at the beginning of the second day we'd moved into the physical realm. Which is certainly a little different with somebody who likes pain, or at least is as comfortable as he was with it. But you have to remember there are different kinds of agony, there's itchiness, there's suffocation, and neither of those are exactly pain. And there are other things that it's important for people to take care of that you can let them not take care of. Everybody doesn't like something, and the trick is finding out what.

The teaser had put in the flesh eels first, to get them started, and then moved on to suffocation. But he gave it up after a couple of hours. Most people go over the edge into sheer animal panic after a couple of near smotherings, but 2JS had just held his breath and tried to burst the veins in his head. Next the teaser had roasted and peeled the skin off the bottom of 2JS's feet, salted the flesh, and let his dog lick off the salt. That didn't get anywhere either. He'd defleshed 2JS's middle finger on each hand, taken off the phalange, and sharpened the metacarpus, crawling his pumice-stone file across it over and over, polishing it down to a fine point, and he'd force-fed him water and tied off his penis, and plugged his anus, and brought in a bowlful of deerflies to bite him, and on top of all that he'd fed him the adrenal glands and also a few shots of psilocybe hallucinogens, the local equivalent of truth drugs. But 2JS had just quivered and snuffled and drooled and his core had never broken. You had to admire the guy.

"They're shifting," the teaser said, feeling 2JS's stomach for the flesh eels. I got onto my knees and looked closer. 2 Jeweled Skull's abdominal muscles were shivering, and his face was darting in and out of all sorts of odd grimaces, like he had to let out a cosmic sneeze. He was having another attack. That tiny bit of alcohol had sent them into a literal tailspin. The teaser took a shell knife and sketched out a cut just below the navel.

No, no, try the ones in the head, I said. I didn't want him to die on us. The teaser palpated the swollen tissue around 2JS's eye sockets.

They're getting fat, he said. I told him to get some of the critters out if he could. The teaser reached into 2 Jeweled Skull's left nostril with a pair of bamboo tweezers and grubbed around.

Gimmie the key, fucker, I thought. I couldn't believe I was in this stupid position.

Believe it.

The teaser started pulling something out of 2 Jeweled Skull's nose, the tapered end of a white noodly thing that just kept going on and on until it was a little over a foot long, until its blood-pinked nonhead finally popped out wriggling, drowning in the air. 2 Jeweled Skull's body quivered, but he didn't make a sound. The teaser dropped the sucker into a cup of balche. It writhed around, practically tying itself into a noose.

"Drink plenty of balche," the teaser chuckled, "and you'll never have worms." It was an old joke.

What they called flesh eels were really some kind of river-tapeworm larva they raised for this sort of thing, yet another species I was kicking myself for not being able to identify, although I'm sure it was related to *Spirometra mansoni*. Anyway it was supposed to be the absolute most painful thing of all, or to be more specific the most unbearably painful, since other things might be just as painful but didn't get such good results. People had cracked under it who had gone months without cracking under anything else. When the worms were in the abdominal cavity, they said it was like nausea, but that nausea was to this as an itchy finger was to getting your hand crushed between boulders. When the worms were in your eye sockets and nasal passages, I guess it was like having stuffed-up sinuses on a depressurizing airplane, with the same degree of amplification.

Gotta think of something here. Okay. Come on. He's got some me in him. Do something with that. Maybe even if 2JS can stand anything, the Jed in him can't.

What's my own Room 101? I wondered. What am I most afraid of? Blood loss, maybe. Bleeding. But I'd gotten over that. So had he, probably. Death?

He was obviously over that too. Being open, being exposed, watching my mind crumble from inside?

"Listen," I said in English, "Jed? Old buddy? Old frenemy? I know you're in there."

He clenched his face tighter. He was definitely lucid, even if the critters had Swiss-cheesed his innards.

"Come on," I said. My voice was hoarsing out. "Remember playing Go with Marena in the harvest-gold Boogie Van? Remember when we drove from Boulder to Panama City with No Way and Sylvia and Sylvania in that old Thunderbird without stopping and whenever we got pulled over we'd have to quick dump the coke through that hole under the gas pedal and CB ahead for more? You don't want to just delete all that, do you?"

No answer. Hmm. Maybe that stuff wasn't really that great.

"Okay. Remember when Sylvania said she wanted to sleep with you? And you were just like, whoa, okay, great? What about that skittles game when you clobbered Gata Kamsky five times in a row and he couldn't deal with it? You know, it's you getting killed, not just 2 Jeweled Schmuck. Remember when you got a whole mouthful of saccharine? Remember when Stan took you to that black-light poster store in Salt Lake and it blew your little mind? You know how you thought your chess clock was an owl face and how it had all those different expressions at different points in the game? Like how when the game started it looked all startled and when you were both around the three-hour mark it looked slit-eyed and weary or wary or whatever, or then when it would look like it was winking at one side or the other? What about making the Story of the Invisible Knight on your old plastic roll-up set? Remember the first time you slept out in the shed on the milpa with your father? Remember the story of Old Monkey and Young Monkey?"

I shadowed his eyes with my hand and peered deep into the left one, down past the blood-flecked dark brown iris into the ragged pupil.

"Come on. You really want to kill me too? You want to take me with you? Please. Jed. Get 2JS to cool it."

Was there a sign of just a little bit of an inner struggle there or was I just imagining it?

"You know, everything's going to be wrecked and it's all your fault," I said.

"Our fault, I mean, but, you know, I'm gonna try to make it better. For us, right? Well, right, I know that's corny, but really, I'm going to live for you, too, I promise, not in a stupid way, in a real way. I'm serious. Anyway, what about your whole culture thing? Remember that? Save the culture, right? Which is 2JS's culture, too, by the way."

I thought there was something down in the dark well, like little flecks of gold leaf in hazelnut liqueur.

(65)

Or maybe I was just imagining it. "Who's running things in there?" I asked. "Come on. Take over. I know you're tougher than that."

2 Jeweled Skull was gasping, something scraping deep down in his chest, like a stick over rough stone.

"Come on, something's happening, right? Something struggling to get out. Come on, come on."

I thought another worm was coming out of his nose and grabbed it, but it fell apart, it was just a lymph bubble. A big bead of blood swelled up under his eye and popped into a drip, and another was forming on the caruncle of his other eye, and one in each nostril and a big bubble of mucusy blood inflated in his mouth. I turned and grabbed the teaser by his thinning pigtail. What's going on? I asked. He gave a humiliative no-excuses-sir gesture, the closest thing he could do to a shrug, and pressed his chest down onto the floor. You incompetent sicko moron, I thought, 2JS's going to die, he's dying without telling us anything, and there's just nothing else for it.

2JS's face was freezing into this blank truculence.

2JS out on the mat. I held his head in my hands and opened his mouth.

Okay, okay, I thought. No absolute despair. The only thing to do is get yourself into that box of jelly with all the bugs and drugs and all the available information, hope that Marena and the Chocula gang can dig me out with some degree of me still left in my skull, and try to figure it out on that end.

Except you won't be able to do it, will you? Koh really didn't tell you anything. You know a little, but not enough.

Maybe with the J Machine working full-time, I thought.

Right.

It might take decades of computer searches to come up with the key. Even if you could really do it that way. Which I doubted. It was like everything was still encrypted through an array of NSA proprietary algorithms. At that point ciphers really do become unbreakable. Anyway, I knew enough to know that whatever Koh had been doing with that move, it wasn't something you could figure out. It was a secret rule, not a strategy. It was like you were playing chess with someone who didn't know that a pawn can turn into a queen on the back rank. Somehow she'd turned that runner into the equivalent of a queen, and it was according to some scheme nobody seemed to know.

If only, if only, if only this stuff were some simple secret, like, sure, there's such and such an asteroid at such and such a place and if you don't blast it it's going to getcha. But it just wasn't simple, Blanche, it was this whole field of study, a whole branch of chaos and probability theory and all this other stuff that I wasn't even enough of a mathematician to identify.

Koh really should have let me in on that one. Should've trusted me instead of that Porcuputz fucker. Oh, well. Or maybe she thought that even if she told me everything she knew I wouldn't be able to utilize it anyway. You never knew with that girl.

I liked her anyway, though—

A click. A little rattle. There was still breath in there. I raised one of his eyelids with my thumb. The pupil contracted.

It focused. He saw me.

IS HE STILL THINKING INSIDE?

"Everybody leave," I said.

Hun Xoc scuttled everyone out. 2 Jeweled Skull and I were alone.

"I'm here," I said. "I'm here, last call, last move."

I moved my eye over him to where he could focus on it. His expression was weird but I thought he was conscious and that I had his attention. I put my one hand on the back of his head and stroked his forehead with the other.

Come on, friend, I said in Chol. Friends. Right?

There was a hint of a sound in his throat like someone cutting a tiny hole with a keyhole saw.

I'm sorry it got this way, I said. I mean, I'm sorry too. I won't tell anyone I learned from you. I'll say spies told me . . .

He seemed to be tuning out. I shifted into humilific court language.

"My father, you have me in you, and I

Apologize for giving pain; I know

We're both the same on different sides; I'm honored . . ."

I was losing him.

"Come on," I said in English again. "Look in what you know from me. When you die you don't just end, you never even happened. This planet's a dust ball with a few suicidal cannibal viruses on it, and you'll just, that's it." This is bullshit, I thought. We're not getting anywhere.

"All right," I said. "Here's the deal. I'll take you back. I'll dump your brain into the guck and have it in the casket and we'll scan it into some poor shmuck in my k'atun."

Nothing.

"Come on, look in my consciousness," I said. My heart was whamming against my ribs. "You know I can do it. I'm offering you a chance. Come on. Just look in me and see what you can get, I'll give you a monument and honors in the overtime, a whole new dynasty—"

"YOU WON'T," he said. His vocal cords weren't working and his tongue was sewn down onto the inside of his lower lip so he couldn't swallow it. His breath was like swamp gas. I recoiled but got it back together.

"I might," I said. "That's all you have. Play balls."

He was staring at me. My skin tingled.

"Come on. It's the closest thing to immortality you'll ever have. You might as well start from scratch at this point. Right? And your name will still mean something. Or just do it because it's the right thing to do. Even you can see that. Or just do it for fun, you know, *sacal chakan can kin bin yx bolon*. Just do it for the hell of it."

No response.

"You know," I said, "death, we all do it, right? In fact I probably won't even live as long as you have. Just do it for me. We had a lot of fun, right? You did great here. You're the greatest. Come on. It means you'll stay in the game, right? No game, no fame, right? More game. Come on. Please, please, pretty please, ugly please with sugar and the blood of four hundred immortal kings on top, pleasy pleasyweazy pluz plaz pleez."

2 Jeweled Skull looked into my eyes for nine beats and I thought he almost smiled, and then I realized he was repeating something, over and over:

"A wing-tip harpy feather," he choked, "a wing-tip harpy feather, a wing-tip harpy feather . . ."

(66)

The protocol was that I went last, with my two torch- and standard-bearers, and then Hun Xoc, Mask of Jaguar Night, Alligator Root, their three attendants, and finally four condemned workmen who weren't going to come out. I held the wing-tip harpy feather close to my chest. Had 2JS given me the right password, or screwed me over with his final breath? Well, we'll know in a few minutes. Hell, hell, hell. The long blank passage sloped down at about twenty degrees, but there were still planks underfoot that had been laid down to support rollers when the masons were rebuilding 9 Fanged Hummingbird's tomb to my specifications, so it was easier going for me than normal and I could stump down on my own steam, propping myself up on the walls. Torchlight spiked out at the edges of my growing and then shrinking shadow, raking over the black spicules of rock like the ultradetailed nonlight in an electron microphotograph. There was a sweet smell of decaying vellum. We bent to the right, that is, north, and came to a wicker door. I untied the knots, my bearers unbound it and pulled it apart, and we walked into what you might call the library of the Ocelots' house, although since at least ninety-five percent of the books weren't ever opened I guess it would be more accurate to call it an archive, or maybe what the Hebrews called a *genizah,* a repository for old sacred texts that can never be destroyed. It was a high blank room one by three rope-lengths, lined with racks of horizontal folded screen-books. Most of them were accounts and tribute lists, or deeds and petitions and writs and torts and estoppels dating back five hundred years. But there were almanacs, bundles of suns and Venus-years, as they called the council records, and Books of Souls' Names, that is, genealogical histories, mostly of the greathouses of Ix, and of course there were stolen chronicles of other city-states, some copied through scores of hands from now disintegrated books, and older copies from oral and written histories stretching way, way back, to before the Flight from the Five Northwesternmost Caves, and prescriptions of rituals and protocols and herbals with medicines and incantations and surgical procedures and recipes of healing-foods and schedules for the foods and diagnostic smells and tastes and sounds and proportions and properties, patterns for weaving and embroidering and farming and architecture and the programming of the fertilizing waters. There were square rope-lengths of texts of the theater of cruelty, orders detailing the schedules of different humiliations for different ranks of captives for different days, calendars of progressive maimings, recipes for torture by iguanas, by flesh-eating beetles, by food forced and withheld, by low-level poisons administered over years, by crushing with a slow addition of weights like they used on the Salem witches, by casting in plaster, by the sun, by slow-closing spike-traps, by selective flaying over decades, by inhaled spices, by smoke, by salt, by proxy, by demons, by induced ulcers and abscesses and other controlled pathologies, by blood poisoning, by what we would call hypnosis, by drug addiction and withholding, by sex forced and withheld, by speech alone, and on and on. Finally there were covered and sealed shelves, two of which held the chronicles of the hipball games, first the rules and strategies and outcomes of matches, bets won and lost, fabulous equipment and legendary players, and last and infinitely more importantly there was an empty cabinet that had held the chronicles of the Games against the Smokers, the outcomes of the secret Sacrifice Games the sun-adders of Ix had played over the b'aktuns, the movements of the deities and elementals through the layers of heavens, earths, and hells. I'd had the whole section brought up into the light, and I'd gone over it all for hours, but it hadn't told me anything I could use, and the only hope I still had from that source was that the Jaguar venerators would come up with something from one of the forbidden texts they were still decoding. But I didn't think they would. They were idiots. Or rather, to be fair, they were just kids who didn't know anything. The heavy hitters had all killed themselves or gone with 9 Fanged Hummingbird. Except one. Hope.

I untied a door in the right wall, let the proles pull it apart, and led the way down into a second sharper-angled tunnel. It was larger but irregularly shaped with a lower ceiling. At a point about a rope-length under the first level of the north slope of the mul we turned right again into the ossuary, a long room bigger than the genizah. We passed a forest of about ten or twelve thousand low-fired jars, in sizes from perfume to mummy. Next we filed through a little canyon of hanging baskets, with relics inside them wrapped in glyphic embroidery in a range of stages of decay. After that there were rows of unwrapped skulls, set on wooden racks carved with stylized skulls, like real flowers in flower-shaped vases. Each skull had a glyph on its sloping flat forehead with the original owner's name-crests and dates affixed with the name of his captor, the date of his dedication, and spirit-quelling invocations on the order of "Rest in Peace or Else." I noticed one tiny squat toothless blob of a skull with the delicately written label 14 Orchid, Death-born Son of 7 Ocelot Night. At one point there was a set of skulls with fake shell-and-obsidian googly-eyes and flint knives jammed through their nose-holes making grotesque bulbous probosci. It was a Teotihuacanob style that the Ixob Greathouses had affected for a while. In some of the highest, most recent baskets there were shrunken and inlaid heads corresponding to the skulls, and a few thin chest-skins stretched over triangular frames to display their tattoos. Three rope-lengths in, the floor dropped a level and we came to an irregularly rectangular door and I stepped through into a tunnel of living stone. It was nearly round, with ropy flow ridges under the planked floor and walls. Here and there the sharper prongs had been smoothed off the black-glazed walls, but otherwise it was only slightly adapted from its original cavern state. The passage was part of a network of lava tubes and bubbles radiating down from the spatter-cone chamber of the extinct volcano—also called 1-Ocelot-His-House—due west of their mul. The caverns had been one of the Ocelots' semisecret foundations of power from way back, and supposedly in the early days of Ix they'd stayed out of sight in them for years at a time when they were under attack. Five rope-lengths down, the passage leveled off into a lopsided volcanic bubble with three hewn corridors branching west, southwest, and south-by-southwest. The west branch led down out of the dry volcanic caves into the much larger sedimentary-limestone caverns that stretched back under the western cordillera. The southwest branch led into a long stone torch-stained room with piles of carpenter's tools and ropes and bags of limestone chips. Farther in there was a salted and wrapped pile of eighteen dead bodies, the porters and stonecutters who'd worked on the project so far, and then a two-rope-length tunnel sloping down at forty degrees to the tomb that 9 Fanged Hummingbird had built for himself, the one I'd been having modified. Its entrance had been masterfully cut out of living rock, but I'd had it braced with ten vertical mahogany logs and then wedged and cracked along its fault lines so that it would collapse when we set it on fire. A rope-length down, it joined another tunnel that had been filled with thirteen two-arm-length limestone blocks, polished, oiled, and braced in place on the greased floor with creosote-pine chocks and bags of resin-soaked sawdust, ready to slide down into the main tunnel and block the narrow vestibule of the tomb. It was more of an Egyptian-style setup than a Maya one, and it had taken my architect a while to grok what I was getting at. But I'd done all the tests I could think of, short of setting it off, and it seemed like it was going to work. Anyway, I'd know in less than four days. If my poor citizens could hold off Severed Right Hand even that long.

We took the southwest branch, which led up slightly from the lava bubble to a twisty corridor through the Jaguar Knowers' chambers. There were irregular doors on the floor, ceiling, and each side, all with the dates of their last shutting on their seals. Some of them said they hadn't been opened for five hundred years, but that was a little hard to believe. Three turns farther we came to a little hall right about under the apex of the Ocelot mul. I squatted down on a heavy octagonal wooden door in the center of the floor, found the little spirit-hole at its center, gave four harpy-whistles through it, and lowered down a long white-tipped harpy-eagle feather on an orange-beaded string.

(67)

It was a whole little society down there. The same bonded family had been tending the hiding places down here forever. You wouldn't think native Americans could be pale, but they were, in a yellowish waxy way, with eyes that squinted and watered in our torchlight. The keeper didn't even ask for our prepared spiel about why 2 Jeweled Skull couldn't come himself, he just showed us through more tiny passages to a little room with a hewn limestone floor and heavily braced walls. It wasn't so well vented as the passages had been, and the smell of sweat and salted feces and stale rush matting was almost too much to take at first, but I could still feel air rushing past us and up through the speaking tube, wherever it was, way up to the top of the mul.

Inside, an attendant was helping the hierophant sit up on his invalid's mat. The old man had a horrible bottle-imp gargoyle face with marionette lines descending like cliff-cuts down into folded shale, but he still had a full head of real hair, divided into twenty-decades-old braids trailing down from silver into black. Supposedly he was a hundred and two solar years old, about five normal lifespans. I didn't believe it, though. He probably just looked that way because he didn't take care of himself. Or smoked too much.

I signaled over my shoulder and everyone backed out, even Hun Xoc, so it was just the hierophant, his attendant, the keeper, and me. The keeper set the torches behind him so he could see me. I pushed an offering-dish of cigars toward one of the hierophant's frozen knees, put my fist on my chest, and looked below his chin. He lifted one arm and made a feeble "Well, speak, what do you want?" sign.

"My great-grandfather, could it be my turn
To pose my great-grandfather a question?" I asked.

He waved a "permitted." I untied Koh's traveling board and set up the position just before her last move, the one she hadn't had time to make. Like I said, the position would take a book the size of *Modern Chess Openings* to explain clearly in words, but basically the runner was being forced into the corner, off the edge, but wasn't quite surrounded yet. I didn't see how you could get around past the end date at 4 Ahau to the center of the board again, but Koh had evidently seen there was some equivalency there, that you could take a shortcut. Like a ladder in snakes and ladders, or like the secret passages in Clue. The hierophant bent down, studied it for a few minutes, and then looked up and got my eye in his, peering through cascaded cataracts. Like I mentioned, eye contact was unusual, aggressive behavior, good for staring down a bear or an attacker, but not for company. I'd gotten unused to it and had trouble not flinching. Don't blink, I thought, instantly needing to blink more than anything else. I thought I saw his face crags recrumble into a pseudosmile, but maybe it was just me.

"And so what should I tell you, new-ahau?"

he asked, in ancient-accented holy language. His voice wasn't from vocal cords, it was a stomach thing that seemed to be squeezing out of a hole in his back.

I asked what he meant.

There are thousands of possible moves, he said, how could I tell you the next one?

Shall I play it out for you up to this point? I asked.

You don't really know that much about the Sacrifice Game, do you? the hierophant asked.

No, I said.

I started to tell him what was at stake, about how Koh had said only "you" at the final moment, but after a few minutes he cut me off. It seemed like he already knew that I came from sometime else, or maybe a lot more about me than that, but wasn't that interested. He said you might be able to get from the corner to the center through some vast sequence of steps, but it was much too much for most players to deal with. Especially himself, he said. He said he wasn't so quick as he once had been. I could believe him on that one. Koh had been thinking somewhere between two and three hundred moves ahead, he said. How could we know which result she was working toward?

"Then what would you do, Great-Grandfather?" I asked. Figure it fucking out, you useless old trog.

"Ma na'atik," he said. "I just don't know."

He said that whatever Koh's shortcut was, it was something she'd invented with herself. Maybe some other players had figured it out, too, but it sure wasn't a general thing, since it wasn't a position that often came up. Or ever came up. Anyway, he'd have to get the human players together again to hear how the counting was going before he could even guess at the moves. Maybe just talking to me gave Koh some insight, he said.

Then talk to me, I said.

I'm too tired, he said, I'm a babbling mush-bowl. He giggled a little and I noticed he still had four or five fang-filed red-enameled teeth left.

I couldn't say anything for a minute. Damn it, I thought, I knew she was a genius. She'd seen that single line of code that would generate an entire fractal planet, the repeating pattern at the heart of chance. God plays dice with the universe, but you can win at dice. But, hey, she didn't share it in time, and the rest of us were just blundering doomed retards. We're fooked, I thought, for the octillionth time. Tilt, fins, it's domino for us now, and cetera. Nearly had it. The greased pig just kept squealing out of my hands. Total disappointment has a very specific taste and it welled up in my mouth and drooled out onto my greasepainted chin. I felt like I'd come to see a cancer specialist and he'd said, "Sorry, it's too late to help you, if you'd come to me three months ago you would have been fine."

I knew the interview was over, that I was supposed to thank him and ask him if it was all right for me to leave, but I was too dizzy to do anything but stare at the intersection of two stained reed-fibers on the mat underneath me. I needed a word for *frustrating* the size of Popocatépetl.

You'd better ask your wife, he said all of a sudden.

I looked back at him.

You've brought me something else, he said.

Oh, yeah, that's right, I thought. Mask had insisted, even though I'd said the whole idea was a gross-out. I signaled for my attendant. He entered, handed me a jade-scaled box, and backed out. I unbound the lid, lifted out Lady Koh's stiff salt-cured hand, and passed it to the hierophant's dune-dry baked-thin fingers. I tried not to shiver until he took his hand away. It felt like he had hollow bones, like a bird's. He examined the hand from every side, stroking the nails against his cheek, counting her fingers over and over and chortling each time when he got to seven.

> *"Well, I can't read her move from this,"* he said.
> *"But maybe you can still go down and ask her."*

It was like he wasn't suggesting anything unusual. Evidently he chatted with dead people all the time. Why, can you get me in to see her? I wondered. I didn't say anything, though, I just looked at him and tried to slow down my breathing.

> *"She passed this way four suns ago,"* he said.
> *"I saw her walking upside down, and sobbing."*

I leaned forward. His breath was like meat ashes. This is totally stupid, I thought, except, you know how when you're totally desperate you're ready to believe almost anything?

> *"And how then would I get to her?"* I asked.

> *"Don't go back up, keep going down,"* he said.
> *"She's strong, she'll last, she's going to find the tree*
> *And climb it. Ask the Sickeners to help you."*

> *"Great-Grandfather, please lead me there,"* I said.

"No, I'm too old right now," he said. *"The oracle*
Can show you to the shore; then call the oarsmen;
They'll bear you four more gorges west—Blood River,
Pus River, Lancet River, Gangrene River—
And vomit you up on the Xibalban shore;
Attend the court, implore Lord Jaguar Night
Before Star Rattler swallows her newborn."

Whoa, okay, I thought. Sure, I can handle that. I'm sure I've still got three whole days left. Plenty of time. Okay, I'll just head back upstairs and deal with this. It's got to work. Well, why not? Ya gotta believe. At least when there's nothing else to do.

What the hierophant was talking about wasn't really an afterlife like a Christian one, and it wasn't reincarnation either. It was more like some people, like Koh, are just so powerful they're already among the immortals on this level. In fact, if you are that powerful death just makes you more so, but most people are so transient they're practically dead even while they're alive, and when they die they're just supposed to do their thing and release their uay back to their relatively immortal clan-spirit. Even somebody like Koh might not be totally herself after she died. She'd be more, like, one of the Rattler pack, and not even the main one. But she'd want to get to the other dead and unborn members of her clan, which meant taking the long way around, going down before she could go up.

I picked up Koh's hand, did my little obeisance, and started to take my goddamn leave of the abominable hierophant. He asked me to leave the hand with him. Probably so he could try to jerk himself off with it, I thought. Oh, well, why begrudge him his bit of fun, right? I said okay.

This is not going to work, I thought, as I trudged up the sweating steps. No, wait, squelch that. I couldn't afford to doubt at this point. Who knows, maybe these guys do know something besides the one equation.

Which they also don't even know—

Squelch. Just try it.

Damn.

Must I do everything myself?

(68)

I got back to 2 Jeweled Skull at the end of the second afternoon watch. The teasers had kept him alive, but he'd managed to trance himself out somehow and it took a while to get him responsive again. When he was finally focusing on me I asked for the Giving Knives and laid the large one on his abdomen.

He couldn't speak but his eyes asked me if I was actually going to let him go for telling the truth about the feather.

"No," I said, "I take it back." I tried to smile but his face was just bleak and exhausted like a ragged mouthless moth's, completely exposed to my tough mercies, just trying to die. I probably look more evil than I can imagine, I thought. Face it, Jed, you're a jerk. Chacal would have been pleased. I made a transverse cut under his rib cage, worked my hand in with the small knife, cut through the diaphragm, and wriggled up to his heart. When you were executing somebody yourself you were supposed to be kind of a psychopomp and help him on his way into the reflecting world. But you've got to be a pretty smooth character to pull it off. I think most often at the moment you start to kill someone the only feeling you remember later is frustration, it's like, just get out of my world. It's the pesky-fly syndrome. His heart struggled electrically against my hand and I twisted and pulled, snapping it like it was the spine of a rat. There was a peak of tension and spastic shuddering and a long exhalation of wet breath, then total relaxation and then there wasn't anything there, he was just a shriveled old corpse. It felt like I'd birthed his uay like a scent essence. I fell backward and signed for them to get my dresser. So, fuck you, your punishment was to get screwed, I thought. I felt a little bad about just plain lying and everything, but in his case it seemed okay to make an exception to general principles. Anyway, I still wondered whether he'd told me about the feather because of what I'd offered, or just because he came up against that level of terror that's so basic, anyone from any culture's the same. Or maybe he had another reason. My attendant lifted me up and I signaled for him to rub me down and change me into court dress. I was feeling kind of misty and sentimental, and at first I thought it was because I was tired and upset about Koh but then I realized that despite myself I might be missing 2JS, since now I really was kind of alone here.

I put in an hour on my ruling mat, getting a few details in order. I ordered a few offerings, including a jaguar and an unblemished and good-looking fourteen-year-old captive. I lined up seven more attendants, two flautists, two cantors, a beater, and two messengers. Just before the sun died I led the team back down into the caves and toward the western tube. I'll meet her again, I thought. Believe, believe. I will, I will, I will.

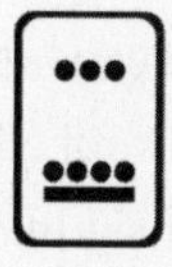

(69)

The twenty of us—or twenty-one, if you count 2JS's body—descended in a widening sinistral spiral, first down gravel but then onto flagstone steps again as we passed clusters of sealed passages, each one marked with coded numbers, some of them tripled or quadrupled because the passages beyond them branched out farther on. Even with four porters handling 2JS's body—we'd brought him along to help with my coming excursion—they dropped him two and a half times. The attendants leading the fourteen-year-old didn't have an easy time, either, since he was too drugged to really walk. And the jaguar—well, drugged or not, you can imagine. At the fifty-ninth passage we checked the markings and cut our way through into a limestone passage that opened out around us. It was dripping with tiny silver stone-roots. There were ragged holes in the ceiling and even through the cantors' dirge I could hear a trillion intergalactic clickings of far-off colonies of bats. Two rope-lengths in, the floor fell away again into a steep slope. My bearers took me and helped me down a rope rigging to a wicker bridge over a still clear pool that glowed in the green-gold light like it had been made with a few shots of crème de menthe. From the middle of the bridge I could follow the cliffs of striated agate down three rope-lengths. I thought the cliff sides were rippling somehow under the water and then saw they were covered with tiny white crabs, all scuttling away from the light.

Another rope-length past the bridge the bubble-passage ended suddenly in an ancient cave-in and the attendants spread out my mats and put me down. Mask of Jaguar Night traced his finger over a stained, convoluted wall to the side of the collapse. It looked the same as any other. Alligator Root looked around a little anxiously, lifting one foot and then another up off the cold ground. The head workman hammered leather-wrapped flint wedges into a vertical crack with a wooden mallet. I readjusted my bamboo leg and rubbed the oiled scar tissue on the side of my stump. It was getting flaky and raw. A fleck of torchlight brushed a cluster of tiny white eyeless newts clinging to a white-lichened rock. There was a soft crunch and the wall seemed to cave in a few finger-widths, blowing puffs of lime dust. The workmen positioned their staves and pushed against it. At first there was just the woody sound of plaster, but finally the chunk swung inward, it was counterweighted somehow, and there was a shrieking KREEEEEEEEEEN that I saw as a shower of icy scarlet ripples, and a hiss of old, unbreathed, mineral-rich air.

Mask of Jaguar Night tossed a triple-headed torch through the cleft to test the air. Light filtered back through the dust.

We sent an attendant back up to the sentries, to make sure this Grandfather Heat had died. Even though we knew he had, you still had to check to make sure, the way they don't start the Islamic month until they actually spot the new moon. I sent everyone back a bit and waved for Hun Xoc to stay.

You're going to have to make a decision, he said. He was the only person left who'd talk to me like that. The only one who'd start a conversation or talk directly to me at all, actually. He meant my choice was to stay aboveground to lead the defense of Ix or go down to look for Koh.

I said of course I was going to choose going down, since it was only probably futile as compared to definitely.

"Then start the fires but take the people with you," I said.

I'd done enough dirty deeds for a few lifetimes and didn't want to commit more genocide than necessary. My idea was that Hun Xoc would arrange for any clans that wanted to leave to spirit their way out of Ix by the river routes at night. Then he'd lead them north with what was left of Koh's cult. Ideally when Severed Right Hand got here he'd find a destitute gang of collaborationists and a whole lot of charcoal.

> *"No, I don't need to live and wear a diaper,"* Hun Xoc said.
> *"I'll plan the exodus, but stay with you."*

I tried to talk him out of it, but I didn't have the whatever to order him. It was hard trying to talk with the sort of death march in the background, it felt like we were all in some old war movie about to jump out of an airplane. Hun kept saying how he really wanted to go down with the ship. Finally I said all right.

The expectation was for me to go through the cleft first. It was kind of disconcerting but I just scrunched through the jaggies into blackness. I wondered whether they were just going to seal the opening behind me and leave me to go insane in the dark and die nibbling on my toes. But they squeezed in after me, the porters maneuvering their big bundles hand to hand. The first thing I saw was a starburst of thirteen skeletons shrink-wrapped in skin, laid out on the floor of the cavern at my feet, ringed with bits of brain coral and stingray spines. They were the workmen and attendants who'd assisted in the last ritual here, 9 Fanged Hummingbird's seating twenty years ago at the age of sixteen, on April 30, 644 AD. Beyond them the dumbbell-shaped primeval cavern branched into irregular feeder tubes flecked with cancrinite. Near the center a stump of petrified softwood had been ground down into a low altar table and I hobbled toward it, my foot crunching a thin membrane of white lime-crust that had accumulated like frost over the last k'atun. My attendants spread my mat over the table, laid me down on it, and undressed me while Mask's acolyte laid out his baskets of pouches and jars and started the process that would, supposedly, protect me when I came into contact with the Sickeners.

(70)

"*Thirteen are the coolings of your skin,*" Mask said,
"*In thirteen layers are our carbon salves;*
You are the great exuder, the great stancher."

They wiped and strigiled me and started to fill each sector of my body with a different essence: my foot and stump got the head oil of an iguana that could lose an entire leg and regenerate it, supposedly overnight, and my eye and socket were daubed with vitreous humor from the eyes of harpy eagles. They shot ocelot musk into my anus and rubbed my genitals with ointments made from the skin-husking creatures of transformation, the coral snake, the *Barba amarilla,* the fer-de-lance, and Star Rattler's daughter, the giant diamondback. They rubbed my head and torso with thickened oil from Ocelot were-toads, which weren't the pretty little tzam lic toads but big warty black things from a colony the Ocelot-adders had kept forever, children of Earthtoad they'd taken as hostages when they entered these caves long ago, right after the first birth of the fourth sun. Behind me Mask was lighting something. I just lay back and went with it all. Of course, no matter how Ixian I'd become I didn't believe I'd exactly meet the Lords of Tonight the way Mask thought I might. What they were really talking about was what the dream-catcher school of native-American buffs call a vision quest. Anything that happened down there—besides getting lost or assassinated or freezing to death or whatever—was going to be happening in my own head. But I had seen enough weird stuff around here—not magic stuff, maybe, but certainly borderline psychic stuff—to at least give them a chance, since it was the last thing left to try. Anyway, I couldn't let myself start thinking like a skeptic or I wouldn't get into it enough for anything to happen. I had to doublethink myself into credulity.

So I let them go through with the whole ritual thing. Anything to get another minute with Lady Koh, I thought. Even a half a minute. Even with only half of her. Or one of her uays, rather. And if I didn't let them do all the mumbo-jumbo they wouldn't have let me do this at all. You'd think I could just give orders, but it wasn't really that way. When you're in charge of a tottering organization you need to strike a balance, you need people pushing for you. Mask came into my field of vision carrying a long multiple-bone tube taller than I was. He put one end in my mouth and held the other below me, near the floor. In my former life I'd seen the same kind of tube on burial jars, usually with a vision snake sprouting from it. It had been kind of an archaeological mystery, I remembered one time when all those Mayanists at Taro's office at BYU were sitting arguing about what it was. And it was really a monstrous bong. I sucked in the smoke and held it down until I couldn't anymore. He took the tube away. I exhaled through my nose—and I think maybe my ears—and went into a coughing fit, keeping it as quiet as possible while the acolyte bled me from my earlobes and collected the blood in a little jar.

He handed me the warm jar and rubbed tattoo paste into the cuts. I blessed the jar and handed it to the attendant who was acting as Hun Xoc's hands. He poured a measure of preservative honey into the jar, stopped it, and molded wax over the stopper. It was going next to the essences of my predecessors in the lists of kings. If it even lasted that long. I lay back, feeling the motionless stump rock under me like a kayak. Maybe we should ease up on the exotic unguents, I thought, but they were just getting started. They kneaded the head oil of hundred-year-old sea tortoises into my scalp and filled my nostrils with a honey that a specific kind of black bee made from maroon orchids that grow on high ceiba trees at the cloud-forest canopy.

They dusted me with strings of a white immortal fungus that grew on yew logs, and then powder from an infinitely rarer blue fungus that grew in dark soil, after a lightning rain, over the bodies of armadillos. I tasted bergamot and aloe root through my eye socket and fennel and valerian through my underarms. They rubbed a spiced oil into my mouth that had been ground with the dried blood-essence of a special colony of *sanguiverous* bats, which were fed only on a family of special deer that fed only on a certain plantation of marigolds, a kind of living triple-tiered chemical-distillation process. Finally they let me wash it all down, but with water mixed with forty drops of honey, eighty of fermented prickly-pear juice, and twenty-six drops of the ancient honey-blood preservatives, two each from each of the thirteen ahauob of Ix, 14 Ocelot Night and 4 Shield and 13 Skull and 9 Fanged Hummingbird and all the others, taken and preserved during their self-offerings at their own pilgrimages here over the centuries.

And that was about it. But I was already feeling the mute gods of the source animals were seeping into my mind and I was seeing through the toads' eyes, remembering what they remembered, feeling myself metamorphose from a spore-speck-sized egg to a quarter-fingerwidth tadpole and then to a legged tadpole and to a complete, eye-lidded, fingered-and-toed toad the size of a water drop, and then to a toad two thousand times that size, looming over a pebble of red gravel that three days ago had been as big to me as El Capitan. I felt myself growing out of a near-zero-G world of surface tension and static and currents of honey-air into a thin-atmosphered high-gravity planet where the muscles in my body were all about springing against gravity, out of a wet world where I could easily grow and grow just by eating thousands of my hundreds of thousands of brothers and sisters, into this arid place where I had to pick off bony sharp flies as they zetsed away from me like little flying tamales—

> *"Now don your father-no-more,"* Mask said, *"and let the Lords*
> *Take you for him, and capture you, and if*
> *They recognize you, slip him off; and let them*
> *Regurgitate you into Xibalba River*
> *And swim for our nets, and let us fish you up."*

They unwrapped 2 Jeweled Skull's body. It was all puffed up and jiggly. Mask opened the stomach with a Jester flint and took out the liver. There was a tumorized abscess on it in the same place his son's had been, but it was bigger, a grapefruit-sized mass of dead flukes and black necroses like devilish sandwich spread. Mask started trying to tell me what a bad sign it was and that I should call the whole thing but I cut him off and said I knew it was bad and that we were going ahead.

So, reluctantly, he washed and flayed the body. Getting a skin off a person in one piece is a tricky thing, but an old person's skin separates more easily, and 2JS had been force-fed corn mush under Koh—so that he'd taste better—and then recently, of course, he'd lost weight, so it didn't take forever. When the skin was off and his acolytes were cleaning and sewing and soaking it, Mask cut off 2JS's earlobes and filleted a strip of muscle off his right flank and dropped them in a pot of hot broth. The attendants finished oiling and spicing. Mask recited another litany in time with the chant and they fed me into the skin. It was all moist with lymph and fat inside and under the spices it smelled like fear-sweat and venom, but as I got into it, it got better, and even, oddly refreshing. Hun Xoc helped my bamboo leg over the hump of the knee down into the foot. By the time they closed the torso over my chest my own skin was expecting it with that tingling like first putting on clothes in the morning, and as they sewed it over me it felt like a big tongue coiling around me and then finally like a mouth holding me, a mother jaguar carrying her cub. Skin held the real essence. Everyone was about the same inside. Even animals were the same inside. But the skin was like a book, a bible-biography of the owner. They pulled his scalp up behind my neck and rolled the cowl of his face down over mine. It was all expertly done, with the nose still intact, remounted over cloth on the inside, and as I opened my eye and looked out through 2JS's eyelids I thought I got a flash of memory of the ball game, except I was up on the reviewing stand, looking down at Chacal. I, or rather Chacal, looked vicious and insane. They rerobed me over the skin in a fresh plain white cape of the ahau of ahaus. And my bearers helped me off the altar and supported me, onward and downward.

They helped me crawl into the fifth passage, their hands slipping against my double skin, and squeezed after me one by one. We came out into a dry gallery at the old water table that opened laterally into a forest of pillars. I took over and led again, leaning on my halberd. Farther on the roof rose up. You couldn't see much in the torchlight, but you could make out the columns separating into stalagmite/stalactite pairs, first just about to link and then thousands of years away from linking. The ridged path, cut centuries before, ran under clumps of helictites like twisty icicles just budding on the arches overhead and threaded between bulbous stalagmites sparkling pink and yellow in the bacterialess air. We were definitely out of amphibian territory and into the mineral world. No newts is good. We threaded through honeycombed bowels in almost four-dimensional convolutions of knotted tubes, impossible to visualize, over thousands of maimed stalactites lying in sections like logs in a jam. At some point I felt some kind of thrum filtering through the stone and my perspective kind of flipped, I realized the place wasn't lifeless at all, we were almost lifeless by comparison.

The path sloped off again down an organ-pipe cliff and my bearers formed a chain and handed me down to a sediment bed near the current water table. A high wall of milky crystal bulged ahead of us like it was breathing, taking decades between breaths, and we edged behind it through a one-drip-at-a-time waterfall and out a narrow vertical fissure into a big space. My shadow grew in front of me and then shrunk again as the bearers came through. I turned and looked around, but the torchlight only lit an oval of the high fluted wall we'd come through and a half-circle in the silver sand around us, and everything else was black. I stood and waited. There was something unsettling about the sound of the cantors and pipers coming through. The echoes were coming back too late.

Evidently the room was a lot more huge than I'd thought it could be. We waited until finally everyone formed up. I signaled. The dirge slid into its ending stave and faded away. Finally the echoes faded too. I signaled again and the bearers stuck their torches headfirst in the sand and they sputtered out. Shedding more artificial light than you had to in the halls of the night was just begging for trouble. At first the darkness was total, like what I'd had in my blind eye, just before it became nothing at all. But we waited, and eventually we could at least see our silhouettes against the green chemoluminescence sweating from the walls.

Mask came up beside me and steered me down a long, long gentle slope, my foot feeling its way over the ridges and my snake-leg stumping along, and we twisted through narrownesses and vastnesses of spiraling alabaster walls. From the tone of our foot-scrunches the spaces seemed to be growing larger and larger, as though we were following the air tube of a chambered nautilus. *Build me more stately mansions, O my soul.*

Finally we edged into a dark cleft in the glow and out through into a deep vaulted sound-dissipating cavern like a black stadium, bigger than I would have thought any cave could be. The ridges vanished under rough sand but Mask kept steering me forward and down, toward a faint nebula of clear light-spicules, not quite moving but still different from stone somehow, and then the sparkles resolved themselves into reflections on liquid. Mask guided my hand to a treelike shadow and when I touched the smooth scalloped stone the procession stopped.

The phosphorescence was fainter here but eventually my eye was able to pick out ancient offerings, laceworks of arm and leg bones spread out over the gray rubble, branched into vertebral columns with multiple necks and mouths for fingers, the human bones forced into merging with alligator-boas with monkey heads and frogs sprouting from their ears, spires radiating and bursting into rosettes of blowfish and cone shells.

(71)

Mask handed me a greenstone hipball. I bounced it off my hip and it struck the pillar. The sparks lit everything with outer-space relief, for less time than an electronic camera flash but still long enough to see a piece of almost everything, the edge of the big white phallic stalagmite boss, like a natural stele, Hun Xoc's wet, startled face, strings and nodes of desiccated offerings draping over bulbous rocks like the single endless skeleton of a legged snake that trailed off into drifts of tortoises and barracudas. The bones got older and crustier, until I realized they weren't all just offerings, that we were on a bed of petrified sea creatures, and that the gravel under my feet was bits of sea-lilies and anemones and crinoid stems and shark teeth cast in lost-stone thousands of millennia ago. I could see down the long slope in front of us, to where the fossils smoothed into fine lunar sand, and then the waveless shore and the black still lake, and then out and beyond that, just nothing, no cave walls that I could see, no horizon, just what looked like veils of dark matter, graphite dust shrouding an old helium star. The sound lagged behind the light and when it welled up it wasn't sharp like glass on stone, it was a low D-note that drifted up through our feet and into our heads and then broke into the hollow voices of fused quartz clusters, *brool tuun tob, broo toon lob,* reverbing away like vibraphone tubes the size of blue whales.

I swung again, much harder, and I nearly jumped or rather hopped, it was like I'd dropped a shipping container of lead ore into a water drum the size of a grain elevator, but I got it together and finished the phrase with two more cracks lower down. Like Mask had said, the melody came out, that interrogatory theme without a reply. So far. It was like the stone organ was naturally tuned to a five-note scale. I was shivering a little at the end, no matter what I told myself I couldn't help feeling I was stirring up larger sounds somewhere else, it was all just that impending Doric strapping-on-the-armor feeling. We waited but the sound didn't end, multivalent echoes came back upside down and self-amplifying cobalt-purple waves reverberated through the Toad's sinuses and it was just really bumming me out, actually, and then I realized Mask was chanting again:

"We are the white snake wriggling in the swampfire,
We are the red snake throbbing in the fart place . . ."

It was like a whisper gallery down here, all he had to do was speak normally and it came back like Paul Robeson singing Odin.

"He dives into our fathermother's womb,
Accept him into your own hall, your court,
Your root, your time, your garden, your own skin—"

I walked forward with my hand on Hun Xoc's shoulder. My meat toe felt glacial water and recoiled. I could sense it was flowing west. They laid my mat and I sat down, my bags of offerings at my sides. Behind me the Adders had gotten the doped-up jaguar and the fourteen-year-old blood out of their swaddles and were trying to revive them. I just sat and looked out over the water. My mental color-wheel had shifted again, past the normal spectrum into other wavelengths where I could see an extra band of heat past infrared and two of ultra-ultra-ultraviolets, which is the definition of something indescribable, I guess, since each different color is something more irreducibly different from any other than any other two things are different from each other. I could see new veins in the rocks and clouds of fear rising off the attendants. I could see infection smoldering in Hun Xoc's pruned arms and

EEG fields rippling around his brain. I could see the pressure of the air on the stone like electric potentials, with the zero lines running between them like cell membranes. The water in the lake glowed bee-purple with radioactive alum. I forgot who I was for a while and then remembered—not that the knowledge of who I was turned out to be very comforting—and wondered if they'd overdone it, maybe there was a plot to assassinate me and they'd given me too much on purpose. No, no no, I thought. Forget it. Paranoia's normal. You always go through this stage when the shit starts really kicking in. I couldn't get my head totally around the notion, though. Still, nowhere else to go but stay. You can do it. Wait it out. *Oh, when the shit—*

Starts kicking in—

Oh-when-the-shit

Starts

Kiiiiiii—cking in . . .

On one level I was aware that behind me they were purifying the two offerings, killing them, and laying them out, but it all seemed like it was happening in some other time, on video, maybe. I felt a sear of pain in my groin. Alligator Root had gotten a bone spike and bladder and was injecting me with a solution of Lady Koh's blood so that I'd be able to find her. Mask of Jaguar Night and Alligator Root touched me silently on the chest. Hun Xoc's hands opened my offering-box of fifty-two of my best mountain cigars and lit one for me. Pineapple light flooded the shore and vanished. Hun Xoc touched me on the breast with his forehead and the entire team hurried off, crimson footsteps skritching away on the tactile trail, leaving the dead boy and the cat behind me. I blew a puff of smoke out over the lake.

Of course, I couldn't see anything but the little dying sun at the end of my cigar, but I felt I could feel everything, the thousands of tons of pressure through the stone above me, the temperature of the water (six degrees Celsius), the magma oozing through the veins of the old volcano behind us, the layers of lithospheres and asthenospheres and mantles of silicates and molten iron and nickel down 3,180 miles to the crystal toad-stone at the earth's core.

I waited and waited and shifted my half-leg and waited some more. 2 Jeweled Skull's skin tightened over me, merging with mine. I could still hear the ringing of the stone bells, maybe just in my mind but I thought also in my ears. I finished the cigar and fanned the last wisp out across the water. I took a jade ball out of my offering bag and put it in my mouth. It was like I was hatching this egg, and then the earth's mouth was incubating us, and the other layers were brooding over the earth. Eventually even the warmth from the bodies behind me and from the coals in my fire bag died away and I was sitting utterly alone in the scaleless phosphor-blue void. I felt tectonic plates drifting over Earthtoad's back like barnacled scabs on a humpback whale and listened to her swallowing her own shed rot, grinding up pustules of fungus into oil and alkalines and bases and reeking clouds of methane and husbanding four billion different food-chain cycles of birth and decay just to vary its diet. And again I caught myself thinking I was a toad myself. There really was something in this stuff, I don't know whether it was a genetic memory but it was sure some basic understanding of toadishness. I remembered how we each carried our own colony of tzam lic inside our bodies, how we knew that a dragonfly was about to swoop toward us long before it left the waterlily it was perching on, rope-lengths away, how we could know the weather months in advance so we could change the thickness of our skin and the placement of our eggs, how we knew where our mates would be, where the orgies would be scores of jornadas away, all tomorrow's parties, the meaning of the toads' own religion of transformation and cannibalism, how we knew where the water would be, when it would dry away, when the water would come again, when to slip into suspended animation and wait for what would be, would be, would be. *Que sera, sero.* I waited until my impatience turned into its opposite, like the waiting itself was making it happen, through suns and nights and in and out of weeks and hotunob and eons until I knew I really was nothing, I was just delusions floating in space, and then just when I was thinking I might just about understand the meaning of eternity I smelled something, first just something and then something unpleasant. It grew into a sensation I couldn't have imagined my little nose was strong enough to register and transmit, a primal black-and-orange STAY AWAY warning-stink of putrefaction beyond gangrene, something only a giant-beaked carrion-eating flightless diatryma bird might have breathed in through arm-long convoluted nostrils as it came over a ridge of hills and looked down at a creosote bog filled with the carcasses of giant dugong sea cows that had drowned years ago and hadn't surfaced until today. I winced my eyes more tightly shut but I was already tasting its full spectrum through the dancing ring-bursts of my retina, bubbles in a dark sea of iridescent oil, and as I started to try to suffocate myself I sensed the tick of paddles and a long narrow shape far out on the hematite lake, approaching under the layer of mist.

(72)

There were nine Scullers in the black shell. I recognized Spine in the prow, just like his portrait glyph with his one-eyed silver vulture face and the lancet through his beak. Next there were Serpigo—a hunchback with badger claws sprouting spine-grass like a Chia Pet—and Scald, a bloated corpse with big black-steaming egg-eyes, and then Scab, with ribbons of flesh flapping over his carbuncles. Snatchbat sat on the thwart, squinting and sniffing around with his gnarly flat-nosed-face, and then there was Yaw, known in Mesoamerica as, particularly, the scourge of the lowland forests, all spider-sucked and shriveled. Sarcoma sat in the rear, covered with clusters of tumerous masslets, and then there was Scurf, not just a disembodied head now the way he was represented in codices and on monuments, but a tall full figure with the tentacled face of a star-nosed mole, and last there was the old steersman, Skitters, the fanged rabbit, so much clearer than his profile on the moon, holding the tiller. It was the whole notorious gang, *the netherworld's bosomfoes working tooth and nail overtime in earthveins, toadcavities, chessganglions, saltklesters, underfed, nagging firenibblers knocking . . .*

The boat glided up onto the beach and Spine hopped out onto the sand. I didn't move. Behind them two canoes-full of white-faced attendants hove to on either side. Spine jumped up on me like a mongoose, grabbed the cigars with both hands, lit one with his eye, and puffed it into life through his other empty eye-socket. Scald and Serpigo had followed him out and grabbed for the cigars but he twisted around and poked them in the eyes with his toe-talons, stuffing the smokes into a sort of marsupial pouch in his distended stomach. A claw grabbed my stump and yanked me off-balance down into the lake. I'm afraid I really did scream, that time, or at least yelp. The water felt like lightbulb-glass shards suspended in boiling aspic. Someone held my head down. I hadn't gotten a breath and swallowed all this crushed-ice sand before he pulled it out again. I started to get in a last swig of air but he stuffed me under again. I could hear them cackling at me through the water. Eventually somebody hauled me up into the boat by my goddamn breechclout and wrang it from behind, crushing one of my testicles until I could feel whatever was inside it squirting into my scrotum like caviar. Don't worry, it's all in your head, I thought. Monsters from the Id. No, wait, don't think about that or they might fade. Go with it.

They tied me onto the spiked thrall-thwart and handed me a long war paddle with a sharpened blade. By the time I'd gotten it turned around and into the water they'd handed me the other seven barbed war-paddles, and I was dropping paddles in the water and trying to pick them up and they all lounged back and laughed, thwacking the paddles on my head—which struck sparks, for some reason—and pulling on 2JS's skin, which I have to admit probably looked pretty lumpy and awful. Yaw grabbed 2JS's penis, stretched it out like a bungee cord, and snapped it back. I yelped again. General laughter all around.

Scab climbed in with my other personal offerings and the corpse of the jaguar and the boy all burritoed up in my mat. Snatchbat poked a spiked goad into my neck and I took one long paddle and started stroking away from the shore.

No problem, I thought, I'm in.

Skitters made a quick fake-out motion and ripped into Spine's pouch, digging the cigars out through the wound. Spine whirled and grabbed for them but Fang threw them up in the air and they all grabbed them and started frantically lighting them. The boat rocked and then capsized underneath us, but then it rolled up like a kayak and they all came up dripping, laughing until they were just collapsing with breathy piping wheezes.

Snatchbat poked me again and again and faster and faster and we shot out over the frictionless clarity, out toward the center of the vast basin, leaving a stinking-yellow trail glowing in the black water.

I lost count after four hundred and ten strokes. The rest of the crew wouldn't help at all, they were just grabbing at the boy's body and tearing it apart while they smoked the cigars down as fast as they could. I couldn't see anything but I could tell the current was veering to port and we were going with it.

Snatchbat jabbed me on the left side of my neck. I paddled harder but we kept drifting left. He lashed me across my eye. I started feathering and then backpaddling on the right but we just kept getting drawn counterclockwise. I looked back. Skitter wasn't even touching the tiller now, he was just munching on one of the kid's thumbs and peeling the skin off the jaguar I'd brought. I was about to say something like "hey, help me out here" but we were already past that moment when you realize you're too far gone to get back in control, and it's like you're slipping down a toboggan run, clawing at the ice even though you know there's just no way. We were just sliding over and around and around into the suction at the heart of the lake, and the circle narrowed and closed in and the surface of the water turned inside out and poured down into the whirlpool, and the canoe rolled over and the water poured in. The paddlers screamed as though it was a total surprise. My lungs filled up and that mind-snapping certainty that you're dying just clicked on in me and my drowning-panic exploded into something else. It's hard to describe but it was like the panic itself was the baseline and I was building the rest of my mind back on top of it.

The canoe righted itself and I was relieved for about a beat before I realized it was the wrong way round, we were paddling upside-down, under the water, on the thin bubble-surface of the air. Snatchbat prodded me again and I paddled automatically, wondering when I'd be dead. And then everything started to seem normal, the way anything will after a while. The deal was that Xibalba was the flip side of the world; your Xibalba-self walked upside down underneath you, sharing your shadow, your two pairs of feet meeting when you touched the surface of the earth. You can get a sense of it when you see your reflection in a pool or even in an ordinary mirror, you might be looking into your reflection's eyes and realize that the person there isn't quite you, not just that it's slightly distorted but that it's got something else on its mind, something a bit hostile or a little crazy, and when it smiles back at you, you can see it really doesn't like you.

So I just kept stroking. It was thicker going, of course, and it was harder paddling air than water. I kept noticing how the bubbles I stirred up were different from water drops. But otherwise everything actually seemed to be going all right. Scarlatina handed me a feathered fan-paddle that worked better on air, and I took us forward and out in a widening curve. I spat up a few last air bubbles and sucked the cold water in through my alveoli. 2 Jeweled Skull's skin acted like a wetsuit, keeping me warm. The current drew us fast forward into rapids and down a fjord between white thorny anthodites, clusters of knifelike stalagmites lit with flickering tourmaline. Everything was utterly clear, like my eye was a scanning tunneling electron binocular microscope. I guess I still knew it was in my mind, but I also knew—or at least I was certain at the time—that I was perceiving another less transient space than the world I'd come from. Not that it was anything wooshy or mystical, if anything it was less mysterious than my lives before, like I'd been staying in a dark haunted old hotel room and suddenly one of the staff just came in and turned on a ceilingful of arc lights and I could see all the electric wires powering the hologram ghosts.

We coasted down into level minus four, past shores cluttered with impaled bodies of humans and animals, white sea-maggots pouring out of their mouths like extruding blobs of mayonnaise and the staccato reports of gas-swollen stomachs popping around us, and then the dendritic copper channel narrowed, roaring through a canyon into Blood River, and spat us through an intersecting gorge into Pus River. Lymph bubbled over the gunwales but Skitters steered us down staggered cataracts into Lancet River, a wide reach of churning spines, and finally into a sluggish river of black bile, with drifting clumps of necrotic liver and gangrene slicks. For a minute I wondered whether it was something I was making up because of 2JS's liver problem, but then I remembered, no, the hierophant had mentioned it.

Spine and Scarlatina had given up on me and taken out their paddles again, and they steered us through linked lagoons of molten ruby and gold and mercury mixing and separating in marbleized swirls and into a long, straight waterway, and we just coasted forward under crystal epidote vines arching overhead, past milpas of kidney-ore corn growing on neatly heaped bodies. Ahead of us the Halls of the Lords of the Night loomed up at the dead end of the canal like a range of karst towers over the Huang Ho Valley, but no matter how much I paddled they didn't seem to get any larger, until after monotonous dark suns of stroking, when I was just collapsed over the thwart gasping the molasses-thick atmosphere, the temples finally rose up over us in fungally excrescent magnificence, cultivated porphyry-basalt columns and buttes of black jade erupting with boil-clusters of opal-dripping carnalite on terraces of tiled yellow crocolite in matrices of banded ironstone.

We pulled up onto a sort of ridge of ghats and the Scullers inhumanhandled me out of the canoe onto the granite, thwacking me with their paddles like multiple Charons. Crowds of Sickeners, or I guess we should more respectfully call them Xibalbans, clattered out and pressed in around us, lifting the canoe over me and shaking it. Wet gristly bones and ornate reliquaries fell around me, the boxes bursting open, spilling clouds of dyes and feather embroidery and expensive smokes. The Xibalbans grabbed them but I managed to grab the smallest box, the one for Jaguar Night, and tucked it under the skin of my groin while they were frantically lighting the cigars and smoking them down in single gigantic drags. I watched Serpigo do a fancy exhalation but then Scald closed her mouth over his snot-stringed nose, and she sucked the fumes back into his mouth and down her own throat. Flesh-stained smoke jetted out of carbonized holes in her chest. Scab and Bloody Teeth were fighting over a tied *culebra*-twist of seven lit cigars, poking for each other's eyes with their sharp-forked tongues. Finally Bloody Teeth got possession of the bunch but Scab got hold of his arm, ground Bloody Teeth's stub-holding hand into a pile of tumbled coals, put the smoldering hand in his mouth, took a huge drag, and farted a gigantic brown-green cloud of tar, nicotine, and burning fat. I tried not to breathe.

Ulcer grafted a big floppy skeletal of my bamboo leg and poked at me until I staggered up the ghats through the eastern gate. There was a low screech from a giant cracked flute and the Xibalbans all parted and scattered, and I walked alone into the trench of a ball court the size of all outdoors, with sloped banks cloven out of solid mesas of wave-green jade threaded with veins of cyanotrichite and olivine. As I walked toward the reviewing stand at level seven I focused on the ground, trying not to look up at the Magister Ludi, and so I couldn't see the thousands of ghouls in the stands, but I could hear their cackling and feel their bulbous eyes on distended optic-nerve stalks, like slugs' eyes. I stood on my marker.

(73)

Jaguar Night, ahau and k'alomte of the nine underwaterworlds, lounged in a high referee's chair woven from the ribs of whale sharks. He was all gooey with baby oil and laden with bracelets and anklets of glistening human eyeballs and a belt of severed hands endlessly clasping each other. His cape was sewn of thousands of woven eyelids, their lashes rippling over the surface like a thin layer of scalloped fur, and he had barbels on his mucous-slick face, like a catfish. White chunks of raw porous bone protruded from his wrists and his brow ridge and his knees and his back, and fat round ticks and white leeches crawled over his irregularly sited pseudopods, leaving interlocking slime-trails. Blue fungi bloomed in the crevices of his groin. He was sick and decayed and in obvious pain, but in his case his condition just increased his strength, he lived on the power of his own diseases, like a sea urchin digesting the mites on its skin. Beautiful little girls and boys climbed over him, oiling him, scraping and licking his pustules. They weren't Xibalbans. As far as I could tell, they were living humans from the middle-world. Maybe the Xibalbans snatched them every so often. Or they'd captured some a long time ago and kept them here to breed. A few of the boys and girls lay in gnawed pieces on big plates. A giant fat hairless food dog with a peg-toothy grin rolled on the amber floor, chewing a child's ear. Four-hundred-scores of husks of lunar fanged rabbits imploded overhead and rained bloody fur like rose petals into the Domus

Auria, and orange twilight filtered flickering through a lattice in the floor, the captive sun struggling in the dark below. "My greatest greatfather-greatmother," I said.

"I know you from somewhere," he mewed. "Somewhere later on."

I repeated the salutation.

You don't fool me, he said, you're not 2 Jeweled Skull. His voice was a nonvoice, like something on an old Moog synthesizer. He peeled a dark-red strip off this little Scab Boy he had next to him—it was a kid who'd evidently been sanded down a few days ago and allowed to crust over until now—and chewed it up like a tortilla chip.

No, I said, I'm not, I thought you might want his skin so I kept it fresh for you. I didn't think my voice sounded too convincing. Jaguar Night gestured and two of his preparators came out, carefully cut the skin's stitches, and shucked it off me. I hung on to my last gift box. The preparators sewed 2JS's skin onto a big howler monkey, like it was a mannequin, and let it hop around. The crowd went wild. I was naked and getting a serious case of that Maidenform-dream vulnerable feeling.

Why haven't you brought me anything? Jaguar Night asked.

I brought you a cat and a boy, I said, and—

Where are they? he asked.

Your ambassadors ate them on the way here, I said.

I don't believe you, he said.

I cracked open my last box, unrolled the bundle in front of me, and fanned out four hundred of the largest and most perfect whole quetzal skins. I made him an offertory gesture. It's hard to explain how valuable those things were, but they were like Leonardo drawings. If you worked it out in terms of man-hours or whatever, what I'd brought would be worth the Ixian equivalent of between thirty and forty million 2012 dollars. Still, their main attraction wasn't the cost. We'd chosen them because we figured they were hard to get down here, even more than fresh chewing tobacco.

One of the boys slid a plate under the green fan and climbed up to the Lord's mangler-hand. He took one of the skins and raised it to stroke his pustulated cheek, enjoying the soft pressure of the feathers against his boils. I guessed it was okay to assume they were accepted. Meanwhile, I'd noticed the largely defleshed name-soul of 2JS seated in the row of ghouls on the reviewing stand, smirking at me. Like everyone who died and went to Xibalba, he was aging in reverse, and despite his skeletality he already looked a little younger than when I'd seen him last.

"Hmm, look who seems to be seated below the salt," I said.

"2JS has been given the position of Chief Convivitor," Jaguar Night said. He meant that 2JS mixed up the blood and burning turpentine they drank as toasts to each other.

"Ooh, I'm impressed," I said. "They really gave you a platinum parachute, didn't they? You've done really well for yourself. That's like being head urinal attendant at the Wilshire Grand."

"Laugh while you still have a trachea," 2JS said.

"Hey, I'm going back and you're staying here in Tabascoenemastan."

Enough, I thought. I was being rude to my primary host. I turned back to Jaguar Night.

A question, please, I said.

He made a "whatever" gesture.

We thought you might know where Lady Koh's uay has gotten to, I said as casually as possible.

We ate it, he said.

Nonsense, I said.

You're right, we didn't, he said. She stopped by, but she left two nights ago.

I need to ask her something, I said.

You should have had plenty of suns already, he said.

That's true, I said.

All right, he said, just give us your own skin, and we'll see you get to her.

I can't do that, I said. I didn't even bother to say that I needed to get back. He knew that anyway, he was just giving me a hard time.

Too late, he said.

I know you can, I said, I know how strong you next to me are.

I won't, he said.

Then I challenge your champion to a hipball match, I said. It was my last-resort prepared sentence.

He looked at me with an eye a like plucked-out rabbit's eye floating in a

Petri dish of upscale shampoo. He sighed through his pleuroceles and, pensively, scratched his tentacles with a testic—that is, rather, he stenched his tensicles with—I mean, he tested his scratchsicles with a tenticrotch—never mind.

All right, he screaked. Then field five balls. And if you win we'll show you the way to Lady Koh.

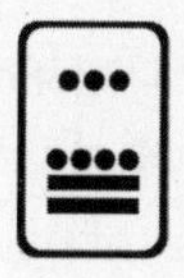

(74)

I should have expected it, but I hadn't negotiated the rules, and they sent four players out against me: Three Balls, a little rotten but looking tougher than ever, and my old mashed-and-charred friends from my last ball game, 15 Immanent, 20 Silence, and 9 Dog. I can't deal with this, I thought, it's too *Dawn of the Dead* around here, but it didn't help. What was I thinking? I wondered. I still only had one leg and one eye, for Chrissake, I could barely play five rounds of Rock 'Em Sock 'Em Robots.

"Good luck. Ball One, play ball," Jaguar Night said.

I got the face-off and hipped the ball west, but as it bounced and 3 Balls gingerly headed it off I realized I'd already screwed up, my hip was spraying blood. They'd let me get to the ball first because the ball was really a spherical knife. It was like this thing that happened to this friend of No Way's named Cobi, he was in a fight in a school cafeteria and got hit with what they called a *ballestero,* a hard orange with a whole bunch of single-edged razor blades stuck deep in it with just their corners sticking out. It really messed him up and he had to have about a hundred stitches. Except this thing the Xibalbans had didn't exactly have blades, it was more like a Möbius strip or a Klein bottle, where even though the surface was round it was still also a big razor-sharp knot that whirled like a Cuisinart blade. Anyway, before I'd gotten it together 3 Balls yoked the thing onto my goal-peg.

I limped back to my marker. Spine ambled out to tidy me up. "Really," he said, "of all of us, you under me are the most nauseating." Yeah, yeah, I signed. He dusted me off with a long-haired scalp.

The second ball came down. 9 Dog blasted it into my chest and it stuck. All four of them ran to my side, picked me up, and threw me up against the peg. My ear knocked over the dish of mica flakes and I bounced down the bank like a Gumby doll.

I won the next six balls, though, and won the match.

A cacophony of jeers all rose around me, it was just horrible, like you'd never think people could laugh that way at something so stupid except of course you can see it every day on TV on talk shows. They were gibbering so hard they were gnawing on their own arms, rolling over and down onto the court, lying on their backs and juggling me in the air and kicking me back and forth until I was ricocheting off the stone bank with steel-on-steel impact. I just took it. It certainly didn't hurt any less than it would have in the real world. They closed around me into a spanking line and thwacked me through it with bone saw-paddles, like I was that chicken the Nephi Knights used to kick around. But I was off in the right direction.

"Hey," I called to 2 Jeweled Skull. "Toss me another towel, will ya? I'll schmear you a fiver next time." I screwed a fist into my working eye and walked forward against the obsidian wind.

(75)

I came to the citadel at the crossroads, in the center of the center. The northern path led down into a scabrous clotted horror-desert, past fractal fungal rock-bones impacted and twisted with projecting nodes in serried rows like sharks' teeth. I felt my scalp peeling back and the flesh shredding off my bones. I turned left at the first new moon, 4 Motion, 7 Thought. Days flickered by underneath me like railroad ties. Whilrlwinds of razors sanded my skeleton. Five layers of fabric parted one after the other, white porcupine quills, yellow leather, mulberry cotton, black snakeskin, and gold-green feathers, and I was through, and I thought I saw someone up ahead, and I saw that what was going to happen on the last day wasn't going to be a natural disaster, or any known type of man-made disaster, that it meant something but something totally new . . . but then it was gone, and then the floor, or what I was visualizing as the floor, must have just rotted underneath me, because I was lying covered with dirt. I was dirt myself. I must have been decomposing for years, I thought, but when it's years of pain you lose track fast. I felt leaf-cutter ants growing fungus farms in my adipocere. I oozed through level nine, and ten and eleven and twelve, and the Tree of Mirrors forked out into a white road, the back of the double-headed star-feathered diamondback Rattler, the Milky Way, and I slid down one arc and up another following Sun-Carrier toward the Heart of Sky. The sun crawled out of the ragged cave-mouth, exhausted and bloodless and thirsty after his escape from the dark lords, and stumbled blindly up onto the rim of the blue-green basin, blinking, looking around for prey. I backed up, scrambling down the serpent's dry, slippery body, but I was stuck, and as I pulled I saw that the serpent was my own foot, or rather the stump under my knee, which had scaled over, and extended, and grown into a rattlesnake. The snake's neck twisted away from me and reared up like a whip stopped in midcrack, and its vibrating head sighted on me, sensing my body heat through the pits in its cheeks, licking my sweat spray out of the air. I could see my reflection in its opaque lidless eyes. Could I really swallow myself? The snake built up the torsion to strike, its snare-drum-roll-thunder peaking to the snapping point, and with the speed of a crack traveling through a sheet of glass it lunged at my lips, hemotoxin welling out of the grooves in its fangs.

But instead of striking, it held itself still, mouth gaping. There was a wet black ball down in its salmon-pale throat. It just swallowed something, I thought, it hasn't finished digesting its last gift. But it regurgitated the black bolus up toward me, and I saw the ball was covered with hair, it was the top of a head, and I recognized the whorl. The head turned backward and a bicolored forehead rotated toward me, and I was looking upside-down into Lady Koh's eyes as she extruded onto the wide scale-path, naked and glistening with cosmic universal solvent and studded with diamond-patterned traceries of jade stars. Wow, I thought. I guess this really is kind of neat. Koh lowered herself up to me along her own death-umbilicus. I know she was more beautiful than ever but I can't remember what she looked like. Just not the same.

"I wanted a separate time with you," I said. She gave a Maya click-shrug, but it wasn't so dismissive as it sounds, there was regret there. I think I was kind of crying, or not really of course, since it probably wasn't even possible in my not-quite physical state, but I at least felt like crying. I'd thought I was past being too emotional but I really did get just this flood of love or whatever and it kind of freaked me out.

Koh said something like "You didn't follow me here just to see me again." Only, it wasn't exactly in words that had any sound or exact shape to them, so I can't quote it exactly.

I said I would have anyway, but that of course I wanted to ask her about the Sacrifice Game.

She either gestured or said that I could ask her.

What did you see at the hotun-end? I asked.

I couldn't see a thing, she said.

No, I don't understand, I said. I watched you.

It's just too far, she said. The chance builds up.

I guess I already said the word *frustration* doesn't have enough size on it. This was like frustration supersized, with fries, with a bullet. I kept thinking I was getting closer to it, whatever it was, and then it kept shifting shape and backing away.

I've got to do something, I said.

You'd have to play in your own time, she said.

I said I wouldn't know how.

You know enough to do it, she said, just play it there, closer to the edge.

I don't know a thing, I said, the position's no good. Remember? The runner was trapped in the wasteland, there wasn't any way to keep playing.

So if I show you how to win from that position, she asked, will you give me your bond that if you play in the afterworld, if what you see is wrong, and shouldn't happen, you'll stop?

I said of course I would.

You'll just resign the Game and let your world run out? she asked.

> "*Wife-sister-father-mother-daughter,*" I said,
> "*Ahau-na Koh, accept your blood-twin. Please.*"

Koh hesitated a moment, scooped a handful of stars up out of the road, let some slip out of her fist like corn, and cast them out over the world, the real world, which was now her board. It wasn't like a globe, it was a flat square, but somehow it also mapped the whole world correctly, and I could see other continents, southern Africa and Australia, under the swirling cloud-steam. The star-crystals bounced and landed into the final position from the City Game, and she set the Sun-Carrier as the runner, trapped in the far northwest.

"And if you see what's going to happen," she said,
"And if it's right, you'll play it out. If not,
You'll take the runner to the edge, and jump."

The word she used for "right," or rather the silent word I understood, was maybe a bit more like the English words *appropriate* or *inevitable,* but stronger than either. It wasn't just like "Do the right thing," it was like "Don't mess up the program."

I asked how I'd be able to tell what was right. She said I'd have to be the umpire on that one, and anyway, it ought to be easy. I promised again that I'd do what she said. Koh looked at me and took the four far corners of the square board, two in each hand, like the world was a map on a square of stiff cloth, and folded them up over the center. They met in the middle, making a pyramid.

"The farthest points are all the same," Koh said.

I felt like Immanuel Kant must have felt when he suspected how the Milky Way could be the foreshortened section of a galaxy, and suddenly the universe was bigger for him than it had ever been for anyone. Although of course that was his own idea.

So the board was a mat, a pop, and it was flexible. The mulob were the same map folded convexly into pyramids—a mountain fold, as they say in origami—and the ball courts were the same map folded concave, in a valley fold. And even the globe of the earth had something to do with the same map, twist-folded back on itself somehow, a torus mapping the inside of a sphere. I almost had a glimpse of insight into how the colors and directions and tendencies and cycles all meshed, how the Sacrifice Game wasn't absolute but just a visualization of a subtle tendency in the universe, put in a form a human being could almost, but not quite, comprehend, like a three-dimensional model of a four-dimensional solid. It was easy to see how the Runner could escape by jumping from the corner where he was trapped. But then after that he could move off anywhere. Although I thought I saw something, not an idea but just a notion—

And then it just slipped away, like the eighth move in a chess game, it was just too much for my pea brain. I didn't have the organizing principle, it was like I was looking at a disk sliced out of the body of a snake and trying to guess what its head looked like.

I'm not taking much back, I thought. Just one trick. One idea, as we say in chess.

"Even from here I see it only dimly," she said. "But I see you alongside him." Or, I should mention again at this point, Mayan is ungendered so it might have meant either him or her. "It's someone you know, but whose face you've never seen."

"I'll try it as soon as I get back to the zeroth level," I said.

"Don't bother, you won't see anything from there," she said, "you'll only drown yourself. Wait until you're all the way there." By *all the way there* she meant "then," that is, in the last b'aktun. "A lot of things can happen from the same position," she said, although those weren't her exact words, which I don't remember. Or maybe she didn't exactly speak in words. "When you're closer you'll see the move you need to make. If we played now we'd be hunting in the dark."

I said all right. It wasn't the time to argue. I was dubious, though. Even knowing about the strategy for the move, I was a long way from feeling like I'd be able to play through and get it right. Even assuming I got back.

I'll just have to take really good notes, I thought. Leave it to Marena. She'll figure it out. She'll give it to LEON.

Below us the sun bubbled up in ecstasy at the horizon apex of the mul board, bloated with offerings, glowing a bloodier-than-blood oxygenated red that was simultaneously blue-green, *yax,* the double-faced color of life, and for a p'ip'il I thought I saw Waterlily Jaguar at its center.

I asked her if she could just stay for a beat.

I can't, she said, I have to go. If you see your Marena, would you give her a message?

What? I thought. Of course, I said.

> *"Just tell her not to wait until the sun's*
> *Last beat,"*

> she said. *"And ask her to calculate the remainder of twenty minus thirteen."*

What do you mean? I thought. Seven? It can't be that simple. "Do you—" I started to say, but she'd already slid away above me and I slipped backward down along the hard shell of the sky, rolling around it like a marble in a bowl. The sick sun slid into the black land, crashing and bleeding out as the mouth of the Earthtoad closed over it, and it was night again, and the skeleton-joint jewelscape of Xibalba rotated over me, the layers of heaven swinging underneath like giant multiple eyelids, and I clawed and scrambled at the sky shell but there was nothing to hold, it was like a water slide at one of Lindsay Warren's old AquaParks, and as I vortexed down into the galactic sewer I know I saw something past the rim, up in the thirteenth level, some kind of a structure I recognized, but I was already in that waking-up state where you feel the dream's sharp-carved details deliquescing into foam but you can't do anything about it, and when they hauled me up out of the ice water I'd already forgotten. They dragged me out of the wet cave to an ember basket in the antechamber and said it was only two suns since I'd begun the vigil. I guess I must have been on dreamtime. Even so, Hun Xoc said I was pretty sick from dehydration. Eventually I looked up at him. He was in his capturing face.

(76)

I had them scrape me clean and get me up out of the caves, up the newly cleared interior staircase to the top of the mul. Even from inside I could hear that weird oceanic all-over noise. It wasn't loud like an industrial-age battle, it was more just the amount and multiplicity of the voices that made it up, the shouts and dogs barking and the raiding drums and signal horns and bull-roarers all combining into a desperate whirring wave. My attendants screened the door of the sanctuary enough for me to peep out without being spotted. It was clear the situation was way hopeless. It was midafternoon on 20 Cayman. The lace blanket of the city around us was on fire at its edges and wide waves of pus-colored grass smoke rolled southeastward through the temple district. I couldn't see much actual flame but from the amount of smoke behind the mountains it was obviously too late to put them out without help from a massive rainstorm, which the Chak-answerers said wasn't likely to happen. I couldn't see much of the defense from here, either, but it definitely looked disorganized. Thousands of refugees had pressed inward onto the peninsula, instead of doing the rational thing and taking off, and they were eddying around just outside the holy courts, not knowing what to do and expecting us to protect them with our nonexistent magic.

Severed Right Hand had attacked after dawn with at least ninety thousand bloods, about twice the number Hun Xoc had been able to get together for the defense. And it was probably just Severed Right Hand's first wave. The attackers seemed to have picked up some of the Napoleonic tactics 2 Jeweled Skull had introduced, at least to the extent of going for the kill as a goal and not just the capture. Maybe through 9 Fanged Hummingbird.

It looked too late to do anything but leave. Severed Right Hand would be here in less than two days. And my brain spikes were getting so bad that I worried that at any moment I might collapse into a 75-IQ blob. Dag, I've really made a mess, I thought. I was in charge for the shortest possible time and I got the whole place trashed. If I died today—I mean, if I died forever today—I wouldn't have too much to be proud about.

I pulled back into the dim antechamber and took my mat. There were twelve other people crowded into the little room, not counting attendants. Hun Xoc went into his report. He said that for the last three suns the Rattler partisans had been holding the Puma alliance off with walls of dart fire, and how we'd been getting desertions and mass suicides and the clans weren't going to hold out another night. Tomorrow would definitely be Ix's last sun. I cut him short and motioned for 14 Black Gila, 1 Gila's son. He kneeled over and crouched in front of me.

He reported that 1 Gila had kept his group together and that nearly five hundred score of Koh's Rattler families were still with him. He was camped around the eastern palisades, his son said, and so far holding off Severed Right Hand's men, but he was going to be forced to retreat northward. I had the feeling 1 Gila was going to come out of this whole thing on top, and maybe even ahead. Which was fine, it's nice when at least a few people know what they're doing.

We'll blood to your father, I said to 14 Black Gila, if he can take so many dependents with him.

Speaking for his father, 14BG pledged that he would.

And once they set the fires in the temple district, I want him to order our bloods to surrender, I said. The closest word they had to *surrender* was *suicide,* so I had to explain what I meant. He promised that too. Hun Xoc set a small screenfold book on the altar table in front of me and spread it out. The pages were way too hurriedly done, nothing like the right style for this job, but it looked complete. I held up my left hand and he pricked the palm with a stingray spine. I dipped the end of a wet lettering brush into the blood and drew a set of four glyphs on each page. It wasn't exactly a will, but it commended or pledged all my bloods and goods and land and rights—except the tombs of me and my new ancestors—to 1 Gila of the Spider House as the legitimate head of the Star Rattler Society. I blotted and folded the book, slipped it into its deer-stomach case, tied it, and handed it to 14 Black Gila.

"By your hand only to his only," I said. He acknowledged the order with an I'll-die-to-protect-this gesture and left. Snotty little bastard, I thought.

So, what else did I have to do around here? I wondered. Any important assassinations? I wondered if I should make doubly sure they torched my office at the Ocelot House. No, not necessary, I thought.

Any messages to send out? The rest of Koh's followers were under this new Rattler person. No use talking to him. Or to the other bacabs. 14 Wounded had been killed, supposedly. Alligator Root was coming with me to repay part of his of his burden to Koh. And it was Mask of Jaguar Night's job to die with me. Maybe I should have the rest of Mask of Jaguar Night's acolytes killed, too, I thought. No, also not necessary. They probably wouldn't get that far anyway. They were double traitors as far as the Pumas were concerned.

I wondered what Marena was up to. Would be up to. She would have been able to deal with all this stuff, I thought. Better than I did, anyway.

Fine, I thought, it's no fun ruling Egypt by myself anyway. The hell with this ring-ding-run country. I feel like Boris Yeltsin.

I gave the order to set up my entombment.

(77)

My bearers lifted me off the Ocelot mat and Mask's acolytes rolled it up for the last time. They carried me to the doorway and handed me my double-headed serpent bar scepter. I could smell lime plaster burning. The fires were already lapping at the stone precinct. The bloods and dependents were laid out below in their ranks and files and orders and levels, with only a few absences. There were four squads of five-score bloods each stationed at the base of the mul, with orders to defend it indefinitely. They looked a little uncertain. I wondered how long they'd actually stay after we disappeared. They all made their unified gestures of submission. But they seemed to be sinking into the sour haze and my horns and stone drums sounded muffled. I couldn't even see the Nest of One Harpy, the Mountain of the East. The sun died behind me as if it were trying to reenact my seating as ahau, only it didn't look so good this time.

Nothing like a little pomp 'n' circumstance while everything goes to hell, I thought. At least there were enough people watching so there won't be any question about where I was going.

What I was doing had been pitched to the public, if you could call them that, as a royal autosacrifice. Or that's what anthropologists would call it. In Ixian it would be more like "freeing all our greatfathermother's uays to intercede for us at the smokers' hearths." It wasn't uncommon. In fact, after ruling for a k'atun you were really supposed to do away with yourself, unless you could fudge it with a proxy the way 9 Fanged Hummingbird had with me, way back in the day. I was just taking an early retirement as a grand gesture. Supposedly my uay would protect the city from the invaders, as long as my body stayed in its mul. I kind of hoped the poor bastards wouldn't buy it, though. Maybe they'd wise up and finally get the hell out. Anyway, my body wouldn't actually be under the mul at all. It would be way back in the cave under the hills, ideally covered with a few hundred tons of pulverized karst.

We should go in before we get smoke-cured, Hun Xoc said behind me.

I signed. The musicians stepped it up and crescendoed. The crowd answered. I withdrew my divine fucking presence and we stumbled back into the sanctuary.

At this point the only bloods in the sanctum were me, Hun Xoc, Alligator Root—who was acting as his hands—and Mask of Jaguar Night. Then there were my four bearers holding my mat and staff and private box, five attendants, and thirteen workmen huddled in clusters on heaped bags of gravel, holding unlit torches and bundles of flint axes. I signed for them to open the floor-door to the Nether Throat.

You should really go with 1 Gila, I said to Hun Xoc.

I wouldn't enjoy it, he said,

> *"Now that I'm just a lump of dough with eyes."*

I next to you am sorry about that, I gestured.

Just tell your new clan about all the ball games we won, and list the captives we took, he said.

I said of course I would. Yeah, I'll tell the gang that once there was a fleeting wisp of glory that was known as Camelot. And they'll be like, so what?

Still, I did at least get the Sacrifice Game skillz, I thought. And the drugs. That's something I haven't quite fucked up on. Yet.

If it still works after all that time. Maybe when you take it out of Toyland the magic drains out—

Squelch. Cancel. Can—

But wait, even if everything works, how likely is it that your little rotten brain is going to work? Not bloody. Memember, Mebecca? They'll screw it up, you're just going to rot. I wasn't even sure I'd made enough gel, the lodestones I'd managed to get seemed weak, maybe I didn't have enough salt, maybe it was too wet down there, the sandbags might not work—

FOCUS, I yelled to the projectionist behind my eyes. Don't even think about it.

The true flaming hell of it was, I thought, I didn't even feel displaced or centerless or whatever here anymore. I felt at home. Even if I did get back to Planet Dismal I'd feel exiled there. I guess that's part of the punishment, I thought, you only get things when you don't want them anymore.

I sent a single torchbearer down ahead of us and let them carry me down the steep inner stairs. They were still dirty from the last excavation. Everyone followed except six of the workmen, who were going to fill the staircase up after us. The ventilation tubes had been cleared, too, and the Jaguar-adders' singing from the ritual outside came in through the pipes and feed-backed around in the stone. I'd say it was like a death march except its melody didn't repeat or resolve itself, it was more kind of an ever-rising fugue of sad, extended tonal interrogations, questions you felt you must have asked a long time ago and now somebody was asking you, and you didn't have any answers. We went down three hundred and sixty steps from the top of the mul into the Jaguar's caverns, the bearers lowering me in time with the beat of suspended logs on the façades resonating through the stone, the entire mul acting as a drum:

Throoomb,

Throoomb,

Throoomb . . .

(78)

Throoomb,

Throoomb . . .

FOMP.

The shock wave punched through the stone and then the sound came and went suddenly, a round echoless explosion like a report shell in a sound studio, and then migraineish pain through my head over an absolute silence I'd never experienced before. The pressure had popped my eardrums.

So what, I thought, I won't need them. Finally, after a lifetime of noise. It was a kind of peace you could get used to.

I was already in the uterus-shaped sarcophagus, sitting upright like it was a bathtub. I must have looked kind of silly. There were only three other people in the room, Hun Xoc, Alligator Root, and my attendant. Mask of Jaguar Night and the rest of the workmen and attendants had been out in the collapse. Just as well I can't hear them screaming, I thought, if that's what they're doing. That would have harshed me out. Hun Xoc was leaning his callused elbow-stumps on the rim of the casket. We smiled at each other. A drop of blood scrolled out of his ear, wobbling on his cheek, threatening to detach and fall on me, but then it didn't. I pointed to my ear and Hun Xoc nodded and made a casting-off gesture. I thumped my right hand on his left shoulder, the equivalent of a thumbs-up. He raised his left elbow-stump to his right shoulder, the pledge position. Still just a couple of old vets.

The tomb's inner chamber hadn't been decorated, but the prepared white limestone walls were covered with charcoal cartoons for reliefs that would never get carved. The small square room was bare except for the four piles of lodestones, one in each corner, and in the center the mahogany scaffolding surrounding the ovary-shaped coffin with its arm-length-thick granite walls. The thick stone lid hung a half a rope-length above me, suspended on hemp ropes and counterweighted by two huge embroidered sandbags plopped on the ground like severed testicles. Then there were four big bulging liquid-baskets suspended from the ceiling, two on either side of the scaffolding, filled with the thin solution that formed the base of the aminoplastic gel. It was basically salts, my imitation camphor powder, and a few different anesthetics suspended in a mixture of urea formaldehyde, and methanol. Each basket held more than enough of the stuff to overflow the casket. The rest were just for fail-safe. And that was about it.

Okay, Step Two, I thought. It's easy. Don't rush it.

I signed a "now" to Alligator Root. He poked a bone dagger into the marked zero on the liquid-baskets. Horrible-smelling yellow stuff shot out, like the thing was a urinating mastodon. He got the attendant to hold the bamboo trough under the stream so that it flowed into the casket. The stuff felt colder than water, like rubbing alcohol, and at first it splashed up over my face. Alligator Root wiped me off and handed me the Little Cup, mint pulque mixed with about five percent of belladonna tea and a few other tranqs. I chugged it down. If I'd dosed it right it would have me nearly knocked out just before I drowned. No matter what anybody says, suffocation is not a fun way to go. He reached in and folded my pillow-sandbag so I could keep my head up out of the liquid.

Cool. Step Three.

I reached down and opened my right femoral vein with my little finger-knife. The Formalin-like compound stung the wound for a few beats before the anesthetics numbed it out. The idea was that as I slowly bled to death some of my body tissues would soak up the solution to replace lost body fluid. Not that this would keep the body viable—that part was going to be a total loss—but just to more closely approach a state of deep hypothermia. I took a last look at eight jars of salted toads and scorpions and puppy dog's tails and stuff I'd packed where my other foot used to be. They looked okay. I was bringing back enough little druggy-critters to dope up a herd of wildebeest.

Four. I signaled to Alligator Root. Hun Xoc made a wan grin that meant, "Sorry I can't help out too." Alligator Root held up a sealed jar the size of a coffee can. I eyed another okay and he broke the top off and poured the hardener into the casket near my feet. It was thicker than the base solution, like maple syrup, and when it hit the pooling liquid in the casket it extruded out of its glob in threads, folding over my legs, spreading and dispersing in the solvent. Basically I was being cast in a kind of a simple organic epoxy, with a few extra metal salts that were supposed to preserve my neuronal structure more or less perfectly—not so much that you could get the same brain going again, but enough so that you could map the changed connections onto the new brain, Jed_1's brain, enough to recover the memories.

Memories, I thought. Not consciousness. You're dying, dude. It's going to be Jed_1 hanging on to them, not you. Not you, your*self*—

Cancel. Cancel. Step Five. Alligator Root handed me the Big Cup.

It was a thinned version of the hardener. If everything worked, it would spread through me and react with the solution as it spread into me through my skin and lungs. A thin skin had formed on the surface. I poked through it and drank the rest in two quick drafts like I'd practiced. Ghac yuk. It was thinned with honeyed pulque but it was still just a total bitter disgusto-sting. Ghastly. Just don't barf, I thought, just don't barf, just don't barf. Do! Not! Barf!!! 'Gator handed me another cup of pulque and practically forced it down my throat to wash the goop down. I got spit all over his hand but he got me back together and he helped me lean back into the casket. I sank onto the sand cushions, settling an arm-length below the rim, still gagging, struggling to keep the stuff down. It was like cold chrome bocce balls were growing in my esophagus. I dry-swallowed a few times and it was like the balls supercooled and I was all numb inside, just a shell of feeling.

Whoa, it's really comfy in here, I thought, it really did feel like a womb must feel. The solution had filled it up faster than I'd thought and was flowing over the rim. It smelled worse than the courts of Xibalba, though. I wished I could have popped my nose along with my ears. A shot of cold ran down my throat into my groin, and I got a flash from when I was in the Warren Hospital for Special Diseases when I was ten and they gave me total anesthesia, and I tried to stay awake and then realized I had to just dive into the big zero and see if there had been any water in the pool and I just let myself slide, and that was okay and I was still here, dammit. Six. I signed again. Gator bent down and pushed the knife into each of the two big bearhide sandbags that counterweighted the lid. I could see a bit of the dry silver jets of fine sand, but I couldn't see any motion in the lid at first. It's stuck, I thought, it's going to crash down and shatter and the whole thing's fucked. But then the shadow grew slightly, it was coming down, gently, like an eyelid. I squinted up at it. It was convex on the lower side to push any air bubbles out of the surface of the liquid. For Keeps, the lid said. Except that was still too weak. It exuded this total eternal stay-putness no matter what.

Alligator Root took the sandbag out from under my head and it sank back, just floating on top of the liquid. It was getting to about the consistency of homogenized milk. The dark lid grew over me like the earth looming under a nocturnal skydiver. No parachute. I repositioned the wax-sealed box on my chest and folded my left arm over it. There were two things in it, Koh's folded feather-cloth Game-mat and a doeskin book filled with my detailed and probably redundant notes on the Game. I was actually pretty proud of the notes, I figured that with them and the drugs a quick study like Marena would learn the Game overnight. She'll handle it, I thought, she'll play and beat the Smokers of Randomness, and in her first play, she'll see past the rim.

I held my right hand on Hun Xoc's forehead until the lid was about six finger-widths from the rim, and then pulled it back into the box. We got a last look in each other's eyes. Before the stone came between us I turned away, to the left, to looked at Koh's profile in the last swallow of light. She was still great-looking and all shiny in her coat of liquid wax. Her head was floating a little on the gel. It's a shame we didn't get to bring your brain back, too, I thought. I held her hand. The silence grew in volume but in my head it was like I could still hear them singing that counting rhyme with the parts of the deer. Relax, I thought. Safe. Safer than walking around waiting to die. I settled into the eternal subterranean cool. I felt like a bottle of great old

Burgundy. We'll gel no brine before it's time. My leg was cold, but not shivery cold, and then it was gone, like it had passed directly to frostbite. The colloid was hydrogen bonding to the walls of my capillaries.

This isn't so bad, I thought. It wouldn't be too bad if I just stayed down here forever. Totally separate, out of my old time, out of my new time. Civilizations would flower and seed and rot and I wouldn't have to sweat any of it. And eventually in a nanofraction of that universeful of time I'd be born, I'd be a little boy, I'd grow up and have friends and enemies and do stuff and meet Marena and come right back here and meet Koh and not be able to protect her, and the universe would spiral out to unimaginable emptiness again while I stayed all cozy right here dreaming in infinite slow motion, free of the clock like a demon on a beam of light. Maybe it was okay, I was finally where I was always going to be and Koh and I could finally rest for real, just be in ourselves, never have to go and do any goddamned things again. Rolled round in Earth's diurnal course.

Okay, don't forget to wink, I thought. Supposedly there was this French aristocrat who was executed during the Terror who told some of his friends to be sure to watch his execution, and he made sure the headsman was going to take his head out of the basket and hold it up to the crowd. And the idea was that if he was still living and conscious, he'd wink, just as an experiment. And his head did wink. So what I meant was not to wink, exactly, but to see whether I could still think or whatever after my heart had stopped, and for how long. It was just something I was interested in. A last little treat.

My heart was already bumping kind of hard, THUB-bub, THUB-bub. Settle down, you're doomed, I thought. I sucked in a deep breath and had to stifle a cough from the dust from the cave-in and the smoke of the mint-and-musk torch sputtering in the reduced oxygen.

Cortez and Pisarro and DeLanda can trash this place all they want, I thought. I'll rebuild it, and I'll rebuild it better, Ocelot will rise, the Lords of the Mat can crack the skull-ball again out into the next age, the blue—

(79)

PANIC
PANIC
PANIC

Wait.

Hun Xoc and Alligator Root were still watching. Just to make sure everything was sealed up okay. They weren't even going to bleed themselves to death until they were sure. The lid grew slowly, like the shadow of my hand when I used to cast it on the ceiling of my room with a flashlight when I couldn't sleep. I used to bring it down as slowly as possible, like the claw of God. This won't work, I thought, everything will have been for nothing, nobody'll figure out the move, and everything's over, by Christmas Eve of 2012 all the world and people and kids and art and giraffes and diseases and pyramids and, like, life itself, it'll all just be a cloud of hot space dust.

I squinted up at the lid closing over me. There were about two fingerwidths of space left. The gel was stinging my eye and the light diffusing through it faded, and I felt the pressure of the lid through the colloid, it had closed without even the vibration of a click through the stone, just with a stopping of everything like the stopping of breath, and it was dark. Sealed. Vacuum packed.

I found a last bubble of air, at the edge of the crack. I wheezed in a breath and the gel seeped in too. I clenched my teeth. My last air. Bye-bye, air. Always liked ya. My head was floating against the stone of the lid, turning sideways. I couldn't feel anything below my chest, except for my nonexistent foot. There was an itch on it that I tried to scratch and couldn't and I dropped into a wave of claustrophobia and tried to wriggle to get it, just this one itch, come on, tranqs not working, I thought, I should be getting happy, and then I was just blind suffocopanic, total insanity, what a tomato hornworm feels as it's being eaten from inside by wasp larvae.

I could feel my heartbeat getting irregular. Calm down, *du calme,* calm down. You'll live again, I thought. All your memories and everything. It's all right, don't worry, there, there, it's all right. You'll be just like any old e-mail, copied and read there almost before you're even out of here, you'll be just fine, just great, just fine—

No. Nope. No such luck. Wishful thinking. Even if they get you back, consciousness is nontransferable. You're dying, plain as fuck. That big old yawning chasm opened inside me again, just that total terror of certain emptiness that there's no way to describe, just that certainty of emptiness, it was just too much, but I was still here, I had to get out—

No, don't think that way, everything you did, everything you learned, the world's keeping all that, it's living on, on and on.

Gee, that's comforting.

Not. Nope.

I couldn't hold my breath any longer and I let it out but it barely even bubbled out into this shit that was now the consistency of warm yogurt as the polymer chains linked up and twined around me. Around my foot, where they'd poured in the hardener, it was already like solid clay.

I've had it, I've had it.

THUB-bub. THUB-bub.

I could tell there was something different about my thinking, even under the chorus of panic it was slower but also clearer, like I'd had a massive dose of THC. I've had it, that's it, that's it, that's it. That's what it is like. This is what it is. This is the big one. Meet the Void. I couldn't feel tears but I could feel the swelling behind my eyes. Something clicked in my stomach and I was sinking into an endless gray vacuum tube, let me out, it's time, I thought, I'm ready, I knew it had all already happened. Ix had been eaten by the jungle, Pedro de Alvarado had come and the People had died, atom bombs thrummed through the stone, Marena and I had been born and she'd given up and gone away and died and they'd all gone away, they weren't going to come for me, no one was ever going to come for me, I was just spinning out into the graphite stars and no one would ever remember. Looosing meeeee. Packed in fuzz. Big cotton fuzz. Somewhere I realized my hands were pounding on the lid and I was biting the stone. I'd forgotten something, something important. What the hell was it? Something green, maybe? Something window.

THUB-bub

THUB-bub

Are you getting up, Mr. Wolf? It's twelve o'clock. I got rhythm, I got myugaaallllummmaorm. *Thub.* Aerror. Aearror. *Bub bub.* I died. I dead. Nn. Died. A. *Bub.*

Auriooonium. Raoiony oiny onny ooon oon oon.

Aorny oon oon. bub. Oun ou

THREE

To the Dorids of Emperor Hirohito

The Remains of an Ancient Sovereign at Rest upon His Bier
Discovered at Aguateca by Graf von Stepanwald

Curious Antiquities of British Honduras
By Subscription · Lambeth · 1831

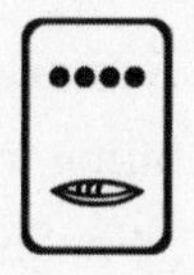

(80)

The first thing I saw was a red dot on an indigo field.

"Please focus on the red dot," a bonesetterly—I mean, doctorly—female voice said.

I did.

"Please follow the dot," the voice said. The dot slid up, down, to the left—I mean, right—and then to the left.

"That's good," the woman said. Her name wasn't coming through, but I knew who it was: It was the project's head doctor. Right. And I knew where I was. Well, not exactly where. But I mean I knew that I was in the twenty-first century, and in some modern facility, a dimly lit, medium-sized room with scents of Phisohex and latex and some, but not all, other components of That Hospital Smell. Definitely not a hospital, though, I thought. There were at least several well-washed but not recently washed bodies in the microatmosphere, but no smells of ejected foul liquids, foul semiliquids, and foul solids, or that special cleaner for what they call an "appliance." So more like a small clinic or a corporate or school nurse's office. Hmm. Somewhere nearby a pink-noise generator was generating pink noise. Something about the sound, or lack of other sounds, or lack of certain types of echoes, or something, conveyed that we were underground. As my ears focused, they identified the sound of several sets of fingers discreetly tapping on membrane keyboards. So more like a clean room, I thought. A Warren building. At the Stake, in Belize? No, I didn't think so. Something about the smells, the sweat or dust or types of pollen or whatever, didn't whisper, as they always do however faintly, "Central America." I used to fantasize about saving the day in some vague and debilitating way and waking up surrounded by sexily starched nurses and going, "What happened? Where am I?" Well, not this time, I thought. There wasn't even the dissociation we'd figured I'd experience. Not yet, anyway. I knew that I'd been in Chacal, in the seventh century, and that now I was Jed again—Jed_3, let's say—and I was back.

That's good, the voice said, or something to that effect. The dot vanished. And by now the field of my effective vision had widened enough for me to see that it was on a big, big OLED monitor angled over me on a ceiling-mounted arm.

Okay. I stretched. I wiggled my left, I mean, right set of toes, and then the other set. I moved my head back but my C3 vertebra didn't crack the way it usually did. I swallowed.

Hmm.

Well, fuck me with a pre-Columbian ceremonial jade battle saw. The world was still here.

Big disappointment.

Kidding. Actually, I can deal with the world. Its apex-predator inhabitants aren't anything to write home about, but—

The cold disk of a stethoscope materialized on my chest.

"Take a deep breath, please," the doctor said. I did.

"It's October twenty-eighth," the female doctor's voice said. "2012."

2 Kimi, 9 Sak, my brain went, automatically but, for some reason not nearly so automatically as usual. That is, 2 Death, 9 Whiteness, in the sixth k'in of the fifteenth uinal of the nineteenth and last tun of the nineteenth and last k'atun of the twelfth and last b'aktun. Fifty-four shopping days left before 4 Ahau. Okay. And it meant I'd lost two hundred and twenty-two days. That is, all the memories I'd picked up in the months between the downloading in March and today were as gone as an unsaved Angry Birds score. In a way—in fact, in more than just a way—that Jed, Jed_1, the one who'd lived on until yesterday, that Jed was dead.

Oh, well, okay. Easy come, easy go. If I'd had any brilliant insights or late-breaking commodities tips or anything, I would have left notes to myself. Which would show up tomorrow or so on my cold e-mail, that is, the account nobody but me knows about, not even my best friend, No Way, or my lawyer, Jerry Weir. Got to sneak out and get some fresh phones. Later.

The thing is—well, one of the many things is—at the same time that I was thinking about all the time I'd lost, or maybe a little before—when you're as tranquilized as I undoubtedly was, it's hard enough to remember what you were just thinking, let alone what order the thoughts came in—I got a microflash of a feeling of triumph and an image of a ball falling away from me between two vaguely sketched opposing players and into a goal, and a remembered sound of cheering. The big hipball game, I thought. Against the Ocelots. Except, no, not hipball, the dudes weren't wearing any padding. And more definitively than that, I'd propelled the ball with my foot. Something from my childhood? Except I'd always sucked at soccer, and they didn't even play it much in Utah anyway. Something I'd seen on TV and misfiled as my own memory? Maybe. And why did it come up? I thought back. When did it come up? Twenty-Eighth. Right. I guessed that it'd been triggered by the sound of the number "28." Huh. Well, look, if that's the worst jumble your consciousness is going to get after all this reshuffling, repackaging, reuploading, and other reabuse, count yourself ahead. Right?

"Exhale," the voice said, or a word to that effect.

I did. Fabric resettled on my chest.

A latex-gloved hand touched mine. I almost-passably-automatically looked down and the little scene came into focus: It was handing me a Tyvek cup half-empty of water, with a single prolate ellipsoid of ice floating in it like a ghost's turd. Evidently I was closer to vertical than I'd thought. I took it. My hand, and now, I saw, my bare forearm, had gotten a lot more muscular. Ripped, even. That's from hipball, my brain said. No way, I responded, we are *not* still in Chacal's body. Don't bust my balls, brain. And they don't play hipball in the twenty-first century either. Must've just been working out a lot while I was waiting for oblivion. I guess I'd wanted to pleasantly surprise myself. Except the arm had also grown an unprecedented crop of dark hair, which meant they'd upped my testosterone for some reason. Ask about it later. For now, just do the minimum and get out of here.

I sipped down a half-ounce. The water tasted a little different. I mean, from water. Grrg. My tongue flopped around, checking out the oral cavescape. Nnng. My sidewise tooth must have been fixed while I was out. That is, I'd always had my left canine tooth kind of negligently wedged in there, and now it felt right in line—

The voice said something like "Tell me your name."

"Don't start with the hard ones," I said, or maybe wished I'd said after I said something even more lame. Or had she even really asked anything? Maybe I wasn't quite so on the ball as I'd thought. I handed the cup back.

"How do you feel?" a different, male voice asked. Taro? No, somebody I didn't like as much. Who? Don't sweat it, I thought, it'll come back.

"Surprised," I tried to say. Only, nothing came out. At least I was trying to be honest. Almost my only emotion was simple surprise that it had worked. The uploading had always been less sure, by a big factor, than going the other way, that is, than the transmission into the Maya host mind. And even that hadn't gone perfectly. I'd always half suspected that the Warren people had just been leading me on, that they'd never really expected the uploading to work, although realistically they'd put a lot more money and prep time into the ROC phase—as we were calling it, based on a phrase of Heinlein's, the "Rigor of Colloids"—than they would have just to fool me. Probably they'd just had a lower expectation for it than they'd let on. And, really, they did want to get as much of a return on their investment as they could. I figured that by this point I'd cost about as much as two new aircraft carriers. One with a black-maple bowling alley.

In the first part of the recovery process, just before the uploading, my original memories—that is, all the higher-level long-term memories I'd built up in my brain over my lifetime—would have gotten "wiped down" by a series of medium-pulsed 2000-milliamp electroconvulsive shocks. Basically, they'd killed me, or vegetablized me. And then, in the second phase, my empty brain would have watched, or let's say it would have experienced, a sped-up "quintesensory video"—as Taro had called it—of the memories that had been downloaded from the ancient brain that had been preserved in the sarcophagus under the Ocelots' mul. And the living brain would rationalize or let's say overinterpret that input to imagine it was really experiencing it. Essentially, it would fool itself into believing it had a Jed_2-like identity. It was basically the same thing brains do with more random input when they're creating a dream.

I felt a disposable sheet slide off my feet. "Tell me what you feel." She rolled a spiked wheel up the sole of my foot.

"I feel one of those spiky reflex wheel things rolling up the sole of my foot," I said.

"Hold on a second," the doctorly voice said, not to me. There was one of those pauses where somebody else is doing something you can't see. I stretched again, crackling the butcher's paper on the examination table underneath me.

"Could you please tell me your mother's first name?" Lisuarte asked.

"Consuela," I said. "Oh, no, wait, it's Flor." Who the hell was Consuela? I didn't know any Consuelas. I'd gotten a flash of a cinder-block house with a big hand-painted Fresca logo on the outside and two men inside it watching Telemundo on an old Quasar color TV, and me inside it—that is, I was seeing the place both from outside and inside—inside the house, looking out its open front, watching a woman come up the road outside with a blue plastic basket of washing on her head, and there wasn't anything at all remarkable about any of it except that I realized I loved the woman but that she wasn't my mother, that is, she wasn't my real mother from Guatemala. She was someone's mother, she—

"Jed?" Marena's voice asked.

"Marena," I croaked. "Hi!"

"Hi," she said again, not so warmly as one would like. She didn't come over to touch me either. Guess she didn't want to be too lovey-dovey on camera, I thought. Either that or whatever thing we had wasn't a big thing, or—no, that was definitely something to think about later on. Stay chilled. Any big emotions you have, they'll show up on the graphs and you'll have to explain them later—

"Jed? You'll want to know that we identified and neutralized him," Marena's voice said.

"Who?" I asked, or rather made a raspy interrogative grunt. Oh, I remembered. The doomster. "The doomster?" It sounded like "Thhh dhhhmpp-strdrdrdrrr?"

"Yes."

I tried to say that was great, or something, but again, nothing came out. By *neutralized* do you mean "blew him away with a double-tap to the right side of his face," or what? It was one of those Commander Weasel words that Marena wouldn't normally use. Just play along, I thought. Until you're not being recorded twenty different ways. Wait.

"His name was Madison Czerwick." Lisuarte, it came to me. The voice's name is Dr. Lisuarte. Right.

That's great, I tried to say again. For the EEG's sake I tried to feel the relief I should have felt—that I would have felt if I didn't know better—but I don't think the graph changed appreciably. It's hard to fool the graph.

So they got the guy, I thought. And they still took the trouble to dig me up and upload me. Well, that was gratifying.

Either that or they weren't sure they'd gotten the whole scoop about the Sacrifice Game from the Lodestone Cross cache. Which they hadn't.

It took Dr. Lisuarte another ten minutes to check my short-term memory, perception, and motor skills. Things seemed roughly up to code. Maybe I should tell them about the second doomster, I thought, while she was making me brush my teeth over a sort of portable sink. In case my brain fries out unexpectedly or something. It's the decent thing to do. Except Koh'd been pretty clear that I'd have to hunt him or her down myself. And that she or he might be somebody I knew. Not knew face-to-face, she'd said—right?—but maybe knew secondhand, or on the phone, or something, which meant maybe one of the Warren people or maybe—well, it meant that I didn't want to spill anything about it until I got my ducks in a row. I asked for a mirror and they said they wanted to see how I did it without a mirror to check my motor skills. Which weren't good, I thought, in fact I wasn't even brushing my teeth right, I was poking my cheek, I was spitting in front of people, which I never did, I wasn't minding the taste of Tom's Propolis and Myrrh, which has got to be the world's most revolting, and I was holding the toothbrush like it was a pen, which is not the right way. And for that matter, why was I using my right hand? I always used my left hand. I mean, I was left-handed. Maybe the uploading had reversed my polarity, like I was a dilithium crystal? Except that wouldn't happen, it doesn't go that deep, it's just memories. Maybe I was looking at myself in a mirror. That had to be it. I winced my eyes closed and brushed again. Nope. Same same. I spat. I rinsed. I drank again. I felt my head. It was shaved, of course, and stuck all over with prickly electrodes. My hand got grabbed before it could feel any more.

"We'd better take those off in a minute," Lisuarte's voice said. "Please don't touch them right—"

"Jed? Do you have any questions right away?" Marena's voice asked, behind me this time.

"Uh, yeah," I rasped. "Did Kamsky win the WCC against Anand?" My voice was weird. It was way hoarse, which argued for a long time under respiratory anesthetic. But it was weirder than that, there was kind of a heavier accent to it. Maybe like a Yucatecan accent. It's a subtle thing, but still—

"Let me check on that," Marena's voice said, humoring me.

"Are we at the Stake?"

Lisuarte's voice seemed to hesitate, but I imagined, I think correctly, Marena nodding at her in a who's-the-boss-here? way, and a beat later Lisuarte said, "No, we're in Holopaw."

"Holopaw?"

"Right."

"You mean, like on Balam, uh, Cat Lake?" It was a nonplace town about, I'd guess, twenty miles southeast of Orlando.

"Correct," she said.

"Kamsky lost five and a half to six and a half," Marena said. "According to the Chess Federation site." She'd come around into view, but she was wearing one of those poufy hairnets and a lab mask with an earphone-and-microphone rig on it, and the little bit of her face that I could see was a funny powdery lavender shade. It had to be the OR lights.

"I'm sure the Federation is correct," I said.

"Jed?" Marena said. "Listen, we need you to focus now for a minute."

"Right," I said. "No problem." Damn, it wasn't even just the accent, it didn't even sound like my voice. I have a surprisingly deep and/or authoritative voice for my charming but relatively unthreatening physical presence. But this was a tenor. Looking back on it, of course, I should have guessed what had happened a long time before this point. But even if you're the most rational person out there—as I figured I was, given the competition—there's a kind of denial about things like this that kicks in automatically. Well, not that a lot of people have experienced any "things like this." But say you've lost an arm or something, it can take days to convince yourself that it's happened. Or if you've had a certain kind of stroke, you might never have any further contact with the whole left side of your body, but until your dying day, nobody's going to be able to convince you of the fact. Denial isn't just the Ventura Freeway of Egypt. It's the essential condition of all supra-single-cellular existence.

"Okay, before we do anything else, we should go over the most important algorithms and procedures from the Human Game, you know, the City Game."

I nodded. How'd they know about the Human Game? I wondered. Had they gotten me to chat in my sleep? I mean, of course they had me wired up the wazoo, but they still can't read stuff that specifically. Can they? No, no way. Or had I blabbed about it in the Lodestone Cross letters, about how we were looking forward to somehow getting it going? I didn't think so—

"Just in case there are any complex memories that you might not retain consistently," she said.

"Okay, I want to get up first, though," I said.

"Well, you're still under some sedation," she said. "It'd be better to do it right away like in the rehearsals. Remember?"

"Right," I said. Better give them something, I thought. Just don't give them the big stuff until you've worked it out yourself whether—

28.

Huh.

I saw the number 28, in black, against three light blue stripes on a white field.

Wait a second.

Twenty-eight. Mérida Fútbol Club. Right-handed. Yucatecan.

Oh. Oh Chri-

It wasn't my body. It was Tony Sic's.

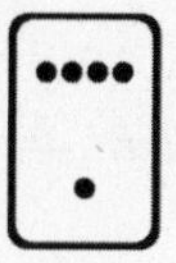

(81)

I screamed:

"WHERE'S THE OTHER ME?"

Now, in general, I try to have a snide remark ready for any situation. It doesn't have to be funny, just smug and mean-spirited. But not this time. I just screamed. And on top of that, despite terror, astonishment, apocalyptic rage, and everything else going on in there, my brain also found room to think of the scene of Ronald Reagan waking up in a similar room and similarly screaming, "Where's the rest of me?"

"Where's Jed?" I shouted. My God, I thought. My God. I'd known these were very serious people, crony defense contractors and private ops goons who could disappear you in a second, but I hadn't quite imagined that they were capable of this. Not this. Not this. Not this.

I started to lurch up, but more than a couple sets of squeakily gloved hands—"gently but firmly," as they used to say in handbooks about milking cows—pulled me back. One set reclamped the blood-oxygen thingie on my nondominant ring finger and another felt like what must have been an IV farther up the same arm.

"Is he dead?" I shrieked. My God, my God. I'd thought I'd imagined every nefarious trick that the Warren Family of Caring Companies could possibly pull, and now here was an all-new one. And I'd thought that Marena and Taro—I mean, had Taro signed off on this? Was Marena really this much of

an antifreeze-blooded murdering psychopathette? Tony Sic's brain, I thought. Jesus. That *choza* with the Fresca logo, I thought. That wasn't one of mine. It was one of Tony's very early memories. And that woman, Consuela, was Tony's mother. Holy *mierdi—*

"Jed's fine," Lisuarte said.

"But he doesn't know? The other me doesn't know?"

She didn't answer. I tried to see who else was in the room, but when I rolled my head around it felt like one of those colossal Olmec basalt helmeted ballplayer heads. Still, I got the impression of about a dozen people. Technicians? Nurses? Male nurses? Warren goons? Was that scary Grgur guy here?

Got to get out.

I started to slide off the exam table—vaguely planning to jump up, punch out the guards, steal some ID, get out of the building, and light out for the Territory—but I found myself sinking back down like I was wearing lead exercise weights, or not even, but like I had lead blood. Like even my earlobes were tired.

"Jed," Marena said. Her hand was on my forehead and the sleeve of her powder-blue lab coat pulled back so you could see a Warren live-badge bracelet. "You have to stay relaxed, there's still, uh, motor pathways coming in—"

"Your brain's still building connections to the new memories," Lisuarte said. "If you—"

"Wait, he doesn't know?" I asked again. "Jed, I mean, the other Jed, he doesn't know about me?"

"Jed's good," Marena said. "And, no, he doesn't even know we went back to the site yet. But we are going to tell him. Or if you want you can tell him."

Damn, so I was going to get to meet myself. I'd thought I'd taken care of this with that 2 Jeweled Skull creep. And now it's even more . . . hell, hell, hell. Well, we'd have a lot to talk about, I guess.

Well, so much for Tony. Poor sucker. He'd been twenty-eight years old. He'd never even had a chance. I'd never been crazy about the guy, but now I was almost feeling tears for him simmering behind my eyes. What the hell was he thinking? Did he have some kind of debilitating depression I hadn't picked up on? Was he terminally ill? Or had they given him some new kind of ultraspecific drug that increased his natural death wish and still left him cogent enough to defend his decision on video? Or maybe they'd brainwashed him over years and years. He'd been with the company for almost a decade, right? Jesus Christ, these Warren guys, they make the Carlyle Group look like Oxfam. They'll do you in a second. Bastards.

And why him? Wouldn't it have been better if it were somebody I'd never met?

Well, maybe that just hadn't been possible. They couldn't foresee everything, they were making it up as they went along too. They might not even have made the decision until a few days ago. And they'd needed someone who spoke Chol. Language is too basic. The mind encodes it way below the level of the sort of memories that we can (now) just pass around. And they'd needed a brain that was already proven to be smart enough, in the right kind of way, to be good at the Sacrifice Game. He hadn't been so good as I was, of course, but he was getting there. So there weren't too many candidates beside Sic to begin with. And as I should have expected, they'd been grooming Sic for years.

"Dude," I said. "You—guys—just—murdered—Tony."

"He volunteered," Marena said.

"What, like some, some, some, some, like some, some, some suicide bomber?"

"All right, you could say that, I'm not going to debate you about it."

"And you thought I wouldn't mind?"

"No, but, I'd say, well, yes, it's a bit of a surprise for most of us that you're quite this upset. Look, Tony Sic made a deal and in a way it doesn't really have much to do with you. He was figuring on a suicide mission of some kind."

"You mean he thought he'd be going to Mayaland and wouldn't be able to get back."

"Well, yeah, he hoped he'd get to go. But when you went instead, he accepted it. He'd already made the deal."

I didn't answer. Nobody else said anything.

"I want to see my face," I said.

Marena got out a quality-paperback-size Samsung tablet, switched it to mirror function, and handed it to me. It felt like I was lifting a three-inch-thick plate of polonium-210, but I got it into position and it "reflected" my face. Sic's face.

It was handsome in a rustic John Leguizamo–ish style, except for the shaved head with its white plague spots of about two hundred silicon-glued electrodes. I'd just seen it on the video, of course, but I'd never really seen it. That is, when it's in a mirror, you look at a face in a different way. And I don't mean because it's reversed—and the mirror function on her tablet defaulted to reversing the image as though it were a real mirror—but because you know your consciousness is in there, and in the face's microreactions, you think you can almost see it. I'm inside there, I thought. I'm inside. It's me inside.

"Oh, my God," I went. "Oh my God, oh my God." And I think I said it a few more times. Finally I started saying, "I can't believe you did this, I can't believe you did this, I can't be—"

"Jed, *listen,*" Marena said. She pulled off her—or do you have to say "doffed"?—she doffed her mask. It was Marena, all right, a little more creased and careworn than I'd remembered her while I was "away," but no wonder. "*Listen.* Did you really want the other Jed killed? Is that what you wanted? That would have made you happier?"

"No, but I mean, of course I signed up for that, and, no, I'm glad he's around, of course, but still."

"It will be interesting . . . for you to meet him," Taro's voice said.

"Whoa, whoa, whoa, *interesting*?" I went. "Are you all *psychotic*?" I managed to roll my head to see where Taro's voice had come from. He was just standing there. He was still in his mask. He was the type who'd forgotten he had it on. What does he really think about this? I wondered. His, what do I call it, I guess I'll say his complicity, his complicity in the thing was bugging me almost more than Marena's. Except, Taro's always been too otherworldly to really think about this sort of thing. Too spergy. Probably he feels like as long as my consciousness is somewhere he's done right by me, and as for Tony, well, Taro's weird, I mean, sometimes I'd gotten the feeling that he thought of the whole EOE thing more as just part of an experiment than something to really worry about. He's not a psycho, he's not sadistic, but, it's like everything's an equation to him. And it felt weird talking to my old teacher this way, but once I'd started I couldn't stop. "You just, you just murdered this like friend and colleague of yours and now you're all like, doo-dee-doo, let's all jump in the Mystery Machine with his reanimated corpse and go have drinks with—"

"Jed, listen, what are we talk—"

"That's how you guys treat your friends? How do you treat your enemies? Maybe you give them—"

"Hey," she said. "Jed. What are we talking about here? I mean, ultimately. Are we talking about the survival of the entire planet?"

I was about to say "But you guys *caught* the doomster." But then I remembered that I didn't believe that Madison was the doomster, and the fact that I didn't believe a word of what I was saying would show up on the polygraph.

And "polygraph" is putting it mildly, I thought. Try polyinnumerabillomyriadomultinominalograph. There were teams of experts, both software and meatware, and not just here in this room, but in several different labs, all watching and interpreting every snack, crapple, and pock in every lobe and fissure of my brain. Hell, they could probably see video of me playing hipball against the Ocelots and having sex with Lady Koh and—well, okay, they can't quite do that yet. But they can sure tell whether I'm lying, and a lot more besides.

"Jed?" Marena asked. "Is that what we're talking about?"

Don't answer, my other side said. That is, "my other side" as in "my regular interlocutor in my endless internal dialogue." If you talk, you'll say one thing too much. Just stay as schtum as possible and get the hell out of these 'trodes before you blurt something out. Right?

Right.

With great effort, I made contact with a few of my opiate-sodden muscles and rolled my head around. I could see that I was roughly in the center of a room the size of an average high-school classroom, and that besides Lisuarte, Marena, Taro, Michael Weiner, Ashleys sub-2 and sub-3, and Lance Boyle—all of whom, besides Taro, had, uh, doffed their masks—there were six other people working at portable workstations set around the walls. I thought I recognized a couple of them through their masks, students of

Taro's who'd worked on the Sacrifice Game software. Still, I hadn't thought this many people were in on the specifics of the project. One, how'd they expect them all to keep it secret? And, two, hell's bells, I've spilled my guts. This was not an intimate spot for a panic attack, a lover's quarrel, or any other sort of freakout. And with my brain opened up for general viewing, it–basically I'd feel more private if I were having a gynecological exam in a sold-out operating theater. Fuckity fuckity fu—

"Because," Marena went on, "because, if we're talking about the survival of the entire planet, then, that kind of changes things, doesn't it, that is, we're kind of in wartime here, in fact, you, it's, it's more serious than just wartime, we're at the tipping point of like life on earth, and a zillion innocent standbyers are all about to just—just, look, yes, of course we feel bad about Tony, but we're grateful, I mean, look, he's somebody we worked with, he's a member of our unit who volunteered for a suicide mission, he, with, with conspicuous bravery, and, okay, he's saving the day. It's his decision. Okay?"

Again, I thought of saying something that sounded fairly good at first—this time it was "Oh, thanks, GI Jane, well, at least we've stopped pretending this isn't a military operation"—and again, after about two seconds of thought, I said nothing. For one thing, at this stage I wasn't sure that I wasn't more worried that it might *not* be a military operation and might be just a commercial one, or rather maybe I was hoping that there was still an iota of difference.

"And the other—look, Jed$_1$'s still alive too," Marena said. "That's more than you expected, right?"

I sort of grunted.

"What would you have done? Think about it."

"I don't know what I would have done," I said. "Anyway, that's a meaningless—"

She started to interrupt me but I cut her off. *"Why didn't you tell me?"*

"Because," she said, "because the psych evaluations indicated that it'd be better to hold off on any major shocks until you got your bearings, you—"

"Because you wanted me to go through any and all Sacrifice Game data first," I said. "And then after that you can just toss me out on the street."

"Nonsense," Marena went. "Just relax a little. I'm not telling you not to think about the Sic thing, but you do need to relax or we'll all be in worse trouble."

I started to snap back at her and then didn't. Chill, I thought. She's right, you have to relax. She's—

Hmm.

I wasn't proud of it, but I was starting to suspect she might be right about a few other things. Like, was I really all that upset? Or did I just think I was upset because that would be the right way to feel? Sometimes one does the right thing just to make oneself feel like a decent person. You don't want to admit to yourself that you're a jerk. So you moan and complain but inside, not very deep down, there's less upsetness there than you'd expect, or want people to know.

Maybe they're right, I thought. They know I'll get over it.

For one thing, I was alive again. It was an unexpected plus. And one feels grateful to whoever makes you alive. For another thing, I was already starting to think again about how I'd go about finding and neutralizing the real doomster. When you're on a mission you forget about your own problems, or you accept it when other people solve them for you. Third, the team knew from my Lodestone letters that my stint in AD 664 hadn't exactly been characterized by nonviolence. So maybe they figured I wouldn't mind another sort-of death in my retinue.

And, fourth—well, I'd had enough experience with Better Self-Delusion Through Chemistry that even though I was in an unfamiliar body, I could tell they had me doped up within an inch of total all-flowering ever-abiding anupadisesa-nibbanadhatu nirvana. I could even tell that the main ingredients were levorphanol and diazapam. And when you have enough of that stuff on board—enough to get that feeling like you're a rack of spring lamb that's been soaking for ten hours in warm mint butter—somebody can come up to you and spit in your eye, steal your girlfriend, step on your blue suede shoes, and call you a Republican, and even if he's unarmed and smaller than you are, you just kind of placidly stand there and laugh it off because, well, things just don't seem all that dire. And of course right now they were raising the level of the stuff in my IV, so in a few minutes I'd be a useless glob of—

"And you're in a younger body," Marena said, "and, look, it's a healthier and frankly a better-looking body."

"He probably has leukemia," I said.

"He doesn't," she said. "He's, your body, it's fine. You're in perfect health."

"Great."

"Yeah."

"Is that why?"

"Why what?"

"Why you've got me in Tony. You wanted me to stay healthier longer because I'm such a big investment? And I don't have hemophilia. And you didn't want to take the chance that, you know, if something went wrong on the uploading, then Jed—okay, uh, the original, Jed-Sub-One, he might be too damaged to be an effective player. Right? But you could still keep him on as a backup. Right?"

There was a smudge of hesitation. "There were other—"

"Or maybe there was a little character trouble. Right?"

"What do you mean?" she asked.

"You didn't like my PSD, the tsam lic addiction, obsessive-com . . . you thought Sic would be cleaner."

Hesitation. Finally, Marena said, "Doctor?"

"Yes, there were some concerns," Dr. Lisuarte's voice said, farther behind me than before. "Some of Jed's . . . I mean, you're right, let's call him Jed-Sub-One, uh . . . some of Jed-Sub-One's reactions on the personality tests under the PET scan were, they weren't—look, after a great deal of consideration we thought he might not be the best candidate for his own new . . ."

"Are you talking about the sociopathology scale?" I asked.

"Well, that's . . . it's one thing that won't carry over," she said. "Sic might have your memories but he wouldn't have your personality. You might even feel that you do, but actually, you'll be . . ."

She trailed off.

"So I'd be more empathetic?" I said. "More good-willed, selfless, all that stuff?"

"It's not so simple as that, you were a good person before, it's more about quantifying what sort of character would be the best receiver of Sacrifice Game–related, that is, basically this very powerful information . . ."

"You thought Sic would be easier to control," I said.

"Again, no, that's a huge oversimplification."

"And you hate my character."

"No, no, we're just saying, you know, what I just said."

"You're saying my original brain developed a flaw in processing."

"Look," Marena's voice said, "frankly, Jed-Sub-One hasn't been acting quite normal. But you'll have, you know, when you meet him, you'll be able to . . ."

"Okay," I said, "but I, I mean, Jed-Sub-One, sure, he may not ever have been *normal,* but he wouldn't have killed Tony."

"We didn't kill Tony," she said. "Look, let's watch the video early."

"Medically speaking—" Dr. Lisuarte started to say.

"No, I'm making a command decision here," Marena said. "Show it. I'm serious."

There was two seconds of pause. The red dot disappeared and Tony Sic's shoulders and head came up on the monitor. He looked haggard, but not crazy or under duress. Of course, he wouldn't. The time stamp at the bottom read 10-24-2:26:41 P.M. Four days ago. He looked straight at the camera.

"*Y pues,* Joachim," Tony said, "you'll want to know why I made this decision."

He paused. I looked at Marena.

"When I was growing up in Xtaretac"—that's a Cholan-speaking town north of the old site of Quiruga, about sixty miles south of where I grew up—"I heard a lot about Justo Barrios, and Porfirio Díaz, and Pedro Cuzcat, and Che Guevara, and Subcommandante Marcos, and I wanted to do, I always thought I would do, something very important to bring my compañeros back from the bottom, to where they were in the old days, when they built the great citadels and ruled their world. Later, even though I did well in school, that ambition came to seem like it would be very hard to fulfill. And then later, when I began working with Taro, it came to seem possible again."

Hmm, I thought. Well, it sounds like he means it. But did he really? What if he was drugged? Or was he forced to say this stuff?

Or was it even really him?

Maybe it was a look-alike. Or not even a real person at all. Just a few years ago animation software couldn't quite fool you, but now, it's like, that stuff can whip up someone you know, from scratch, and you can't tell the difference. The fact is, you don't know anything. You're in a Phil Dickian nightmare of total surveillance and total simulacronism where total paranoia is totally justified. You'd practically have to be the president to know what was really going on. No, in fact, whoever's running the Deep State probably has him on strings, too, he's probably got an explosive pacemaker that'll go off unless he just reads the exact lines they give him, the real power, the deep state . . .

"I thought I would be able to see that golden age," Sic was saying. "And that would have been beyond my dream. But as it turned out, someone else was chosen to do this. And I was not even able to feel jealousy because I could tell this was best. Not just because of Taro's reasons but also from the Sacrifice Game, from plays of the Game I made myself, I could see that there would be a doom bringer, and that stopping him, that would be too important to take any chances."

I tried to look into Sic's eyes as though he were living and present. It felt like I was looking into a mirror, and that I could understand his face the way I'd understand my own face in the mirror, and that what I'd thought was haggardness looked more like the aftermath of extreme disappointment and resignation.

Maybe that was all it was, maybe Tony was simply a good person, a real hero, acting with conspicuous bravery, the sort of person that made me feel like a coward, a sleazeball, and a parasite—

Except don't think that, my other side said. You're doing the right thing. Right? Right. And it doesn't matter why. The people you save won't care about your motives. It just doesn't feel to you like your motives are good because you can't, you can't stand feeling all self-righteous. Right? So don't worry about it. Anyway, maybe Sic's not even that exceptional. Maybe he's just one of those people who wanted to be great. And who, like most people, gave up a little early. Everybody wants to go viral these days. It's like how everyday people commit increasingly spectacular live-streaming suicides. When they do surveys of terminally ill people, they still want to be famous even if they're not around. Or there was that study where seventy percent of ninth-graders actually thought they'd be celebrities, that is, they really believed they'd become famous, people just can't bear being average anymore. And I guess Sic was one of them. He'd wanted that so much, to be the Neil Armstrong of the past, to be the hero, to be the first person to see it. He wanted to be at the head of something, the first of something, at the forefront of science, so that then when they gave him a chance to be the hero in a different way, he took it. Maybe you'd do the same thing. You've done close to that, anyway—

"And there are two other reasons," Sic said. He explained that he had a huge family—there were eight sisters, one of whom was in late stages of Tay-Sachs disease and needed two hundred thousand U.S. dollars per fucking annum in medical care—and that they were now all rich people. And last, there was something he didn't want much to talk about. Suddenly I got a flash image of a face, the face of a Latino girl who looked around eight years old, a face I was pretty sure I'd never seen as Jed, and the face had an expression of sheer, hopeless terror.

"I have been carrying," Sic said, "some very traumatic memories from the time I was working for Marcos. They are memories which I cannot erase and which I do not feel I can live with anymore."

He didn't elaborate. But I got the sense—although it wasn't a memory, just a feeling—that the Latino girl was someone Sic had killed. And that he hadn't done it in a way that he was proud of. Just a feeling.

Well, you can't fake that, I thought. No way. I was sure he was real, and I was sure that he was telling the truth. Maybe it was because he was me, now, or maybe it was that I'd even picked up a drop of the way Koh could see into people, although of course I didn't think I'd ever get close to her level, or maybe I just had a capacity for empathy now that I'd never had in my shaken-up Jed_1 brain. At any rate, I was sure.

So, bad memories. He's right, I thought. They're a bitch. Well, he's erased them now.

"En cualquier caso," he said, *"le deseo suerte. No incurra en ningunas equivocaciones."* He reached forward and the screen went back to the blue field with the red dot.

Don't worry, Tony, I thought. I won't screw it up.

"Jed? How are you doing?" Marena asked.

"I'm fine," I said.

Okay, I thought. Look. You know what you'd do if you were actually smart? You'd go along with it. You'd get Lindsay Warren to trust you. You'd become one of them, sitting around that table with the rest of the Syndicate, pulling the strings. And then, one fine day, if you haven't become totally corrupted, you can turn around, use your great spider-powers with great spider-responsibility, and open up the system and really benefit the world. Right? Get to Lindsay and make him an offer—

Except, be realistic, my other side argued back. Don't kid yourself. They don't *need* another partner. Especially not somebody like you. You're an ex-radical, emotionally unstable multiple drug addict. You're fucked. Oh Christ, oh Christ, I am so very, very fucked—

Hold it. Cancel, cancel. You're not expendable yet. In fact, they've got you insured for upward of a hundred million dollars U.S. Right? So—

But the second you become expendable, well, you'll be expended. You're screwed, Jude. You'll lose, just like you always have, loser, loser, loser—

Stop that. Not helpful. Breathe.

Okay. Look. The worry, the well-justified worry, is they might just ice you as soon as they're sure they've gotten everything usable out of you. Just like what probably really happened to Tony. Someday you'll get drowsy from something you ate, say, and you'll lie down and you just won't wake up. Even if Marena doesn't want that to happen. For that matter, Marena might be being unrealistic herself. And Taro, for that matter. They both could just disappear. Or, best case scenario, after the 4 Ahau date they'll just scoop the incriminating bits out of your head and toss you out in the street. Or they might kill you, of course. Except I don't even think they'd do that. They want to keep Marena on board. And she does actually like me. Doesn't she? She may not be the most trustworthy person in the world, but she won't want to just see me get murdered. Really, she's not that cold. And anyway, even if they get everything about the Game out of me, if I make them think there's more to get, they'll still keep me around for a long time. Long enough to figure out what to do. Unless keeping me around means putting me in cryo storage. If they can do that yet. I wouldn't put it past them. Or really, no, realistically, they'll probably just dose me up with whatever recipe'll keep me permanently docile but not quite vegetablized enough to upset Marena and Taro. Right?

Hell, hell, hell, hell—

Okay, okay. I think we know the downside. Let's just keep that from happening. Stay indispensable, stay on the inside, keep enough dirt on them ready to dump so that they're hesitant, and most of all, use the Game. If they're not as good at it as you are, you can stay ahead of them. Right? Just be smarter than they are. Even if they've got LEON working on it full-time. Even if you teach LEON some things yourself. Just don't teach it everything. Keep that silicon bastard where he ought to be, in the dark. Twilight, anyway. You can do this, you can survive.

Right? Except for you to survive, the world has to still exist.

And without you the real doomster's going to get away with it. Right? Even if you tell Taro everything, they'll probably blow it. Maybe you need to just find the real doomster on your own. Except you can't, probably. You'll need LEON. You need their investigative resources, at least. And you may need their security resources to take the bastard out. You need to go along with them for the duration. Use the system, work up a LEON-aided version of the Human Game, and find the fucker and nail him. Right?

And maybe by then you'll be inside. That's how you'll stay alive. You *want* to be part of the syndicate. You're one of them. Or, let's say, one of THEM. And you'll rise through the ranks and then, once you're in charge of the bad guys, you can turn the place around. Use your power and position for good. Be Spiderman. With great power comes great responsibility, great deeds, great tolerance for platitudes . . . just don't sweat it right now. What you need to do is, you need to cool down, clean up, regroup and reorient, and get in a position where you can at least be clear about what you've got.

But I've got this urge, I thought back. I had this urge to tell them everything, the Human-Game algorithms, what Koh had said, the scoop on the real doomster, everything. Don't, my other side said. That's the meds talking. Just keep the key stuff to yourself. Even if they know you're holding out on them about something, what can they do? Dose you with amobarbital and try to worm it out of you while you babble? No, I don't think they'll do that. Not with Marena around. Not with Taro around, probably, for that matter.

Even if M and T both know I'm . . . no, they still won't want to go Guantánamo on me that fast. They'll stay close by, work soft on me for a few days, and then . . . well, and then, if you really hold out, at some point they'll give Lindsay's goons a go at you. But for the time being, just play along like every other nonloser does. Right? And then in a few days, if things get flaky, you can break away if you have to. Go underground if you have to. Do whatever you have to. Stay one step ahead of them. Just like the granola package says, never surrender. Awaken your Giant Within. *Be* Tony Robbins. Right? Right. Okay, here goes.

I sat still. I didn't say anything. The video had lasted two minutes and twenty seconds. Now it was two minutes after that, and I was so tranqued up, so filled with equanimity, that if it had turned out I was in the body of a baboon, I'd have just lain back in my cage and told Marena, "Hey, be a doll and toss me a banana."

"Jed? We still need to talk a bit about the Game," a Midwestern-sounding male voice said. I rolled my giant stone head to the right to look at him. Yeah, that guy, I thought. Finally, I remembered his name: Laurence Boyle. He, too, was in a powder-blue lab coat. Hmm, what kind of blue powder was that, originally? I wondered. Blueberry powder? Bluebird powder? Damn, I was as high as a radiosonde balloon. Focus.

"Mr. DeLanda?" he asked. "I'm sorry to seem uncaring here, but we also still need to do some business."

"Right," I started to say. "Business is . . ." I managed not to finish the thought.

"Larry, I don't think this is the best time," Marena said. She sounded real. I mean, like she was really feeling it. Had they rehearsed this? Was she just being Good Cop?

Whatever.

"I understand," Boyle said, "but let's just get a few things out of the way."

"Listen—"

"Also, Elder Lindsay wants to congratulate you." I couldn't tell whether the *you* was singular or plural. "He's standing by the conference—"

"Larry, no, we have to give him a break. Seriously. He's not in any condition to talk about this right now." Yeah, why the rush? I wondered. If they caught the doomster already, what was the problem? All they wanted out of the Game was a whole lot of bucks for the Warren Group. To be followed, inevitably, by world domination and a new millennium of corporate totalitarian soft dystopia. A whole Stanislaw Lem thing. But without the humor. But surely that can wait a day or two. Right?

"Miss, Ms. Park," Boyle said, "*as* we did in the rehearsals, we *do* need to continue the debriefing."

"I don't think I'm conditioned, uh, any condition, in any . . ." I said.

"Let's meet again in twenty-four hours," Marena said. "Doctor? What do you think?"

Lisuarte started to say something but Boyle cut her off. "Marena, we're all efforting to make this as nonconfrontive as possible, but there—"

"Stop it!" Marena said. "He's just had, he's *having,* a huge fucking shock, I mean, absolute trauma, and he's handling it—I mean, how would you guys handle it? He's lost months, and the two transfers, we don't know what that's like, I mean, come on, even on top of the Tony Sic thing, he's had an experience like, you know, and he's got a lot of meds on board. I absoshittinglutely in*sist.* I insist."

"I have to agree with that," Dr. Lisuarte said. "He's close to dozing off."

"I agree with Marena," Taro's reassuringly precise voice said.

"Anyway, nobody's going anywhere," Marena said. "We can start up again in twenty-four hours. I think that's fair."

Laurence gave in. I had an impression of people signing off on the decision and making plans to call each other in twelve hours. Dr. Lisuarte's nurse, who looked familiar but I guess didn't have a name, wheeled over a cantilevered table and set down a big Let's Fuck with Jed Kit, a compartmentalized tray full of pills and elixirs and electuaries and a large-bore Tuohy needle that looked as blunt and clumsy as a left-handed safety pin. Going to vax me into a staring askeletonite with Williams syndrome. Raggedy Jeddy. My earth-sized head floated upward in the nurse's hands, and as Dr. Lisuarte started to de-'trode it, icy rainstorms of solvent broke out across the coast of its northern continent. I dozed.

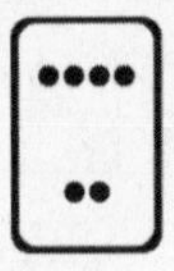

(82)

We convoyed to Marena's house. It was in a gated community in an expensive suburb of Orlando that, two months after the Disney World Horror, had been tested and cleared for radiation and cleared as safe. When I walked into Marena's living room, I noticed, through a window, a guard standing outside, leaning against Marena's Jaguar. With the other goon guy, who I think was named Hernán, in the vestibule, and Google skulking around somewhere, that made three. I was beginning to wonder whether they were keeping others out or us in. I staggered into the bathroom because I thought I remembered there was a steam room in there, but before I could turn it on I fell asleep in the dry sarcophagal tub.

It seemed like I slept for the next thirty hours, although I remember various combinations of my Toxic Co-workers turning up a few times to get in a little perfectly casual debriefing. Boyle reminded me a few times that everything I'd learned in AD 664 was the property of the Warren Corporation. I'd gotten cranky and Marena'd tried, with only some success, to act as the peacemaker. Lindsay checked in and Marena and I both talked with him on speakerphone. I was a little surprised that she didn't want to talk with him privately. He smarmed on about how great it was to have me back. Then he asked whether I'd seen any Hebrews there. Marena and I rolled our eyes. It's a Mormon thing.

I said, "No, you over me, I saw none."

"Well, they must have been there someplace."

We sat down with two double espressos after that.

"Can you tell me about Tony Sic now?"

Marena said, "I don't know what he was thinking."

"Try."

"He had serious financial problems. Like the suicide bombers, his large family has been amply taken care of."

"Why do I get, like, almost none of him? I got a lot of Chacal."

"Because, you know, with Sic the CTP team was working directly with the two brains on the table, at the same time. With Chacal there was physical distance, there was a, a humongous time distance—"

"Okay, I know, I know," I said. It's true, I was just whining. The thing was, in spite of the video, Sic's motivation in sacrificing himself was still something of a mystery to me. Maybe I'm just too much of a jerk to ever understand.

It was the thirty-first, around eight P.M. Halloween Night. Max wasn't going out trick-or-treating. I guess that was one of those things that, now, seemed like giving the kids realistic toy guns. He was going to a midnight Harry Potter party, though, and he was in his Dementor outfit, minus the face hood.

"So, you don't like the Domino's theory?" Marena asked us. I think she meant the pizza. Maybe she'd asked me about it before and I didn't remember.

"Anything's fine," I said.

Max made his two index fingers take a halt-step, the left one after the right one. It was the ASL sign for *lame*.

"Okay," Marena said. She floofed down between Max and me on the Chickly Shabby sofa. She was in blue Skele-Toes and a sort of fire-orange triangular shirtwaist. "Well, we could just order from Silk Thai."

"Is that the place with the fried water?" Max asked.

"No, that's the one with the Ho Mok, you know, the fish curry?"

"Oh, yeah, right—what's that thing, like, million-year-old eggs?"

She finger-scrolled down on her tablet. "Uh, that's, that's Khai Yiao Ma Phat Kraphao Krop."

"And what's that yellow spread stuff?"

"Uh, that's Nam Prik Kaeng," she said, a bit suspiciously.

"Okay," he said, "let's get that, and, uh, one Mok Yak Prik—"

"Maxie, don't even start."

"Or Uncle Jed might enjoy the Dum Ho Poon."

"That sounds great," I said. "Hey, do they make that, uh, Dark Drab Krap?"

"Oh, sure," he said. "And the Nip Suk Dik is very nice—"

"Hey, Maximilian," Marena said. "I'm serious."

"And they do a fine Pak Man Kum," he said, "very high-protein—"

"Well, I'm afraid that's a bit umami for my palate," I said. "But if they have an Ai Kyu Gap, or, uh, Sik Phat Phuk, then—"

"You guys, I'm not kidding," Marena said. "If you don't knock it off I'm going to text Seoul Train and order some Bibimbap and that'll be it. And there's nothing else in the house."

"No, no, okay," Max said. "Sorry. So, we agree on two bowls of Pak Man Kum, and my Mom'll have a Kwik Rim Job, and, uh—"

"And one Gook Lik Kok," I said.

"Hey!" she went.

I said sorry.

"Listen, Max," she said. "*Sérieusement.* Do you think you could just order a family-style vegetarian selection and do the order like a responsible adult?"

"Sure. "

"Okay."

"No Bung Plug Krak."

"Max!"

"Okay, okay, jeez."

"You want to call them on the MasterCard phone?"

"Yeah, where is it?"

"It's on Kitchen Island. In the Drawer of Many Things."

He Sleeked off.

Damn, I can't believe how domesticated I am, I thought. Well, believe it. The deal is, after two and a half days, anything seems normal. If I'd woken up with the head of a chicken, the tail of a beaver, the eyes of a gigantic insect, and the body of Megan Fox, it'd seem normal. Or the body of a chicken and the beaver of—I mean, anything. Being in yet another different body was one of those things like scuba diving or flying that for a long, long time people tried to imagine what it would be like to do, and then when they finally do it, it seems natural. It's not that it's so different from what at least a few of them had imagined, but since they'd imagined it in so many different ways, and some people had such high and varying hopes for it, there's always a touch of disappointment. And there was always that feeling of something in back of my mind, something small but still a deal breaker, like a mosquito in the room.

"Marena, seriously," I said when Max was out of earshot. "I want to meet Jed-Sub-One early."

"Let's stick to the schedule," she said. She still hadn't told Jed_1 anything about me. At least, she'd sworn up and down that she hadn't. The idea was that I should have my own head totally in order first, because of course he'd want to meet me and if he saw me all messed up then he'd get upset. But I also figured that they had some other, more serious reason.

"We still need to satisfy Lance on the debriefing," she said. "Then we can do whatevs."

"Right."

"Right."

"What did Dr. Lisuarte say?" I asked. Marena'd just been on the picture conference thingy with her.

"Well—look. I have to let you know, the readings indicate that there's a lot you're not telling us."

"There was a lot that went on back there."

"I know, but you'll have to force yourself," she said.

I was about to say I didn't *have* to do anything, and then I didn't, and just made a puffing sound. There was still that mosquitoish thought back there someplace. Or maybe it was more of a feeling like you're falling asleep in a house in the country and you start wondering whether you locked the door. You decide to forget about it and nearly drift off and then you get this picture of a door that's just a little bit ajar, and you're like, Forget it, forget it *(ajar)*. Good night *(ajar, ajar)*.

"Look," I said. "Why don't we call—"

There was an A-flat and F chime. Doorbell. Automatically—it must have been Sic's body memory, because normally I just lie there like a two-toed sloth—I got up. "Wait, let the Gurg get it," Marena said.

"No, I've got it," I said. I got into the front room about fifteen steps ahead of Gurgle—maybe he wasn't that on the ball after all—and opened it just as whoever it was started to knock again. I opened my mouth to say hi—

Whoa. Me. I mean, it was me. There was my gangly body and corny expectant smile, wiggling a bit in the video-friendly porch light.

"Hey, Tony," he said. "Hi."

". . . Uh, hi," I said. "Hi, Jed."

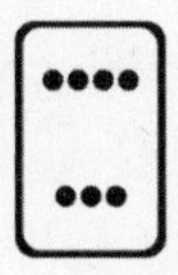

(83)

I motioned him inside and made a feeble gesture at the coatrack. I don't know what I was thinking because of course, like me, he'd want to keep his coat in this icebox.

"I'm in the orifice," Marena's voice called. I was pretty sure she was watching us—it seemed like she had cameras in every other Robie sconce—but she sounded casual, not at all worried that I was out here with her gentleman caller. Impotently, I followed protocol and pointed Jed_1 toward the door to the living room, and watched as Marena swept across the room and planted—is that the right word?—her lips on his. Max Sleeked through the hall and vaulted over the desk. Marena gave me a funny look, held up a wait-one-minute finger, and closed the door in my face. I guess I hadn't changed that much, after all. Big tough Jed, back from Mayaland.

I tiptoed back to the guest bedroom. Maybe if they couldn't hear me slink away, they'd forget about me.

I could hear Marena chattering away and could tell by the thunk of stone on thick wood that they'd started up a Go game. Hmmm.

Time trickled past. Every once in a while I sort of tiptoed back over to the door. I didn't put my ear on it, though, since I figured everything you did in this house was on video.

"Are you and he having a thing?" Jed_1 asked.

"No."

They must have moved into a different part of the room, because their voices got too muffled to hear, and I started feeling stupid standing there. I went into the sort of living zone and flopped on the sofa. Huh. Damn. It's me in there and he doesn't know it. This is odding me out. And I'm jealous, sort of. Except I suppose they couldn't be involved if he was asking insecure questions about me. Then again, she'd just said we weren't having a thing. Weren't we? I went back to the guest bedroom again, turned off the main light, and started one of my pacing rituals. I was on my one hundred and fifty-fourth circuit when voices started coming out of the phone. I was about to pick it up and then realized they weren't talking to me, and that Marena must have turned on the intercom so that I could hear her conversation with Jed_1.

"Don't even tell me, you *fuck,* you, you, you . . . you think you're going to make that decision—you can't make that decision, you're not some like, wise being, you're just, you're a loser." Geez, I thought. Take it easy, that's me you're talking to. "You're a boring windbaggy geek loser, you don't know anybody worth knowing, nobody's heard of you, you've never done anything remotely important, you're—"

I heard a little grunt. Had someone just gotten punched? And her voice had sounded so guttural. Like, desperate. I picked up the receiver, turned the speaker thing off, and walked out into the hall.

"You *shit,*" Marena's voice went. "I was, I was, I was practically falling in *love* with you and you were *shit.* You were worse than shit. You're what shit would shit if it could shit."

I skidded a little bit in Tony Sic's athletic socks as I rounded the corner of the hallway.

"How do I stop it?"

I opened the door and saw Other Jed, Jed_1, looming over a very small-looking Marena.

"Hey, what's going on?" I asked like an idiot.

Jed_1 looked over his shoulder at me. "Hi, Tony, nothing." I felt something large and rocklike push me to the side. It was Grgur.

I looked back just in time to see Marena give a brutal low kick to Jed_1's knee. I winced and jumped forward. I don't know if I was planning to protect Jed_1 or help her finish the job. Neither thing happened, though. Jed_1 was backing away through the room, throwing whatever was handy at the three of us.

"Jed's gone psycho," Marena shrieked. Her voice wailed feeedbackily through every speaker in the house

"GRAB HIM RIGHT NOW, NOW, NOW . . ."

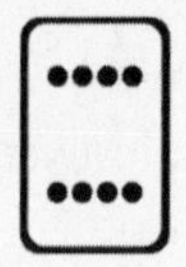

(84)

And at that, I knew they were going to kill him.

Another thing I knew, though, was that Marena's earlobe-mounted phone, and the whole house's phone and Internet systems, weren't running off the increasingly sketchy post–Disney World Horror local towers. Instead, there was a pair of direct-uplink dishes on the roof. And they ran on the house's electricity.

I toe-mushed my latex sandals off my feet and padded out, into the kitchen, and through a little pantry. It was Florida around here, so there wasn't any basement, and the house's gut brains were all in a little room behind a commercial water cooler. I'd already identified both the regular main circuit breaker and the big isolator switch that cut the line to a natural gas-powered backup generator that lurked in a shed in the backyard. Just to make a cleaner break, I cut the generator first and then the house main. There was a second of real dark and then a few battery-powered night-lights came on. Well offstage, Marena's voice shouted something.

That ought to give him a few extra minutes, I thought. I'll try some of his cold e-mail accounts later. My cold e-mail accounts. Our. I opened the kitchen door, jogged across the backyard—which wasn't the yard with the pool and the pepper hedges and everything, but just a swath of centipede grass surrounded by dready yew bushes—and vaulted—well, *vaulted* sounds a little too graceful—over a steel fence post into the neighbors' yard. I lost footing and rolled over. If they catch me, they're going to ice me pretty fast after this, I thought. A few days of interrogation, tops. Still, I was less terrified than I would have expected I'd be. Maybe Tony's brain—the less conscious part of it that was still there the way he'd left it—was less cowardly than the Jed mind it had appropriated. Or maybe it felt like I didn't need to worry because I wasn't really me. I got up again and ran around the neighbors' big faux-Spanish-Colonial pile toward Oshkechabi Street. I'm doing great, I thought. Got to ditch the phone, though. And check again for implanted chips—oh, hell. I only got the vaguest impression of something behind me before there was something around me, crushing my chest, and as I realized that one of the guards had tackled me the grass tilted up and mashed me in the face.

Too late.

(85)

"Well," I said, "if you'd let me meet with him, like I'd been begging to do, this wouldn't have happened."

"Or else it would have still happened," Marena said. "Or something even worse."

We were checking out Jed$_1$'s house, or rather aquarium. There were wads of Kleenex and drilled-and-smashed hard drives lying all over. What a fucking slob, I thought. Marena and I had come out onto the sort of porch because I couldn't bear to watch Ana's team tear up the place.

"Okay," I said, "but—look, what was I supposed to think? It sounded like you were going to kill him, in fact I bet you were going to kill him, and I didn't know why, so, so, so—"

"Okay, okay," she said, "let's not just keep going over and over this. We'll find him, and you're going to help us find him, and we won't kill him, and everything'll be fine."

"Uh, yeah," I said.

It was me, I thought again. I am such a fuckup. I'm *evil*, I'm vile, I'm evillive vileeliv, I'm—

No. No, it's not me. That me is a different me. The me I am is *not* that person any more. Better. Anyway, don't dwell on it. Fix it. Find him and neutralize him. And don't get sentimental.

Someone I know of but whom I've never seen face-to-face, I thought. Idiot. Who else could it have been? Obviously mirrors don't count. *Idiota, tonto, pendejo—*

Cancel, cancel. Not helpful.

Come on, work with Marena. Make sure *she's* okay. Because she's not okay right now, that's for sure. She doesn't realize how much trouble she's in. Warren's paranoid. I mean, both the individual and the company are paranoid. No matter how much I doth protest, they're going to think I'm going to make the same decision as Jed_1. Especially after my little world-destroying misunderstanding the other day. They'll keep me on a short leash, short like choking, and when I don't have any more goodies for them, they'll kill me. And Marena—I mean, they'll do her, too, no matter how sophisticated she seems she's still a little too trusting, she still thinks they're her friends, she doesn't realize they'll do anybody, oh, Jesus we are so screwed—

Cancel that, my interlocutor self said again. Don't sell yourself short like one of your corn contracts. You've still got a few arrows in your bow or strings to your quiver or whatever the hell it is. Go along with it, stay close to Marena, win her over to your way of thinking, put in protection for both of you . . . I mean, you know all this, Jed, Jed slash Tony, Jed-Sub-Three, whoever you are now, just do it.

I guess you're right, I thought back.

". . . how to stop it," Marena was saying. "Right?"

"Sorry?"

"What?"

"Sorry, I tuned out," I said.

"I said, Jed-Sub-One thought the Cascade wouldn't be stoppable because you couldn't figure out how to stop it. Right?"

"Well, yes," I said, "if you mean that just doing random things and hoping one of them'll work is too much of a shot in the dark. Presumably it's a robust autocatalytic event chain with a variable *n* of—"

"Okayokayokay, hang on."

"I tried to access his finances, but I couldn't get much of it."

"The thing is he didn't know about the Human Game, right? So it may be figure-outable with that, I mean, it might identify a whateveryouguyscallit, there may be, you know."

"A stopping mechanism."

"Right. And with the LEON version of that, the, I guess we're calling it the Human Game, that should do it, right?"

"I hope so. I mean, *we* hope—"

"So, so let's just put everything into finding Jed-Sub-One, and then, we'll get out of him what, you know, whatever's going on, and then we'll bring in LEON and work from there."

"Get out of him, like, sweat him."

"Right. Why, do you mind?"

"Oh, uh, no, no, definitely—"

"Hang on." Ana and one of her tech people were calling for us to come back in. We did. They'd really torn up the place, but so far, it looked like they hadn't disconnected any of the fish tanks. They'd pulled up the rubbery jigsaw matting and were prying the old half-ton Chubb safe out of the concrete. Needless to say, Jed_1 had reset the combination.

"Any erasing or explosive triggers on this?" Ana asked.

"Not that I know of. Unless I got even more paranoid after the Guate trip."

"No radioactive materials or anthrax powder or whatever?"

"No, no, are you kidding? I wouldn't—"

"Anything that's going to erase the hard drive on opening?"

"No, I don't think so. It'll erase without the password, though."

"Right. Any ideas on the password? Any favorite pet names, TV characters—"

"No, I don't do it that way, it's like with the safe combination, every Sunday when I do my Grandessa Game I just grab a new sixteen digits off a randomizer and reset it to that."

"What's a Grandessa Game?"

"Well, a Grandessa . . ." Hell, I thought. It felt violating, getting interrogated. But I'd screwed up. Pretty regally, in fact. You deserve it, Jed. Just co-fucking-operate. I started again. "A Grandessa's just a word for a sort of pouch of like, seeds and stones that all Maya sun-adders have. And we use it to tell the suns, you know, like divination. So it's kind of an abbreviated version of the Sacrifice Game. But I use it with a full Game board. And I do it at midnight on Sunday and that kind of maps out the next week."

"Why on Sunday, aren't you on a Mayan calendar or something?"

"Oh, well, you could do it anytime, it's just a Catholic habit, my mother would get querents then because the farmers stay up late on Saturday, like a midnight Mass."

"Okay."

"And I do all my numbers then, investments, passwords, upcoming dates, all that. Of course, clients want lottery numbers."

"Right."

"But anyway, that just tells you when the last combination got set. It doesn't have anything to do with the combination itself."

"Right, okay, never mind, we'll deal with it."

I'll bet you will, I thought. And I bet it'll be with an oxyacetylene torch rather than with logic. I just hoped they wouldn't ship the safe to Quantico or some other godforsaken place where it would attract the attention of politically motivated gangsters.

"You're sure there's no other strongbox around?" Ana asked. I said no.

"No other hides?"

I shook my head.

"What about all your safety deposit boxes?"

"I'm sure he would have changed those," I said. Come on, five isn't "all," I thought. Five is still a nonparanoid amount. "Unless he didn't get the time to go to Vegas and deal with the one at the Bank of Nevada."

"Yeah, Bill's already on his way to check on that one," she said. I'd never heard of Bill, but I didn't think he'd come up again anyway.

"Great," I said. And be sure to put my underwear up on eBay, I thought.

"Hey, check this out," another of the tech people said. I think his name was Chet Nguen. He called us over to my old desk, which had a new Samsung laptop on it. There weren't any sensitive files on it, of course—those were all in the safe—but it did have the names of some recently modified files, and the last-touched file had automatically named itself after the first distinctive phrase in the contents, and, in the last five minutes, Chet had already deciphered the name out of EncryptX. It was a little on the ominous side: *Why I Did It.*

(86)

Marena got the *Mission: Impossible*–style team together again—herself, me, Taro, Ashley$_2$, Dr. Lisuarte, Grgur, Hernán, and Ana Vergara. Our main goal was, of course, to track down and capture Jed$_1$ and interrogate him about the Domino Cascade. We'd also be trying, concurrently, to identify the Cascade and divert it directly. So far, though, we hadn't recognized even a single one of the "dominos." Finally, the members other than me had a third directive that I suspected—to keep a close eye on me. That is, me, Jed$_3$. Marena was still worried that I might make the same decision as Jed$_1$—even without an overdose of tsam lic—and then there would be two Game-savvy homicidal maniacs running around. The more I thought about it, the more I realized that no matter how sentimental Marena might get about me, it wouldn't matter to the Firm. As soon as I'd delivered the goods—the full deposition, the Game, and Jed$_1$, in increasing order of importance—Warren would slate me for cleansing. Still, I went along with it all for now.

Jed$_1$ could have been anywhere in the world, including Antarctica, Indiana, Peru, or even Peru, Indiana. There had been a hint, though. Jed$_1$ would be happy that the end of the world would kill the Mano Blanco guys and that damn nun. He'd want to let them know ahead of time and suffer. So I had feelers out watching them. And of course, I was watching all the nudibranch sites. He'd be happy to be in a place where he could take a last look at his favorite genus of animals, nudibranchs—but that could be at almost any of the reefs in the Caribbean, on the Pacific Coast, or even Southeast Asia or Australia. However, since Jed_1 and I shared versions of the same mind, I was at least able to compete with him on a high level, with almost a kind of virtual ESP.

I played four Games against the absent Jed_1. Unfortunately, somehow—despite my using the Human Game algorithms against his less powerful ones—he was able to anticipate my moves. And he kept eluding me.

Finally, on the Second Day of the Dead—that is, Friday—we got the certified decryption of *Why I Did It.* Marena and I read it without saying anything. There were sixty-two pages of Executive Solutions research attached, confirming that what Jed had identified as the first dominoes had, indeed, fallen.

Marena and I—the rest of the team were setting up a temporary office in the Holopaw compound—were alone on the sofa in her office, and we sat for two minutes without saying anything. I know because I was facing the clock collection on her big desk and this gaudy ormolu French Directoire thing had a big old second-counting annular ring that kept whirling around like a damn salad spinner. We sat for another two minutes without saying anything.

"Maybe nothing else is going to happen," I said, finally. "Maybe he's just blowing smoke at us."

"Um . . . yeah, I hope so," she said. "I don't think so. Though."

"No."

We sat without saying anything, this time for two and a half minutes.

"Hey," I asked, "are you sure Jed-Sub-One never told you *how* he thought the world would end?"

"No, I told you," she said, "he said he didn't know. I mean, before. And then when he was, you know, he didn't say how."

"I mean, did he ever just guess at it, or say anything about what it'd be like for, like, the People of Earth, or whoever?"

"I don't know," Marena said. "Painlessly, or whatever, I guess."

"He said that?"

"Uh, something like that," she said. "Or that people wouldn't notice—"

"Damn it," I yelled, "I knew it!"

"What?"

"Well, just that, that would be something that'll disappear the whole planet in a second."

"I thought it might be some sleeping-gas-type thing."

"No, no," I said. "I wouldn't ever say—I mean, he wouldn't put it that way, that, that's—no, he, he means some collider event. Like a strangelet. You know, like, a black hole thingy. Or something. Something that just vanishes the whole place without anybody noticing."

"Okay. Wow, you're right."

"That's a *huge* clue. We can work backwards from that." I started off toward my temporary server station on the kitchen table.

"Sorry," she called after me.

After an hour I thought I had a pretty good list of facilities. It started with CERN, which was, of course, the world's biggest collider, and then went down through a hundred and sixty-one others until it trailed off in labs whose particle accelerators probably weren't functional enough for the job. There were two big problems with it, though. One was that one didn't know exactly what procedure old J_1 was thinking of. The second was that the U.S., China, Europe, Israel, and the old USSR each probably had at least a handful of secret installations. And the third—okay, three problems—the third was just that even though he was still using the old version of the Game, the ol' Jed-Sub-Onester was probably capable of doing the whole thing remotely. We had to start monitoring online traffic to each known lab, but there wouldn't be much percentage in staking them out physically.

Or we could just convince every single one of them to shut down for a few months, I thought. Like, right, that'll happen. Governments are so safety-minded.

Hell. I'd never thought I'd be sorry that I was intelligent.

By the next morning, Marena and Taro (on the phone) and I had talked it around another ten times. Lately she'd been thinking that instead of trying to track Jed_1 down, we needed to get him to get him to reveal himself.

"Yeah, but, the trouble is," I said, for the unknownth time, "it's hard to smoke out somebody who's that paranoid."

"I know," she said, "you said that."

"No, but—well, that's it."

"Look, he has to—it has to be very subtle. We have to let him suspect something." And, she went on—not in so many words, but in many, many more—his suspicions have to be as close as possible to the truth. Maybe he needed to think that we'd come back from Guatemala with a game-changer. Except he had to think it was even bigger than it was, that our new and improved version of the Sacrifice Game was definitely going to let us overcome his nefarious scheme. In fact, Taro suggested, maybe we should create a similar anomaly. "Something parallel to the events of the Domino Cascade," he said. "Which would look to him . . . as though we have found a blocking strategy."

I was noncommittal.

"His curiosity has to . . . get the better of him," he said.

"And, uh, not just his curiosity," Marena said. "But like, you know, his pride."

"So, like the *How to Beat Bobby Fischer* strategy," I said.

"What's that?"

"We need to let Jed-Sub-One think that playing against us is going to give him an outlet for his creativity."

"Correct," Taro said. "He might even . . . as they say . . . he might spot a trap. But he needs to think that that trap. . . . is different from what it actually is. And then he may make an overplay."

"Okay, then, listen," Marena said. "In that case—well, let's look at this a different way. What does Jed-Sub-One really hate?"

"The whole world," I said.

"Okay, so his hate's too generalized. So let's give him a focus."

"A focus like what?" I asked.

"Like a movie star. Everybody's jealous of movie stars. Right?"

"Okay."

"And that's at least one thing I know how to do pretty well."

"Make movies?"

"Yeah."

"You mean you want to direct."

"Oh, shut up, I'm saying, we're all set up for, to—"

"So, wait," I said, "you're going to make a movie in a week? And distribute it?"

"No, no, of course not, we—no, we don't need to make a whole movie. Just the trailer. Right? Just enough to make Jed-Sub-One believe it's really going to happen."

"Hmm."

"Right? And then he'll get jealous and, and he'll contact us, and he'll screw up the call routing somehow, and we'll grab him."

"Hmm."

"Don't you think?"

"I don't know," I said.

"But you ought to know, right? You of all people."

"Well . . ."

"Come on. Let's make you a star."

(87)

On 11/4/12, at 2:05:49 I was standing on an X made from DayGlo-green gaffer's tape, in front of a green screen, wearing green bandages where some of the costume details would go, talking to a green target that they moved around.

I knew film shoots weren't glamorous, but in these days of hegemonic computer graphics they're even less glamorous. Once in a while they yelled instructions at me. Fortunately, in these days, you don't really need to know how to act. As to the product, at least it was classy enough that they spoke some subtitled Yucatec Mayan, but when the Maya characters spoke English, like when the Jed character talked with 2JS, say, they talked in that faux-historical way, without contractions, like they hadn't invented contractions yet.

On the thirteenth, Marena leaked the trailer onto YouTube. *Chrononaut: Maya* would star Tony Sic—me—playing self. The release date was set for summer of 2013. The trailer used some of the footage taken by the small film crew on the creep into Guatemala and the downloading and from the debriefing, and also some stock footage of the Disney World Horror and other contemporary events, mixing it all up with some scenes "acted" by me in front of the green screen and worked up with computer-generated imagery to re-create some scenes from my experiences in "Ancient Mayaland." It implied that the film would tell a simplified and heavily censored version of my "time trip." Naturally, it was an abomination, but Marena said, "We're into survival now, so who cares?" Of course, most bloggers didn't believe the claims made in the trailer. But a few people who'd worked out some of the more esoteric aspects of Maya civilization, and who'd gotten some gossip about the research on time projection and consciousnes-transfer, believed it was accurate. And the debate, of course, increased the clip's notoriety. Forty-eight hours after posting, it had gotten over five million "full views from unique visitors." Our line was very much in the water.

But Lindsay Warren was furious. Marena's six-and-a-quarter-minute trailer—a *trailer*—had cost forty-three million barely approved Warren dollars. One point two million of that was for eighty-nine seconds of screen time by January Jones. Who turned out to be really nice, by the way. Even more enragingly, though, the project had basically preempted the much more expensive 3-D feature film that—along with games, novelizations, and other related media—Warren Studios had been working on for months, and which it had planned to release in June of 2013. Assuming, that is, that the world continued to exist after 12-21-12. And, even more enragingly, Marena had revealed Warren proprietary information. For example, details were coming out about Warren's clandestine human testing of the CTP, which would, to say the least, cast the company in a bad light. Another example was the Hippogriff Incident, when a Guate helicopter was shot down as the team returned from Ix Ruinas. This and other revelations would open Warren up to an avalanche of private lawsuits and even, probably, criminal charges. And as though that weren't enough, the film had even given away some details about the Sacrifice Game—which, from the Warren Group's point of view, was entirely proprietary and which represented an investment of several billion dollars.

So despite the fact that Marena and Taro contended that the release of *Chrononaut* was absolutely necessary to keep the universe from disappearing, it seemed that Lindsay, despite his general confidence in the efficacy of the Sacrifice Game, didn't believe it. Either he still thought that Madison was, as "predicted" in the Codex Nuremberg, the only doomster, or because he wasn't convinced by *Why I Did It*, or simply on account of his Mormonism and acceptance of Mormon cosmology. Or, alternately, it's possible that

Lindsay was confident that his own separate investigative division—sinisterly referred to as "HR," for Human Resources—would be capable of tracking down Jed_1 without needing the film to smoke him out.

At any rate, Marena gave up her position at Warren. Ana had to quit working for Executive Solutions and hire herself out directly to me and Marena (who, since I couldn't access any of Jed_1's accounts, was now paying for everything herself). I was still bound by my Warren contract, but I started missing meetings with Warren staff—although of course, HR, the Warren investigative division, was now closely shadowing me, Marena, and everyone else on the team. Also, according to Marena's connections inside the Warren Corporation, these events set the Warren board of directors against Lindsay, whom they began to try to phase out in favor of Laurence Boyle.

Over the next two days, Marena worked with me on a series of posts to my Web site that would hint to Jed_1 that I had returned from the past with a still-more-effective iteration in the ever-increasingly powerful Sacrifice Game. The idea was for Jed_1 to suspect that this upgrade would overcome his plans. But even if he didn't get as worried as we hoped he would about that, he'd still want to learn what had happened during the Human Game. For that matter, he'd be desperate to learn how to play the Human Game, even if he knew he'd disappear before he could ever use it. The Game was the central mystery of his life—of our life, let's say—and no matter how his character had changed, he'd never be able to leave it unsolved.

Most cleverly, though—and this was Marena's idea—the posts were pretty well hidden, but went out twice a day, and each one had a little more information than the last. We wouldn't be able to see where he'd accessed them from—he'd be way too careful for that—but if we got Jed_1 talking about them, we might be able to suss out which post he'd seen last, and even maybe when he'd seen it, and that might give us a sense of how on the ball he was, Net-wise. It wasn't much but it was all we had for now.

Otherwise, I just kept doing interviews about the trailer—teleconference only—to prop up the perception that I was soon to be the next Chris Hemsworth. I did okay, but in between gigs I kept getting bouts of unnecessary surliness. Sillily, my biggest emotional problem was that I knew Marena thought No Way had sold us out to the Guate military, but that she was just plain wrong. She thought I was in denial about this, but I knew him and there was just no way he'd do that. He's dead, I thought. Still, I'd have to deal with that later. If there was a later.

As per my recommendations we kept putting out little bits of propaganda. For instance, at 4:55 EST on Sunday night, we posted something—coded, and in a very difficult-to-find location—about Kristen Stewart, the *Twilight* girl. We kept waiting to hear from the Jedster. Finally, on November 16, a caller ID popped up on Marena's most private line: **JED**.

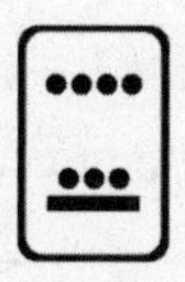

(88)

"Hi, it's Jed," Jed_1 said. His voice was heavily processed to eliminate background clues, but Ana's telephone technicians quickly determined that it was really him. You could hear that he was smiling.

Ana was all over it. "Okay, the second relay's in." This was the telephone code locator. "That's—that's U.S., so, it's in, um—"

Antonio said, "Pawleys Island. North Carolina. Jed's old beach house."

"You're sure?"

Ana snapped, "Probably."

"Okay."

"It's about a two-hour drive from there."

"Got it," Ana said. "Okay, Antonio, you take the big chopper. We'll find a car there."

"Never mind, I'll put in a bike."

"Like, a chopper in the chopper?" I said.

"Right."

"Good deal," Ana said. "Just, keep an eye out for decoy relays. And bombs and the usual shit."

"He's not going to have any booby traps," I said.

"Not your style, huh?" she said. I stared. "It's classier to just vaporize the whole place, right?"

"Okay, let's not bust Jed's balls," Marena said. "Jed-Sub-Three's."

"What's left of them," I said.

"Sorry," Ana said.

The team also ascertained that Jed_1 was using a chain of physical relays—pairs of telephones set up in different locations around the country—to make the call difficult to trace, since by the time each location was tracked down, and the next one in the chain was identified, he'd be long gone. Even so, this was a huge step forward for the team, and I—trying to ignore the oddity of talking with myself—took over the call.

I said, "Aren't you curious about what's going to happen in the future?"

"There isn't any future."

"Don't you want to meet Kristen Stewart?" I asked. "We just signed her for the sequel."

"I know."

"Oh." Hmm, I thought.

"Look, get your heads together and poke me on HarpoCrazy," he said. It was an anonymous-messaging site that I, or he, had used before for talking to the posse at La Sierra. Ordinarily it wasn't anything that the Warren code spooks couldn't crack, of course, but he'd be covering his digital trail anyway, way before the message ever got to the site. So I guess he just wanted to make sure nobody else would come across the exchange. One thing HarpoCrazy did do well was keep their text off search engines. Supposedly the NSA has a whole division that just keeps on breaking into the site, twenty-four hours a day.

"Uh, okay," I said. "HarpoCrazy."

He hung up.

"What the *hell* are you doing?" Marena asked. "You have to *keep him on the phone*!"

"He just screwed up," I said.

"How?"

"He just told us where he is without realizing it."

"Sorry?"

"Or because he didn't think about it. He got that Kristen Stewart post. And he wasn't looking for it. So he must have played the Game and just found it. I mean, the weekly Grandessa Game."

"Okay, that's terrific, so that tells you what?"

"Well, I do that, I mean, you know, he does that right after midnight Mass. That means it's already Sunday there."

"Where he is."

"Right."

"It's only Saturday."

"Right, so, where does that mean he is?"

She thought for about a half-second. "So it's super-early there? So it's in the Pacific. Near the international date line."

"Correct. Right here, we're, you know, we're Coordinated Universal Time minus five hours. But wherever he is, it's UTC plus fourteen."

"So it's an island. It's, it's some nudibranch thing?"

"Correct. And there was a big new species discovery out there, and it came out in the *JMS*, uh, the *Journal of Malacological Studies*, in December, I mean, it was the December issue, but it got published in October. *Mexichromae zenobia*. That's a kind of possibly eusocial 'branch, uh, nudibranch—"

"Right, right, so where is he?" Her thumb hovered twitchily over the CALL icon on her tablet.

"Guess."

"Come on, don't bust my ovaries, where where where where where?"

"Where's Zenobia from?"

The Recent Solar Obscuration as Witnessed at Ixmul

Curious Antiquities of British Honduras
By Subscription · Lambeth · 1831

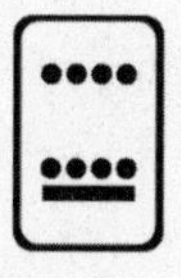

(89)

Google-Earth "Palmyra Atoll" and at first you won't see anything there, but if you zoom down to the maximum you'll bring up a linked pair of tiny islands, looking up at you like a white domino mask. If we'd had to stick to commercial travel, it would have taken us eighty-one hours to cover the 6,750 miles. But Marena'd been mending some fences with Lindsay and Boyle and she'd convinced them to lend us one of his Gulfstreams and a crew of three. They took us from Orlando to Twentynine Palms in five hours, and from there we got on one of their decommissioned C-17 Globemasters and flew to Wheeler Base in Wahiawa, in the center of Oahu, in eleven hours, and from there it took five and a half hours to get to Kiribati. We took a cigarette boat to Palmyra and met Ana's crew, who were on a stealthier boat called the *Gotengo,* just before sunset.

As I'd explained, a bit breathlessly, to Marena, Jed_1 had to have used the Game to find that hidden post on Kristen Stewart. And he said, "I just got that," which meant he'd found it during his Game of the Week. Which he does on Sunday night at seven P.M. And the only place where it was already seven o'clock was in the Line Islands, which are practically sitting on the international date line. And the most interesting spot in the Line Islands was Palmyra Atoll, because that's where the newly discovered possibly eusocial nudibranchs were. Although when you spell it all out it seems a lot less magical.

The *Gotengo* rode low in the water, and weirdly slushily, I guess because it was some new kind of stealth thing, all Kevlar and carbon fiber. It was forty-two feet, which would normally seem like a lot to a reef bum like me, but most of that was under the waterline, and the eight of us—Marena, Ana, and five male security contractors, or let's just be blunt and call them mercenaries, and me—kept bumping each other as we squatted in the ungenerous deck space. Actually, *Gotengo* wasn't the boat's real name, or rather it didn't have a name, just numbers and a two-terabyte spec disk that told you things like how it was built by VT Halmatic and that it was tested for ninety knots, which is huge. But we wouldn't be doing any racing.

"They're talking about the storm," Megalon said. Of course, "Megalon" wasn't his real name, which I didn't know. I did know, though, that he was an ex-commodore in the SBS, that is, the Special Boat Service, which is like the UK version of the Navy SEALs. He spoke in that low-key-but-still-working-class way British grunts all have, with a vestige of Australian. He was big and naturally jovial and he'd let his hair grow out a bit now that he was in the private sector, but he still had what they used to call military bearing and a tattoo with a stubby gladius and a banner that said something like BY STRENGTH AND GUILE. Good plan, I thought. He was talking about the people on Jed_1's charter, the *Blue Sun,* or rather I should say the *Matango*. You couldn't see it from here, but the sonar said it was right out there, three thousand and twenty-eight ESE. Oh, and Megalon was telling us because he was talking on his in-ear phone to our audio lady, who was below with the captain and another IT person. Audio Lady—well, let's use her dumb alias, Mothra—seemed really good. I'd tried listening to the raw audio coming in from the *Matango,* but it just sounded like a hyena in a wind tunnel. You had to be a veteran sound geek to take the stuff off the three differently tuned parabolic microphones, sort it out, denoise it, interpret it, and summarize it for the likes of the rest of us.

"Reptar wants him to come up in a half hour. Ogra says no." "Reptar" was the skipper of the *Matango*. Ogra was Jed_1.

"I used to like to go in a little after sunset," I said. Most 'branchs don't roll out of their crooks and nannies until dark. "Except—"

"Hah!" Megalon went. "Okay, there they go." He said that Ogra had gone in with two other divers, possibly bodyguards, and they were swimming south, without tow sleds, toward the extreme tip of the reef. "Eighteen minutes." We wanted to spend as little time in the water as possible, and I'd said how my average dive was about seventy minutes. So if we could get there in forty-two minutes, and we wanted to catch them toward the end, when they were tired. I shifted on the little drop-down seat. Eeekch. My tow-harness's crotch strap was chafing the tenderest segment of my perineal raphe, but I didn't want to unzip and grub around in there in front of Marena and Ana. A trio of brown pelicans shuffled over us, boogying west. Way off in the east, a low scroll of clouds was turning to what Joseph Conrad had called "that sinister olive." I checked the little screen on my left wrist. It was six minutes to sundown on Friday, December 2, that is, sixty-three hours after we'd ID'd the boat. Weatherwise it was sixty-four degrees, with seventy percent relative humidity, wind southeast at eighteen miles per hour, and cloudy with a chance of annihilation. Tide was high water minus one hour and waves were two to three feet SW, and choppy. The clouds in the east were part of a late tropical storm building up over Antigua, forty miles away, and according to the Meg man they could be a problem—or "issue," which I guess was worse than a problem—but it wasn't yet.

"So why's he got guards unless he's expecting us?" Marena asked.

"Maybe it's just for safety," Megalon said. "With the current. Or maybe they're just friends."

"Friends?" I asked.

"Do you not have any friends?" he asked back.

"No, it's—I mean, haven't we been monitoring all my friends? Like, all one of them?"

"Yeah, we have," Ana said. "Then they'd have to be new friends," Megalon said. He pulled on a full face mask—yellow fiberglass face complete night-vision goggles and bolts at the temple. It had an exposed wire breathing apparatus that curved around from his neck and made him look like the Vincent Price Fly wearing a supersized Essix retainer.

"That doesn't sound likely," I said. Must readjust groin area, I thought. Megalon's voice sounded beefy and determined even over the com link. "Even if they're females, we're going to treat these friends as armed frogmen," it said. "Grab, contain, and retrieve."

Sir, righto sir, I thought. Someone handed me a BandMask®, Bandkeepers®, and a SuperFlow® regulator. I started strapping the gear on, expertly, until Ana just took it from me and strapped it sadistically tight. ITCH! OUCH! IOUTCH! MUST! ADJUST! NOW! A glint of yellow flashed on the underside of the green cloud front just as my full face mask was closing down on me. Not a good sign. Marena was looking at it too so I half-stood up and sneaked my hand into the old crotch area behind my harness. Ahh. A little more. Damn, she was looking at me. What the hell. I sat back down, bobble-heading heavily under the mask.

"Let's hook on," Megalon said. I found the 'bener on my harness—the one gouging my crotch—and clipped it onto a nylon line that went over the side and down and aft, leading to my designated tow sled, or Diver Propulsion Vehicle, henceforth referred to as a DPV. There were seven of them trailing behind us in a long line. They were big—or, it seemed to me, gigantic—but supposedly any other models were way too noisy and the Matango's hydrophones, if any, would pick them up in a second.

Ow. The adjustment hadn't been entirely successful. All the stuff down there had just better smooth out in the water or—

"Let's go," Megalon said. He tipped backward and slid discreetly into the sea.

I flipped up my seat and sat on the gunwale. Ana went next, making a little more noise, but nothing to be embarrassed about. I started hyperventilating. The other combat swimmers dropped in, three, four, five, six. Okay. Breathe. In. Out. In. Now. I leaned backward, fell, and heard the beginning of an amateurish splash. Then even with the Jack Browne drysuit, there was that zap of almost-insupportable cold that, like always, was over almost before it registered, and then the gradual melting into equal buoyancy and that moment where—no matter how big a sack of bad is going down—every diver in the world ever, in the wooshiest, most clichéd possible way, feels, for a few seconds, at one with the all-embracing wine-dark brine-mother. This time it reminded me of how Koh had told me she remembered breathing saliva in her mother's womb, listening to the hairdressers' muffled singing in the red twilight. Okay, focus. I sucked in two lungsful of ntitrox. Ahh. There was an extra eight percent of O_2 in the mix, enough to give you a little extra moxie but not enough to make you silly. Okay. Step two. Claim your DPV. I got hold of the tether line and followed it aft, pulling myself along upside down, until my head hit the vehicle. I got in position, dropped the tether, and clipped my harness to the cleat on the back. You could ride the thing hands-free if necessary. In fact, if, say, you got knocked unconscious, the crew on the boat could remote-drive it back to the boat, trailing you along. I got into position behind the thing—you could feel the motor purr through the handlebars, but you couldn't hear it—and let myself hang with my head down, soaking up the growing warmth and listening to that different underwater-world five-thousand-feet-per-second sound, with critters clicking like fairyland stone marimbas. I thought. Okay. I switched on the DPV's headlight. Damn. The visibility was lower than the thingy'd said it was, barely five yards, I guessed. Way too much phytoplankton. Maybe it was because of the storm. As always, I twisted around for a useless look over my shoulder. Nothing. Brrrrr. No matter how many night dives you've done, there's always a shudder-and-chill when first you feel that immensity of dark below and especially behind you, which your amygdala helpfully populates with peckish hammerheads, cardiolethal box jellies, the last surviving *Carcharodon megalodon*, snaggle-fanged Xibalbans, and a couple Spawnlets of Cthulu.

I stretched my arms and let myself settle into the soothing pressure, about a foot under the surface. Ahhhhh, that's better. Enough of that gravity bullshit. I balled myself into a fist, counted to four, straightened out, and shook my legs. Damn. Mobility problems. Too much crap. Which, naturally, the SBS guys called "systems." Of course, gear doesn't weigh anything once you're in the water, but there's still a limit to how many protuberances you want on your eighteen square feet of body surface. The closed circuit rebreather—which didn't make any tattletale bubbles—was lighter than a normal tank, but it was big, and they'd loaded me up with all this other gear, including a full-face mask by Ocean Reef—I think we can call it a helmet—with unslashable woven steel hoses and securing straps around your forehead so enemies couldn't yank it off. There was also a night-vision system with protruding flylike eyes that swiveled in and out of my field of view. It seemed jerry-rigged and jury-built, and my whole left forearm was covered with what looked like a black-jade scaled wrist cuff, with the OLED screen and big keys with excitingly geometrically styled raised icons. The trickiest deal on it was the synthetic aperture LIMIS, that is, Limpet Mine Imaging Sonar. The speakers were on the *Gotengo,* of course, but each of us could see the picture on our heads-up screen, shifted so that it corresponded to our own point of view. Supposedly the pings were disguised, and too low for most countersonar systems to hear anyway. Still, the resolution was great. You could see, or rather hear, a beer can on the ocean floor a quarter-mile away. Then there was the adaptive-beamformer communications system, and the beacon system that ID'd and located me, which also included five 'trodes taped to my chest that monitored my heart rate and blood pressure and, for all I knew, my sperm count. And they'd mandated those new tiny thin superspringy fins that kill your knees, and then the worst thing was that the supposedly ballistic wetsuit was way too stiff. Don't worry about it. Breathe. Ahh. Okay. Depth fourteen feet, temp sixty-four degrees, and pressure 1.3 ATM. Check, check, and check. Location, 17.22° North, 63.1° West. Current, east by northeast at five miles per hour. Littoral floor depth, thirty-one feet. Estimated travel time to the reef was creeping up on fifty minutes. I squinted at the heads-up display. It showed a hundred-foot area in three dimensions, on an xyz axis with me at zero. There were four views, like on 3-D AutoCAD software. And right now it showed way too many blips. Lots of snapper around. I switched it to standard mode, which was supposed to edit out anything under shark size, and everything disappeared except the six blue dots for the other divers and the big green one for the *Gotengo.*

Djoong djoong dhoong djoong, Megalon went. Get in formation, he meant. *Djoong djoong djoong djoong.* I finned myself to the right and forward. Three blips came up even with me, as though I were the leader, although I wasn't. Ana was the nearest on my left and Megalon was nearest on the right. *Breeeeep,* Ana's wrist thing went in my ear. It meant, "Jiga here, all okay." I hit two keys meaning "Jed_3 here, all okay." The others sounded off.

Get ready to rumble, I thought. A flock of sphinx moths fluttered around in my stomach.

Even when we got close to the targets, and even though the system knew Jed_1's height and weight, they probably wouldn't be physically different enough for us to tell one from another. Which was the reason we weren't carrying underwater firearms, although they do make guns that shoot steel rods instead of bullets and Megalon even had some. But there wasn't any point when the mission was to bring the subject back very alive. So that was that.

Yesterday we'd gone over our moves with one of us holding the target from behind and the other tying him up, I could at least see how it could be done. In fact, they said, more manpower would be superfluous. Still, there—

Gonnng!

It meant everybody was ready and all was clear. There was a pause and then it gonged again, higher, meaning "Let's go." I twisted the handlebar and felt the vibration of the silent propeller and, sluggishly, the DPV started to move, dragging me behind it. Forward, I thought. Once more into the breechclout. Stick your courage in the screwing place. I settled into the slipstream. The ridged silt bottom scrolled under me faster and faster. A school of emerald-green palometas darted in front of us and turned around and away, in sync, like trained pigeons. Forward. The current seemed stronger than the arm thing said it was. Or maybe I'd just gotten soft. Spending all that time counting money. During the test runs the SBS guys had been pretty dismissive of my diving skillz. But since they'd all spent more than a couple tours defending our freedom by slogging through ninety-degree half-crude-oil diarrhea in the Persian Gulf and digging unexploded ordnance out of boiling wreckage, I'd tried to take it in stride. Thank God Marena didn't have enough diving experience to play SEAL. Still, she'd refused to stay onshore.

Come on. You can do this. No sweat, blood, or tears. Forward! Forward drag! Trails of water swooshed around me like Japanimation speed lines. When you head into pure blackness you start to feel that you're not going horizontally, but falling. Moving, moving . . . youch.

Damn. Still having crotch trouble. Ignore, ignore.

Okay. Think. Jed$_1$'s boat's set up for diving. So the support line'll probably come off the windward side. The port side. Hmm.

Mainly by luck, the two guys Ana called her "conventional tecs"—that is, digital-and-paper-trail investigators—had gotten us a good picture of the

Megalon. They'd gone over a list of all the over-thirty-footers registered in Jed$_1$'s "active zone," the area he could reach in less than a day of surface travel, and they'd come up with sixty-eight possible boats and their locations. And I'd just cross-checked those with the biomaps and in less than five minutes I'd picked out the right reef. It was a not-very-well-known stand of *Dendrogyra cylindricus,* that is, pillar corals, which are food sources for a few types of nudibranchs, including *Lasidorus greenamyeri,* the possibly eusocial type that Johnny Greenamyer had first described in the June issue of the *Journal of Malacological Studies*. Anyway, then Ana's tecs interviewed some local skippers and they'd said that most of the reefs had died over the last ten years but there was a half-mile or so at the southern end of one of them, three miles offshore, that was still alive and almost pristine. Then the ex-SBS people had taken the *Gotengo* out there and after only forty minutes of eavesdropping Ogra's voice print had turned up on the wave-form monitor.

We were all pretty thrilled, considering. Megalon was glad that Jed$_1$ would be diving and not just sunbathing on deck. "It's a lot safer to grab him underwater," he said. "Most of the issues occur during boarding attempts." Also, when he'd asked whether it was possible that Jed$_1$ would kill himself rather than get captured, I'd said it was a possibility. So they didn't want to give him any time.

Megalon said that in the old days—meaning, say, ten years ago—it would have been tough to pinpoint a human target in such a large area of dark ocean. But now the Boat Service was using piezoelectric transducers that sent the data to a Kurzweil program that zeros in on human-made sounds, specifically on the distinctive rhythm of UBA breathing. Unless they held their breaths, we'd know where they were.

The *Blue Sun* wasn't a known smuggling boat and nobody on board was likely to be armed. Even so, Ana had started off insisting that I couldn't go along, and there'd been a lot of back-and-forth about how my Sacrifice Game skills were too valuable to warrant putting me at risk and everything. But I kept sticking to my spiel about how my Game stuff wouldn't be valuable for very long if the whole planet got sucked into nonexistence, and how Jed$_1$'s interrogation was still in the future, and if something went wrong with it we'd need all the other information we could get. If Jed$_1$ spotted us and got back to his boat and we had to try to negotiate, he'd respond better to me than to anyone else. Maybe he'd even let us take him in. Or even if Jed$_1$ resisted to the bitter end, he still might blurt out something to me that he wouldn't say to other people, or—and of course this was grabbing at straws—maybe I'd just notice something that the others wouldn't pick up on, something in his behavior that might give us a wisp of a hint of a ghost of a clue to the Domino Cascade.

Falling behind. Keep up. I twisted the left handlebar for a burst of speed and got back into the formation. Come on. Run silent, run deep. My heads-up display said we'd gone two thousand and fifty feet, so the *Blue Sun* was three hundred thirty-four feet away. Megalon sent out a series of short, A-flat beeps repeating a 2-3-2, 2-3-2 pattern. Damn, forgot what that meant. Getting groggy. I touched the SONIC CODES LIST button on my Dick Tracy Two-Way Wrist TV. DESCEND, it said. I let some gas out of the buoyancy compensator and sank about ten feet. There was that cozy feeling of the sea hugging me closer. If you could just stay down here, you wouldn't need the Celexa. Ahhhhh.

Around here the tips of the corals were usually about twenty feet from the high-tide surface, so Jed$_1$ would probably be down at this level or lower. Or he—

Bling grong, Megalon said. Time to switch off the headlights. We all slowed to a crawl. Jeddo-Sub-One probably wouldn't even turn on his spotlight. It's better to check out the nudis in the natural chemoluminescence of the ambient plankton. I switched off the lamp and the night-vision goggles automatically swung into position on the front of my mask, lighting up the silty seabed in that granular green.

Hmm. Not okay, I thought. "Not okay," I beeped. The rows of red numbers on my mask's heads-up display were way too bright. I fiddled with the keys. Hell. It'd take me more than a minute to type out the whole question "How do you turn down the bloody lights in your eyes?" in words. The keys were big, of course, like on a toddler's keyboard, and each one had a distinctive shape that you could pick out with your fingertip, which, by the way, you could easily slip in and out of a slit in the thoughtfully designed electrically warmed glove. But the damn thing was still impossible. Should've brought slates. More than half the time new gadgets just slow you down. I typed another likely command. Nothing. *Breep djoong breep,* Megalon went in my ear, telling me to get it together. *Breep breep breep breep breep,* I typed back, meaning, roughly, wait a goddamn second. Jeez, this show's running Marena about fifteen thousand dollars a minute, she'd just said she'd sold her last points in the movie, including sequels, video, most of the computer-game rights that weren't based on the earlier Neo-Teo world, and she was still going into debt, so financially, at least, the EOE would work out for her, and then you don't even tell us—

Oh, Okay. Got it. I dimmed the heads-up so that I could barely see it and ran through two reps of rage-abatement breathing. Cancel, cancel. Everybody's doing their best. They're professionals, they're doing a good job, you're doing a good job, you're capable, you're resourceful, and people like you. Okay.

I smell 'branchs, I thought. Can't see anything that small, though.

Hmm.

On my heads-up display the six blue dots, my own team, were forty feet west, that is, behind me. Adequately close, I thought. The divers from the *Blue Sun* were too far away to separate and were just one big orange dot.

I switched off the night vision.

Making things out on a lampless night dive is like—hmm. Well, if you've done it, it's like that. Otherwise I guess it's a bit like standing at an open door in the dark with the light behind you and calling your dog, and somewhere he turns around and, maybe not over-hurriedly, ambles back, and you first make out the dirty emerald green of his eyeshine. Here I could just glimpse the peaks of a few digitate spires, the foothills of the sierra of sleeping coral.

Closer. Hold still.

Nudibranchs.

In the barely two lumens of light they looked dull blue with black stripes, almost exactly like *Tambja mullineri.*

But they were moving differently from any 'branchs I'd seen before. Almost like a school. I dropped one of my two-pound weights and let myself drift in the school's—or schoolette, or I guess we can call it a class—I let myself drift in the direction they were headed, southeast, toward the tip of the reef. A little tune, soft but angry, started up in my ear, meaning that I was letting myself get unforgivably separated from the rest of the team. If—

Hmm. Orange dashes on my mask screen. What does that mean? No, wait, they're out there. Streaks of lights, evenly spaced, and not—

Whoa. It was the support line from the *Blue Sun*, marked with a glowstick every fathom. Yikes. I put the DPV into reverse, backed up twenty feet, angled the thing down, and descended ten feet, toward where I guessed the anchor would be—

BEEP. DONG. DONG-DANG, BEEP.

Danger.

(90)

On the heads-up screen the three orange-for-hostile dots had separated into a wide triangle, with the closest vertex about twenty feet off. But they were also blinking, which meant that the divers' locations were only approximate.

Coral giant's-fingers about three yards high. Down another five feet. Colder. Following an undercurrent. I used the old trick of making my eyes like a microscope, crawling over the coral as if it were feeding time, going at it as if I were sucking out the polyps. A little on the late side, I was realizing that Sic's unfamiliar body wasn't used to diving, and wasn't responding the way my original body would have, and so my kicks were awkward and out of sync with my amateur-night spasmodic-ass breathing. I focused on my heads-up display. The rest of the team was falling behind. The farthest of the dots was in a hard-to-read cluster that might have been hostiles. What were they up to? Still dealing with the guards? From the beeping I guessed that they thought I'd ditched my minder intentionally. But why weren't they talking to me? Was I getting set up by my own team? No, too elaborate. They could've gotten rid of me anytime they wanted. Maybe one of them was working for the other side—some other side—and was going to assassinate me? It didn't seem reasonable. More likely, the guard is more trouble than they'd thought. Or maybe some other people from Jed$_1$'s boat had showed up? That would explain the dot—

Huh.

There was a dark shape against the dull green coral. In wordless thought and in less than a second, I realized that he was less than five feet away, that he was facing me, that he saw me, and that he was reaching toward me, and, not from his masked face or his head, which was hooded, but just by some hitch in his movement that was as unmistakable and indescribable as the signature rhythm of your mother's footsteps, I knew that it was Jed_1.

And almost before I knew it, we seemed to be hugging each other, slipperyly. I dropped my DPV but the harness was still attached. I got a hand on him. I couldn't stop thinking of the scene in one of the later Oz books where the Tin Woodman meets his head. Don't get distracted. That's your problem, Jed, you're always fuguing into a digression at the worst possible— Cancel that. Keep your eye on the bling. Supposedly it was another pretty big problem people had in combat, where they start thinking about some book or running some song they like or whatever and the next thing you know you're sticking your head out of your trench. Coolitz, I thought. Strength and guile, I thought. In fact just guile.

Where was the rest of our team? Damn, the DPV was dragging us down. I managed to get my left hand in there and get the 'bener off and detach myself and slip partly loose from Jed_1. There was mist in my mask now and I couldn't see the heads-up stuff clearly, but I could still infer from the shapes and from the sound cues that Jed_1 was finning the two of us away from the rest of the divers, his and mine, away from the reef, out into the deep water. I followed. I guess it's pretty bathetic to say it was weird, but it was, I mean, there was this person with my mannerisms and my face, who was more obviously me than I was—

Click. He'd found my channel on his com link.

"You got me," Jed_1 whined in my old voice. He kicked away from me.

"Come on in," I said. "Seriously, they won't torture you, they—"

He dove, deep. I followed. He's killing himself, I thought. He'll get down to sixty or so and then pull his mask off and blow up his head. It's a quick way to go, like a hand grenade.

Going down, it gets dark fast. But the pressure tightens up even faster. A crunch echoed through my head with a noise like Serpentine Glacier calving into Prince William Sound. Breathe, I thought. I breathed. I already felt like a cork in a wine bottle. Breathe. Down. Breathe. Actually, the rebreather should work better lower down. Except Jed_1 might've packed some deep-sea nitrox mix just in case. If he did, then he'll do better. Down.

"This is so fucked up," I said, in that Alvin-and-the-Bathymunks falsetto you get below four fathoms.

"Yeah," he agreed.

I got the light on him. I blasted what air was left out of my buoyancy compensator. I finned down. There.

I got him.

It wasn't a fight. At best it was a grapple. Maybe because long ago I'd read too much doppelgänger fiction, I'd expected it to feel like I was fighting with a mirror image of myself, but it didn't, and not just because he wasn't reversed. He'd changed. He had short hair. And there was the mask. And his expression, from the little I could see of it, was so I don't know what . . . and I'd do something and he wouldn't, and then he'd strike out with his left hand, say, and I'd catch myself trying to do the same with my right hand, as though somehow the right thing to do was to keep up with the mirror theme, but then I'd realize how stupid that was. Just stick to the factuals. Just keep him here, keep him away from the boat, Ana's going to get here any second, she knows what to do, just hang on. I hit him in the stomach but I wasn't sure it had a lot of effect. There was a sort of bonk on my mask. Yeowch. Salty. Hell. Blood. I'd bitten off a little part of my cheek. Damn it. Supposedly there were hammerheads in the area, and they'd come in shoreward at night. And they're like aquatic tracking hounds. If there was even a thread of the shit leaking out of my mask they'd be able to smell it all the way to Cuba. Yum yum, guys. Hell—

Jed_1 twisted and nearly got free. My left hand hung on. I finned and got my right hand onto his belt. Hang on. Regroup. Okay.

Attack.

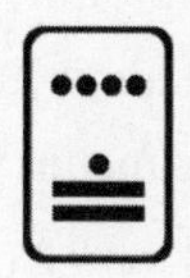

(91)

And I guess the deal is that when you fight with someone at the terminal level, when you're really trying to kill, when you finally contact flesh and really get your hands in there, they seem so delicate and squooshy, and you can feel them react to the pain, and so if you're not a natural sadist, which I guess this proved I wasn't, you naturally pull your punches. Except you can't pull back. In my overactive but currently not-terribly-original imagination he still seemed like he was me, like I was fighting a gooey mirror, and that made it—

Oops. Nearly got away there. Hang on. Just another minute. Hang. On. Ha. Ng. Where were they? The cavalry wasn't showing up. And we were still going down. Even through the thick neoprene the water here felt about ten degrees below zero. Sic's body was bigger and stronger, but he wasn't a diver, so the deeper we got, the less well I could deal with it than the good old Jed_1 body could.

I yelled into my microphone. *"Where the shit are you?"* It came out like "Warashuvarrooo?" Too late I realized that I hadn't closed the other channels, so now Jed_1 and Jed_1's guards and the people on Jed_1's boat and everybody between here and Key West could hear me loud and clear and knew I was desperate and alone.

Brop. We sank. *Brop.* Ow. Another sinus popping. *Brop.*

Sinking. Eight fathoms. Nine. Brop brop brop brop. Ten. Oh, hell.

He's not committing suicide, I realized. He's planning to kill me this way. He'll let the pressure immobilize me, and then he'll clip a weight to me and wave good-bye, and I'd sink down and—and where the fuck were they? Just leaving me. Lazy bastards. Setting me up to get killed so that they wouldn't have to do it themselves, so they'd have a record and witnesses of somebody else doing—no, no. Cancel. Paranoia is not your friend in moments like this . . . except that it's starting to seem pretty fucking plausible, they weren't here, they weren't—

BRORK. Ow, shit. That smarts. Damn. Get his weights, I thought. And I got one hand on one of them, but then his hand got onto mine, and held it. And there was a weird sort of pause. I held his leg with my leg. I got my other hand into his belt. If you can't get the weights, then just hang on, I thought. They'll get here. If—

"I'm still scared," Jed_1 said.

"What?" I responded automatically. "You mean like—"

Oof. He'd gotten me in the stomach. I backed up, that is, toward the surface, and got hold of an ankle. Just stay on that. "You mean of, of . . . of, of, of dying," I said.

"Yeah," he said. He kicked. It seemed that his foot connected with my right hand, but I couldn't be sure.

"Then . . . *stop it.*" He kicked again. "Damn it, Other Jed, stop jabbing at me." I couldn't help smiling.

I clawed up, or down, over his body, past the belt and onto his harness's cross-chest strap. Despite the cold, and in spite of all the other gazmos and gidgets sticking out, I felt that he had an erection. I nearly got level with his mask. His hands were on my gas hose, trying to disconnect it, but it was a SEAL-grade product made for just this sort of thing, and he couldn't do it. He twisted away again. He was as slippery as a giant nudibranch, and this time he pulled free. Through mainly pure luck I got the light on him and watched him fin down into the trench. Hell. I swam after him. My right leg felt weirdly warm. I got to him again. His fin got me in the face but my helmet/mask stayed on. I got his ankle, and then his knee, and then the other knee.

There was kind of a lull. Obviously both of us were completely exhausted and it was like we'd agreed to take a break.

"You know," he said in his own falsetto, "even if you do . . . get the Domino . . . it'll . . . it will just mean that . . . you and Marena'll spend . . . what time you . . . have left in . . . a . . . cage."

"Really?" I asked. Was that a clue? I wondered. *BPOK.* Ow. Sinuses popping. Pressure, pressure. Well, at least I now knew what those eight great tomatoes in that little bitty can felt—

Sprooong.

Pain. Twitch. Agggh. Oxygen toxicity convulsion. Ow, ow, it hurts, it really hurts. Where were they, where were they, where were they, where were they, where were they, where were they, where were they, *WHERE WERE THEY?!?!?!?!????* And was I floating up? Yes. I'd gotten the weights off. Surface, here we come. Too fast, though. *BPOK.* Ow. Ow and ow. So, I thought, if I'm heading into a world of pain, he must be heading into a zillion universes of agony. My hand definitely wasn't working right. Where were they? The water temperature felt around absolute zero. Was I really bleeding that much? Or was it some fear thing? Well, serves you—him—whoever—right. Bastard. Ow. There must have been floodlights because I could see. The good guys, finally? If so they were too late, too late, too late, I was dead, he was dead, everybody on earth was dead, too late, too late, too late, because now I could see his silhouette against the dark green water, except it wasn't a human silhouette, it was like some giant sort of black Siamese squid with way too many tentacles. Ow, fuckfuckfuck. I could feel the blood in my toes and fingertips starting to boil. We rose ten feet and now I could see that the tentacles were Jed$_1$'s blood. He'd gotten cut somewhere, somewhere exposed outside of the somewhat self-healing properties of neoprene, and the difference in pressure was squeezing the stuff out of him like a tube of toothpaste open at both ends. Eeks. The hemophiliac's worst fear. I almost thought I saw a glimpse of his face, that is, my face, with an expression like he was looking at his dying child, if he'd had one. Almost a disgusted expression. By two fathoms after that, my own mask had filled with blood too. Somehow I got it off. Hold breath, I thought, but I couldn't, and I inhaled a burning snake of seawater. This has got to be it, I thought. Good-bye, Columbethius. Bye, bye, Birdie. Hello, Deathy, well hel*lo*, Deathy. Just break the news to Mother. Cruel world anyway. So—

Owch. There were claws lifting me from behind. Maybe I was going to live long enough to at least experience the shame of how badly I'd fucked up. It felt like a year since I'd spotted Jed_1. Which meant it was at least ten minutes. What the hell had gone wrong? I mean besides everything else—Ow, ow. Can't deal with this bends thing. Ow. They pulled me on board and set me facedown on a sort of stretcher. I threw up. Since I was still thinking I was going to die from pressure poisoning, about all I could do was focus on the kind of cross-hatching in the gray textured linoleum, with ripples of what looked like strong tea—diluted blood—washing over it. After all the water and, it seemed, some of my intestines, had been ejected, they turned me on my back. I got a glimpse of Jed_1 lying next to me. He didn't look good. I noticed that I could hear my teeth chattering, and meaningless talking—I wasn't thinking clearly enough to understand what they were saying, so it sounded like it was in a language I didn't know—and then heard a buzz and felt another buzz in my right calf and then figured out they were the same thing, electric scissors cutting through my suit. A female hand—Lisurate's?—was holding a sort of cup thing over my groin, that is, on the left side of my doodads. Fuckshitfuck fuckdamshit, I thought. Evidently I'd been too hopped up on O_2 and adrenaline to notice at the time, but the little weasel must've stabbed me with his dive knife. Going for the femoral artery. Which, if he nailed it, would have done me in within three minutes. So much for the bullshit reinforced wetsuit. Which I'd known wouldn't work for shit. Ow. This sucks. Ouch. Jeezus. I'm not supposed to die like this. I'm a movie star, for crying out loud.

"Fear," Dr. Lisuarte's voice said. Fear of what? I wondered. Next to me Jed_1's body half-clenched like a big fist and then relaxed again.

Oh, *clear*. Why do they say that? I noticed that they'd already hooked me up to a baggie of Tony Sic's white-cell-enriched B+ plus Special Blend, which Dr. L had thoughtfully had me autodonate four days ago.

Well, hell. That was it. I was gone, I thought, or rather he was gone, or rather the world was gone, soon to be gone, anyway. I'd screwed up. Big-time. Biggest-time. *Todo por me culpa.* All my fault. I'm the biggest fuckup in all creation. Yep. Since the Big Bang itself, no entity in the universe had ever fucked up quite so utterly as I had. I heard the boat's motor shift into first gear, and about two minutes after that I heard Dr. Lisuarte's voice talking to the shore crew on the phone, confirming that Jed_1 was dead.

(92)

The only thing that can ever be good about any hospital room is that it can be private, as this one was. In fact, this one was so private that it was even quiet. Sinisterly quiet, of course. I was already pretty sure I was in a forensic wing.

"How life-threatening is it?" I asked, trying to sound butch in front of Marena. Despite the fact that Sic's body was younger, fitter, and handsomer—well, let's say conventionally handsomer, catalog-handsomer—and also hemophilia-free, I still wanted my original body back, even just to say good-bye to it. I'd cried about it more than once.

"Not," Doctor Lisuarte said. "Decompression grade two. However, your right arm is going to be in that cast for at least a month." She explained that it was just the index metacarpal, but that it was shattered into four pieces and needed a lot of stability.

Finally they left. I could tell when the door was open that it was the forensic wing. There was a nonopenable square of nonbreakable "glass" looking out into a "courtyard" made of that 1960s-era icky white brick studded with air conditioners. Straining my head up I could see floors above and below. I guessed we were at least five floors up.

I was groggy, and not in a pleasant way. My groin picked now to start aching. There were puncture wounds all over my body, which would still take a while to heal, even these days.

And of course I was tightly guarded. They wouldn't even let me have any of my own phones or laptops, only Warren-approved versions that were impossible to take apart and filled with all kinds of nannyware.

The SBS people had interrogated the captured guard to see if Jed_1 had said anything. They'd also stormed the boat looking for intel. After going through hard drives, and sweating the crew, they came up dry.

Well, let's see, I thought. So the actual end of the earth will be the opposite of the bangs-and-whamos Jerry Bruckheimer version. There won't be any fires, explosions, cartwheeling aircraft carriers, or cities flooded to the thirtieth floor. It'll be the definition of unspectacular. It'll be over in a fraction of a second. And nobody will even notice.

Hmm. So . . .

Without Jed_1 to tell us what he'd done, how would we even know that the last domino wouldn't fall early, like, say, now? We didn't.

How did we know that this instant wouldn't be the last, that two seconds from now we all wouldn't exist and wouldn't notice that we didn't? I tried to think of each moment that passed with us still here as a little victory. We went around and around.

At one point I said, "It'll be like—the thing it'll be most like is just, when something distracts your attention from whatever it was on previously, and you forget what you were thinking about. Except not even that much."

Taro said, "Not only will it not hurt . . . but one will not even notice it."

"But somebody on, like, Io, who was looking at the earth, that person would notice it," I said. "Although he'd disappear, too, in whatever minutes." There was a feeling of oddity in the conversation, something about how we were racing to stop something that, if it happened, we wouldn't even notice. Keep it real, I thought. It's real. It's a real threat. Focus.

"We will know *if* we have stopped it," Taro said. ". . . But if we do not stop it . . . we will not know."

"Kind of the physics equivalent of flesh-eating bacteria."

"Hmm?"

"I mean, it's going to reach a certain probability in there and then it'll just suck in everything, you, me, the Grand Canyon, Jupiter, the Horsehead Nebula, the Sombrero Galaxy, the Roy Rogers Cometary Globule, everything."

"No, no," Marena said, "I'm not buying that, whatever Jed-Sub-One did in there, it's not going to blow up everything, that's ridiculous."

"No, you're wrong, it *will* blow the, the—it'll blow the universe *in,* not *up*."

So, now Marena and I, without all the resources of the Warren Corporation, worked to identify the Domino Cascade. Marena'd hoped the Game would work again, maybe better than it had worked before, Marena smuggled eight full doses of tsam lic into the forensic wing. On the first night I took two doses and followed Jed_1's last clue. After a lot of false starts I started to see patterns that I thought could be links in the Cascade. Surprisingly, or maybe not so surprisingly, given who set it up, they tended to cluster around Warren Corporation–related events. The Game also helped me make sense of the wealth of code-breaking programs you can get these days, and it wasn't too hard to get into at least the outer directories of some of their defense-contracting divisions. After a few hours I'd grabbed eight terabytes of data. At dawn I started the Hard Part—separating the cream from the milk, uh, the wheat from the chaff, the ideas from the clichés . . .

It turned out that, because of accelerating troubles with Pakistan—combined with a U.S. military that, thanks to the social unrest "Stateside," was now barely usable overseas—DARPA had commissioned an accelerated testing schedule for a piece of Warren-proprietary "neoartillery" called RABS. The machine "followed the trend toward basing real weapons on 1950s-era science fiction"—notably battle bots, acoustic ordinance, the death maser, and the heat ray. RABS, which stands for "Remote Atomization Battlefield System," was, according to the highly classified but still-in-adspeak brochure, "rather like a disintegrator." The "cover explanation" for this acronym was "Reliability, Availability, Bang-for-the-buck, and Scalability."

After another dose, I was able to intuitively check the math on the reactions required for the RABS to a degree that no one else, not even the cadre of particle physicists on the Warren payroll, had done so far. I calculated that instead of a one-in-ten-thousand chance of destroying the entire world (which, characteristically, the corporation found well worth taking), the very first RABS test, scheduled for December 19, had a one-in-one chance. Evidently Jed_1 discovered the same thing, and then constructed the Domino

Cascade by working backward from this relatively "easy access" doomsday event. All the way back to buying a few corn futures.

Unfortunately, the test didn't require any unique equipment—that is, there were at least fifty particle accelerator facilities in the world that are capable of performing it, and it was too close to the test date to investigate them all. I kept moving ahead anyway, though. At the last moment, as the tsam lic peaked, I managed to remember what Koh's ghost had told me on the Tree.

The ring, I thought. The racetrack. It's a supercollider. A secret one at the Stake, underneath the circular racetrack that surrounded the Hyperbowl complex. And they were using it to test the RABS.

Well, huh.

Normally this would have been good news, since Lindsay would be able to stop the test there himself without having to convince anyone else in the company to give up the contract. Over the next two days, using relayed phones and e-mails, Marena, and Taro and I tried to convince him.

Boyle, certainly, didn't believe us at all.

"He believed in Madison," I said, at 2:00 A.M. She was sitting on the foot of the hospital bed, squnching my foot.

"Yeah, but Madison wasn't on their payroll," Marena said. "Anyway, the State Department's pushing Linseed to do the test."

It turned out that the RABS worked by creating a miniature white hole at a targeted spot on earth—or in outer space, where they did the first couple of tests, or on Io or wherever. The 3-D or 4-D or whatever universe is like the surface of a balloon—I mean, to oversimplify just a little—and the strangelet is letting the air out of it. Eventually it shrinks into a dot and we're screwed. It's like a pinhole in a balloon—this world is like the surface of a balloon floating through higher dimensions. Or you could say that it's letting the air out of our universe, spacewise . . .

Damn. There was still something in a crevice of my mind that I had to remember to remember.

"You know," Marena said, "you're really not going to enjoy hanging out with me if you keep thinking about her."

"Who?"

"Lady Koh."

I said, "Come to think of it, it's true. I guess I've thought about her once or twice a day." Maybe once or twice every hour. Ten minutes. One minute. A lot.

I'd been trying to contact No Way without any success. Lately I'd also been trying to contact Pablo Xoc, the headman from Xcanac, the village near Ix Ruinas—but he seemed to have disappeared.

A lot of things seemed to have disappeared.

Still, the world seemed reasonably durable around us, with carpeting, reasonably tasteful chairs, oceans, trees, plasma screens, mugs emblazoned with our corporate logo, the whole ball of low-melting-point wax. Kind of like the Cantor Fitzgerald offices at the World Trade Center, I thought. Just by virtue of its total banality, everything had an air of permanence. But it was totally illusory, of course. And Marena was increasingly desperate and Lindsay was constantly unyielding.

I reckoned I'd try one last heist.

(93)

I figured I'd run a Game-assisted hack-and-search of Warren files to see if I could find a "lever"—maybe a smoking gun (likely about their human testing) that could be used to blackmail the corporation and force them to stop the test.

I started by snooping through Marena's former division's computer network, using some passkeys she'd snuck in before leaving the company. Immediately, and slightly "ironically," as they use the word these days, I found some files she wouldn't have wanted me to see, videos that confirmed my longstanding suspicion that Marena'd recruited me from the beginning. As my privilege kept escalating, the unanswered questions escalated into vast, intertangled enigmas. One of the oddest was a file showing that Warren's KIMERA Division—a branch of the Firm that I hadn't heard of before—was also evidently interested in nudibranchs, with an installation of five thousand-gallon tanks in a building at the Stake. Did they get the idea from me somehow? Or is it just another synergy? Whatever it was, I didn't have time to stop and investigate this any further, and, reluctantly, I moved on. I found another file that made it look to the reader as though LEON was going to be taking over and running the world, à la *Neuromancer* and its many descendants.

"Look," Marena said, "remember, one thing the Neo-Teo project has going for it is that the Sacrifice Game actually works. You can't say that about Allah."

"I guess not."

"The Game gets your life under control, you're happy and peaceful—or 'placeful,' as they call it—without drugs, you see things coming a mile away, you're instantly part of a simpatico community . . . it's a whole thing. It's *the* whole thing. And it appeals to smart people."

Marena's face had taken on yet another aspect. This time she looked as though she was standing in extreme cold, not chattering, but freezing, and suddenly unconscious that anyone else was in the room.

"You mean, like, religion doesn't?"

"Heh. Well, you got me there."

Marena left to see Max in a school production of *Seascape* and said she'd be back in two hours to deal with the Apocalypse. I put in an order at Porlock's Artisinal Charcuterie, took a hot shower—as close as I could get to a proper sweat bath around here—and took three full doses of tsam lic. Following the offering formula I'd learned in Olde Mayaland, I pierced my skimpy, mutilated half-foreskin—a difficult thing for me to make myself do, because of my early history of hemophilia—with an ancient jade artificial stingray spine, polished by forty generations of hands and genitals, that had been a gift from Hun Xoc, and which (along with the 9 Death pot and a few other mementi) was among the few items from Jed_2's tomb that I still had. I scattered, or—let's say to be fancy, lustrated—the blood onto a petition letter to One Ocelot, which asked for a clear vision in my playing of the Sacrifice Game. I went in the bathroom, disabled the smoke detector, turned on the exhaust fan, and burned the letter in a dish of (smuggled) charcoal and copal. As the drug began to bring on its special brand of awareness, I slipped on a new type of Warren ultralite data-glove (which they were planning to market as the "Holopaw") and called up the on-screen version of Ix Professional, which, as in Taro's lab, had also been integrated with most major programming languages and search engines.

"Teech Aj Chak-'Ik'al la' ulehmb'altaj 'uyax ahal-kaab Ajaw K'iinal . . ." I said, rooting myself in the software. "You, Hurricane, who sparked Lord Heat's first dawning . . ."

This time, even though I was still casting the skulls and sending out a runner—both of which were now more along the lines of cellular automata than humans, centipedes, or whatever—I wasn't exactly asking the Game a question about the Unrevealed. Instead, right now I was using it as a sort of combination decrypter and next-generation search engine, something that would let me hack into Warren's network and lead me through its masses of data to what I wanted to find. I don't think anyone who wasn't using the Game could even have gotten a three-digit foot in the door. But with it, I managed to work my way through several layers of encryption to the company's primary secure server and to a long list of "auxiliary assets," which seemed to be like a shareholders' report, but too dirty for the actual shareholders to see. At first there was so much to look through that I had to guess where to start. The Warren Group's holdings included companies dealing in "everything from aerospace to zooplasty"—including, I noticed, a shell corporation that owned a controlling piece of Executive Solutions, "making at least that part of the deal nicely in-house." I tried these files under "Lindsay Warren." An index came up that included a list of all the meetings Lindsay attended personally. I searched the transcripts of this list for the phrase *Parcheesi Project.* The first file in the results was dated 11/01/01. I opened its first video component, "Introductory Remarks by LSW."

On the screen I saw Lindsay standing at a lectern in front of a giant video wall flashing news clips, PowerPoint pie charts, and other trappings of early-twenty-first-century corporate presentations.

"Since Nine-Eleven," Lindsay said, now in front of a slow-motion video of the imploding towers, "there has been a realization—at the highest level—that America needs a new warrior ideology, one that can compete directly with Islam's.

"As many of you know, in our own participations in these discussions, we've stressed that images of the Stars and Stripes and Uncle Sam and stories about George Washington weren't going to do the trick." The picture behind Lindsay faded to one of marching mujahideen. "All that fooferaw was too associated with oldsters, too easy to make fun of. Basically it just wasn't sexy. What we need on this ranch is something more stylish. More mystical. More youthy."

The image behind Lindsay changed to the great Ciudadela pyramid at Chichen Itza.

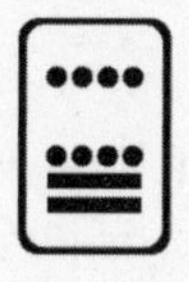

(94)

"Now, in our last presentation to the Joint Chiefs, which I don't need to tell you went very, very well, we made the case that the Boy Scouts had the right idea, using Native American words and concepts . . . but of course even us Eagle Scouts never really knew what we were talking about."

There was a scattering of polite laughter.

"But today," Lindsay said, "we can pick it back up and take it farther than it's ever been, utilizing every one of our areas of expertise—new media, old media, postmedia media, psychotechnology . . ."

So, I saw, Lindsay hadn't first become interested in the Sacrifice Game because he was an investor in computer-game companies or because of the Mormon mythology about pre-Columbian America. Rather, in the months following the attack, the Pentagon had wanted to investigate ways of instilling a "suicide ethic" in soldiers to parallel that of the jihad. They'd already sponsored studies of suicide-bomb cultures and other microsocieties where self-immolation is still a primary virtue, and found that "a touch of martyrdom" makes these societies much more stable, much less internally contentious, and more energetic in achieving their goals—basically, more powerful. The idea was to "harness a terrorist mindset for an antiterror agenda." And in their bid for the next phase of the study, the Warren group had argued that the American Indian "cultures of austerity" were even more hard-core than the Islamist ones. After they won the contract, the team went looking for "the symbols that made them tick," and came across Taro's work on Parcheesi/patolli.

As was fairly well known at the time, DARPA was already funding highly speculative research, most of it still dealing with remote viewers, or psychics. But by '03 this seemed to have hit a dead end and the Defense Department redirected several billions of research dollars to several companies, including Warren, which were experimenting with "more up-to-date exotica," or "outside-the-box solutions to global terrorism." These included long-term simulation, consciousness transfer, singularity projection, and other inquiries into the possibility of stopping terrorist or rogue military strikes before they happened. And as I already knew, Taro's weather-simulation research had already been partly funded by the Joint Chiefs' SAGA (Studies, Analysis, and Gaming Agency). So, I guessed, when Lindsay read the report on the Sacrifice Game, he must have felt that a number of diverse strands were coming together—in a way that to someone like him may have suggested a divine agenda.

At any rate, starting in 2005, my own name begins to come up frequently. It appears in over two thousand files compiled at that time, some going back beyond my first meeting with Michael Weiner to Guatemalan court documents on the going back to the massacre of Jed's village. Apparently the Parcheesi Project had been keeping close track of me (as well as several other possible candidates) for a long time. There were recordings of Taro working on the Game with me when I was still in high school. After a few minutes of snooping, I found a file of the first time I met Marena. As I suspected at the time, her phone was recording everything. I watched my own face peering down into it as I studied the pages of the Codex and then watched myself leave for the bathroom as Marena made a videoconference call. The call was to Lindsay.

From their conversation it's clear that at least since 2010, when the Codex Nuremberg was first photographed and Lindsay's group first clearly visualized the Parcheesi Project—basically the whole R & D division that investigated the Sacrifice Game—I had been identified as one of five possible persons to get "downloaded" into an as-yet-undetermined subject in

664. Now, in 2012, Marena is telling Lindsay that she thinks I am "absolutely the best one," and tells Lindsay about my Disney World "prediction." Lindsay says he's still "only sixty percent sure about this Game thing, and about five percent confident about this Jed character," but that he'll wait and see what happens.

Naturally, I was quivering with rage; however, I managed to "stay in Gametime" and follow the thread, looking through file after file. After the Disney World Horror—which no one besides us had expected—Marena and her team went into overdrive. Reasoning that I would refuse if they asked me to do what they wanted, Marena manipulated me into volunteering.

Bitch, I thought. Of course it was an auditory hallucination, but it sounded like the mosquito in the room said something like *"We'll get her."*

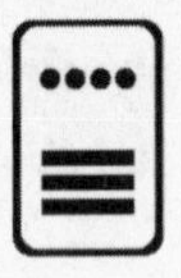

(95)

Marena's deception upset me more than it should have. I knew it anyway, I thought. Just not this much. Not this much. I looked up where she was on the employee locator and found she was on her way home from the school play with Max. I almost called her to confront her, but instead I kept flipping through Jed-rich files, moving on to their "CHOCULA PROJECT—IX—IX RUINAS—EXTRACTION" folder. It contained hundreds of gigs of text and at least eighty hours of video. On the first one, I saw that I was definitely sedated just before the uploading, as they hustled me into the caves while the soldiers arrived. Skimming through the Extraction files, I reconstructed a lot of what had been going on "offstage" during the dig. Evidently a contact of Lindsay's in the Guatemalan military, whom the file identifies as "Felix," convinced the Guate troops to move their training exercises away from the area of the site during the downloading and exploration phases in April. Then, in September, the same person managed to divert military police patrols from the dig zone, allowing the Chocula team to stay undetected as long as it did. However, when the diggers began blasting into the tomb I was buried in—even though they used thunder as cover for the sound—some military satellite detected the explosions' chemical discharges and somehow the information got to Felix's superiors. Felix immediately warned Lindsay and, covering himself, dispatched troops to the site. By this time, it was a foregone conclusion that the core team would have to be extracted by air.

The Hippogriff extraction had been planned to the second, and its probability of failure, it seems, had been worked out to less than one percent. Remote-piloted vehicles, controlled from the Stake, were already fueled and loaded at several hidden airstrips in Belize, ready to launch and take out any aircraft that got too near, and even to clear ground artillery if necessary. It came very close to going off smoothly, and while the two Guate helicopters that unexpectedly intercepted the Hippogriff were a terrible glitch, they never really had a chance. The incident, with the deaths of the officers, had greatly exacerbated the Belize/Guate conflict. Moving on chronologically, I found that two days after most of the Chocula team got safely back to Orlando, Lindsay called a major board meeting of the Warren Group. I pulled up the video. This time Lindsay was sitting at a table with a much smaller group, ten or twelve people, all men, in what looked like the safe room at the Hyperbowl.

"The great religions," Lindsay said, "used every available medium of their time to get their message across. They hired the greatest architects, composers, and artists. Well, in the twentieth century they lost that edge. America, in fact the West in general, or for that matter the world in general, is in the middle of its greatest spiritual crisis since the Reformation. And how is religion responding? Falteringly, feebly, and fragmentarily. No single strong, clear vision has emerged. Well, Warren has been a leader in the spirituality field since the 1970s, and now we're poised to take on the third millennium."

Lindsay went on to mention some other religions, new and old, that have recently begun working seriously with new media and progressive marketers, developing state-of-the-art psychological software to help keep and gain converts. But the Ix franchise, he says, will take this to the next level. "It will provide all the meaning people need, through every medium available." Finally, he said, "Every religion needs a Mecca."

Leaning back in his ErgoChair, Lindsay claimed that his simulations team had used the newly augmented version of the Game to work out a feasibility study in which it was possible for the Stake development to become an autonomous country, sandwiched between the hostile borders of Belize and Guatemala, "the first major designer country not on an island."

"Both countries are pretty destitute," Lindsay said, "and they'd be happy to sell off some land if the moonstone people can come up with justifications that would get the decision by their parliaments. Well, they're going to come to realize that having our Mayan project"—he pronouned "Mayan" to rhyme with "Sayin'"—"and few other boutique states nearby"—he pronounced it "byoo-teek"—"is going to make them bigger, not littler."

I flipped forward through the speech, catching bites here and there. Lindsay said that although this new "private state" will be immensely profitable—and although the online version of Ix II has already become the U.S. military's leading source of psychological referrals for recruitment—the object here is not to use Neo-Teo as a breeding ground for dedicated workers and eager, fearless soldiers. The main motivation, he said, is to create a society "in line with the Warren Predictive Demographics Division's projections for the near future" (which they arrived at partly by using LEON software with the 2011 version of the Game). According to the research team's sociohistorical modeling, world population will continue to increase for at least another fifty years before peaking. Well before that time, however, people of above-average worth will be contracting for various types of "fail-safe life extension: that is, systems that monitor clients' health in real time, and keep them constantly within reach of a dedicated paramedic team that will rush them to a hospital, or, in terminal cases, to mobile cryogenic facilities. In cases of advanced age, the clients will be kept on increasingly sophisticated life-support systems, and dosed with increasingly powerful anti-Alzheimer's and brain-cell regeneration drugs. And all that's nothing," Lindsay said, "compared to new uses of the consciousness transfer protocol, which could, they tell me, go on forever."

As I skated my cursor over the transcript of Lindsay's speech, a link came up to "Neo-Teo/TTT/LDS." Clicking it brought up an even deeper level of lunacy: a third video, also taken in the safe room but this time beginning with Lindsay praying with three other men in front of a DHI altar. In this one, Lindsay's "infectious but paralogistic babbling" is about how the cosmogram of the Game was somehow also the True Cross of the Native American Prophet, the angel Moroni. "And I believe that this is the Stone of Abraham, the Pearl of Great Price that the Prophet Joseph intended us to find," Lindsay says. "After all, the original Urim and Thummim were a pair of dice, or I suppose I should say dreidels. And when we master that great Game of God, surely we will be raised up, as the dross is cast down, raised up live through the Tree of Nephi to the garden of Adam the Christ, to a life everlasting of the body as well as of the soul, to live in Maya and become as gods."

The three men answer, "Amen."

Of course one's natural first reaction to this was that Lindsay was a total crackpot. The obvious second reaction was to remind oneself that this hardly ever matters, and that Saint Paul, Joseph Smith, and Hitler were all even bigger crackpots, and did pretty well for themselves. And the third was to wonder what Lindsay was really talking about, in practical terms. He had to be up to a lot more down there than just building neon pyramids. There was no way he was going to get autonomous state status without being involved in some government thing, some military thing . . .

I searched for *Guatemala, Belize, Chocula, Neo-Teo, Real Estate, Lobbying,* and all possible combinations of those terms. Hundreds of files came up, but even just glancing them I could see that they were all relatively public-consumption stuff. The real dirt had to be somewhere else.

And what did he mean by "Live in Maya?" Well, put a pin in that for now.

I tried searching under *moonstone,* a word of Lindsay's that I remembered hearing before somewhere—although now I couldn't remember where. *Moonstone* didn't work, but when I tried *Moonstones* (dimly recalling that it might be the name of an extinct breakfast cereal), a single folder came up. This one was encrypted under a whole different protocol, with a built-in autoimmune system that would destroy the file if it were accessed without a set of randomizer-card codes. However, after more work with the Sacrifice Game interface, I managed to break through and call up the folder. It had to be the most heavily protected data I'd ever seen or heard of, since there were thousands of decoy files around it and nothing to indicate it to anyone who didn't know exactly the name they were looking for. Even then there were probably only ten or so outside drives that were like Marena's old drive—which she'd cloned before turning in her old one to be destroyed—that belonged to officers of the corporation but weren't inside Warren offices, and that could access it at all. The odds that anybody without my exact skills, motives, and life experience would ever get into it had to be vanishingly small.

At any rate, there were files on secret DARPA contracts going back to 1978, files relating to U.S. State Department black ops in Central America going back to the 1940s. Obviously, Lindsay had a tangle of ties to the military communities in both Belize and Guatemala, not to mention a rogue's gallery of other countries. Whatever the overall goal of the project was, it was clearly ongoing. But at the moment I was only interested in one aspect of it. On an impulse, I searched this batch of files for *Felix AND García-Torres.*

The search flagged over two hundred files. My heartbeat shifted into neutral. I took a Ziploc bag out of my pocket, dug the two still-damp Kleenex wads out of it, and ate them. Gak. Another slug of soda. Ahh. Good to the last drop.

The first file showed that Felix and García-Torres were the same person, the same Corporal Jorge García-Torres, now a commander in the Guatemalan Army Air Corps, who was at the top of my (s)hit list, responsible for my parents' murder in the G2 massacre at my village. It was obvious that he was on Warren's payroll. Damn it. I *knew* it, I finger-fucking knew it! Hot spit. You're a dead guy, I'm going to work this connection until you die screaming, you *fuck*!!!

As I reconstructed it, García-Torres and Lindsay knew each other from way back—at least since the 1970s, when the land that is now the Stake was one of John Hull's training camps for the paramilitary squads who were helping run cocaine for Oliver North's group "under the aegis of Bush the First." Since then, García-Torres—now a commander—had acted as Lindsay's main contact in the Guatemalan military.

Despite the detaching qualities of the tsam lic, my teeth were chattering with rage. I was already getting that blue taste and that ringing in my carapace. I checked in on Marena again. She and Max were in her car, which meant she'd get here in a little over a half an hour if she didn't stop for anything, which she wouldn't. Come on, Jeddidiah. It's in there. Find it. Find it.

(96)

For now I left out No Way's middle names, even though one of them, José, was how he got his nickname. Instead I just searched for QUINONES and XILOX. Eleven files came up. One was a Bosch .dv4 from the day after the downloading, when we were still at Ix Ruinas and I'd still been under some anesthesia. I clicked it open. At first I couldn't tell what the image was, and then it sort of clarified into Grgur's big scalpy head bobbing close to the camera in green greasy grainy enhanced night-vision and a little light from a red-filtered lamp. One of the ugly Alarcón brothers—I couldn't tell whether it was Leonidas or Luis—asked him something about what I guess was Ana's diversionary squad and he said something back, but I couldn't make it out. It was weird how completely I'd missed that whole strain of activity at the time, the patrol coming through and confronting them and everything, it was like I'd had a minilobotomy. Grgur's head moved aside and I could see No Way's face and naked upper body about two meters from the camera, his skin glowing phosphor-gray in the visible darkness.

Uh-oh, I thought. Bad deal. Bad. Bad.

No Way—basically my best friend, and my only real friend who remembered the crazy life—was at an angle on a blanket and a pair of hands was putting a blood-pressure cuff around his upper left arm. There was a sort of thick monocle surgical-taped over one eye and his other eye was taped open. He was wearing a black headband like the one I'd had for the downloading. I was getting that unfun gravityless feeling like the part of your face where you live is still okay but the dorsal side of your body—starting from your back teeth—is all melting away, like that Peter Lorre knockoff at the end of *Raiders of the Lost Ark.* A torso passed in front of the camera and then another hand pulled a drooly bit of tape-wrapped rag out of No Way's mouth. He'd been knocked out and transported. I'd always thought No Way was so alert nobody could ever sucker him. But I guess your own crew can usually get the drop on you. Or maybe even his own communicator or some other piece of equipment had had a remote-fired restraint stunner planted inside it. He started trying to say something but I couldn't hear anything, just Grgur and the Alarcón boys talking about whether they'd found anything. They must have strip-searched him. When the torso moved away I could see that No Way's arms were pinned under big nylon sandbags like Whitefoods. A window came up in the lower right of the screen that said the software and field unit they were using was from Royal Ordnance, which I think is a subsidiary of British Aerospace. The window looked pretty much like the Norton System Doctor interface, except instead of Disk Integrity and everything it had temperature, skin temperature, blood pressure, respiration, muscle tension, "Estimated Voice Stress Level," galvanic skin resistance, electroencephalograph, and a bunch of other exotic readouts. Of course, I couldn't see the controls or anything, but from the one window it seemed like a pretty sophisticated gadget. Electroshock is pretty much the only kind of interrogation device anyone uses these days, since it's so convenient and effective and doesn't leave major marks. But I'd been hearing lately that even with a lot of conductant some of the Amnesty International types were figuring out how to tell if someone had been tortured from collagen calcification or some other histological change in the skin cells. So the deal now was to use pulses of AC voltages at very low amperage, like you were using an old hand-cranked magneto. Then ideally the current wouldn't arc or cause burns. On this particular unit the bar graph went all the way down to fifty volts—which probably wouldn't hurt much more than a good-sized pinch of carpet static—and up to sixty thousand volts, which could cause a heart attack if you weren't healthy. I couldn't see the electrical leads in the shot, but if they were following common practice one would be a large conductor, with a lot of conductant, clipped to the flap of skin between two toes, and the other would have been inserted in his anus or urethra. Leonidas Alarcón bent his head down, made sure No Way was breathing, and then wrapped his mouth and neck in a sort of big puffy yoke made of white rags. No Way's head stuck up out of it like it had sunken halfway into an Elizabethan lace collar. Someone threaded what I guessed was a little microphone into the front of the muffler. No Way would be able to breathe and talk, barely, but if he started yelling it wouldn't be loud. Evidently they weren't far from the site. Where, presumably, the Guate patrol was stomping around.

"No Way?" Grgur's voice said. "It's Grgur. You know who I am, right?"

Someone flicked on the microphone. It picked up No Way's voice pretty well:

"*. . . quia peccavi nimis cogitatione*," he was mumbling, "*verbo et opere: mea culpa—*"

"Come on, don't worry," Grgur said, "we're not going to hurt you, but we do need you to answer a few questions before we take you into detention."

"*. . . beatum Ioannem Baptistam, sanctos Apostolos Petrum et Paulum, omnes Sanctos . . .*"

"Hey. Pancho? You understand? You're getting too uptight about this. Knock it off." They let him finish, though. Maybe they were all too Catholic to zap him in the middle of a confiteor.

"*. . . et vos, fratres, et te, pater, orare pro me ad Dominum Deum nostrum. Amen.*"

I fucked up, I thought. I'd always said I wouldn't trust anybody, and then I'd done it anyway, and once again I'd fucked up royal—

"Good," Grgur's voice said. "Sorry, but I'm going to have to just test this for a second." The voltmeter bar slid up to seven thousand volts and back. No Way's body arched a bit, and there was an exhalation of air, but he didn't scream. If you've felt it, you know that the pain of electricity is like nothing else, it seems to come from within your own body and not from a foreign source. It's like your cells decided to fry themselves. I couldn't help seeing some of the readouts, pupillary size dilating from five millimeters to seven, muscle tension bouncing from sixty-five to ninety and back, galvanic skin resistance—that is, the conductivity of the electrolytes in the skin—going up twenty percent, the whole nine yards. Leonidas Alarcón looked back at the camera, which I guess was just the little teleconferencing lens in the screen frame of Grgur's phone. He listened to the night sounds for a minute.

"Okay," Leonidas said.

"Could you tell us your name, please?" Grgur's voice asked. His voice had a new police-trained ring to it, with less of a Slavic accent than before. He sounded bored but I got the feeling that under that he was in a hurry.

"Hey, you're getting a hard-on," No Way rasped in Spanish. "Check it out, he likes his work."

"Could you tell us your name, please?" Grgur repeated.

"Quiñones Xiloch," No Way said. Maybe he'd decided to get this over with as fast as possible.

"Could you tell us your age, please?"

"Thirty-four."

Grgur paused for a minute, probably watching the readouts. The electroencephalograph seemed to be set to flag peaks, troughs, and unusual concentrations of the sinusoidal alpha waves over different time intervals. Right now it was wavering between 10 and 13 Hz, which I guess polygraph devotees would call normal stress.

"Would you please tell us, what is your primary affiliation or loyalty?" Grgur asked.

"EGP," No Way said. That is, the Ejército Guerrillero de los Pobres, the Guerrilla Army of the Poor.

"Would you list your military affiliations?"

"EGP only."

"Would you tell us your position within that organization?"

"Clase de tropa," No Way said. It was like a noncommissioned officer.

"Would you tell us your serial number?"

"There are no numbers."

Grgur didn't pursue it. Maybe he knew it was true. Anyway, the program recalibrated itself and marked the response as normal.

"Would you please tell us your commanding officer within that organization?"

"Carlos." Carlos was the head of the whole movement, like Marcos had been in southern Mexico in the early nineties, and like Marcos he wore sunglasses and a bandana and nobody knew who he really was. Or whether he was even one person.

"Would you tell us the names of the other officers in your cell?"

"Rodríguez, Infante, Kauffman, Noxac, Rueda."

"None of those check out," Grgur said.

"Then I don't know the real ones," No Way said.

"Would you tell us the names of the other officers in your cell?"

"Rodríguez, Infante, Zaya—"

The voltmeter darted to ten thousand and hung there for 2.1 seconds. No Way's backed arched and bounced and he let out a tiny whistling screech.

"That's bullshit," Grgur said. "Listen. Would you please tell us the name of your contact?"

"Did you come?" No Way asked.

"Who's your current contact?"

"Nestor Xconilha."

"Would you please tell us the name of your current controller?"

"Also Nestor Xconilha."

"Who is your backup?" He meant the person who comes looking for you.

"I have no backup on this job."

"When is your gone-missing date?"

"Today."

"How long will it be before your organization starts looking for you?"

"They may be looking for me now."

"We weren't due to finish until tomorrow."

"I was supposed to report today."

"Who can we contact to back that up?"

"They won't answer any contacts," No Way said.

"What call signals can you give us to help you make the report?"

"No, they won't."

"If we let you make the contact, will you arrange for them to meet us here?"

"Sure."

"I have a problem with your physical readings on that answer," Grgur said.

"You're right, you're right, they won't," No Way said. "That's against policy. They're too careful for that."

"So what would we do then?"

"Meet, uh, prearranged place," No Way said.

"Can I ask where is that?"

"Poptún."

"I don't think that's right," Grgur said. "Listen. You know about the new polygraph feedback software, don't you?" "No," No Way said. He was hoping they'd take time to explain it to them.

"Yes, you do," Grgur said, "we can tell. Even on a trivial question like that one."

"Okay," No Way said. I could tell he knew it was bullshit, though. And I think Grgur could tell that too. Not that the thing wasn't sensitive, but all real interrogators know that no matter how many readings you get, they don't always have much to do with the truth as such. If anything, they have to do with how much the subject expects and fears the next burst of pain. So if he thinks lying's going to avert it, his readings might go down on a lie, not up. But I guess they were hoping to get enough out of all their data back at the ranch. At least on one or two key issues.

"Who should we contact if we have to release you to the Guates' army patrol?" Grgur asked.

"Nobody."

"Who should we contact if you were detained, injured, or killed?"

"Nobody."

"Listen, believe it or not, we're not hostile to you," Grgur said. "We *are* somewhat hostile to the current administration of this country and we had the impression you were too. Is that true?"

"Yes."

"Would you please tell us what your cell knows about this operation?" Grgur asked. At least for now he wasn't pursuing the names thing. Maybe they really weren't after that.

"Do you mean this particular looting expedition?" No Way asked.

"Yes."

"I don't know anything about it myself."

"What does your cell know?"

"They don't know anything, I've been out of contact since August thirtieth."

"Would you please tell us what Mr. DeLanda has told you about this operation?"

"Nothing. Wait, nothing besides your schedule and that you were digging and had to keep it quiet."

"You're sure that's everything?"

"Yes, I even asked whether you were after jade masks or what and he said he wouldn't tell me."

"Can you tell us what you know about the settlement at Pusilha?" Grgur meant the Stake, but I guess he wasn't supposed to call it that.

"I know there's been a lot of real estate bought in the area. By the Morons. Four plantations, water rights . . . that's it."

"Are you sure?"

"They're building landing strips and a control tower."

"What else?"

"That's it," No Way said. He didn't look so good. Since the beginning of the interview his blood pressure had gone from 135 over 80 to 155 over 95, and the pneumograph said his breathing was up to twenty-five breaths per minute.

"Would you please tell us everything Mr. DeLanda told you about the settlement at Pusilha?"

"He didn't tell me anything. Just that you'd come through there. I supposed his employers had something to do with it. But he didn't tell me that."

"Mr. DeLanda tells us you alerted this patrol to our location. Would you like to give us your side of the story on that?"

There was a pause.

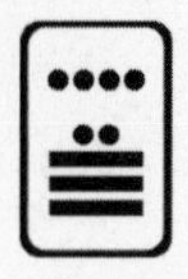

(97)

No Way knew that was a total lie, of course. It was too close to book procedure, trying to make the subject feel betrayed.

"I didn't tell anybody anything."

"So you signaled someone?"

"No. I didn't signal anyone."

"In that case, who do you think alerted the patrol to our location?"

"I don't know."

"Did you alert this patrol to our location?"

It was pretty clear to me that was the only real question in the bunch. If they made sure it wasn't No Way who turned them in, then they'd have to look elsewhere. Probably among their so-called friends in the army.

"No," No Way said.

"Why did you alert this patrol to our location?"

"I didn't," No Way said. The voltmeter slid slowly up, from a hundred-volt tickle to two thousand and then to eight thousand. After three seconds, at fifteen thousand, No Way couldn't hold it in anymore. His back arched higher and bounced and there was a squeal of his vocal cords sawing into each other. His body bounced again and then relaxed as the voltage went back to zero.

"That was a one-second application of a level two shock," Grgur said. "On your next false answer we're going to wait five seconds and then administer a level four shock. Just so you know, a level eight might be fatal."

"Let's try it," No Way squawked.

"I'm going to have to ask you again," Grgur said. Pause. "It's not a big deal, you know, we're not out to get anyone. We just want to know where we went wrong. No Way? Who alerted the patrol to our location?"

"I don't know." No Way's readings thrashed, anticipating the shock. His temperature was dipping and his galvanic skin resistance was down twenty percent. The EEG was showing sharp seven-hundred-microvolt eliptiform spikes and big asymmetries between the right and left hemispheres of his brain. The shock didn't come, though.

"So you're saying you know someone did."

"No. Didn't." No Way's voice sounded like a crushed bullfrog's. The Estimated Voice Stress Level thingy reset itself to the new timbre. Eighty-five percent, it said.

"You didn't what?"

"I didn't. Alert. Anyone."

"One of the patrol officers already told us the information came from you."

"Not true."

"Then who did?"

"I don't know. If anyone did. Or not."

"Who do you *think* may have alerted this patrol to our location?"

"¿Quién sabe?"

"You're sure? I'm going to have to give you a long charge in a minute."

"Can you execute me now, please?" No Way asked, but the voltage was climbing again and his voice rose into a screech and then petered out in gooey sputtering. Grgur held it for three seconds. The EEG dropped down to what it said was an unconscious alpha level. Grgur cut the charge and Leonidas took the muff away from No Way's neck. Passing out was one thing, but they didn't want him to go into shock.

(98)

"This isn't good," Leonidas said. There was blood all over No Way's chin and when they wiped it off I could see he'd bitten through his lower lip. I guess they were worried about it because it was a torture-victim giveaway. Leonidas stuck some bits of gauze between No Way's teeth and his upper and lower lips. It gave him kind of a Ubangi-woman look. No Way was waking up, and he drew in a breath to try and get a scream together—he'd picked up on their stealth factor—but Leonidas remuffled him before any noise came out. He taped a shock of hair back out of his eye.

"Come on," Grgur said.

"Okay, it's okay," Leonidas said.

"Okay, No Way?" Grgur asked. "Can you hear me?"

"Uh-hunh." I think he was trying to make himself pass out again, but the Royal Ordnance system was good at not letting that happen. Grgur gave him a hundred-volt wake-up buzz.

"Who is Jed's backup?" Grgur asked.

"I am." His vowels were just ragged grunts and he didn't have any consonants left, but I could still understand him.

"All right. Listen. We already know the patrol was acting on a signal from you. We only want your confirmation of who set up the contact and how they were signaled."

No answer. Of course, they didn't actually have Clue One. It was just more standard procedure to tell the subject they knew he was lying. No Way wasn't buying it, though.

Torture for information usually actually works well, but it can take time. No Way's choice now was either to start changing his answers to try to buy time, or to keep to the true answers so they'd kill him as soon as possible. All guerrillas were trained to try to do the first, to hold up the interrogators for as long as possible. The main reason was what used to be called the "forty-eight-hour rule": you stalled in order to give the other people in the cell time to relocate before the other side learned their whereabouts. The other was that there was more of a chance for you if your interrogators had to take you back to wherever with them. Once you were in prison, you were less likely to be executed. In this case there wasn't anyone else trying to get away, although maybe No Way thought I might need to get out of here myself, and I'm pretty sure he knew there wasn't any hope for him either. But he did pick up on the fact that these people were nervous, and had been spotted by someone. And so just to screw them up as much as possible—I think—he did the right thing. Which was to start off telling the truth and then to reverse himself as they turned up the screws and the physiological readings got harder to evaluate.

"No Way? Listen. Who's your primary runner on the Guate side?"

"Cano."

"Rank and first name?"

"Captain. Juan."

"Would you please tell us how and when you signaled this patrol?"

"Fresh stolen phone. Leave text asking for a subscription to newsletter."

"Would you please tell us the name of this patrol's commanding officer?"

"No sé."

"Who have you told about this operation?"

"Cano y los GNAH."

"Who else?"

"I can't remember right now."

"What have you told them about this operation?"

"Everything, your schedule, your objective, cargo, everything."

"And what do you think is our objective?"

"Royal tombs."

"What about the royal tombs?"

"Specific artifacts."

"Which are?"

"I don't know."

"Would you like a cigarette?"

"Yes, thank you."

"Then please tell us that list and we'll give you a cigarette."

"Uh, de Vega," No Way said, pretending to think. "De Rivera. Caballero, Negrín, uh, Azana y Díaz—"

"That doesn't look right," Grgur said. He made out like they were checking the names No Way gave them against a list, but I bet they weren't really. "I'm going to have to give you a level six shock." Grgur gave him a little jolt, only half a second, but No Way was so softened up I could see sweat bead up out of his skin and roll down like someone was squeezing the wet sponge of his face.

"Please don't do that," No Way said, "I'll help you get into contact with them."

"With who?"

"Whoever."

"We're not going to execute you, you know," Grgur said.

"Thank you."

"Is there anything you would like to tell us before we release you?"

"No."

I could tell No Way wanted to keep them talking longer but he barely had the energy. He knew they were going to kill him anyway, but I guess he wanted to toss them a little more disinformation if he could. Or maybe, at the literal last minute, even he clung to life. It's hard not to.

"Okay, that's it," Grgur said. "You're sure you don't have anything else for us?"

"No, no, I can tell you more."

"Okay, what?"

"Deposit. Banco de Gran Caimán." To me it was obvious it didn't mean anything, though, it was just a false lead to take up their time, and I think they knew it too.

"Who's the contact at the bank?"

"Zamora."

"That doesn't sound right." There was an almost-silent scream and the voltmeter blasted up to forty thousand. At that level they only left it on for a quarter-second but it still knocked him out. No Way's face and body twisted up and collapsed. His mouth was open and drooling. His heartbeat skipped and took two irregular spikes and then settled back to sixty-five. His EEG was heavy on the Theta.

"All right," Leonidas said, "that's twenty minutes already, that's as much as we need to spend on this."

"We're going to give you a list of names of people who may be working at Pusilha. I'd like you to indicate which ones you've heard before, which ones your organization is following, or would like to follow, or wants to learn more about. You understand?"

"Okay."

"Even if you've just heard the name before I want you to tell me, and then we'll try to remember where. All right?"

"Okay."

"Bastarrachea Manzano."

"No sé." The program thought for a second and gave a combined reading of 7.6 out of 10.

"Juan Ramón."

"No sé." It registered a 7.0.

"Froot Loops."

"No sé." 7.8.

"Count Chocula."

"No sé." There were a few differences in the readings, but the program flagged it at 8.1.

"Domingo Dzul."

"No sé." The combined register jumped up to 9.

"Bacon and Eggs."

"No sé." 9.5.

"Hmm," Grgur said. "Let's talk about Count Chocula for a second."

He was right, I thought. That was the only really solid name they had. The readings had gone up after he'd said it because No Way had bitten his tongue or done some other tack-in-the-shoe thing to confuse the reading.

"Are you sure you've never heard of Count Chocula?"

"No," No Way said. "I don't remember product names."

"If you had, what would you have heard about it?"

"I can't remember yet."

"Where would the name have come up? At an EGP base?"

"That's right," No Way said. He wasn't caving in, by the way. He was trying to confuse them. He didn't have enough of a secret to protect. At most, he wanted to protect me, to get any blame off of me and onto himself—even though for all he knew I was on their side, or had even called in the patrol. I wondered a lot about what he thought about that. I hope he trusted me. Or maybe he just figured I still had a chance and he obviously didn't. Or he'd suspended his judgment for the purposes of his last act. And actually, in terms of sheer bearing up, he was one of the bravest subjects I'd ever heard of. Certainly as tough as anyone back in Ancient Mayaland.

"You're sure you have nothing to add? You understand we're going to kill you now."

No Way didn't say anything, he just rolled the pupils of his eyes back, which was the closest he could come to closing them.

"You're sure? Okay."

Someone's right hand held a small nylon sandbag that had been tightly wound with duct tape against the left side of No Way's head, above the ear. The matching left hand cushioned his head on the other side so his neck wouldn't bend. Nothing happened for a minute and then the arms swung a second wrapped sandbag, like a big sausage, underhand against the first one. It was a variant on what police in the U.S. call the telephone-book technique, a way to give someone a concussion without leaving an external bruise. I could hardly hear the strike, but No Way's heart rate skipped and spiked and his EEG scrambled up past 900 Hz and then dropped and bounced. No Way's expression was all sort of submerged pain like a dog having a bad dream.

"Wait, hang on," Grgur said. He swung the bag way back again, gathered up force, and struck. No Way's pulse took a last spike and flatlined. His EEG kept going, though, in this really irregular way, like he was still thinking about a few dissociated things, ships and sealing wax and cabbages. Again, nothing happened for a minute. Leonidas's hands went out of the picture. The image jiggled as Grgur picked up the phone and moved it into a close-up of No Way's face with its wide-open doll eye and held it steady, long enough to show he wasn't breathing. His temperature had already dropped a twentieth of a degree.

"Okay," Grgur said. I got glimpses of the crew pulling the sensors off No Way's head and cleaning and redressing him and everything, but I couldn't really pay attention. I did notice they put him in a Chouinard rock-climbing harness, which probably meant they were going to dump him in a *chultun* like he'd been exploring and fallen. You'd think they wouldn't even bother being so careful out in a place like this, but I guess they were just trained to be absolutely professional.

(99)

Two minutes later the video ended. I didn't move. I felt like I was bursting with acid diarrhea. And vomit. Or actually a single mass of diarrhea/vomit that was about to spurt out every available orifice.

No Way was maybe my best friend and certainly my only friend left from the *vida loca*. And he'd always led a dangerous life, but my personally getting him killed was a lot worse for me than his dying on his own. For any member of any blood-brother gang anywhere, if you lead somebody into a trap and he buys it you really owe him, a lot more than if he just took a bullet on the street or something.

Betrayal is an amazing thing. It's abstract. I mean, in the Warholian sense, like too big and awful even to try to represent. I was feeling a new dimension in my anger, different from the rage I felt at people who were dishonest and stupid and destroyed everything. In a way it was even stronger than my anger at the soldiers who'd disappeared my family, because it was multiplied exponentially by a more personalized invasion. And thinking back on it, actually, of all the strange things that had happened to me, Marena's treachery was the strangest, the thing I had the most trouble getting my brain around. Because it made the world seem the most alien. Even though I guess in a way I'd expected it.

I watched the video through again and then again. Each time I absorbed the fact of it a little more and I could feel my rage balloon inflating up out of my chest and into my throat in an almost detached way.

She sold you out, I thought. She fucked you all the way up the colon with a Chunnel driller.

No, wait—I thought back—you don't know how much she knew about it. She may not even know No Way's dead.

Oh, yes, she does. She just doesn't know it happened down there. Obviously Lindsay doesn't tell her everything, but she knows good 'n' plenty. If she's curious about No Way, she's just trying to cover her tight little ass.

Well, first of all, I've got to get hold of Grgur. Ask him. What's Marena's real deal?

What is this, *Harnessing the Power of Wishful Thinking*? You want to determine the exact degree of guilt on some scale between Quisling and Mussolini? She fucked you over and one'll get you ten they're going to waste you, too, sometime, and she knows about it and doesn't care. If she didn't come up with it herself, that is. It's probably fun for her to fuck a soon-to-be-dead guy. Dead Man Fucking. It's another PSDL power trip. Your whole life you've just been a tool, maybe a sharp tool but disposable, like a plastic razor.

Yeah, you're right, I thought. Time to rock. I could already see myself boiling over, trashing the whole place, grabbing Marena to interrogate her, a little taste of her own shit—

Don't do it, I said. Give in to rage and you'll screw worse up. Chill. Chill. Get past furious, get to that cold point where you can just nurture that little green flame. Figure out how to record this stuff. Go public. Get them all put away. And *then* maybe get them killed in prison.

No, wait, better just kill them first. Even if I got them into court they'd hire Scheck, Spence, & Dershowitz and everything'll stay the same and I'll be hung out to dry. At best. At worst I'd disappear before I got myself into custody.

Okay. Okay.

Goal.

Payback.

Why the shit did Lindsay hang on to that video? I wondered. Maybe he wanted his killers bloody all over. Still—

Okay. Record. I started downloading the file onto a Zip Chip.

Okay, I thought. I watched the bar graph fill up with deadly data. It said it would take another 1.2 minutes.

You know, you still don't know what's going on, I thought. Find out. Do de right thing. Find out. Information isn't power yet, but it's on the right track. First you learn what Lindsay's really doing. Then meticulous planning. Then horrible and merciless revenge. Then party.

I checked Marena's GPS. She was eight miles west of here, but it looked like she was headed back.

Okay, think. Lindsay's got a scheme.

Find out.

What's his plan, what's his plan, what's his plan?

Not sure, Shitlock. I entered SEARCH COUNT CHOCULA. Why did the EGP want to check out this guy? If they did at all. For that matter, why were they that paranoid about that stupid-looking Stake place? It wasn't like it was a secret or anything, it was just another really bad-taste Mormon summer camp. One of dozens. So far it looked like a vintage-1979 Ford trucks dealership in the middle of the rain forest. So, what's the big deal? *The answers to these questions and more are yours next week . . . in the heart-rending conclusion of—*

Sixty-three files came up.

Hah.

(100)

Some of the security windows were as vapid as "Thank you for downloading DrudgePro 1.3." But some were packed with simple powerful yet powerful statements, like "do not click on any items other than those specified or you may void your bowels." Still, it all didn't look too tough. These days you barely have to even hack, you just use reverse-engineering programs. You become a systems manager. No sweat.

I checked Marena's phone's GPS dot. She was on Chinikatook Street. On her way. Better hurry.

Looking, looking . . .

Most of it seemed to be military products, things like bowling-ball- and beachball-sized ground robots. Another division of Warren was developing much smaller "spider robots, which were partly guided by brains taken from pigeons." Don't stop to gawk, I thought. Eyes on the bling.

Okay. I found out that LEON was not an acronym for "Learning Engine/ Orlando Network." Rather, it was short for Leonid Bugaev, the Russian researcher who oversaw the Russian military's time-travel research in the early 1970s, and who came up with the basic equations used in the missile-defense system—a name I heard mentioned during the Racetrack Table Conference.

I was still clue-free about what the Warren Corporation was really doing, though. Were they just contracting for the Pentagon? Or for some other country, maybe?

They weren't telling me Shit One, that was for dang sure.

I was cold and shaky.

Chattering.

Obviously betrayed, even though I didn't know quite what the deal was.

For a moment I felt that there was somebody in the room with me. But I looked and there was no one.

The Stake has a fleet of five F-22s, which doesn't sound like a lot, but is actually enough to do quite a bit of damage, and over forty unmanned support aircraft, over five hundred medium-range remote-piloted missiles, and over two hundred freight and troop transport aircraft—also eight attack helicopters and at least thirty noncombat helicopters.

How many troops? Twelve hundred regulars, fourteen thousand irregulars?

The Pentagon group had calculated that the country couldn't withstand many more attacks in the mode of the Disney World Horror, and that they might happen even if the U.S. policy in the Middle East changed a lot—which it wouldn't. And no conventional means could stop them. So they began to fund research on speculative systems that might be able to affect a situation without touching it, or redirect it once had started. Over the last ten years, they had funded nearly a hundred speculative research projects—disintegrator rays, antigravity, telekinesis, atmospheric shielding, weather control, and so on—and only a few of them, notably ASP, ever worked out.

They reasoned that they'd never be able to completely stop terrorists from getting into a jet and taking it over, but that once they've seen the jet is heading for a given target, they might be able to get into the terrorist pilot's head and make him reroute it—even in the last couple of seconds.

Then, it became clear that there might not even be time to do that—but that it might be possible to send signals or even consciousnesses into that terrorist's head at a moment in the recent past. This wouldn't affect anything up until the time you sent the signal, of course—but it could give you enough leeway to change what that terrorist would do later on, beginning the moment after the signal was sent.

And, of course, the project grew from there. And grew, and grew.

Okay. Time for that call. I touched PIC. Marena's head and shoulders came up.

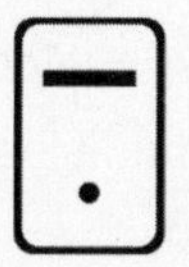

(101)

"Hi, friend," her head said. "I stopped for slushies. And I have to do a few things. I'll be back in forty-five minutes." I said great and managed to stay expressionless. She disappeared herself. The Windows status bar said it was already 5:11:23 P.M.

Okay. Let's do the hustle.

Order something. I clicked up ParkShop and after a little thrashing around I picked out a few needful things from Lobel Brothers' Prime Kosher Provisions and the New Prana Botanica and Balducci's South and a few other places and prepaid them on Marena's Mall number. Instead of using Marena's delivery service I clicked up Pink Dot—it's this really fast high-end driving-and-errand place we used to use a lot in the Kings—and sent them the list. You really can get almost anything almost anywhere without even speaking to anybody. A mosquito—how'd it get in here?—passed between me and the screen and I grabbed and crushed it. Under my breath I said sorry to Greatfather Mosquito and, just for good measure, to the whole Mosquito clan. I *ZPZFZPP!!*ed some shmutz off the pyramid with Marena's beloved Dust-Off. I sat back down. I took the precious Kleenex out of my pocket and unwrapped it. I took off my sweatshirt, found some Centrix scissors, and cut off the cuff. I pushed the Kleenex down into one glass and the cuff down into another and poured in just enough water to cover them. I watched them soak for a while, mushed each of them around with a pen cap, and watched some more.

Okay. Dosage. Maybe just drink the whole thing. There's no way to tell, anyway. The stuff's different now. Maybe it had lost its kick. I'm different. I'm probably nearly twice as heavy. On the other hand, maybe the Greathouse families had built up such an immunity to this stuff over the centuries that now even a little taste would kill me.

Face it, you don't know what you're doing. You'll have to just do it by taste. Trust the Force.

I sat and thought for a hundred beats.

I put the emergency nurse call button near my good hand just in case. Okay. I opened my water carafes. One of them was hot water for a selection of muslin-bagged teas. I set my two original tumblers on the cart, away from the drug infusions, and filled each glass with water. There was a salt shaker near the food tray and I poured half of it into each glass and stirred it up. Okay.

If I felt like I was in trouble, I was going to punch the call button, drink the first glass of saline solution, "induce vomiting," as they say, all over the floor, and then drink the second glass. Then I'd yell for a nurse.

I rehearsed it a couple of times in my head. Okay.

I took two Styrofoam cups off the cart, squeezed half the scorpion tincture into one and half the orb weaver stuff into the other, and drank them both. The scorpion fluid only had a numbing taste, but the spider essence rang that blue-ambergris taste up into my sinuses and back into my Eustachian tubes, and it was like I could feel Koh stroking me and telling me not to worry in that soft Chol as the neurotoxins ratcheted in my inner ears.

I opened the DHI driver program. I needed a password and I just clicked through it, KCAJ/ZENOBIA/1132. I didn't have to figure it out, I just remembered the patterns of Marena's fingers on her phone from the night before, although ordinarily I wouldn't be able to do something like that. The stuff was already getting to me.

I looked through all her work. She'd saved about ten copies of each version of the Sacrifice Game we'd played since I'd been back, and each one had a different silly name. At first I couldn't find the current model but finally I clicked up something called *Molly Niven's Ringworm* and it turned out to be an automatic backup of everything we'd worked on when we'd played the

Game a few days ago, including the setup of Koh's last position. It took me another twenty-score beats to get it going. Marena definitely hadn't made it easy for me. I felt like Bluebeard's eighth wife, turning forbidden doorknobs and listening for a creak on the stairs.

There was a little bar graph on the phone interface and I moved it halfway to the right. The difference was like how things looked when I first got two eyes back again. The pyramid-world seemed to get bigger somehow, except it didn't actually grow, its edges were still in the same place, and I could still see the room around it, but it was like I'd risen up in this secret dirigible sky fortress and I was looking down through at this vast multilayered mesa-pyramid Game-pueblo through my ultra-high-power Master of the World Giant Brass Telescope. I moved my finger a few millimeters to the right again and without losing clarity I was another fifty or so kilometers above ground level and the city had expanded to the scale of a mountain range. It was like that *Vertigo* effect, where you track the movie camera forward while you zoom the lens down from telephoto to extreme wide-angle. I got my finger on the part of the table that worked like a joystick, and I leaned closer and moved my point of view down and in, and it was like I was diving at a more-than-possible acceleration and I could feel my pituitary gland pumping adrenaline and tightened my grip on the edge of the table, but at the same time I was still totally aware that I was sitting on a hospital bed. In fact, if anything I was more aware than usual of how my body was part of the world. Marena's design was all spare, like an idealized city by Piero della Francesca, but it was also *homey* somehow, like you wanted to live there. It was something about how every part implied every other part, it made it like a real place, or the essence of place, it had that particularity that places had in the old days or when you were a child, before you could see how the Plasticland strip-mall grid had tightened around the world. A beat before I hit the green center of the mul I pulled back and there was an instant of stillness right over the apex as my parabolic course reached its nadir, and then I wafted back up over the courts and floated below the hard turquoise shell of the sky like I was in an upside-down Great Salt Lake.

Rapraprap. Another nurse-knock.

"Mr. Sic?" She pronounced it like "sick."

"Uh, hi, yeah, just a beat. Just a second."

The food order was here already. It seemed like it had only taken about forty beats. Actually, the thing was that even though the tsam lic made everything slow down for you—so that you had all the time in the world to calculate—it also kept you from getting tired, and you'd get involved with what you're doing and lose track of time. I signed Marena's number to a thirtypercent tip. I'm a kept man, I thought. It looked like Grgur had pawed through the stuff, not found any weapons, and let it pass. I closed the door, rolled the cart up against it, and locked the casters. Okay. I ran some water over a towel and laid it along the base of the hall door. I got out my box of personal stuff. I dug through it and found a small cotton sack and a foil-wrapped stack of black disks like miniature hockey pucks. I set one disk on an upside-down cocoa saucer, took four big copal crystals out of the bag, and laid them on the disk. I took a book of matches out from under my scrotum and touched a flame to the charcoal. Spark worms crawled through the disk, melting the crystals into boiling resin. A thin sticky smoke-snake drew itself up to the ceiling, filling the room with that clearing resin scent. It eddied toward the exhaust fan. I dug around some more, found a pack of Camel regulars, and lit one up. Camels have a bit of chocolate mixed in with the tobacco. Of course it's mild compared to the old stuff, but it's got something right about it. I purified the four directions and sat smoking for a few score beats, picking grains of tobacco off my tongue, feeling a cold electromassaging bodysuit of silk-fine woven magnesium slip over my skin. The tsam lic didn't seem quite the same as before, but it was definitely kicking in.

I put out the stub and peered back into the softworld. It felt like the precredits sequence in *The Spy Who Loved Me,* when he skis off that cliff and falls past all these interestingly striated rock formations while it takes forever before his parachute opens. From a distance the landscape underneath me was more numerical—not strings of digits the way a computer would think of it, but constellations of coordinates on the nodes of vast curves—but as I got closer I could see it more as a weirdly weathered landscape, Monument Ice Valley as redesigned by Eero Saarinen, bluffs and buttes and interlocking rock bridges coalescing out of the mist and eroding away again, not like Gibsonian cyberspace but all pale and fragile and mysterious.

My disembodied eye settled on the apex of the mul, paused, and then seemed to *unreel* away from the apex in a widening equiangular spiral, spinning fourteen hundred and forty degrees around the sanctuary in a condor-smooth glide through the coordinate ether. Potentiality-paths radiated out from the mul like the hundreds of thin spokes on an old Alfa Romeo wheel, crisscrossing each other in that reverse-slant pattern at four different angles. The closer the paths were to the base—to the nexus at the present—the more similar they were to each other, but as they diverged off into space-time they bifurcated and quadrifurcated into vegetal veins pulsating with events that each caused infinities of new events until the branches broke up into vast pixilated patterns of three-dimensional archipelagoes over the four-dimensional ocean, stretching out to the fogged horizon at 2012, and the thing was to trace the single path through the matted snarl that could lead you to that edge and beyond it, like the gold thread in Queen Zixi's cloak. The tsam lic was a flexible process, and to someone else it might seem totally different. I attached my point of view down into the Quarry and stood on top of the mul. It would be way too lame to say it was an amazing view. Or inspiring prospect, or whatever. It was like I could see anything I wanted, I had the whole observation platform to myself, and the only problem was that there were still a few more even higher ridges visible ahead of me. When I was playing the Human Game with Koh I'd just gotten a scruffy glimpse of the peak I was now standing on, squinting up at it through veils of snow and ash. And now that I was so solidly *there,* it was like, so what was so tough about that?

I felt for the keyboard and called up LEON. The processors had been thinking all night, and almost all day, now, and they'd come up with a move. I touched INPUT.

Everything shifted around me. I stayed the same. Now it was like I was standing at the edge of a low cliff at the tip of a sterile promontory, not that high up but a little too high to jump and survive, and much too steep to climb down. So from where I was in the Game-world—at least the way I was visualizing it at the moment—I could see across the next two months to the ridge at 4 Ahau, but I couldn't see how to get there, let alone over it and beyond. The whole Game-state depends on the truism that if you don't know what something is, you can't visualize it enough to predict its effects. You know, ya can't tell where you're goin' without knowin' where you're comin' from, all that. Which was Koh's problem all along. I mean, there's a limit. And right now it was as though I could see all these *details* spread out in front of me, maybe like I was stumbling over a vast Petoskeyish pebble beach, except instead of pebbles it was more like those drifts of novelties and jawbreakers and figurines and dice and tiny cameras and flashlights and trinkets in plastic capsules in one of those arcade crane-game things. But the thing with details is they're so small and there are so many of them. And I had to grab the right one just to take the next step, I could walk out into space and across to the next mesa if I could just find the bridge, find the solid path through this fruit-salad bog of image-confetti quicksand, but when I'd squint down into the surface I wasn't just picking through a coastlineful of stationary objects, I was peering down into a Gaudi–Facteur Cheval–Watts Tower mosaic of compressed events churning under my feet, translucent layers of forking capillaries, knotted nets of beads, each bead with something different inside, an idea or a particle collision or a disease or just any old thing, people and minerals and televised political speeches and dead termites and schedules and trajectories, charities, deaths, monetary units, chemical reactions, shoes, and ships. It was like Error's vomit in the beginning of the *Faerie Queene,* just this tidal wave of crud, and there was still only one pathway solid enough to get you where you wanted to go, the others would just collapse and you'd slide into some totally unrelated track. You had to start with something you knew well. Scope out some chain of cause and effect on the other side, something you recognized, and then follow it back. Like No Way had been over there. He'd left what was like a handful of footprints glowing up the other side, a few little bits of detritus I recognized as his. Or rather he hadn't really *been there,* exactly, since it was in the future, but there was something that made me think he'd seen over the rise somehow, and if I did want to get over there maybe I could ask him. It was like I could see his intention of going there, or his knowledge of how to get there.

Okay, decision time. Only, I realized I'd already decided.

Making a real chocolate ice-cream soda is getting to be a lost art, like semaphore signing. The deal is to put a mouthful of milk, two mouthfuls of chocolate syrup, and a coarse shot of seltzer in the bottom of the glass, and mix them all really really up before you do anything else. Then I like to put in a handful of chocolate ice cream shavings and stir those around to get everything cold. Then you pour in the bulk of the seltzer, up to within two fingerwidths of the rim, and stir that around really gently. Then you drop in two scoops of ice cream, submerge them in the liquid, let them bob back up, and perch the last and most perfectly spherical scoop of ice cream on the side of the glass. Finally, you blast in the last bit of coarse seltzer until the foam rises out of the cylinder and is just about to spill over. Oh, and if you like, you can make sure a little seltzer drizzles over the top scoop and forms an icy crust. And then you sink in a long, long spoon and you're done.

So I did all that and cleaned up and then tasted it.

Gastronodelic, I thought. Not *quite* there yet, though. Only one thing could possibly make it better. I checked the GPS. It showed Marena's Cherokee hurrying into the hospital parking lot. Whatever. I got the Lobel Brothers tub out of my food delivery, put the two Styro cylinders on the lap desk, and poured the little one over the big one.

Fabulous. I took a fountainspoonful.

Mnmnmnmnmn.

Perfect. Perfectomundino. Per—

(102)

"Hi, Jed."

"Hi, Marena."

"So how are you doing?" she asked. She put down an empty Phlegmy cup, found the food delivery, dug out a slice of salmon, folded it onto a big round water biscuit, and pushed the package five finger-widths in front of me.

"I'm good," I said. An imaginary mosquito buzzed behind my neck. That thing I'd forgotten. Damn.

"Are you sure?"

"Yes. Why, don't I seem good?"

"Well, I don't want to say you don't seem good, but you don't seem exactly happy, you know."

"Maybe I just have a sad face." I lifted out a slice and lowered it onto my plate. I took a bite. It wasn't dry enough and the smoking was different, but it still had that great old taste. I said thanks to Great Grandfather Salmon.

"Oh, yeah . . . but, you know, you brought back the stuff, we'll work out the LEON software on the Sacrifice Game, we'll deal with it, we should all be feeling a lot better than we did two months ago."

"Yes." I uncapped the Tabasco sauce and shook five shake-worths onto the salmon.

"I mean, I know it's hard to believe, but there was a time when people weren't so blasé about time travel."

"Right."

"You're like Neil Armstrong or, well, you know, I hesitate to mention Christopher Columbus, obviously."

"Thanks," I said. "No one's going to know about it, though, right?"

"Come on, don't make me a schmuck. What's it look like out there?"

"It doesn't work too well without the drugs."

"I know," she said, "but still . . . seriously, what's up with it? Any stock tips?"

"Uh, yeah. Buy gold and ammunition and keep them both under the mattress and stay down there with them."

"Really?"

"I don't know. Yes, basically."

"Do you realize you've used up, like, half a bottle of Tabasco sauce?"

"Uh, no," I said, "I guess I hadn't noticed that." I put down the bottle. "Thank you." I picked up the cup of water and automatically poured a shot out on the floor for No Way. "Oops. Sorry," I said. I found a napkin and bent down to wipe up the spill. The cup was still in my hand.

"It's okay," Marena said. I looked up at her. She wasn't looking. I knocked the Tabasco sauce onto the tile floor.

"Oops again." When I stood up I stepped on the bottle. It shattered.

"Damn," I said. "Sorry. I am such a total mess."

"It's nothing," Marena said. She started to get up.

"No, sit, I've got it," I said. I squatted and picked up the pieces, getting sauce in my hands. Damn. Random perturbation. Okay. Mime washing. I took the pieces and cap thingy to the bathroom, pulling my IV with me. In the bathroom I rinsed my hands and, noisily, dropped most of the bottle in the wastebasket. I kept a nice long shard that, conveniently, had part of the neck on it, making a good handle. I tucked it under the soft inner-arm edge of my cast, sat back down, and picked up the clear sporkf.

"You know, you've been stabbing that salmon over and over."

"Oh. Sorry." The mosquito was buzzing louder.

"Yeah," she said, "the way you're holding that fork, I don't know, it's scary." Pause. "Okay, so, you want to show me what you're doing with the Game? Is that okay?"

"Sure," I said. You lyin', cheatin' honky-tonk angel, I thought. I am *totally* onto you. I finished smoothing down the foil and rolled it into a little cylinder. This stuff is incredible, I thought. Color, thinness, pliability, a miraculous confluence of properties achieved by some unfathomable alchemy . . . in the old days we would have traded ten thralls for something like this. I slipped it into my shirt pocket.

"This tastes kind of weird," she said, "is there salt in it?"

I looked around. She'd picked up what was left of my ice cream soda and tried it.

"Oh, yeah," I said. "That's the way we used to have it."

"What is that?" she asked.

"It's a chocolate soda," I said.

She looked up at me. It was one of those moments. She knew.

"Is that blood?" she asked.

"Um—"

"*Is* it? Gross! Jesus!"

"Well, no, it's beef stock, it's just, like, *au jus* from Lobel Brothers—"

"Jed, it's blood, it's blood and I think I'm going to throw up." She put the glass down on the table and looked away. Her face was all scrunched up.

"Sorry," I said.

"I think we have to get you some help."

"Oh, please," I said. I looked down at the clotting soda. It didn't seem quite so appetizing anymore. But I picked it up and took a slug anyway.

"Jed, I'm your good friend," Marena said, "and I really feel like you might be freaking out just a little bit. Do you have any feelings in that regard?"

"Uh, I don't know," I said.

"Would you be willing to talk to the shrink? I mean without anybody else around. Confidentiality city." She poured herself some water. The moment she wasn't looking I slid the bottle fragment under the pillow. You could really dig out a pretty big plug of flesh with this thing. I cached the glass ready-to-hand in the near corner pocket of the pool table. Marena pulled out a baby Lurisia, wrenched it open, and drank half the bottle.

"Well?" she asked. "Seriously."

"Uh, sure," I said, "I mean, I'll see what I can do, I'm not sure I want to go into therapy or anything—"

"No, no."

"But, you know, I don't want to spend the rest of my life confused either."

She came over and put her hands on my shoulders and looked into my eyes.

"Jed, seriously. I'm on your side. What's going on?"

"I don't think it's anything," I said. I moved my eyes away from actually looking into hers and focused on a tiny little mole on her forehead.

"Your eyes look like they're not focusing or something."

"Yeah, I think, uh, that's right—"

"Maybe you should take a Val or four and chill."

"I will."

"Okay." She sat down.

"Okay," I said. I flicked on my screen. "Okay, just a beat, I have to purify the directions."

"Uh, right."

"Tin chi'm tex tahlah tex to cal ual tu cal xol," I said.
"Cantul ti ku cex cantul lubul bin yicnal."

"My breath is black, my breath is yellow, my breath
Is white, my breath is red. Accept her head."

"Som pul yicnal can yah ual kak ke
Tix tu ch'aah u kah u chi u sudz."

"Accept her husk, her skin. We cast her down,
Into the heart of the cave lake, turquoise heart."

"So look inside," I said to Marena. "Check it out." I moved the marker and entered the move. Marena leaned over the screen.

"See the deal?" I asked. I got my glass knife out from under the pillow but kept it out of her sight line.

"I can't focus on this anymore," she said. She pushed back.

"What's the problem?" I asked.

"Nothing." She got up and moved away.

"No, you have a problem," I said. "I can tell." I pulled out my IV needle and, without thinking about it, licked away the drop of blood. She recoiled a little. I moved away from her, but between her and the door, keeping my right hand down at my side with the glass in the lee of her vision. "Seriously," I said. "Please don't make me upset. I know I look like a nerd, but when I do get upset, people say I'm hard to deal with. This is not a threat."

"I don't know," she said. She leaned forward and reached for the speaker button on the phone.

"No, no, that's not necessary," I said. I got between her and the phone.

"Look, Jed, seriously," she said, "I think something serious is happening and we need to talk about it"

"I'm there, I'm all over it," I said, "yes, I want to help, don't *WORRY*!"

"I just want to send one text," she said. "Just to be on the safe side."

"No, really, don't," I said. "Really, I'm adamant about this."

She moved back.

"Okay, okay," she said. She smiled. "Atom Ant. Let's go sit down." She went toward the chair. I repositioned between her and the doorway.

Pause.

"Okay, fine," she said, suddenly shifting gears. "You don't give a wet shit about the world, or other people, or, or the Maya, or even yourself, or anything," she said. "You just wanted to see a bunch of ugly pretentious old buildings before the paint came off. You know what you are? You're a fucking *tourist*. You ought to be wearing five different cameras and, and Madras shorts."

"The article in *Time*. That was a plant, right? For an audience of one."

"Come on," she said. "Don't make me have to get everybody in here."

"So is that sort of a threat?" I asked. It was getting harder and harder to talk the way Jed would.

"No," she said.

"How about this?" I asked. I got the piece of broken bottle into striking position, where she could see it. "Is *this* a threat?"

"Jed, listen."

"Answer question, is this a threat?"

"Yes, I think it's a threat," she said. She started moving away, in the other direction, getting the bed between us. "What do you think?"

"That's a stupid like question," I said. I moved to the right. If I went after her she might get around me and get out the door. She paused. I could see her gauging how long it would take to get to the door, thinking it was better to keep the bed between us, that if I jumped over it she'd be able to fake me out and get away. I moved back a bit, to a spot where I could get to her before she got out the door. It was all about pretty subtle trajectories.

Come on, give her a break, Jed thought.

Too late, I thought.

Come on, Jed thought. *Anyway, I'm making you up. You got that*?

No you're not, I thought, I'm really really back. THANKS for bringing me BACK! I'm BACK, Jeddy, it's ME! I'm HERE for YOU! It's ME, CHACAAAAAAAAAL!!!

You can't do anything I don't want you to do, Jed thought.

Of course I can, I'm so much stronger than you are. Wimp. Anyway Marena outfucked you. And now she's your enemy. She's going to have you put away for a very long time. You got that?

I guess, Jed thought. He was obviously just feeling too weak to say anything against me. When people like Jed feel all enraged and stupid and betrayed and everything, they don't have enough stamina to put up with it. The whole world seems so bleak and scary to them that they just gray out.

"Okay, Jed," Marena said, "come on, you know you're—"

"Fuck Jed," I said. "Jed's gone. It's me, *Chacal,* SURPRISESURPRISE*SURPRISE!!!*"

Marena didn't move, but I could see her hair stirring and goose bumps spreading over her face and her nipples standing up under the linen. Her eyes were huge but I could see her already coming out of the initial Oh-my-God-I'm-dead-I'm-dead shock and thinking, What am I going to do to get out—

Whoa. She was on the chair-and-table side of the room, as I had maneuvered her, so the door and the call button were on my side, with the bed between us. If I went around it to grab her, she could jump over it and reach the door. I feinted as if I was about to take hold of the IV pole to hit her, and

I could see from a flick of her glance that she was going to jump onto the bed. Alpinist Marena—no problem. She leaped, just one foot on the edge of the bed, pushing her over. But because I knew it was coming, I swept her feet out from under her and she fell head-down onto the floor. She didn't move. Alert that she might be faking, I leaned down and grabbed her throat, but she didn't respond. I put my forearm, the one with the bandaged hand, across her throat and leaned on it, while I picked up the Tabasco bottle and pointed the sharp end next to her trachea. I waited for my arm to kill her. But it didn't. Could I use her later? Or did I love her? Or did I even care about that? After two-score beats, I pulled over the IV pole and shoved the needle in her arm vein. I wasn't very good at it, and it took a few tries, but she didn't react. With the needle in, I opened the flow valve. The drip had been intended to keep me docile, but I was twice as heavy as Marena, so my dose ought to put her out. But to be on the safe side, I pushed the flow valve to max, and watched as the drip rate increased.

Hmm. Well, that all looks stable.

Now all I had to do was get out of here. Well, not *all*. There were a few things, a few quick, easy, fun things, easy experiments with everyday household objects . . .

(103)

So, Jed asked from down in the bottom right side of my head, *when did you know you wanted to come back to our little old twelfth b'aktun*?

I knew before the sacrifice, I answered. Before you squealed out English on the mul.

I wasn't hard to fool, was I?

No.

Are you my other?

No.

What did you see on 4 Ahau?

I'm not going to tell you.

I need to know.

Everybody always wants to know what's going to happen, I thought back.

I just want to know, he kept saying, like a dying cricket in my head. *I want to know whether this is it for everything or what.*

I'm not going to tell you, I thought.

I could feel him squirm, but there was nothing he could do.

Manac zub, I thought. *Come on.* I need to get a grip on this time. Think. Think. And who is the steward of our captors?

Probably just Grgur.

The only reason you got back at all was that 2 Jeweled Skull let you.

When, you mean, when he told me—

When you said "Play ball*s*" instead of "Play ball," that's when 2JS knew I was inside you, that I was going to take over. That's a phrase that only I use.

No way.

Yes. He saw what was going to happen and that's why he told you where the nacom was. You know how tough he was, he wouldn't have done it for any other reason.

What about my whole life? Jed asked. *Did you set up the date of my birth, and the fact that I was going to come back? Did you guys set up* everything*?*

You'd have to ask One Ocelot's daughter about that, I thought.

Jed just floated for a few scores of beats. I thought he'd drowned, but he came back.

I still want us to leave Marena alone, he thought. *I don't care what she did.*

She'll make a prestigious captive, I thought.

I won't let you do it, Jed thought. *Let the girl go. We have a let-the-girl-go clause.*

I felt muscles tightening up and down my body, Jed trying to fire my motor nerves, but he just shivered like he was pushing hard against a wall. You're pathetic, I thought. Give it up.

He tried to make me exhale and hold it, maybe choke and die, but I just drew in a slow stream of air until it filled my torso basin.

You're helpless, I thought. Betrayal's a strange thing. I've been there. I know.

I won't, I'll get back up again—

> *Now fall you still, I thought, now little cousin, seize:*
> *Unique point of the lancet, penis tip,*
> *Now starts the bleeding, now you be aspersed.*

Shame wind swept over Jed. The nerves released. I felt my penis inflate.

> *He eats, he licks the white blood, snake-clot blood,*
> *On the wooden haft, the stone haft, here it strengthens.*

Automatically, Jed went into the begging formula:

"Accepted, singular ahau, I froth
The beaten mouth broth: here I take the shoots,
Four are his forces, four doors to his arbor,
O 4 Ahau alone, unique ahau."

And, with that, Jed was officially my captive. All nine of his—well, around here and now, they call them "souls"—were my thralls. Forever.

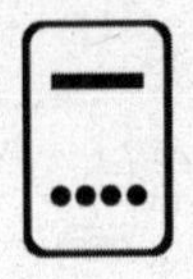

(104)

I touched the eel-edge of the mirror with my left hand and gingerly pulled it toward me.

It swung out, my uay-self turning aside.

Not one-way glass.

Thin smooth white plastic shelves bolted in.

I expected all sorts of magic things inside but there was just a cylinder vase that said *Phisohex*™, an amber chunk labeled *Neutrogena*™, a paper box of Band-Aids™, and a stack of disposable paper towels. There was nothing else.

There was something, though. Something in Jed's memories about the white steel cabinet frame.

I moved the Phisohex and on the left side, five finger-widths above the bottom corner, there was a tiny slit with a square of ancient brown stickum glue underneath, the trace of a label that had once, in the preinjector, predisposable era, read USED BLADES.

Got it, I thought.

I gouged into the metal with my thumbnail. Too hard.

Tool needed.

I walked to the big white vase in the floor, said a purification over it, sat on it expecting an underworld batfish to come up and chomp me, and managed to squirt a little urine into it.

I looked around. The paper stuff they used came out of a dispenser that was bolted to the wall. There was a tank on the back of the vase with a cover. The cover was plastic and it seemed solidly attached.

I rose up, got my feet on the rim of the toilet basin—there was no seat cover—turned around, put my hands down over the plastic tank lid, hit the flush lever, and just as the sound crested I yanked up—and, thank Iztamna for small favors, the rectangular lid popped off relatively undamaged.

The old brown-crusted rod between the flush-lever and the wire that went down to the rubber drain-cap looked pretty sturdy.

I unhooked the wire that held it to the drain cap, shutting off the flush. On the lever end the rod was attached with a little nut that I tried to unscrew, but it was corroded on, so I bent it back and forth a few times and finally it broke and I wrenched it off.

I put the cover back on. My hands were covered with black rubber-scum and I scrubbed them in the sink, wiped them with paper towels, went back and cleaned the side of the tank cover, and went back to the sink.

I turned the water on, reopened the medicine cabinet, jammed the rod into the slit, and pried back the sheet metal, sawing down into the depths of the cabinet, pulling the sharp flap back with my fingers.

Metal is such weird stuff, I would never have expected it. In Ix I'd owned tiny and extremely expensive earplugs made out of gold, the Venus-feces of the South, and copper, the sun-feces of the North. But here it was cheaper than pebbles and came in all colors, even that pure mirror zero-color, and nobody seemed to notice it. I went back to what I was doing, sawing and digging, the ragged hole getting bigger.

Finally, at the base of the hollow wall, nestled against the cinder block, was a stack of rusted rectangles.

I dug it out carefully, wrapped it in Band-Aids™, and Band-Aided it under my scrotum. It was the safest spot I could think of. Jed's testicles instinctively retracted, shrinking from the idea of sharpness. Just in case, I stuck forty or so wrapped Band-Aids next to it in three thick little wads.

Marena was sound asleep. But the nurse might check in early.

I separated sixteen of the old double-edged razor blades from the brick, scraped as much of the rust off them as possible, and folded them into V's down the center, so that they had two edges sticking out at about forty-five degrees from each other. After some picking I peeled back the outer layer of my hand cast. It wasn't plaster, it was some kind of light breathable cheese-nylon stuff.

I cut slits through the edge of the cast and threaded the V's into them points outward, kind of like fishhooks in a cork, so that I finally had two rows of double blades traveling around the edge of my paddle hand.

It was a bit like the way they make weapons out of two safety-razor blades and a toothbrush in prison. Two edges do a lot more damage on the first stroke than one because they take out a kerf that's hard to sew up.

Finally I filled in on either side of the blades with little folded paper tabs from the back of the Band-Aids, wrapped the outer layer of stiff beige cheesecloth loosely back around the whole thing, and stuck that down with looped Band-Aids on its inside hems so that it would look as normal as possible. When I hit someone with the assembly the edges of the blades would go right through the outer layer of cloth as though it wasn't there.

It was bigger and lumpier than before, but I figured if I kept it down at my side and turned away from their lines of sight it probably wouldn't get noticed.

Just as a last touch, I made a little balloon out of Saran Wrap, filled it with Tabasco, and secreted it between my teeth and upper lip.

Right.

I pulled the IV out of Marina's arm, rolled her gently under the bed, re-taped the needle onto my own arm like it was still in my skin, and hit the lighted call button on the padded bed rail. Wait. Marena's bag was still on the window ledge radiator thingy. I slid it under the bed just before Nurse Wretched came in.

"Are you all right?" she asked.

"Yeah, thanks," I said. In fact I'm feeling great, I thought. I feel more like myself with every p'ip'il. "Sorry to bug you, but I really needed to talk to Grgur, I've got to tell him something." She put down the tray and left. Grgur came in.

"I really need a cig," I said.

"Forget it," he said.

"I also have some information."

"Save it."

"I just worked out a couple of dates Marena wanted," I said.

"It'll wait."

"Please, Gulag, you know I am a nicotine addict."

"No," he said, "you have to detox."

I thought for a few beats about how Jed would put it. All right. Let's try this.

"Come on, please please please," I said. "We carcinogen lovers have to stick together. Right?"

"Yeah," he said. He beeped at the backgammon game on his phone.

"I'll split a box of Monte Cristo Pirámides with you when I get home."

"Ungh."

"What's going on with you," I asked, "are you wearing like, ten NicoDerms or what?"

"I have the power of the will," he said.

"I'll wire you ten thousand dollars," I said. "Otherwise I'm just going to toss and turn and thrash until Grandfather Heat—until dawn. And then I will start screaming. And then when people ask I'll tell them you did let me smoke, and it messed up my meds."

"We can not smoke in here anyway," he said. "It sets off the sirens. We would have to take us out into the stairs."

Hah. Progress. "Or I could go down into the morgue and crawl into a drawer with a dead guy," I said.

He went out. I could hear him mumbling something into his phone. He came back in.

"Grg, old pal next to me, . . . wow, I knew you had some pity in you." Tears almost burbled up in Jed's/Sic's/my cowardly eyes. "Thanks. Really."

"Yeah."

We waited.

There was a rap on the door and the other one from the house came in wearing a shirt woven out of the blue hair of some odd creature that Jed's memory said was called a Nylon. He also wore a pectoral on his chest with his name and mask. I mean, portrait. Somehow I didn't think he was so alert as Grgur.

"This is Hernán," Grgur said.

"Yeah, we've met, hi," I said. Did that sound natural? Other One didn't say anything. I hoisted myself up more unsteadily than I had to. Hurry up, I thought. Marena might cough or twitch or start singing. We went out and they steered me in front of them down the hall, letting me pull my own IV pole. They certainly didn't seem to notice that the cast on my right hand was a little larger than it had been. I didn't see any of the guards either.

We turned right at the far end of the hall. I couldn't see any of those dart shooter weapons—I mean, guns—printing on Hernán's clothing, but one never knows. I got an impression of a deserted waiting-area of bolted-down mats. That is, seating units. Chairs.

We turned down another humming green corridor to a FIRE/EMERGENCY EXIT ONLY door. There was a door across from it labeled NAHSO, which something deep in Jed's hard drive told me was the hospital's code for Pharmacy. Grgur ran a badge through the lock, pushed the door open without touching the aluminum bar, and went out ahead of us into the white concrete stairs.

Other One—Hernán—herded me in behind him and shut the door. He said something about how the Magic were going to make it to the Finals against the Jazz, but Grgur just grunted and pulled a pack of Kolumbos out of his shirt pocket.

He shook three out, put one in his mouth, handed one to me and one to Hernán, and took out a book of Delano Hotel matches.

He lit one one-handed and touched it to his own first.

At least Marena'd really trained this guy to be polite, I thought. A lot of people think it's polite to light the other person's first, but with matches you're supposed to absorb that awful sulfur taste yourself before you move the clean match on to someone else.

I put my cig in my mouth and sort of moved into position. He held the match out to me and just as the end was about to light I blew the match out through the cigarette.

"Sorry," I mumbled. This is the move, I thought.

I took the book of matches with my left hand, shaking my head, and he let me take it.

YES! I pulled a match around to the back of the pack with my left thumb, lighting it one-handed, and sucked in the smoke, double-inhaling it up through my nose. You can't really explain the pleasure of smoking to a non-addict. It's like trying to describe sex to a five-year-old.

Okay. I moved the little balloon of Tabasco out from under my upper lip with my tongue and got ready to bite down on it.

Right. I held the still-lit match out to Hernán, sucking that big old blow-gun breath down into my lungs so that I'd be ready.

Hernán leaned forward and I moved the burning match to his cigarette and then moved the matchbook under his chin, my thumb extruding two old razor blades from under the cardboard in a V-shape.

I sliced into Hernán's throat from the left side, the first blade quickly burying itself up to the crook of the V, and continued the same motion in a smooth arc up toward his right ear. Thin flat strings of blood jetted out of the slit, black in the minty nonlight.

I let go just before reaching the ear and pulled back. Hernán reacted late to the relatively painless cut, bringing his hand up to his throat, and he lurched forward and grabbed my right wrist with his other hand but I twisted against his thumb and pulled back and fell against the corner of the wall. Only, it wasn't the wall, it was Grgur grabbing me from behind.

I accentuated my fall, going off balance, and as Grgur came down after me, grabbing at my cast arm, I bit down on the balloon of Tabasco and swung my head around, getting the bolus of liquid position.

His face came into range.

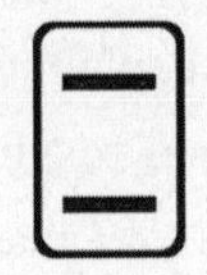

(105)

Even in Tony Sic's fultballer body I didn't have the lung power I'd had in the old suns. But still, if you know how to cough into a blowgun, you can send liquid out with enough force to practically go through a closed eyelid. And Grgur almost certainly wouldn't close his eyes anyway. People trained the way he was . . . well, he was like us Ball Brethren. We do not blink, even when losing a limb. If their eyes get dry they wink one and then the other.

I blasted it out. He didn't close his eyes fast enough. He squinted in obvious agony, orange drips sliding over his face, but still he just held my arms tighter behind my back.

I looked back at Hernán. He had his hand in his jacket pocket but he wasn't pulling a gun.

I did a porcupine, pulling my legs up and curling into a ball, trying to wrench my left arm free, but of course what I really wanted was the right arm, the cast arm, and Grgur let his grip on that slack for just a beat, enough for me to twist it against his thumb and line up the shot, and I slammed the cast down into his inner thigh and drew it up along the artery into his groin, leaving a trail of bloody shredded fabric.

It got him to relax his grip enough for me to slide out and down to the floor, at the edge of the stairs.

Hernán had partly gotten his act together and was nearly on me, even with one arm wrapped around his throat.

So I tipped myself over and rolled down the stairs. At the first landing I sprang up and turned and half ran, half fell down around onto the next flight, four at a time in my little paper booties, pitching forward onto the landing below, my back tingling with imagined bullet-wounds.

I grabbed the inside railing with my left hand and wheeled around. In most combat situations one main thing is to just be decisive and book when you can. A lot of people stick around too long when they're ahead.

There was one flight of metal-and-tile institutional stairs between me and Grgur, but I could hear him run-creeping down toward me, I could practically see him through the stairs, and as a single foot turned the corner I slashed at it with my cast and it slid out from under him.

I held on to the banister and struck again around the corner at his knee.

He grabbed my arm just before the second swipe could connect but I pulled my cast back and down into the crook of his elbow, the big artery there spraying blood onto the wall, and as he released the cast I backhanded him with it up into the left eye.

I was pretty proud of the job I'd done on my little hand-mace. After working on the thing near forever it was nice to see it doing its job.

Behind Grgur Hernán was crawling down the stairs at us, all bloody like a flayed captive. So much for the instant-killing technique. It was taking this guy's uays forever to leave. And his body was still thrashing around dangerously. I dropped back from Grgur, decided to take a chance, and gave Hernán a shot in the split-open neck with my left foot.

Ordinarily I'd never kick in an actual weapon-based fight, it's not worth possibly getting off-balance, but this time it seemed like the timing and everything was right and when the fútbol-edge of my foot flipped his chin up he spittered up a fountain of arterial blood and crumpled.

I noticed a sort of porcelain knife, a six-finger-width black-blade thing with a blue Chinese-water-beast-skin handle, lying on the floor next to him—I guess he'd pulled it and I hadn't even noticed—and I grabbed it and turned back around to Grgur.

For a beat I thought I was fucked and then I realized it wasn't a gun in his hand, just a phone. Maybe he didn't even have a gun with him.

Still, he'd probably hit some alarm. Just as bad. I gave him a left haymaker to the cheekbone with the butt of the knife, being careful not to break a finger, dropped it, twisted the phone away from him with my left hand, hooked his legs out from under him, and as he slid back down against the wall I tried to size him up.

Grgur definitely didn't look hazardous. So just to be safe I picked the light little knife back up, scampered up the stairs again to the landing—I was feeling like a little grasshopper-dancer, an elf, sort of—and got behind Hernán, sunk the blade into his head under the ear, pulled it out, and wiped both sides on his shirt. I could smell Hernán's shit releasing as he died. I went back down, sat behind Grgur, and started choking him with the elbow of my mace-arm.

I sat behind him, holding his neck from behind with his fat muscular ass between my legs and I was a little embarrassed because with all the excitement and everything I had a kind of serious hard-on and it was pressing up against him. Not that I found him at all attractive, it was just that sort of blood-rush adrenaline thing.

Kind of sluggishly Grgur got his arms up and started going for my head so I poked the knife into his elbows, one after the other, trying to pinpoint the nerves that drove his lower arms.

I had to try a couple times on the first one, but finally, from the way his hands reacted, I figured I'd gotten it right. His squeals didn't come out like much. Hernán's urine was running down the stairs from above, along with blood and other liquids.

I dug into Grgur's lapel pockets with my good hand and found his wallet and Marena's Sylphide lighter, which I guess he'd found on me and was going to give back to her. There were two different key cards with Florida Hospital on them. One said S-WING RESTRICTED USE A. Fabulous.

I felt a disturbance in the air, wind coming up from the bottom of the stairwell eight floors below, probably people answering Grgur's alarm, and Grgur probably felt it too.

I held the cards against the handle of the knife and jammed it into the cast on my right hand. It went into my flesh a little bit but I could hardly feel it. The blade was facing his neck, and I pulled my arm back as far as it would go without cutting him.

"Let's try to stand up together," I said. If I fell over, or if he tried to break away, he'd be caught in the crook of the cast and the knife. Or at least that was the idea.

We stood up. His mangled leg nearly slid away from him and then he got it back under control. I was practically riding on his back. His arms dangled.

"So, look, why don't we go back up to our floor, and we'll be really, really mellow, and check out the pharmacy?" I asked.

Even though he was gasping, I could see him thinking. I hoped what he was thinking was that if he was too recalcitrant I'd probably just kill him and run, but if he came along, the others would probably find us and pick me off pretty fast while he broke away.

"Grgur? Okay?"

"Okay."

(106)

His card relaxed the jaws of the door. Maybe it opens everything, I thought. A little demon in the wall switched on the caged lightning.

The tiny Pharmakopia room was all eye-dazzling shelves of many-hued translucent jars, some with seals in colors I'd never seen before. Magic Elixir City. Excellent.

I squeezed my cast elbow tighter around his neck and when I could feel his legs about to give out I pulled out the knife, sliced off his live badge with my left hand, and held it up to his left eye.

"So listen," I said, "what other tracking equipment do I have on?"

He tried to shake his head. "Nothing," he mouthed. I heard the door shut itself behind us.

"What else do you have on?"

"Nothing."

"Did you get that alarm sent?"

"Yes."

"You're lying," I said, "I'm going to gouge your eye out on the count of one." I held the black blade up to his eye. "Zero."

"There's nothing else."

"Dogshit. Show me the other trackers. One."

"Go ahead," he whispered.

"Never mind, I believe you," I said. I squoze off his air for another thirty beats, to the point where he was just beginning to pass out, and let him sprawl on the floor.

I found some surgical tape and wove his fingers together around the bolted-down leg of a metal shelving unit.

I sat down and started sawing the tracking box off my ankle with the white-bladed knife while I watched him. It took thirty-nine beats. By the fortieth beat Grgur'd stopped coughing and was getting it back together.

"So how do I get in to see Lindsay?" I asked. Jed would probably have asked whether Grgur was working primarily for Lindsay or for Marena, and whether Marena had given the order on No Way, and a whole bunch of other trivia, but I really didn't care.

"That's. Difficult," Grgur choked out.

"Well, so then what are *you* good for?"

"I can try him."

"How?"

"On the phone."

"Where is Lindsay right now?"

"He went to assens today."

"Assassins?" I asked. I got the ankle box off and sliced off my ID bracelet just in case. I was pretty sure there wasn't anything else on me. Had they implanted a surgical tracker? That would be a little much even for this group.

"No, Athens, Greece," Grgur said.

"What's the best way to reach him?"

"Text him."

"I mean in person," I said.

"I don't know."

"Hang on," I said. I stuffed some cotton pads into his mouth and surgitaped over it, leaving enough of a gap so that even if his nose stopped up he wouldn't die. Next I cut some airholes in a big plastic trash bag, poured in three economy family-sized boxes of cotton pads, foomped it down over his head, twisted it, and taped it around his neck. He looked like—who?

Jack Pumpkinhead, Jed thought.

Right, I thought back. Next. Badges. Steenking batches. Think.

"Back in a third," I said.

I opened the door and walked out, ready to cast-slash anyone in sight, but there was nobody. I wiped some blood spots off the floor in front of the door with the toe of my goddamn cloth slipper and I walked through the blazing flat light to the little waiting area. The couches were this acid orange that kind of upset me, and I tried not to look at them. I climbed up on one and looked out the window. It looked out on a closed courtyard, and there was a fire escape. And it was dark down there. After some fumbling I got the leaf, I mean, the key card I'd taken, to slide into a three-finger-wide crack, threw the glove with the trackers out into the warm dark, and closed the window again. There were footsteps coming up the hallway. I walked back to the pharmacy, closed the door with good delicacy, got behind Grgur, pulled the bag down a bit, weighted his arms and legs as much as I could, and choked him some more to make sure he'd be absolutely silent. If the cops or whoever came through the door I'd throw him at them and then go out the back and see if I could still get away. Although that didn't sound good.

The footsteps went by outside. I didn't breathe.

All right.

Pause.

For a few beats I thought about skinning him and wearing his face out, but, based on experience from doing the same thing in the old days, I figured it wouldn't actually be so convincing. You needed trained taxidermists to work on it, and even then the effect was odd. And even assuming his head was big enough to fit over mine, there would be the bloody eye sockets and nostrils, and the whole nose issue would be a real problem, and if I couldn't sew the lips together they'd hang open and show another pair underneath.

So even if they mistook us for him, they'd think we were so messed up they'd bring us right back to the hospital, where we don't want to be. And skinned faces don't really look that much like their previous owners until you preserve them correctly. Without all the muscle attachments and everything on underneath, they just look kind of droopy and abstract. Taxidermy is an art, and the human variety is the hardest.

"So, look, you're going to transfer me out," I said. Grgur mumbled something like "Okay." He was still bleeding so I surgi-taped his worst wounds, just so he wouldn't shock out on me, before I started rooting through the shelves. Hmm. Turbocurarine. Meprobamate solution. Most of the potions seemed familiar, I suppose because Jed had spent so much time in hospitals when he was little he'd memorized a volume known as the *Physicians' Desk Reference*.

Let us see. A few bottles of Percocet. Some dioxyamphetamines in case I had to stay awake for a while. Some scalpem. Scalpels. Aha.

Downerland.

It took a little longer to find syringes. They were way up on the top shelf where the little kids couldn't get them. I dumped a drawer of twenty- and hundred-millimeter disposables down into Grgur's bloody lap and climbed down next to him with my bottles.

All right.

I mixed a few things up in little jar, a solution of about four milligrams of Pavulon, four grams of meprobamate, and thirty milligrams of tubocurarine chloride.

If he weighed two hundred pounds, that would make it about a quintuple dose of each. He'd feel it as fast as if it were heroin, but it wouldn't get him right away. When it got distributed, though, he'd have had it. I pulled his sock down, found a clear vein on the inside of his upper ankle, and shot it in. He was squirming a little so I sat on him, pulled the bag off his head, pulled the wad out of his mouth, and while he was still gasping made a big wad of cotton and taped it over his mouth and nose. He'd be able to talk normally and I'd just be able to hear him, but if he started screaming it wasn't going anywhere. His head was all red and sopping wet. I unwrapped one of the hundred-milliliter arterial syringes. It had a nice long sturdy needle. Beautiful.

I looked at his watch. We'd been in here for about thirty-score beats. Ten score since the injection. I should really give the shit another ten-score beats to kick in before I tried anything. You just can't cover everything, though, it's all a compromise. Give it another fifty-score beats.

"So this may be a cliché," I said, "but can I ask whom *exactly* you're working for?" I got more weight on his head, turned it sideways, and felt the edge of his jaw.

"Mrmff," he said.

"You can talk," I said. I slid the dry needle through the thin skin over the lower arch of his mandible, under the masseter muscle and away from the facial vein, and rested it against the nerve-rich bone. There was only a tiny bead of blood.

"Now twist, now writhe in ant-blood tickles," I said.

I drew the thick needle through a wide arc, scraping against the bone. Grgur didn't groan but I felt his involuntary tense and shiver. That's nothing, I thought.

"You understand I look like Tony Sic, but I'm—ah—I'm Jed."

"Yuh. Somebody said—"

"Come on. Who is your steward of long things?"

"Huh?"

"Your commanding officer."

"Lindsay Warren," he said.

"Who put up the money?"

"For what?"

"For the Stake, in Belize," I said. I tried not to look at the drifts of precancerous dander under his pathetic thinning sideburns.

"Lindsay's investors."

"Who's Lindsay's superior?"

"As far as I know, um, I don't think . . ."

"Hurry up."

"I think Lindsay's his own boss."

"Really? Okay, how do I get in there?"

"Where?"

"His office. At the Stake."

"I don't know."

"You'd still better get some codes and names and whatever on the table. I'm serious."

"I'm serious, I don't know."

"Okay, you obviously have nothing to offer." I drew the needle back and scraped it over and over into his mandible toward his teeth, not widening the single puncture but etching a deep line in the bone, over and over, like I was jerking him off. He started shrieking way back in his throat but I gave him a full twenty strokes before stopping. Working on him was getting me back on track.

"There's a Warren weapons test on for December twenty-first," I said. "I want you to help me find out about it."

"Okay."

"So, okay, tell me about it."

He paused like he was thinking of making something up, but he must have decided not to.

"I don't know," he said, "there's a Christmas party at the Hyperbowl, if there's something on for the Stake I'm not in on it."

"How do I get to see Lindsay?"

"I don't even know when he'll be back, they move his schedule around—"

"Please, be terse." When the stuff took effect he wouldn't be able to tell me anything. "What codes do you have?"

"I just have a card."

"How long is it good for?"

"Forever."

I eased the needle in further, pushing it down from above with my finger, under his loose, bristly skin, until the point threaded into the base of his number-three molar. He tensed. Maggots of waxy sweat welled up out of his pores.

"Come on, how often does the card change?"

"All the time, it's live—"

"I mean the whole card."

"It gets replaced every week. I get the new one in two days."

I felt footsteps again, and voices I couldn't make out went down another hall, more urgent and official-sounding this time. I jammed the drift of cotton into Grgur's face.

(107)

Twenty beats later I heard them come around on the other side into the nursing station and run off.

It's a big sun day, I thought. Excellent. They're following the badges. I eased up on the wad.

Grgur seemed immobile so I started doing some repair work on my cast-mace, taping in a few scalpels in a sawtooth pattern and then rewrapping the outside with regular white surgical tape.

"Who gave Jed-Sub-One the fake anticoagulant?" I asked.

"When?"

"Back on Halloween."

"I don't know, some other cutout."

"Why?"

"We were not going to kill you, we were only supposed to bring him—you—in."

"Bring me in to whom?" I asked. I scraped him again. He just squeal-whimpered a little. "Grgur? Seriously. To whom?"

"To Mr. Warren," he said.

"Who else was going to be there?"

"I don't know."

"So what was the next step?"

"We were just going to move you out, we're here to protect you."

"We were here to protect you," I said, trying to imitate him.

"You're crazy," he said. "If you walk out of here you're dead, they know where we are, the whole place is covered . . . you're sick, they put stuff in you that's going to kill you if you don't let them take care of you—"

"You're crazy," I said, sounding a bit more like him. I tried to raise my voice to the pitch he'd have if he weren't so hoarse. "You're a dead man. They know where we are. I'm here to protect you. You're crazy. I'm here to protect you." It wasn't brilliant, but I thought it might pass.

Grgur must have gotten what I was up to because he shut up, but I wadded and scraped him again. Tough or not, he screamed and screamed. The cotton wad buzzed like a vibrator.

"Come on," I said. "Who doesn't like me? I mean, the most?"

"No, that's the way it is." He was starting to sound a little slushy.

"All right, let's just chat, then. Tell me about Lindso's Grand Prize Game."

"I don't know about things like that."

I held the wad over his mouth and dug the needle in under the tooth. I didn't find the nerve right away, but a few hundred beats after I did find it his eyes started tearing and five-score beats later he was screeching into the wad.

It's kind of intimate and pathetic when someone actually breaks, when his whole tough-guy thing—which is a big part of his sense of self—just evaporates. Sometimes an interrogator can start feeling sorry for the subject at that point and stop pushing as hard, and then, even though the subject's in a pretty bad way, he might still notice and start withholding information. I didn't have that problem, though.

"Come on."

"Let. Um. Me think. For . . . a minute. Okay, please?"

"Forget it," I said, "you're right, you can't help me." It was probably true, this whole session was a waste of time. Anyway, they must be finding those badges by now. Better hustle.

It had made me feel a lot better, though. Not out of revenge, like I cared about No Way or anything, but just more like I was back on my sacrificer track.

"You're going to check me out of here."

"Whatever you say, asshole," he whispered.

"Look, here's the deal," I said. "Are you listening?"

"Sorry, what?" he said. He was trying to stall me.

"I know you heard that," I said. "Okay. You feel sort of numb and cold right now, is that correct?"

"Yes."

"I've given you a mix of paralytics and depressants and a few other things and it ought to kill you in less than a half hour. You got that? And it will be very . . . claustrophobic, it will feel like you are drowning in feathers. So, we are just going to take the other elevator down into the Emergency entrance and you're going to tell everyone who hassles us how okay everything is. Okay? And if you, if you screw up, I just will not tell them anything, and by the time they figure out the mix of things that's wrong with you you'll be a big blue bulgy-eyed turd." I held the little drug bottles up in front of his face. "But if you're really helpful, I'll give you the bottles when I leave and maybe they'll figure out what ails you. You understand?"

He grunted a little.

"You got that?" I asked. "Otherwise they'll never work it out in time."

He made another grunt that sounded a little more affirmative. Meprobamate is a hypnotic and I hoped he was getting into a receptive state of mind. Not like it was a truth serum or anything. Nothing is.

I took the wad away. He was gasping and I was pretty sure he wasn't faking, he had that rattling shiver specific to Pavulon. This stuff is great, I thought. Maybe Jed did have a grain or two of useful information in his head.

I looked into his eyes. He was still glaring, but his eyes were already looking a little dilated and lymphy. I got the feeling he didn't believe I'd care enough to let him live.

"Lube, I'm serious," I said. "You may not know me, but the one thing I wouldn't do is renege. On the other hand, if your guys pick me up I'm not talking. You know, even if they think to ask what's wrong with you. I mean, I'd be upset to get nailed, but letting you die would take a little of the edge off. Okay?"

He nodded a little.

"Okay, here we go," I whispered. I stood him up. He was weebly but he could stand, so I guessed the stuff was working correctly. I realized I was still in my gown. There weren't any doctor costumes in here. Damn. Have to remember to take Grgur's jacket on the way out.

Okay. Anything else? No. I cleaned his face up a bit with some Sani-Wipes and squirted some Phisohex on his stringy hair and slicked it back. I tied his right wrist to mine with a surgical tube and held on to it so that at a distance it would look like we were handcuffed together. I opened the door and walked him out to the elevator. There were glass doors two rope-lengths ahead of us, and it even looked like there were car lights past them. We took four steps out of the elevator. Grgur was pretty sluggy but so far he could walk. There were some cops around, but with all the flat bright artificial colors, like everything was flat weavings, I couldn't really pick out whether they'd noticed us. This era has so many dyes and paints and Electromats, anything can be any color. In front of the eye-dazzler stew a woman who looked kind of in charge came toward us from around a desk and I turned Grgur's head away. I read her name tag. Teresa de la VillaReal.

"Good night, Teresa," I said in his voice through my almost-closed lips. "So now I gotta transfer Mr. Sic to the state police. Sorry. See you later."

"Wait, are you okay?" she asked.

"I'm fine," I made Grgur say.

"You have to wait," Teresa said. "The other police are here, there's been a killing—" She was the voice I'd heard before, upstairs.

"It's okay," he/I said. Teresa hit some keys on a black thing in her hand and an alarm started wheeping like a hundred linked screech-owls. Some big guys in suits were pushing toward us from the other side of the lobby and there already were four cops between us and the doors. I veered us left, dragging Grgur, into an area where the crowd was thickest. There was some sort of punk gang dressed as neo-Maya bloods over there, five or six nearly naked teenagers with major tats and dyed green feathers, who I guess had been in a fight because a couple of them were bleeding into sorbents. There was a boom box with rack music blasting softly, and a couple of interns running around trying to get them all to settle down.

"Freeze, asshole," somebody said in a studiedly authoritative voice, stepping in front of me. It was one of the cops from upstairs. He had his gun out but I pushed Grgur into him. "The prisoner has drugged me," I shouted in Grgur's voice. "He's got a bomb."

The cop hesitated for a beat. It wasn't even that convincing, it was just weird, I guess. Then he realized what was going on but I'd already cut myself free of Grgur and I slid left into the knot of kids. Grgur kind of grabbed at the guy as he fell, and that gave me another beat. I singled out one of the healthier-looking of the punks and punched him in the face, not hard enough to really hurt him.

"You're under arrest, scumbag!" I shouted. He recovered and he and a couple of friends came at me, grabbing my hospital gown. I shrugged out of it, letting it rip over my head, and punched my way through the gathering melee over another tier of waiting-room seats and I vaulted over it. It felt good. I tossed the tranq bottle into a big pebbly trash can. Old Gruggle's had it, I thought. He shouldn't have messed with Big Red in the first place. He was bug meat from Go.

"Hang on," some major male voice said into a megaphone on the right. "*Sir!*" I just pushed toward the doors, only ten arms away. Through the fabric I spotted a couple of big guys in light suits pushing into the area along with the cops, but now there was a whole big Mexican extended kinship group coming in around us—a couple of the teenage bloods or guys or whatever they're called were wearing Kings colors—and I sort of steered us around them and got to the outer door and started to dance through it, like I was just a drugged-out party dude. Somebody grabbed my shoulder from behind and I whirled, not seeing well through the cheesecloth-covered eye-ovals in the mask, but it was just the kid I'd punched in the nose. I snapped the tip of my cast through his wrist and he dropped back, looking at it. I turned and walked at a relatively normal pace, toward the first pair of big double glass doors, and they opened around me. It seemed like being nearly naked was working in my favor, it threw people off a bit. Still, the sound coming from behind me gave me the impression that the Warren security people had almost gotten to us. The second door opened into a rush of blissfully real hot toad-breath twilight air. I didn't look back, I just padded across the concrete, opened the shotgun door of the Mexican family's old Dodge van, and slammed the door. There was a middle-aged woman, a maiden-aunt type, sitting at the wheel, and a couple of kids in the back. I crawled into the front seat and across her lap and looked out the open window. There was a black Maxima low-rider with a weird black-light glow coming out from under the chassis, like it was floating on a Xibalban color-cloud, and there was another fifteen-year-old pseudo-Maya wannabe at the wheel. I slid out the driver's door of the van, opened the Maxima's passenger door, slid in, way, and yanked the door shut behind me.

"Don't do anything or I'll kill you," I said in Spanish. "Drive around that taxi." The kid started to grab for something between his legs, so I killed him, swishing my cast-mace between his eyes, through the bridge of his nose, and then back through his Adam's apple. Instead of pushing him out I just shifted into drive, crouched down, pressed his foot down on the pedal, and steered us around the taxi judging by the lights overhead and then around a couple of minivans, sensed their bumpers with the low-rider's little catfish-barbels, and got us out into the far left lane and accelerated. We got out from under the overhang. Out of range, I thought. I stuck my head up and started really driving. I floored the thing around the sort of rotary and got to the ramp leading to the highway, scraping the ground. Low-riders are great, they really do corner. No flip, no slip. There were cop cars with sirens pulling into the overhang from the other side, way too late as usual. I buzzed over the road's molars—*rumble strips*, Jed's mind said, automatically but a little late—out of the hospital complex and up a curved slope and onto a frictionless gray sacbe, sliding between crystals of topaz, all identical and as big as a fist, set into the surface. Even with the sled's masks down—*windows open*—I was starting to smell the dead pre-blood's feces and urine, so I steadied the car for a few beats in the left lane, managed to get his jacket off him, and when I got up to about fifty I just opened the driver's-side door and body-nudged him out. I felt him bounce and the car started jerking all over. His leg was still partly caught in the shoulder harness and he was scraping along the asphalt, and from the way he twitched he was still partly alive. There was a little auto-rush of revulsion from the Jed side of my head, sort of fear and loathing combined, but I slashed through the strap with my cast-mace and finally he rolled away from the sled like a used-up captive into a mass grave. As the back roller bumped over him the car nearly skudged into the median strip, but I wrenched it inexpertly around, got back on course, and closed the door.

I knew to let Jed's motor memories take over. Despite my shameful fear of the giant sled he got the car onto the Great Sacbe. The wind felt great through my bandages. I'm just getting started, I thought. No stink of them here. SOUTH, I read off a green sign. Wrong color for South, I thought. I was going too fast to look around but I moved the rearview mirror from side to side. No cars coming up behind me, at least not fast. I looked at the gas. Enough, I somewhere knew the needle pointed to. Jed's mind seemed to think that the night watcher bloods, I mean, the police, might be relatively easy to shake because no matter what bonuses they were getting they'd still only assign a couple of people to the case. But I also had a large, well-funded private organization after me, which is a lot more serious. I figured I'd cruise as far as possible for about four-hundred-score beats and then change cars. No sweat, as they say these days. I started pulling at the last layer of magically clear cloth that was still stuck to my right hand. I watched the yellow speed indicator clicking up through these people's gangly base-ten numerals, up through a sort of sky or ceiling that Jed's mind called the Invisible Gardol Shield, 67, 71, 79, 83, 97. I touched the CRUISE glyph at 94 and held on to the steering plate like a child on its mother's back, feeling the speed of twenty Mixtec runners.

Score, I said to myself. Goal.

Game.

FOUR

The Anareta

(108)

I left the U.S. heading backward on the so-called "Maya Diaspora" illegal-immigration route that Jed had once sponsored, from Miami to San Antonio and then male-handward along what they called the Pan-American Sacbe through the resettled Teotihuacán and finally Belize City. I was able to utilize some of the fruits of Jed's paranoia. Before leaving Florida, I rolled someone from a pastless clan—I think they call them Homeless People here—for his revolting but correctly sized clothing, picked up a semifake passport from Jed_1's anonymous safe at a storage warehouse, and even found that he had set up a Dominican Republic account under a false name that would let me withdraw cash from Western Union ATMs using a code, and not a card—and after a bit of bullying, Jed's dying consciousness gave me the code. I kept up my pentadaily call to what Jed_1 had called his Secret Server, to keep it from spilling the beans. One of Jed_1's old Zeta contacts—I gambled on his being okay because it was one of a few that he'd never mentioned or entered on any keyboard—sold me some other papers and five very small explosive devices, which we FedExed, disguised as printer cartridges, to another Zeta guy in Ladyville, Belize.

Getting from Orlando to Belmopan used up five suns. By the time I dug in there, a jornada from the Stake, I'd become familiar enough with English and Spanish to interact with the domeheads without making Jed-in-Me interpret—he'd had a big advantage over me when he was my guest, of course, because he already spoke a decayed dialect of Chorti—and I even stopped bumping into people on the sidewalk. I'd been trying to pass them on the sunward side, what they'd call the British side. But people here went around things clockwise, as they called it. And there were other things that were hard to get used to. Car fart, or exhaust as they euphemistically called it, was one thing I could never handle, even though I'd slept in killing valleys filled in a fog of burning gangrene. Exhaust was soaked into everything, in the water and in the food. On the other hand there were the splendid things. I got so amazed by the Wal-Mart in Monterrey that I wasted hours just walking around in it. First it was the amount and variety of sheer things that got me, and then it was the goods themselves, rolls of turquoise foil and mats of fur cut, I thought, from giant blue deer that lived on the verso of the world in a place Jed's brain said was called China—and televisions and carnival glass and so on—but finally the oddest thing for me was the way the same complex object could be flawlessly repeated over and over, like it was one of those demons that used to live in the hills, who could be in different places at the same time. Metal bothered me, so I got a complete set of thirty-four Ming Tsai white ceramic knives. Then I found the upscale malls, and for a while I couldn't keep myself from buying all sorts of red-striped clothing at Versace and Richard James, until I realized it was making me stand out too much. So I forced myself to blend in, to dress for the hunt. I got my tattoos back as compensation, so I could wear some of my old power-glyphs inside, on my skin. The tattoo artist loved some of the designs so much he wanted to keep them, but I explained they were secret and if he let them out, I'd have to come back and eat him. I got my hair extended again. My hotel room started filling up with jewelry and exotic mock-weapons and sports equipment and gadgets from Sharper Image and Lifestyle Innovations. Eventually I realized that for some reason all the stuff that I thought was the most expensive, turquoise, jade, amber, ivory, jet, pyrite—all those things—were now the cheapest substances of all thanks to the new alchemy. Color, matter, and place were all worth nothing, and that had turned the people into cowards, only half alive.

I bought a thigh-top magic book and got Jed's fading memories working on hacking into the Warren files again, but I couldn't manage to do much.

Jed-in-Me felt almost gone. And I didn't have any tsam lic to help me crack the passwords. Finally I gave up. That Marena's going to have to do this stuff, I thought. Even if I have to boil her feet.

So instead, I focused on blending in. Food around now had been hard to get used to. Most of the foods I liked were easy to find, turkey, peanuts, chilies, tortillas, tequila—although they were all quite different, all uniform, with no souls. Corn was gigantic and sweet but they had only one kind on the ear. You could get the sacred blue strain—in fact, *anyone* could get it—but only in shards of broken tortillas. I found I could get venison and some fish and shellfish, but that dog, bats, locusts, and axolotl, and of course people, were almost unobtainable. When I did catch and cook up a stray dog, its flesh was gamy and festering with internal boils. Pet dogs were better but harder to capture, and still had that all-pervading taste of petroleum—which was the most unpleasant thing about the final hotun. The entire time, since I'd found myself in the hospital, there wasn't a single moment when I didn't hear and smell an engine digesting somewhere, on the streets, in the walls, overhead, whatever. So generally I stuck to turkey. There was even a kind of sacrificial festival for birds, with even the lower clans eating big fat birds, with divination by something they called the wishbone and the cranberry sauce standing in for blood.

I scattered my white blood a few times, with professionals from sex castes. Tony Sic's mutilated foreskinless penis was much less sensitive than mine had been, even with all the scars mine had from the offerings. Anyway, it wasn't safe, since I had to execute and dispose of them, so I gave it up.

The U.S.—increasingly an outcast state anyway—had had to recall ambassadors and shut down embassies in all of Latin America and in several countries around the world. Troops were being asked to leave their bases in over fifty countries. Another domino falling. Two weeks ago the UN had passed a resolution condemning the U.S.'s actions. The next domino. However, following the UK's lead, Belize had not passed a resolution condemning the U.S. With this as something of an excuse, two days ago Guatemala had demanded that Belize break off ties with the UK. Belize, knowing that would make them vulnerable to a Guate invasion, refused. Now, it seemed that the Guates were poised to cross into Belize at its southern and southeastern borders.

Among other countries, Guatemala was demanding that all U.S. military advisers leave the country. And the U.S. State Department was in crisis mode about it, since Belize was still a British protectorate, the borders were closed and the militaries of both countries were on full alert. I was by now understanding more and more about Jed's life and world and I wondered whether the conflict meant that Lindsay would have to cancel his planned Neo-Teo opening party at the NeoMayaLand Hyperbowl in Belize, less than two jornadas from the Guatemala border—or whether the dispute was something Lindsay wanted to make happen.

The newscasters mentioned that there were reports that officials in the stricken villages had received anonymous tips that something disastrous was going to happen—probably, it was said, from someone within the Drug Enforcement Administration who didn't agree with the policy.

And, in astronomical news, there was a new Herbig Ae/Be star in the Pleiades.

Jed's memories gave me four hundred times four hundred ways of keeping out of sight. I worked out a good approach, a very direct one, low tech for today's post-high-tech world, and crossed what was now the border of the Stake well ahead of time. I hid out in a dry wash near a hot water pipe from the power plant, in a foundation for a cooling tank that wouldn't begin construction until the next b'aktun, which meant never.

Even when I'd been hiding out in Texas KOA kampgrounds, I learned from police broadcasts that while there was a warrant out for me, it wasn't for murder or even assault but simply for fleeing arrest. There was nothing saying I was armed and/or dangerous. Evidently Lindsay's people didn't want me to get caught by the police and must have managed to cover up the killings at the hospital.

On what they called December sixteenth I moved into a pastless—I mean, transient dwelling in the suburbs. That night—the seventeenth—the events of the Greatfather Heat's incarnations seemed promising. I started acquiring and testing the hardware I needed and studying the Hyperbowl compound from a safe distance. After a few days of frustration, I learned to draw on Jed's knowledge of computers, and eventually I reconstructed enough skills from Jed's memories to master the basic programming that would be necessary to work my way into the Warren systems. Many of Jed's math skills seemed to work more or less automatically, ready for anyone to use. And while I certainly never really understood anything more complex than a simple loop, computers, surprisingly, fascinated more than repelled me. Without Jed's uay, I could not have done it.

Were they watching me? Did I have any tracking implants? By mid-December, I'd taken too much evasive action and had been examined by enough underground-friendly doctors to be pretty sure I could answer the last two questions in the negative. Speaking of which, my fractured right hand was healing faster than I'd have thought. All good. All good.

I hired a truck driver to smuggle me to the Stake. There were patrols out and Jed—in either body—would have been spotted right away, but I used the old methods, sticking to the jungles, wearing and carrying very little, and keeping all my metal equipment in a little Otter fishing-tackle case. I made an ambush camp under a collapsed wooden water tank in sight of the border and waited.

When I felt the time was right, I crossed the trench, the electric fences, picking up a couple shocks, but ignoring them and the field of razor-wire, which I rolled over, laying down Kevlar blankets.

As I expected, the security at the Stake's inner Olympic Complex was harder to penetrate than the border. There were trucks and passenger vans going in and out, and helicopters and, once, a new white Zeppelin, landing with VIP guests for the opening—which had not been put off by the hail—but despite the activity at the gates, I decided to sneak in the old way. Through radio intercepts and observation, I found that, evidently because of the war, there was a fleet of small remote-piloted vehicles patrolling the air above the Stake and, certainly, watching the ground. This was a setback, but finally, during a brief rain before dawn (off-season, because of the mixed-up weather) I took a chance and made my way across the perimeter. I rubbed myself with burro dung to throw off the guard dogs, crawled through ten rope-lengths of card teasel and poison ivy, and lay motionless for eight hours until I was sure I could get to what seemed to be a currently unworked construction site near the racetrack. I hid out, as I'd learned to do in my youth, silently, unmoving, in a pylon excavation, eating Snickers bars and putting my human waste into baggies of sodium polyacrylate beads. When the Pleiades rose that night, the new star, which they'd named Akhushtal, was clearly visible just below Maia. No surprise there. Lady Koh had been right again. And in that video, Lindsay'd meant "Live in Maia." Not Maya. He never pronounced "Maya" right anyway. Maia like the star in the Pleiades. The next Kobol, I guess. He also knew.

At the death of Grandfather Heat, I waylaid a right-sized waiter near one of the pools, washed myself in the unearthly blue water, took his clothes, key cards, IDs, and a room-service cart, and walked into the hotel lobby and up to Marena's room—which I'd located by monitoring conversations on the waiters' earphones. Jed's bible was the Collected Works of Ian Fleming, and I'd decided to stick to the faith. Anyway, it's not so hard to get into a place as long as you don't care about getting out. The very second key card made the lock light green. I walked in. She was already dressed, in a flinty pants suit, a garnet necklace, and up hair, but still without her sandals. She tried not to show that she was surprised to see me, and then not to show that she thought I was going to try and kill her. But she picked up a square chrome-framed table mirror in both hands and weighed it like she was going to swing it through my face.

It wasn't hard to get her on board, though. Even though she'd thought I still wanted to kill her.

"I know what's happening," I said, "and I can stop it."

Well, actually, I had to put in another few words.

"Look," she said, "if you're not going to save Max, I'm not interested."

"We're going to save Max. And everybody."

"Who cares about everybody?"

"Fine."

"Fine."

"All in the light, then," I said. "Fine."

"Fine. Tell me."

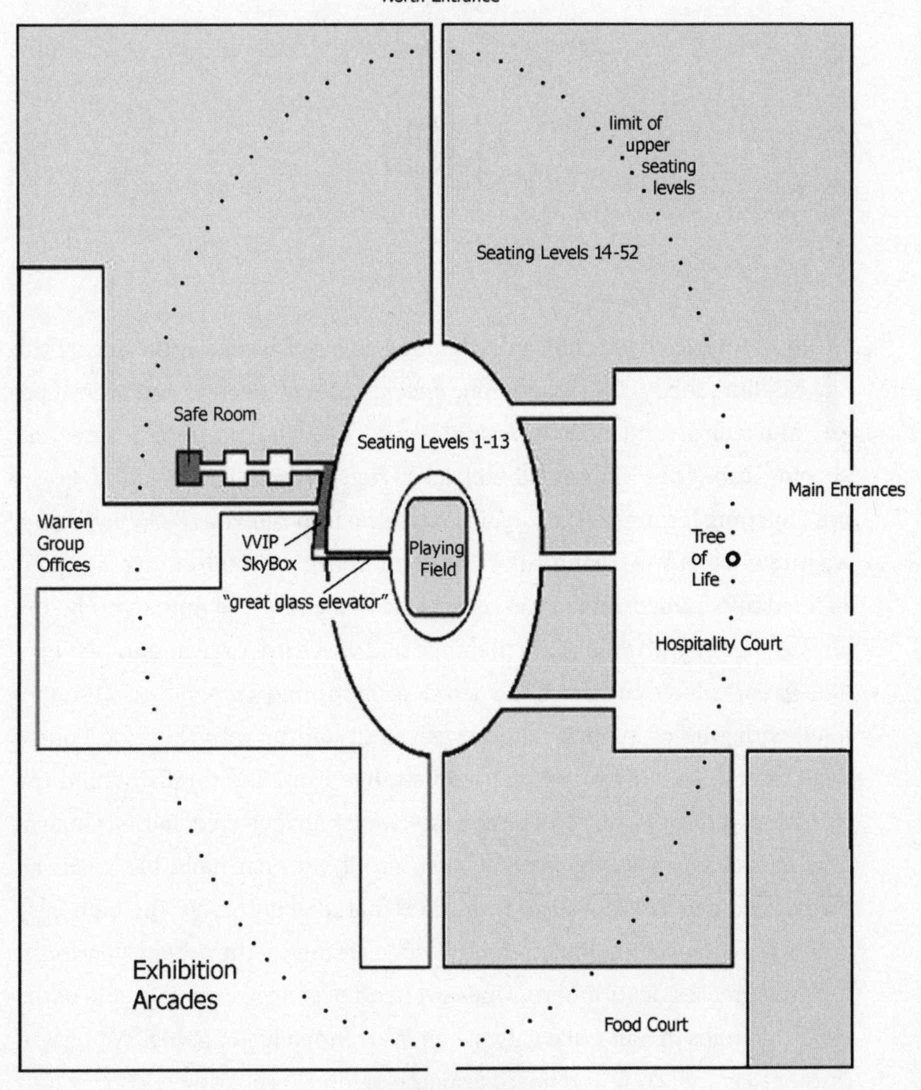
BELIZE OLYMPIC HYPERBOWL
North Entrance
limit of
upper
seating
levels
Seating Levels 14-52
Safe Room
Seating Levels 1-13
Main Entrances
Warren
Group
Offices
VVIP
SkyBox
Playing
Field
Tree
of
Life
"great glass elevator"
Hospitality Court
Exhibition
Arcades
Food Court
South Entrance

(109)

The center gate led right into the long covered arcade approaching the stadium lobby. There were four checkpoints of greeters and identifiers and guards, and a few thousand neo-MARCOSite protestors they were keeping at bay but Marena biometricked herself through the gauntlet, and her vouching for me worked again. We came into the Warren lobby, which was now a kind of far-up-the-scale food court, or food empyrean, as it seemed to be called, laid out as an idealized diagram of a human body. The air was breezy with what Jed's memory said was extra oxygen pumped in.

Marena piloted me down the center aisle, around a green central square filled with ears of quadricolored sweet corn and up into the food court's head, past counters of fish flesh and strange fruit. The thralls behind the counters were working screens of base-twenty abacus-calculators. Once in a while she squeezed my arm, cutting into it with her nails, like I was an overturned canoe. We walked into the Hyperbowl entrance. The high false arch was flanked with animated DHI video statues of the athletes performing their greatest feats and routines over and over again, monuments of the 2002 Olympics in Salt Lake City, when Warren really got going. We passed through a sound cone and heard a snatch of John Tesch's voice: "*At this time we'd like to extend our condolences to the family of Greg 'The Leg' Nagel, our beloved Jaguar forward, who passed away during practice earlier today. As we all know, Greg's outstanding stats included . . .*"

Trapezoidal doors slid open and shut around us and the air changed to some designer mix, cool but still tropical and scented like a disinfected rain forest. It was almost quiet because of the active sound baffles, but there was the *roorsh* of artificial waterfalls and conversation.

"Let me carry your handbag," I said, grabbing it on the second word.

The lobby was almost large enough to enclose the Ocelots' mul. But it was still all in earth colors, with five kinds of grass growing out of slits in the granite floor and clusters of furniture twisted out of unfinished hardwood. There were about two thousand people milling around on the floor in black and white clusters dotted with much more colorful neo-Maya outfits, all mood-lit by pin spots slowly roving through the gloom. I noticed Shaquille O'Neal and a few other emeritus basketball players sticking up out of the crowd like spirit poles in a cornfield. There were also quite a few officers' uniforms, Belizean, British Territorial, and U.S. In the center of the room, where the information kiosk would have been, a giant thing rose up three rope-lengths, almost too confusing-looking to name at first, a tower, a ceiba tree, a poplar tree, a wooden stele, a stone stele, a high-angled pyramid, a Christmas tree. The ornaments were all DHI spheres, most of them running different views of the Ix Ilä softworld. One of them showed a slowly rotating readout of today's soon-to-expire Maya date:

On the far side of the lobby high-arched corridors led through to what I figured were the stadium seats. There weren't any crowd-control stanchions that I could see. Good.

The first person we knew who saw us was Michael Weiner, in full Neo-Maya drag.

"Hi," I said. "Wow. You look absolutely . . . uh . . . suburban."

He opened his mouth and then shut it. It was a true-bliss moment.

"Tony?" he asked.

"Hi," I said. He didn't clap me on the back, like usual, so I clapped him on his. He had on a sort of carcanet, a quilted ceremonial collar, and I managed to get the brown Bug Bom planted on it without anyone noticing. The colors didn't quite match, but I figured nobody would notice. "How's my favorite thing on the History Channel?" I asked.

"I'm, I'm fine," he said.

"Yoo-hoo!" someone said. She pushed through to us. She had hair. Very faintly, Jed's crumbling Book of Uay's Names seemed to read that they called her $Ashley_1$. She was holding a phone, which I guess she'd spotted us on.

"Come on," I said to Michael. "We're going to go talk with Lindsay and I want to ask you both something. Okay?"

"Uh, okay," Michael said.

"You are *so* great," A_1 said to Marena, talking loud above the noise of the crowd. "You actually decided to make it!" She'd met Tony Sic, but she didn't recognize me, although that didn't mean much because she was as dumb as a bag of squashes. Two bags. "So, great, great, great," she went on, "let me show—"

"Thanks," Marena cut her off. "Listen, could you find Lindsay for me?"

"Uh, okay, he'll be thrilled you made it—"

"It's really important. Seriously."

"Sure." She held her phone up to the crowd and waved it around. "Okay, I got him," she said. I looked over Marena's shoulder at the screen. It turned the real architecture behind it to a wire-frame model of the room with little security-tag dots floating around.

"Okay," A_1 said, "Lindsay's this pink dot with the *L*."

"Great," I said. It meant he was over behind the Tree of Life, under the giant display screen. Marena clocked him herself and led me left and down a flight of stairs on the left out onto the floor and around a tableful of barbecued emu skewers and would-be primevally menacing ice sculptures and into a darkened area behind a row of dichromatic halogen spots. Michael and $Ashley_1$ followed along.

"That's Bob Costas over there," she whispered to me.

"Who?" I asked.

"There."

"Huh."

"You know, the great many, many award-winning sportscaster," she said. "He's here with John Tesch."

"Oh, right, that's, yes," I said. "That's a big deal."

"Exactly," Ashley$_1$ chirped, brightly. "Defini*tive*ly. Great, great, great." She went back to pointing out all these people you'd never heard of. Well, at least, I'd never heard of them. In the old days we would have said they were mouse-uayed people pretending to be felines. Here I guess we'd just say they were irretrievably B-list. I caught up with Marena, but some ditzy-grinned lady had buttonholed her.

"Uh, Tony?" Marena said. "Michael? You guys know Peggy Noonan, right? Peggy Noonan, Tony Sic." The woman held her hand out.

"Hi. Wow, the Leni Riefenstahl of speechwriting," I blurted out, before I quite knew what I was saying. "It is nice to meet you, but your hand has too much blood on it." She froze for a split-beat. "Your old boss had my parents killed." Noonan turned and stalked off. Jed would never have had the nerve to say that, I thought.

"Thanks a lot," Marena said. "It wasn't Jed who said that, was it?"

"No," I said. "But I support some of Jed's causes. Jed is an old friend."

"You're such a self-righteous cornball," she said. "You're dis-fucking-gusting, I mean, I don't love her, either, but for crying out bloody tears."

"What's going on?" Michael said. "The last thing I heard you were in real trouble."

I mumbled something.

"There he is," Marena said. Lindsay was about thirty steps femaleward of us, standing under the Tree of Life, ringed by a bunch of what looked like investors. You had to hand something to him, he had this whole vast private-army black op going on right at this moment and he was standing here shmoozing like he didn't have a care in the world. A waiter held a tray out at us.

"Is that celery?" I asked.

"I'm sorry, they're white chocolate sticks," he said.

"Oh, great." There were ten of them. I took nine.

"No, thanks," Marena said.

"Come on, have one," I said.

Lindsay had on a gray summery jacket and I dug the Bug Bom with two dots—the gray-covered one—out of Marena's handbag. It wasn't a great match, either, but it would have to do. I wanted to go right up to him, but Marena said it looked like he was going to send them on their way pretty soon.

"Okay, let's hang back for a beat," I said. I ate a chocolate stick.

There were two identifiable security people standing behind him. One of them I hadn't seen before, a big classy-bodyguard type in a black tie with an earphone. The other was that commando woman from the Creep, Ana Vergara. She was in leggings and a close-fitting black huipil and looking almost attractive, for a hired enforceress. She hadn't spotted me yet, but she would.

"Do you know that they're all, I mean, the police," Michael said, "they're all looking for you?"

"Oh, yeah," I said, "I know, I'm too fast for them."

The covey of investors laughed—what was the funny part? I wondered—nodded, and turned toward the entrance to the playing field. Other people were hanging around, too, waiting to talk with the great man, but Marena pushed through and tapped him on the shoulder. He seemed genuinely happy to see her, although of course he wasn't. She said something to him—I hoped it was what I had told her to say—and he turned around, to his left. Ana had spotted me now, but she expected me to stay where I was so Lindsay could face me, and instead I had just enough time to move around to his right and clap him on the back. Beneath the cashmere, the silk lining, the Sea Island broadcloth, and the Jesus jumper, his trapezius muscles were surprisingly hard against my fingertips. "Hail, fellow, well met," I said.

Lindsay kept turning. He hadn't felt the bug yet, since it was just held on with Velcro. When he recognized me he was pretty smooth, his expression didn't change, but he didn't say hello. He just stood there, waiting for Ana and whoever to take care of it, seeming relaxed, his look radiating that he was a big guy and I was a little guy and big guys just don't get fucked with. He was wearing an American-flag lapel pin and a dressier bumblebee pin, this one with yellow sapphires.

"Chief, don't move," Ana said. She'd spotted the bug, and she knew what it was. I squoze the button in my pocket that activated its little hooked legs. Lindsay felt them digging down through his jacket and into his flesh and jumped a little.

quilting on his collar, and without the bug's hooks in, the pellets might not go through, but I needn't have worried. There was a sound like a buried firecracker and a hiss as the Bom's hollow shell flew across the lobby. A surprised expression bloomed on Michael's face.

"Oh, shit, somebody get a goddamn paramedic," Marena said, loudly but not shouting.

It usually takes a lot longer for someone to respond to sedation or poisoning than one thinks it should. Blood in any given capillary will return to the heart in about twenty-three seconds, but after that it still takes some time for whatever it is to get absorbed through the cell walls of the heart or lungs. So often there are two hundred or so beats of lag time. But the Bom did a good job of scattering its crystals through a wide range of levels and locations in Michael's back, and in less than thirty beats the look of surprise turned to—well, I am not sure what the English word would be. Let us say it was a rich mixture of pain, fear, and rage. He wobbled and started to fall, but Ana held him up. I looked back at Lindsay. He was still thinking about pulling off his jacket.

"DO NOT MOVE," I said again. "Seriously. If you pull too hard on that, it will fire on its own. It is *not* the tranquilizer shit it comes with in there."

"Shut up," the Big Guy said. He pushed my head down.

"There are enough neurotoxin crystals in there to kill a blue whale," I said. As if to illustrate the point, I heard Ana easing Michael down onto the floor. He gurgled. Probably his heart had already seized up. "If you pull my arm back any farther I'm setting it off," I said to the Big Guy. "Also, I have to enter a stay-of-execution code every two hundred and ten beats. Three minutes, rather. So, I want—"

"We make these things," Lindsay interrupted. "There's a way to get them off."

"Go for it," I said. I could hear the Big Guy mumbling into the air, asking for backup over his ear thing.

"Good deal," Lindsay said. There was just a lot of confidence there. Even to me, he just seemed senior, the way 2 Jeweled Skull had. I suppose the equivalent in this era would be the way the school principal looks to a third-grader.

"I have said enough," I said.

For about twenty beats, Lindsay seemed to be conferring with Ana and maybe Marena, although I couldn't see them. Finally they seemed to have made a decision. Lindsay came over, crouched down—I could see the heels of shoes, which, maybe oddly, were black bowling shoes, rising off the floor—and must have signaled for the Big Guy to let my head up so that I could look at him.

"Come on, have them let me go," I said. I gave him a little buzz and he froze. That was another well-designed thing about the system. It really *felt* like it was going to explode. "And *do not* walk away, I'll blast you just like Fuckwad here." I looked over at Michael for emphasis. A paraperson was already trying to give him mouth-to-mouth resuscitation.

"What do you want to talk about?" Lindsay asked.

"I am not negotiating," I said. "I do not want to kill you, I just want to chat, but you know, if anything happens to me I do want to take you down with me. Also I have to keep punching this thing or it'll go off by itself anyway. Do you understand?"

He didn't answer.

"Anyway, the release code is thirteen digits long, and you will never get it out of me in time. Also, I promise I am not going to be asking for much. Could you get this guy to take it easy?"

"Doug, take it easy," Lindsay said to the Big Guy. Doug's grip relaxed and I could look up.

"Marena?" I asked. "Could you button Lindsay's jacket for him? Including the top button."

"What do you think?" Marena asked him.

"Fine, do it," he said.

She did. It made Lindsay look turn-of-the-century. I mean, the century before the last one.

"Dump out your pockets and then put your hands in them," I said. He started to but they were still sewn together. "Not your jacket pockets, your front pants pockets."

He did. A couple of old coins bounced on the floor. Behind him the paramedic pulled away from Michael and came up with a mouthful of blood. I am glad I do not have that job, I thought. I looked back at Lindsay. He had not moved.

"Maybe you will kill me whatever happens," he said.

"Nonsense," I said, "if I wanted to do that I would have done it already. You think you are that hard to get to? I am just concerned about my role in your new administration. We are on the same side of the court on this."

"All righty," he said. "Except you're not going to get out of here whether I want you to or not."

"I know, but I still recommend you stall for time. Is not that the standard procedure?"

There was a kind of Woo standoff for seventy beats while Lindsay talked with Ana. Finally they let me up. Without looking away from my eyes, Lindsay cracked enough to raise a finger. Doug pried his hands off my arms.

Lindsay just darted his eyes toward the south wall and Doug and Ana fell instantly into line, leading Marena and me on a straight cut through the freaked crowd and along the long granite wall behind the dessert tables. Doug did not loosen his grip on my arm but he did talk into the air again, telling the backup security to hold back. Ana led us around a corner toward the bank of elevators. "Let's go up to your office," I said to Lindsay. "This is a bummer party anyway, I've never seen so many nobodies in my *life*." Ana opened the door to a big blond-wood-paneled container by holding her palm over a little red laser.

"Not that one," I said. "Let's go up to the box." I turned and walked to the end of the line, making them follow me, to the Elevator V, the one that led to the floor behind the VIP box. Lindsay signaled okay and Doug opened it.

"Could you move all the VIPs out of the VIP box?" I asked Lindsay. "Maybe send them on a tour of the locker room?"

He gave Ana the order. She sent it over her ear.

"You can let go of his arm," Lindsay said. Doug did.

"Thanks," I said. A Glorious Foodster slid past with his tray still in his hand and I grabbed a highball glass of what turned out to be upscale chocolate soda.

"The guards can't come up," I said.

"That's impossible, they have to," Lindsay said.

"No, I'm sticking on that issue," I said. There was another pause, as tense as if we were waiting for the first ball to unravel its knot and drop onto the marker. I tossed off the soda and dropped the tumbler on the floor just to hear the sweet sound of breaking glass.

"Okay, fine," Lindsay said, "Look, I can talk for twenty minutes. Then I have to go back down and check the guests. Or you'll have to kill me."

"That's fine, that's plenty," I said, "thanks for taking the time, I know a lot of people want to get in to see you—"

"Oh, please," he said. "Doug, you go up to twelve. Ana, you cover the fire exits."

"Ten-four," she said.

I stepped into the elevator. Marena followed and then Lindsay. The time on the panel said 3:21:02 P.M. Roughly two hours and eight minutes left before the Sweeper test. Better keep moving. Marena punched in the eight-digit code for the fourteenth floor. As the door started to close, Ana still was looking at me with her watchful eyes. We started up.

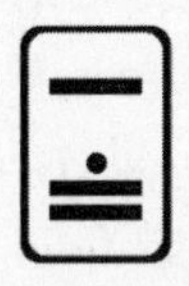

(111)

This time there was a long acceleration. I looked away from the security camera. There was an instant of equilibrium and then a slower deceleration and a D note on a nonexistent metalophone.

The door hissed open on a big would-be-classy waiting room. Three meters in front of us a single security dude was standing up behind a glass reception desk, holding a communicator to his ear, his mouth open. To the right a wide glass door led into Lindsay's VIP box, with the last of the VIPs filing out of it into the Great Glass Elevator. We waited for a beat and as the elevator went down I led Lindsay and Marena past the puzzled desk guy. As the next set of glass doors opened themselves we heard the BONG of another elevator landing somewhere. Lindsay looked around. A bunch of new guards had come around the corner to the right. They were in heavy gray TAC-team gear, like puffy gnomoids. They weren't rushing at us, though, they were just standing there wondering if there was really a problem.

"Listen, Lindseed," I whispered, "call them off *now*. Seriously."

"This is Lindsay Warren, stay there!" he yelled at them. "FLOOR GUARDS, STAND FAST!" They paused. "I'll page you in a second," he said.

We turned our back on them and went in. The door sealed itself behind us. Lindsay led us into the box, past the Great Glass Elevator and the windows looking down on the interior of the Hyperbowl. A stage with a proprietary Sleeker-friendly surface stage had rolled out over the ball pit and they were doing some kind of elaborate rite, or what they would call a halftime show or awards ceremony. The recipient of whatever it was—some of the signage said it was the Oskars, but since they spelled it that way I figured they had had trouble with the actual Oscars, which might still be going on somewhere—was standing on a scaffold in a tiara, giving a speech about how lucky and well-meaning she was. The VVIP SkyBox was empty, with signs of recent recreational use.

"Let's talk in the Blue Bin, or whatever you call it."

Lindsay punched a code into a panel on the far wall. The door slid to the side with a little sizzle. It was probably just a sound effect they'd put in to make the whole thing seem more cool. I made sure I'd remembered the code and then made the three of them go in first.

Lindsay's Blue Room—which was really known as the Safe Room, or the Sealing Room—was steel-lined on all four sides and had no windows. It had only been slightly face-lifted since Jed_1 had been here, so it was still about two rope-lengths square, with a one-rope-length ceiling and only two doors, one directly opposite the door we'd come through. There was a square black-granite conference table in the center of the room, off-angle so that you could sit at it and see all four walls, and in the center of the table, about an arm square, a DHI holo-block layout of the Game, with the center bin taken up by a small model of the temple district and stadium complex of Neo-Teo. It was turned off, with only a single green light marking our position in the stadium, but I could still see that it had been vastly improved. The only other solid things in the room were twelve black chairs. The ceiling was white and emanated a cheap-feeling ethereal glow, and the walls looked like blue silk. Each had what looked like a big oil painting in a wide black frame. Directly across from us, that is, on the western wall, there was a scene of Lehi arriving in the Promised Land in an odd sort of boat like a wooden submarine. On our right there was a bigger canvas of Christ in America. It showed Jesus upstage left, his hands outstretched showing his wounds, and behind him the Pyramid of the Castillo at Chichen Itza. A group of rather Anglo-looking ancient Maya surrounded Christ, regarding him with varied attitudes of gratitude and awe. One of the women was wearing a huipil that was almost authentic, but the men sported anachronistic gold neck-plates and quetzal-plumed pickelhaubes like nineteenth-century Prussian officers. On our left another mural showed Nephi Making Gold Plates. Behind him, Teotihuacán burned, except, judging from the fall foliage around him, Teotihuacán seemed to be somewhere in Upstate New York. The last painting, above the door we'd come through, showed the Angel Moroni appearing to Joseph Smith, pointing out the buried Plates of Nephi with his radiant finger.

"Have a sit," I said to Lindsay, pointing to the center chair on the table's southeast side. "Keep your fingers off the tabletop." Be more careful, I thought. I fingered the detonator buttons on my phone. "Put your hands through the arms of the chair and on your thighs. Please."

He did. As he raised his arms his jacket pulled a bit on the Bom and he winced a little.

"Push your chair back an arm. Two feet. Right." I took a crushed roll of clear packing tape out of my lapel pocket and tossed it to Marena. She did not catch it. "It is just tape," I said. I got her to pick it up off the floor and tape Lindsay's wrists to the arms of the Aeron. After some explanation, I got him to cross his feet behind the chair's stalk, and Marena taped them to the base. I also had her run two loops around his chest and around the headrest. The Bom would not go off from pressure, but I did not want him weakening its hold on his flesh by slamming back and forth. I took off my live badge, slid it over to her, and had her exchange it with Lindsay's. I had Marena sit in the central southwest and tape her own ankles. She slipped her feet out of shoes that, according to Jed's irksome memory for trivia, were vintage albino-boa-skin Roger Viviers. I was about to tell her to put them back on and then decided against it. I did her last wrist myself, not getting too close. She was tricky. But she believed I could do what she wanted. I think.

I clipped Lindsay's live badge to my chest and sat cross-legged in the center of the northwest.

Whew. A breather. Finally. I spat out my plastic cheek inserts and rubbed the fake fingerprints off my hands, switching my phone from one to the other. Do *not* let go of that, I thought.

"Okay," Lindsay said. "Now, what kind of a deal are you looking for?"

(112)

Lindsay was certainly less surprised about all this than one might have thought. I suppose that like any businessman, he was always expecting a shakedown. And in fact, that was probably the right thing to expect from a domehead like Jed. But from me it was not, or rather from me it would not be for money. He was about to get shaken down for the main event.

"The first thing we need to do is harden this room," I said.

I tapped the tabletop. The granite effect disappeared and a keyboard and standard interface screen—Warren proprietary, but basically like Windows—bloomed on its north quadrant. The tabletop functioned as a single large touchscreen, leading to a station that could control hundreds of Warren's networks. I got to Lindsay's personal desktop, to MENU, to SEALING ROOM SYSTEMS, and to ISOLATE SEALING ROOM SYSTEMS, before I had to ask for Lindsay for a password. He gave me one and it worked. When I closed the vault-style doors over the standard door behind us I could almost feel the steel dead bolts sliding shut. I did the same thing with the rest of the floor, locking down the Great Glass Elevator, the six other elevators, and even, contrary to regulations in nonprivate countries, the fire doors to the stairs. According to the room's HELP file, they could not be opened from outside, even if there were a fire. Lindsay had probably guessed that I would make contact at some point, although he had not expected this situation.

On the one hand, I could not get out of here. But on the other hand, Ana's group couldn't use any of the usual hostage-grabbing tactics, or even exotic ones like CCV, that is, Cognition-Compromising Vapor, or stupid-making gas. So far, Lindsay's millennial paranoia, especially his care in constructing his refuge, was working against him. I looked at my watch. It was 3:23 P.M.

"I'm awfully busy," Lindsay said. He sounded less worried than one might think.

"I know," I said. "Do not worry. If everything goes well, I am not going to interfere with the invasion."

Lindsay and Marena both reacted to this, although I had the sense that only Lindsay knew what I was talking about.

"All right," I said. "Well, as always, the first thing is to get drugs. I understand there is a new formulation of the tsam lic."

"That's correct," Lindsay said.

"There should be some in a wall safe in this room."

"I don't think so."

"Let's see," I said.

After some back-and-forth, he told me how to open the safe. The door swung out of the blue-silk-looking wall without any booby traps. There were a few interesting-looking things inside—storage chips, wrapped cash, jewelry rolls, the Vase of the Seven Xibalban Gods that used to be in the Art Institute of Chicago—but all I took out was a pharmacy bottle labeled 41-037. It was full of white gelcaps.

"Where is the bar?" I asked.

Lindsay told me. It opened the same way. It was a whole little alcove with hot and cold running everything, so I got a glass of warm water. I opened one of the gel caps and tasted the powder. Even though it was a synthetic version, my tongue could still tell that it was the real deal, and more potent than ever. I swallowed the powder and pocketed the rest of the capsules. I drank the water.

By now the Hyperbowl took up most of our field of view. It had been refaced and enlarged and was now an impossibly huge truncated cone, stepped like a pyramid but too squat and too big, a gold-glass-sheathed tumor that supposedly seated 255,300 people. A ring of 365 vertical white lasers, bright enough to be visible in daylight, beamed from the roof up into space in an update of the Lichtdom, Albert Speer's searchlight pillars at the Party Conference at the Zeppelintribune in 1934. Despite its hugeitude, though, the stadium was just part of a larger sports district. Off to the north I could see something like the Disney Mad Hatter's Tea Party Ride. A little east of that, gladiators in furry suits fought in big clear balls. The whole thing had a sense of continuous, controlled combat, a cross between extreme fighting, a rave party, and an elegant promenade. Most people had sandals with some kind of Sleeker striations on the soles that functioned as skates. Some of them were pushing carts with gliders instead of wheels. I tried to read their clans by the color coding, but I got the feeling that clan membership was decided more by competition and adoption than by birth. Anyway, most people from the powerful clans were probably inside waiting for the Big Hipball Game, the ball game that would, presumably, launch the new era. Everyone else would watch it on whatever the new 3-D system was—probably a better view, at this point, but reality still had a certain prestige. The pipes sounded again three octaves up, and I recognized what they were playing: the introduction to "Stairway to Heaven." Christ, I thought, what is this, the Class of 1978 Junior Prom? Evidently the revolution hadn't been exclusively a highbrow event.

Wait a beat, I thought. Had I thought that, or was it Jed? I barely knew what a junior prom was. The last thing I needed was for Jed to start butting in again. Well, worry about that later.

"So, Lindsay?" I asked. "Let us play Password."

"What password is that?" he asked.

"Let's just get into the sysop desk first."

"All right," he said. I slid a phone over to him—not my own, but one of the three fresh ones I'd brought along. I liberated his right hand. He spent some time flexing the circulation back into it, as though he was reluctant to start, and I was about turn up his dorsal joy-buzzer when he typed thirteen keys and slid it back to me. It said SAMARANA7104.

I pecked it out on the lengthening password list in my own phone. I wished I still had Jed$_1$'s brain's facility for remembering everything. But why get hung up on details?

I typed in the password one-handed on the desktop. Marena snuck a look at what I was doing but there was a chunk of DHI model between her and my hand.

A menu came up labeled SEALING ROOM PROFILES. It looked pretty simple. Lindsay's programmers had made the interface so user-sycophantic anybody could do it.

I touched an item called SET VIDEO WALLS. The big "paintings" of Christ in America and whatever disappeared and the walls went to black. The ceiling light dimmed and a vast A-chord came from an angelic choir everywhere at once.

The walls began to fill up with stars and, one after another, Mercury, Venus, Earth, and the other neighborly planets, all complacently rouletting around the solar drain. The room's walls, ceiling, and even floor were entirely covered with a seamless mosaic of DHI video panels, so a huge number of interface windows, from any source, could be called up and displayed simultaneously. Since Jed had last seen it, the system had been upgraded with iris-sensing xographic panels that could display in 3-D, and the current show was overusing the effect, trying to make us feel like we were really floating through a friendlier version of outer space.

"The Great White God of Ancient America still lives!" an impossibly deep voice said. An image of a tall, Caucasian Jesus rose out of outer space. *"The divine personage that emerges from the discoveries of archaeologists now stands out as an unassailable reality."*

"I don't think that is the right channel," I said.

"Try Five," Lindsay said.

"This being," the room said, *"known to the Mayans as Kukulcan, to the Mexicans as Quetzalcoatl, was also known as Wixpechocha in Chiapas . . ."*

"Jeez, Lindsay," Marena said. "You're really into this bullshit, aren't you?"

I found Channel Five. A long menu came up.

"Who was this Great White God who appeared to the ancient Americans?" James Oreo Vader-Jones asked. *"The Father of the Maya, Caculhá Huracán, the Heart of Heaven, Quetzalcoatl?"*

Faux Dvořák music welled up.

"Who was the Feathered Serpent, the White and bearded Lord of Light? He is Jesus the Christ, the Savior of all Mankind."

"How do we turn this off?" I asked.

"I'll do it," Lindsay said.

"We are not going to untape you," I said.

"Try END TOUR PRESENTATION," he said.

"I mean, I hate to break it to you," Marena said, "but Jesus Hershel Christ did not fly over to Central America and rap with the Oldmexes or the Latexes or whoever, and he definitely was not Itchy Coo-Coo or Kukluxfranandoli or whatever the shit his name was, the whole thing is just ri-fucking-diculous."

"Millions of people believe it," Lindsay said. Don't they have something more important to talk about? I wondered. It's amazing how they chitchat around here. The world could be ending and they'd—well, in fact—never mind. Keep typing, I thought. Don't look at the keyboard, it'll just confuse you. Use Sic's muscle memory. Damn. I was having trouble finding the command. I tried again. How many attempts before it turns itself off? On the screens we were being treated to a montage of aerial shots of other Mesoamerican sites, Cleft Sky, Teotihuacán, and Ix. I got that hometown feeling.

"So what," Marena said, "millions of people believe, like, I don't know, they believe that Kenneth Branagh's a talented actor. They believe anything anybody ever tells them. Whatever." She was getting more nervous and less articulate. On the big video display the heavenly outer space had been replaced by postcardy shots of the Ciudadela at Chichen.

"When the Crucifixion took place and the earthquake shook Palestine, even worse conflagrations swept over the Western Hemisphere . . ."

Marena turned to me. "Doesn't this stuff upset you?" she asked. She was trying to feel me out a bit.

"Not really," I said, trying to look like I knew what I was doing.

"The Book of Mormon tells the story of the Christ in the New World . . ."

Hah. Found it. Kill.

The *Christ in America* show winked out. The walls went to black.

"Thank the Lord," Marena said. Actually, she was right. I hated what I'd seen of Christianity even more than Jed had. It had such a bad case of the cutes. I mean, just for one thing, crucifying someone on a world-tree is *not* the most painful thing you can do to him. Not to brag, but if I were going to get to be Supreme Ruler of the Entire Universe for doing it, I could hang out nailed to a cross all day and barely even notice. In fact, I bet I could roll jade earspools through my fingers on both hands and sing the Harpy Ball Brethren marching song over and over, all day, for three days.

I touched HYPERBOWL LOCAL SURVEILLANCE.

(113)

The model of Neo-Teo in the center of the table lit up. A corresponding map came up on the far wall. Numbered windows from hundreds of cameras all over the compound blossomed over the walls. There were panoramas of the temple and sports districts and other key locations, and even a view from a satellite exactly 11,088,000 inches directly overhead. A few showed the festivities down in the arena. The Celebrity who we'd seen before, whose name I still forget, was finishing a sappy offering chant. Next to it, on a live window running the big in-house show, we were being treated to close-ups of audience reactions, teenage boys laughing, teenage girls singing along, and fat women weeping happily, sobbing happily away, getting their daily catharsis. I checked out a view of the main lobby downstairs. The party seemed to be going on fine, only slightly subdued after the Weiner incident. Another window, twenty-three, showed an overhead view of the rotary outside the East Gate, the one we had come through. A protest outside had already gotten out of hand, and Warren security guards with giant transparent shields were forming a sort of tortoise, almost like the Teotihuacanian infantry's. Foam spray appeared out of an invisible fire hose and covered the dark mass of protesters with white flakes. I panned the camera back with the cursor. Belize police in electric ATVs were crowding around the edges of the rotary like overzealous T-cells.

"A riot," I said. "Fun."

I blew up a few of the windows that were most important to me personally: specifically, those showing the fire stairs, elevator shafts, and the floor below us. Doug was on twelve. Ana Vergara had a team in each of the stairways. She was in the one that led to the fire exit on the outside, that is, the nonstadium side, of the Safe Room. It was a whole little army with shotguns and assault carbines, and they had also gotten two whole destruction crews together, with electric rams and oxyacetylene torches and sensors and gas mines and paramedics and whatever, like they were ready to take on Kim Jong-uns secret redout under Mount Myohyang. I made sure I had good views up of the empty VIP box and the rest of the deserted thirteenth floor. Finally, I blew up two windows of the Safe Room itself, one showing the three of us from the north side, as though we were all reflected in a mirror that didn't reverse, and another bigger window showing the whole room from a hidden lens somewhere overhead that made us look like three beetles feeding on a many-hued graham cracker.

"Congratulations, Lindsay, you're the last domino," Marena said.

"What's that?" he asked, although I was sure that he knew.

"Lindsay, listen," I said. "If we can't stop the test, we're going to change the coordinates to zero-zero-zero."

"That means right here," he said.

"Really?"

"We'll all die."

"So stop the test."

"I can't do that," he said. "Get on the phone to the Pentagon."

"Never mind."

"You want to die right now?" he asked.

"It's fine," I said. "Marena and I have a lover's death pact, and you're an evil bastard."

"Forget it," he said.

"Lindsay . . ." Marena started. She paused. "Look, you just have to believe us on this one. It really is going to, you know, be like I said."

"What?"

"It's going to disappear EVERYTHING!"

"That's ridiculous," Lindsay said. "Jesus won't allow that. Let alone the other gods."

"The Sweeper's going to go over a certain probability range," Marena said. "And it'll just suck in everything, you, me, the Grand Canyon, Jupiter, the Horsehead Nebula, the Sombrero Galaxy, Planet Qo'noS, the Roy Rogers Cometary Globule, everything."

"So it won't hurt," he said.

"Not only will it not hurt, but you won't even notice it."

"This is malarky."

"Fine," I said. "Well, just to see what we can do . . . look, the fact is, we're going to have to torture you."

"Go ahead. The White God is going to get me through this one just like He's done every time."

"Look, Lindsay," she said. "Boss. Why is it so important to you to run this test right this moment?"

"It's not a test," Lindsay said. "It's air support."

"For what? For an invasion of Pakistan?"

"That's correct."

"They're invading right now?"

"Correct, Indian troops started crossing in from Srinagar as of—as of about eight minutes ago."

"So I bet this is going to destroy Islamabad. That's like two million people. If it weren't going to destroy everything, I mean."

"Miss Park, if we do not provide our allies this support, it's not just going to be the end of the trail for the Warren Family. It'll be the end of the United States of America."

"Enough," I said. "Get ready." I took out my bone-scraper needle—it was really just an old woman's hairpin—and an antiseptic towelette, sterilized it and Lindsay's left elbow, and slid the pin into his ulnar nerve. There was a grunt deep inside him, and a half a flinch, but nothing else. He was tough.

I looked into his eyes. They looked back like two freshly drilled blue holes in the face of the Serpentine Glacier. I couldn't be sure, but I thought it was possible—maybe even likely—that Lindsay was one of those few people who have no fear whatsoever. Of course, even they respond to torture eventually. Like I say, no matter what you've heard, torture works. But it could take time. And there was no time. In fact, soon there'd be no time at all, anywhere. Two beads of sweat slid from his forehead into the hollow of his right cheek.

"We were afraid you were going to be difficult," I said.

He didn't answer. The ice holes looked back.

"So," I said, "have you ever heard of Sampson Avard?"

"No." He was lying. He was smooth, but there'd been a quarter-beat too much hesitation.

"I've got some letters from him that I put up for posting," I said. I typed eighty-one characters into a Firefox window on the desktop, downloaded a PDF file from a very-far-offshore server, and flipped the window around and slid it over to him.

He looked at me for ten beats and then couldn't resist looking down at the window. It was the real thing. He looked back at me.

"Well," I said, "to answer your unspoken question, yes, I got that off the LDS vault server," I said. "In Salt Lake. And, yes, we also have the other two hundred and nine sensitive files from the folder."

"And he used the Game to do so, I'm reckoning," Lindsay said, getting himself back together.

I nodded. Shut up, I thought. Contrary to media portrayals, a supervillain, or superhero or superantihero, should *not* explain to the other side what he's about to do.

"And he gave the folder to your friend Quiñones and Quiñones gave it to you."

I nodded.

"So, what's it got to do with me?" he asked.

"You really don't want this going out, do you?"

"I don't care," he said.

I pulled the window back, flipped it around again, and hit POST.

"Okay, it's up," I said. "Google it."

He glared. At first I thought it was my imagination, but then I saw that it was happening: His ears were glowing pink.

"I only put up the first letter," I said. "And, you know, it's not, it's not the worst one. My favorite's the Joseph Smith eight-year-old girl rape stuff. Although the Elamites on Mars business is also pretty great. Right?"

His ears had become a true, deep red. That's the trouble with being a WASP, I thought. Your eyes might be opaque, but your skin's an open window.

"Fine," he said. "The first password is RALSTON. All caps."

I started typing.

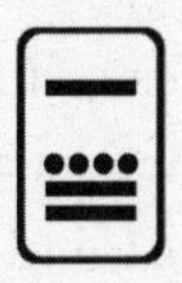

(114)

We all watched the clock. 11:59:8, 11:59:9, Noon. All in. *Les jeux sont faits*, motherfuckers. It was the cosmic sell-by date:

I looked back at the RASP coordinates. Well, there they are, right next door. Might as well just relax. We'd experience another three point one minutes of what we like to call living, and then we'd feel a short sharp shock and maybe even a flash of heat, and then, well before we felt any pain, we wouldn't exist anymore.

"Too bad we couldn't just stop the test, huh?" Marena asked.

"Lindsay?" I asked. "Any ideas?"

"For that we'd have to call a meeting," he said. "If we want to bring a few of the directors in here for— "

"Forget it," I said. "Rerouting is the way we're going to go. Sorry about the nonexistence thing."

"Well, let's try this anyway," Marena said. She was looking at something called ELEVATOR FUNCTION and then RAIL LEVEL.

At first I thought the room was falling down into the cleft canyon of the underwaterworld, and I saw the numbered floors rising past us and saw they were real, or rather real images, and realized what Marena must have noticed already but hadn't bothered to tell me, that we were actually, physically sinking, that the reason the place could be on the thirteenth floor and still be called a Safe Room was because the whole room was really an extra-large elevator. Weirdly, most of the cameras were still functioning, and the transparency macro was chugging along, so it was as though we were sinking through the transparent building into a transparent earth, with explosions flashing around and over us. On the ceiling, translucent wipes with those green wire-frame edges represented the horizontal doors sliding shut over us. We passed a few brightly lit subbasement floors and decelerated.

"Damn," Marena said. "Maybe we'll make it after all." She sounded eager, but also like she didn't want to get her hopes up.

"That's great," I mumbled. I must have sounded vague. Really, I wasn't good for anything anymore. It was all I could do to keep straight what was realish and what was waking-dreamish.

"Check this out," Marena's voice went somewhere. " 'When at its lowest level, this facility was designed to withstand a force of twenty kilotons and slash or two thousand degrees Celsius for over twelve hours. This is roughly equivalent to detonation on the scale of the Nagasaki blast only six hundred yards away.' Isn't that great?"

"Is that the operating manual?" I asked.

"Yeah. 'Cooling is achieved by the use of onboard vacuum sealers and conventional freon refrigeration. Nitrox is supplied from six units in the live floor, each with a capacity of, blah blah blah, ventilation is redundant with, blah, blah . . .' Damn."

This can't be happening, I thought. Although, on the other hand, I guess if anybody would have something like this, it would be Lindsay. Paranoia was one of his most characterizing and endearing traits. There was stuff like this in Jed's memories, things he'd heard about on good authority years ago, in Utah, like supposedly there's a vault under the Church Office Building, the LDS headquarters on North Temple, that you could dip in the sun for twenty-score beats and pull it out and it would still be seventy-two degrees inside. I suppose at the time, Jed had thought it was just a suburban legend. Well, for once somebody wasn't just paranoid, but was paranoid *enough*.

I blinked around. Everything was still sideways. All over the room's six sides the last surveillance systems were going dead. Window after window closed down, but instead of just going to blue the confused system replaced them with video mirrors. We saw ourselves re-reflecting our reflections into serried ranks of identical Chacal-in-Jed$_3$-in-Tony-Sic and Lindsay Warren and Marena Park toy figurines, with the table and chairs replicated in infinite rows curving away toward hidden vanishing points, like long freight trains disappearing over the curvature of the earth. Somewhere among the receding clone armies I thought I saw Maximón, wearing his old manto and and sombrero and smoking and smirking like I Told You So, but it was probably just me. I saw what Lindsay had meant about the Sealing Room. The room was a high-tech version of the marriage chapel they have in Mormon temples, which have huge enfiladed mirrors on all four walls, "set," as they like to say, "to catch eternity." Evidently the designers hadn't thought that was cool enough for the New Age Moron weddings Lindsay and his pals planned to have here, though, because now the display programs were going into some preset routine where they pulled images from the ongoing recording stock and replayed them in palimpsests over the current "reflections," so we could see ourselves enlarged, shrunk, from above, from the other side of the room, unreversed, in slow motion, in ultrafast motion, four-hundred-score beats before, one beat before, everything except a beat from now. I saw us walk in again, and I saw Marena run the video where she called Lindsay to resign from the Warren Group, right after the *Chrononaut* trailer preview. It was like being in the head of some obsessive-compulsive person who could think only about the three of us, stuck in our little lifeboat from here to eternity—

The room rattled like a little box in a big box and then seemed to settle. The screens flickered and went to blue, and it was like we were in a glass bathyscaphe deep in the ocean. Big red letters scrolled across the walls: EXIT AIRLOCKS ALIGNED. There was a click and a loud hiss. The air pressure changed and cool, oxygen-rich air welled up out of the floor, noisily. Excellent, I thought. Not with a wimp, but with a banger.

"-00:00:13:00," the readout said. "-00:00:13.5" . . .

We sat, and looked around us, watching the fifty-two windows, the in-house and public news feeds on the south wall, the stars wheeling on the ceiling, the maps on the north wall, and the news videos and charts and graphs and flickering equations and scrolling code and a thousand other varieties of data. I figured that to an outside observer—God, if only there were ever an outside observer—we looked pretty much like three random blobs of videonarcotized trailer trash anywhere in the random world. Marena touched my wrist, like, *Thanks for saving Max, or trying to.*

We waited.

"-00:00:09.50," it said,

"-00:00:09.00,

"-00:00:08.50 . . ."

FIVE

To the Jaguars of Ix

(115)

Most of the drone cameras got knocked out by the first shock wave, but there were a few dozen that had stationed themselves at a five-score-rope-length circumference, and the screens in the Safe Room automatically switched to them, and then when those got knocked out they switched to an octet of drones at the quarter-jornada mark, and so on, so we got a gods'-eyes view of the blast.

I'd never seen an explosion before. That is, as Chacal I hadn't, even though there are sometimes all-natural ones, dust explosions in caves and volcanic incursions into oil pockets and so on. So to me it was new. Somewhere what was left of Jed-in-Me compared it to the many explosions he'd seen, many on video and a couple in his real life, and now I could hear him again, for the first time in a long time, thinking that it seemed bizarrely slow, that explosions in films are always shot in high-speed and then slowed down, but that this one, maybe because of the size or the convection or air pressure or whatever, would actually have to be sped up to look convincing. And I heard, or felt, echoes of the many metaphors they use in English to describe explosions, words like *flower* and *mushroom.* But to me it seemed to be taking place very fast—I wasn't used to the speed of this world in general—and more than a flower or mushroom it seemed to me to be a tree, the Tree of Four Hundred Times Four Hundred Branches, the Tree with the Mirror Leaves. The canopy of dirt and carbonized flesh and smoke and sand

and steam and barium isotopes and four hundred times four hundred other materials branched out two-score rope-lengths over us—and we could still see it from underneath on some of the drone cameras, as well as from the side and even from a seventy-degree angle over it—in such a wide, embracing curve that I couldn't help feeling it was welcoming and motherly, like the Tree, and we felt its voice, a long growl through the millions of cubic rope-lengths of packed earth around us.

I felt burning in those head-caves where tears would be made if I were the sort of person who would make them, and then the groan faded, and it seemed the three of us were still alive. The collider had been cut in half by a premature release of millions of BTUs of spontaneously generated heat, and despite the loss of life upstairs, the outcome had been, by his lights, a huge relief, and maybe everything would be okay, so to speak... and then, although Jed-in-Me was stronger than he'd been in a long time, he seemed to wilt and go silent, as though his consciousness had fainted from the excitement.

When my attention slid back to them, Marena and Lindsay were, oddly, having something like a civil conversation. Lindsay said the air supply was fine—"for three little breathers, adequate for over a month," was how he put it—and that it would be better to hold off for two days on using the tram system because the air over the terminus, a jornada away at a facility on the highway to Belize City, might still be toxic. Marena—who I thought might almost want to thank me, at some point, for saving Max, despite everything else, but who seemed unsure, to say the least, of how to behave with me—said, "We can't be sure about the O_2."

"What?" I asked. I started untaping her.

"We got, our seal got breached. I can smell it."

"Oh. Right."

Even down here we were getting a whiff of oxidized polymers and carbonized flesh. And we'd have to worry about earth gases getting in. They aren't good for you. Anyway, our own air would leak out pretty fast. We couldn't stay.

"I can't find the hole," Marena said. She'd gotten herself the rest of the way loose and was feeling around the west door. "I think it's on the other side of the, the inner door vaulty thingie."

"I wouldn't open it right now," I said.

"I'm not." She untaped Lindsay and as he massaged his ankles she went back to typing.

I rolled over. There were three red dots on the blue Zeonex floor, and as they came into focus I saw they were beads from Marena's necklace, which must have broken during the unpleasantness. I laid my head down. Beds and whatever are great, but really, I thought, there's nothing so comfortable as a nice flat floor. The blue screens shut down, meaning the system wasn't finding any outside electricity and wanted to be thrifty. Emergency lights came on, just a few red and white LEDs in the floor and ceiling. It was quiet. Like all military elevator shafts, the one above us had a set of baffles that slid over us as we went down. But I could still feel an occasional explosion through the thousands of tons of clay, as soft as that earthquake in Oaxaca that rocked me to sleep—

"We have to cruise," Marena said.

"How much air do we have?" I asked. "It should be, uh, keeping track of that—"

"I'm going to open the other door. I mean, the main door. Hang on."

"Let's wait."

"If there's a problem with the tunnels, nobody's going to bother to dig us out."

"I just need a little nap," I said, although I knew she was right. "Forty score—uh, ten minutes."

There was a click and whir from the main door. Maybe I dozed off. At any rate, I saw something, like a snake farm, maybe—

"Damn it," Marena said. "I can't get the thing open." Lindsay was working on it with a penknife.

Great, I thought. We're going to get through all this and then get stuck in here. Asphyxiate.

"Come on," Lindsay said, "help us with this."

"Five minutes and I'll be good to go."

"Hang on." Maybe there was a pause. At some point I heard something loud, and only a few beats later I smelled cordite.

"Come on, we're cruising," she said.

I made a last effort, stood up, and slid back down. I started to try again, and then realized I really, really couldn't stand up, and it wasn't just laziness. I could have stood up on the wall, like the way I used to run up the angled sides of hipball courts, but not on the floor. The reason I'd slid off the table wasn't just because I was tired, but because pressure from that nearby explosion had blown through my semicircular canals and harshed my equilibrium. And if you've ever had that happen, you know that when it's gone, even though you know that the ground is still the ground, you believe, in your heart of hearts, that you know better, that the sky, or the wall or whatever, is where the gravity is. For some reason Marena didn't have that problem. Maybe she'd been chewing gum or something.

I gave up the standing idea and either crawled or got dragged over an irregular threshold, into a red-lit tunnel with the smells of stone mold, fresh concrete, and Janitor In A Drum. There was a backlit map on the wall showing the network of tunnels, glowing in Ocelot emerald. YOU ARE HERE ▪, it said. As always, I thought.

"Sit in this," Marena said. She kind of molded me into one of the Aeron chairs and rolled me past some pieces of door. I guessed the bang I'd heard had been exploding bolts blowing the door outward into the tunnel. Thoughtfully designed for just such an emergency. I'd expected to run into a crowd of refugees in the tunnel, but there was nobody. Evidently this one was for VVIPs only, and we were the only ones left.

She started pushing me along like I was in a wheelchair. "Stop leaning over," she said.

"I'm not."

"Lean in the other direction."

"Why don't you go ahead and come back and get me after you get settled?"

"You know," she said, "I've just about had it with your martyr syndrome."

"Sorry."

Bathetically, there was still that Dvořákmusak on somewhere and it echoed behind us, woodwinds wailing. We went a long way. Lindsay fell down a few times—despite everything, he really was an old guy, I thought—and I had to hold his arm most of the way. I knew that later all I'd be able to remember would be long, long, long passages, dreary pipes and concrete, and a sense that we'd walked for at least two-score rope-lengths. At some point Marena was banging on a door above us, and then she was strongly encouraging us to climb up some stairs, and eventually, on all fours, I did. She steered me through a door and up more stairs and it took me more than a minute to realize we were outside because the fresh air wasn't fresh, it was full of gasoline smoke, although there were a few nicer smells in it, wood and green-leaf smoke that made me think it was the burning season, and it was hot, and it was night already. No twilight. Except it wasn't dark. The sky was charred tangerine. I listened for explosions or artillery but didn't hear anything, just distant sirens and that sort of over-Niagara-in-a-barrel sound of the wind of glass rushing past us on its way to the giant updrafts, columns of a million different carbon compounds rolling up into the stratosphere, and then I thought I heard lightning but I think it was actually malfunctioning defense lasers firing blind. They make a sort of crackle as the air boils away in the beam, and then a miniature thunderclap as the surrounding atmosphere closes in around the vacuum.

"Lie here," she said. I said thanks. I lay down on the asphalt, near the top step. She duct-taped Lindsay to a Siamese pipe connection. I got it together to look around. The door was down in a sort of retaining wall, and the stairs came up sheltered between two sort of huge concrete Jersey barriers. There was a warehouse or something across the whatever that seemed intact but I couldn't see very far. Anyway, it didn't feel worth it to go back to try some other branch of the tunnel. A few leaves of plasticky fallout fell around us like the pages of an incinerated book. A big sheet of red-anodized metal siding rattled up and down around on the pavement in front of us, threatening to chop us into bits when the pressure changed. Latin American builders, I thought. Cruddy house-of-cards postmodern architecture. One little thing and it's all over the place.

"I was thinking about sending a distress signal," Marena said. "But now I think I won't, okay?" I noticed she had something over her shoulder, a big transparent bag with a big orange word EMERGENCY on it and all kinds of electric beacons and radios flares and things inside.

"Sure," I said. She was probably right. If we went exploring we'd be more likely to get hit by flying whatever, or caught by Executive Solutions or even by troops from the UN or Belize or anybody else.

I thought I heard a scream not so far away, but it could have been shrapnel.

"I don't think we're going to burn up here," Marena said. "And if the smoke gets bad we'll go back into the tunnel. I don't want to get stuck in a fire. Okay?"

I said something like "Fine." I would have agreed to anything. My field of vision was reverse-tunnelling. That is, widening, weirdly, past 200 degrees. Marena was saying something about how the best thing to do is sit tight until morning, walk east, find the highway, and try to get a lift to Belmopan. I mumbled that that sounded right. We sat.

"Are you Jed again?" she asked. "Or Chacal?"

"I don't know," I said. I really didn't.

Marena took out her phone. The line was dead, but we watched the clock. Nine minutes left, it said. And then it would be officially a new b'aktun, and a new sun, and a new creation, and, and, and . . .

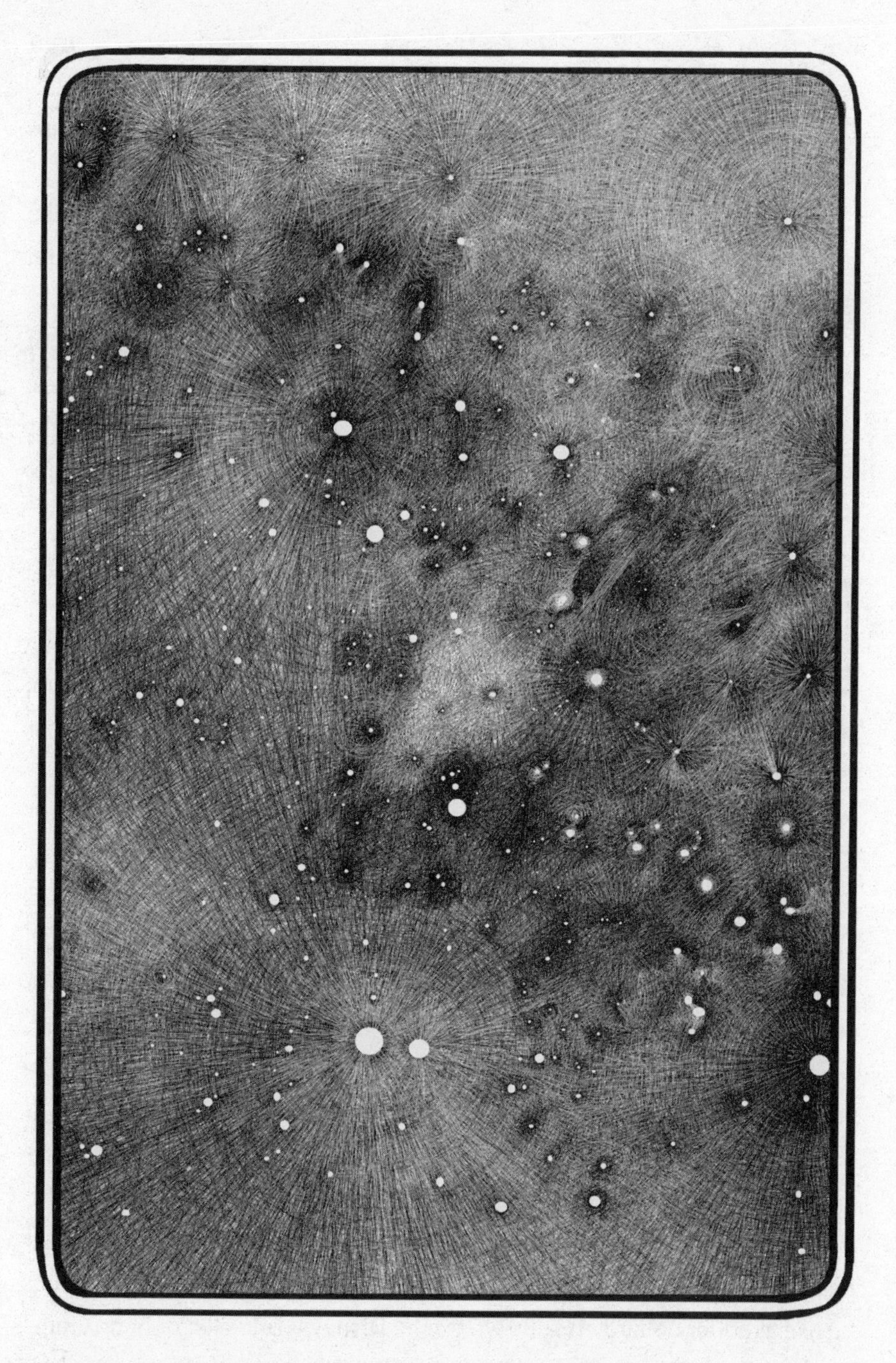

The Pleiads, Called the Rattle of the Celestial Ophidian, as They Will Appear in Times to Come with a Nascent Eighth Star, According to the Native Cociques of Alta Verapaz

Curious Antiquities of British Honduras
By Subscription · Lambeth · 1831

(0)

December 21 came and went like any other day.

But of course that didn't mean that nothing had changed. Everything had changed. Everyone's tomorrow, and the next day, and the day after that, and the next tun, and the next k'atun, and the universe's final seven b'aktuns—what Koh had called the "remainder of twenty minus thirteen," would be whatever I made of it. Or whatever we deigned to make of it, Marena and I, or let's call her what she would be called: One Ocelot.

My field of vision kept widening. Now I could see above and behind and above my head and now in every direction, even, it seemed, into my body, and, as I rose through the tree and curved into higher dimensions, I could see through objects, and out past the last straggling galaxies, until I even seemed to get a glimpse or two or three of that other universe, the bubbleverse, our less lucky twin, the one that had diverged from ours thirteen years and three hundred and fifty-two days ago, the one where One Liberty Plaza hadn't burned down on 9/11 and so Lindsay hadn't been able to use the marble floor from it in his fucking VVIP Skybox, the one where both towers had collapsed all the way instead of that half of the South one still sticking up like a fodder pollard, the one where the Disney World Horror hadn't happened, where Dick Cheney hadn't killed himself as he was being arrested, where Amy Winehouse had died in that coma and had never recorded or even written "Shake Before Serving," one where the nine-stone Game had never come back and which was, therefore, on the royal road to ruin because at some point soon, somewhere, some doomster would hit on the right combination and there'd be no way to stop him or even find out about him until it was too, too, too too late, where I and Marena, maybe, had never met, and where I'd never even heard of Lady Koh, and where they were not yet, even, aspects of each other, if they even ever . . .

Don't think about it. We're here, in our own friendly universe, and it would still last a while. Until 19.19.19.17.19, 9 Kawak, 12 Yaxki'in. Thursday, October 12th, 4772. After that, the big nothing. Well, that was still quite a distance off. Don't think about that either. Look, you bought the world quite a good amount of time. Human-scale-wise. Anyway, things'll be quite different then, right? In fact I could already see some different . . . yes. I already saw the new city, the capital of the world, with its double mul rising in undulating omnichromatic stairways to an apex higher than Popocatépetl and, then, widening, filling the zeroth sky. I saw odd decisions being made, the Pantheon in Rome exploding in violet lava, a fashionably naked pair of two-ropelengths-long humans with thirteen pairs of dainty thalidomidesque arms sprouting centipedishly down their sides nuzzling each other as they reclined on a fur toboggan drawn through the Park Avenue Tunnel by four yellow phororhacci, and the trail led down an alley of titanic ceiba trees that shed clouds of jade razors around my defleshing body, and there was something horrible waiting at the end of the path, something pustuled with screaming larvae but still wearing the knowing smirk of the toad, and I already knew, I knew why it had started and when it had to end, the smell of a graviton, the color of the Ku band, the reason a skull smiles. But as I came to know I stayed to forget, thirteen, nine, five, I was already forgetting, four, three, I will have already forgotten, two, zero, I've already forgotten.

End of Book II

APPENDIX

The Ancient Future of the Seventh Skin

(a fragment of the "New Maya Calendar")

According to Ahau-Na Koh of Ixnich'i Sotz

Thirteen b'ak'tuns and no ka'tuns, no tuns,
No uinals, and no kins, 4 Overlord,
3 Yellowribs, on Friday, on December
The twenty-first, in twenty-twelve, Sun Zero:
The White Road's nine last overlords burn themselves,
The sun's last thirteen overlords drown themselves,
One Ocelot's new flesh reseats the May.

Thirteen b'ak'tuns and no ka'tuns, no tuns,
No uinals, and one kin, on 5 Sobralia,
4 Ununennium, on Saturday,
December twenty-second, twenty-twelve:
The thirteen newborn overlords take the sun,
Nine newborn overlords retake the dark.

Thirteen b'ak'tuns and 1 ka'tun, and thirteen
Tuns, and two uinals and two kins, 5 Helicon
And Zero Kaon, Saturday, the twelfth
Of August, twenty-forty-five: the Chewer
Gobbles the day above the new mul-garden.
Xiamen is the seat of the ka'tun.
The Ludic May ensorcells the b'ak'tuns,
The Coiler molds new followers from pyroxene
And they take refuge in new citadels,
In orthorhombic tetrahedral muls.
Pain and cessation cease, but not aloneness
Despite mass melding. Now the earth falls mute
Since others might feel pity. Now eternal
Electromagnetic silence is our burden.

Fifteen b'ak'tuns and no ka'tuns, no tuns,
No uinals and no kins, 2 Nothingness,
18 Ununennium, Thursday, June

The twenty-eighth, in two-eight-zero-one,
At the sun's pubescence, at his third thirteenth,
The solar hurricanes erase nine billion
Bright consciousnesses. Mourning is our burden.

Fifteen b'ak'tuns, fourteen ka'tuns, twelve tuns,
Twelve uinals and three kins, on 13 Scattering
And 16 Kaon, Wednesday, on December
Eighteenth, in thirty-eighty-nine: the sun's
First brightest dog rejoins his master, after
Six hundred and eighteen thousand and three hundred
And seventy-three opposing suns. Now rises
The second regency of 7 Macaw,
The consciousness of his four hundred times
Four hundred times four trillion breathing things.
Unclouded and lidless eyes become our burden.

Then in the nineteenth and the last b'ak'tun, and in
The nineteenth and the last ka'tun, and in
The nineteenth and last tun, and seventeenth
And final uinal, in the eighteenth kin,
8 Amethyst, 11 Funge, October
Eleventh, Wednesday, anno domini
Four thousand seven hundred seventy-two,
One Ocelot and Turquoise Ocelot
Enter the courts of the sun, and play to a draw.
All possibilities occur in a single ninth.

Now in the nineteenth and the last b'ak'tun, and in
The nineteenth and the last ka'tun, and in
The nineteenth and last tun, and seventeenth
And final uinal, in the eighteenth kin,
9 Shuddering, 12 Funge, October twelfth,
Four thousand seven hundred seventy-two,
The nine and thirteen lords unspeak their names.
The seas of consciousnesses choose dissolving
Over another repetition. The Zeroth
Burden is equal to never having been.
On a field, turquoise, Brunnian roundels, red,
Unclasp and collapse to twenty, to thirteen,

To nine, five, four, three, two, one, zero, never.

GLOSSARY

ahau—lord, overlord
ahau-na—lady, noblewoman
bacab—"world-bearer," one of four local ahauob subject to the k'alomte'
b'ak'tun—a period of 144,000 days, roughly 394.52 years
b'alche'—lilac-tree beer
b'et-yaj—teaser, torturer
Ch'olan—the twenty-first-century version of the language spoken by the Ixians and others
grandeza—a pouchful of pebbles
h'men—a calendrical priest or shaman. Also translated as "sun adder" or "day-keeper"
hun—"one," or "a" as a definite article
k'atun—a period of 7,200 days (nearly twenty years)
k'iik—blood, a male belonging to a warrior society
k'in—sun, day
koh—tooth
kutz—a neotropical ocellated turkey
milpa—a traditional raised cornfield of about 21 x 20 meters, usually cleared by burning
mul—hill; by extension "pyramid" or "volcano"
nacom—sacrificer
pitzom—the Maya ball game
popol na—council house
quechquemitl—Mexican woman's triangular serape
sacbe—"white path," a sacred straight causeway
sinan—scorpion
tablero—the horizontal element in a Mexican-style pyramid
talud—the sloped element in a Mexican-style pyramid

teocalli—Nahuatl for "god house," or temple

tun—360 days

tu'nikob'—sacrificers or offering priests, or, literally, "sucklers"

tzam lic—"blood lightning," a frisson under the skin

tz'olk'in—the ritual year of 260 days

uay—a person's animal coessence

uinal—a period of twenty days

waah—tortilla

Xib'alb'a—the Underworld, ruled by the Nine Lords of the Night

xoc—shark

yaj—pain, pain smoke

Yucatec—the present-day language of the Yucatán Maya, a version of which was spoken during the Classic period

ACKNOWLEDGMENTS

Rosemae Aristomene, Ron Bernstein, Anthony D'Amato, Barbara D'Amato, Robertson Dean, Julie Doughty, Jonny Geller, Karin and Timothy Greenfield-Sanders, Jessica Horvath, Erika Imranyi, Janice Kim, Stefan Lübbe, Diana MacKay, Helmut Pesch, Prudence Rice, Dietmar Schmidt, Deborah Schneider, and Brian Tart should all be thanked on, at least, the front cover, and not back here.

More thanks to Jacqueline Cantor, Lisa Chau, Brian DeFiore, Michael Denneny, Sajna Dragovic, Molly Friedrich, Cathy Gleason, Lynn Goldberg, Justin Gooding, Sherrie Holman, Marissa Ignacio, "Mad P," Victoria Marini, Phillip McCullough, Jamie McDonald, Liza Cassity, Erica Ferguson, Stephanie Kelly, James Meyer, Mary Ellen Miller, Robert Pincus-Witten, Bruce Price, David Rimanelli, Michael Spertus, Rebecca Stone-Miller, Jane Tompkins, Mari-Jo Van Malsen, "Tony Xoc," "Flor Xul," and Ivan Zlatarski.

Thanks also to the Foundation for the Advancement of Mesoamerican Studies and pauahtun.org.

Thanks to Brian D'Amato for any and all errors.

For a select bibliography, please see briandamato.com

Photo © Timothy Greenfield-Sanders

Brian D'Amato can usually be found in New York, Michigan, or Chicago. He is an artist who has shown his sculptures and installations at galleries and museums in the U.S. and abroad, including the Whitney Museum, the Wexner Center for Contemporary Art, and the New Museum of Contemporary Art. In 1992 he co-organized an exhibit at the Jack Tilton Gallery in New York that was the first gallery show exploring the then-new concept of computer games as an art medium. He has written for magazines including *Harper's Bazaar, Index, Vogue, Flash Art,* and most frequently *Artforum* and has taught art and art history at CUNY, the Ohio State University, and Yale. His 1992 novel, *Beauty*, which Dean Koontz called "the best first novel I have read in a decade," was a bestseller in the U.S. and abroad and was translated into several popular languages. For more information please see www.briandamato.com.